DANCE OF
SHADOWS

THE RAAG OF RTA SERIES

Sons of Darkness
Dance of Shadows

Dance of Shadows

GOURAV MOHANTY

An Ad Astra Book

First published in the United Kingdom in 2025 by Head of Zeus,
part of Bloomsbury Publishing Plc

9 7 5 3 1 2 4 6 8

A catalogue record for this book is available from the British Library.

Cover design: Micaela Alcaino
Maps: © Gourav Mohanty

ISBN (HB): 9781035900275
ISBN (BROKEN BINDING HB): 9781035916948
ISBN (B&N HB): 9781035915231
ISBN (XTPB): 9781035900268
ISBN (E): 9781035900299

Printed and bound by CPI Group (UK) Ltd,
Croydon, CR0 4YY

Head of Zeus
First Floor East
5–8 Hardwick Street
London EC1R 4RG
WWW.HEADOFZEUS.COM

To the mother who nicknamed her son
'Prince' and let him write his own legend
(and perhaps spoiled him along the way).

Hi, Maa *waves*

ABOUT THE AUTHOR

GOURAV MOHANTY was born, and currently lives, in Bhubaneswar, the City of Temples. A connoisseur of mythologies and momos, he's been certified as a nerd ever since he graduated as a gold medalist from law school. He keeps things interesting by daylighting as a lawyer, moonlighting as a stand-up comic and gaslighting as a storyteller.

gouravmohanty.com
X: @MohantyGourav7
Instagram: @thekingbeyondthewall

CONTENTS

AUTHOR'S NOTE

The events of *Dance of Shadows* take place alongside those in *Sons of Darkness*, like a shadow trailing a particularly dramatic hero. So if you're reading this and wondering, "Wait, didn't I already hear about that battle?" – congratulations, dear traveller, you've been paying attention. You see, while the main cast was busy waving swords, making speeches, and doing their level best to destroy the world, far more sinister deeds were unfolding just beyond the edge of sight. *Dance of Shadows* is that story, the one beyond the veil, the one where vengeance sets sail.

Gourav Mohanty

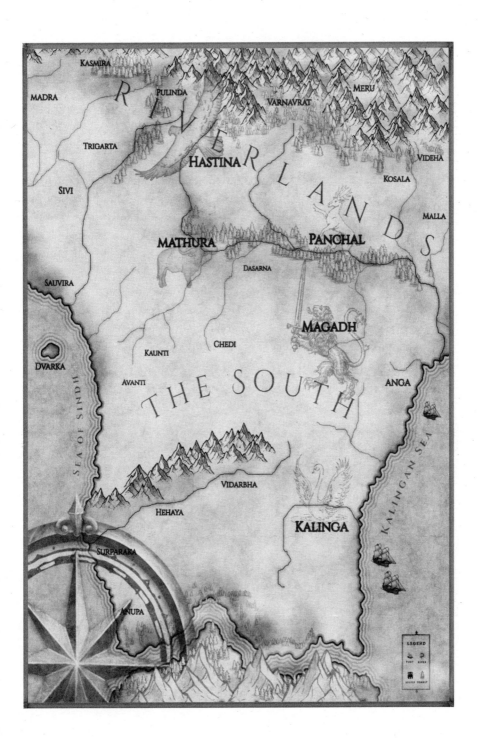

DRAMATIS PERSONAE

EMPIRE OF MAGADH

Jarasandh	Brooding and brutal Emperor of Magadh
Saham Dev	Crown Prince with a weak spine and cruel mind, Mati's husband
Mati	Unhinged Empress-in-Waiting and former Princess of Kalinga
Chalakkha	Ambassador desperate to find himself in Emperor's good books
Dantavakra	Lover of women, contest favourite, Shishupal's brother and bane
Dimvak	Unfortunately, Dantavakra's teacher
Shishupal	Dantavakra's shy elder brother, former Commander of Claws
Gorin	Mercenary attached to Chalakkha, with bad teeth
Isa	Warrior in the Imperial Army
Milani	Visiting noblewoman with the airs of a goddess
Runaan	Revelmaster who is petrified of Unni Ehtral

Mair	Dantavakra's rich stableowner friend, Milani's brother
Vishwakarman	Famous architect tasked with retouching Virangavat
Whisper	Silver Wolf prisoner rescued by Chalakkha to shield him
Sidestep	Greedy Silver Wolf prisoner rescued by Chalakkha
Itch	Silver Wolf prisoner who was foolish to get caught
Fidget	Silver Wolf prisoner who was foolish to try and rescue her friend
Amala	Lowborn handmaiden to Mati, with a secret
Anaadi	Owner of Tulips Tavern, with a gambling problem

UNNI EHTRAL

Narag Jhestal	High Priest of Unni Ehtral
Bhadrak	Priest of rank Acharak in Unni Ehtral who is obsessed with purity
Sarai	Priestess of rank Maekhela in Unni Ehtral

KINGDOM OF BALKH

Vahura	Bookmoth Princess of Balkh and granddaughter of Bahlika
Bahlika	A pyredodger King of Balkh and Vahura's grandfather

Somadatta   Dead son of Bahlika
Bhoorishravas   Warlike Prince of Balkh and grandson of
                            Bahlika
Old Ella   Warlike governess in Vahura's service

TREE CITY OF KAMRUP

Bhagadatt   Mysterious Tusk of Tree Cities and Remnant
                            Monarch
Baggy   Friendly Marshal of the Tree City
Sokarro   Tusk's Bloodguard whose nose and ears were
                            sliced away by men
Shurpanakha   Founder of Tree Cities and sister of mythical
                            Ravana
Aindri   A young Yogini with a penchant for mischief
Zubeia   Sultry Mistress of Ravens and head of Yoginis

LIBRARY AT THE RIM OF THE WORLD

Asshaye   Master of Stratagem
Orym   Master of Potions and Machinations
Kalay   Master of Human Sciences
Toshad   Master of History
Ailmar   Master of Cataloguing

UNION OF HASTINA

Duryodhan	Heir apparent and tortured lover of Mati
Karna	Brooding Highmaster of Anga and finest archer of his time
Sudama	Murdered nephew of Karna
Yudhistir	Duryodhan's funless cousin and rival to the throne
Bheem	Yudhistir's brother and a gifted wrestler
Arjun	Yudhistir's brother and a gifted archer
Nakul	Yudhistir's brother and a beautiful horsegroomer
Sahadev	Yudhistir's brother and a gifted lawscribe
Shakuni	Master of Spies, the Queen's brother, an angry soul
Bheeshma	Old Lord Commander of Union, the White Eagle
Dhritarashtra	Blind King of Hastinapur
Gandhari	Blindfolded Queen of Hastinapur

HOUSE OF DEVADASIS

Meenakshi	Real name, Marzana. Devadasi Prime and Gurumaa's daughter
Gurumaa	Comatose matriarch of Devadasis
Badi Dee	Seniormost superseded Devadasi with a penchant for politics
Damaya	Meenakshi's sister and a gifted dancer, about to become a Devadasi
Jalapa	Patron who enjoys being dominated
Labang	Servant boy who loves to gossip
Old Khai	Highest-paying patron of the House of Devadasis

THE RED ORDER

| Parshuram | Founder of the Red Order and impatient, immortal teacher |
| Nala | Parshuram's apprentice and irritated, inquisitive student |

SAPTARISHIS

Vyas	Acharya of the Orange Order and teacher in Meru
Masha	Sister of the Black Order, excited to explore the world for the first time
Nar Ad	Acharya of the Blue Order, Pathfinder and horrible singer
Shree	Nar Ad's apprentice with a Taint in her voice
Nomnom	Shree's handsome pet rat
Ajath	Mute and deaf mercenary attached to Vyas, with black-dyed teeth
Taksha	Migrant Naga attached to Vyas who believes he'll find the Messiah
Balthazar	Warrior of the Iron Order, with a bald head
Tamasa	Acharya with a grim frown
Tapasa	Acharya with a gleeful smile

KINGDOM OF KALINGA

Chitragandh	King of Kalinga and absentee father
Matakshara	Wraith of Tamra Lipta with eyes only for gold
Handsome Haram	Peacekeeper of Tamra Lipta
Asanka	Dwarf boatswain on the *Gilded Lion*

SIGILS AND WORDS

REPUBLIC OF MATHURA

Deeds, Not Birth

EMPIRE OF MAGADH

We Do Not Bow

UNION OF HASTINA

Law Above All

KINGDOM OF PANCHAL

Death Before Dishonour

KINGDOM OF KALINGA

Voyage and Valour

YAVANAS

Arete and Kleos

TREE CITY OF KAMRUP

Seeds Don't Die in Dirt

KINGDOM OF BALKH

Forge in Faith

SAPTARISHIS

In Chaos Lies Cosmos

PREVIOUSLY ON RAAG OF RTA...

To the benevolent remover of obstacles, Lord Ganesha,
Hearken and heed my caution before you read further.
While I offer a glimpse into *Sons of Darkness*, brevity dictates this
be but a mere whisper in the wind, leaving many a tale untold.

Perhaps I should begin with an age long past, when the immortal
Daevas slit a woman's throat. But bound by a vow they could not
break, they locked her brother, Muchuk Und, in an ice sleep instead.
Fear guided their betrayal, fear that Muchuk Und would wake the
Elementals from their rest, an ancient force so loved, so absent, so
mercifully dead.

Or perhaps it is wiser to speak of the present, where Masha,
an oracle, seeks the Son of Darkness, the serpent prophesied to
strangle this Age. Instead, she finds dubious heroes dangling by
threads of fate. Take, for instance, the leaders of Mathura, Krishna
and Satyabhama, who, under the frail armistice with the Magadhan
Empire, are gifted a moment to breathe. But wars don't end simply
because swords are sheathed. Bloodied but unbowed, they scheme
to spirit the Mathurans to safer shores before the Empire, bolstered
by new allies Kalyavan and Bhagadatt, bring monsters to make
Mathura a feast for the gods of slaughter.

Or take Mati, the Pirate Princess of Kalinga, betrothed to
Prince Duryodhan of Hastina. She turns her devotion to him
violent by not only murdering a thorn in Duryodhan's throne as a

token of affection but by mistakenly bedding the lowborn Karna, Duryodhan's closest friend.

And how can we forget Shakuni, weaver of schemes, sowing discord in Hastina, hoping to see it bloom into a civil war between Duryodhan and his cousin Yudhistir. His noble work, however, is rudely interrupted when a captured Daeva, sighted after centuries, is discreetly rescued by none other than Karna, Betrayal's favourite poem. Wracked with guilt, Karna plans to go into exile with his nephew, only to abandon his designs when Duryodhan's cousins, Yudhistir and his brothers, are burned alive.

To sway public opinion and forge alliances, Shakuni urges Duryodhan to pursue Draupadi's hand at her swayamvar. But Duryodhan, led astray by his love for that unhinged Mati, names Karna as Hastina's champion at the last moment. Things looked promising until Draupadi, with Krishna's whispers in her ear, bars Karna from the contest for being lowborn.

Unaware of Duryodhan's loyalty, Mati, in a fit of rage, seduces the Magadhan prince into slitting Draupadi's throat. But chaos erupts when a lowly priest, none other than Yudhistir's brother, Arjun in disguise, wins Draupadi's hand just as Mati's assassins descend. In the mayhem, as Karna clashes with Arjun, a stray arrow from Arjun takes the life of Karna's nephew. But the world has no time to weep for a lowborn when highborn scandals shake the realm. After all, Yudhistir and his brothers are alive, and Draupadi has been wed to all five.

Turns out Yudhistir, on Krishna's advice, had staged the arson, with a tribal girl, Nala and her kin offered up as sacrifice. While Nala's family burned to ash, their charred remains passed off as Yudhistir and his own, Nala herself survived, patched up by Parshuram, the immortal warrior-sage. She begged him to take her under his wing, to polish her rage and turn her into a knife. And old Parshuram decided to give Nala her purpose. But things took a turn when Parshuram was summoned by the Saptarishis to hunt down the Son of Darkness.

Meanwhile, before Krishna can complete his exodus, Kalyavan, the Greek warlord and the Emperor's ally, lays siege to Mathura before the Armistice expired, bold enough to do it alone without waiting for the Empire. You know how these young things have strange hungers. Krishna's only hope lies with Hastina, but Hastina has its own mess to handle: Arjun's trial for the death of Karna's nephew. How do the Gods choose? Whose prayers do they refuse?

Arjun is acquitted, naturally, much to no one's surprise. But Sahadev, Yudhistir's brother, seizes the moment to stake Yudhistir's claim as the rightful heir of the Hastina over Duryodhan. With Duryodhan and Karna both supposedly attending the Conclave in the East, Shakuni struggles against Sahadev's legal manoeuvring until word of the Battle of Mathura reaches him. Knowing Yudhistir's wife and brother are trapped are trapped in Mathura, Shakuni forces Yudhistir agree to a partition of the Hastina Union, with Yudhistir winning a measly slice in exchange for Hastina rescuing his brother and wife. An even trade? Only time will tell.

But, the Battle for Mathura... such beautiful carnage. I wish I could take a crowbar and pry out the broken pieces of heroes from under Mathura's debris. Be it Satyabhama, bless her, who locked in a tense duel with Kalyavan, fell with one fatal misstep. Or her Silver Wolves, ever loyal, who charged into certain death to buy the civilians time to flee. Or Krishna? Consumed by grief, he stayed behind and freed Muchuk Und, the man with a wound centuries deep, the man who was trapped in an ice prison beneath Mathura. The same man who awakened the Elementals, incinerated Kalyavan alive, and turned Mathura into a smouldering ruin just as the Hastina forces arrived to rout what remained of Kalyavan's army.

I know you may claim the battle was won by Krishna. I disagree. The history of wars may gild his name, but all he cherished lies in ruins and flame.

Now I am certain you have questions, My Lord. What became of Karna and Duryodhan? Why were they absent from the Trial of Arjun? What happened in the Conclave in the East? Did Mati disappear into the mist like a wisp of smoke, or did she have more schemes up her sleeve? What of Parshuram's task to thwart the Son of Darkness or Nala's road to avenge her sorrows?

Lend me your ears then, and let me take you to the cradle of our civilization. As the Saptarishis say, in chaos lies the cosmos.

Yours in bemusement,
Acharya Vyas, Orange Order of Meru.

PROLOGUE

I

Some soldiers forsake their oaths by fleeing the battlefield, some by unlatching the gates, others by seducing a superior's darling, but only the chosen commit treason by accidentally pissing on their king.

'They're ready, Sir,' whispered Asun.

Marshal Ethari withdrew his whistle and wiped it. Felt like the hygienic thing to do. 'I'm aware, soldier,' he said, hoping he had infused some nonchalance into his tone. Nonchalance, after all, earned a Marshal respect, or so his mother reminded him every day while she violently combed his unruly curls. 'I can hear them,' he added for good measure.

Judging by the noise behind him, there was a considerable number of spectators who'd been lured to the battlements – a considerable number that was steadily rising. It put Ethari in the mind of the mob's uproar back in the Day of Exodus: Seven Tribes, hundreds of voices raised in delighted devilry as they bid farewell to Iyran Machil forever. *Wonder if they'd survived. Wonder if they were up to something better than overseeing a piss-the-farthest contest.*

Ethari would have very much liked to follow the Seven Tribes out. They were bravehearts who refused to live any longer as ageless refugees in this realm and returned to the Surface at great peril. He wasn't without sympathy for their cause, after all. However, he didn't fancy the idea of drowning, either. Not to forget he had sworn an oath to the Realmseer. Not to King Manu directly, of course, but, you know, he'd sworn it even so. He had been happy to swear it when he was rescued from the great flood, and supposed it would be rather unsporting to unswear it now simply because he was bored. What kind of a Vachan would it be then? His superior had assured him last week that Manu promised a new beginning, a new world where they would want to eat again. He missed eating. You never truly appreciate how negotiable starvation is until you've spent a few centuries without an appetite.

'Sir?' Asun asked.

Disturbed from his contemplations on digestion, Ethari glanced at his men and women spread thin along the walls of Iyran Machil. What a flimsy little blue line they cut. Perhaps thirty archers and ten spearthrowers. All useless. The wall was barely high enough for a fall to end in a fracture. Not the architect's fault, of course. Who do you defend the city walls from when your city is the only settlement in the realm?

Bored, Ethari whistled without overseeing.

With a hearty cry, he let forth the first stream. His comrades, not to be outdone, followed suit, and soon enough, like feeble spigots in a garden, waters of sunlit hues streamed down the battlements to the ground below. A windkeeper, captained by the Archmarshal, hovered in the air above – judge and jury of this ungodly contest. Someday Ethari would be up there in the sky, judging the arc of pees himself. *Any decade now.*

Meanwhile, the mirror clouds above the windkeeper cast their gaze on the wall in grand detail. Oh, how he loathed those clouds! Especially when they conspired to reflect his face, enlarged and uncomfortably close, as though the heavens themselves were holding a looking glass to his soul. It might have been tolerable if these clouds reflected the truth but he was firmly convinced that mischievous sprites lurked in the sky, who spun mirages of the mind, twisting and distorting reality. See, even now there drifted a mirror cloud, its reflections mimicking his every move until they showed him tumbling headlong off the walls.

A scream caused him to drop his whistle to the ground. The symphony of splashes from the bladder brigade now interrupted, some of the contestants turned about in alarm, startling and showering their supporters behind instead. He, on the other hand, stuffed it inside his trousers, a growing patch of dark on the crotch the only evidence of his folly. But Ethari was past caring, his mouth turning dry as he deciphered the contents of the scream. His jaw, along with his trousers, dropped simultaneously when he confirmed it from the reflection on the sky.

They'd been relieving themselves on Manu, the Realmseer, their King, the Father of Mankind, by whose name the entire human race was now known. And Ethari had allowed this to pass.

Difficult though it was for him to admit, Ethari was having a hard time staying nonchalant. On the contrary, he was on the brink of squealing for his mother. He hadn't been trained for this. They don't train you for what to do if you accidentally douse your probably unconscious, probably sleeping, hopefully dead king with urine. Does he run? Does he call for help? Does he blame someone else? Does he blame Asun for rushing him to whistle?

Almost as if running out of time to decide, Ethari went with the evidently self-incriminating choice. 'On me! To the Realmseer!' His soldiers glanced at each other, stirring uncomfortably, but to their credit and his relief, they followed him down the steps.

Ethari heard the Realmseer before he saw him. Heard his heartbeat to be precise. How could he hear the Realmseer's heartbeat from such a distance! Was it his own? But the sound of the Realmseer's heart faded in Ethari's ears when his eyes saw the Realmseer's body.

Manu was lying face down. Wheezing and leaking red all over, his hair, his back, his arse, all seemed damp. Ethari hesitated, whispered a prayer, and then delicately turned his king over, and fell back in horror.

Arteries bulged out on Manu's face, much like they did on his sculptures. The Orb of Agan Mian, carved into a hole in the centre of the king's forehead, glimmered weakly, its shine dimmed. But it was Manu's eyes that petrified Ethari. Strange golden specks in his brown eyes, starlike, were merging into each other even as Ethari observed them.

Ethari had never seen Manu in such close proximity but he did not need prior intimacy with his king to know something had gone horribly wrong. Was it because of the piss? The specks in his eyes were the same colour as it! *Oh Mother, I'm dead.*

'Summon the windkeeper!' Ethari snarled. 'Now, you bastards!'

Ow! Ethari rubbed his eyes. Perfect. Just the time for dust to make its entrance. Now his eyes would turn red, and his soldiers would think he was weeping. Of course, Ethari wanted to but he wasn't. He will be damned if he let his underlings see him so. Fucking ingrates that they were. Pissing off the walls! What kind of a soldier does that? Now he'll be blamed for their bladders!

While thoughts of fairness raged in the poor Marshal's head, the windkeeper descended. A heavily robed healer pranced out, followed by the Archmarshal.

'Report,' the Archmarshal, a short, diminutive woman with two slim swords peeking over her shoulder, commanded. The little fucker. Kaksi, her name was. Ethari would have followed the Realmseer into hell. But not this arsehole, this bitch with her wooden fragrances, her fine accent and her nonchalant jaw. *Why am I so... angry?* That question was, however, buried by the knowledge that he was glaring back at the Archmarshal.

But before the Archmarshal could take offence, the healer spoke. 'Clots in the blood vessels leading to his mind. He should've perished... but the Orb of Agan Mian, or perhaps the poison of Velas Kalein, is stopping him from—'

'Do you want to climb to the battlements and announce your lack of knowledge to the world?' Ethari barked, not believing the words coming out of his mouth. Why was he so angry? And why did his eyes hurt so? He turned back and looked down to find Kaksi nodding at him.

'We will take the Realmseer to his palace,' Kaksi ordered.

In this suspended state between sickness and health, Manu was carried by Kaksi and her men onto the windkeeper. The engines roared to life. Soon it would ascend over the walls of Iyran Machil, passing the floating mirrors and the flying D'rahis, to take the cloud street straight to the palace. Not once did Kaksi look down to thank Ethari. If she had, she might've saved herself from his dire fate. She might've even saved this world.

II

Manu was dying. Rupa looked at her husband's diminished figure, his eyes rolled back to reveal only the whites, his hands scrawling gibberish upon the parchment on his chest. His hair remained black as ever but his face was the colour of the linen he lay on. The orb on his forehead was still the brilliant red of cooling lava but with a touch of blue at its centre, like an ocean inside a drop of flame. It no longer shone as it had for centuries past. What other evidence did she need? She branded the thought on her mind again: Manu was dying. How could he abandon her to shoulder everything alone, especially now? For the grim reports she had received over the last three days since Manu was brought in painted a red picture of Iyran Machil. Even by conservative estimates, the toll of the unprovoked riots was far higher than it had been during the Exodus a century past. But what was worse was the uncertainty: why was this happening? What did they want? A wave of frustration crashed into her followed by another wave of rage. *Wake up, Manu!*

The deep current of sorrow beneath those waves sought to drag her under but Rupa clung savagely to the splintered plank of her anger. *He will rise,* she told herself, *he will rise and pull us through this.* Only then would she pause and permit herself to feel. For now, she dipped a cloth in warm, neem-infused water, and gently wiped his shaking arms. When they had first steered the ship of humanity through the Great Tears, her two palms had not been able to span the mighty arm of her husband. Now that arm was a limp twig wrapped in slack flesh. No. It was hard to find any trace of the man she had known and loved for centuries.

He stirred lightly under her touch but did not waken, his lips simply quivering those same words he had spoken when they had discovered him on the windkeeper, all his guards aboard, ripped to pieces. 'Make the Choice. Make the Choice.'

Rupa spat great, wet blotches of red betel into the spittoon, her teeth orange with chewing. What choice? No one knew. The only time Manu had risen from his tormented dreams, he had addressed her with veiled eyes and incoherent words. 'When I was in the sky, Rupa, caging this spider in my eye, I felt it weave a strange web of iron threads and golden strings to pull my ears open and make me hear things. No, don't! Hear me, my love! You see, something whispered! I did not know the language, though the punctuations were full of suggestions. Anonymous in origin, apocalyptic in design. Awake in the dark, waiting for me to see them... maybe they were the future, my divination powers in play perhaps, I know not. But these visions, these suggestions... won't spell themselves till I blind myself to the care of the present – Oh, no, I can't! Iyran Machil needs to be saved!' It had been a long speech for a sick man. He had stopped to breathe, and then turned to her, eyes still trapped shut. 'If I do not use this new power to tend to the city now, it will be bruised, but if I do not see the future now, we will walk to it none the wiser till the world ends in ice and fire. My people or my race? How do I make that choice?' He had asked like a starving man might ask for food, and so Rupa had answered with what she knew Manu had wanted to hear.

'If this were my final day on this earth, my first act would be to plant a tree. A civilization grows only when leaders fell forests to shape lands they'll never live to see bloom into a city,' Rupa had said, realizing a touch belatedly that the metaphor did not quite suit Iyran Machil, a city that hadn't witnessed corpses for centuries. But she had pressed on, 'Do what you must! The world will see the value of your sacrifice when your deed becomes a memory.'

Manu had nodded weakly then, demanding a scroll and a quill, before slipping into his white-eyed slumber. That was three days ago, and his condition had not changed since. Suddenly frowning, she wiped at his beard. That clumsy daughter of hers, Akuti, had let him dribble kheer all over himself. It was as if the girl just didn't care to learn to be a woman. Akuti would ascend the throne one day, hopefully on the day when Manu took them back home. But a Queen who cannot manage her own house could hardly steer the dwindling remnants of the human race to a brighter dawn. Rupa had hoped seeing her father sick would spark the sense of duty Akuti needed but little changed. She obeyed orders she was given, but not with anything resembling grace or sincerity. Yesterday when Rupa had asked her to drip lavender drops in her father's eyes, Akuti had looked stricken. She had shaken her head, fiercely and mutely, her eyes closed shut until Rupa had ordered her off. Perhaps Akuti was seeing how far she could push her, knowing Rupa would not leave Manu's bedside. Well, she'd find Rupa Vaivasvata of Iyran Machil was not a woman easy with the whip.

Rupa shook her head, and put Akuti and Iyran Machil out of her mind. She had other, more pressing matters to attend to. She left him to write in his sleep. It was all she could do for him now. Keep him clean, replenish his quill, and leave him to die.

Bitter memories of all the plans they had discussed together trickled unbidden: when they had conspired until sunrise as they flew the skies on their windkeeper, their helms thrown aside, their faces flung open to their reflections in the clouds. 'I'm this close to finding it,' he'd promised her, 'finding a way to rid us of the poison of this foreign realm, of finding a way to harness the furies to help us build another civilization. Similar to Iyran Machil where we remain untouched by decay but different in that we can grow, where we can die, we can hunger, where we can be only half-deities, half dust.'

'Like the Daevas, the Children of Light?'

'Just like the Daevas, my love. Would you fancy that? A world a bit like theirs, a bit like this.'

'I'd rather return to the Surface,' she'd replied then, 'return home with you, have you beside me to see seasons pass. We only left to save what we could of humanity from the deluge. I know most of the continents are still under water but there are lands which remain, which have risen anew from the ocean's reign. We could join the Seven Tribes and help them rebuild. We could toil under the sun, where our reflections will be private, where we can be afraid of age and loss again so that we never take each other for granted, where we can tend to the trees with orange blossoms because we grew them from earth and not from magic, where we can be... humans again, mortal and flawed.'

'You want to return to the Surface,' he had asked with a bite in his words, 'where we will open our doors to disease, to decay, to death, where we will know suffering again?'

'Suffering is the only metric by which we can measure happiness. Either way, just divine us a way out. I cannot bear to see my girls stuck in their pigtails playing with wooden toys for another decade. I want to see them wedded and start with their own families, ruling humanity alongside their husbands. And I want *my* husband on this bed till I'm heartily sick of him.'

Fate found a cruel way to fulfil her wish.

She sighed, moving silently into the anteroom to settle herself at her desk. She looked at the reports the Marshals had brought for Manu. Those poor soldiers. Over the last three days, their expressions had slipped from comfortable to anxious, and then to what Rupa had come to think of as petrified. A hundred different tales clouded the riot's beginning. Ethari's killing spree. A coup by the Seven Tribes. An assault by the D'rahis. A sudden shortage of this or a deficit of that. March of the living dead. Perhaps none of these things had occurred. Perhaps they all had. But the riot had destroyed half the houses on this far side of Iyran Machil. It had then somehow spilled into the grand libraries, where, judging from the smoke, it raged on unchecked. Manu's garrison had set out into the streets to launch a savage campaign of pacification. In times past, Iyran Machil had been easily cowed by a few dozen cracked skulls. But not this time. It seemed they had had enough, and they fought back. The reports went out almost as swiftly as they came in, and always it seemed like she was asking a Marshal to hold the city for another day until Manu recovered. Rupa realized she could no longer believe her own lie. It was time to take matters in her own hands. She unrolled the first scroll, its contents written in a small, imprecise hand. She bent closer still, frowning at the mention of the words 'plague' and 'eyes' when she shuddered. She could no longer hear the words *'Make the Choice'* from the other room. Was… he gone?

'Rupa…' Manu's voice was like a rusted hinge breaking free. At the first sign of his senses, Rupa rushed into the room, a river of curses spilling from her lips as her foot found a fallen quill. Ignoring the pain, she reached to fetch the opium, but Manu shook his head. 'I made the wrong choice, Rupa. I was meant to find a way, and I thought I had. But this… this is something else. I now fear this creature I tried to control. I have chained it in my eyes but it has gone through my mind like thread through a needle. Everything I see is now stitched with its colour. It will soon escape and I can do nothing to stop it!'

Creature? What creature? What was he rambling on about?

'I can't control the visions, I can't control the creature!' Manu curled into himself, a sack of bones shivering, breathing in like a bellows and exhaling through clenched teeth.

'I do not understand, Manu,' Rupa said as she gently pulled the red-stained cover from over him and screamed. His chest was mutilated with a glass shard, defaced with words she dared not read. Manu suddenly seized her wrist, eyes finally open, eyes finally seeing her, one eye, the warm brown of the Manu she loved. The other, where the pupil had dissolved into a topaz ocean, that other eye belonged to a monster.

'Please, Rupa…' Manu whispered, his breath hot, his word cold. 'Run!'

III

Slices of their conversation buried themselves in the back of Manu's neck long before their footsteps reached the room. His hearing felt unusually alert. Nicked wide open by nerves, perhaps. It felt nice, a refreshing change, to feel this exposed, this alive, as he turned to face his daughters, who had escaped their mother's captivity, their mother's last desperate stab at keeping them safe… from him.

The orange glow of the fires in the reflections outside the window picked up the hollows of Akuti's face even more starkly than usual. Manu sympathized with his daughter. So much lost. So much gone. Though he could not understand if it was sadness on her face. Anger, maybe. No… it was understanding.

'You can sense it, can't you?' Manu smiled warmly. 'Akuti, you have always been special,' he said animatedly. 'Is that why you neglected your poor father in his sickbed? Out of fear?'

'Something infected you…' Akuti confessed tonelessly, eyes still on the floor.

'*Someone* infected me. A fatal mistake on their part – they thought it would end me, and it nearly did before it severed the chains that bound my Chakras instead. And now the… pestilence is chained inside my eyes.'

'Why… did you not destroy it, Father?'

'I could've destroyed it but why destroy a weapon when you can wield it. Look at me. Look into my eyes, Akuti. I am a martyr. You still don't believe me? Just look around you,' Manu spread his bloodied fingers wide, gesturing to the walls dripping with red. Red runes, red words, red symbols, all gouged and clawed into every inch of available space. 'All this is nothing compared to what I have wrought outside the palace. Akuti, do you still not see? I did it. I turned their weapon against them. I saved the world. I see the future, and I will change the ending.'

'Your heart…' Her voice trembled.

'Yes, it still races faster than it should and that was a challenge but the Orb…' his fingers tapped the smouldering gem on his forehead, 'helped me wrest control back to save the future. The future, Akuti! Now all those corpses that litter the city are not wasted deaths, but sacrifices.'

Akuti's steps faltered, her mouth making soundless words. More shock than suffering. She clutched the side wall for support, its paintings now red-spotted, and made a wailing sound. More suffer-ing than shock, this time.

Manu didn't blame her. Rupa probably didn't look like Maa now. She was propped against a wall. Her face, collapsed under his sledgehammer, looked like minced meat moulded into the shape of a bread. It certainly didn't look like a face that would be attempting to stop her husband from saving the future.

'Why have you scribbled all over the walls? You have dirtied them! You will be in trouble!' Prakruti said, in a sing-song voice. 'Oh, oh, this effigy is dressed like Maa! Can I smash it too!' saying which his younger daughter mimed the motion in the air with a 'Hiyaaah'.

'You can watch,' Manu said as he swung the sledgehammer to smash Rupa's face again. Prakruti cheered on.

'But if you are already infected,' Akuti said, 'that means… I am infected as well?

Manu let the sledgehammer fall with a dull thud. He stepped toward Akuti, wrapping an arm around her shoulders, guiding her towards the mirror. But as she lifted her gaze, he found himself distracted – not by her yellowing eyes, but by his own reflection.

Had he aged in a day? No, there were no fresh wrinkles. Then why was his hair silver? It wasn't silver, he realized. It was bleached. So were his brows and his lips. The only thing of colour that remained on his body were his grey armbraces. And of course, the red slashes carved across his wrists and his chest. He ran a finger along the cuts on his chest, feeling the script etched into his skin. The mutilation was a poem in an ancient script all but invisible on the bleeding canvas. He wiped at the blood, clearing enough to reveal the words beneath. '*Son of Darkness*? Who is that?'

'Akuti!' Prakruti called her sister, her own eyes by now had yellowed like a sky catching up with the sunrise. 'What happened to her, Father? Why does she not move?'

Before Manu could answer, the floor shook. Something had fallen – or rather, been hurled – from the sky and crashed into the palace. The roar was loud enough to separate membranes in the middle ear. Paintings slipped from their nails. Toys drifted off shelves. The concussion sent the floor wavering beneath his feet, and Manu flung his arms out for balance. Out in the hall, the crystal pendants of the chandelier chimed madly. He sessed down the palace. Felt it tear off like a rotting plank in the hands of a carpenter, the pins exploding out in puffs of sawdust. No time to spare. He scaled the window sill and, facing the pyre of Iyran Machil, jumped.

He sessed out, palms stealing grey from his own armbraces, as he channelled Wind. Air surged up from the earth to cradle his dive, but it vanished as suddenly as it had appeared. The armbraces, now bleached of all colour, had given their final offering. The dive became a fall.

When the pain of fractures became familiar enough, he dragged his gaze to look up at the reflection of the palace ruins in the mirror clouds. *Oh*, he realized when he saw himself lying alone. He had forgotten to save Akuti and Prakruti. Little was the time to dwell on remorse, however, for through the sky above, Justice was making its descent. The Seven Tribes, who had left Iyran Machil in the Exodus, had returned.

IV

Iyran Machil took seven days to devour itself. It was the seventh day.

Trisiras was impressed with Iyran Machil's resilience against his plague. The city thrashed endlessly in a futile dance of defiance, an immortal fish tossed alive onto a bed of hot coals. For far away, the purge raged. The vile and the virtuous burned together as vast sections of this diseased world were destroyed by volunteers from the returned Tribes. Heroes, all. Their sacrifices had been instrumental in chaining the plague to this realm. Just as he had predicted.

He would've still liked to witness their brave efforts but this was more important. The Judges from the Seven Tribes had by now drifted down to their tall vaikunshard chairs. Those chairs had been fashioned by a lost race to resemble the face of a creature, an aspect of the dead God. Eight aspects, eight seats, each facing the centre. The tallest seat, reserved for the Father of Mankind, remained unoccupied, as he himself was the one now chained on the floor.

'Iz the aa-oh nez-zery?' Manu rasped. Speech was still difficult. Understandable. An arrow lodged in your jaw did not lend itself to pleasant conversational skills.

One of the Judges continued his lament as if Manu had not interrupted him, 'You had a chance to stop it. You could've stopped it. Letting the present rot to save the future isn't my style, no insult to those that do. We all got our reasons. I try not to damn a man on his choice of goals to die for. But your own Codes, Realmseer… erm, I never was good at it. What was it, Janai?'

'*Dereliction's a toll,*' the woman named Janai said. She was the only one amongst the Seven who had done a neat job of blinding herself. The other judges had turned their eye sockets into hollows of horror. '*A derelict monarch foregoes the ring and bears justice's cruel sting.*' Her head snapped to the west. 'I sense uninvited visitors approaching. Manu, Shepherd of Humanity, for your crimes against the Iyran Machil, we, the Seven, condemn you to—'

Trisiras was rudely startled by Manu's answering scream. He sessed zinth course through the madman's nadis in a bid to loosen his anguish on the world.

'I was told there was no colour,' one of the other Judges said. 'How is he drawing power?'

'From his organs,' Janai said. 'He is bleaching his lungs! Such raw power cannot exist.'

'And it will not,' the Judge replied. 'Now!'

Six arrows flew from six bows through Manu's neck, through Manu's chest and through Manu's waist to make a reclining throne for the Father of Mankind. And that was that.

Funerals and farewells, in Trisiras's experience, were like watching paint dry. He would rather return to the City and marvel at his art instead, and of course, meet the uninvited visitors Janai had keenly sensed. Fortunately, his cheeks were as dark as midnight, as was common with the race of Danavas, the Children of Dark. And midnight was a charming colour, not only to set off his purple eyes but to conceal him as he escaped into the Iyran's shadows.

He slunk down streets scattered with slaughtered children, disabled horses and strewn insides. Soon, rutted mud turned to straw-streaked dirt, to cobbled stones, to new paving, till he finally found a tower untouched by the carnage. When he reached its terrace to take in the sights, he was not disappointed.

Iyran Machil had become a city wardrobed out of a fevered dream. The carcasses of four D'rahis lay strewn in a ragged row, their wings torn apart. Where their blood had spilled out, it had fused with the lifeless soil to grow taloned roots of the largest tree in this realm. Perhaps a thousand reaches tall, its trunk stood mighty, a tapestry of intricate patterns on it resembling coiled scales, a legacy to the legendary creatures whose blood gave it birth. The marigold flowers on the tree, their petals brushed with hues of fire, fanned out in a reminder of the flames that burned down Iyran Machil.

Trisiras hummed a tune as he jotted down his observations for his manuscript on mankind. Occasionally, he paused to admire the sky, which hung heavy with clouds to serve as twisted mirrors.

He cut a stocky, stout, weathered figure in the reflections with his layered snowy hair but the star markings splashed across his face like freckles made him look very young and handsome, despite being eternities old. True, his shoulder and his neck were charred by the fire from Manu's staff when Trisiras had infected him, but it was a trifling price to pay to see how his invention would yield fruit. *Or flowers*, he chuckled as he absently sketched a marigold in the margin of the page. But his reflection did not chuckle back, rather it broke into tears. Disturbed, Trisiras returned to his manuscript.

From what Trisiras had gathered, the Seven Justices planned to sacrifice themselves after sealing Iyran Machil from the outside world. In the days to come, the trace of the plague would be erased. The ash-ridden winds would salt Iyran Machil's ruins. Nothing would be allowed, spirit or scribe, to speak of the horrors of this day to any passing bard. Survivors, if any, would perish out of starvation after Manu's death and death of that damned gem on his forehead, and with that, the destruction of Iyran Machil would be complete. A good plan.

Hopefully the Daevas, who he now sensed approach from behind, would feel the same way. Still... who approached? Faraladar? Merene? Vosei Rune? Curiosity made him turn rather than wait for the answer. *Interesting.*

Anyone acquainted with Thorin Drazeus, King of the Daevas, the Children of Light, would have pictured him hunched over his lunch directing at a blameless aubergine a look of such hatred that the poor vegetable would have sizzled beneath it. He had favoured mankind over other races of mortals after all. Therefore, it surprised Trisiras to see Thorin going about the place with a beaming smile and a spring to his step. Especially when his pristine white clothes were sheathed in the gore of the infected humans who had probably attacked him on his way. Only the marigold petals stuck in his hair gave any contest to the rest of the stink from him.

'Trisiras!' Thorin laughed. 'In a single night you have turned a city of promises into a pyre of carcasses. See what the Light and Dark can achieve together? How far back do you think this has pushed their civilization by?'

'The pestilence, perhaps by a few hundred years. But the burning of books, scholars and acolytes ordered by Manu in his madness,' Trisiras exhaled, 'all the way back.'

'All the way back,' Thorin repeated, grinning. Trisiras could not remember the last time he had seen this wide an emotion on a Daeva face. 'I like that. Your gamble paid off, I see.'

'You may throw dice with their fates, Thorin. I play *Shatranj*, and that is a precise endeavour.'

'Shatranj?' Savitre Lios appeared. 'May your Night be Bright, Your Grace,' Savitre greeted Thorin before turning again to Trisiras, 'Hope the others don't find out you've been using two queens all along.' His voice had that light veneer of humour that he used to avoid admitting how horrified he truly was.

'I care not for the game but the result,' Thorin declared. 'Manu had known too much already.'

Trisiras nodded amusingly. 'But it was Manu's greed for knowledge, his thirst to know the future that came in his way, or else he would have undone my gift all on his own.'

Thorin raised his golden eyebrow in a blend of awe and anger. 'Men and their filthy Chakras and their filthy Gems.'

'Why don't you deploy the cure now?' Savitre prodded, the patterns tattooed on his lean ivory arms glowing faintly. When Thorin shot Savitre an odd glance, he hastily amended, 'At this rate of destruction, there will be no one left to harvest.'

'There is no cure,' Trisiras said. 'Besides, the Seven Judges have already contained it in the Chaining and the yellow dust I blew into Manu's eyes was the only sample,' he lied. 'It will take decades to brew another.' That part, at least, was true enough.

'One time was all that was needed,' Thorin said. 'A push to guide these lost souls.'

'This will force the mortals to forge alliances,' Savitre warned. 'They will war against us.'

'They will lose,' Thorin said. 'With this,' Thorin snatched the scroll that Trisiras had been scribbling on, 'with their secrets exposed, we know now their weaknesses. Let them band together. It will be easier to destroy them in one great war rather than countless small skirmishes.' He casually tossed the journal back to Trisiras's lap, missing the flash of rage on his face. 'All thanks to...' he turned to Trisiras, 'what are you going to name this beautiful plague of yours?'

Trisiras looked up at the colossal marigold tree's reflection in the mirrored sky, and just smiled.

The three sat there for a long time watching the city crumble. Iyran Machil, the cradle and now the grave of a civilization, was the evidence of the lie in the immortality of a world. Worlds, it seemed, could be slain.

Even the world of the Children of Light, Trisiras mused as he plotted to rally his Danavas against the Daevas in the future. He just had to bide his time.

But everything always goes exactly as planned, said no one ever.

Unfortunately for the Daevas, the mortal races did band together, just as Savitre had foreseen, and drove the Daevas from their realm in the Siege of Tyrants.

Regrettably for the Danavas, before Trisiras could unleash his plague on the Daevas, along came a descendant of Manu by the name of Muchuk Und to sever his head on Thorin's behalf. Thorin would later betray Muchuk Und, plunging both the plague and the warlord into the murk of legend. Alas, for the realms, legends had other plans, for they both were found again.

AEONS LATER

TAMRA LIPTA

6 MONTHS BEFORE THE BATTLE OF MATHURA

The woman billed as Matakshara 'Wraith' Harran received a fair share of unsavoury correspondence but this was the first time a request for murder had arrived carefully pinned to the robe of the same girl she'd been petitioned to murder. The two clergy who'd escorted the blindfolded lass had refused to explain at the door. When pestered, one o' them had simply tugged at the ragged robe about his neck. The sight of a crimson scarf stitched with runes from the North had been enough. Matakshara made a mental note to reward the man later for keeping his wits and admitting them without further ceremony.

Matakshara, however, did not need to see red to know the Order these pious gentlemen belonged to. The shiver crawling up her spine on the heels of an abandoned memory reminded her of their pedigree. Still, Matakshara did not rise, and rather leaned back, one hand behind her head. The other emptied the arsenal of knives from her belt on the table.

The gentlemen, who she'd named the Twins, settled into their seats without greeting her. One still carried that hospitable smile which hid a world of harm behind it. It was he who took the girl's hand, and ushered her forward. Though blindfolded, the girl used her hands as a lantern to guide her. Stubbed her toe against the table but gracefully hid the evidence of the pain. Using the table's edge as her mooring, she finally arrived on the other side.

Matakshara ripped the envelope from the girl's robe, leaving the pin obediently clinging to its button. Just then, two servants brought her guests cups of tea with lumps of sugar on the side. But the cups remained on the desk, untouched, growing cold as Matakshara read the letter. She skimmed over the contents, any prediction by its author of horror in the reader failing miserably. Matakshara lingered only on the relevant facts: that the girl was now in her custody, that she was carrying an ancient affliction and that it fell on Matakshara to deliver her to her destination.

'A delight to deal with fellow professionals,' the Twin with the grin said to his brother. 'Didn't I tell you? The Sealord of Tamra Lipta in the flesh! She did not flinch once!'

'Would that help?' Matakshara asked.

'No,' the grim Twin answered. 'Possible for you, pirate? In the manner orchestrated?'

Matakshara leaned back, exposing her loose black vest decorated with cuts that had more to do with close calls than the latest fashion. 'The price for something of this magnitude… and well, given how it is personal, would be what you fancy greens call exorbitant. Savvy?'

The Twins did not respond in words. One grinned. The other scowled.

'Good.' Gold was never a concern for the Red Order of Meru. Quite fair, given how their misdeeds were never of the simple stock. Planned by their oracles, each death was a link in an unseen long chain that shackled the realm. This girl was no different – a butterfly soon to flap her wings, unleashing a storm that would lay waste to half the realm.

She escorted the girl to a secure room, not knowing what else to do with her till the time came. Such a little girl, such a heavy burden. But the sea has neither conscience nor mercy. Fortunately for Matakshara, this girl was mightily well behaved. She perched on an uncomfortable chair without a murmur, did not move, did not fidget, her hands folded still in her lap, her poise at complete odds with the line of framed bills advertising the current bounty on Matakshara Harran.

'You seem like a butterfly, my dear, so I'll call you that, alright?' It would become evident later that it wasn't. Despite several attempts in the following weeks, the girl adamantly declined to acknowledge anything other than her name. Princesses were a pain in the arse.

In her moments of solitude later, Matakshara would wonder if she had ever hurt a princess. She couldn't recollect any. Princes, a fair share. Kings, aplenty. No princess. *Hold the sails.* Matakshara recalled a time when she damn near sent her First Mate to the Ocean Goddess. Aye, she'd definitely hurt her. *Surely that counts*, for the said First Mate had been a Princess once. *Empress,* she corrected herself with a smug smile. *Mati is an Empress. For now.*

The thought upset Matakshara. Mati did not deserve it. But then again, 'deserve' had got nothing to do with it. It was just Fate's hand that Mati had unwittingly drawn the card marked 'Marigold Mold'.

ADHYAYA I:A

THE SWAN AND THE SLUT

RAJGRIH, CAPITAL OF THE MAGADHAN EMPIRE

3 MONTHS AFTER THE SWAYAMVAR

6 MONTHS BEFORE THE BATTLE OF MATHURA

'The willing are led by fate, the reluctant dragged.'
—Cleanthes of Assos

MATI

I

Mati was staring at a stranger. Eyes the colour of a storm, a crescent-shaped bindi between them, and a bruised nose, slim at the bridge, broad towards the end. All this she recognized. Yet she saw how wifehood had changed her. Wind-tousled short hair that once just about tickled her jaw lay combed to her shoulders, perfumed, and neatly parted, with a slash of vermillion marking the centre line like a stripe on a sacrificial lamb. Collarbones once free to frolic with the breeze were now buried under golden chains, and wrists that wore rope bands now jingled under the weight of golden bangles as heavy as shackles. She caught sight of her wedding gift in the reflection of the mirror, a tapestry of a monstrous swan locked in a skirmish with a majestic shark, and wondered, not for the first time, how in this fairy tale had the bloody Black Swan transformed into the Bedecked Duck?

'My love,' Saham Dev breathed from behind, his arms snaking around her waist. With a tender touch, he swivelled her to face him. By now Mati had arranged her hair to conceal the itchy red welts on her cheeks. 'Oh, just look at the state of you! I am a wretch! Can you possibly find it in your heart to forgive me this time?'

Who wouldn't want to forgive that face? Not out of a melted heart but a mortified one. The face of the son of Jarasandh was strangely soft and had only grown softer since his ill-fated decision to part with his beard. If not for the delicate wisp of vegetation above his upper lip, the Crown Prince might've even passed off as pretty, the sort of pretty Mati sold off as slaves in the Golden Islands.

'You know I only want the best for you,' Saham Dev said with genuine concern. 'The Conclave is nigh, a few full moons away, and here you were, still feasting on the dinner table like a marauding pirate.'

'I reckon I did tell you, eatin' cabbage plasters my face with hives.'

Saham traced the scaly rashes on her face. With the edge of his sleeve, he wiped a hint of vomit from her lips. 'I stand corrected, don't I? If anything, this fortifies the bridge of trust between us. I thought you were just being a spoilt brat. You know how you Kalingans are, indulging in raw fish straight from the seas. A jest, of course! But what is true is that eating vegetables is what distinguishes us from the primitive man, and yet, you never touch anything green, Bhanumati. I daresay that is why you've spent the last three months in a most disagreeable state of gastric distress.'

Mati. But she did not correct him. Not now. Not when, for the past week, for every single meal, Saham had her served cabbage and had his Rakhjai see to it that Mati remained seated until the last leaf was swallowed. The first time, Mati had flung the cabbage soup at the Rakhjai's face. It was at that moment Mati grasped the finer point of Rakhjai etiquette: while striking royal blood was strictly off-limits, royal spouses, it seemed, were fair sport. So, Mati, with a bloodied nose and bruised pride, had retched her way through the ordeal instead.

'But dinner was… Your own wife! Why did you…' Mati couldn't help but cringe at the memory. Of how her eyes had softened when Saham Dev had brought to her side a bucket with his own hands and softly suggested she use it if necessary.

'Why did I what?' Saham Dev asked, unbelievably clueless, and then pouted when he saw Mati's expression. 'I am sorry, my moon. But surely you know just how unsightly I found you then! There is a regal way to retch, Princess. You cannot expel food so without shielding the scene of the crime. At the very least, once you're through, wipe your lips. The way you slouched against the chair after, the droopy grime on your chin, it was so revolting! I nearly lost my own lunch just from seeing your lips.'

'And so you commanded your dog of a guard to thrust my head into the bucket and wipe the fucking bottom with my face till you concluded your meal!' As Mati gave vent to the words, her hand groped for something sharp behind her on the mirror's desk while her mind desperately tried to scream caution. *Remember your vengeance.*

'I know, I know, I have been excessive.' And then his expression darkened. 'But why must you always knowingly act so barbaric to stir my ire so, my love? Do you derive some perverse pleasure from provocation?' Saham Dev closed his eyes and took a deep, dramatic breath. 'I do not wish to let my passions turn red again. Just come here!'

He suddenly kissed her cheeks, lifting her in a half-circle spin. Mati would've preferred the cabbage. She soon landed, and looked up to find her reflection again, whispering soundlessly in the mirror. Two fingers below his ear, twist at the right angle and her husband would drop dead. *Do it! Just... fucking do it! Just—*

'Let all that be in the annals of the past, my love,' Saham Dev interrupted his death. 'Now we are square, are we not? The Rakhjai was my favourite. Yes, *was*. I know what you did. He was simply following orders because I would never, ever lay my own hands on my wife. But do you see me throwing a fit at you for murdering him?' He left the hug only to press another tender kiss to her cheek. 'No. I swept that affair under the rug, and now, none will get wind of it.'

Saham Dev was not wrong. The consequences for murdering a Rakhjai would've had her facing a sight worse than a pail of her own vomit. Crucified in that ghastly arena of theirs? Rolled down Yama's Hands into the fire pits? Blinding? Mati vented a sigh. Saham Dev was good as her guardian, as her bulwark, as someone who had her back against the world. Why did he have to be such a rat bastard though? And the worst part was that all this rat-bastardry was such an unwelcome surprise given his illustrious reputation as the most celebrated coward of Magadh. After all, the entire court called him Saham the Spineless behind his back. A formless drop of water which would trickle down any slope that offered itself. But turned out that once he shut that door to his room, this drop of water curiously froze into the shape of a limp-cocked warlord, knowledge only his wife and his personal staff was privy to. How lucky was Mati! *You are no prize, either. Or have you forgotten?*

'Nothing to say, my sweet?' Saham Dev prodded.

'Should I thank you?'

'You never have to, my sarcastic butterfly. You will be Queen of the World. All I do,' he scowled at a stray speck of filth in Mati's hair and plucked it out to flick it away, 'is to civilize you. And I know just how to make you happy. Behold!' He plucked out a shiny key with a flourish. Rather small in size to make Mati happy. 'The verification of ownership lineage is complete. Can you believe this tiny trinket is a Rakshasan Relic? The Empire in a gesture of benevolence will return this cultural treasure to the Tree Cities and mark my words, the Leeches will be grateful. And who knows? Maybe toss a few more airavats our way.'

Mati was adrift in the sea of Saham Dev's chatter until a recollection bobbed to the surface. It was all Saham Dev talked about these days. The Emperor had secured Bhagadatt's support in the Yamuna War. A pact inked in the ill-fated Panchalan Swayamvar. Airavats were to hoof their way from the East, gold in return. This grand alliance was to be solemnized at the Conclave of Monarchs in the Tree City of Kamrup where Saham Dev, much to Mati's surprise, was chosen to champion the Empire's cause. And then, once winter waned, Mathura would either be trampled underfoot by airavat-mounted Magadhans or burned alive by blazebane-hurling Greeks. Or both.

Though Mati wondered how the Empire's new ally, Bhagadatt, would take to Saham Dev's use of slurs against the Rakshasas should he accidentally let one slip out at the Conclave. Execution by airavat? Tossed off a cliff? Life in a Seed Pod? Imagining the diverse ways Saham Dev would be killed soothed her, allowing her to give the key the attention it deserved.

The key was a fine thing. It could fetch a tidy sum in Tamra Lipta's black market. The surface had a tapestry of delicate filigree work. But it was the flawless sapphire nestled in its heart that was the prize. Around it, symbols of Elemental wind were etched in silver, legible enough to leave a seasoned Namin of the Orange Order, the priests who studied arcana and history in Meru, weak in the knees. 'What does it open?'

'Nothing important, I assure you, or else we wouldn't be parting with it. But what is diplomacy if not a dance of hollow gestures. I am still pinching myself over the fact that Father chose me as the envoy! Come, let me open a bottle of a Vidarbhan vintage to celebrate this.'

Ale. The master key to her heart. *Kill him... Run away, Mati...* The voice faded this time without any effort. It was becoming easier with time to silence it. 'Cause even if she did, who would she run to? The world, after all, had disowned Mati of Magadh.

The thing is when Mati had seduced Saham Dev into wedding her, it had been to find a man more powerful than Duryodhan to cook her that sweet morsel of payback at Panchal. Vengeance was sustenance. But here was the rub. It caused indigestion when heated over haste. Blinded by rage, she had not realized how marrying into the Magadhan Empire that had tamed the freedom-loving, rule-breaking pirates of Kalinga was a crime amongst the Kalingans second only to setting sail without a cat on board. She'd still reached out to invite them – her friends, her old crew, her former lovers, her doting father – invite them to her wedding to explain. Pirates understood vengeance, after all. But her ravens returned empty-taloned. She had done nothing wrong, Saham Dev had said, and if the Kalingans were going to be ungrateful curs about it, they best be left tied outside the gate till they learned their manners. 'Don't force them to want you. Let them miss you instead.' Hard not to see merit in that. But to see none of her trusted shipmates make the journey for her grand wedding had caused a great pang. At least dear old Father had graced the occasion, if only to dole out dowry to the Emperor. But blessings for his own flesh and blood? Those were in short supply.

Fuck her friends. Fuck her father. Fuck Kalinga. She had no time to mourn the indifference of heartless pirates. She would be too busy in the enthusiasm of her new subjects. She was the future Empress, after all. People would be lining up to win her favours. Surely one of them would be of moderate intelligence or beautiful enough for Mati's friendship. Even when those queues turned up empty, Mati refused to lose heart. They all were naturally intimidated. A captain doesn't make friends, she reminded herself. She lures a crew.

Mati made anonymous donations to the local Ehtral temple. The handmaiden Saham Dev had gifted her artfully let slip Mati's identity as the mysterious benefactor in the right circles. Oh, how Mati had loved her plan! Was there anything more delightful than doing a good deed in secret only for it to become public later. It certainly would've been delightful had the temple not returned her donation when they found out the funds were, in their words, 'tainted'.

Turns out the subjects who Mati was destined to rule disliked her as if she were one of Krishna's spies. And it was only when Saham Dev comforted her did she learn that her unpopularity had nothing to do with her résumé of murder and mayhem.

The power-hungry noblemen disliked Mati, laying the blame for Kalinga's sudden ascent from a protectorate to the First Family squarely at her feet. Understandable. Jarasandh had built the Three Walls of Mathura for his last son by law. This time, he'd been a touch less theatrical, settling for exempting Kalinga from tributes for ten years.

The pious clergy scorned Mati for her choice of deities. Again, understandable. The Greens were fools, ignorant of the truths of the ocean and the skies. The gossiping ladies of the court despised her for... well, women had always despised her. Nothing new in that. Who cared about those women? To think of it, who cared about the gentry? She would win the hearts of people. They were the only ones who mattered.

But when on her inaugural court appearance Mati saw fit to break the nose of the darling of Magadh, all her plans went awry. To be fair to Mati, the lady in question had complained about soaring fish prices when Mati had passed her by. What else did they expect Mati to do? Stuff jasmine in her pits? *Perhaps I should've.* Little had Mati realized a single punch would unwittingly fashion her own gilded prison. The Emperor had Mati banished from court and confined to her tower until the woman's nose healed. The woman ended up serving curdled milk to her infant that night, who succumbed to dysentery. Overwhelmed by guilt for having been unable to sniff out the spoiled dairy (because of her bandaged nose), she jumped to her death. Now no one in their right mind would blame Mati for the tragic, unforeseeable chain of events. Unfortunately for Mati, no one would argue that the Emperor was ever in his right mind, especially not when that woman had taken her life in the same way his own daughter had, a year past.

And so, here Mati was, perched in her tower, the loneliest woman in the world with a newfound passion for puking. Granted, it wasn't much of a loss. Stepping out to enjoy the city, where the favoured pastime was stoning the disliked, was hardly an enticing prospect. But still, it was hard on her to discover the difference between solitude and isolation.

'Princess Bhanumati?' Saham Dev intruded upon her thoughts. 'Drink?'

And when one is marooned all by themselves on an island prison, what choice do they have when the warden offers a drink?

'Lead the way, husband.'

II

'Putrid drinks at night, privy dungeon in the morning, that is the rule.' Her eunuch guard chimed in with the other servants as Mati dashed into the necessary in the morning. Mati could hear the giggles even as she lay hunched over the basin, hurling food out. 'When I had balls,' the guard continued, 'I could empty a barrel without a burp. But these days...'

An old woman, in charge of the cushions, protested, 'Wine doesn't gift you the bad squirts in the head.'

The eunuch snorted. 'That is rubbish. It all depends on how much you drink.'

'It is not the Princess's fault,' a little girl said. 'The Prince egged her on. To celebrate, he said. Celebrate what, he didn't.'

'Hush, child,' the eunuch warned even as Mati stumbled out the door.

''Tis because I'm definitely growing older,' Mati settled the debate as she brushed damp strands of her growing hair up from her forehead. 'What I drank last night was barely an indulgence compared to what I can swallow. And now. Even the thought of ale... oh, here it comes.' She gagged and heaved but nothing trickled out.

False alarm. She could not believe she could no longer hold her ale. With age was supposed to come wisdom but somewhere on the way the wise mind swapped places with a weak liver.

Mati, eyes closed to thwart the head spinning, dismissed her guards and made her way alone to the designated room for her clothes. By now Saham Dev's private palace had become her ship, and the fortress around the palace a perilous sea she could not swim in. She was used to navigating the palace with the familiarity of a circus acrobat. But today the climb up the stairs to the closet room seemed a lot steeper. She would have rested against the wall when she reached the room if she hadn't been so furious at how weak she had become. She was about to find a weapon to throw at the golden chandelier when she heard a polite cough to interrupt her tantrum.

A strange woman came in bearing a fresh set of clothes to replace the one Saham Dev had thrown his glass of wine at. Another new attendant? Another replacement? Her handmaidens, all Magadhans, had been changed on almost a weekly basis. Mati should just ink a manual on how to behave as a Kalingan's handmaiden, to save her the trouble of training yet another one.

'Your Grace.' The servant woman raised her hands, a hanger suspended from each. 'The pink sequined blouse or the stringed red one?'

Mati ignored the damn blouses for a comfortable linen shirt from her wardrobe. When she opened it, she found an organized tailor's private collection rather than her dishevelled, badly folded clothes. Her new handmaiden beamed behind her. 'I took the liberty to make sure all the clothes in the wardrobe were cleaned, pressed and arranged as per colours on your shelves.' Mati shook her head as she picked out a white shirt and put her hands through it. But when she struggled to close the button at her waist, Mati's rage returned. Her callused hand backhanded the handmaiden hard. 'Listen, you laundry hag, if you shrink another one of my shirts, I will shove the eunuch's gobbled parts down your mouth, savvy?'

'I did not shrink it, Your Grace! I swear, I did not!'

'Well, it had to be one of your ilk then, wouldn't it? Or are you saying I have turned fat?'

The servant's face went slack with horror as the implications fumbled their way into her head. 'I would never, Princess! Your beauty poisons the Magadhans with envy. You are—' Before the servant could complete her bumbling apology, Mati darted for the privy again.

'Princess, are you alright? You look dreadful,' the servant said as she peeked inside.

If one more member of the royal staff uttered their concern, she would lose her breakfast on their face. Mati rubbed at her chest furiously as she bent over, hoping she could keep the nausea at bay. When had she turned so weak? Her stomach used to be lined with iron. And then the servant's words rearranged themselves into an epiphany. *Your beauty poisons the Magadhans with envy.* Mati's whisper was a cold breath, 'Someone is poisoning me.'

III

'No one is poisoning you. You are just growing used to finely cooked food and fine condiments. So, stomach in, chin up. Come, I've brought you a present,' Saham Dev whistled. 'I know you are used to slaves in your part of the world and it certainly doesn't help that the handmaidens here have not been trained to serve a woman like you. Well, we don't have slaves or at least, we don't call them that, but I found you a solution.' He winked. 'Come, little girl. She is a high Resht, one of the girls from my school for orphans,' he whispered, 'so while she is well-trained in home remedies and herbal concoctions, she is uneducated in the manners of a royal household. A perfect match, don't you think? Amala, come in.'

Another handmaiden? *Storms.* The girl who entered had a soft face as sad as the first time Mati had seen her dusting the chandelier in their room. Her arms were willowy, decorated with flowery tattoos that twirled out from the Resht mark of the spade on her neck. She was the youngest handmaiden Mati had been gifted so far, and definitely the first lowborn. Maybe she would be less of a bore.

Saham Dev continued. 'She will...' he waved his hand over Mati's face and stomach, 'fix this. Fret not, my love. Alright, I must go on my disguise-walk. Tonight, I head to the Tulips. Let's see what the officers gossip about the Empire when they think no one is listening.'

'You're going without a Rakhjai?'

'Well, I can't find a replacement as swiftly as your hands thrust the knife into his side, now, can I? And I don't want the ones loyal to Father. I need my own man. But worry not. No one has recognized me in the last few months,' he said as he kissed her cheek and walked out the room. Mati doubted anyone would recognize him even without a disguise.

Mati tossed herself on the bed for a nap, paying no mind to Saham Dev's gift. But the moment Mati cocooned herself inside the blanket, her intestines rebelled. Again.

'I just came from it!' she complained to her stomach as she crawled her way out of the blanket. It did not matter. All her innards suddenly found the privy to be a far better place to spend time in than on her majestic four-poster bed. When she returned, she found Amala scooping up the wicker basket at the foot of the bed.

The little girl had never met her eyes before, and she did not change that now. Mati felt her heart thaw a bit for her husband. Despite his faults, the maniac cared for his people. These weekly sojourns, the adoption and employment of Resht orphans, his donations to the families who found themselves homeless after the Ehtral Edicts, all these acts of charity did much to save his life every time Mati came close to stabbing him. Mati sighed as she looked at Amala and decided to let her feel useful.

'Girl, comb my hair? I do a terrible job of it.' Mati missed her short hair that she could comb just with her fingers. But in return for the gifts he gave, all Saham Dev had requested was for her to keep her hair long. *Not a single woman in Magadh wears her hair like a man,* he had said. *You can't be a queen of the masses if they are not bewitched by what they see.* And so, she had relented. When she had to tie her hair into a short pony for the first time, she felt she had died. No. That was not tragic enough. Death was not a tragedy. The tragedy was what died inside of you while you were still alive.

But what could Mati do? A small request of her husband. A small retreat by the wife. How long before the tide washed over, and there was nothing left of the shore?

Amala took Mati's tangled hair gently in her hands and began untying the knots. Mati watched Amala in the mirror as she did this. The girl's face looked so innocent. But she was not innocent, was she? She was a Resht. Born in the gutters. You don't survive the comforts of the gutter – the filth, the pain, the hunger, the injustice and the betrayal – by remaining innocent. *Not true. Karna was innocent till you corrupted him.*

'I still feel sick,' Mati said suddenly, dismissing that thought. 'Food that doesn't stay, waist that doesn't stop. You Reshts have any home remedy for this?' Amala shook her head. 'Is it perhaps a season of flu in Rajgrih, then?' Amala shook her head. 'Thought as much. Enough with the hair. I need to take a stroll on the terrace. Help me with this kamarband.' *Another gift.* 'I will cinch in my waist, and then you hook it.' Mati stood up and inhaled deeply. She observed the girl's careful touch in the mirror as she wrapped the kamarband around Mati's bare waist in the saree. 'Tell you what, you find a potion to rid me of the purges, and this—' Amala squeaked a gasp to cut her offer off. Mati chuckled. 'I've not even mentioned the reward yet.' But Amala did not respond. She left the kamarband on the dressing table and went on to sift through the room's wicker baskets.

'Girl, what are you doing?'

'Thousand pardons, Your Grace.' Amala went on her knee and bowed after she was done with her raid. 'But there is something wrong with your flows, isn't there? Up until last night, I was in charge of the waste baskets and the chamberpots on this floor, and I don't remember taking out any bloodied muslins in a long while.'

Clearly this girl hadn't the faintest notion of how to talk to a Princess, which Mati found rather refreshing. Perhaps they might just get along. 'Not that I keep a tally. They have always been moody ever since I took to ship life. Now why, pray tell, are you asking about my bloodied muslins, lass?' she asked, smiling.

Mati could hear the ill squelch as Amala swallowed. 'You are with child, Princess.'

IV

Mati's heart was beating with considerable urgency. She might not have liked how her body looked now in the mirror but she had been wrong to doubt its competence. She thought it hadn't worked! Oh, had the nausea been a sign? What would she know? Her mother had left before she had bled. And her father, well, he'd never treated her as a daughter but as his First Mate, the old salt. Even her conversations with the other women in ports had been confined to plunders and lovers, not exactly the stuff of maternal guidance. Such oversight had been careless of her but understandable. Between wooing Saham Dev, hiring blades to kill Draupadi, abducting Duryodhan and arranging supplies for arson in Panchal, Mati had had little time to read a book or chat up a midwife. She now needed to gather all necessary intelligence about these wretched doldrums she would be navigating for the next nine months. Or was it six? No matter. She would sort it out in due course. But for now, she was going to celebrate and thank the Ocean Goddess! What she had been waiting for had finally happened. And about time.

Not one to let anger trickle away, Mati had dammed it. It did not matter if it submerged whole valleys of her soul. But given how *charming* her married life was turning out to be, that dam had been on the verge of collapse. The humiliation, the anger, the rage all leaking away through the cracks… until today. For her plan had worked. Fate had not only mended the dam but also dug a small channel at its base to let the stream of molten resolve irrigate her fields of vengeance.

But first, she had to take care of a possible locust.

'It is not possible…' Mati found Amala whispering as the Resht darted nervously about the room. Amala's eyes widened when she learned Mati had already emerged from the privy and that perhaps what she had been whispering was not something to be muttered out loud. Her fear was well founded. Mati's arm snapped out to grasp Amala's collar. The Resht gasped as she was hoisted off her feet and then slammed against the wall.

'Speak,' Mati demanded in a low voice. When Amala shook her head, Mati squeezed harder. 'I'm sure you've heard how I skewered a

Rakhjai and got away with it. Do you think they will complain if my hands are wet with the blood of a Resht? You will be just another handmaiden Saham Dev will have buried in the backyard.'

Amala's feet dangled, her slippers kicking against Mati's shins. Mati lifted her higher, as if she was no more than a sack of sails, before tossing her to the floor. Amala gave a shuddering groan, stretched out a quivering hand asking Mati to stop even as Mati calmly lifted her heel and dug into Amala's palm on the floor. Amala bit her other hand to choke her scream. Smart girl. It was definitely not her first tryst with torture.

'Speak.'

'We *know*.' These two words, spoken between sobs, carried with it the force of a spell to temporarily unlock the Black Swan's cage.

Kraken take me! 'Take me to the Prince.'

Amala, sobbing, led her to the Prince's chambers. Along the way, Mati dismissed the servants in waiting, who scampered away. Outside, Mati waited as Amala hesitated at the Prince's door, and then disappeared inside. She emerged within a matter of heartbeats, almost looking relieved, and beckoned Mati inside. Mati walked into the room to find Saham Dev frowning, face only half concealed in cosmetics to disguise him as a Resht. 'Did Amala disappoint you in any way, my sweet?'

'Is there anyone else inside the room?'

'No.'

Mati grabbed Saham Dev's collar. He protested but Mati struck him. Hard enough to snap his head to one side. Blood spilled from his mouth. That made her happy, but she could not let herself be distracted. He spat, coughed and then spat again as Mati pushed him on the bed. She straddled him as she held his wrists together over him with one hand. Saham Dev's short height made it easy for her to do so while simultaneously unlacing his breeches. She spat in her palm, rubbed it all over his shaft, and then stroked him with a religious fervour. The sheath kept getting caught, the movement not fluid enough, the shaft not iron enough. Saham Dev struggled in her grip, but he did not shout. He would not. What would he complain to his guards? That his wife was forcing him to bed her against his will.

She spat more, spat so much that her mouth ran dry. But it did not work. 'Sail, dammit!' She used every trick in the book, she used her nails, she bit, she pulled air as if she was drawing venom out of a snakebite. It did temporarily stiffen but then it flopped out. 'Fuck!' Mati cried out and stared at Saham Dev's face with raw fury. The cruelty behind Saham Dev's laughter in reply robbed her of her breath and her pride.

And with that, her gambit failed. Mati released her hold, panting with the effort. One would think a lifetime of swinging through ropes would have kept her arms in a finer shape. Saham Dev rose softly and used the sleeve of Mati's loose white shirt to wipe her saliva off his cock. Mati knew she would be punished for this later. For now, Saham Dev returned to his mirror to complete his disguise.

Feeling an uneven dread grate through her throat, Mati wiped her lips and rose to leave. Before Mati left the door, Saham Dev called out, talking to her through the reflection in his mirror. 'My love... you know seducing a man is not difficult at all when the woman is feminine and divine. But impossible,' he scoffed as he said it, 'if she acts like a hyena in heat. I thought I had come a long way in civilizing you. My mistake. More work is needed.' He laughed as if suddenly realizing. 'You know something. I can see why Duryodhan gave up on you. Not because he fancied Draupadi. No, no. It was simply because he did not want *you*.' He laughed again at his epiphany. 'Wise man, your love.' Saham Dev's laughter cut Mati like broken glass.

This time she decided to cut him back with the shards. 'You're going to be a father.'

V

'I'm sorry, Princess, I'm sorry,' Amala pleaded. 'But please don't do this. I... I did not mean to, I cannot... I will be condemned to be reborn as a termite, please, Princess, I don't want to sin—'

But Mati's attention was not rooted to the present. Saham Dev had not said another word. He hadn't even moved his head to show he'd heard when Mati had told him that Saham Dev was going to be a father. The silence had stretched out till Mati had decided and demanded she needed house plants for the baby. Saham Dev had only said the word 'Amala' and then returned to dabbing tar on his face. *Storms*. Mati should've tried to fuck him again before revealing he was going to be a father. Or sourced silphium juice and laced his milk to consummate their wedding when he fell unconscious. But the urge to hurt, when hurt, could cripple your wits. So much for damming the anger. It was only her good fortune that there was no Rakhjai currently employed, or Mati wondered if she would've left the room without a miscarriage.

'Please, Princess, I don't want to sin—'

'What are you babbling about?' Mati asked, irritated.

'Belladona? Hemlock? For house plants!' Amala fell to her knees, Mati's list still in her hand. 'These are poisons! You are going to poison your unborn child.'

Mati looked at Amala for a long while, contemplating whether she should smother the girl. Mati's eyes went to the mark on Amala's neck again. Perhaps, there was an easier way. 'Is there someone you want saved, Amala?' Mati asked, slowly, enunciating each word.

Amala, for the first time, looked up to meet Mati's eyes. 'I... do not understand.'

'Seems rather self-explanatory. Do you want someone saved?'

Amala squinted at Mati. The poor thing did not know if she could trust Mati but little girls, no matter how early they are forced to grow up, do not leave their naïve habits behind. Mati should know. 'My mother,' Amala confessed.

'Weren't you an orphan?'

'I... Mother thought it best...' She looked down, ashamed.

'Ah, the better life. Commendable. Where is she now?'

'She is a cartwoman. Carts dead bodies from the Ehtral temple to—'

Mati's eyes raised by a fraction. 'You are no Resht, are you? You are an Untouchable.' Amala recoiled back at the word. 'Hey, there, little girl. I'm a Kalingan, remember. The Magadhans think of me worse than you lot. So you're in good hands, lass. You do as I say, and I will have your mother working in the royal kitchens as a help. Do we have an accord? I mean, a deal?'

Amala nodded, hope flooding her eyes and the corners of her lips. 'Yes, Princess. Anything.'

'Anything. Just save my mother. What do I have to do, Your Grace?'

'Good. Help me brew this poison.'

DANTAVAKRA

I

The wooden board hung precariously on the wall, camouflaged in the shadows of an ornately framed painting and a tall wardrobe on either side. But the dagger found its target each and every time it was thrown – a bill clipping pinned on the top corner of the board.

The clipping was a cut-out from an acta gazetting the important social events of the lunar year. The only reason the girl snoring on the bed behind him was able to get her hands on it was because it was dated almost six months ago. The colour of the bill had waned but his resentment only waxed to a sharp crescent.

The dagger spun over and over to puncture the bill where the name 'Dantavakra' was painted in clear bold letters. The said gentleman, Dantavakra, followed up in the wake of his dagger to retrieve and remove the blade gracefully. He walked back with a glass of summerwine in one hand, only to turn swiftly on his heel and let the dagger fly again.

The sound of steel on wood finally roused the girl from her nap. She wearily walked to the basin at the edge of the room. Using a cloth soaked in rosewater, she dabbed her face and then the insides of her thighs. As he admired her attending to her chores, he wished he could remember the exact turn of phrase he had used that fetched him an invitation to her bed. The servants had kept the cups brimming all night. By the time the moon began its descent, Dantavakra had been drunk on wine and giddy with glamour. He'd danced with many a beauty on the floor. Probably sung a few ballads with the hired singers. But as drunk as he may have been, he had still been the soul of courtesy. He'd talked to the high nobles and their ladies with respect, showering them with undeserved compliments. He'd swapped morsels of court gossip and explained his japes on the Crown Prince. He'd posed with other eligible bachelors and damsels of the Capital while the hired artists captured them with a quick brush to bring it to life later. It was, after all, the Lord Chamberlain's Winter Ball to introduce his daughter to the distingué society and, to be invited to it had been a high honour. He remembered it all but he could not remember the words he had used on the girl. He had to remember! How else could he use them later! A faint memory finally floated at the edge of his eyes but his recollection was interrupted by the same girl's hysterics.

'You have to go, Danta!' He found the girl staring out the window, panic-struck. 'He is here! How is he here a day early! Oh, Danta, go run! As fast as a Raksha! Oh but where will you escape from? Can you jump out the window?'

'Three floors down. Not likely.' What was he? Karna? And what did that phrase even mean: As fast as a Raksha. He had met a few Rakshasas in his life and he could outrun any of them without breaking a sweat. Dantavakra returned his attention to the board instead. The sentence that held his name on the clipping was the same one that had ruined Dantavakra's mood to the point of bill-mutilation. A single sentence. Described him as a man of noble birth. *Correct.* A handsome bachelor by all accounts. *So far so good.* Finalist of the Imperial Contest. *Finalist.* Was there any word more bitter! A pity-fuck was what it was.

Most warriors would be flattered at finding their names on the royal acta. Most warriors would ignore the next line where the news of the upset in the arena (when he had lost) had caused many enthusiastic wagermongers to suddenly find God. Most warriors would hire the artists from the Lord Chamberlain's ball to reproduce a likeness of the acta, and then discreetly spread it to the parks and cheek-painting houses where the finer gender was known to frequent. But not this particular warrior.

Yama forfend! *Finalist.* He hated the word. Absently, he began scribbling with a quill on a stray parchment on the table. The dagger, retrieved again, had already flown across the room, over velvet carpets of peacock feathers from Meluha, passing perilously close to the decanter of summerwine. The handle turned over in the last breadth of a second to let the blade bury itself in the wooden board once again. This time it pierced the now nearly shredded bill, completely obscuring the word 'Eklavvya'.

By all rights Dantavakra should have won the Imperial Contest. He should have been basking in the glory of his victory. When the Emperor asked him his boon, he would've prayed to lead the next charge on Mathura or better, be elevated to a Marshal. He cherished stories. And stories which earned genuine awe in his audience, those he loved the most. Genuine awe, and not courteous applause. If only he had stopped Eklavvya from toppling him mid-fall when he had leaped at him from his horse, he could've gravelled his place on the Walk of Fame. *No, not this again.* He had tormented himself with hundreds of what-ifs from that day, and for the sake of his own sanity, he could not put himself through that again.

'Danta! What are you doing?' the girl asked as Dantavakra stopped drawing and began now to casually rip out the drawers of her wardrobe and fling her clothes behind him as if in the midst of a raid. 'And where is my saree!' Dantavakra paused his ransacking and turned to look at her. By now, the girl had buttoned up her blouse and tied the petticoat around her waist. A generous display of her midriff was interrupted by a bite-bruised cleavage when she bent down frantically to pick up the strewn clothes.

Dantavakra returned to his thoughts. The Future was all that mattered. He was young, and had time on his hands, he thought as he pulled a drawer all the way to let it fall on the floor. He had been swimming in the moat every day since, at least every day that did not follow a night of dandiness. For all work and no fuck does not make a man. If he wasn't swimming, he was running the Colonnade all the way to the Crimson Tooth and back. And every day before he met his friends by the pier, he would spend two hours swinging the trident. Yes. He would manifest his destiny. The next acta would describe him as the winner of the Imperial Contest, the God of the Trident, the Pride of Magadh, the—

'Woman of the Hour!'

Dantavakra turned towards the voice. It came from behind the door, where a panting man had paused to catch his breath.

'Where is my lovely?' The door opened. Just as the master of the house entered, Dantavakra flicked the dagger at the door frame, the handle humming to match the popping veins on the startled Lord Chamberlain.

'What!' His moustache brimmed like an angry caterpillar. 'Ser Danta. What are you doing?'

'Finally, the loyal son of Magadh returns,' Dantavakra said, casually rising, running his hand on the scattered papers on the desk. 'I was just about to find it. Perhaps, you can help me.'

The Chamberlain's eyes bulged with indignation. 'Find what? What is the meaning of this?'

'Books on equality amongst castes. Or as the Drachmas call it, contraband.'

The Chamberlain swallowed hard. Surely a man as connected as the Chamberlain had friends who were scholars, and surely some of these friends had been acquainted with the cosiness of a cell in the recent spate of arrests. 'This time I have a confirmed tip,' Dantavakra said, 'and I'm going to find the contraband and, Yama help me, finally fetch me the promotion to Marshal.' By now the Chamberlain had the look upon his jowly face of one who, having opened the door to find a stranger, would have preferred to discover the man in bed with his daughter rather than accusing him of such blasphemy.

'Ser, ser,' the Lord Chamberlain raised his hand, 'I know not who gave you this tip, but I swear on my daughter's life, it could not be further from the truth. Uurvi, tell him!' he urged his daughter, who had by now fashioned a makeshift saree from the linen sheet on the bed.

Dantavakra interrupted him. 'Whatever Lady Uurvi had to say or *do*, she has done. You stand accused of blasphemy, My Lord. I cannot believe it. Because of you, I could not sleep all night. What is worse is, because of you, I did not even let your daughter sleep.'

'I am a loyal follower of the Ehtral Edicts.'

'Are you? Then what is this?' He plucked out the sheet on which he had been scribbling. A doodle of a woman with serpents in her hair. 'This is a likeness of the Ocean Goddess. A relic perhaps to be prayed to. Even holding it so taints my spirit.' Dantavakra waved the sheet before the Chamberlain. 'Just because the future Queen is from Kalinga, will you forsake the truth and start worshipping these false gods? *Tch. Tch.* I had expected better.'

The Chamberlain tried to snatch the paper from Dantavakra to inspect it himself but Dantavakra pulled his hand back.

'And now you're trying to tamper with evidence!'

'Ser, no! You know me. We dined together just last night!'

'And that should shield you from the rigours of justice? Was that feast a ploy for you to convert us?' Dantavakra gasped with a big O as if he had uncovered the plot of the century. 'Is this drawing a secret code amongst your brotherhood of traitors?'

By now the Chamberlain's voice had reached a pitch only the bats could make out clearly. 'It must be a silly drawing by this silly girl.' He held the shoulders of Dantavakra with the familiarity of an old friend and beckoned him to the side of the room. 'It is just a silly sketch. How about we...' The Chamberlain dipped his hand in the pocket of his coat and extracted a velvet pouch. 'How about ten...' He commenced counting the silver in it.

'Ho, what are you trying to do?' Dantavakra asked, incensed. 'What are you counting, eh?'

'Nothing, nothing.' The Chamberlain abandoned his arithmetic, and handed him the entire pouch. His daughter gasped behind them. 'Keep quiet, imbecile!' the Chamberlain seethed.

Dantavakra grunted. 'Be careful, Lord Chamberlain. And be mindful of your surroundings. Stay true to the Empire, and to your daughter. Don't consort with scholars. Don't claim you are going for business for two days, and then *return* a day earlier. Men may be above the law, but they are no longer above Gods in this city. I will turn a blind eye this one time.'

'Oh, you are a blessing, Ser! You must attend my next ball! I will save the finest spot on the table for you,' he said, unexpectedly hugging Dantavakra, even as the future Pride of Magadh winked at his daughter.

II

Dantavakra wished his friends had been privy to that delightful exchange. What a beautiful day it was turning out to be. The fact that he woke up in the morning without the usual ale aches, despite having fallen asleep without drinking water, was a good omen. And thanks to the Lord Chamberlain's untimely entry, he had been able to leave without awkward farewells and uncertain promises. And the most splendid of all, he was on time for his training. Feeling rather pleased with himself and the weight of the purse that hung from his belt, he strolled towards the sand pits at Mane's Turn – or whatever new holy name the black-clad priests of the Unni Ehtral had changed it to. He had come within a street of the pits when his path came to a sudden halt.

Not just because the street was filled with emaciated people, fouled with excrement, welts and sores. Yes, that too. But the sight had become common ever since the slightly richer Reshts, the slightly more agnostic Magadhans, the slightly more liberal Namins and the slightly more independent women of the night had found their houses torched by vigilantes. The destitute packed the street like abandoned children, lost and forlorn, blinking in the harsh morning sun, waiting for justice before the law courts that did not open their doors till noon. So yes, Dantavakra did reel back on being assailed by their stench but the real reason why he stopped short stood ahead, distributing food amongst the recently homeless.

Ordinarily Dantavakra would have dashed in the direction that would have diminished his chances of an encounter with the man his mother had made the unfortunate mistake of birthing first. Dantavakra still harboured a suspicion one of them was adopted. For they did not look alike one bit. Dantavakra was soft silk and elegant dagger. Shishupal was rusted nails and boiled leather. But as he eyed Shishupal handing down leaf plates, Dantavakra could not help but remember an old friend. That ill-fated goof, while attempting to escape his creditors, had tried to pass right through them by wearing a wig and a saree, only to have his wig swept off by the wind. The look on his friend's face then was the same one on his brother's now.

'Oh, it is you,' Shishupal said when Dantavakra interrupted his charity walk. Shishupal's tone left little room for doubt that recent tragedies in Shishupal's life had not altered his opinion that he had so long held that his little brother was a smear on the Chedi royal bloodline.

'Aye, me. Why do you resemble a bereaved beaver?'

Shishupal eyed him curiously. 'You are wearing what you wore yesterday when you left for the feast in honour of Lady Uurvi,' and then Shishupal closed his eyes, as he always did when life became too much for him to bear. Traumatic experiences in the past had taught Dantavakra that run-ins with Shishupal meant scoldings and sermons, and he braced himself again, driven by sheer muscle memory, to meet with defiant denial whatever accusation was about to be hurled at him. Dantavakra was a firm priest of the God of Denials, if one existed. So when Shishupal smiled at him, Dantavakra felt deeply unsettled.

'What?'

'Nothing. Sometimes I am envious of the troubles you cause. They seem so mundane in the grand scheme of things.'

Dantavakra was unsure whether to take it as a compliment. He decided to stay mum till he had a better grasp of things. 'Alright, then.'

'I am going away, Dantakhandiya.' *Dantakhandiya*. Crooked Teeth. A mutilation of his name to tease him for misshapen front two teeth. He did not care. The imperfections only made him more endearing, more believable. And the silky hair and the sharp jawline more than made up for the imbalance – *I hate that name!*

'For another swayamvar?' Dantavakra gave it back. Shishupal shot him the elder brotherly glare that Dantavakra was accustomed to keel before. 'Apologies. Too far. Where? Chedi?'

'Mathura,' Shishupal said. 'Or rather, Agran. Spy on what the Usurper is up to.'

Dantavakra frowned. Shishupal was the Commander of the Crimson Cloaks. Not a lowly spy. And from what he knew of his brother, no one could accuse him of having the stealth or conversational skills or charm which he supposed were essentials for espionage. Understanding soon followed.

'No,' he said. 'You exiled yourself? I thought you were just moping around with all that nonsense! Brother, you fool!'

'I hope you are never acquainted with the need for atonement, little brother. The Emperor agreed with my request, and assigned me... this. I should be back before Armistice ends.'

'You'll be away for six months!' *Yes!*

'In the meantime, it is on your shoulders to keep the Trident proud. Do not do anything from which I cannot rescue you, for this time, I truly will not be able to.'

There was his old brother back.

'I like bringing roses to the cheeks of fair maidens, big brother. It is no crime.'

'If only their mothers shared your sentiment. Remember, not for ourselves alone are we born but for the men and women whose protection is cast upon us. Take care of your men, groom them as your Marshals groomed you. You are fortunate to have been knighted so early in your life. Use this time well. Where were you bound to?'

'The pits.'

Shishupal shut his eyes again. It was as if, if Dantavakra were to vanish, Shishupal would finally lead a happy life. 'Let go of the Imperial Contest. You have already proved to everyone you are a distinguished warrior. You are a knight now!'

'What is the point of being a knight if the only thing I command is my horse? I want to be a Marshal. From there, a Rathar. Have my own chariot. And who knows, if I prove myself in the next battle, I might become a Paladin.'

'You just want to skip the queue.'

'And be something even you couldn't achieve.'

'I hear dark rumours, Danta, about the next Contest. I do not want you hurt. Think truly and deeply. Is there any meaning to risking your life again in that blasted arena?'

Dangerous thoughts. If he started looking at his life from the eyeglass of meaning, there wouldn't be much of a life to lead. But it wasn't worth the breath to explain this to Shishupal. Shishupal did not understand how badly Dantavakra wanted people to cheer for him when he walked, fawn over him behind his back, and hang on to his every word as if it were gospel. He wanted children to bicker over who got to play Dantavakra in their mock duels. And this view was only offered by the highest rank in the army a Ksharjan could attain: a Rathar. Rathars were knights who paraded into battles with their own chariots, and who sat comfortably just below a Paladin and a Rakhjai in the hierarchy of heroes. And he did not want to wait to rise through these ranks. What was the point in being an old Rathar? What would he do with the glory and gold then when he would be too old to spend it on anything but horticulture? No. He wanted it all now. *So no, thank you, big brother. The only way out of the Imperial Contest is by diving in.*

Shishupal was still droning on. The man was heading on an exile but you had to give him credit for taking out the time for a lecture. 'And stop ruining maidens for their future husbands. Seriously, Danta.' He stared at the sun in the sky. 'Look at the hour. I must leave now.'

Thank Yama. Dantavakra savoured that delectable taste of peace which comes to men of ambition when their elder siblings have had their say and are ready to depart. For unlike the masochistic soldier in Shishupal who had taken considerable pains to avoid the Uurvis of this world, Dantavakra was a man about town, a man who had spent his days at court in the company of the debonair, the strong-willed type of women and was never happier than when knee-deep between the legs of baronesses and barmaids. Perhaps slightly happier when wielding a trident in the arena but it was a close contest. The Capital might cheer Dantavakra for the red he spilled on the arena but the Capital truly thanked him for painting its taverns, theatres and tiger race courses that cheerful colour instead. So let his father, and his brother and his distant cousins consider him a pain in their necks but Dantavakra was a man of the masses, happy in the love he received from less austere quarters of civil life.

'It was nice talking to you, brother. I feel a lot better about your exile. Are you certain you do not want to extend the trip?'

Shishupal clasped the back of Dantavakra's head and touched his forehead to his. 'Farewell, brother. Be good.'

'It is just half a year. Do not be so dramatic.'

Shishupal smiled as he crossed Dantavakra and returned to handing over food packages to the destitute. Dantavakra turned once and called out his name. 'Shishupal,' he said, 'the death of that boy was not your fault.'

'I know of at least one man in the Union who would disagree. Be nice to Lord Dimvak. He is the only one in the royal court who still stands by you.'

III

'I must confess, Danta,' said Dimvak, 'that I apologize for having failed you.'

Dantavakra said nothing, massaging the bruise on his head, aware an explanation was on its way.

'I thought with the Contest right around the corner, I might ease up the regimen. Fewer classes, fewer jogs, fewer bouts. I hoped that without an outside hand, you would blossom under the sun on your own. Find your own steelsong,' Dimvak said as he slipped the mace under Dantavakra's leg to trip him, 'but instead of a flower you've turned out to be a worm, content at digging for scraps in the soil.'

'Tarry a little, Lord Dimvak,' said Dantavakra, face buried in the sand. Stripped to the waist, he shivered at the wind's cold caress. Sand had peppered his chest. With one hand, he brushed it off, and with the other, he flexed his fingers on the long hilt of the practice trident. A narrow band of braided leather held Dantavakra's long hair back from his face as he turned to Dimvak. 'I am here at training, right? Have I missed any session for the last few months?'

'Only been late to them all. And that hardly forms one ninth of the routine I had the scribe write for you,' said Dimvak, disgruntled. 'Not to forget the tidings I've heard from the Tulips. You spend more time in strange beds than wandering monks. Certainly more than you spend practising your trident routines or learning to command your squad. You need to be creative on the field when bested by a foe stronger than you, and nothing destroys creativity more than comfort and convenience. Nothing destroys Dhyana more than debauchery.'

Dantavakra rose to his feet grateful that his attempt at conversation had distracted Dimvak long enough for him to rise to his feet without a bludgeoned face. Young as he was, Dantavakra was taller than most boys of his age but Dimvak... Dimvak was so tall he could use a giraffe as an arm-rest. Court gossip flourished around the possibility of giant blood in his veins but Dantavakra knew if there had been any truth to that, he would've been the first man the Ehtrals would have hung in the square. Good luck finding a rope that would hold Dimvak's weight though.

A chorus of giggles made Dimvak turn and scowl at Dantavakra's audience. As was common in his sparring lessons, children cheered from tree tops around the sand pit while women peeped from corners of the half-constructed brick walls. Dantavakra wanted to lie to himself that he was barely aware of the crowd, that he had evicted the tenants squatting in his thoughts, that he was knocking at the doorstep of Dhyana, but the truth was that the shakes from last night's ale made that damn door move every time he came close.

He could not believe he had been tricked by his mind to think he would survive the day without an ale ache. He cursed himself again for forgetting to empty a gallon of water inside before pulling the sheets. Rather Dantavakra had lost whatever water had remained in his body thanks to the Chamberlain's daughter. So here he was swinging his trident at Dimvak like a blindfolded kitten trying to catch a fly. He needed to buy time to will strength back to his mind if not muscles.

Fuck Dhyana, Dantavakra cursed. He could not empty his mind and fight the Lord Commander of the Rakhjai at the same time. It had been a stupid idea to begin with. He liked the flurry of thoughts that plagued his mind, the very thoughts that allowed him to think of the hundred ways his teacher and tormentor would attack him.

'It isn't the stretch of the time but how much I stretch in the time that determines how limber I am, My Lord.'

There was an eerie silence that followed his words. Dantavakra would blame last night for the miscalculation he made in quoting Dimvak back to Dimvak.

'You pus-eating archon of arrogance,' said Dimvak, growling louder with each word, 'you infected-arsed, shit-bathing mosquito!

Do you have any idea what you've been given? How much your brother has sacrificed so that you could be here gallivanting your arse through whore-alley. How many vassal-borns do you see rising to your rank so early, eh?'

Dantavakra meant to offer a word of assuagement but the briefest flicker of Dimvak's gaze sewed his lips shut.

'A year under my tutelage,' Dimvak's loud voice made the ale aches worse, 'learning my stances, nurtured by my hand and my time, and you lost last time because you leaped off that infernal horse at Eklavvya! And even then, did I beat you for it? Did I throw you in the pits to get you buggered by the worst inmates?'

Dantavakra winced. 'Of course not.'

'Then validate my faith right with your weapon, not your words.'

The practice mace in Dimvak's hands glided smoothly and surely as he flowed from one stance to another. Dantavakra searched for a pattern in the way Dimvak's mace moved, hunting for any hint of the direction from which the strike would come. It came from above, and Dantavakra had been ready.

For a long minute, the trident's swish and the mace's thuds filled the pits. Dantavakra made no effort to attack Dimvak. A practice trident was blunt-ended and posed no danger to anyone. A practice mace on the other hand left a circle of pain where it hit flesh. Not to forget that in Dimvak's hands, the distinction between a practice mace and a real one was a line drawn in sand, a fact Dantavakra knew all too well. Even as he parried an attack, one such circle burned his shoulder. So, audience notwithstanding, all Dantavakra's self-imposed task of the day was, was to leave the pits without wearing any more of these decorations on his body.

He barely got the trident up in time to stop Dimvak's mace from smashing his face to pulp. Could someone please inform Dimvak that he was not on the battlefield and that Dantavakra, despite his charming looks, was not Krishna? The Chedi did his best to ground himself against the onslaught of the mace, to dispel the force of the blow evenly across his hands, and then through his body onto the sands below. Even so, his legs trembled. Either from the impact of the blow or the five hundred squats Dimvak had put him through, he couldn't say. All he knew for certain was he was not looking forward to a trip to the privy.

'What do you think this is all for?' asked Dimvak. 'Why am I here when I could rest in my off time? Is it so you can laze around and lead astray girls who should know better into nameless orgies?' Dantavakra laughed one of his quiet laughs at that word. Dimvak pressed on, 'You can drink and dice when you have made something of yourself, Danta. Till now, your face is your only achievement, and that is a gift from your mother.'

No quick quip ever made could stand before the storm of such chastisement.

'And so, I humbly beg your forgiveness for my own failure,' Dimvak said as he switched the mace to his weak hand, 'for allowing you to reach such a petty state of affairs that you're more a sailor than a soldier. Time for me to redress the wrongs. Are you ready?'

Ready? They had been at this for hours already. What did he mean, *ready*? The man was a fiend. It did not help matters that Dimvak absolutely relished the opportunity to spew out words of motivation every time Dantavakra pleaded for a break. 'The only rest you deserve is the rest you earn,' he sermoned when he swung his mace at his head. 'You will stop when your body turns a slave to your mind and not the other way around,' he roared when he forced Dantavakra to duck under an almighty swing.

'Yes, thank you for that motivational quote, Master,' Dantavakra said as he jumped back and curved the trident through the air like a ribbon to the applause of the onlookers. The wind rose again, wafting the scent of roses to his nose. One of his onlookers was a woman of high birth waiting with a garland of roses. That errant thought was flitting through the darkness of his focus like a whimsical firefly. Now that he knew there was a high-born woman watching him move, he used it to energize himself. 'I was struggling to find the strength to roll my eyes today,' he said loudly and was pleased with its reception in the audience.

Dimvak just stared in response. Clearly his Master had woken up on the wrong side of the bed. *So glad I came on time for this.* Dantavakra shook his head in a bid to throw off the aches. Dimvak charged with his mace. Dantavakra stepped smoothly into the mace's arc, shifted the trident, ensnared the mace-handle between its two prongs and twisted hard. The pressure wrenched the mace out of Dimvak's hands and sent it with a dead thud on the sandy pit. *What? Did I just best*— The thought remained unfinished. In executing that manoeuvre Dantavakra had stepped into hugging proximity of Dimvak, which predictably ended with a tender rib and bruised pride.

'Is that how you are planning to duel in the Contest? By gifting your soft ribs to your foe to plant his dagger. Why not just turn around and bend over?'

'Master,' Dantavakra said, massaging his ribs. 'May we just take a moment to savour the fact that I disarmed you. It's official now. Pigs can fly, Reshts can read and Dantavakra just disarmed Lord Dimvak.' The children erupted in applause and the women gifted cherry nods.

'No japes, Danta. This is grave. Always keep your eye on your foe, not his weapon. A momentary lapse and Yama will haul you over his chariot before you have time to say *Claw*,' Dimvak advised as he hoisted Dantavakra to his feet. 'Is this how you plan to defeat Eklavvya should he contest again?'

It wasn't a battle at the Three Sisters. It was a duel in Virangavat. No one died in the arena. The scene of crucified children flashed before his eyes to correct him. Well, at least not the contesting Ksharjans. It was forbidden to kill. But Dimvak would not be Dimvak without a touch of the drama. The man would have flourished in a theatre troupe.

Dimvak, who hadn't relinquished his grip on Dantavakra's hand, yanked his elbow. He sniffed the air and caught a whiff of ale from Dantavakra. And then the worst thing that could happen in a day came to pass.

Dimvak smiled.

'We are going to have a little fun, you and I, from tomorrow.'

'Master, no, please.'

'Come sunrise tomorrow, you will jog the circuit of the Wall of Rajgrih every alternate day in the hour of the roost. All the way to Yama's Hands. On the days you do not run, you will swim the moat where the Emperor has ordered for the public baths to be built for the outers.'

'Master, a teacher should know his student's limitations. Sunrise?'

'Fret not. I will knock on your door every day to wake you up. It is the least I can do for my prized pupil. If you do not open the door or if you are not home, I will torch your quarters. Understood?'

'Aye, my Lord,' croaked Dantavakra as he made a mental note to resign from the Contest that very night. But then what would people think of him? What would his father think of him? His father, despite his private complaints, had been boasting to any noble who came to his court about how excited he was to see his son fight in the centre of Virangavat before the Emperor. Last year, his father's disappointment in the letter to Dantavakra had crushed him. If Dantavakra threw away his chance this time, he could say goodbye to ever rising before his father's eyes or in the army's ranks for that matter. His superiors were too envious of him to promote him. Say goodbye to a life of bribes and rest.

'And no more revelry till the Contest. Or I will sign you up to guard the Unni Ehtral without your consent. Where I failed, perhaps they will set you straight.'

Ah, Dimvak had finally landed at a good incentive. 'There will be no need of that, My Lord,' Dantavakra said, fear colouring his voice.

'So, you will stand victorious at Virangavat?'

'Yes, my Lord.'

'And will give up rioting, revelling and carousing?'

'Yes, my Lord.'

'Completely?'

'Completely.'

IV

Late that night the door of Tulips banged open. Loud sounds of music and dancing washed out at him like a siren's call, coaxing him to return. Dantavakra resisted the lure, his steps unsteady as he soldiered out of the tavern with a half-finished bottle in his hand. A shape flew out of the tavern and crashed into Dantavakra's back as they both fell in the mud.

All Dantavakra had the strength for was to pray for someone to get the lout off him and then he wondered why did he not have that strength himself. His mind was foggy, his thoughts muddled by the copious amount of winter mead that sloshed inside his liver. But as he lay there in the mud, a memory began to emerge from the haze.

He remembered the warmth of the mug in his hand and the soft whispers of a woman. Ah, his friend Mair, whose family ran the local horse races, had hosted a tavern meet to introduce his first cousin to Rajgrih's nightlife. She had been visiting the Capital for the first time from Nalanda. Dantavakra had thought he would pay his respects along with his other friends and be gone but the first cousin's beauty made for a convincing case to stay for a little while longer. The officers had ordered round after round of ale, toasting her, singing raucous songs, with each man competing for her attention, while Mair had tried to ward off an army. The ale had flowed freely, warming their hearts and loosening their tongues, one of which had complimented Dantavakra for being able to find a sponsor in Dimvak.

Dimvak's name had had the effect of clearing the cobwebs in his mind. If the legends of his time in the Yamuna Wars were true, Dantavakra had no doubt as to Dimvak's arson abilities. Dantavakra loved the way he had designed the interiors of his home too much to test it. So, he had offered his apologies to his friends, paid his compliments to the indifferent first cousin, and then swaying, stumbling and staggering, he had finally walked out of the tavern. But clearly the Goddess of Good Times, if there was any, would not let her favourite priest leave.

'Alright, alright,' he slurred as he tried to shake off the dead weight on his back, 'I will stay but can you get him off me, please, Goddess!'

No one answered. No one was there. It wasn't early enough in the night for patrons to be still strolling in and it wasn't late enough in the night for the patrons to be thrown out. A voice inside warned that if he were caught in the mud bent over with a man atop, it would not bode well for his reputation in a thousand ways and one. But just when Dantavakra had given up hope, the weight suddenly lifted. 'Thank you, Goddess.' He turned behind to give a lecture on liver etiquette to the drunkard but stopped when he saw what the man wore.

A nondescript brown, loose-fitting tunic cinched at the waist with a slender leather strip was paired with jute sandals. A turban, fashioned from the same brown cotton, was wrapped loosely around his head. The mark of the spear on his neck was the only sign he was permitted inside but for all intents and purposes, he looked like the lowliest of Reshts. How did they even permit such a man to enter Tulips? Seriously, the Ehtrals had the right of it. The privilege of free entry was a rather abused one. By now the man had half risen, and was clutching at Dantavakra's robes with one hand, and his throat with the other.

'Oi, what do you think you are doing?' Dantavakra asked.

The lout made a wheezing sound in answer. Dantavakra's eyes cleared as training took over and he stood up to take the man by the shoulders. 'Easy, good sir, easy. Too little food and too much ale, eh?' Dantavakra poked a finger inside the man's collar to let air in.

'Yama's horns,' he said. The man's throat had swollen up as if a whole guava was stuck inside. He summoned Dhyana or whatever the closest was to it to keep the ale's stupor inside him away. Took hold of the man from behind. Positioned his arms around his waist, just above his navel. And then applied firm pressure with his hands. He felt the man's sternum and ribs beneath his fingers and pushed harder. It did not work. The man struggled in his grip – the sounds from his throat an instant curative for the inebriated. A couple who opened the tavern door saw the scene, snickered and darted back inside before Dantavakra could scream for help.

Blast this! Dragging the man by the arm, he slammed the Tulips' door open and let out the Imperial whistle. Officers and soldiers, at least the men who had not succumbed to the floor's embrace, snapped to attention. Finding the source of the whistle, they scampered to Dantavakra's aid, half tossing the snickering couple from earlier aside. 'He is choking but I don't think it is food. I need you to – hold still! – clear a table and, you, I need you to hold him from the legs.' The man was flailing against Dantavakra as though Dantavakra was the cause of his troubles. Dantavakra tried pounding the man's chest but all that did was turn his cheeks a dark shade of purple. By now the man's eyes had rolled all the way back in his head.

'Is there no healer!' Dantavakra asked.

'What is happening to him?' someone shouted.

'Hold his stomach from the back and heave, Ser!' someone else barked. *Already done that, dogballs.*

It is up to you now. Dantavakra squeezed his eyes shut to drown out the voices. Clutched at the man's wind gullet with one hand and, with the other, slipped out a knife from the back of his belt. Holding the knife in a scalpel grip, he forced the man's head back sharply as he pressed the blade down on the man's throat. Ignoring the protests and cries of the patrons around him, he traced the point below his throat's apple. The muscles on the man's neck stood out like the face of a cliff but, with gentleness, Dantavakra cut a delicate slice on the skin. *How drunk am I? Or is that blood purple?* Purple-stained blood bubbled from the cut and then ran in a river down the sides of the man's neck. The protests suddenly ceased as the word 'poison' began to spread like wildfire through the crowd, many of whom turned accusatory fingers at the innkeeper. Many of the patrons tossed their drinks at the innkeeper but Dantavakra had no time to pay attention to that.

'Reed! Scroll! Does anyone have any of these?' Dantavakra shouted.

Everyone searched their pockets, their sleeves, their bags, but none stepped up. How was it that in a tavern full of officers not one had a goddamned scroll on him? 'Are you serious! Does no one—'

The innkeeper's boy darted into the room holding a bouquet of hollow reeds in his fist. 'Will this do, Ser?'

'Good lad,' Dantavakra said as he mellowed down. He took another swig from the beaker of ale. Inserted the reed stick into the incision he had made on the man. Men and women gasped. Someone even whispered 'Murder'. *Well, this better work or that whisper will soon turn into a war cry.* In a matter of three seconds, whatever abscess lurked in the lout's wind gullet was bypassed. Air navigated the new path to the poor man's lungs. In a wet gasp, the man coughed out with an ear-scalding cough as he twisted over and retched a stream of purple liquid. After expelling the filth out to his lung's content, tears streaming down his face, he turned back to thank Dantavakra, and then fall unconscious on the table. The man's face was still a ghastly shade of plum but on the road between breathing and dying, it looked like the man had now turned in the right direction.

Dantavakra flopped back into a chair, his focus all but depleted. The stupor he had held at bay returned with ill intent. He became aware only a little later of the commotion around him. *What now?* Blinking open his eyes, he turned to see the onlookers staring at him. Each and every patron had stood up to clap for him. *Oh, Adoration, thy milk is my elixir.*

He rose unsteadily but bowed graciously. He had enough practice after all. As he returned to the chair, his eyes closed on their own and he began to wonder if he could add 'master of reed sticks' to the scrolls his mother dispatched to distant royal ladies for courtship. Perhaps he could start a side venture as a wind gullet instructor, or maybe even join forces with a Drachma to launch a line of branded reed sticks. The possibilities seemed endless.

'Why did you save him?'

Dantavakra peeled open his eyes and tried to focus on the speaker through bleary vision. The words came from a woman with skin the colour of rich mahogany that seemed to be glowing unnaturally. Long, raven-coloured hair peeked a little from under the hood she wore. Caught in the thrall of her beauty, he felt his heart and his pants swell with desire.

'I beg…' the voice came out as a squeak. Dantavakra burped as he climbed to his feet. 'I beg your pardon, My Lady.'

When the woman's face finally resolved itself into a coherent drawing before his eyes, he felt as if a war hammer had just smacked him squarely in the chest – breathtaking, yes, but with the distinct possibility of some cracked ribs. Just the sort he relished, at least when it came to women. Who was this enchanting creature? How had he not seen her before? Was she new to the Capital? He could definitely pitch himself as her new tour guide.

'Why did you save him?' she asked again.

'Erm.' Dantavakra stood straighter, confused. 'Just my duty, My Lady. If you were in my place, you would have done the same,' he said, hoping he was still able to flash a winsome smile. From the corner of his eye, he felt the first cousin – why couldn't he remember her name? – stare daggers at them.

The woman let out a chuckle that brought to his mind the most heinous of child snatchers he had seen on stage. 'No, I most certainly wouldn't,' she said. 'You've gone and spoiled all the fun.'

'My Lady.' Dantavakra attempted to keep standing but his grip slipped on his chair and he collapsed back into his seat. He chuckled but the sound died in his throat as he met the woman's bluish-grey eyes. Eyes that looked profoundly... sober. 'Are you saying you would have left him for dead, My Lady?'

'What? Oh, no,' the woman said, her expression softening, though it did nothing to sheathe the hardness behind it. 'Haven't you heard of a woman wishing her husband dead before?' she said with a grin that revealed the most perfect set of teeth he had ever laid eyes on. Maintained in excellent condition, white and all. Lips, too. No trace of white webbings on them. While he couldn't smell the beeswax from her lips, he assumed she must have dabbed her lips with olive oil instead. Why couldn't he stop staring at her lips? Look somewhere else. Anywhere else. Wait... did she say husband?

The woman, it seemed, was regarding him carefully. Her eyes stopped on Dantavakra's brooch. 'Chedi infantry, then. Bloody Greens. Never able to handle their liquor.'

'Ser,' someone called him.

'Not now.' He waved the someone off. Just then another hooded girl approached the woman and pulled at her sleeve as if to leave. 'I am a knight, My Lady,' he beamed with pride, 'also a...' the word didn't sound as bad as it had sounded in the morning, '... a finalist of the Imperial Contest.'

'Ser,' the someone insisted.

I will kill you, arsehole. He took a deep breath and smiled at the woman. 'A moment, My Lady.' He turned behind, and then again turned back to the woman and the girl. 'Please do not leave. I will be done in a minute.'

'I'm sure you will.' The woman laughed as she said that, but in a friendly way, and it made Dantavakra feel more at ease. He turned around again to see who had disturbed him when he was just about to fall in love. Had to be his brother. Such terrible timing was Shishupal's sole domain. But it turned out to be the boy who had brought him the reeds. He stood there like a goat with a tankard of ale. 'Ser, compliments of my master, the innkeeper, for saving his inn.'

'Anaa… adi?' Dantavakra stuttered. 'Where is that degenerate gambler? He owes me – wait? Saving the ma… the man, you mean.'

'Yes, but you also saved the inn,' the boy leaned in to whisper. 'Do you not know who the man you saved is?'

In Dantavakra's extensive tavern experience, people knew him, not the other way around. He shrugged. 'Who cares? I did my duty as I would whether he be a pauper or prince,' he proclaimed loudly, and slowly, to dilute the slur, hoping the dark woman was eavesdropping.

'But Ser, he *is* a prince,' the boy whispered. 'You just saved the life of Saham Dev, the Crown Prince of the Empire. My master, Anaadi, is eternally grateful to you.'

Behind him the woman and the girl had vanished as suddenly as a shadowed dream fleeing the light.

MATI

A light, warm rain danced down around her, causing the mud of the streets to generously ink her sandals and ankles. It seemed only natural that the Storm God would drink up the sun and start pissing the moment Mati got a chance to step out. However, she remained defiant. The last few hours of Mati's life were not going to be spent in dry dread. So, she scuttled up and down the local bazaar in her mud-caked disguise to make the most out of her remaining time in Magadh, or rather in the world.

A soft hand clasped Mati's finger in the crowd. Without a flinch, she glanced down and was met with Amala's bobbing head. With the palace occupied with nursing Saham Dev back to health for the last few days, no one had noticed when Amala had slipped out with Mati through Saham Dev's secret passage, the same passage he used for his nocturnal escapades.

'Thank you again for saving my mother, Princess.'

Mati had an utterly unfamiliar urge to gather Amala in her arms and let the girl's head rest on her shoulder. *Storms! I refuse to get maternal!* She waved her hands dismissively. 'Thank you for saving me from boredom. Now come.'

They scurried behind small squads of red-caped Crimson Guards marching ahead. The crowd parted to give the soldiers a wide berth, allowing Mati a serene stroll through the city. But not everyone was so accommodating. Black-robed, single-eyed Ehtral priests, walking in the opposite direction, stood rooted before the soldiers, each faction contesting their right of way. Mati could see a clash of wills looming in the future between the Thugs of God and the Enforcers of Emperor's Peace.

She swapped her swagger for an obscure awkward stance that would scream 'harmless' to both the agents of chaos as she slipped to the side. Seemed like other members of the audience had the same idea, and soon ample space circled the black and red teams. It was evident that a walk through the streets of Rajgrih these days involved a certain measure of adventure absent in Jarasandh's early days of blissful neglect.

Not Mati's Empire. Not Mati's problem. She had things to splurge on.

Mati came out of a Drachma store later, her list of whims considerably shrunk, when she noticed Amala eyeballing the alley that opened into a local fair. Mati nudged Amala with her purse. 'Go enjoy. Use the remaining coin. Buy something.'

'The Prince will not like it, Your Grace,' Amala said, accepting her purse but still not meeting her eyes despite her newfound status as her co-conspirator. Mati had been surprised when Amala had agreed to poison Saham Dev without resistance. Saham, for all his faults, doted on the pups of his orphan school like an adoptive father. And to think Amala had been so horrified at the mere idea of ending Mati's unborn. Perhaps Amala could stomach better the idea of being a kingslayer rather than a cradle butcher. Or perhaps children could do anything for their blood mothers... she wouldn't know. Her own mother was a kraken.

'When he wakes up from his fever, he will most likely have other concerns. Like how to kill us in the most imaginative of ways. So let us momentarily set aside the Prince for just today and relish the time we have left. How about that, kid?'

Amala nodded.

Upon Mati's pat on the bum, Amala skipped down the alley to the fair. Mati, left behind, watched her go with a fond smile, all the while inwardly railing against that wart of a knight, Dantavakra. A show-off who just had to swoop in and save Saham Dev from a perfectly respectable demise. Couldn't he have been more like Karna? Karna had just stood there dumbfounded on the *Fat Mistress*, even as Prakar Mardin had succumbed to her poison. *Fucking heroes.*

'Remember your resolve, old girl,' Mati interrupted her own tirade.

'Make the most of your day. It could very well be your last.' With a firm nod, Mati gathered herself and set off after Amala.

Nostalgia makes hallowed shrines of mundane places. It felt like a dream to be back under the open sky even if it was in disguise, on wide streets even if so clean, and bargaining with stalls even if so green. Given that Mati would not live to see the light of the day once Saham Dev woke up, she intended to hold tight to this dream.

And so the future Queen of the Empire, disguised and decidedly pregnant with its heir, dived deep into the Magadhan Fair. In more ordinary times, the great plaza sometimes served as the execution grounds, sometimes as the staging arenas for plays, and sometimes as the grounds for the royal parade, but now it stood transformed. It was as if a second great bazaar had sprung up overnight, a bazaar of silk not stone. Merchants and zookeepers, the primary customers of pirates, sold hides and hawks, feathers and fruits, exotic animals, spices, incense, figurines, totems and all manner of illicit goods. Puppeteers, body painters and magicians wandered amongst the Magadhans plying their trades – as did scarlets and cutpurses. She avoided the *madira* vendors pushing terracotta cups towards her face while barely sidestepping a livestock trader, whose scent suggested he'd been fraternizing far too closely with his wares. But her moment of pride came when a juggler – clearly in the early stages of his career – managed to fling a jug in her direction. With a nimbleness that harkened back to her pirating days, she ducked, causing the jug to sail over head and drench the livestock trader instead, an act for which surely the cattleman ought to have been grateful. The juggler, looking more alarmed than apologetic, offered her a frantic bow and sprinted off before the trader unleashed his oxen on him. Mati laughed freely for the first time in days as she weaved through the riot of colours and sounds.

Behind the rainbow-coloured splotches of humanity, the walls were smothered with bills. Indictments, incitements, religious bluster, old victories, endlessly pasted over by the new. Some of the torn and dog-eared ones caught her eye. They showed a woman's body with the head of a fish. Mati realized with a smile that it was meant to be her. Over it was boldly painted: *Voyage and Villainy*, a clever twist on Kalinga's honour words: *Voyage and Valour.* If it was meant to offend her, it didn't. Villainy suited Mati a lot better than valour.

'Are you more agile than my hen?' cried a wild-haired woman holding a traumatized bird over Mati's head. She beckoned Mati with animated eyes. At her feet lay a set of spoons and a basket of lemons. 'Lay your bets! Test your balance against this hapless hen! The first to reach the finish line in this lemon race wins! Hen versus Human. Easy peasy! One copper a try! Oi! Surely you think you're faster than this hen!'

I wish.

Afternoon came with gifts of heat. By now the rains had disappeared as if they had never existed in the first place. The enthusiastic sun drove most of the Magadhans away from the streets. Dogs slept in the shade. Peacocks took shelter in the trees. Her body wanted her to return to the palace as well but she had been desperate to escape the screams of maids being interrogated.

Storms! If only her second attempt at poisoning Saham Dev in the tower had worked! But it had only led to deaths of two innocent maids and turned the Claws' suspicion to the royal staff instead. How long before her name featured on their list of suspects?

Not too long, if the healers did their jobs right and Saham Dev opened his eyes.

Even now she felt the gazes of two Crimson Guards drilling into her back as she walked down the bazaar, and Mati wondered what they had been ordered to do to her. Had Saham Dev already woken up? Time would tell. They followed her through the city's marble heart, past the friezes of legends, and the arches on which vines, both live and sculpted, climbed and coiled. They followed her across practice pits and prayer halls, along the high wall of the elephant stables, through insurance streets and the maze of caravanserais loud with horses, and over the green waters of the Prapti Canal, thick with a traffic of trade barges. Sheer pirate instinct made her consider darting down any of the alleyways she passed, into the palm-lined residential societies, but then what? Where would she go next? Mati's last three attempts at escaping from the city had failed miserably. She did not take her failure as a stain on her own competence. In a city she did not know, in a city gripped with fear, in a city whose citizens hated Kalingans, in a city where even the Kalingans hated Mati, a girl had few options. She had no way to find the underworld who ruled the gutters of Rajgrih. She wondered if an underworld even existed in the righteous Rajgrih. She wondered if she even had the wits and the blood to find them. The whelp brewing inside her had sapped her of her vigour. The Mati who had burned down a ship and caused a deadly stampede to escape in Chilika only a few months past was someone she could only reminisce about, not resurrect.

Even the Rakshasan Key Relic she had tasked Amala with appraising via the local gemsmiths had offered scant satisfaction. An ancient but an ordinary key, they had called it. The sapphire in the key may have fetched her enough to buy a horse but not escape with it.

Tired of walking, Mati stopped at a mango seller's stall and joined the queue waiting to buy one. With her nausea diminished, her appetite had returned with full force. Or perhaps it was because attempts to murder made Mati hungry. Either way, she waited impatiently for the seller to stop arguing with a poor man who wanted a discount and hand over her slices, damn it. Meanwhile, the two Crimson Guard soldiers drew near behind her, and Mati pricked her ears to gain some clue about their intentions. They were just chatting idly about mangoes. They hadn't been following her. Mati let out another sigh, this time one of relief, but didn't stop eavesdropping.

'Don't know why you got so excited over this blasted rain! It's just Yama sprinkling a dash of water on dry ground, like a cook splashes water on a hot tawa before he flips a paratha.'

'True, true. I never learn, do I?'

'If you got your mind out of your fantasies about Panchal's harlot and her five husbands, maybe you'll have a chance.'

'Forget the North,' the first guard said, wearily. 'Our own Cub is rumoured to be headed to the Conclave to forge so-called iron bonds with our new friend, the Leech of the East. For an exchange of ideas and knowledge, Lord Dimvak calls it.'

'Gold and airavats, most like,' the other guard snickered. 'The Empire don't care about ideas and knowledge. Look at the scholars hanging from the public posts.'

'Now that I don' mind. These so-called scholars and the academics is the first ones to sow paths of treason. How they love fashioning misery out of peace! Live our life, and they would know!'

'Parasites who feed on protests. With them behind bars, I love how our duties in the City have gone down. Or do you think we could have come to buy mangoes in the middle of the day?'

'Might just end up being a curse, friend. I am more worried about whether they is gonna haul our arse to protect those two in the East. I tell you if that happens, I am resigning and joining the Ehtrals themselves. East! Land of bogs and swamps. Not me!'

Funny how these fools were defaming the beautiful Tree Cities of the East while squatting in Rajgrih. A bard's first impression of Rajgrih, Nar Ad's account had told, was that of a magical banyan tree, its perfume one of jasmine and sandalwood, its birds' laughter, the sound of lovers' chimes. Mati suspected that Nar Ad must have sunk one too many bottles. Or perhaps he had visited in a different age. If Magadh was a banyan tree, it was infected with root rot. Its perfume stank only of soot and smoke. And the only sound she ever heard were the damn temple bells of the Ehtral Temple of Death.

The guards might have been under the impression that with the execution of a few scholars, they had successfully stamped out all forms of protest. However, they were rather overlooking the minor detail that schools had vanished in the process as well. One only had to glance at the abandoned establishments on either side of the road by the canal to grasp the full picture. Saham had enlightened her about the purge carried out by the Ehtrals. Many of these ruined buildings, if not all, had once been conservatories run by the culturally inclined Drachmas and Ksharjans and even by a few liberal Namins. Tales of such places had even reached Kalinga. Stories of tiny gurukuls dedicated to studying anything that was useless in the real world: paintings that survived the Second Age, occult Astra science, subjects named *moral relativism* and *alchemical astrology*. Some even devoted classes to understanding unplayable musical instruments of Daevas and reinventing themes of historical fashion of the thirty-third century. Now they were nothing but whispers of crumbled mortar and fragments of sand. Not surprising. When men of God seized power, men of Scrolls were the first to be thrown to the pyre.

Mati bore no love for the school of these destroyed institutions where spoilt children learned much *about* but nothing *from*. But if the custodians of such useless arts were killed, it would spell the end of a thriving black market, and the pirates would have to return to stealing horses and spices. Robbing a painting drawn by some pissant in the Second Age yielded far more value for effort. You needed the rich to grow bored for the pirates to thrive. One could not exist without the other, much like a jester without a court.

'I don't trust the Leeches,' another man with the caste mark of scales on his neck, who seemed to have joined Mati in overhearing the guards, chimed in. 'But their Tusk, Bhagadatt or some such name, has finally come into a bit of coin now that he does not have to send tribute to the Usurper in Mathura this year – thanks to the Emperor's largesse in putting that condition in the Armistice agreement. With the Leeches now cosying up to the Lions, we can expect a flood of their exotic wares. Just imagine the fortune we could rake in by selling those to the other vassals.'

'As if having a foreign Queen weren't enough, now we need foreign goods too. Piss off!' The guards broke the line and snatched their mangoes from the seller without settling their dues. Mati watched them swagger off, bought her mangoes, and then left the main thoroughfare to let the street take her on its whim. It delivered her to the high bund of a tank. She climbed it, loosening her shirt, but it did not help with the heat. Mati descended down on the other side of the bund wall to a flat wash rock beneath the shade of a banana palm. The tank was full after the day's rain, and children were scrubbing themselves in the shallows. Ahead, a herd of labour elephants were rolling and plashing, their mahouts swimming fearless amongst them. Over the water, bright flashes of cranes strolled around in search of fish. There, under the shade, she settled down to enjoy her rich and ripe mango and the cool that rose from the waters. It felt good to inaugurate her rekindled relationship with food by sinking her teeth into the wet wedges of sunlight.

The sound of clothes being beaten against stones drew her eyes to the nearby washerwomen, who were rinsing their laundry along the banks, beating it against rock to dry and then laying them out like a display of colourful paintings. Mati caught snatches of their gossip. Incomplete stories spoken in hushed voices of the flogging of children, of the blinding of uncooperative Vedan priests, the hunting of leaders who stood up against the Ehtrals, of torture and the deliberate disfigurement of prostitutes, of scholars found hidden and executed as spies, of houses searched and looted and burned for hiding relics of false gods.

Mati crawled like a retired spy into deeper shade to ignore them, and watched between her eyelashes as a brahminy starling preened on a low branch. It was a small fawn-coloured mynah with a long wispy crest whose blue bill was dipped in yellow and whose dark tail was dipped in white. It had the exact markings of the starling Duryodhan and Mati had spotted in Chilika together. She turned to the side to ask him to look and then remembered Duryodhan had abandoned her. Mati smiled grimly, feeling that flutter of rage again, and shut her eyes to see herself standing over his corpse. Just as she rehearsed the seventeenth imaginative scenario for his untimely death, her daydream was shattered by a whistling crowd.

Mati opened her eyes angrily to see an audience gather around a boy who had trained a monkey to perform acrobatics. He held the cord that collared the animal as it danced and cartwheeled on the grass while asking it scripted questions.

'As the idea of you heading East starts to seem more and more likely, Appu, what's got you most excited about it?'

Appu chattered and screeched.

'What was that, Appu?' she boy translated Appu's gibberish, 'Oh, you want to bring their airavats here, and even the bark from the ghastly Everwood Trees? Brilliant idea! What else? Anyone amongst you fine noblemen and ladies – can you tell Appu what he should do when he meets the Leech King to really seal the deal between Magadh and the Tree Cities?'

A woman with a screechy voice butted in. 'That'll never happen. The East is not savage because of their deathly bogs and deadlier marshes, it is savage because of its people. Horned Asurs and Grey Rakshasas! Have we forgotten the ship raids, the attacks on convoys, the arrests of our diplomats, the sprawling slave camps by Narkasur?'

'The Son does not mirror the Father, Appu says,' the boy coughed, realizing he needed to moderate the Empire propaganda of getting the Magadhans to like the Rakshasas before it got out of hand. 'Bhagadatt is the first Rakshasa in a thousand years to venture into the heart of the Riverlands and attend a swayamvar. If this is not an olive branch, Appu says, then he doesn't know eggs from his turd. And I agree with Appu. The East may be a savage land but as the Greeks and the Valkans have shown us, under the guidance of the Empire, they can serve the realm. An Empire is only as strong as its borders, and the Empire is not just for preserving civilization but spreading it. And if they don't behave, we can always bow before them even as we sting them with our tails. Those who will not treat the lion with respect will sleep with the manticore instead, deals be damned.'

His audience exchanged knowing nods. Mati absently applauded him as well, her mind buzzing with the boy's words. Bow and sting. Yes, bow and sting! She was just going to do that. When the Prince woke and came to arrest her, Mati would bow in penance and then drive a dagger into his chest, her plans be damned. Let the Lions feast on her then. At least they would eat the Black Swan rather than whatever she had become. Yes! Mati clenched her free fist. *The Black Swan is back!* No sooner had that thought crossed her mind than black-robed men grabbed her arms, pulled a hood over face and abducted the future Queen of Magadh in broad daylight.

DANTAVAKRA

I

Water cascaded down a stone wall, flowing into a small shallow pond filled with koi. The scales of the koi glowed in the sunlight, bright stars of orange and blue in the dark green water. Dantavakra and his companion, the lovely first cousin from the tavern – or as she preferred to be called, Lady Milani – waded into the waters and held their hands out against the wall, letting the cool water frolic over their fingers even as they pressed their feet against the coin-laden floor beneath. Milani withdrew her hand to delicately pat it against Dantavakra's arms – an intimate gesture – even as a battalion of koi danced a merry jig on their feet. Dantavakra could only hope Milani revelled in having the dead skin from her feet expertly discerned and dispatched by fish as much as he did.

They talked about the state of the weather and the latest high-society scandal as they strolled through the park later once their feet had dried. The scandal being, of course, how Dantavakra had saved the Crown Prince from the brink of death. There were a few who had decried Dantavakra's use of a blade on a member of the royal family, but Milani advised him to ignore such noise. After all there was a limit to how loud their envy could squawk before it started to sound like a parrot that's lost the plot. Dantavakra could not agree more.

He could not shake the thought that his dear old mother would give Milani the wholehearted nod of approval. Perhaps it was because Milani had herself planted the idea by unsubtly suggesting it. Or perhaps it was because Milani, like his mother, possessed a fondness for carrying an endless supply of snacks which ended in Dantavakra's belly on the grounds of 'Eat more, you're too thin'. Either way he was pleased Milani had reached out to him through her cousin despite the said cousin's counsel against such rashness. Dantavakra particularly relished how beneath her shield of propriety, she was not averse to a spot of rebellion. And now that he could see her with the sun behind his eyes and above his head, he saw she was very young, quite sharp-eyed and heavy in all the places he liked. Dressed in a skirt trimmed with golden lace and a blue crop jacket over her blouse, she knew the fashion of the day, and the way that sun veil lusciously dangled from her cap left no doubt that back in the country she was from, she was used to crowds parting before her.

As they approached another pond, they were greeted by a flock of ducks, quacking about in the water as if they seemed to agree with Dantavakra's assessment.

'Look, ducks!' said Dantavakra. 'They are said to be a good omen. Oh,' Dantavakra pointed at a rather dishevelled-looking specimen on the side of the path, 'that poor chap appears to have lost his way.'

Without a second thought, he bent down to pick up the duck, but to his surprise, the bird began to flap its wings wildly, splashing mud and water all over his trousers and his recently exfoliated feet. Milani stifled a frown as she looked down at his soaked trousers in dismay.

'Well, I suppose that's what I get for trying to play the hero,' Dantavakra said with a wry smile and then turning to the duck, he added, 'and this is living proof one can look adorable and be annoying at the same time.'

'Indeed, one can,' said Milani, unimpressed. 'Perhaps next time we should just leave the ducks to their own devices.'

'Point well noted, My Lady.'

And with that, they continued their romantic stroll through the park, mud-spattered trousers and all. Milani held on to his arm with the territorial tenacity of an Easterner, less out of possessiveness, more out of a show for the other ladies who mooned at Dantavakra as they passed him by. Partly driven by fears of diminishing his market value before these other ladies, Dantavakra guided Milani to a bench secluded by giant hedges. He whispered a thanks to the gardeners committed to the cause of illicit lovers in need of privacy, glanced around to confirm the absence of any other lady he might've kissed in the same place, and confirming there were none to be seen, heaved a sigh of relief. But before he could continue the conversation about ducks, Lady Milani's palm found its way to his crotch.

Eyes widening, he turned to look at her, and then due to sudden nether pressures, closed his eyes instead. Dantavakra was nothing if not a cautious man. He borrowed her sun veil with her permission and deftly placed it over his lap to build a linen Mathuran Wall to keep his tower safe from prying eyes.

He whispered, 'Someone might catch us.'

'Doesn't the possibility of being caught make it far more thrilling?'

'You are… extraordinary.'

And while Lady Milani was tending to Dantavakra with her gracious touch, a winter breeze washed through the park, carrying the fragrance of spice from the market over the wall, together with the stench of putrefaction from inside the wall. Dantavakra winced as he discovered the source of the rotten perfume, half softening under the sun veil. In clear view from where he sat, beyond the hedges and up above the gates, a head, impaled upon an iron spike, played audience. What remained of the man's head, at least. The crows had already plucked out his eyes, leaving two dark holes which made it seem from the distance as if he was surprised. The expression was complemented by the man's mouth which sagged open as if to express outrage at the open display of debauchery in his garden. Dantavakra shivered when he realized the head was not charred, which meant his body had been denied cremation. The worst fate to befall anyone. Ever. He would not wish it on anyone, not Krishna, not Rukmini and not even his old governess who, in his tender years, had resorted to unorthodox bathing techniques involving forcing his face between her legs.

Unfortunately, Dantavakra recognized the eyeless head. It formerly rested on an old Acharya who'd been heard preaching sermons against Narag Jhestal, the High Priest of Unni Ehtral, and championing the worship of all the Seven Gods of the Pantheon

instead of just worshipping the Ehtral Gods of Life and Death.
Naturally, swift justice was dispensed. All good, yes. But couldn't
there be a spot designated for impaled heads? While Dantavakra
would never admit such sentiments in public, he grumbled to his
friends all the time as to how the entire city aesthetic was being
marred by rotting heads, turning wooing into a woeful affair.

He did feel a twinge of sympathy for the other Acharyas though
who must now be living in constant fear of the sword. Unlike other
kingdoms which typically had just one Acharya assigned by Meru,
the Empire had fourteen to steer it on multiple aspects of gov-
ernance. And in the time since the decapitation of their colleague,
half those Acharyas had jumped ship from the Seven to Unni
Ehtral, though quite what differences lay between the two was not
something he was willing to ask anyone. He pitied these turncloak
priests for their lack of courage and conviction in their beliefs. Such
a shame the Namins were built so differently. Not so for Ksharjans.
The warrior blood that ran in them—

Dantavakra let out a sigh as Milani began moving her hands
furiously to bring him back to the moment. His spirits, along with
his trousers, experienced a noticeable elevation until a shadow fell
upon him. A reed-shouldered man, dressed in loose linens of the
Ehtral fashion, loomed over him. 'May I sit?'

There are those who might not be afraid if the priest of a murderous cult walked in on them while their lady friend was inspecting
the flute inside their pants. They might tell the priest to bugger off
with a stiff upper lip, immune to the whims of fate. But Dantavakra
was not one of them. He felt the proverbial snake of ice climb up his
leg. He did try to shake the snake away, but it was rather difficult to
do so with his pants unlaced in a public park.

'Of course, Your Worship,' he said as he felt Milani continue to
move her hands. Was the woman insane? Oh, wait, she did not
know much of the Ehtrals! She was an outsider. He tried to squeeze
his thighs shut to encourage her to stop but that only motivated
her further. 'I… I was just sitting here to admire the gardens,' he
stammered.

The Acharak nodded as he sat beside them. Dantavakra tried not
to gag. There was something incredibly faecal about the Acharak's

fragrance. 'The head of the wicked here does add a certain charm to the garden, wouldn't you concur, Ser?'

Much akin to how a congregation of Reshts adds a certain charm to a temple procession. 'Quite so, Your Worship,' he said, stifling a moan. 'The grotesqueness of his sin blends with the beauty of the flowers to constantly remind us of the two roads that lie before every man. How his soul appears at the end of the road depends on the path chosen. A plant of rose or feed for crows, the choice lies within the man himself.' He turned animatedly to Dantavakra. 'Do you know of *Samsara*, Ser?' He took his time arranging his robes on the bench.

That was a good sign, wasn't it? Ehtralites did not talk theology with people whose heads they intended to use as gate decorations. Dantavakra nodded. 'Endless cycle of rebirths.'

The priest smiled. 'Not endless, good Ser. A dog may be destined to chase its tail but with discipline it can be instructed to chase the stick instead. Such is the way with souls. The goal of every life is to break free of this cycle. And to break this cycle, one needs to unshackle the dormant Chakras in the body. The Namins, being the Firstborn of Yama, are blessed with ancient power in their blood to cast off these chains from their Chakras by—'

'Severe austerities! Yoga. Penance. Even meditation,' Milani answered excitedly even as she circled her thumb around his tip. *Yama's harem! Stop talking, woman! No. Stop stroking, woman!*

The Acharak nodded. '*In the still mind, in the depths of meditation, the Self reveals itself: Scriptures VIII.* Ksharjans, like you, Ser, carry blood in your veins that gifts you the power to achieve nirvana through death on the battlefield. But I daresay the finest warriors in a cruel irony, by their very skill, are denied this route. They die undefeated, old, pissing their bed, decrepit men whose biggest battlefield then lies in their privy. I am afraid to admit that it is the same fate for Namins who choose the household life. Their austerities lie in arranging funds for a good dowry for their daughter or which sacrificial ceremony to choose to dispel the bad aura around their clients. What of these good folk? How do they break free? Don't they deserve liberation from *Samsara* but are unjustly denied?'

Dantavakra shrugged as he made a constipated face. He was close. 'Wait for the cosmic lottery to be reborn a priestly Namin or a warrior Ksharjan?'

'Karma, Ser. The Yoga of Karma. Selfless action is the only key to free yourself from the bondage of *desires*.' He stretched the last word out. 'When the good you leave behind far outweighs the sins, the scale of life will tilt, and you will rise on it to dine in the feasting halls of Yamalok, the Abode of Yama.'

Dantavakra was the kind of person the world might call an optimist. But even these fools have their limits. Look at the circumstances the poor knight found himself in. He could be forgiven for believing that he was not breaking free of any *Samsara* for a few thousand years even by a conservative estimate. Not that he wanted to. He loved his life on earth too much to be a lowly dining guest in heaven. 'I'm afraid that ship has sailed for me, Your Worship.'

'There is another way, of course.' The Acharak turned to him. His blue eyes were sharp icicles in a wrinkled face. 'Martyrdom.'

Dantavakra swallowed the lump in his throat and was surprised he did not end up coughing.

'Is *that* a sacrifice?' Milani awkwardly pointed at the rotting head before them. Dantavakra groaned. Did she not know you never ask an Ehtral priest follow-up questions?

'No. Within their kind is just winter, ice and despair. *The crookedness of the treacherous will destroy them: Scripture VII.9*. Denied cremation by the fire, the souls of these blasphemers are now damned to the dark ends of the earth to live with old horrors.' Milani squeezed his cock in cold fear. *Good Heavens. Why was he stiffening?* 'Sadly, blasphemy is not the only route through which souls find themselves at the ends of the earth.' And then he glanced pointedly at Dantavakra's lap, hidden behind the sun veil, leaving no room for even the most delusional to continue deceiving themselves. Just at the brink of his release, Milani jerked her arm free and hid her damp palms in the folds of her odhni, her legs fidgeting with the nervous charm of someone who had just confessed.

'I... I can explain,' Dantavakra started, the frustration at having been denied a dive at the cliffside of pleasure competing with his fear of decapitation. The Acharak raised his hand.

There is nothing to explain. Young love is like a seesaw. One rises, the other comes crashing down.' He smiled kindly. 'Tell me, Ser, are you an ardent faithful to the Seven in its true form?'

He had no inkling of what true form meant. 'Yes, Your Worship.'

'I would hope so. My meeting you was no happenstance. Your presence has been commanded by the Emperor in his throne room. You are to be there before the hour of the nightingale.'

The Emperor? Wanted to see him? Why? Did the Chamberlain complain? *Oh, I'm so dead!* 'Have I done something to be in trouble?' The potential answers to that question could fill a book.

'No.'

'Then what awaits me?'

'That depends.'

'On what?'

'How high can you fly?'

Dantavakra blinked his eyes in confusion till the Ehtralite gestured towards the gate. 'You do not want to keep the Emperor waiting, Ser.'

'Yes, yes of course, Your Worship.' He turned to Milani. 'Come, My Lady, the hour is late upon us. I will escort you to your residence on the way.'

As they both rose, the Acharak cleared his throat. 'You need not bother, Ser.' Dantavakra felt an ugly twist of fear in the pit of his stomach as the Acharak rose to join them. 'You should hasten. Time is of the essence after all. I would be happy to take your place and accompany the Lady if she will have me.' He smiled. A kind smile that belonged on a grandfather with a secret basement. 'She is new to the city, I believe, and I would be happy to give her a tour of the delights our city has to offer. You were headed to the Winter Fair, were you not?'

Before Dantavakra could object, Milani spoke. 'It will be my honour, Acharya.' *Not Acharya. He isn't a Namin priest.* Milani whispered to Dantavakra, 'The Emperor wants to meet my dashing hero face to face. Maybe I am turning out to be your lucky charm. Off you go, grace the Emperor with your presence. I will be fine. And perhaps afterwards, we can finish what I started.' She whispered the last course of action in his ear.

'But you don't—'

'I will handle the priest,' she cut him off. 'Women are trained to manage old men from the moment they blossom. Nothing I can't handle. See you on the morrow.'

II

She will be fine. It is just a walk, he thought resolutely till his resolve wavered. *Yama, old friend, please let her be fine.* He shook his head violently to let in the cavalry of optimism. *Of course she will be. The Acharak just wants to deliver a sermon on ethics to Milani. He did give him his word, after all, that he would return her safely to her residence. Should I find a way to convey her whereabouts to her cousin?* No, no. *That will just add hot sauce to a curry.* He was not even sure if Milani had clued Mair in on her rendezvous with Dantavakra. Judging by Mair's possessiveness in Tulips last night – highly doubtful.

Everything will be fine, he told himself for the hundredth time. Come the morrow, he would reunite with Milani and jest at the Acharak's expense, and the woman would finish the half-done job. They'd all share a good laugh, and with the benefit of hindsight, come to view the escape as a tavern-worthy tale.

Provided of course the Emperor had not summoned him to have him gelded. The thought purged him of any lingering concern for Milani and slipped urgency into his boots. Ploughing through a crowded archway into the spice-market, he scarcely spared a glance at the Lion, Stag and Eagle puppets performing on his favourite puppet stage. So lost in thoughts was he that even when a great palanquin was heaved in front of him, he ducked under it absently, nearly knocking one of the carriers over and making the whole thing teeter.

And in this oblivious state, the skirtchaser of Rajgrih ambled into the Imperial Palace. He zigzagged through the maze of huge white marble columns that rose to join the leviathan paintings on the vaulted ceiling. Sunlight poured through the narrow windows that dissected the walls. The Crimson Guard, the ones not busy ushering the supplicants, gripped tall spears and stood beside these windows. He had often played and cheated them at decks in the evening games by the harbour. If, by a miracle, he lost this year's Imperial Contest, he would, with his connections, join the ranks of the Crimson Guard in a matter of a few years. Would they be the same soldiers who would drag him by his heels to the cells today? Dantavakra's steps faltered at the thought, and a Drachma merchant behind trod on his heel. He righted himself only to be intercepted by a Royal Page.

'Ser Dantavakra of Chedi?' the Page inquired.

'Don't pretend you don't know me, twat. What is it?'

The Page scowled. 'I'm to escort you to the throne room.'

People were huddled in clumps about the wide stone steps, biding their turn until ushered through the doors below to meet their Emperor. Another sprightly Page bellowed instructions to them. 'Lords and Ladies, you are commanded to kneel at the approach of the Emperor of Kings, His Imperial Highness...' As he droned on the titles, Dantavakra glanced around the room. A rather sizeable gathering today. All manner of people lining up to seek the Emperor's Justice.

But clearly Justice would have to wait, for the human tide parted to let the Page leading him pass. That brought a smile to Dantavakra's face as he began to feel rather self-important. The Page must have noticed it for he made a show of glancing up at the wall behind Dantavakra and then staring at him, and then back again at the wall. He finished the performance with a feigned snigger. Dantavakra, scowling, turned to find a tapestry of the God of Darkness and Death: Yama, who stood with his hands outstretched, his kind sister, Xath: Goddess of Light and Life, nowhere to be seen.

Fuck.

The hanging bore a likeness to the stone sculpture of Yama on the outskirts of the Capital. Same alignment, same pose. Yama's palms faced up to the sky but sloped down to the ground, so that each of the heretics' children could roll down them and fall into the gaping fire pit. It had grown to become a popular winter spectacle for the city's amusement. Dantavakra did not feel amused now. Was it this that awaited him?

As he passed the candle men and waited at the corridor that led to the richly ornate throne room, the Page curtly instructed him to wait. Dantavakra, hands clasped behind, fidgeted on his toes. Peering through a crack in the door, he saw that the candelabras inside had not been all lit, and the flickering torches, along with the evening sun, were the only source of light in the throne room. From here, Dantavakra could spy two figures who sat at the far end of the room. The Emperor, slouched on the throne, seemed to be ageing ten years a day if his face was used as a calendar, even if his hulking arms thoroughly disagreed. In the flickering shadows, the many scars on his bare skin stood out like dark tattoos even from this distance. There was also the vague form of someone else shrouded in the shadows behind them. All of them were in the midst of a discussion which if not by the volume but by its sheer content seemed like a heated one, one Dantavakra knew he should not intrude on. But intrude he did.

The man in the shadows squeaked. 'My liege, see not sacrifice as the lessening of souls but as an emboldening of a society. Scholars, prisoners of war, criminals, all give us their lives to nourish our own. Did not their blood fed to the soil turn it fertile to keep our soldiers fed through the winters?'

'Why do you think I said naught when you buried their maiden daughters alive at Virangavat's base. But I am not going to sentence my own.'

'Did it not help complete your arena of desire, My Emperor?'

'I have spoken, Jhestal.'

There are moments when one is glad for not having consumed too much water before a grave meeting and this was one of those times. It would not have boded well for Dantavakra to wet his breeches even before he entered the throne room. Why was Jhestal here? What did Jarasandh mean by *sacrifice his own*? Was Dantavakra going to be sacrificed? *Oh, My Lord! Fuck. Fuck. Fuck.* He could not believe he was stupidly fantasizing about becoming a Paladin one day when he was going to be buried with those maidens under the very arena of his dreams. Stupid Shishupal had to obviously leave the Capital when such misfortune befell him! *He* was the unreliable sheep of the family, not Dantavakra. *Shit. Shit!*

'... Your Grace, Ser Dantavakra of Chedi,' the Page's voice echoed. Dantavakra hooked a finger inside his stiff collar and tried to coerce the air into moving in with little effect.

The gilded doors heaved open and the crack of light in the middle widened hauntingly. Dantavakra pulled his shoulders back in what he hoped was the bearing of a man who had committed no crime. He threw on his best smile as if he were posing for an artist, realized how enormous a breach of etiquette he was about to commit, swapped it for a solemn *tired-after-a-day-of-righteous-living* frown and stepped through.

It was far from his first visit to the throne room, of course. He remembered being so excited when his father had brought him here from Chedi to surrender Shishupal as a ward, being impressed when he'd been introduced by Shishupal, then Claw in the Imperial Army, to the Emperor, and being enormously bored when he'd attended as a squire for a Paladin in a property dispute.

Dantavakra went on his knee, and then realized that he'd done so at least fifteen steps behind the designated circle. The Royal Page was no doubt shaking with laughter behind him. *I will kill him.*

Dantavakra raised his head awkwardly to have his worst suspicions confirmed. It was indeed Jhestal. His condescending pout was hidden behind the mask that left only his stern eyes for a man to gauge his mood. But if he was petrified at seeing the High Priest, he turned almost catatonic on seeing Dimvak, Lord Commander of the Rakhjai and his mentor for the Imperial Contest. Was he being summoned for missing the morning lessons? Oh, Seven Hells! It was bad enough Dantavakra was going to be hanged but for it to be done before someone who believed in him was rather discomforting. It was far easier to bear an insult before strangers rather than before friends.

'Your Grace,' Jhestal turned to the Emperor as if in a last bid to change his mind, 'there is still time to—'

The Emperor spoke over him. 'Danta, you are Rakhjai now. You are to guard Saham Dev.'

Being a seasoned customer in the betting business, Dantavakra faced whatever Fortune threw his way with the calm indifference of a princess in a swayamvar. However, at the words emerging from

Jarasandh, a spasm definitely shook Dantavakra's legs and caused his facial muscles to dance in a way to make a jester envious. His look, as he stared at the Emperor, was the look of a man unable to believe his ears.

'Your Grace?' Dantavakra was as confused as a dog looking for the stick his master had not thrown. 'To be Rakhjai, one needs to be a Paladin,' he explained as if divulging valuable inside information.

The Emperor did not respond and let Time do the work. Time took its own sweet time but soon Dantavakra's eyes widened in proportion to the surprise. 'I… I am now a Paladin?'

'So it would appear,' Dimvak grunted. 'Now, Ser, what do you say to the Emperor?' he prodded Dantavakra like a mother prodding a child to thank guests who brought toys.

The sound that emerged from Dantavakra's throat seemed to have originated from the very soles of his feet. It transcended the boundaries of a sigh to a groan. It was the sort of groan that might have been wrung from the reluctant lips of an ambitious Resht at the stake.

But it was only sound that found its way out. No words. Dantavakra said nothing. Could say nothing. To any chronicler given to snap judgments, a vassal lord's second son, a thorough shame on his family, who hadn't even participated in a real battle, being elevated out of turn to the most exalted position within the Empire probably seemed an enviable one. 'Lucky!' the chronicler would say to himself as he wrote a history of the Empire in his cramped quarters. In many cases, of course, he would be right. But not in the case of Dantavakra of Chedi.

The issue here was quite different. This poor boy had, poetically speaking, a pebble in his rice bowl, a Resht girl in his line of suitors, a strand of hair in his spiritual tea.

Where. Was. The. Fucking. Celebration?

The fireworks? The cheer of onlookers? The envy of his friends? The lust of his paramours? He had been bestowed the honour that even the greatest warrior of the Realm, Arjun, had not earned. Not his own brother, not that upstart Karna, none from his generation. In a heartbeat, he had become the greatest warrior of the Realm but he did not feel so. His ability to forget that in his head he had been moments away from death was something stoic philosophers could learn a lot from.

'Uh, uh…' he stuttered.

Were the Meru philosophers right? Was the only thing worse than not achieving what you want, achieving it? Is suffering the only thing that lends victory its value? He had no doubt that he deserved it. Who else? But he had the constipated look of man who, having visioned climbing the tower to save the distraught princess, had found her lounging in the garden instead. Dantavakra was all in for honour-without-hardwork but reward-without-anticipation felt humdrum at best.

'Ser!' Dimvak almost spat that word. 'Do you know what an honour it is for a boy of your age to be elevated so? And all you have to say is *Uh*.' Dantavakra, whose ego competed with his mother's chinaware, would have liked to ask what he meant by the expression 'boy of your age' but he was offered no opportunity to ask. Like most murderous teachers, Dimvak was not easy to interrupt mid-monologue. He waxed eloquent about Dantavakra's insolence and his complete disregard for rules. He suspected Dimvak had veered a little off-topic.

'Yama's teats,' Dantavakra murmured under his breath after Dimvak made a remark about his drinking, and then froze stiff with a fear that by some wind magic it had carried across to the throne. 'I… I am honoured beyond measure, Your Grace,' he spoke quickly as if to drown out the echo of *Yama's teats*.

'Spare him a moment to absorb it, Lord Dimvak,' Jhestal said. 'Rise. Lord Dantavakra. Lord Dimvak, if you will, please.'

Dantavakra stiffened as Dimvak stepped down from the dais and approached him. A rolled piece of clothing was tucked securely under one arm. He was almost confident he would be slapped in a few heartbeats.

'Ser Dantavakra of Chedi,' Dimvak intoned, his voice carrying across the hall, 'you have shown great valour and skill in the service of the Empire.' *Have I?* 'You have…' Dimvak hesitated for a moment before continuing, 'fought bravely and upheld Ksharjan honour in times of peace.' Dantavakra did not fail to notice how the words *fought bravely in battle* had been suitably amended. 'It is now my privilege to bestow upon you the honour of Paladin under the aegis of the Seven.' He then whispered, '*The way you saved the Crown Prince, you made me proud, you undeserving lucky bastard.*' Dimvak then summoned an Acharya of the Orange Order, who hastily mumbled that he was ready to administer the Vachan.

Oh... is that why? Dantavakra swallowed hard as Dimvak drew his sword, the metal singing as it left its scabbard. Pure Assyrian unbreakable steel, charred at the ends from Dimvak's legendary skirmishes in the ice peaks of Mai Layas. The Lord Commander of Rakhjai held his thumb against the sword edge and swiftly slashed it against the blade. Whispering a prayer, he placed the bleeding flat of his thumb between Dantavakra's eyes.

'In the name of Yama,' Jhestal said solemnly as Dimvak drew a tilak on his forehead, 'who art glory and law, and in the name of Xath, who art fairness and life, will thou set yourself free from vain temptations of chance desires and give unto the Empire your soul in the spirit of sacrifice?'

How often had Dantavakra practised the lines of this Vachan before the mirror when he was a child? Then why did his voice quaver when called on to scream those very words? His eye caught the slowly retreating figure of the Page behind him. Ah, now the Page will know his name, won't he? *On how high you will fly.* The Acharak was right. This was his destiny. How high would he fly? All the way to the bloody sun. He drew strength from the thought and gave voice to the millennia-old Pledge of the Paladin.

'On the holy Xath and just Yama, hear in witness and my vow remember,' the words rang out true, 'here do I swear fealty to the Empire, to be the light to guide the herd, to be the rod to reprove the err'd, to use my heart to shield the blood of my Lord and my hand to shed the blood of his foes, to do as my Lord asks of me, to keep his secrets and to never flee, from this moment henceforth, until death takes me. So say I, Dantavakra, son of Damogjosha of Chedi.'

'Witnessed,' Dimvak said, and the Acharya nodded.

'Witnessed,' echoed Jarasandh and Jhestal both.

'Rise, Paladin,' Jhestal said.

As he rose, he could not help but feel a twinge of disappointment as the rumours about a Vachan's ability to strengthen one's nerves proved false. There was no surge of newfound sensations. He felt nothing new. Nothing strange. Even the fleeting rush he had felt while taking the Vachan dissipated when he felt hands encircling his neck, turning it with a firm grip. Dimvak looked smug as he unfastened the bronze clasp and whisked Dantavakra's knight vestment away. With a flourish, he threw around a rather heavy weight of gold-trimmed white cloak behind Dantavakra and affixed it to his shoulder with a crimson lion brooch. 'And now you are one of us. One of the Rakhjai.'

That was it. He had achieved his life's finest dream. He could send in bards to check but he probably was the youngest Paladin in the realm. All reasons to celebrate but all Dantavakra could wonder was *what next?*

He began to follow Dimvak as he returned to the dais, had a momentary panic as he wondered whether he should have taken the Emperor's permission, and decided to wait till someone who knew more instructed him on what to do. The realization that now he was the *someone* who was supposed to know the most evaded him tenaciously.

It was Jhestal who finally addressed him, the calmness in his voice still as unnerving as the first time he'd heard it when he had sentenced those children to be crucified. 'Ser, Winter has kissed our skies, and we are on the last rung of the ladder – the last battle of the Yamuna Wars. As we flip through our metaphorical paintings, reminiscing on the darkest moments to plague the Empire – there are so many to consider after all – we often forget to turn to the paintings of the Future. Sibyls have seen the future in the entrails of the sacrificed and as is common with the Future, it is a mixed bag of happiness. The skies above Mathura were red and green. Smoke and ash blotted out the sun. The trumpets of airavats filled the air. There were other disturbing signs.'

Why is he telling me this?

'Wars in the Riverlands as millions fight over water freezing in the Mai Layan glaciers.'

Aren't they glaciers? Water is always frozen there.

'Mathuran refugees flooding into other kingdoms struggling with plagues.'

Didn't that already happen in the second year of the War?

'Kalingan coast subsumed by the sea.'

Isn't Chilika already under water?

'All these events are bound to happen but what is not known is how our realm would respond in absence of one shepherd to guide them all. The Realm is in need of a strong, firm hand to guide it through the apocalypse that awaits us, don't you think?'

'Erm, yes, Your Worship.'

'Ah, glad we think alike. I do think the Conclave offers a grand opportunity for the seeds of this idea to be planted. Mathura's end is nigh, and with the Usurper soon out of the way, the Empire can do what it was born to do. Save the World.'

'Pardon, Your Worship,' Dantavakra finally mustered the courage, 'but what has this got to do with *me?*'

'It has everything to do with you, Ser. We are sending the Crown Prince and Princess Mati as envoys of Magadh. Royal blood needs Rakhjai, Ser. You are to protect the royal couple in their endeavour to build a bridge with the East. The Crown Prince himself requested your services as a Rakhjai after the way you saved him from near death.'

The Crown Prince requested Dantavakra! Brilliant. But wait? Did he mean East? The East! The fucking East! The Leeches! Savages and blood-drinking barbarians who still had not faltered towards civilization. The weather! He vaguely remembered hearing the Eagle from the puppet show scream of how even the trees of the East sweat. Dantavakra did not deal well with humidity. His face cried a river even in the dimmest of summer. The air there was rumoured to be so thick with humidity, one could cut it with a knife, if one could find one that hadn't already rusted. Holy balls of Yama! He even forgot about the bugs. The bloody buggy East! What had the Lion in the puppet show growled? The national sport of those dark fiends of the East was arm wrestling with the mosquitoes. And the land! Growing up, his father had always used the threat of sending him to the land of marshes and bogs to keep him from making a nuisance. *No, you have to wriggle out of this! Remember!*

You convinced a father to let you go even after he caught you with his daughter. Find a way!

Staring at Dimvak for support, he said, 'But a Rakhjai can never leave the Emperor's side.'

Dimvak's stern eyes pulled an I-told-you-so roll before answering. 'Royal Blood, Lord Dantavakra. Not Emperor. Royal Blood. So best make preparations for the long journey ahead. The nights will be long, the days will be wet and the rains will be arrows if the monsoons rear their ugly head. Now off with you, *Rakhjai*. The throne room will now open to the supplicants. Best not get caught in the stampede.'

What? That's it? He wouldn't even get to stand behind the Emperor? How will the Capital know of his elevation? It would be horrible if he had to tell it himself to his friends. And what would he say? That he had been elevated to Paladin and Rakhjai in one day to guard the Cowardly Cub of Magadh on his journey to the rotten arse side of the Realm? *I don't want to go.*

Dimvak cleared his throat loudly.

Droopingly, like a man on whose future the oracles had closed their journals, Rakhjai Dantavakra of Chedi, having given his Emperor one sad, reproachful look, left the room to find the worst secretkeeper amongst his friends to share the news. But on his way back, he saw the Page behind the gilded door bowing gloomily. Dantavakra's mood returned to its soaring heights like a falcon. One can't let immediate concerns ruin one's plans for the future and one can't let future concerns spoil the fruits of the present. And didn't someone say the best way to cheer yourself up is to ruin the day of someone who crossed you.

'Ah, Page, I have been meaning to talk to you,' he crossed his hand over the simpering fool as they left the throne room, 'I like you. You have guts. Guts that are wasted here. Guts...' he eyed the Page mischievously, 'that would be rather suited in a squire to my royal mission in the *East*.'

'Please... no, my Lord,' the Page stuttered.

And like the monstrous Rakshasas of the East, Dantavakra found his humours returning with each drop of blood that drained away from the Page's face.

MATI

I

Mati straightened in slow, stiff jerks, having been bound hand and foot for hours in the cart. Rough hands seized her arms as they escorted her over rocky, wet floors. Her captors had to be amateurs the way they kept fumbling with her. Not that Mati was to be blamed. She had not resisted it once. In fact, she was looking forward to it. Mati knew the orchestrator could not be Saham Dev. He liked his violence in the bedroom behind closed doors, delegated to his loyal brutes. It had to be Duryodhan on the other side of her blindfold. Maybe he was repaying her for his abduction in Panchal. Wouldn't that be poetic? She would be rescued from being charged for her husband's murder by her lover. A classic Black Swan adventure.

It could be Krishna wanting to ransom her from the Emperor. Wouldn't that be nice? The Emperor would, of course, scoff at such demands, especially if Saham Dev were to reveal that Mati had poisoned his son. And then she would be left to her fate as Krishna's hostage. Maybe she could seduce Krishna to be his fourth wife. Given he had three of them already, Krishna was surely a one-man pleasure parade. Virile and vigorous. *Get your mind out of the gutter.*

'Ow,' one of her captors winced.

'Twenty-one steps, Balloo. Twenty-one steps. It's that simple.'

'Maybe for you,' he rasped. 'My feet are larger.'

Some other day, Mati would've smirked at the mention of large feet. But... practice had shown her the lies in that myth. *Damn me to the depths! How long have I gone without being sailed that all my thoughts seem to spiral around a mast?* Before she could answer, she heard the sound of a door opening ajar. The smell of camphor descended on her. Her escorts stumbled again, causing Mati to nick her toe against a doorframe. 'Mind yourself, maggots!'

'Sorry, sorry,' the man, presumably Balloo, fumbled.

'Don't say *sorry!*' the other one winced. 'We are her captors. We aren't sorry, Princess!'

Who would hire such idiots? They were taking the thrill out of the abduction. A girl's faint cry from the distance strangled the humour of the situation. *Amala?* The girl wasn't being raped. The cry was different, a cry of unbearable, continuous pain. Torture. So... not Duryodhan. 'Gents, if anything happens to Amala, I will have your eyes plucked out.'

'That is indeed an interesting threat,' a voice sweetly addressed her. A strong musky perfume filled her nostrils. She sniffed deeper. The last time she had encountered this foul fragrance was on her wedding day.

'Acharak,' Mati addressed the man who had officiated the union between Saham Dev and Mati, 'you Ehtrals have a fine way to treat a Queen.'

Her captors gasped but the Acharak allowed himself a languid chuckle. '*Princess*, once again, you rob mystery of its charm.'

'The only mystery is why you bothered with the blindfold at all. It was fairly easy to trace the steps from the bund, down Lamp Lane, past the sweetshop, down a flight of stone stairs hundreds if not thousands of years old, to wherever this cavern is.'

There was a moment of silence before the Acharak cleared his throat. 'Well, standard procedure, I suppose. At any level, it is helpful when our guests resist. The anticipation helps break the ice. But you spoiled the fun.'

'Terribly sorry for not screaming. Etiquette has never been my strong suit.'

The smell of his perfume grew stronger. She could feel his skin upon hers as he went behind her. The Acharak untied the blindfold with one hand and returned to stand in front of her. She untied the rest of it, preparing to wince at the blast of light but only darkness greeted her.

'Cosy.'

The Acharak chuckled and slurped something deeply. 'A religion worshipping Life and Death isn't much without the symbolism. Dark décor, dark robes, bright hearts.' He gestured with a finger. Flames rose on their own from the clamshell niches low on the walls.

Behind the Acharak now stood the two acolytes of the Unni Ehtral, her amateur abductors. One was spiky like an underfed hound with greasy hair and scrubby grey beard. The other was a slender boy with good teeth, the sort that should be playing around in a park. The two clearly belonged to different worlds, except for the one thing they shared in common. Both had one of their eyes neatly gouged out. The Bats, her handmaidens called them. She did not know of their rank in the hierarchy for the Ehtrals kept their secrets close to their empty sockets but the bandage on the boy's eye was still wet. Newly elevated, then. He must've been the lad who had stumbled all over himself, no doubt still getting used to perceiving depth and distance in the darkness with one eye.

As for the Acharak, unsurprisingly, he was dressed all in black or some blasted dark hue, sipping chai directly from a saucer instead of a cup. His wrinkled face was disappointingly plain. Just another bony old man. But it was his blue eyes, both very much present and always in motion, that suited the Ehtral reputation. To Mati, they reminded her of an owl who was unable to decide whether it was hungry or bored.

Another scream rang out in the corner. Resolve swirled in Mati's eyes to keep them perched on the Acharak. The scream was haunting, but Mati didn't want the Acharak to know she was getting the shits.

'I suspect we aren't here to discuss theology, Acharak. What are you doing to Amala?'

The Acharak smiled as he poured more chai from the cup into the saucer and savoured another sip. 'The lowborn girl is safe, I assure you. Your turn. Why haven't you consummated your marriage with the Prince yet?'

She knew the Empire used spies on its enemies but it seemed future Emperors weren't exempt. 'I am not well aware of your Green laws but I'm sure I would have known if this was any of your business.'

The Acharak plucked a biscuit from the folds of his robes and dipped it into what remained of the chai in the cup. He lifted the biscuit and turned it for Mati to see. As seconds passed, the biscuit surrendered to the tea, softening, yielding, sagging under the weight of the liquid. No longer sturdy, no longer hard. The Acharak smiled as he squeezed gently and the biscuit broke.

It was clear. The Acharak had already cottoned on to Saham Dev's lack of appetite for Mati.

He just wanted to see if Mati would lie, or perhaps he wanted Mati to know that he knew. 'As I'd suspected. Princes don't usually reach a marriageable age without scattering a few bastards first, and the Prince has been remarkably virtuous in that aspect. It isn't an ailment of the body, if you were wondering. The Emperor's seed is strong.' He chewed the biscuit slowly, deliberately, deviously.

Mati shrugged. She had no knowledge of how potent her father by law was but she had caught his son touching himself when he had returned exhausted from his orphan school. He had passed out on the sofa between their rooms. He had probably thought she was fast asleep. But she had watched him, and all his parts seemed to have worked fine then. She had then assumed him to be a sword-swallower but had found no evidence to support it. Haunted past? Perhaps. Overthinker? Definitely.

But Mati would be damned if she was going to let a bat breeder insult her bastard of a husband. *Why the mixed feelings! Damn the Prince to the Depths!*

'It is plain as day to anyone – the Prince is fond of you but he does not wish to—'

'Fuck me?'

The Acharak ground his jaw at her choice of words. 'Yes. And yes, it is because he does not find you desirable.' *Tell me something new.* 'And yet, he labours day and night to better you, but unlike the Prince, you and I both know a lifetime of savagery is not undone by a day of penance.'

'Look, Acharak. I see that you are a little pervert. I don't care. I am an exhibitionist by nature,' Mati said, relishing the rediscovery of her sharp tongue. No one in the Empire would dare speak to even an Acolyte in a rude manner and here she had called the Acharak a pervert! Oh, it felt so good! She continued, 'But if you think calling me savage is a clever way to stir me to share a bed with you, you'll have to do better, Your Worship.'

'How I wish I could twist your spine until all the ungodliness is squeezed out of your pores.' The Acharak licked the last drop of chai clean from the saucer, and startled her by dropping it and the cup on the floor. He stepped over the broken shards, rubbing his bare feet on them, left-right, left-right, making Mati almost wonder if it was arousing the mad man. 'I should not have spoken so, Princess, and that was my penance. You see, even an Acharak, at the end of the day, is only human. But Narag Jhestal is not. He is an Ascended. And he has need of you.'

'Lucky me.' Now that she knew he wouldn't hurt her, it felt less dangerous but no less fun to needle the priest.

The Acharak took a deep calming breath. 'Yama is stern but just. You cannot be blamed for being such a mannerless infidel. You cannot be faulted for what you were never taught. Still... Geography might have made us foes but I hope necessity will turn us into allies.'

The Acharak gestured Mati ahead to join him for a stroll. They climbed up the sloping floor for thirty or so paces before the floor began to dip again. The light was dim but enough for Mati to see the paintings in yellow and ochre on the walls. Outlined in white, extinct beasts were being chased by stick like figures, a struggling attempt by an ancient race to paint their own forms.

'I bring good news for you, Princess. I have no doubt you miss the sea. You will be pleased to know that the Emperor has decreed that you shall sail with the Crown Prince to the Tree Cities for the Conclave. The Conclave is of paramount interest to the Empire. It *needs* those airavats. But the journey on road is fraught with perils. The Empire is not one to underestimate Krishna. I would not put it past the Usurper to steal our airavats on the way and prolong the War by another decade. That leaves only the sea, and I need not tell you how dangerous the East Coast is. The Emperor saw it fit, seeing your experience with the Three Eyes of Elusa on the Kalingan Sea and, of course, the Tree Cities, for you to not only captain the *Gilded Lion* to Kamrup but also attend the Conclave as the Empire's envoy to... handhold the Crown Prince through the discussions with Bhagadatt. I am assured Lord Shalya of Madra will be present as well to aid the Empire's cause should complications arise. He was the one who helped negotiate the deal in the P—'

'I know of the warbroker,' Mati said. Until yesterday, she had not so much as set a toe outside the Palace in months. And now, she was being asked to set sail to the Rim of the World for what was, by all accounts, the most important assembly of monarchs in a decade, if not longer. Thoughts, plans and propositions flooded her mind but with a mental flick of the wrist, she built a dam across them to hold back the deluge, preferring to first see where the Acharak was steering this conversation. 'What else? This revelation is not abduct-cavern worthy.'

'His Grace has ordered the Crown Prince to consummate the wedding and bless you with child before you both return from the East even if it is at the cost of your consent. The Emperor has expressed dissatisfaction at the news that you've yet to sire an heir, and he aims to dispel any doubts on the fertility of your fields.'

Reckon the Empire doesn't know everything its priests know, Mati thought as she absently rubbed her harvested stomach. The Acharak made nothing of it. 'Isn't the Prince lying unconscious?' Mati scoffed. 'Doubt he will be up for the chore.'

'The Prince has woken, and seems quite keen at the prospect of travelling with you.'

It was an effort but Mati managed to stop her face from betraying her feelings. *He is awake.* 'And? What do you want from me? You know spreading my legs isn't the issue here.'

'We need you to ensure he does not impregnate you.'

Now *this* she had not seen coming. 'Does *not*?'

'Here, you both remained under our watchful eyes but away on the seas, we know not the nature of storms. To put it in legible words, Narag Jhestal is concerned you will try and rape Saham Dev.' The Acharak cleared his throat and added, 'Again.'

As long as the Acharak remained in the dark about her attempts to murder Saham Dev, she couldn't care less for her complicity in any other shenanigans. But right now, Mati felt the need to tread with care and for that, she needed to put on a show of outrage. She ignored the faint cries in the background and said coolly, 'You will mind your words, Priest. It isn't rape when he is my husband. It is just his duty, his obligation that I'm helping fulfil. And what is it that you seek with your grand plan? You want to break my marriage with the Crown Prince? Brand me barren? I had underestimated how badly you Lions don't want a Swan for your Queen.'

'Your obsession with yourself is your blindfold. A malady of your generation, we have observed. The Ehtrals don't think in weeks, months, years, we think in decades and centuries.'

'A low-scale production of the Saptarishi play, I see.'

He flinched. This had touched a chord. Mati made a mental note of it and tucked it away for consideration later.

'The answer to your question is—' he exhaled to extinguish his temper '—Yama, you do test people's patience! And the answer is a no. We don't care whether you are Queen or not. What matters is that the Emperor's first grandchild must not be sired by Saham Dev.'

If Mati's compass was askew before, it went haywire now. Had these bats stumbled upon a way to resurrect the Emperor's twins? 'Then who do you desire,' she turned her voice grave to mimic the Acharak's, 'to sire *the Emperor's first grandchild?*'

'Jayatsena, the Defender of Darkness, the First Unmade. Jayatsena, the Firstborn of His Highness Jarasandh.'

II

The Emperor had another child! How was this salacious piece of gossip never spoken of? If she still had any friends left, she would've been bursting at the seams to rush back and tell them this. Damn the gossip of the Harlot and her Five Husbands! *This* was the kind of news that could draw a crowd around any table. But friends or not, she needed to delve deeper. And the first rule of listening to gossip is to keep a nonchalant face till the final act.

Mati looked at the Acharak teasingly. 'You sound like you are in love with this... Jayaena.'

'Jayatsena.'

'Yes, Jayatsena. That is a lot of titles for someone whose name I have never heard—'

Another cry cut off what Mati was about to say. This time the scream was so brutally raw that she felt its heat in her own throat and her eyes slipped in its direction. *Barnacles! So much for nonchalance.* The Acharak caught her look, smiled and beckoned her to follow him as he pulled the curtain to a narrow crevice that led to another cavernous chamber. Mati, hesitant at first, rubbed her toes inside her boots, steeling herself before following him.

'It is New Moon today. On this day, new beginnings are made, new journeys are charted and... new souls are born,' he pointed to a bed, '... ever ready to serve the one True God, Yama.' At the Acharak's gesture, one of the Acolytes lit and set a lantern on the bedside table cluttered with instruments of torture.

A girl lay on the bed, her hands and legs manacled, her naked body wreathed in sweat. The manacles seemed as if they were weeping blood. She had been pulling on her chains, seeking to squeeze her hands through the shackles. Upon seeing the Acharak, the girl started alternately chanting Yama's name and Xath's name, pleading to be released. The Acharak took a winterbind cloth from the table and wiped the sweat from her forehead in a fatherly gesture.

Mati frowned. This was the same girl from Tulips who had been eyeing Dantavakra when Mati had approached him. Two older girls, Ehtral Acolytes, hovered around the girl's bed, one at the head, humming a soft lullaby; the other, by the leg of the bed, her head obscured by whatever she was up to between the girl's legs. Were the Ehtrals healers in their spare time?

'Are you cutting a fetus off her?' Mati asked, confused.

The Acolytes by the bed gasped and spat in the air twice as they made a holy sign of death.

'That would be a crime against Xath, Princess,' he said, evenly. 'No, this is the Resurrection.'

'Another ritual of yours?' Mati asked.

He nodded. 'Humans are helpless. But some of us are so far gone, that the only way they resist temptation is by yielding to it. Temptation is the root of all evils but in some cases, temptation spreads to the branches, to the leaves and to the fruits. Look at you for instance. Months of marriage without the carnal pleasure but have you fallen wayward? No. You may be a heathen but in your own twisted way, you are pure. This is the Way of Ehtrals. Water?'

The Acolyte by the bed handed him an unstoppered flash. He set it to the girl's pleading lips. The girl drank mouthfuls of it, coughing, water spilling on to her chest.

'I caught this poor girl succumbing helplessly to this demon of temptation in a public park, in a public park, mind you, when I was seated right next to her. I could not see her suffer so. She comes from a far-off place but that does not mean we cannot let her have our gift.

The manacled girl's back arched like a bow and stiffened half in the air as the knife did its work, her screams muffled behind the Acharak's iron clasp. 'The Resurrection will wring away desire and restore control to her, as is the aim of Unni Ehtral. Restore control to humans so that we can together achieve *greatness*. And for that, some pains are worth it.'

Mati clenched her fists hard as she realized that whoever the true God was, Yama or Indra or the Storm God, he was not just invisible but deaf and blind as well. 'And not just women, there are men who don't even need their eyes to sin, their spirit is that tainted. Look at that innocent boy sleeping on the bed by the corner. Dragged away by his body's evil desire and enticed, his mind's shackled itself to his flesh. His mother trusted him to our care so that we can teach him ways to master his body in a way that is holy and honourable. Temptations may well be abundant, but so are paths to endure them.'

'What did you do to him?' Mati asked, wondering why she wanted to know the answer.

'We sliced the sheath of his sin into three,' he said, smiling, 'so that every draw of his sword brings a taste of the fires awaiting him should he wield it for a purpose profane. But we wander away. Where were we?' the Acharak asked as he examined the bloodied lump of the girl's essence before tossing it aside on the floor. 'Yes. Jayatsena. The annals and histories are silent about it because Jayatsena's name was deliberately struck off. Thankfully, memories are more reliable than parchment. The estranged child of the Emperor was exiled before the Yamuna Wars. Probably even before the wedding of the twins.'

Mati strained to pull her eyes away from the carved-out pieces of the girl on the floor, and turned to him. She pressed her thumb against the edge of the Rakshasan Key inside the folds of her pockets, the pain doing its bit to clear her mind. 'What will happen to her now?'

'Sewn up and made as good as new,' he smiled. 'Do not worry, Princess. We do not forcibly convert anyone.' When Mati stared back at the Acharak with dead eyes, he clarified further. 'She can even relieve herself easily, you know. A small hole will be dug carefully into her after she heals. After that she is free to lead her life as she wishes. We just gifted her a chastity belt.'

A chastity belt stitched of her own scarred flesh. Mati's eyes took in the instruments of torture and was calculating how long it would take to kill each and every person in the room, when the Acharak put a hand on her shoulder.

'I have always wanted to ask you this, Princess – the Yellow Wedding – did you actually witness it? The arson? The stampede? Rumour has it, three hundred people were crushed. I have always found stampedes a sign that humanity was not meant to inherit the realm. How can so many people be shortsighted together? Just cease moving. Isn't that a cure for a stampede? I can't fathom how the survivors endured, unable to even raise their arms for help, dragged off their feet and welded into a block of people while the world behind them went up in flames. Was it truly that dire?'

The water in her mouth turned to dust. *Point duly noted, Acharak.* 'So you want Jayatsena to be the Emperor.'

The Acharak feigned surprise at the sudden diversion in the conversation before sparing her a smirk. 'Those who stay in straw houses should not carry a torch to a protest.' He rose from the bed and beckoned her to follow. 'Back on course, then. Jayatsena has been… ritually shorn from the royal ties to Emperor Jarasandh. It is as if Jayatsena never existed. So Jayatsena will never be Emperor. But it has to be Jayatsena's blood, Jayatsena's line that ascends to the Empire next. The War of Pyres looms on the horizon and from the ashes of kingdoms will rise only one power to rule over them all: Magadh. It will be the centre of the world, and it cannot be so if Jayatsena's line is not the firstborn grandchild of Jarasandh.'

The War of Pyres. *Storms and Sirens! This damn cult is a believer of sheep's entrails and star dust. How can the Greens be such lackwits? A sheep's entrail is only good to fertilize a plant and a star is only good for guiding ships.* But that was good, wasn't it, she asked herself. Fools so deep in their delusions were the easiest to steer against the wind.

'But... why not just kill me?' Mati asked.

The Acharak smiled and Mati understood. They had considered it. But then why not? Something else was at play here. The Acharak was not behind this ship's helm.

So, what were her choices? She still needed the might of the Empire for her own plans, and she knew how easy it would be for the Empire to discard Mati if she was proven to be barren. A glance at the whimpering girl on the bed reminded her she could not refuse the Ehtrals. But to manipulate this Acharak, she needed to learn more. 'And how will you return Jayatsena to the fold?'

'You may not be well aware of our *Green* laws but you were right, you'd certainly know how it works if this were any of your business.'

'But then why tell me of Jayatsena? Why tell me of your plan? You could have simply threatened to hurt me. I can see you are rather good at that.'

'We are not barbarians, Princess. We hurt no one. We tender justice. You are, at least after your marital vows have rendered you anew, innocent of your past, and we harm no innocents.'

There might be a hundred different laws in the hundred different kingdoms but in none of them would Mati be found innocent by a court of law.

'And as I said, we would rather have you as an ally, and trust is the cornerstone of an alliance. What say you, Captain? It is not as if you're fond of the Crown Prince. Why not be fond of power, instead? True power.' Mati only shrugged in response. 'Just because you can't see how I seek to profit out of this, you don't trust me?' The Acharak smiled as he said it. 'Eyes blinded to acts of pure love will see conspiracies everywhere. So, let me explain. Maekhela, gag Lady Milani. Her cries offend my ears. Come here, Princess.' The Acharak ushered Mati outside the room. Once they were outside, the Acharak beamed again. 'If there is one thing we can agree on, it is perhaps that Equality is the world's greatest lie, wouldn't you say?'

Mati nodded.

'Good. Our ancestors knew of it and ushered the Golden Age by uniting the races of Men against the other tribes. Not because they meant to hurt others then but simply because the Men of the Golden Age had wisdom.' She had heard these sermons often from her room as Saham Dev's tutor had waxed eloquent on the subject of social contracts every day. The same nonsense about the pathetic Rakshasas and of how they fell to Ayodhya, of the Nagas who were chased to the bowels of earth, of a world cleansed of leeches and snakes.

'Now the vile races are gone, our Golden Age is past, because as is common with every empire, be it that of the Children of Light or the First Empire, our realm has passed from Pinnacle to the inevitable stage of Decay and Decadence. Comfort has ruined us. Equality has spread its cancerous hands again, preaching of evenness amongst castes, and what is worse, the high bloods are letting it pass. In all this posturing, humans now think they are the end of history. No doubt the Elder Gods thought the same. No doubt the Ksharjans thought the same before Acharya Parshuram. Look at our Age now. In the North, the Reshts have risen. Their Red Blades threaten to return. The Drachmas rule in all but name. And now these Northerners are flooding Magadh. Do you think these coincounters or shitpickers will save us when the Daevas come knocking? No. It will have to be the Namins who discover ancient secrets and the Ksharjans who wield scythes on the warfield who will be our salvation, the highborns. But all a Namin cares now about is which kingdom he gets assigned to from Meru and all a Ksharjan cares about is making himself richer through trade deals. And so, we have a hundred kingdoms with a hundred gods and therein lies the problem. There can be no Seven anymore, Princess, not in the face of what looms. There has to be just One. One Faith. One Emperor. One Fist.' The Acharak clenched his open palm into a fist. 'United in pain.'

'And Saham Dev ain't pulling his weight, is he?'

'Saham Dev is a noble soul, for sure. But he is weak. Weak by the torment inflicted by time. He lost his mother when he came to the world. The Emperor blamed him for it and by the time he knew better, the Emperor was deep in the Yamuna Wars. So Saham Dev came of age, alone and abandoned. That is why Saham Dev craves desperately for childhood, and a child cannot be a Man. But even if he were one, it does not matter. It cannot be Saham Dev's line that spreads the strength of the Empire beyond its borders, as has been foretold. If Saham Dev's line ascends to the crown, it will be the downfall of our Age.'

'I care not for the world,' Mati said, tired. 'You want me to captain a ship around the Three Eyes of Elusa to the Tree Cities and you want to ensure the Crown Prince does not impregnate me before you magically bring this Jayatsena to court. Correct?'

'Yes. And I see the tide of your thoughts. Tell me. What do you seek in return?'

'In return, I want you to hold off an attack on the Hastina Union for the next ten winters.'

Now it was the Acharak who did not see it coming. 'Not attack Hastina? I thought you would want us to attack them forthwith. You continue to surprise, Princess Mati.'

'And I will remain Queen of the Empire till Saham turns five-and-thirty, after which we will attack Hastina, I will do a bit of revenging and once I am sated, you can install anyone you please. I want the Ehtrals to swear they will not turn any cannons at me in this interlude. I will choose the crew for the voyage to the Tree Cities. And I want none of the Prince's current personal guard to accompany him.'

The Acharak considered Mati for a long uncomfortable while before nodding.

'Tarry a little,' Mati said. 'How will you agreeing make the rest of the Ehtrals or, for that matter, the Empire agree? I need it written and sealed.' Mati was not a fool. She knew that even if they gave her something in writing, it could never be enforced by the Empire. However, it would be evidence enough of Ehtral misdemeanour should these Bats turn on her.

'The truly blind can never understand what it means to bind. I am their Acharak. My words bind each and every one here as their words bind me. We are one organism.' He raised his hand and uttered a wolf howl. Suddenly the entire underground including the two Acolytes, including the poor wretched girl on the bed, howled together. Mati took a step back, the eerie feeling making a living out of the horror in her spine. 'And do you honestly doubt our influence on the Emperor?'

Mati managed to shrug again but this time it looked rather pathetic. The Acharak only smiled. 'Even so, let me inspire your trust with something far deeper than a piece of parchment. Time to escort you to the Inner Sanctum. Seal our understanding in a Vachan.'

Kraken's balls!

'A Vachan?' Mati tried to keep the tremor in her voice down. A Vachan! A ritualistic pact that would annihilate her if she even dared to betray it. Fuck. Suddenly the words she had released to the wind on the *Fat Mistress* returned to her on the sails of a ghost ship. *The only way to keep promises is by not making them.* 'Why?' Mati managed to ask.

'Surely you would not trust the word of a pirate, would you? Come.'

While that was sound logic on the Acharak's part, what was she to do? How could she make a Vachan of not bearing a child in her belly when one was already making itself comfortable there? Mati followed the Acharak, numb, realizing that she was moments away from being roasted alive.

III

The door at the end of the corridor led her into a beehive-domed central chamber, its spoked branches leading off to lesser rooms

shrouded in darkness, felt only by the echo of whispers and footfalls. After another half-dozen heartbeats of indecision, she stepped
through. The air in here was still and motionless. She stretched a
hand out to brush with fingertips the faded friezes on the side. On
the friezes were scarred and chipped images of chariots crashing, of
men and women sparring, of lions eating the insides of a tiger, every
bleached, dusty frieze intent on murder.

Within this space, young children sat naked upon the cold stone
floor beside a pool, like a congregation of penitents. Their eyes were
fixed upon an aged Ehtral priest clad in flowing black robes. The
timbre of the priest's voice carried its conviction.

'The Pantheon came out of worship of the first elements of
existence. Light, Dark, Volcanoes, Oceans, Earth, Wind and Life.
Many other Gods erupted since the First Empire as the faculty of
thought and imagination grew but god-worship mostly ebbed and
flowed between the Seven. Most of these Gods are a lie.' Some of
the children gasped. Their names were noted by the senior pupils.
'In their essence, everything is a duality of Life and Death. A
volcano that does not erupt, can it be said to be a Fire God? No,
it is dead. A desert where nothing grows, can it be said to be an
Earth Goddess? No, it is dead. Death is the only true God and his
twin, Life, his balance. Darkness is an aspect of Death, and Light
is an aspect of Life. These two – the first, the greatest, the purest,
Yama and Xath – are the only Gods worth worshipping. This is the
Ehtrals' mission. To pledge the realm to the True Gods! To bring
our children together for the War of Pyres!'

The children repeated the chant. 'We are the Unni Ehtral, the
patrons of the dying and the diseased, of desolation and ashes, of
Father Yama, the God of Death and Darkness, and Mother Xath,
Goddess of Life and Light.'

Upon seeing the Acharak, the priest and his pupils retreated to
the shadows, lending Mati's eyes more room to take in the ruins.

Ahead, a sledgehammer had been taken to the idol of a God
on the altar. The shattered stones, even if they were of an old God,
seemed to confirm her suspicion. This temple had not always
belonged to Yama and Xath. A man crouched by the altar, manacled in chains which were loose enough to allow him to pore over

papers and scratch on parchment with a quill. As she drew closer, she saw his face was all twisted. He looked more ogre than man, shoulders covered in bristly red hair, a large head assembled on a short neck, a head framed by a pair of beautiful curving horns that spiraled elegantly. As she squinted at the first Asur she had seen in Magadh, the Asur turned, his eyes glittering dull as rough blades.

'Meet Mayasur, Princess. Squire of Lord Shishupal. Perhaps you know him? Lord Shishupal left for his exile thinking Mayasur had safely escaped the clutches of the Empire. But this wretched thing was too curious for his own good. We caught him trying to study the edifices here. Yama saved him from justice by making him quite useful as an architect. He will turn this altar of Skanda into a fit Temple of Life and Death.'

Skanda... Mati had come upon his idols in the black market, for his faithful had become, over time, followers and were now a cult, his idols now relegated to collections. It was because of her experience in this trade that she remembered that Skanda was the forgotten God of War. How strange it was that the ancient Temple of Skanda no longer existed in the memory of Magadhans. Much like the firstborn of Jarasandh.

'It feels odd here.' The air had become solid, difficult to breathe.

'It takes getting used to. Some keepers of the flame from the past think Rajgrih stands on top of a ley line. I find truth in their words. Ley lines were conduits between Gateways of power, and Rajgrih reigns over the most powerful city of them all. It was our pursuit of such a Gateway that led us to find this abandoned temple.

'And seeing how the God of War had walked out, you conveniently turned it into a new house of the God of Death.'

'All Gateways from War lead to Death, don't they?'

Mati barely heard him. She stopped paying attention to things she did not understand. She remembered she had more pressing concerns. Taking the Vachan would be a great fucking risk. A gamble of life. And now that she had agreed so easily to the arrangement, she could not back out. Fuck. If she did not play it right, she would perish here and now. If she did not take the Vachan, the Acolytes in the darkness would kill her now or worse, do things to her to

ruin any chance of her ever having a child. An inconvenient route
but a necessary one when seen from the Ehtral perspective. Mati
shuddered at her imagination that placed her on that bed instead
of that poor lass.

No. She had to find a way out. She rolled her tongue over her
gums as her mind sailed through an arsenal of horrible ideas till she
stumbled upon the least bad one.

The Acharak urged her to sit round a decorated pavestone in
the centre of the room on which was inscribed, with a stylus, an
intricate mandala. A Namin joined them, this one clearly one of
the Orange Order. His hands were manacled as well. Made sense.
Duryodhan had once explained to her how Vachans could only be
administered by the consent of the Seven, and very, very few priests
of the Orange Order were trained in the ritual. And no priest of the
Orange Order would ever assist an Ehtral priest... voluntarily.

'Securing these Vachan-priests comes at no small cost, Princess.
Ideally, this man should be attending to a new Rakhjai at the
Imperial Court but I've brought him here expressly for your needs.
Vachans can be rather untidy affairs, no?'

Bastard.

If Mati had had the time, she could have tried seducing the
Namin to do her bidding but short of flashing her tit at him, she
had nothing. The Namin asked them to close their eyes and before
Mati knew it, he started chanting. The ritual had not been explained,
but in those whispered words, there was something coldly beautiful,
a dark eloquence.

Unable to resist, she opened her eyes. The air around them
wavered, as though alive with something malevolent. A mist began
to coil and twist, its spectral tendrils creeping toward their clasped
hands, wrapping tighter, like fingers around a throat. The mandala
beneath them flickered to life, glowing with a sinister, pulsating
light, as if thousands of fireflies had been snuffed out and their
dying embers were trapped beneath the surface.

Mati rubbed her eyes with her free hand, desperate to shake off
the vision. When she opened them again, the mist was gone. The
light too, extinguished in an instant. *Light playing tricks on your*

imagination, nothing more. But she closed her eyes resolutely this time.

Soon it was time to say the words. *Fuck.* What does she do? Could she make a run for it? Just then Duryodhan's words wafted to her ears from the deepest recess of her memory. *Law is malleable. What is not expressly forbidden, is impliedly allowed.* She smiled. And so, over the next few minutes, Mati played the gamble of her life.

IV

Mati felt the effects of the Vachan instantly. Her tendons stretched farther, her nerves fired faster and her muscles contracted differently. There was a sweet burn in her muscles as she flexed her arm which had now become corded. How badly she wanted to shake someone's hand and pulverize it. She also felt heavy, as if she was carrying armour over her tense mass of hard muscles, an armour she felt could contract and crush her at any moment.

'It is done,' the Namin in chains said. 'Now the Vachan binds you to your words as you have bound yourself to each other.'

'Excellent.' The Acharak rose, flexing his arms, and strolling to the broken altar to wash his face from a pail of water. 'I will see you later, Princess. Stay awhile. Admire the view.'

'A Vachan, like the Codes, is a precise endeavour,' the Namin whispered to Mati once the Acharak was gone. 'It focuses too much on form rather than substance. For instance, if one carefully words her oath to not consummate her marriage and become pregnant in the future, the Vachan does not necessarily cast a net over her if, say, for instance, she was *already* with child.'

Mati looked sharply at the Namin with alarm, her eyes widening like a sailor spotting a jagged reef. How did he know? Mati's disguise was as baggy as a bard's trousers, leaving no hint of an extended waistline. Had the Namin truly deduced it merely from her artful twisting of her Vachan into the future tense? Or perhaps the Namin was a healer with an uncanny knack for these things? The Orange Order was known to supply these male midwives.

The Namin continued, 'That is why it is always advisable to engage a well-read Namin when dealing with such tricky affairs.' He raised his wrists to show the chains around them. 'Too bad the Ehtrals think I know nothing of what I write about. I'm still surprised how that fool of an Acharak did not catch it. But don't worry, Princess. Your secret is safe with me. I hope you make their lives very, very difficult.'

They both nodded at each other in respect. He was going to keep her secret, and that was the dolphin's fins as far as she was concerned. Mati smiled at how she had just dodged the Ehtral's God of Death. Words were a precise game, and constantly twisted by lawscribes in Hastina. That is what she had learned from Duryodhan when they had met over trade deals the first time. And it suited her perfectly.

By the time she showed in a way that could not be stowed, she would already be on the sea, far away from these bats. Her ninth month fell a week after the Conclave. She would push out the damn baby in the Golden Islands and bring him back to the Empire as its heir. While this meant she could not kill Saham Dev now, he could not kill her either.

Saham Dev needed her to save him from the Ehtral plot. Mati would tell Saham Dev about Jayatsena and the Ehtrals. He would no doubt find common cause with Mati, and things would turn for the better. They would return from the Golden Islands and reveal the Ehtrals' plan to the Emperor before this damn Jayatsena could do anything about it.

Once her child was anointed heir, Mati would finally unveil her sinister scheme. A scheme she called *best served cold.*

V

Duryodhan had been right. *Even the Gods must bow before a good lawyer.* But little did he realize that a lawyer eventually dies. Gods don't. The Acharak by now had left the Inner Sanctum to the erstwhile throne room of Skanda, which was armed with vast tapestries onto which were woven grandiose battles that were forgotten. The Acharak could see his Master's smudged reflection in the polished black marble of the floor.

'It is done?' Jhestal asked.

'Yes, Your Worship.'

'You have pleased me, Acharak.'

'We have sworn to not do anything to hurt her or her position as the future Queen of Magadh.'

'As expected.'

'... and not to attack Hastina for the next ten years.'

Jhestal raised his eyebrow at that but thankfully nodded in agreement. 'No harm will come to you, my child, for what you have promised binds me as well. We do not lie.'

'I am not afraid of burning.' The Acharak bowed. 'Will she still die, Your Worship?'

Jhestal smiled. 'They all will,' he said with a twinkle in his eye. 'Now bring me a white raven. Time to send word to the Seven Saptarishis that we have duly complied with their request.'

INTERLUDE

VAHURA'S ADVENTURES

OUTSKIRTS OF KAMRUP, CAPITAL OF PRAGJYOTISHA

A FEW WEEKS BEFORE THE BATTLE OF MATHURA

I

Rain had woven Vahura's hair into ropes after her parasol had abandoned her like her family had. Water coursed down her neck, onto her jacket, her satchel and her boots. Winds shook her in a piecemeal manner, a bone here, a cheek there. If an oracle were to peek inside her heart, she would see that Vahura, at this moment, would be more than happy to set aside saving the world to settle for a dry blouse. She regretted not heeding her assigned Curator's advice to purchase local.

A few more steps, she reminded herself, hunching her shoulders and squinting at the temple ahead, the clouds pissing on her eyes. *Oh, Indra, how much did you have to drink?* She stared up at the gloomy heavens hoping for Indra to be shamed, but alas, the Rain God made no special dispensation for a princess or a librarian, or in this case, both. Not in the wettest part of the world, where it rained as if the clouds had something to prove. The locals called it *lap bah* — rain so heavy and eternal that it was the mightiest rain of all.

If Vahura did return home alive, her first act of patriotism would be to consign the Royal Sunshader to the dungeons. The

Sunshader had pinched his neck to swear that her parasol and her jacket could withstand a tempest sent even by the Gods. It had certainly cost her a godly amount. Her parasol rested in the heavens now. And her jacket's seams had unravelled after the first drops of rain. So now, here she was, drenched as if she had taken a swim in the river with her clothes on. *Oh, Janak, how I am going to enjoy watching you squirm in the dungeons... you blot on the profession of tailors.* The only truth to spill out of the Royal Sunshader was of how Vahura had cut quite the figure of a veteran explorer, which she had to admit she did, just like those heroes she read of in her books.

Even before Vahura's mother had killed herself to save their kingdom, Vahura had never considered her stay in the palace to be temporary. She had never longed to witness the places her mother brought home in books from the Library of Takshashila – the breezy shores of Kalinga, the impregnable walls of Mathura, the snowy pinnacles of the Mai Layas; places she was more than happy to explore on parchment, in silence and solitude. She was a reader of magic after all, feeling most alive in worlds that never were. The only toil her feet undertook were the long walks in the book aisles. But her mother's sacrifice had nudged her off the cliff of comfort to pursue her nightmares. And that infernal tailor had used her fear of the far as a master key to her purse. She wouldn't have minded the manipulation if it had borne dividends.

More than my parasol, I hope my plan bears dividends. Her nose was running now, and she could no longer tell if it was water or snot. She abandoned the lessons beaten into her and hiked ahead in a rather unwomanly fashion, much like a crab, to keep her thighs from chafing against her trousers and against each other. Any more friction, she would have sparked a fire between her legs. But the chafing of thighs was nothing compared to the agony of her cherry tips which seemed determined to spear through her shirt, becoming an unstoppable force against an immovable wall. No one could predict the victor but what was plain was that Vahura would suffer. The whole affair was infinitely intolerable. Those bards truly blew the whole business of travel-the-world out of proportion. What she would give to linger in bed a little longer, sip tea with hot scones, read a good book by the fire and gaze out the window with not a care in the world.

Oh, books. How long had it been since she had closed her eyes on reading a beautiful sentence, ruined her covers with tears over her favourite character's death or slapped the charming rogue in her daydreams? Of late, all her reading had shown her was the shadowy realm of miasmas and diseases. Not that those volumes were easy to come by, either. Most of the scrolls she had read on the subject had once belonged to her mother, who had bequeathed her bows to Vahura's brother, her gold to Vahura's little sister and her library to Vahura.

She longed for that library. It had been a sanctuary of beautiful tomes – illuminated folios, vintage pamphlets on philosophies, miniature prayer books – but nothing had changed Vahura's life more than the scrap of silk she found, clenched in her mother's cold fist.

The dying words brushed on it were in iron gall ink, but Vahura had still used alum as a mordant to secure the words. Perhaps it had been Vahura's way to ignore her mother's body, dead and blinded by her own hands, lying beside the corpse of a slain assassin. Or perhaps the urgency arose because it started with the words 'Dear Firefly', the name she was fond of calling Vahura when she used to whisper stories to her in the twilight hours.

She was nearing the temple now. *Shake it off.* To maintain appearances, she trotted up the terraced steps with elegant strides, but her sole and soul were far from pleased. But wasn't pain always relative? Vahura's favourite way of seeking solace was to compare her current torments with her codex of supreme ordeals from the past, and use the difference to soldier on. Granted, the list wasn't diverse, featuring bullying in its various avatars over the years. The boys had bullied her for her grotesque height and broad shoulders, the girls had cowed her for her wild untameable red hair, and the teachers had tormented her for her memory. A spot of foot discomfort hardly measured up now, especially when she considered where she was.

The roofless Temple of Kamakhya, the temple of the Yoginis, stood on the high Nilachal hill on the outskirts of Kamrup, the

Domed City. The hill itself was barren on all sides. It had been difficult to spy it through the grey curtain of rain. Now closer, she noticed the temple's enormous cyclopean walls, looking like they had been given a hearty shove from the inside by ten thousand stone hands. Airavat fossils, arranged as pickets, covered the grounds outside the temple like a garish necklace. Totems, stolen from the corpses the Yoginis no doubt looted for their rituals, fashioned a chaotic arch over these pickets. When Vahura reached the great door, she paused and turned to look at the place she had hiked from.

From the vantage of the hill, she could see the forested Dome in its full glory – shielding within its green walls an entire city. From here, the tall but comparably tiny trees outside the city resembled an ocean having a go against the brown-green trunks of the Everwood Trees that formed the Dome. Even the towering green foliage of the Everwood looked different from the outside, luminescent and light, the hues of freshly bathed parrots. From within the city, however, when one looked up at the Dome, the Everwood leaves wore a deep and dark sheen, the hues of ancient emerald pools.

To coerce the mighty Everwood Trees into forming a natural wall over and around a city using songs made it worthy to be an abode of Tvastr, the God of Forge, himself. What Vahura wouldn't give, if she had anything left, to unravel the workings of those songs. She squinted at a stone tower, the only structure that jutted out of the green foliage-ceiling of the Dome like a chimney. *Wish you could have seen this.* Leafsong, the palace of Bhagadatt – the Tusk of Kamrup and the Remnant Monarch of the Tree Cities – shone against the backdrop like a stone at the heart of a poisoned green apple.

I am here, Mother. Even now the silk letter she had left behind lay nestled close to Vahura's heart, carefully slotted into a small, slender wooden case that hung from a cord around her neck. Vahura gently clasped it, her thumb caressing its sanded surface, before she turned to face the temple.

She rapped thrice on the door in the instructed pattern, the fat rain drops stinging her bare-knuckled fist like sling-stones. She shivered, clutching the collars of her ruined jacket together with

one hand and sheltering her satchel inside it with the other. A
hopeless exercise seeing as she was already as soaked as a quill left
in an inkpot.

A *cham cham* melody from an approaching anklet on the other
side of the door hastened her heartbeat. *Distract yourself.* A page
fluttered open in her mind's eye from *Maneaters: The Cult of 64*
drawing her to a line she had charcoaled with hue ink:

'Yoginis decapitate intruders the moment they cross their
temple's threshold.'

Thank you, Mind, for that. Well, if her last chapter was to end
today, at least it would be a predictable and glamorous ending –
death at the hands of death-priestesses. A far cry from those
embarrassing demises she had narrowly dodged. Just last week, she
was hounded by a colony of firetoads outside Kamrup, only to be
rescued by her governess. Her mother had always frowned that she
was much too dependent on Old Ella. Her father, in fact, had even
gone so far as to call Old Ella her keeper. Well, why not? She was
a genius, her hero in a prim and proper saree. *Not this time, though.*
In the tapestry of order, Old Ella was a master weaver but even the
Gods were helpless before a bout of cough. In ordinary circumstances, Old Ella would have never let Vahura venture out on her
own but time was slipping away like a pickpocket in a crowd. The
Yoginis might not have opened their temple to her any other day.
When Vahura had made that argument before Old Ella, all her
governess had done was fix her with a disapproving stare, such as a
connoisseur of reds might've directed at a caterpillar he discovered
in his goblet. But there were times when the domestic staff needed
to be told off. Vahura respected Old Ella in the matter of hairpins,
blouses, rings and rescue plans but Vahura would've been a curse on
the Ksharjan spirit if she let Old Ella muscle in and edit her plans.
So Vahura had mustered her feudal courage and slipped the old hag
a special poultice for her sniffles, laced with dreamwine, and tiptoed
past her defences when she had passed out. *I will be fine.* It was just
a temple after all.

A short woman opened the door, holding a large umbrella made of palm leaves, papyrus and peacock feathers. Her face was streaked with white ash, and her hair was matted, filled with braids, perhaps almost as long as Vahura's own. A garland of pigeon skulls dotted her neck but it was the marks of runic symbols on her exposed midriff that caught Vahura's attention. The Yogini was breathtaking in every way, be it of cloth or contours. She held her hand out to Vahura, beyond the cover of her umbrella. Not a single drop of rain kissed her wrist. Those that managed to come close suddenly changed their mind, and along with it, their direction, as if her hand was surrounded by something impenetrable.

'Princess Vahura of Balkh?' the Yogini asked.

Vahura nodded, twisting her shoulder slightly to swing her satchel bag to the front. Plucking a scroll from inside, she handed it to the Yogini, who curiously sniffed it instead of reading it.

'I am called Aindri. If you ask anything about our sex rituals, I will burn your tongue. Is that understood?'

Vahura nodded, wondering what kind of conversational experience would have led to this being the first words out of her mouth. No doubt the train of humans flooding the East for the Conclave would have made the Yogini Temple a mid-day spot. She wondered if the Yoginis begrudged the Rakshasas for lifting the ban on the race of Manu from strolling around freely in Kamrup.

Aindri clicked her fingers to yank Vahura off her dreamscape.

'I apologize, I was just awed,' Vahura lied. 'An inspiring construction, this temple of yours. I have never cast my eye on a hypaethral temple before.'

'It allows the Yoginis to take flight to the skies.'

Vahura politely laughed at the jest but Aindri cocked her head to let her know she did not mean it as one.

'Perhaps you might see it for yourself,' Aindri smirked. 'The ritual of *maithuna* is quite a spectacle. We permit no strangers, but for the gifts you have made to our Coven, I have been instructed to tell you that it would be our honour to host you.' Aindri motioned her to step inside. 'The ritual shall unfold its splendours in a few weeks when we celebrate the menstruation of our Goddess. Rest assured, we won't hold it against you should you not wish to attend. Our Dance on the Dead has never been easy for the world to understand.'

'I would be honoured to attend,' Vahura said, neatly omitting the detail that if she failed in her quest, the whole world would be dead in those few weeks.

II

Vahura scarcely had a moment to appreciate her head still being attached to her shoulders as she crossed the threshold. The blinding brightness inside the temple caught her off guard. It was then that she realized she had been ambushed by a savage sun in a clear, blue sky. Of the grey clouds and murderous rain that had so diligently harassed her for hours, no trace remained.

'Did the rain truly cease in the matter of heartbeats it took me to cross the threshold?' Vahura asked, pulling off her damp gloves. She shook them gently and was startled when they dried instantly. Even as she stared at them, her rain-soaked skirt followed suit, the blackish blue drying back to the colour of glacial ocean. Had she not just forded a small river to get here?

'Shall we, Princess?' Aindri asked, ignoring her question. 'Matrika Zubeia, the Mistress of Ravens, awaits you in the Demoness Dancing Hall.'

Alright. Those names raise no concern at all. She willed her mind to cease the theatrics. If only she could coerce the same obedience from the other Yoginis who had materialized outside their rooms. They observed her with eyes as dead as doornails while Vahura walked past. Their heads pivoted from left to right in perfect unison, making Vahura's neck prickle. *You have read about this. It is just a hive mind they share. You were braced for this. Steady on.* She nodded at them respectfully but still whispered a prayer to Tvastr when she saw more Yoginis, standing guard on the temple walls, turn in perfect synchronicity to fix their gaze on her. There were so many of them, all breathtakingly beautiful, but the uncanny unity in their movements made Vahura's skin crawl.

Vahura turned, a decision she came to rue. On a dais in the central courtyard, framed by four massive, cut stones etched with arcane symbols, corpses were being sensuously washed in milk, honey and sandalwood by two Yoginis. Vahura gulped. 'I would be honoured to attend...' She left the sentence midway to rush to a niche in the wall. 'Is that...?'

Frowning, Aindri followed. 'Yes, this is Matangi. The First.' Aindri bowed before the sculpture of a buxom woman with the head of a goose. And then she turned to Vahura as if she expected her to remark on the aesthetics.

'The detailing on the goose is marvellous,' Vahura said. The Yogini rolled her eyes, and hunched her shoulders in a gesture. 'Oh, oh.' Vahura bowed. Satisfied, the Yogini turned to Matangi again.

'Yoginis were sorceresses from an Age we lost, an Age the orange-clad baboons in the North call the Golden Age. Do you know why it was called the Golden Age? It was because it was ruled by women. Men, dear Princess, used to be just tools created so that women could spread the race, a secret convoluted by time.'

'Women ruled? The entire realm?' Vahura had her doubts. If Vahura were being overly modest, she could call herself 'well read', and she had never even heard whispers of a matriarchal society at the helm of this realm.

'Aye, before the Saptarishis, there were Saptamatrikas, the Seven Matrikas, who guided the realm to peace and prosperity. Alas, they sought to do it through pleasure, through happiness, through the beauty of chaos, till the Great Tears cracked the structures of the society they had built. Through the holes, men crawled out like maggots, with their vision of peace and prosperity through pain, through war, through the cage of order. They descended on the Saptamatrikas, killing all, wanting the secrets of our powers to themselves. They were held back by the last Matrika, Chamundi. Wearing a garland of skulls of men and holding a trident and a drum, she sacrificed herself in slaying the men who came after her, buying her daughters enough time to escape into hiding. Matangi was her eldest, and the one who founded our Coven.'

Every truant child who had been scared by a mother using the threat of a Yogini knew that the death-priestesses had stayed hidden for centuries. But what they did not know was the Yoginis had been hiding from their persecutors, waiting to be forgotten till... they were. But when they emerged, the world had turned so corrupt, even the Yoginis, with all their powers of love and persuasion, could not convince them to a better path. The die was cast. Order had spread its dirty veins through the fabric of the civilization that Chaos could just not purge. And the new world that came to be... feared the Yoginis. And what Men fear, they hang. But still... Saptamatrikas? She doubted it.

'The Rakshasas, bless their demonic hearts, gave us this dilapidated estate outside their city as a home. Someone else might've been offended at being treated as pariahs but we understood it was not personal. Tree City laws forbid human settlements inside their Domes. So, we complained not. Our wants were few, you see. Our memories of when we lived in trees, hunkered down in caves and shacked up on funeral grounds, fending off men who wanted not our wisdom but our bodies, made us look at this run-down temple as a palace.' Pausing before a pillar, Aindri swooped to snag a clay cup and hand it to Vahura. 'Here,' Aindri said as she poured from an earthen pot an aquamarine drink with a purple orchid floating on it. Vahura, with cold certainty, knew to not ask the obvious question if she preferred peaceful dreams but Aindri explained anyway. 'The traditional welcome drink. Concocted of dry ginger, lemon bark, blossoms, jaggery water and just a smidgen of human blood.'

'I thank you, revered Matrika.' She could've lied about a fast, but after that yarn about lost heritage, Vahura could not risk offending her. Closing her eyes, she took a swig, doing her damnedest to let the drink reach her throat without touching her tongue. It burned her throat, and she turned her face away to shield the storm of frowns on her face, only to find corpses being turned over now for a backside cleansing. *By the Forge!* The blood must have been from one of them – and with that thought, she had to hold a pillar to suppress the gag that threatened to bring her down and her food up.

'Curious about those bodies?' Aindri asked. 'It is for the *maithuna* ritual. Their heads will be chopped off in single strokes the day after, and it is on their headless bodies that our practitioners will join their bodies and spirits. Till then, it is our duty to keep them fresh...' the Yogini stopped short when she realized Vahura had stopped following her, dazed. Unknown to her, Vahura's mind had flipped open another door of her memory palace to read the pages of *The Secrets of Tantra* by Acharya Vasa Yana.

'Maithuna, where Shakti and Shaiva twine in a union of spirits divine, is a rite where carnal humours are caged throughout the ceremony of coupling only to be ritually ingested after. It allows its sadhakas, the practitioners, to attain temporary divinity in the physical bliss of kama and spiritual liberation of moksha. The seed...'

'It is fraught with peril,' Aindri raised her voice to bring Vahura back from the world of tantra to the world of the undivine, 'to hunt for fresh corpses on the day of ritual. What if none perish on that day? Goddess knows death is final but never determinate, and especially with healers aplenty, death is often stalled outside the door. So, we make prior arrangements.'

As a librarian, Vahura would never admit it but she did see the wisdom in early shopping. 'Of course, it is only cautious,' she stuttered, hoping Aindri would just take her to Zubeia but she was too polite to interrupt.

'Glad you appreciate it.' Aindri leaned in closer, as if whispering a secret. 'The older Yoginis frown on our ways. Why don't *they* go and steal fresh corpses from the City then—'

'Because they do not favour the easy over the necessary,' a soft voice called out.

Aindri shut her eyes with the air of a thief caught with her head in a locker. 'Yes, Matrika Zubeia!'

Matrika Zubeia, the head of the death-priestesses of the Coven, wore attire much like Aindri's but it was her face that held Vahura's eyes. The artistry on it was enough to take Vahura's breath away. Three distinct flower-pigment rows of purple, black and purple again split either cheek diagonally into two striking halves. Tiny blue runes wove above and along her eyebrows to disappear into her unruly, silver hair that cascaded long on the left and was clipped short on the right. She seemed as young as Vahura, 'seemed' being the key word. Zubeia's face bore the weight of wisdom, her eyes too knowing.

'My, you are a tall one, aren't you?' Zubeia stepped across the door's threshold and gave Vahura a hug. Not a formal, polite one, but a bear hug that allowed Vahura to feel how full of curves Zubeia was, how citrusy she smelled with notes of sandalwood and jasmine. Vahura suddenly became very aware of the wet, sweaty areas of her own body, despite having dried off, and tried to pull away but Zubeia held her for a beat longer before releasing her.

Feeling Zubeia, all soft angles, made Vahura acutely aware of the lack of proportions in her own. Vahura had inherited her father's height, a height to intimidate the tallest of knights, and her breasts, when they arrived rather early, were a cause of mockery in classes but only till she bled. With a face that never caught up with its nose, made worse by a constellation of freckles which reddened easily under the Eastern sun, Vahura was not a person who made doorknobs turn. Her only feature the royal artists enjoyed painting was a pair of large, wide-set eyes but Vahura knew it was only in poems that a pair of eyes could compensate for plainness.

Matrika Zubeia turned to Aindri with a gentle smile. 'There is a difference between a guest and a prisoner, Sister Aindri. Would you venture a guess what forcing the Princess of Balkh to listen to your rants and,' Zubeia spared a pointed glance at the other Yoginis, 'your pranks make her?'

Aindri giggled, an improbable sound from a woman of her demeanour, and bowed, before stalking off to her chores. The rest of the Yoginis pirouetted in synchronized turns to return to their respective rooms. Vahura's skin threatened to crawl off her flesh again at that sight.

'Swarmsense,' Vahura said. 'I had only read of it. It was… almost ethereal to observe.' Vahura meant to say petticoat-pissing horrific but diplomacy lessons over the years had lent her an edge in using polite antonyms.

'You're a braver woman than most,' Zubeia said. 'But I do apologize for the behaviour of my sisters. More than a hive mind, they share a taste for pranks.' The iron ring through her nose shifted as Zubeia smiled.

'They are fascinating,' Vahura said, 'and so different in age and race and colour.'

'Some of them were little girls thrown into cellars by their fathers, some of them were women of science who were black-faced and marched on mules around the village, some of them daughters of mothers who shouldn't have died, all of them women punished for wanting something they shouldn't. That is what we Yoginis are in essence: women who wanted too much. Like you. I would have shown you our world, but now that Aindri has eaten through your patience, perhaps our conversation can wait. Why don't I escort you to the one you have come to meet? It is high past noon, and it would bode well for you to return to the City before dusk. Not safe for someone from the Race of Manu to lurk in the East after dark, especially not the Princess of Balkh.'

III

The lower levels of the ancient temple descended into the ground like a warren. On and on she climbed down the spiralling stone steps, passing underground cells that had not seen any use in centuries. Despite the seemingly sturdy drainage, the handiwork of rain was evident in the way floods had inundated this level, smearing the walls with thick silts, and the fragrance of stagnant water.

She wondered if now would be an appropriate time to ask Zubeia. *Just ask her. Ask her, Vahura. Stop finding comfort in hiding.*

'Is there something you want to ask, Princess?' Zubeia asked in a voice that could calm oceans.

Vahura gulped. 'Do you know... what... or who is a Steerseraph?'

'Steerseraph?' Zubeia mulled the word, savouring its taste on her tongue as one might a fine vintage. 'I am not familiar with the word, child, even though I feel I have heard its echoes. Where did you come upon it?'

'Just… something I heard from my mother once,' Vahura managed. 'I have always wondered its meaning. It doesn't matter,' she lied, even as the memory of silk in the wooden necklace pressed against her ribs again. It seemed to have filled her lungs, for sometimes when she took a deep breath, it caught on her mother's dying words, leaving her breathless.

> *They infected your sister with Marigold. Your father will end her to save Balkh for she is now a threat.*
> *She is now terrible.*
> *But you be bold, be shrewd. Remember what makes her beautiful. Conceal her while you seek an Astra. An Astra will have the cure for this curse. Find it and save your sister, Firefly. You have just a year before your sister succumbs to madness.*

Blood, Vahura guessed, from her mother's self-punctured eyes had sullied the other three lines but thankfully left the last paragraph for her to weep on for weeks ahead.

> *You are going to make the universe so proud, my darling and I salute you for the trials I am going to put you through.*
> *I am sorry for my silence, I am sorry I did not tell you about me.*
> *Yours, Steerseraph.*

She remembered staring at the letter dumbly for a long, long time. The words had fallen into her like stones into a well, and while she could hear them hurtling down her memory, they had not made any sense. They could not possibly make sense.

That was then. This was now. The cure she had been hunting for across the world had to be here. No other option, right? Didn't Acharya Oram say that in a labyrinth of choices, when you've worn out all paths but one, the last remaining path is the true road to the treasure.

And Vahura had trodden all other paths. Starting with the path of trust, which she regretted now. After wordlessly staring at her mother's corpse for what had felt like the passing of seasons, she had found her sister blindfolded with a strange alchemical cloth, crying under the bed. Her little sister. Her mirror. Her little accomplice. Her midnight companion, and her confidante. Her sister who loved to roll down the dunes and tell Vahura all the things she loved about the world. They shared a thousand jokes, and her sister laughed at each of them so easily, without worry. They would bicker too, as sisters are wont to do, Vahura often wishing she were an only child when their mother would scold them with the words, '*Someday, it will be you two against the world*', not knowing how soon it would come true.

But Vahura had not hidden her sister as her mother had asked. Where would she hide her? Who would she hide her from? Vahura had presented the silk fragment to her father instead.

A decision she came to rue.

Her devastated father had only agreed to not painlessly poison her sister when Vahura had threatened to stab her own eyes like mother had, despite knowing she did not possess the courage to do so. They had compromised. He had consented to caging her sister for a turn of the sun at the end of which Vahura would not only marry a man of his choice but would herself feed her sister the poison. This Vahura had sworn beside her mother's pyre, and a fragile truce was made between father and daughter. Afterward, her father took to the secret hunt for those who sought to wound Balkh with a plague while she began to… read about the plague.

From there, days had become weeks, and then a month while Vahura did nothing but read and pace and worry and feel useless. And the more she read, the more she realized that the Marigold Mold could destroy Balkh not just by its miasma but by its mere name. Perhaps that was why her father had cloaked her mother's murder in the guise of an accident to stave off panic in the masses. If the world knew the incurable Marigold was not a myth but a stranger knocking on the door… it did not bear thinking of. She had no choice but to find the cure. But she could not find a way or even think of a way. What her mother had asked her was a job for a hero, and Vahura did not know how to be one. She lay awake at night, writing letters after letters to colleges, to temples, to citadels but ended up chasing only phantoms. She made dramatic plans in the darkness only to discard them as daydreams. She would do this. She would do that. She would... she would...

Apparently, she could do nothing by just sitting in her house. Every course of action in her head where she just sat in the palace ended with her sister dead and her mother disappointed. That was until she decided to play reckless and confided her new plan in her retired governess, Old Ella.

'It's a fool's quest and we'll probably die,' Vahura had said.

'Oh, well then,' Old Ella had said, 'I always enjoy those.'

And so Vahura had set off with Old Ella on a tour of her kingdom. Being a librarian and... an unwed princess of one of the richest kingdoms of Aryavrat, doors opened easily for her. She scoured every shelf in the Tower of Taxila and hunted down every tome in the Citadel of Nalanda. And while the Citadel of Meru, the academy where young boys grew up to be Acharyas, barred women from their libraries, they did loan her the books in exchange for a generous donation.

But her entire quest so far had just been a collection of dismembered almosts. Every tome, every book and every scroll she devoured seemed content with speculating on Astras as exaggerated figments of an idle mind, as if the Astras had never existed. Most of these scholars believed that when things are too splendid to be true, they aren't. Even the accounts of a few bards who extended some credibility to the Astras ended their accounts with a brisk mockery of the whole thing, as if to dodge the risk of being mocked themselves.

She was left with no choice. She had to commit adultery as a librarian by placing her trust in legends instead of books. And they helped some.

Songs of forgotten tribes spoke of these 'Astras' as celestial gifts carved out of the body of a dead god to arm the mortal races against their immortal landlords: The Children of Light, the Daevas. It wasn't, however, just in their destructive power that the magic of an Astra lay. Hidden within the rumours were whispers of how the Astras bonded with their wielders, healing all manner of maladies of the body and the mind. The Lost Heroes who had wielded them were said to have heralded a new age, an age free from sickness for eternity.

But Eternity ended aeons ago. And now, nothing stood between her sister and death, perhaps even between man and annihilation. Nothing except a nervous wreck of a bookmoth.

It was not a life Vahura would have chosen of her own accord. However, no one, be it her father, her grandfather or even her brother, had heeded Vahura's warnings. It was as if she were an oracle fated to never have prophecies believed. With Vahura's father threatening to lock her away should she persist in her foolish pursuit, she had found herself with little choice. Desperate, she had agreed to accompany her grandfather and her brother to the Panchalan Swayamvar, only to fall sick and retreat to Balkh mid-journey.

Or so the tale she had spun to her grandfather went.

What she did, in fact, was pawn the jewels her dead mother had set aside for her dowry to pay the greatest living bard, Nar Ad of the Blue Order, the Third Order of Pathfinders, to meet her for a turn of the hourglass on her way back to Balkh. Vahura considered confiding in him about the Marigold Mold but memories of past attempts to warn men in power of a plague on the horizon stayed her tongue. She kept her inquiries confined to Astras.

While Nar Ad hadn't been well versed in Astras, he spilled rumours of a Daevic scroll – a study on the secrets of the human body by Daevas. Similar, he said, to how the Acharyas of today pored over the sonar of bats or the buzz of bees. Deep in his bones, Nar Ad was convinced the Daevic Scrolls held the secrets of how Astras bonded to mortals. For a peck on the cheek, Nar Ad even disclosed its last known location: the Citadel of Meru. Splendid! One more charitable donation, and she would have the Daevic Scrolls. But the Acharyas weren't wrong. When things are too splendid to be true, they aren't.

The Daevic Scrolls had been stolen by the Rose Coterie many years ago. Turned out Nar Ad had only found out about the Daevic Scroll while writing an unfinished book on the exploits of these legendary thieves of fortune. No one knew who the Rose Coterie were. Of the ones who knew of their existence, some said they were a defeated king's men, some claimed they were bored priests, and some championed them as Resht heroes... everyone had a different answer depending on the mark on their neck. All that was known was what the puppeteers claimed.

The Rose Coterie believed there used to be a Goddess of Rogues, Lavannai, who was slain by the other Gods but her realm supposedly remained. The Rose Coterie were sworn to sustain this realm, well, by filling it with looted treasures.

Nar Ad had shown her pages of his signed interviews of the victims and witnesses of Rose Coterie but with none having actually seen the thieves, he had left the book unfinished, much to the relief of the Seven. For the Citadel of Meru, or rather its overlords, the Saptarishis (the Seven), had spent considerable gold sovereigns in transforming the Rose Coterie into a mere fable. The Rose Coterie was Meru's rotten secret after all, a black stain on the white robes of the Seven who ran it. It did not do much for the reputation of kingmakers if highway gangs could pilfer from them with impunity. Games of the Seven aside, if anyone was privy to where those Daevic Scrolls were tucked away, it had to be the Rose Coterie. Though, Nar Ad did warn, the Rose Coterie had not been heard of in decades. '*It was as if they had just vanished into thin air,*' Nar Ad had mused. '*Or perhaps they are dead.*'

And that was another reason why Nar Ad had left his book on the Rose Coterie unfinished. For there was simply not enough known to write more than a page on them. All he had of the Rose Coterie was the banner on which the band of rogues had drawn a rose, a rose they left at the scene of every crime which eventually lent the thieves their name. Nar Ad was confident that the mark had been smeared by the Meru wherever it had been left, pillar, stone or rock, making this banner perhaps the only tangible proof that the Rose Coterie ever existed. While Nar Ad had refused to part with this artefact no matter the coin Vahura offered, he did concede to permit his blue-lipped servant girl to let Vahura read the interviews he had taken, in exchange for another peck on the cheek.

Vahura, in the days that followed, had waded through a sea of pages. Nar Ad's interviews were a concoction of the bizarre and the downright absurd. Amidst the chaos, she found the only semblance of coherence in the account of a tavern-woman, who had grumbled of how the Rose Coterie had bragged about their exploits in a tavern and left without clearing their dues. In the hay of their boasts was a mention of an ancient parchment that was born of a light that did not illuminate. The woman had even demanded a reward from Meru for her information along with restitution for unpaid bills, and Meru had responded with the threat of a Shrap.

But like a Namin whose rosary never left him, Vahura's memory never fled her. The curves and swirls on the unnamed woman's signature on the account mirrored the signature on the letter a raven from the Library of the East in Kamrup had brought to her in Balkh weeks ago. A letter stating the library shelved no books on Astras but would still appreciate her donation in the interests of good conscience.

And so here she was at the Rim of the World, chasing after a lost hope, her only hope that this tavern-woman turned keeper of scrolls might point her in the direction of her salvation. Even when she discovered that the Library of the East had been rented out to a perfumer, and was a library only in name to keep receiving funds from Meru, she was not disheartened. For the letter had come stamped with a seal.

A woman standing on a decapitated body while sipping blood from its severed head.

The holy mark of the Yoginis.

So engrossed was Vahura in the memories of her journey that she startled at the soft touch of Zubeia's hand against her shoulder.

'Should I send a rope to pull you out of the sea of thoughts you are drowning in?' Zubeia asked.

'My apologies, Matrika,' Vahura lied, 'but the world around here is so different from anything I have ever seen before. I am just overwhelmed.'

'I do not enjoy lies, Princess.' Zubeia's gentle smile felt like a whip across the back. 'Though I will grant that you are excellent at it. No matter. I do wish you came at a better time, Princess. With the Conclave around, tensions are high.'

How was Vahura to know that the damn Tusk would win the bid at Panchal to host the Conclave? No one ever bid for the Conclave. It was a liability. Just her rotten luck. Now the entire roster of monarchs was on their way to Kamrup for the first ever royal meet in the East.

'We are here, Princess,' Zubeia said when they reached the foot of the stairs. The sounds of men and women enjoying themselves drifted out from the other side of the door, laughter and singing. Zubeia knocked gently. The door remained shut for a long time and the sounds from the other side did not cease. Zubeia raised her fist and banged it again on the ancient door. The door rattled, threatening to drop down from its hinges any moment.

Slow footsteps clicked the floor on the other side of the door. A few clumsy coughs later, the door budged a little. A face more ancient than the door peered out of the gap and squinted at Vahura. The old woman's face was lit ominously over the candle she clutched in her withered hand.

'We don't want to join your sex cult, girl.' The old woman broke into a fit of coughs. The wrinkles on her face were more extensive than a Nar Ad map. Her hair, however, hadn't thinned at all. Just a few streaks of white and grey. 'No orgies, no climax, no nothing. Do I look like someone who wants to bend a full circle to suck someone's cock? That being said, there was a time not too far away when I did not climb to the bed with just one man or one woman. So many parts of my body to touch, and a pair of hands are just not enough to—'

'Lady Asshaye,' Zubeia said sternly, still clinging to the calm smile, if only barely. 'I have with me the Princess Vahura of Balkh – she is the one who made a generous contribution to the library you *don't* run.'

Asshaye frowned as she opened the door. She wore a voluminous grey robe that hung loosely on her shoulders. 'Ah, but I was told some librarian would be visiting, to fund our request for books – dire books on cosmetics – required to save the world! Some Vura.'

'Princess Vahura, Lady Asshaye. And she is… that librarian.'

'A princess who is a librarian?' She smiled, revealing a clean set of teeth. 'Oh, it feels good to be surprised at our age.' She turned around to walk with her candle lighting the way. 'Follow along, flamehead.'

Zubeia turned to Vahura. 'Your funeral awaits.' The Yogini gestured her inside, and closed the door ominously behind her.

IV

'The Yoginis are no death-priestesses. Sex-crazed witches is more like,' Asshaye prattled on, not particularly concerned with if she even had an audience. 'Can you imagine they claim true orgasm needs no climax? Pray, what matter of nonsense is that?'

'Perhaps—' Vahura tried in vain to get a word in.

'All hogwash I tell you. It is the potions of ecstasy they smoke that turn their unions orgasmic without orgasm. And they are rather discriminatory, you know, for the women can orgasm when they want, but it is the men who are compelled to hold their orgasm back. Well, I stand for it, but it just feels unfair in principle. What say you?'

Vahura was no fine-nerved, sensitive prig but hearing the word 'orgasm' five times from an old woman in a matter of seconds, turned her ears bright red. 'About ehm orgasms? I...'

'Don't tell me you have no experience. Oh, darling, you need to attend their *maithuna* ceremony the month after. It will do you good.'

'Perhaps if I have saved the world by then.'

'Ah, right. Here I am talking about erotica when you have emergencies to handle.' Asshaye stopped by a wall to hang the lantern. 'Come. Meet the others, and then you can tell us what we can do to earn your silence about the library.'

'Where are we going, Acharya?'

'To the Great Hall, dear,' Asshaye said. 'If you come around the time for dinner, you can expect us to be eating food.'

Dinner? Wasn't there still a few hours till sunset? Vahura smiled. She liked old people. From their correspondence, she'd gathered Asshaye was assisted by four other Acharyas. Five old crones, all of whom had detailed out in their individual letter what they had wanted as donation. From onyx robes with a predetermined hem-length to zoology tomes that had the fur of its subjects stitched to its pages, their demands made them come across as half-mad hags, which she only figured out later had been their intention.

They soon entered a cavernous chamber, lit by a modest fire. Shelves, burgeoned with ancient leather tomes, ascended on every wall, disappearing in the darkness of the high ceiling. The portions of the wall mercifully unclaimed by the shelves were sheathed in large maps scribbled with hand-drawn circles and lines. Even the floor was not left alone. Books were messily stacked in leaning pyramids that teetered at the edge of destruction. Certain death would befall anyone who came under them. A hazard a librarian courted every day on the job.

The candelabra was the only furniture that seemed it had been bought rather than pawned. Hung low over a longtable, it was attended to only by a few candles. Seven chairs were on the other side of the table, though only four were currently occupied. The table itself was crowded with a spit-roasted fox stuffed fat with grapes, and silver platters of smoked prawns in glistening bamboo chilli glaze. The dishes were attended by a transparent decanter that held scarcely watered wine. This was not dinner. This was a feast. They were celebrating.

Asshaye limped over to stand on the opposite side of the table. The rest all stared curiously at Vahura and she had the nagging feeling she was standing on trial. Perhaps she was.

'We modelled this longtable after the House of Saptarishis, designating seven Acharyas in a fashion after those dynasty designers,' Asshaye said. 'We are two short. But, well, replacements are in short supply.'

'Liar,' said the man closest to Asshaye. He was half a head shorter than Asshaye, pale skinned and brown eyed, and nearly round but in a way that had yet to sag. 'Meru sent a few a decade ago but Asshaye can be heartless in her interviews. Just like she was heartless with us when we were boys falling in love with her.' He dabbed his sauce-smeared lips and approached Vahura to take her hand and kiss the air above it. 'None ever gets through.'

'This man who foolishly believes he is charming is Ailmar, the one who should have catalogued our damned trinkets. Maybe you can teach him something. But he isn't wrong. Meru always sent pillocks and ninnyhammers. Even Ailmar would be a thoroughly undeserved nomination if not for the rest of this pitiful company around this table. Come now, old men. She is a librarian and a Princess from Balkh and, and most importantly, a *donor*. Make your proper introductions.'

'I am Toshad,' said an old man with a bone-white face who wore a jacket liberally dusted with hairfrost. He didn't deign to stand and merely bowed from his seat. 'History,' saying which he returned to his prawns.

'Don't mind him,' she whispered. 'He is senile.'

'But not hard of hearing, Asshaye.'

'It is *Acharya* Asshaye,' she said.

The wrinkled scowl opposite her deepened.

'Not again, you both. I am Orym, the youngest of the lot. Master of Potions and Machinations.' Orym could not have looked more an Easterner than perhaps a Rakshasa himself. A halfbreed with a skin shade leaning towards humans, this one had pierced everything – earlobes, nostrils, eyebrows, tongue – the ruby ornaments a startling contrast to his pale face. A Grey Shaman. Not an Acharya. True, he was younger than the rest but by no means young.

'Kalay,' said another man with optics perched on his curving beak of a nose. 'Human Sciences. You are so tall. All signs of selective mutation. Originated from one girl in the Age of Treta. I have studied them. There is a potion—'

'Yes, yes, the human body is a marvel. We know.' Asshaye snorted. 'Remember, we agreed not to boast about our fields before her.'

'What?' he shouted.

'Good grief,' Asshaye turned to Vahura, 'he is hard of hearing. Let me convey it to him.' She dragged a stack of square papers from the centre of the table. Vahura observed the table cluttered with papers in Kalay's general direction, all scribbled with messages, all scribbled in upper case. No doubt their preferred medium of communication. Asshaye took a quill and scribbled *Shut Up*, in beautiful calligraphy despite her quivering hand. It was in the same style she had signed Nar Ad's account decades ago.

'Acharya Asshaye, what study do you look after?' Vahura asked, somehow knowing Asshaye had been waiting to be asked.

'I study geography, Princess. Maps, topology, mountains and whatnot. Did you know that in the future the Mai Layas will rise to be higher than the Vindhyas in the South?'

'All predictions without an ounce of evidence,' Kalay said.

'Better than stating the obvious, Acharya Kalay,' Asshaye said. 'Oh, your hair is black. It means your mother's hair was black. What a science!'

'How is it different from "O, there is a mountain there. Its height is –"' Kalay said, emphasizing it, 'Nobody. Cares.'

'Acharyas, now, now,' Orym said, 'what a sorry figure we must be cutting in front of our benefactor. Please, Princess. We are all very passionate about our sciences, as you can see, and we understand the books we each have requested you to graciously donate cost a ransom. So… take your time.'

Asshaye passed a goblet of ale to Vahura. 'Have a glass first to wash away the vile human blood the witches no doubt made you drink. The patronage of leeches has turned these Yoginis into one. Let us raise a toast.' It was a while before each one present raised their glass in the general direction of Vahura. 'I am grateful to the Conclave that brought the young Princess to our shores so that she may decide which of us to reward with objects of our desire. Let us raise a toast in her honour. To Princess Vahura.'

As the glasses clinked and turned, Vahura looked at the shrunken faces in front of her, eyes clouded, decrepit backs, trembling hands, living as far from human civilization as possible, lonesome, crotchety and, perhaps, even ignorant of the world outside.

'You honour me but shall we raise a toast to the Gods instead? Who do you swear by, Acharyas?'

'Oh, we are of diverse beliefs, Princess,' Ailmar answered. 'Toshad and I worship the Seven, Kalay worships the Forest Spirits and Orym believes in some Eastern rubbish about a no-god. Who do you light the candles for, Princess? We can raise a toast to your deity,' saying which Ailmar dissolved into a coughing fit which faded into the chatter around the table.

'As you will, Acharya,' Vahura said loudly. *Here goes.* 'Hunchbacked Lavannai, Goddess of Thieves,' she called out loudly. Silence sliced through the grumbling chatter around the table but Vahura soldiered on. 'I fear no noose for the knots you have taught me to untie,' muttered Vahura, closing her eyes to hold back the slipping courage as she poured a libation on the floor with her left hand instead of the traditional right. The unholy hand for any Vedan. A thief's gesture against Order. 'Goddess of Stealth, I will rob the other Gods of their heirlooms without fear, for you sheathe the sounds I make. Goddess of Chaos, I will fear no law, for without it no prize will be worth the take. Ever and forever, I will seek in lairs and steal from heirs, treasures that were never theirs.'

When she opened her eyes, four of them, Asshaye, Ailmar, Kalay and Orym stood straight, their drooping shoulders suddenly erect, their rheumy eyes suddenly fiery, their smiles suddenly savage. Each of them had a crossbow pointed at Vahura's throat.

It made Vahura the happiest woman in the world.

'You took going underground quite literally,' Vahura said as she took in the dark décor around her. 'It is an honour to finally meet you, Rose Coterie.'

THE DEVOUT COMES TO DEVOUR

MALENGAR, A CITY STATE KINGDOM BETWEEN THE MAGADHAN EMPIRE AND HASTINA UNION

6 MONTHS BEFORE THE BATTLE OF MATHURA

'And if thou gaze long into an abyss, the abyss will also gaze into thee.'
—Nietzsche

THE HANGED MAN

I

Out through the shroud of moonlit mist, the thrice-cursed archer stalked forth to hunt down his friend. Twigs crunched under his fraying boots. The sighing wind twisted into a wail. The only other light came from the Temple of Kaamah ahead, the flickering flames of a thousand camphor lamps casting a dull orange glow on the girl about to die.

She was fewer than thirty paces away from him, a slight figure with ribbons fluttering in her hair, her small hands wielding a stick as a makeshift sword against the tall grasses. He recognized her as the daughter of the local priest. Just this morning the townsfolk had flocked to hear him make his speech about letting the Reshts build their hovels within the comfort of city walls. Where was he now? Why had the priest left his girl alone when he should have been here, with her, protecting her from the shadow bent on slaughter?

The memory of his nephew summoned by that thought was sharp enough to cut himself on. The unruly hair, the warm voice, the foolish hope and the look of sheer disbelief when the arrow pierced the boy's skull, lashed at the archer like the frantic beating of an eagle's wings in a snare. His composure trembled. He squeezed his eyes shut as if in a bid to banish the past.

But memory is a malady that cannot be cured, only ignored. With practised hands, he unfastened a small leather vial from his belt and squeezed two green drops of Abyss into his right eye. *Sweet, sting-ing embrace of oblivion.* The gnawing pain of remembrance dulled, receding into a haze as the effects of Abyss washed over him. His breath steadied, his mind settling into the numbness he hungered for. Feeling better, the archer waited.

Darkness deepened.

The clouds took their time in releasing the moonlight they had concealed, teasing it out in thin, reluctant beams. But it was enough. Through eyes blurred by the sting of freezing tears, the archer watched Bagheera advance, his fur kissed silver by moonlight, a green-fletched arrow buried deep in its flank. *It is time.*

The arrow he had chosen was obsidian-tipped, black-fletched, long and heavy enough for what he needed to do. The woods fell silent. The wind stopped whispering in his ears. Even the snowflakes seemed to hang motionless in the air, suspended as if unwilling to miss the tragedy about to unfold. And in that moment, he realized his life had once again boiled down to the single question: could he bring himself to extinguish the flame of an innocent to save others from a fire?

A twig snapped beneath one of Bagheera's paws. The girl froze, darting glances in every direction, searching for the source of the sound. Bagheera, his body so perfectly blended into the shadows, sank into his haunches, muscles coiled. Positioned downwind, the girl neither saw nor smelled the panther, but something in her marrow – a primal instinct – must have warned her of the danger that lurked just beyond her sight for she began to sob.

'I can't do it,' the archer lowered his bow in shame, his golden eyes glinting with cold tears like the tips of melting ice, 'I just… can't. Bagheera is innocent.' *So is that girl.* He tried raising his bow again but his fingers continued to revolt. 'I just can't.'

'THEN UNLEASH ME,' a voice, trapped within the archer's chest for years, growled forth, clawing its way into his consciousness.

'No, not you…' the archer panicked, his heart a fistful of thunder, but it was too late. The darkness inside that had threatened to escape during the Panchalan Swayamvar had found a jade key to its prison.

II

A single black flame ignited in the Hanged Man's consciousness, burning his fears, and along with them his fetters. The flame grew until it enveloped everything, becoming too large to contain. And just like that, it burst into a thousand tiny sparks, scattered like gems in the dark, leaving behind iced clarity. Sure, at the edges of his awareness, mercy and morals flickered, but rage and anger? They spread across his mind like navy blotches on a damp parchment.

The urge to save the Namin girl skimmed across his thought's surface like a pebble across ice. But he didn't. He watched on as the panther sprang from the bush in a flash of silver, his fangs gleaming. A marvel of beauty and brute strength. The girl didn't stand a chance.

The Hanged Man waited patiently for the panther to maul her face beyond recognition. What had her father brayed at the fair today? That the Kingdom of Malengar was kind in how it endured its Reshts. Endure? You endure the gutter slush that spills over the streets in monsoons. You endure the mosquitoes in the summers. You endure what you wish would simply vanish. There was no honour in being endured. *Let the priest pray tonight he can endure the nightmares of his daughter's half-eaten face.*

It is time. His arrow struck the panther's side and it howled in pain, releasing the girl's neck, her hair snagged in thick tufts between the panther's fangs. Hackles raised, the panther bounded towards him in great leaps till recognition seeped into the beast's wide, blue eyes, and it stumbled to a stop.

By now the Hanged Man had already drawn another arrow. The panther didn't even try to dodge it. As if it would rather die than attack him. 'PATHETIC.'

His arrow went clean through its eye all the way in up to the goose fletching. The panther collapsed to the ground, legs twitching as its low whine sliced through the wind. When the Hanged Man reached to pluck out his arrow, he was surprised to find the panther alive, pawing weakly at the ground. He reached for the beautiful creature and turned it to the side. 'FAREWELL.' He stamped his boot on its neck repeatedly to put the Fool's friend out of its misery.

As for the poisoned green arrow still protruding vulgarly from the panther's flank, he cautiously plucked it out. The exercise merited utmost care to avoid scratching his skin against the tip. He spared a moment to appreciate the serpent etched upon the shaft as he wrapped the poisoned arrowhead before neatly pocketing it.

The Hanged Man rose to look at the panther whose cradle had been his shoe. After all, his better half, the Fool, had taken the panther in when he had rescued it as a cub. Its mother had slipped to her death in a ravine, and the cub had been only a misstep away from following her. The Fool had named him Bagheera, after a beloved beast from a lullaby his mother used to bribe him with. The Fool had needed a friend, one he believed he could neither betray nor endanger, especially after the regrettable incident with the temple whore. So even though it was a cub, and even though he had no experience rearing jungle cats, the Fool latched on to the furry orphan and spent the rest of that night beside the apple tree, talking to the cub. And before he knew it, a friendship had blossomed.

From that day forth, the Fool's dawns were spent watching the big cat pounce at snowflakes or chase after firefly glimmers. His nights were spent meditating beneath towering pines, the panther curled up contentedly at his feet. They would hunt game together, brave blizzards together and the Hanged Man was sure, if time had let them, they would have probably brought forth a litter together.

And now, even in death, the panther would keep both of them warm. The Hanged Man could only hope the Fool would not mind him skinning his pet so. Seemed like a dreadful shame to let such precious fur go to waste.

Once done, the Hanged Man wrapped the bloody side of the pelt around a branch to retrieve it later before hoisting the skinned beast across his shoulders. The trek back to his cottage was long, and he couldn't risk leaving a blood trail that might lead anyone to him, especially that fawning village hunter hiding in the bushes, so he frequently changed directions. When he reached home, he strolled past it to the towering oak tree where the Fool used to strangle hens and toss them to the panther. It took a will of his shoulder to let the panther gracefully rest against the oak's roots. Even skinned, the beast's lone eye now stared sadly at the night sky. The Hanged Man wondered if he felt any remorse for the poor beast. He did not. That was the Fool's job.

One would think the Fool would be a changed person after having spent three months in a new, different place. Wasn't that the whole point of a self-imposed exile? But the Fool never learned, did he? *To love is to perish*, the Hanged Man reminded himself as he stacked the chopped wood, seriously considering inking it on his wrist as a daily reminder for the Fool. Perhaps, later.

The Hanged Man tossed the skinned carcass on the wooden blocks. Unfortunately, the panther made for very poor kindling and took hours to turn to ashes. The wind moaned mournfully through the trees as the pyre crackled into the night. He waited until the charred remains became indistinguishable from those of the camphor and reeds that burned beneath it, using the fading light to admire the green arrow that had driven the panther mad. He smothered a smile as he recognized the brand. By the time the Hanged Man was done with them, perhaps some of those women might survive but for those who did... that would be the worse outcome.

The voice of the trapped Fool echoed in his ears. *'Revenge will not bring you happiness.'*

'I HAVE NO INTEREST IN HAPPINESS.' The Hanged Man's lips finally pulled back in a malicious grin. 'I WILL SETTLE FOR SATISFIED.'

THE TEMPLE DANCER

Marzana, known to the world as Meenakshi, wished she could choke Damaya with the ashes of the dreams she had burned, even as the oblivious nine-summer-old fastened her ankle bells. Marzana was the finest Devadasi of her time. Now at three-and-twenty, she should have been in her prime. But she knew she was no match for Damaya. Marzana was not even from Malengar. She did not know where she was from. She was sold off in some far-flung desert country, and then she was passed from broker to broker until she ended up at the temple, barely more than a child. Perhaps that was why her mind still bore the rot of the outside world, the rot that permitted illicit curiosities. She was an outsider, after all. Not Damaya, though.

Damaya had been born in this temple and raised by Badi Dee, the current matriarch of the Devadasis and Marzana's rival. Even though Damaya was Marzana's blood, she was Badi Dee's pride.

All the Devadasis, the servant wives of Kaamah, the God of Love and Beauty, served him through their divine dance: Nritya. Nritya was poetry inked by feet, and a Devadasi was the poetess of this floating world. But Damaya, with her Nritya, created sculptures with every form and pose, a timeless moment of creation that was so fleeting that it was visible only between blinks. In a couple of weeks, once the Royals of Malengar returned from the Conclave, they too would know this truth. It would be at that time, a priest would choose an auspicious date for Damaya's arangetram, her dedication to Kaamah. Badi Dee had already hired a gifted singer to serenade the occasion when the world would finally witness Damaya, the sister of the famous Meenakshi (Marzana), dance. Marzana was tired of hearing the messengers spread far and wide how Damaya was her mirror reflection. Same milk-pale face with the same eyes of a lucent green that seemed to fracture in the sunlight. That part was true though Damaya's nose and low brows came from Damaya's father. And unlike Marzana, Damaya did not need to dye her hair black to look Vedan.

Badi Dee impatiently patted her palms, startling Marzana out of her thoughts. The drummers took their seats. Damaya stepped meekly to the centre of the mandala on the floor, nervous for her training. All part of the ploy, Marzana knew. With the first *ta tha* of the cymbal, Damaya became her other self, the self that could create universes with her hands and legs, and annihilated them too.

Today, Damaya honoured the forest with her Nritya. As the drums beat like a heart thudding on a woman's first night with her groom, creatures manifested wherever she willed them into existence with her wrists, palms and eyes.

She twisted her arms. Two snakes entwined. She arched her back. A crescent moon loomed overhead. Raising a leg, she stared furiously, mouth agape in a snarl. A roaring lion.

Her ankle bells punctuated her creations, chiming in harmony with the cymbal beats, her entire self, perched on the edge of her toes, like dew on the tip of a leaf. Damaya bent her elbows, conjuring the symbol of thick Eastern forests, then she sculpted a river through them with her palms. She broke apart, then closed in, she flowed, she stood rigid, and she turned her back. Old magic streamed out of the movement of her eyeballs, her palms and her feet.

Ignoring Badi Dee's instructions, Damaya began improvising her dance with slight surprises. Surprises that added to the Nritya's charm much like the dimple on her smile. Badi Dee, who would've skinned any other youngling for such disobedience, grinned. For Damaya's improvisation did not mutilate the centuries-old dance form. Her dance remained straight and cold, carved, like a line of High Sanskrit etched with a stylus but etched over a pliable palm leaf instead of stone.

Marzana just knew the Gods in the heavens were watching Damaya dance. But then, so were the devils on the ground. Many eyes twinkled, lusted and sparkled. The gazes roamed over

Damaya, swallowing her alive. But the one whose searing glare charred Marzana was Old Khai's. As the richest landlord in Malengar and Marzana's own patron, Old Khai, the self-styled Prince of Circuses, had earned a right to attend these training sessions through hefty donations to the temple coffers. His eyes cut Damaya like a flaming discus, letting off sparks as they imagined cutting through her blouse. But Damaya did not look at him. She looked at none of them. Lost in the ecstasy of the holy dance, her eyes flowed over her hungry supplicants like honey, draping them all, settling over none.

For a brief second, Old Khai's gaze, as if summoned by the voice screaming inside Marzana's skull, slipped to her. Marzana's memory of him inside her, flowing loose and liquid, crawled over her skin like a line of ants. But Marzana just smiled and nodded with her eyelids, as if giving him permission to go astray. Pleased, Old Khai turned his face back to Damaya.

Marzana wondered if she was blaspheming. Her discomfort didn't stem from familial concern for Damaya, but from jealousy. Not jealousy because of Old Khai. Old Khai was a man. Worse, a rich man. *They want what they want when they want it.* Marzana wasn't even sure if he knew or cared that Damaya was his own daughter. Not that there was anything wrong in it. *As long as he pays and prays for it, he could have anything.* The wisdom of the grandmother, the wildness of the mother, or the blood of the daughter. Patron's pick. The jealousy arose because Marzana was no longer the dancer she used to be.

The cymbals reached a crescendo as if to agree with Marzana, signalling the end of Damaya's performance. Afterwards, when Damaya retreated behind the curtains, Badi Dee cleared her throat. Fine and thin as parchment was her skin, and white with wisdom was her hair, but the way her eyes shone like nails, grey as screws, Badi Dee was now pride personified.

'If any can oust my Damaya in a dance, barring Kaamah himself, I will shave my head and walk tar-faced in the town,' Badi Dee said. 'I wonder when the Royals will return. We need to set a date for her arangetram,' she added offhandedly, knowing Old Khai would be tempted further by the chance of losing her to someone more powerful, someone richer. Secretly tonight, his private bid would rise.

'No surprise there. She is the sister of Lady Divine Meenakshi after all,' Old Khai said. They all nodded as one towards Marzana, who smiled a thorn.

'But can she vanquish a Vishkanya?' teased another landlord, who had spent an entire urn full of gold to earn the privilege of a seat.

Thick coils of smoke rose from Badi Dee's hookah, wreathing her beautiful aged skin in cloying fumes. 'I meant humans, not heathens, Lord Jalapa.'

Marzana wondered how the most feared assassins in the world would respond to Badi Dee's remark. They would perhaps not care. Their vipers' nest was as old as the temple itself, and one did not grow old in Malengar if one was offended too easily.

'You are the bravest woman I know, Badi Dee,' Jalapa said. 'Even Gurumaa never traded words with the Vishkanyas.'

'Why, they're mortal women, same as us. They eat, they age, they die. They can be killed, can't they? And they don't take men for their husbands, same as us. Only, we are married to our God, and they are married to their vials. Why should I fear them?'

Marzana sensed Badi Dee was seducing Jalapa. Jalapa liked his women to turn him into a servant in bed, and turning this Ksharjan bear into one, needed steel in the tongue. Marzana could only hope Damaya was not listening and learning the wrong ideas. Yes, the Vishkanyas were mortals and yes, they could be killed. But if you killed one, the entire clan dropped what they were doing to hunt you down. What they did to you and your loved ones made the House of Oracles seem a dollhouse for little girls. She had heard Old Khai say self-immolation was preferable.

'I agree,' Old Khai said, evidently forgetting the tales he had scared Marzana with. 'Damaya could vanquish anyone.' That declaration fell like stone on Marzana's lungs. It was no longer a rumour. Marzana's time with Old Khai was at an end.

Unable to bear the humiliation, Marzana slipped out of the dancing hall to her house, easily accessible through the back door in the temple wall. Most of the other Devadasis resided in the Devadasi compound on the same lane but Marzana had been gifted her fine house by Old Khai. She could only hope he did not take it away now. *He wouldn't. Damaya stays in this house too.*

When she entered the anteroom, she found her birthing bed, lately transformed into a death bed, smelling of urine and decay. She stepped in cautiously, gazing at Gurumaa's diminished face, and wondered how many days remained for her to live. For Gurumaa, the true Matriarch of the Devadasis of the Kaamah Temple, was dying.

She removed the folds of Gurumaa's saree, and cleaned her legs and everything in between. Carefully replacing the soiled sheet from under her, she substituted it with a crisp, new, dry sheet. Gurumaa stirred faintly under Marzana's ministrations, but did not awaken. Marzana did not expect her to. Marzana had dropped Abyss in Gurumaa's eyes twice today already to keep the woman who had adopted her sane through her pain.

Once Gurumaa had been cleaned, and the stench of the room began to dissipate in the air rushing in through the open windows, Marzana gazed down into Gurumaa's face. It was hard to find any trace of the Gurumaa she had adored and loved since she had been bought by her. Keep her clean, drop Abyss into her eyes and leave her to dream. That was all she could do. Kaamah bless the Inkspeller for his gifts. *Not gifts,* she reminded herself. *Loan.*

Even now, with the candles snuffed out, she felt the Inkspeller's presence behind her, hearing him, feeling his breath against her ear.

'Meenakshi…' Gurumaa groaned, eyes still shut.

'I'm here, Maa,' Marzana said. 'Sleep.' She swallowed her ire as she spread a blanket over her mother's shivering body. Gurumaa was not of her blood. But she was of her soul.

Gurumaa's warm kiss had dried little Marzana's wet tears and stilled her troubled heart when no priest had offered to buy Marzana, a Mleccha, to be a girl of the temple. Since then, Marzana had become the sunshine of Gurumaa's days and the north star of her nights. When Marzana grew older, she became Gurumaa's ally and arm in the politics of their little empire within the temple. Marzana had often asked Gurumaa why she had chosen her out of all the other girls in the slaver's stable. Gurumaa had had no reason to bid on a mongrel. The palette of the Devadasis of Kaamah

Temple ranged from faces the colour of sunlit soil to hands the hue of cocoa's richest depths. Marzana, on the other hand, had been too sun-spit, too fair to fit the accepted shade of ivory south of the Ganga.

But she was still taken in by Gurumaa, not just to learn to serve Kaamah himself but also to learn how to *bless* the scions of the Orange Court, seduce the patronage of the great Drachma Houses and, at times, even instruct the women of the royal household in the Art of Sighs. Years passed in this manner, pleasant and demanding, spent in the company of other girls, each walking the path of burning coals that was the ritual of Nritya. The Namin priests assigned to the temple were kind, and took shifts to instruct the younglings in the ways of the Seven, and the prayers of Kaamah. Knowledge of the world as it truly existed, however, was kept from them, be it the study of stars or the politics of kingdoms. Nothing mars pleasure more than awareness, and Kaamah being the God of Pleasure, nothing would offend him more than current affairs.

The older dancers of the temple taught Marzana the skills of the body: song, pouring tea, preparing bed chambers and painting life-size portraits. And every week, following the great prayer ceremony, the Inkspeller – not the present one who was extorting her, but his predecessor who had painted the Devadasi mark of the whispering aetherwing on her back after her arangetram – brought Marzana gifts in the secret grove by the stupa. In return, he only asked to borrow poetry books the priests lent Marzana to read in her free time.

The education had only been a complimentary tool to accentuate the Nritya, and in Nritya, Marzana had grown so popular that her reputation had transcended beyond the casual 'wah wahs'. Each night, as Marzana fastened the bells around her ankles, the Orange Court's elephants clogged the narrow lanes outside the temple. Even the loftiest nobles and rich landlords had to cough up hefty donations to secure admission. Rumours abounded that anyone bewitched by Marzana's dance courted ruin to his house for the pleasure of her blessings could only be had as long as one had a treasury to deplete in the bargain.

Drunk on success, Marzana had often urged Gurumaa to appoint her the next Matriarch, superseding the elder Badi Dee, so that Gurumaa could rest comfortably before Badi Dee snatched Gurumaa's reins. Gurumaa knew the Devadasis were Marzana's home, her sanctuary, and that Marzana would never let harm fall on the younglings who Marzana had rescued from the bidding market. The Yamuna Wars, however, rattled Marzana's plans.

'Oh, there will be time enough for that,' Gurumaa had said, when urged again. 'Once the war is over, Damaya is grown and our debts are paid, you shall ascend. I want you not as a name on the lips of my creditors. This will be my gift to you along with my time. You'll be heartily sick of me before my time is done. I can foresee it. Meenakshi, you will be begging me to go back to teaching girls to dance and let you both rest with your lovers.'

As prophecies go, it was a poor one. The Yamuna Wars lingered. Gurumaa fell sick. Marzana ended up taking care of Gurumaa while Damaya fell into the clutches of Badi Dee. Gurumaa did come to her home, but woeful Kaamah, what a way for Marzana's wish to be fulfilled.

When Gurumaa, too sick to even move, finally handed the keys of the Devadasi treasure to Marzana, Marzana had mistaken it to be a reward. It was only when Marzana opened the locker that she realized that it was not just her own life that Gurumaa had put in her hands but the lives of the Devadasis as well.

In the years under Gurumaa's leadership, the House of Devadasis had prospered. There had been bad patrons, runaway girls, plague, wars both early and late to contend with, but always, a good festival had offset the loss of patronage. Had their coin not been hoarded by the Namin priests in charge of the temple's coffers, the Devadasis would have rivalled queens in wealth. Or so Gurumaa claimed. Even as it had been, if not coin, they'd been comfortable with the gifts of jewellery from their patron that the Namin priests of the temple could lay no claim to. Pawning the jewellery had bought them a year or two from knocks on their door. But this war, the one the bards called the Yamuna Wars, did not cease. The Mathuran Republic simply refused to die at the hands of the Empire, and the realm suffered for Krishna's obstinance. And it was into this whirlpool of debt that Gurumaa bequeathed Marzana the responsibility of stewardship. An inheritance of loss.

In those middle years of the Yamuna Wars, the wealth of donations filling in temple coffers had slipped for in uncertain times of war, no one prayed to the God of Pleasure and Love. Especially not when a new God of Darkness and Death was rising just south of Malengar's borders in the Magadhan Empire.

Things would change, Marzana hoped.

Oh, they did change, but for the worse. As the Yamuna Wars tightened trade across the realm, Marzana reluctantly relinquished one parcel of holding after another to forestall the Drachmas from seizing maidenhoods as mortgage. A few of the Ksharjans had even begun to solicit the services of the harlots rather than the blessings of the Devadasis, Ksharjans who had been promptly blacklisted by the temple's priests, much to the woe of the Devadasis. The harlots, who had been on the run from the Magadhan purge, were more than happy to feed on temple rejects.

Temple rejects like Haridas – an old patron who had gifted her an emerald navel ring just to have her to bless his newborn child. She supposed Men had needs, and Haridas did what he had to do to keep himself sated in hard times. He had told her as much when he had solicited the grace one of the lesser temple dancers named Kamala. Haridas had all but suggested he would give a small slice of Kamala's profits to Marzana if she let Kamala accompany him on his business trips to the North. Kamala had no patrons. She lived on the donations the priests allocated the Devadasis. No personal wealth of her own. The offer was good even if Kamala would then cease to be a Devadasi. Marzana did not like to think of how sorely she had been tempted to take that offer.

In hindsight she had been glad she did not have to make that choice. The Yamuna Wars only grew worse, and with the worsening war, the Devadasis somehow grew richer again. It dawned on Marzana then, that it was only when things turn truly wretched for the world that the men in it turned to God. Uncertain war, and temples flounder. Certain war, temples prosper. Wealth flooded in alongside prayers for prospering ventures, safe return of boys off to war and leaving Malengar out of the eye of either the Empire or the Republic. Every Devadasi was finally happy and safe save for Marzana.

The difficult decisions she had made to keep the Devadasis afloat during the tough times (while acquiring Abyss for Gurumaa) had diminished her popularity amongst the Devadasis. They cursed Marzana for the orchards she sold. They blamed her for the Resht servants she had let go. The colour of Marzana's skin, long forgotten, suddenly turned into an eyesore for the girls she had grown up with. Without Gurumaa, a pillar of her power had already turned to dust on the ground, but now with Damaya's rise, Marzana was no longer even the finest dancer. It was an open secret that Old Khai had now eyes for Damaya. Even Damaya, who Marzana had neglected while striving to save the Devadasis, favoured Badi Dee over her.

And that was when Badi Dee, leveraging Damaya, orchestrated the coup and seized control of the Devadasi household. Though credit must be given where it is due. The manner in which Badi Dee had played her cards, she deserved to be called Lady Krishna. Pitting sisters against each other before one patron was brilliant. There was something about women of the same blood that allured a man. Something perversely incestuous lay in conquering them both. Badi Dee had infected Old Khai with this desire, brandishing Damaya as the cure, and Marzana as the discarded. And Damaya had been more than content to play along.

Marzana wondered if Badi Dee would have been able to plant the seeds of poison the same way if Damaya had known she was not Marzana's sister but Marzana's daughter by Old Khai himself.

But she could not blame Badi Dee for doing what was in her nature. It was not her fault. It was not Kaamah's fault either that Marzana had faltered. It was her own. She had let herself be consumed by care for Gurumaa and the Devadasis. She had let herself be trapped by the Inkspeller. And now she had let herself be distracted by love.

A shout outside her window caught her attention. She took a jug of water to throw it at the ruffians who always gathered outside to steal a glance at her. But it was the local hunter, armed with a catapult, squatting and shooing the crows from descending over something hidden to her eye by the tall grass. 'Oi!' she called out from behind the windows. The hunter, startled, turned and, seeing the Devadasi, bowed. 'Did the panther kill another?' Marzana asked, shuddering at the thought of the maddened maneater having crept so close to her home.

'Yes, Your Divineness,' the hunter said, 'a girl this time. But its reign of terror is at an end. The panther is dead.'

'They slew the beast?'

'He killed it, Yer Divineness. A clean shot, right in the eye. Quick death. Perfect kill. Before I could even bow to the archer, he was off, draggin' the panther's carcass behind him. I gotta go now, take the girl's body to the priest. It's bad enough these beasts are gettin' bold, comin' close to the village, but killin' the priest's daughter? Malengar'll be wearin' a shroud of unrest for a long time.'

'Tarry a little. Did you see more of this archer? Did you speak to him?'

'I thought 'bout followin' him, but... he was like pure fury, Yer Divineness. I seen him yank a green arrow outta the beast. From where I was, looked like one of them Vishkanya arrows. I saw the archer tuck it away. By then, forgive me fer sayin' this, he looked mad, proper mad. His eyes were all amber, his face twisted, and he laughed – gods, that laugh, it was like the damn bells of the underworld. Weren't no sense left in him, none. That archer, he musta been Yama himself.'

No. The archer was no God. He was a demon. The same demon she had fallen in love with. And if he was angry... she had to save him. *And save the others who come in his way.*

A knock on the door timed to match her decision. It was one of the castrated servant boys. 'Lady Divine, the Granary Lord seeks your audience. He sends a pair of earrings in the shape of peacocks as a token of his—'

'Not now, Labang.' Marzana chastised herself, knowing she could ill afford to return gifts. Not when her daughter was slowly preparing to snatch everything from her. 'Tell him the moon river is flowing. Tell him the midwife is called. Tell him to come back in a few days. No, wait! Don't tell him about the moon river. Tell him, she is not in the mood today.'

Labang bowed. No one would doubt Marzana's reason. It was one of the first lessons the Devadasis were taught. Refuse the first small gift to be gifted treasures later.

A few minutes later, Marzana slipped out from the back entrance of her house to find the archer, happy and sad that no one in the temple would notice her absence.

THE UNMAKING OF POISON

I

The Hanged Man flung wide the tavern door, the breath of the cold stars, their harsh indifference and their coldness of regard trailing in his wake. The fur of a panther, thrown over his shoulders, was long enough to flirt with the floor behind him. By now the effect of Abyss had receded but he did not care to fill the blank spaces in his memory.

He drew attention to himself from the patrons. Sure, he looked unmistakably rich with that golden armour but it was only the rich who were found in Vasuki's Nest. He was undeniably beautiful but it was the beautiful who bartered their bodies for bottles in Vasuki's Nest. He was unquestionably a man in mourning but Vasuki's Nest was already overflowing with them. No, there was something different about this man with the bow. He was the diamond glint on snow.

The Hanged Man found himself oddly taken with the ambience of the tavern. Tall stone urns, brimming with waxy green leaves and pink oleander, marked the corners of the bar. Vine-draped pillars held up the ceiling. Ale spills damped the carpets. And where the carpets did not reach, the ale had puddled the uneven flagstones of the floor, forcing giant salamanders to slither out and drunkenly mate with people's toes.

Jade-hued smoke wreathed overhead, veiling the low rafters, blunting the light from the torch sconces. His nose twitched at the dense odour of Abyss. Abyss was the priciest elixir in the realm, outlawed in every kingdom but here in the tavern run by its brewers, the air itself was Abyss. No wonder so many of the townsfolk frequented Vasuki's Nest to be able to sleep unburdened by their memories. The poisonous vapours of Abyss were just enough to coax some sleep, all the while keeping their memories at bay.

Even as he passed, some of the patrons collapsed on their tables. The closed eyes of the ones already on the floor, whose ears were being used by the salamanders for carnal bliss, dreamed behind their darkened sockets.

Only the women with the green paints around their eyes sipped their drinks stoically on their tables. Four of them. Any more, and there would have been casualties. For the poisonous Abyss in the air came not from burning alchemy or a broken cauldron but from the breaths of these women who the world feared as the Vishkanyas, a word of High Sanskrit that meant 'Poison Maidens'.

'What is your poison, lad?' the barkeep asked, her raven hair tied up and pinned.

Interesting choice of words. He jerked his thumb to the flagon of winterale on the counter.

The barkeep wiped her hands on her apron and filled a chipped earthenware carafe, smiling. Perhaps education in the mapping of faces made her feel for him as one would for a lost puppy. The Fool's face had that effect on people. Perhaps that was why she felt the need to caution him about the tavern's peculiarities. So when the Hanged Man gruffly informed her that he already knew, he enjoyed her stung expression as she curtly slid the entire carafe his way along with a clay glass.

Taking a swig, the Hanged Man turned. His eyes took in the colours of the arrows peeking out of the four quivers in the room. The fact that the owners of those quivers were staring back at him with their placid eyes did not dissuade him from his raid. He found the colour of the feathers he wanted, and looked up at the woman who owned them.

Sleek and muscled, she was swathed in a diaphanous saree of pickle green. Around her bare waist, a black leather harness held two naked-bladed daggers, and on the side rested a quiver full of green arrows with jade fletching. She smiled at him with silken lips, and he smiled back. He gestured to the barkeep to buy the woman a drink. The barkeep shook her head sadly as she filled a vial with a glowing turquoise liquid and slid it across the smooth counter. He caught it and strolled over to the woman with the green arrows.

'Blue Fairy, my favourite.' Her lips, painted a dark juniper, parted to reveal a set of perfect teeth and exhale tinted air. He remained unfazed in the gust of her poisonous breath, making the woman frown at the cold disregard. 'Have a blocked nose, Mister?'

He shook his head.

'Who are you?' the woman asked in a deep and mellow voice, and then stepped forward, running a finger across his neck and flicking his hair behind him to reveal the mark of the spade. 'Ah, there you go. A Resht. A lowborn. The only difference between a squirrel and a mouse is that of a mark. One you feed, the other you cage.' Her gaze, as blank as a rattlesnake's, slipped to the man's own bow and quiver, her lips curling into a smile. 'Now what is a Resht doing with such a fine weapon? Don't tell me that Old Khai wants Resht warriors now in the brewery of his.' When he did not answer, she pressed on. 'You must be a Resht brewer. Is that it? You escaped your overseer, and now you want the one damsel who would kiss you because no one else will?' She paused. 'How desperate do you think we are?' she asked as she wet her lips.

He knew they were. Who didn't? These Vishkanyas were girls born with a fault in their stars that foretold death for any man who took them for a wife. Most of these infants were drowned in vats of milk but some were bought by assassin guilds to be weaned on poison and antidote alternately. Reared to turn immune to venom. Most of the girls did not make it. But the ones who did were trained in the arts of seduction and dance to become the finest assassins in the world, their breath, an unseen blade, and their sweat, a caress filled with perilous promise. The poisonous breath these Vishkanyas exhaled caused mind clots but even the smallest dose of their saliva brought the long night. Anything more led to the pyre. It was their saliva and breath that the Black Acharyas bought at great expense to craft the draught of Abyss, which when poured into the eye temporarily purged the taker of his unsavoury memories.

The short-lived brewers, working in their cosy contaminated surroundings were the only ones who could bear to kiss a Vishkanya's lips without collapsing. So... yes, the Vishkanyas were desperate. But it wasn't their lips the Hanged Man was interested in but rather their quivers. Their infamy for using poison-tipped arrows to finish their assignments was what made these Vishkanyas so expensive to engage.

Without a word, he reached for one of these arrows from the Vishkanya's quiver, twirling it between his callused fingers. He examined the intricate craftsmanship, the symbol of a snake etched on the wooden shaft and the green shaft. The Vishkanya was startled but she did not object. She simply watched, her curiosity piqued.

'Perhaps you think you can withstand my touch?' she asked, snatching her arrow back from his hand and returning it to her own quiver. When he did not respond, she stared at him, deeply this time. 'You are a looker behind that beard, aren't you? To the kiss of death, then.'

Lust danced in her eyes as her slender fingers curled around the vial. Before she could take a sip, he pulled out her green arrow from his jacket pocket and used it to impale her palm to the table. Admirably, not a shriek escaped her lips though her eyes widened as she stared at the arrow and then him and then back again to the arrow. The others did not move.

'YOUR ARROW,' the Hanged Man growled. His voice, too heavy with baritone as if two voices were holding court together. 'GO AHEAD. ASK ME WHERE I FOUND IT.'

She hissed. He poured the Blue Fairy from the vial onto her palm, and this time, she cried out.

'ASK. ME.'

'Where did you find it?' the woman finally screamed, her hand burning.

'FUNNY YOU SHOULD ASK. I PULLED IT OUT OF A PANTHER,' he growled, twisting her arrow deeper into her palm, the wood pleasantly grinding against bone, 'THE FOOL WHO HUNTED THE PANTHER LACKED THE WIND TO FINISH THE JOB. THE POISON OOZED FROM THE ARROWHEAD INTO THE PANTHER'S VEINS, THE AGONY TURNING IT MAD. IT TORE THROUGH THREE BEFORE I PUT IT OUT OF ITS MISERY.'

'You best leave.' Another Vishkanya pulled back her chair. The sound of bangles and the aroma of mandrake filled his senses. 'Or I will stuff you with so much Abyss, you won't even remember your mother's name.'

The Fool would love that, wouldn't he? Abyss severed you from memories, yes, but what many didn't know, it severed you from caution as well, allowing you to act on impulse rather than reason. That's why Abyss was such a gift. It blinded the eyes to the consequences. Another Vishkanya rose behind him, no more than three paces away. She had washed-out blue eyes on a hooked face. 'Leave, lowborn. We don't like to kill if we don't get paid for it,' she said in a lazy drawl.

'It was just a blind arrow shot in the air!' cried the Vishkanya in front of him, the wound in her palm throbbing. 'The beast was foolish to get hit. We don't eat meat. Why would I be hunting...' She paused mid-plea when her eyes nudged her to stop.

His face had turned pale, as if the memory evoked from her words soured him with a venom, a venom different from her usual arsenal. A memory of a little boy falling to the ground with a blind arrow jutting out of his skull.

The Hanged Man's face turned vascular, flushed with visible arteries and veins, and his heart thundered so loudly in his chest that it was faintly audible even from afar.

A Vishkanya raised a hand. 'We enjoy immunity from prosecution, mongrel. Ahalya's breath took the life of a groping ambassador and not an uff was heard from his family. The vials Vasuki forgot in the gardens slipped to the river and caused an entire herd of royal stags to perish. The King said nothing. Who are you to get riled over three children?'

'FUCK THE CHILDREN. YOU SHOULD NOT HAVE HURT HIS PET.'

'What pet? Just who are you, Resht?'

'HALF CORPSE, HALF GOD.'

'He is senile.' One of the Vishkanyas smirked. 'End him.'

He slid like smoke into the midst of the two Vishkanyas. A blurred sliver of obsidian-tipped wood.

His left hand went for the lipless Vishkanya. She twisted and pranced back, her daggers thrust out to ward him off should he seek to close in. But heat spilled down her cleavage, her throat slit by his arrow. She staggered forward. Met his bare knuckles. Her daggers skittered on stone. Stunned. Fell on the ground. The last thing he saw of the Vishkanya was a salamander climbing her gurgling throat.

With his right hand, he had already severed the tendons in the arm of the bangled Vishkanya. She screamed and dodged back, holding the mess of arteries in her mutilated arm.

He alighted on his feet in a crouch, raised the arrow with which he had slit the other Vishkanya's throat and flung it across the room like a dart. The arrow cleaved through cornea, bit into the pupil, and was then through, bursting into the barkeep's retina. The barkeep's unfired crossbow crashed on the counter with a thud.

Behind him, the bangled Vishkanya with the bleeding arm rose. She slashed with her good arm but he entered the arc of her cuts. Wrestling an unused dagger free off her belt, he spun to slash at her face now. He missed for she threw her head back to dodge but her head crashed into a low-lying rafter. A heavy thud. The Vishkanya sagged on watery knees on the floor. He settled for stabbing her cheeks instead.

Instinct made him elegantly sidestep a poisoned spit by the first Vishkanya. The spit pellet landed on a hapless salamander on the floor, searing through its skin. With a swift pivot, he turned only to find that the first Vishkanya had already pulled out the arrow from her palm and was readying herself to use it as a dart.

He seized that wrist just in time, sinking the dagger from his free hand into the Vishkanya's left hip bone. He pressed down against the hilt, the dagger chewing through her lower intestines. Her wrist holding the arrow slackened in his grip. He shifted his stance. His right hand now anchored firmly on her shoulder, his left reversed its grip on the dagger, and thrust upwards. Through her abdomen, alongside her heart, through her lung. The blade burst free just below the curve of her clavicle.

'BEAUTIFUL.' The Hanged Man wet his lips with her splattered blood. Too bad none of the patrons were awake to witness his artwork. Perhaps a gentle rousing was in order, to ensure they didn't miss the chance to appreciate his talents first hand. *Enough!* The Fool screamed.

II

Poisoned blood ran like fire in the veins of his mind. He struggled against the monster, its awareness like a scalding noose around his neck. He somehow tore the sleeve of his shirt, folded it into a bandana and bound it tight round his head before he staggered out of the tavern. The alley reeled in his vision. As the monster inside waned along with memories of what just transpired, he saw a gold haze, and in it his nephew, his friend, his brother, his teacher, his mother, every one he had loved and let down, and behind them, the face of his nemesis, handsome, bitter and steel. 'What... happened?' His own voice seemed to come from far off.

It was the sound of wet slippers that woke him. He saw bobbing lights hurry. Coming to kill him, no doubt. Given how much he had borrowed in his life, he was surprised that someone took so long to collect.

That someone called out to him. His name. Sweet and full of concern. That someone asked after him, cradled his head on her lap and dabbed at a wound he did not remember earning. She called him. She called his name. A name that belonged to one of the greatest and noblest warriors in the realm. A name that belonged to a cruel murderer and traitor to the realm.

Karna.

MEMORIES OF THREE MOONS

I

THREE FULL MOONS PAST

His diary had garlanded Marzana with his story three months past. *Garlanded*. That was the right word, wasn't it? For his story had no beginning, no flow, no ending. Just a stitching of different lives, like marigold, jasmine, roses and margosa leaves, strung like blooms on end. A tale of grief over a child lost was sometimes retold as a story of his failure, and sometimes, as a plan for revenge. He veiled wrath for a whore as concern for a princess. He wrote of angels who meant to bring harm to the world, and how the world that had cursed him thrice, deserved it. He bared his guilt for his only friend, one he had betrayed over and over, each treacherous step inching him closer to the knowledge that he, Karna, had earned his fate, that he deserved his death.

Other pages she discovered, lines scratched, something about being the best. Perhaps the basest of his emotions, certainly the most boyish, this desire to outwork, outdo all, but also the most lacerating of his secrets if these were the only lines he had scratched off. Each page was a world of dew, and within each dewdrop, a world of struggle.

She had dried her tears by the time she closed the diary, chiefly because it would have been a mark of false piety to mourn for Karna.

For it was not luck that had led her to Karna's secret spot by the abandoned stupa. She had been tasked to shadow him by the Inkspeller, and from the trail Karna had left in his wake, it had not been hard to discover the loose brick behind which he stashed his secrets. Days of stalking had followed, waiting for him to leave, to steal his life from his diary in his absence. She had often wondered why, despite staying alone in his workshop, he chose this place to bury his life's tale but she knew not to question her blessings.

After turning over the last page of the diary, she had waited. To tell him he could trust her. To... be his friend. It had not started well. Discovering someone waiting in your sacred space had naturally not been a sight that inspired confidence. Waving his diary at his face had not helped either. The flash of anger in his eyes had made her skin crawl but the anger, seemingly fatigued, could not stay aflame long when she, a high-caste Devadasi, had broken every law on earth by bowing to him.

Marzana had lied then, telling tales of how the stupa had once been her sanctuary, a refuge from the lecherous priests, claiming that the brick which concealed his diary had come loose, and that she had mistaken his diary to be a merchant's ledger, a means and flee her wretched life. Karna had sipped every word of hers without question. Trust came easy then, as it does between skilled deceivers and innocent believers.

But friendship... now that had taken time. She had to purchase it, paying with her own secrets and her stories, with her real name of Marzana, not Meenakshi. Though, was it truly payment when given so freely? She had told him of her life as a Devadasi, of Gurumaa, of the weight of debt in her life. To veil the Inkspeller's hand in her autobiography, she had conjured a few thorns out of thin air to cloak the stem holding her flowers aloft. The thorns had been enough to prick Karna, and friendship had bled forth from him then.

Over time, secrets concealed from paper began to fall off Karna's responses, the way cats lose bits of fur when petted thoroughly. It started with a tour of his workshop, hidden under his uncle's skin-wright shop. His uncle had been a skilled designer of caste marks, guild marks and tattoos on the human canvas, who had moved from Hastina to Malengar to ply his trade as an inkspeller when Karna was a child. But his uncle was lynched years ago by a mob on the suspicion of pilfering holy books from the highborns, and he was replaced by Marzana's Inkspeller.

While the empty clay inkpots, the bronze needles of varying thickness and carved bone handles still spoke of the shelves' past, that is where its memories ended. The workshop had been now filled with the pungent aroma of wood shavings and a hint of rosin from the bows.

'I speak languages more fluently than I read or write them,' Karna said. 'There is something in the feel of the sounds. But when I write it or read it, the letters scatter like startled pigeons. Hence, the diary. Trying to better myself in it.' He had smiled when he said that. He looked more his age when he smiled.

'May I ask you something?' Karna asked. Marzana nodded. 'Why is it that you do not mind my caste? The other day I saw a turbaned merchant scold a Devadasi for allowing a Resht's shadow to graze her, an accusation that seemed to petrify the woman. Did my mark not bother you when we met?'

Marzana had discovered then what Karna's greatest weakness was. Kindness. It turned him a slave. So, she had answered him truly.

'It bothered me. It still does,' she said. 'When you come too close, I recoil. It is the order of things the Divine etched on a scroll. I hope you can forgive me.'

'You have nothing to be forgiven for,' Karna said. 'A Devadasi, wife of the Gods, is in the workshop of a Resht. It is a marvel I would scarce believe from another tongue. It's surprising, but I don't mind a good surprise. Although I am still curious as to the *why*.'

It was a fair question. Devadasis were second only to priests in the hierarchy of mankind. Of course, not everyone held Devadasis in such high regard. That disdain, however, was born of ignorance. When the local headman had taken a Mleccha Yavana as a mistress, he had held a big feast. Naturally the temple priests and Devadasis were invited. When introduced, the Greek woman had smiled, all pretence, and badly done pretence. No doubt the Greek woman thought she was talking to one of those low-caste Magadhan harlots who painted their face with garish colours, who stood under trees and beside fields at night, who were indecent, foul mouthed, who consorted even with the poor and the Resht, the spreaders of disease. The Devadasis did no such unholy work. To earn a Devadasi's nod was a God's blessing. They were paragons of politeness. Their weapons were the rules of grammar and the softness of their poetry. Their dance was a delicate tapestry woven with passion and years of discipline. Devadasis were custodians of traditions, holding the key to a forgotten era where Apsaras walked the earth. Even if now their position was such that they needed patrons, the Greek should have known that it made them more alike than different. They both were kept women. Only the Greek would be discarded later for she was married to a Man while Marzana would simply find a new patron for she was married to a God. But the memory of the Greek gave her a lie she could season with the truth to answer Karna.

'Because over the years of my glory I had forgotten I was an outsider. I dye my red hair raven. I am a Mleccha. A Mleccha who has been sanctified by wedding to the God but a Mleccha nonetheless. My daughter, who believes she is my sister, torments me now. I am half pride, half agony. Her success has peeled the Meenakshi off my skin to let Marzana breathe again. And *Marzana* has secrets. And…' she had looked up at him, believing every word she said, 'I think if I gave you my secrets, you would treat them tenderly.'

Karna's soft eyes had seemed brighter, then, in the afternoon sunlight that shone through the windows, eyes the colour of honey made by black bees.

'Thank you, Lady Divine,' Karna said.

'Marzana,' she corrected him.

Karna nodded as he turned to cook himself lunch. Marzana, naturally, could not partake of any food cooked by a Resht. But she listened and talked. They did not speak of their past or their caste again but spent most of the meal discussing his fear of ships and her fear of irrelevance. The pauses in the conversation never grew awkward. The silence held a language of its own. And this was how Karna and Marzana's forbidden friendship grew.

Almost all of a Devadasi's *padams* are about love at night and of how the rising sun separates the lovers, but for Karna and Marzana it was the opposite. While everyone was asleep in the noon heat, they came together, and it was always dusk that separated them. Dusk that brought her back to her house behind the temple where she took a long bath to purify herself again.

But the setting sun wasn't the only thing that had forced them apart.

The Inkspeller had been waiting for her.

II

TWO FULL MOONS PAST

In the second month of their secret meetings— no, that does not do it justice. On the sixtieth time they met to talk, Karna asked her, 'Why haven't you asked me why am I here?'

Marzana had considered this thoroughly before she had responded. 'Because I do not wish to know what made you sad till you feel comfortable sharing. I would rather see you smile instead.'

'You want to have my smiles?' Karna had paused before continuing, amused. 'You can have them, if you can find them.'

For reasons unknown, the sentiment had delighted Marzana so much that she had not been able to properly respond, and had only smiled. Karna had lifted a hand, hesitated, then clenched his fists to let the strand of hair she had deliberately let fall across her face stay there. His callused fingers scraped against his knees instead, awkwardly.

She had known it was foolish to even start down this road but she could not help herself. 'I could prove you are wrong about every thought that just went through your head.'

'Can you, now?'

She gave a sly smile that made landlords stutter. 'You could even choose how I tell you,' her eyes flickered once to his jawline, 'teeth or tongue.'

'You are vile!'

'And you are virtuous. The finest songs are those where the vile and the virtuous burn together!'

He laughed.

'See... I told you I would find those smiles.'

They had walked back then in secret, courting death with every second because of their different castes, going their separate ways only once they had reached the temple. She could not wait to meet him again.

But Karna had missed their next meeting when he had been chased out of town by a gang of spoilt highborn boys. When Marzana did meet him the day after, she tied an amulet around his wrist to safeguard him from the evil eye. Her fingers had hesitated before touching his skin, like a pair of scissors before a white chrysanthemum.

But can scissors ever resist a gardener?

Karna had said nothing. He had just stared at his wrist with dead eyes, the dark circles beneath bearing a striking resemblance to one of those pandas one heard about from beyond the Mai Layas.

'Won't you tell me what ails you, what tugs at your dreams?'

Karna had bared his soul to her then, told her of how Sudama, his adopted son, his nephew in truth, had once saved coppers to buy and tie a similar string around Karna's wrist. He told her of how Sudama had fallen in the Panchalan Swayamvar, and how Karna had not been able to sleep since that day for he always found Sudama waiting in his dreams. 'He asks me the same question again and again. *Why did I let him die? Why did I abandon him?* I fled Hastina to come here to escape the memories but I cannot seem to outrun them. I knew I was a cactus, pricking anyone who tends to me. I had always known it. But with Sudama's murder, I was uprooted and cast to the winds. This is what I am now, something ugly, drained of all that once made me whole, bled dry of even the last drop of sap.'

Marzana had hesitated then. But why the pause, why the delay? This was the moment she had been instructed by the Inkspeller to wait for and it was here. Karna had finally spoken of Sudama. Do not hesitate, Marzana. *But he is so kind. He has suffered so much.* Had she forgotten? Lust is a thought, blood runs in the veins. When the Inkspeller cuts, guess what will flow? Remembering the first time the Inkspeller had collected his debt, she prayed for forgiveness and turned to Karna.

'You don't have to show leaf and petal to be living, you are soil and root.' Saying this, Marzana had lured him into taking the Inkspeller's gift. She had herself emptied the vial of Abyss into Karna's eyes to follow the Inkspeller's commands to the letter.

Little had she known then that she had unleashed the horde of locusts hiding inside Karna's heart. She only witnessed the aftermath during one of their walks through the forest around the stupa. There, they stumbled upon a gang of Namin women, mercilessly whipping a Resht for covering her bare breasts with her drape. The Reshts were forbidden from covering their chests in Malengar. It was known. The girl, however, had swathed a scarf over her little breasts. Marzana, nay, the whole town knew she had done so to dodge the advances of the astrologer. Perhaps, the astrologer's wife had discovered her husband's fascination with the girl, and unable to rebuke him, had directed her wrath at the victim instead.

It had been a strange voice that had growled beside her then. Karna... no longer looked like Karna. He had looked feral as he had stalked ahead to greet the Namin women. His voice, like two knives scraping against each other, had her toes curling in her sandals. Marzana, petrified by both Karna's turn of shade and the peril of being caught in a Resht's company, had melted away, vowing to never meet Karna again. The Inkspeller could languish in hell for all she cared. This had not been part of her debt.

By sunrise the next day, her resolve had only hardened when whispers of the disappearance of three Namin women had swept through the town. The temple drummers reckoned they had eloped with their common lover, the astrologer, who had also disappeared overnight bequeathing his wealth to the Temple of Kaamah. Did they vanish or did they perish?

That afternoon Karna had thrown a pebble at Marzana's window. When she confronted him, she was staggered to find Karna had come to request more Abyss. He remembered nothing of those Namin women. When reminded, he had been confused, almost disoriented, and for some reason, Marzana had smiled. *Just when I was beginning to believe someone could be perfect.* The Inkspeller had been right. Karna had caged darkness within him but there is the darkness that is restful and then there is the darkness that frightens. The man she had seen stalk towards those women was not the glow of a candle but the silhouette it cast. And what was worse, Karna did not know. Did not remember. Or had suppressed the memory.

Realizing her heart left her no choice, she had stayed with him. And that was when she realized that while she had set out to trap Karna, she was now in return trapped by him.

She hated how she could not think of him without turning him into a metaphor. She hated how she was not even allowed to be in the physical shadow of a Resht let alone yearn to caress his callused palms. And the most grievous reason of all. She was supposed to be the ocean drowning everything Karna had inside, not be burned alive in his fire.

She had thought then of confessing to Karna but by then it was too late, and she resigned herself to the pain of having never spoken up at all. She feared losing him too deeply in her bones to be honest to him. Sometimes life was like that, wasn't it?

Was this why she had not tried to wrangle back Damaya from Badi Dee's control? After all, it would take just a whisper of another confession, and Damaya would return to Marzana. Her power would be restored. Was Karna the reason why Marzana never unsheathed that dagger because she wanted to spend time discovering Karna even if she could not touch him? She hungered for the sound of his laughter more than the sound of cymbals. She hungered for the divine game to make him slip his soul out of his skin and sleep in her palms rather than the domestic sport of who holds the key to a locker box of meaningless jewels. And she knew she would be able to do none of it if she ascended to be the Matriarch of the Devadasis. So she decided to give up on the Devadasis. Little had she known that Karna was going to leave her the next day.

The sun had been hanging high in the sky when Marzana had appeared by Karna's side while he strung a pair of chicken corpses. 'Most would hunt the panther down, you know?' she said. 'You could let me sell it and fetch good coin for its fur. You could use that to set some of those Resht children in the hound races free.'

'They will just be replaced by other Reshts,' he had said absently. 'This is an orphaned cub. Finding him would be tough but I intend to make sure he lives a long life.'

'Could you at least lace the jerkin up to your neck. The whole world knows you are a Resht, and seeing you with a bow would help no one.'

'So would seeing me with a Devadasi.'

Marzana scowled. Karna had then obediently laced his jerkin up at the neck. 'Is that better?'

'It is perfect,' Marzana said though her gaze had remained on his smile.

Later that day, Marzana had not even been able to spot the cub against the cliff, it had been that beautifully camouflaged. But Karna had approached him like a mother. The cub, afraid at first, had stared warily at Karna's outstretched hand, till he had drawn closer and licked his fingers. It could not have been older than eight months. Karna had then tickled the cub's ears till it snuggled in his palm, and Marzana witnessed a bond take wing.

'How...?' she had asked, when Karna had returned to her, the cub trailing.

'I have a way with them... Discovered it in Meru. Animals like me for some reason—' He was interrupted when Marzana climbed on her toes to hug him. His body listed momentarily towards hers as he let her consume him. She wrapped her hands around his chest to never let go, to take him whole, with his awkwardness, his vulnerability, his laughter. And just then Karna's fingers spread vines across her back, sprouting flowers on her spine, turning her bones fluid. It was so perfect, that moment. Fragile and frozen.

Just then the cub let out a soft rumble, and Karna pulled himself away. He had stared at her with longing and loss, then disappeared with the cub into the hills without a word. Her head had been still swimming so it took time for her to realize... she had driven Karna away.

III

PRESENT

When the Inkspeller inquired later about Karna's whereabouts, she had spun a tale, adulterated with truth, claiming he had left to rescue a cub. The Inkspeller had believed it, harbouring no doubt that his spy had fallen in love with his quarry. The Inkspeller was certain Karna would return, and for the time being, as reward, had let Marzana see her son.

Devadasis of Kaamah were forbidden from bearing sons. Sons held no place in a Devadasi household, and faced the same fate as third daughters did around the realm – Death. But Marzana had birthed twins. Damaya. Dhanush.

Dhanush was rescued by the Inkspeller to be placed in a high-born home. The Inkspeller had not once called upon Marzana to repay the debt. Perhaps she could have settled it had the Inkspeller not also saved the Devadasis from financial ruin with his gold or Gurumaa from eclipse with his Abyss. Even then, when the Inkspeller had knocked on her door with his favour, Marzana had refused the idea of being in the same room as a Resht, an action for which she paid with the body of her firstborn son when the Inkspeller broke his elbow and cut off his thumb before her very eyes. After that day, she would have damned an army of Reshts to eternal pain to save the life of her boy.

Good thing Karna was gone. She prayed he never returned even as she pined for him.

But today when she heard stories of a maneating panther on a rampage, and then heard of a godless archer who took it down... she knew. Karna was back. And he wasn't back alone. The Darkness in him had returned as well. She wondered if she would even return alive from her foolhardy trek to find Karna.

Only one way to find out.

IV

Marzana discovered Karna lying on the walkway outside Vasuki's Nest, curled up, so covered in blood that he might have been a figure moulded from mud. His eyes were open and staring, his amber pupils flecked with green Abyss. *Don't be dead. Please, don't be dead.* The slow rise and fall of his chest brought watery relief to her eyes.

'Karna, please wake up, please tell me you are alright.' Marzana poked his ribs with a twig.

'Ow.' Karna smiled without opening his eyes. 'Is that you, Marz? I think I sinned. Again.'

'No, you didn't.' A moonbeam, moving through the street, caught a shine of the gold on Karna's chest and for an instant Marzana could see Karna's clothes clearly. She had experience with blood. Some patrons were not known to be delicate. They were hanged later by the town council for sacrilege but Marzana was the one who dealt with the stitches on the girls. The same experience told her that most of the blood on Karna was not his own.

Marzana turned to the door of Vasuki's Nest that was ajar. Even from the walkway, she glimpsed silhouettes of toppled chairs and tables inside. An army of flies lay unmoving at the threshold, their entry denied by the poisoned air within. But what had lured them there?

'You did nothing wrong, Karna. Just stay here. I will be right back.'

Summoning courage from Kaamah, she ventured inside the tavern to find out. Moments later, she staggered out, hands pressed against her nose, stumbling into the middle of the alley. Murdered. Four Vishkanyas. All murdered.

Even Karna, with his legendary skill, wouldn't stand a chance against the entire Vishkanya army. *And that is assuming the Malengar Marshals don't get to him first.* He would be— wait. Should she not let that come to pass? Could it not rid her of her plight? With Karna dead, the Inkspeller would release her. This was the solution to all that ailed her! She laughed. If it were that easy, the world would be free of love and regrets.

But what could she do? Unbidden, the tale of Mati of Kalinga from Karna's diary surged before her eyes, unbolting a floodgate of ideas. Muttering a prayer to Kaamah, she returned to Vasuki's Nest. As she threaded her way around the drugged and the dead, her eyes caught the glint of a shattered bottle of Blue Fairy on the counter where the barkeeper lay dead. She borrowed a match from a table on which three men lay sprawled, the pipe they shared empty, their faces drooling and dreaming. *There are still other people inside, Marzana! Innocent people just addled and dreaming, too lost to wake up. Like Gurumaa.* She couldn't do this!

Would that have stopped Mati?

V

Karna followed her like a gentled mule. *Bless Kaamah for his benediction.* From the tavern to her house behind the temple, she prodded him with a long stick. Behind her, the clouds, faintly reflecting the fire consuming Vasuki's Nest, hid the moon and its court of stars.

Even now, in the safety of the anteroom in her house, she wrapped him in her own shawl so that there was no contact between their skins. She clutched the shawl tightly before holding his arms to guide him. Becoming flushed and distracted with the knotted muscles, she tossed him on the floor beside the bed. A glance at the catatonic Gurumaa, still sleeping on the bed, likely as drugged as Karna, confirmed she was still passed out.

Feeling soiled, she took a cold bath to wash off the sin of Resht and poison from her skin. After, she ran a comb through her wet hair before a mirror. Half her cheeks were dully illumed in a warm yellow light from the window. Aware of the source, she ignored it and climbed on the bed to draw a sheet over her face and forget the night. Before she closed her eyes, she peered over the bed to check on Karna, only to find her shawl had slid off his chest.

It was not the first time she had seen him bare chested, yet 'bare' seemed a liberal description considering his chest was hidden behind… she did not know what to call it, a half-sleeved golden skinplate, perhaps. But for the first time she could openly study him without fretting over whether he had noticed her gaze. And what she saw made her… thirsty. That was so strange. Marzana had always preferred dark, rough, hairy men and Karna being fair, woman-skinned even if muscled, was not the flavour of sherbet of which she partook.

So what overcame her?

She slipped down her bed and… with closed eyes and trembling anticipation, traced his forehead with her fingers. It felt hot. It felt unholy. Even though this touch might have sealed her fate for a thousand rebirths, she thirsted for more.

'Water…' Karna's faint groan gave her the excuse she needed.

She returned to Karna with a glass of water, her movements hesitant, as if each step were a silent prayer. Carefully propping his head with the blanket as a barrier between their skins, she guided the glass to his lips. Half the water slipped past his mouth in agonizingly slow trickles down his neck and over his gold-plated chest. Karna managed to swallow a few sips before turning his head away as if seeking refuge from the world. Marzana, fingers shivering, wiped the water from his mouth. His lips were as soft as swansdown. Gooseflesh whispered all over Marzana, and she danced around the need to let out all her breath on his face. A thrill surged through her veins when she, instead of discarding the glass, raised it to her own lips. To even touch the glass was sacrilege. But when, with the tip of her tongue, she captured the tiny pool of water lingering at the bottom, she knew she was lost. It was just water but as it misted and condensed on her tongue at the same time, her fingers grazed over the line that led along one thigh and found the dew between her legs. And when she swallowed the water, the dew turned to rain.

Perhaps now there wasn't much difference between Marzana and the priests of her temple. Those Namins, unable to afford the grace of a Devadasi, slipped out at night to the huts of pariahs. Unequal until death, yet equals in bed. It was this thought that let her sleep peacefully beside the poisoned lowborn, her hands around him committing blasphemy punishable by death with each passing breath.

Sleep peacefully, that is, till two pairs of hands banged loudly at her door.

VI

'Unless your eyes and ears have been stitched shut with boar hide, you could not have missed it,' Badi Dee said nonchalantly, sipping winterale under a canopy of wildbriar and jasmine flowers, her head turned to the horizon where blue-yellow smoke rose in sinuous coils. Their temple terrace had earned them a good view of the town on the other side of the River Ganga where the fire had transfigured the river to molten gold. Marzana's heart chirred like a glowmoth. 'Told you they were just mortals,' Badi Dee said, much to the relief of Marzana. 'They burn just like anyone else. With all those Abyss addicts in their tavern, I am surprised it took so long for a fool to set it ablaze.'

Marzana saw Damaya step onto the tiled floor of the terrace. Damaya went to Badi Dee like a child to her mother and buried her face in Badi Dee's chest while Marzana sat ignored to the side.

'Here, have a grape, light of my eyes,' Badi Dee said as she carefully plucked a purple grape from the platter piled high with Vidarbhan fruits. 'Prince Viren had all this brought to you from across the borders,' she said. 'He thought you might like a small reminder of the exotic towns he intends to take you to if you choose to favour him over Old Khai.'

'But so many dead,' Damaya sobbed. 'Labang told me fourteen men and four women...'

That many... The smoke was far away but Marzana felt it rub her throat raw as the weight of her crime descended on her.

'Vishkanyas aren't women and you'd do well to remember that,' Badi Dee said. 'Girls who should have never made it past their childhood. All I now care about are the remaining Vishkanyas. Hope the rest move their nest somewhere else and leave the good folk of Malengar in peace. What else did Labang say? He just stutters before me.'

'Something about Blue Fairy, the smell of the flames, it was a fire caused from some liquid—'

'Understood,' Badi Dee cut in, spitting the last of the betel leaf on a potted plant. 'First, the maneater. Then this explosion. More will be flocking to the Temple. Good for your arangetram. And send for Labang when you head down. Meenakshi, see to it, he receives fifteen lashes for corrupting young ears with talk of ale.'

'Yes, Badi Dee.'

'What a nuisance,' Badi Dee said, smiling hungrily.

A eunuch guard came charging to the terrace, panting and looking as though he'd seen a ghost. *Oh, Kaamah!* Had they discovered some trace that tied her to the fire? Had she, in her haste to save Karna, let slip a piece of jewellery? Had the fool stumbled from her chambers like some clumsy oaf? Perhaps it would be wiser to cast herself from the terrace now and be done with it.

'Spit it out!' Badi Dee demanded sharply.

'The Prince is on his way to the Temple!'

'Be more specific. Every man in the Orange Court fancies himself a prince. Which prince? The Prince of the Granaries? The Prince of the Wells? The Prince of the Sandalwood Market? Or is it Old Khai? The Prince of the Brewery,' she teased, tickling Damaya, much to her delight.

'*The* Prince,' the eunuch guard said, 'the Prince of Hastinapur and Heir of the Hastina Union. Prince Duryodhan.'

VII

The sanctorum of the Temple of Kaamah had been given such a cleaning as had seldom been seen by Marzana in the past decade. The bases of the eight pillars had been polished, the *dwarpalakas* guarding the entrance scrubbed, the mosaic floor waxed until it gleamed like satin. Legions of sanctified Reshts had cleared a year's accumulation of soot from holy fires etched on the friezes along the gallery. Slowly the virtues of Devadasis had brightened on those friezes, colours emerging anew from beneath the blanket of grime. The dancing area itself had been decorated with oil lamps crafted from clay, all aglow, emitting the scent of cotton wick dipped in ghee. Upon this area, Damaya danced, which was most unorthodox, given she was not a Devadasi yet.

The gathered lords and nobles broke into spontaneous applause once Damaya was done. With the King and his eldest son away in the East for the Conclave, the Orange Court's finest nobles had assembled at the Temple of Kaamah in haste to make Prince Duryodhan feel welcome. Malengar was, after all, a tributary of the Union. But unlike the rest of the righteous Union, the Malengars took pride in the culture and arts of their kingdom, and found it fitting that the Prince had chosen the Kaamah Temple of Malengar as his inaugural visit. The choice signified him as the Man of Gods, a reputation that had diminished lately due to his Resht Reforms.

None of them even noticed how the said Heir refused to be hypnotized by the dance of Damaya's bare ankle and slender arms.

Duryodhan had even dismissed the girls who had been waving the palmyra leaf fan gently over him.

Even when Duryodhan asked a servant girl for a glass of butter-milk, the assembled Namins did not make much of it. But when the Prince thanked the servant girl and asked her to hand the glass to him, the Namins turned as one. And when Duryodhan sipped from the glass, the rim touching his lips, the Namins shivered until Badi Dee leaned over to whisper to them that the servant girl's caste mark had been hidden from the Prince due to the angle of her positioning. Marzana wondered if the priests had believed that lie. But she could see why Karna could do anything for his friend.

'Your Grace.' Old Khai passed a freshly rolled betel leaf to the Prince with both hands. His cheeks were sallow but his bearing regal. He was wearing a chain of the most beautiful workmanship over a string of pearls as big as hen's eggs. 'These Devadasis are the finest in the realm. The Old Gods themselves reside in their ankles. But if my Prince wishes for an entertainment of a modern nature, might I request your august presence in my mansion tomorrow?'

Duryodhan nodded gratefully. 'If time permits,' he answered Old Khai politely.

'Your Grace, I must commend you on standing up for the down-trodden. The Trial of Prince Arjun is—' Prince Viren said.

'Most righteous.' Old Khai said.

Viren frowned. 'Yes, most righteous. You are a—'

'Man of the people!' Old Khai finished.

'Man of the people, I say,' Prince Viren said quickly as if he came up with it first, casting a sidelong glance at the merchant-noble, and then he leaned closer to Duryodhan. 'Is the outcome, however, decided, Your Grace? A small fine, no doubt,' he asked, speaking as if Duryodhan and he were milk brothers.

Duryodhan rose in response, and requested a word with Badi Dee. The rest of the patrons sniggered as they excused themselves from further conversation, content that even Prince Duryodhan was a mortal man like them. All except Old Khai. Marzana could not help but chuckle. He would not get the first night with Damaya after all. Not that Old Khai blamed the Prince. The Prince was a man after all but Old Khai did appear resolved never to delay his bid again. Little did anyone expect the twist fate had in store.

Badi Dee's plans and Damaya's pride fell and broke into petals around them when Duryodhan requested a *tour* of the Temple with a Devadasi named Meenakshi instead. Tours of the Temple of Devadasis seldom involved an exploration of the divine architecture as much as replicating the postures of divine love sculpted on it.

And just like that, Marzana urf Meenakshi was restored to the pedestal of prime dancer of the temple over Damaya without having so much as graced the stage that night. After all, who wouldn't covet what the Prince of the Union desired?

Marzana felt that familiar net of glances being cast her way, a sensation she had long since surrendered to Damaya. But Marzana was no novice. Without letting any surprise show on her face, she rose with delicate grace to lead Duryodhan without a word, relishing in the restored power as if it had never slipped away in the first place. She might as well enjoy it for as long as it lasted. Marzana knew that what the Prince of the Union wanted with her had naught to do with her charms but everything to do with her company.

VIII

Spots of colour glowed on Duryodhan's cheeks and shame lent an awkwardness to his words. 'You misunderstand me, Lady Divine,' he said when Marzana led him outside the temple to her house and locked the doors behind him.

'Make yourself comfortable, Your Grace,' she said with absent courtesy. When he did not move, she glanced up, meeting Duryodhan's gaze. As if reading an entire book in a fleeting heart-beat, she knew none of her wiles would work on him. So she asked him straightaway, 'How did you know he is in Malengar?'

'Spies.' He did not blink. Eerily so. 'Where is he?'

'Has he not suffered enough on your count? Why do you want him?'

'Curious, the question I was going to ask you was strung of the same words.'

How much does he know? 'I am wed to a God. And that ranks me higher than you, Prince. Not to forget you are in my house, and as such are a guest. Guests don't make demands of hosts.'

'Guests are the only ones who do. And wed to a God you may be, but from what I hear, Gods aren't kind on adultery of the heart.'

'A subject with which you are well acquainted from what I hear.' That found flesh. Duryodhan's expression dropped a scale. She decided to dig her dagger deeper. 'And I also heard of your acts of kindness towards Karna,' she scoffed to let him know what she thought of him. 'There is a saying amongst us Devadasis: The dogs you feed in your front yard never shit in your front yard. They guard them instead.'

The set of his jaw betrayed his displeasure. 'Karna is *my* friend.'

'He is *mine*.'

'Seems like Karna should have some say in the matter.' Karna's weary voice startled Duryodhan and somehow even Marzana as it came from the other side of the bed. 'A wife of a God and the future King of the Union vying for the affection of a Resht? The revolution is here.' Karna rose, coughing, massaging his temple, looking every bit the murderer without a memory.

'Karna!' With a will, Marzana lied with the touch of silk, 'I imagined you would be insensible for days. I was uncertain whether you had an ague or some unknown pestilence had—'

But Karna wasn't even looking at her. 'Karna,' Duryodhan said.

'Prince,' Karna replied drunkenly.

Duryodhan and Karna stood facing each other, no arm shakes, no greetings, just standing there exchanging wordless messages of comfort as if in their private language. Marzana could not help but feel envious. She thought only she had known his language. The silence was only broken by Gurumaa's cough.

'Aye,' Gurumaa's voice grated. 'Two handsome men. Meenakshi, you have finally ceased being a prude.'

It was the longest speech she had given in the last two years. Gurumaa paused to catch a breath. 'Remember, gentlemen, view it not as a contest but a team race. In this race, the one who comes first is not important. It is—' She turned her weary gaze to Karna, whose tactless shock at Gurumaa's suggestion was writ large on his face. Gurumaa gave a feeble cough as her dull eyes focused on Karna. 'Oh, this one has the mood of a pebble in rice. Remember, lad, a triangle of love is nothing but a threesome delayed.'

Her voice wound down, and in the end her words were lost as the poppy Abyss Marzana fed her carried her dreaming mind back to the centre of the temple where she danced, hopefully, with the three brothers she spoke of.

'What are you… doing here, Karna?' Duryodhan asked.

'Where is… *here?*' Karna slurred.

'A Devadasi's quarters behind the Temple of Kaamah.'

'Ah, I was wondering. This room smells too much of jasmine flowers to be mine.' He tried to move but stumbled.

'You aren't going anywhere now,' Marzana said.

'Prince…' Karna said, ignoring Marzana. 'I don't remember why am I here? I either drank too much or got hit by a chariot. I remember chasing Bagheera, I mean the panther.'

'If I were a wagering man, I would say you're drunk,' Duryodhan said.

'I think I am poisoned.'

'He is a wither head,' Marzana pantomimed sprinkling a powder into her eyes from an imaginary vial, 'addicted to the Abyss.' She drew a sharp eye from Duryodhan and Karna. *By Kaamah!* She had forgotten who Duryodhan was and more importantly, why Abyss was forbidden by the edicts under the Codes.

Abyss took birth as an elixir when a Black Acharya, while treating a wounded Vishkanya, had stolen her sweat and saliva to see if he could create their poisonous breath in powder form. Scores of experiments later had seen the Vishkanya's bodily extracts bubble in a vial in his hermitage but in a world destined to be cruel, a powder that could temporarily sever memories to sharpen focus had to be a camouflage for general unpleasantness. No one ever knew when the enjoyment of the elixir turned to a want, and then deteriorated to a need. But the world was littered with enough war veterans, old assassins, young broken-hearted lovers and accident survivors who had become so dependent on Abyss that they felt the world owed them the drug. Often at knifepoint. The Malengar King had forced the Black Acharya to eye-wash his own weight in Abyss to turn him into an addict so that he could be more motivated to find a cure. Three weeks later, the Black Acharya slit the throat of the Princess when the royal physician refused him access to Abyss. And that was the end of it. Drachmas plying the Abyss-trade were hanged by the dozens, properties of the families of Abyss addicts were confiscated by the Kingdom if they did not report it, and in only three years, the elixir went from being displayed on a shelf to being hidden under the counter. 'I jest. A poor jest, admittedly. He is poisoned – not drugged,' she said, unconvincingly.

'I don't remember there being a difference when it comes to Abyss,' Duryodhan said.

'I think Gods give us friends like you so death won't come as such a disappointment, Marz,' Karna told Marzana and decided to feel for the wall behind him to keep him standing lest he fall. He missed it and did fall. Both Duryodhan and Marzana instinctively stretched a hand to help him, and seeing each other, stiffened, withdrawing their hand, leaving Karna with no help at the end when he passed out on the floor.

Duryodhan turned to Marzana for an explanation.

'He walked into a Vishkanya tavern to punish them for killing his cub, and in the brawl, a Vishkanya set fire to their own tavern.'

A pregnant pause.

Duryodhan cleared his throat with a sound that could only be described as a prelude to an epiphany. 'Women and Fire, or rather Women-who-cause-Fire do seem to follow Karna where he goes. For once I would like to meet him when he isn't hanging on the brink of death.'

'My theory is he attracts deranged women if they are in a radius of one league around him,' Marzana said.

'Agreed,' Duryodhan said, a touch of sly in his eyes. *I walked into that one.* 'Jests aside, he isn't on Abyss now, is he? It is a crime, not just against his being, but against the Codes.'

'No, he isn't,' Marzana lied. 'Though he does behave like he is on it. Why are you here, Prince? To put Karna through another round of your chores so that he would end up actually needing the Abyss?'

Duryodhan seemed rather struck by this breach of etiquette. 'You forget yourself, Lady Divine.'

'Did you look at Karna? Look at him, really. It is like gazing at a faraway star. It is shining but the light is from thousands of years ago. The star doesn't even exist anymore. Whatever war or conspiracy you need him for, he is ill-equipped to stand beside you.' *What are you doing? Why urge him not to take Karna away, you fool?* With him gone, her woes would fade, the Inkspeller's grip at last unmade. *Release him, Marzana. Relinquish him!*

'I need him as a friend not as a Highmaster of the Union,' Duryodhan said.

'For Princess Bhanumati?'

Duryodhan did not possess a face that lent itself to shock, but Marzana saw it. A flicker in his gaze. 'Reckon he trusts you more than would be considered wise.'

'Yes, he does. But he did not tell me this. I happened upon it in his diary when he wasn't looking.'

Duryodhan's eyes widened but he said nothing. Marzana should have chosen silence then but recklessness had seized her speech.

'Tell me something, Prince. Didn't Princess Mati make her choice with the Crown Prince of the— Oh, Kaamah! I see the madness in your gaze! Has the Princess even asked to be rescued or is it just your longing in disguise?'

Unsettled by how easily he had been disarmed, Duryodhan spoke with a raw candor and pain, as if Marzana had uncorked the words he had bottled up. 'My letters must not have reached her for I have received nothing in return. The Black Swan, a harbinger of unkind verse, doesn't miss a chance to use her quill. She's never been a siren of silence, Mati. I fear something is amiss—' and suddenly realizing who he was speaking to, Duryodhan ceased his confession midway.

Marzana said nothing in reply, pointing at the long seat against the side of the room. 'You can sleep there on the diwan or rest on the swing. The world will think we made love until dusk, or dawn, however long Karna needs to completely recover. You can help him escape this street, then.'

Duryodhan was uncomfortable with the idea but took the diwan. Marzana doused the two remaining lamps in the room and then climbed into the bed beside Gurumaa, wondering why did she ask them to sleep in her room instead.

'Why did you ask that question?' she heard Duryodhan ask, frustration unmistakably colouring his voice. Marzana smiled at how the Prince of the Hastina Union and Old Khai had one thing in common after all: a crippling insecurity that needed a voice to tell them they were on the right path. Be it the path between her legs or between the legs of the Empire.

She knew better than to say something, pretending to be asleep instead. It was not her place to mock him for wanting to say goodbye. She had witnessed this in the young girls who had run away from the temples searching for closure only to come back empty handed. The word 'closure' was an empty word behind which lay no meaning. The end only came from forgetting, a habit perfected over years of harrowing repetition, a music so often listened to that the ear turned it into the noise of the wind.

Marzana could only hope she would remember this lesson when Karna left her. *When or... if.* She saw all the ways her heart could bruise in the space between these two words.

THE TRUE FRIEND

I

Karna, still lying on the floor, twisted and turned when the sound of morning prayers polluted the air, and parakeets sparred over the berries of the neem tree outside. Marzana had evidently risen with the lark. Her saree was in disarray from sleeping in it. When she raised her arms to twist her thick hair and pull it into a knot at her neck, Karna's eyes trespassed, without his consent, on her bare waist and lingered for a moment longer than they should have before they heard his mind and rose back to her face hastily.

'Not a morning person, I take it.' She looked at him as she spoke, and he inched away. Her gaze made him too aware of how close to her bed he was.

'I am,' he said. 'But I can't talk to anybody until I've had my tea.'

'Explains your manners.' Marzana rose to open the curtains.

Did she mean his staring? No, it had only lasted half a heartbeat. Would she think him a lecher? Or worse, would it have rekindled the fire he had doused by running away? Then who would be to blame if she burned not just in, but because of, the fire? For a Devadasi to even exchange words with a Resht was more blasphemous than facing the moon while defecating or kicking a cow. Anything more did not bear thinking of. Not to forget, nothing good had ever come from a woman's touch on Karna. The first time, a man was murdered, a ship sunk and a port burned. The second time, men were murdered, a swayamvar sunk and a city burned. There are men who can smile as they dance on corpses but Karna was not part of such a cult.

He massaged his head. He desperately needed tea.

'You can always tell him no,' Marzana said. 'I know it is difficult for you but muster those words – N. O. Just pull them from your gut and say it out loud when he asks. I know the bereaved look in the eyes of high-caste men when the torch of consequences does not light their path. I noticed the same look on Duryodhan last night. He will take you down.'

'What are you on about, Marz?'

'I'm talking about your friend and whatever mad caper has driven him to seek your aid.'

Oh right. The Prince was here, sleeping on the other side of the room. It's a marvel how a mind could stash away crucial information under a rug during a night's sleep only for one to trip over it come morning.

'May I go on?' Marzana asked.

'No!' Karna was busy playing his favourite game again: to figure whether his headache was from dehydration, poisoning, Abyss withdrawal, heartache, exhaustion, his high ponytail, his lack of sleep or a cheeky tumour in his skull.

'No?'

'No. I haven't had my tea.'

At this moment Marzana rustled up the good old beverage and handed it to him gruffly. 'I did not mean for you to make it!' Karna said, aghast. Apart from his mother, no woman had ever gone to the bother of brewing anything for him.

'Will you just take it?' Marzana held Karna's palm out with one hand and placed the tea cup and plate on it – there was surprising strength in her grip – and her skin felt like... jasmine flowers. Something softer, smoother. Karna shivered as he realized their skins were touching each other. Snatching the tea hastily, he spun away. *Gods, how could anyone's skin be so soft?* Memories of their shared kiss flooded back, causing Karna to turn red as a beetroot. *Just drink your tea.*

Karna sipped on it with a glad moan. After a couple of loud slurps, the world seemed a bit brighter. Even the morning prayers didn't offend the ear as much as they had a while back. The sunlight felt softer too. By the time he had finished the first cup, Karna was a new man, so much so that he not only permitted but encouraged Marzana to continue and complete the rest of her treasonous chastisement, and even went so far as to agree with the soundness of her fourth warning. She was still mid-monologue when a sudden silence pricked their ears, and he noticed that Duryodhan had stopped snoring.

'Tea for me,' Duryodhan ordered.

'Brew it yourself,' Marzana said.

Duryodhan, in the middle of stretching, looked up at her and then at Karna. 'Why discriminate between guests?'

'Karna is my friend.'

'*Friend*, it seems,' Duryodhan scoffed. 'Karna is my friend, and we never made tea for each other.'

'Perhaps something to reflect on, then, Prince?' Marzana narrowed her eyes at him.

'I will make it!' Karna rose before his friends drew their daggers.

Marzana raised her hand to silence Karna. 'There is some left over in the pot,' she said, adding a lot of undue emphasis on *left over*. 'I will pour it into his cup.'

'My gratitude, Marz.' While Marzana prepared another cup of tea for Duryodhan, Karna asked directions for the privy and made his way there. As Karna crossed Duryodhan, Duryodhan mouthed, '*I do not know what you see in her*.' Karna chuckled as he entered the privy. His headache persisted, and he blamed it on a hangover. One could get used to everything but not a hangover, especially when it emerged from a blackout. It was an eternal virgin experience. *Just what was in that poison of the tavern?* He ought to be grateful that Marzana rescued him though he knew he was more likely to obsess over how she managed it. Some primal instinct drove him to close the window before he got a better view of the day's past.

But his hand still quivered. Unearthing one memory from the past threatened to pull the sheet from over a host of buried recollections. He badly needed a release, just this one time, just this once. The circumstances were special today, after all. Bagheera was dead. Marz had to rescue him. Now even Duryodhan was here. And most importantly, it was almost the end of the month. He would start afresh next month, a new month, a new resolve.

His hand had already slipped past the false bottom of his rucksack to find the vial while he had been still debating it in his head. Out came the vial, half-filled with powder the colour of brilliant green. Orphan's delight, Vishkanya's Piss, Abyss, Moongrain, many names for many hues. Karna started at it, remembering how Marzana had offered it to him the first time.

He was glad he had put his trust in Marzana. The way she had looked at him, told him it will be fine and that he deserved forgiveness. Forgiveness in the form of forgetfulness. An unnoticed tear tricked down his cheek as he threw his head back and dropped the powder on each of his eyeballs, and then rubbed the eyeballs directly with his thumb.

Fire spread from his eyes throughout the rest of his face as the alchemy began to shroud his memories with a black blanket. The only way his life could be spotless was if it was all dark. Abyss slowly drained away the faces of the ones he loved, smeared the ones he had lost, wiped the tales of his betrayal. Draupadi. Sudama. Savitre Lios. All gone. That was the beauty of Abyss—

'Have you decided to settle inside? Should I fetch you a book to read?' Duryodhan asked.

II

After a while, the carriage slowed down and slid to a halt outside massive gates flanked by stone posts. Beyond the gates, the imposing dome of the stupa rose out of the forest, its sides barely visible behind the branches crawling up its sides. Doves roosted in those trees, sacred and unharmed. Under the trees, Karna waited for them at the stupa's base.

If anyone had seen Karna when he woke up, the portrait retained would have been of a nervous sack, eyes redshot and cheeks slackened. He had exhibited all the evidence of a man even the most trusting of dogs would avoid. Enormously different was the Karna who stood before Duryodhan now. Composure seemed to drip from this man's every pore. His face might have seemed a little flushed, his eyes a little green but there was a spring in his step and his face was stretched in a smile to signify he was ready to return the roses into Duryodhan's cheeks. Whatever Duryodhan was here for, whatever he needed, Karna would do it. Such was the power of Abyss.

'Good morning, Highmaster,' Duryodhan said in a mocking tone. 'Seems like you had a pleasant nap on your way here?'

'Don't start, my Prince,' Karna groaned.

'So that would be a no? How's the view from up there?'

'Let's find out,' Karna said.

If Duryodhan thought climbing the stupa would be his way to get rid of Marzana, he could not have been more mistaken. A dancer's feet could give any climber a contest in grip. But soon after they began the climb, a light drizzle broke. It made the climb hard. The stupa's bricks were crumbling and loose, slipping away like butter in her hands. But the thick vines draping it made for good handholds.

'Did you know if not for Jarasandh conquests,' Marzana called up to Karna between breaths, 'this would've been the largest stupa to Agni (the God of Fire) in the world. The old Rock King wanted the fire burning here to be visible from the borders. Can you imagine?'

By now they were halfway up, where thankfully the slope levelled out. Karna strode ahead, striking down thorns and scrubs with a sugarcane machete. Raindrops wet his white shirt, allowing bright patterns of the golden armour beneath to shine from within.

'If they had built a wall instead,' Duryodhan said from behind her, not out of breath at all, 'maybe they would not have lived in fear.'

'And just imagine the number of Reshts it took to shift all this earth and brick. Ten thousand and more. When the workers died, they did not stop. They built around their bodies. This isn't a monument, but a mound.'

Marzana groaned. Karna laughed. Handling one Karna was bad enough, two of them were a headache she had not bargained for. Not to forget the barbs these two shared from time to time. General incivility seemed to be the bedrock of their friendship.

When they reached the top of the stupa, they sat down, with Marzana sitting closer to Karna than was necessary. They ate the tiffin Marzana had brought: rotis, lentils and tender cauliflower curry.

'You detest vegetables,' Duryodhan suddenly remarked.

Sensing Marzana's back stiffen, Karna spoke hastily. 'Used to hate. Perhaps because we Reshts did not get our hands on grains as easily as the rest. But Marz does something to them to make the taste pleasing,' he said, smiling, as if it was the finest compliment of the world. 'What is it you do to them?'

'I add masala,' Marz declared in a way to turn something said as a matter of fact, murderous.

Karna smiled while Duryodhan said nothing.

'So what brings you here, My Prince?' Karna asked.

III

When Duryodhan was done telling where he was bound to, Karna wondered where the line drawn on the sand was, and then decided he cared no longer. 'The idea of you reuniting with Princess Mati brings to my mind the inside of a cat's ear,' Karna said. 'With respect, My Prince, she is an unhinged fiend.'

'I prefer *creative* and *passionate*.' Duryodhan's white grin flashed in the dark face.

Karna frowned.

'Well, I'm heading to Magadh and I thought I'd tip you off before you hear it from someone else,' Duryodhan said.

'Where else would I hear it? From the bard staging a play called *Foolish Men and their Fantasies*?' Karna was certain he'd be the star of one act of that production. To think Karna had naïvely believed the days of Mati's dark wings shadowing their friendship was ancient history. Of course that insufferable woman had to peck his peace again. 'I cannot believe you want to rescue a woman who you discarded, a woman who is married to the Crown Prince of the bloody Empire.' *A woman who does not deserve you.*

'She left me alive when she could have killed me, Karna, and I did not deserve that mercy, you know that. I'll just enter Magadh and find out if Mati is in distress. Should I receive reassuring words that she still smiles through the streets, I will leave without any face-to-face. I'll accept that she is happy without me, and that will be my karma to shoulder for life. But she has responded to none of my ravens. If trouble's brewing, I will ferret out the source of what ails her, and arrange an audience with the Emperor to redress it, as her friend, of course.'

'*Of course*,' Karna seethed. 'I wager the war-loving Emperor would love to chat about his son's wife with his son's wife's former lover.'

'You have always been biased against her. Need I remind you she saved your life too.'

A life she put in danger because she murdered a man, for which I was and still am blamed. But Karna couldn't very well confess to Duryodhan about his lady love's curious idea of a wedding gift. 'But why would you write to her, Prince? That chapter was over.'

Duryodhan said nothing for a while, taking on the role Karna usually played in their conversations, one of silence and secrets. He absently traced the neatly groomed beard on his face and exhaled deeply, as if to extinguish a battalion of candles. 'A wound unmended often suspends time, Karna. The truth is that we had no proper ending. None of us said goodbye.'

'I suppose thrashing a lover within an inch of their life and tossing them into a river does lack the finesse of a traditional farewell,' Karna said. 'You just want to rescue a woman who hasn't even asked to be rescued.'

'No, it is not like that…' Duryodhan said. 'I would just rather not spend my life wondering what might've been if I had only tried.' After a moment, he added stiffly, 'And not all who need to be saved ask to be rescued.'

Mati? Need saving? The woman always looked like she had just returned from having committed some unsavoury crime, which in her case was not just a look. Karna decided to attempt an alternative approach.

'How did Lord Shakuni ever permit this? The number of *ifs* in your plan could give an Acharya of Language a lasting headache.'

'What he knows not cannot hurt him. He believes, like the rest of Hastina, that I am on my way to the Conclave, which, to be fair to me, I am. I am just taking a longer route. And tarry that, what is wrong with your eyes?'

'Don't turn the subject. Prince, this isn't the idle dreams of a romantic youth. You are not Krishna.'

'I say there's a touch of romance to it,' Marzana chimed in. When Karna turned to stare at her at a dramatic, slow pace, she added, 'Wounded recognizes the wounded, Karna. Why, what else would you call this?'

'The beginning of a scroll that ends with the line *"And then he turned the sword on himself"*.'

'Behind your sad, tragic beard lies a flair for exaggeration,' Duryodhan said. 'Listen, Karna, I did not come here to debate. I came here to inform. I just want to see if Mati is doing well, and *if* possible, bury things with Mati, and *if* needed, help her out. *Without any law-breaking.*'

Before Karna could protest, Marzana stepped in. 'Let me try, Karna. Prince,' she said, 'let us assume that Princess Mati finds herself in grave peril. Your plan to carry her off—'

'Why carry off?' Duryodhan asked, eyes narrowed at Marzana.

'Would you prefer *seize*? *Snatch*, perhaps?'

'What's wrong with *rescue*?'

Neither Karna nor Marzana could hold a straight face at the thought. Marzana suggested 'spirited away' and they settled for it.

'You should be prepared, Prince, truly prepared from your heart to do the right thing because no matter what you tell yourself, what you do to save Mati will be unlawful,' Marzana said. Karna smiled as he understood what Marzana was doing. Telling Duryodhan to go on the path he wanted while letting him know what he would have to lose to stay on that path. Karna's own mother had often used that ploy to dissuade a young Karna from taking on Ksharjan archers.

'There is no such thing as an unlawful right,' Duryodhan declared.

'Given how there are lawful wrongs, there has to be a balance,' Marzana said. 'There are moments when even princes find them-selves at a crossroads, having to choose between honour and the right thing to do, between law and dharma. Having walked that bed of coals, I can assure you the aftermath of such a choice is a life of blisters and open sores. It will be no different for you. Let me paint the images in your head. What if the Princess is in trouble? What will Your Grace do then? Flee with a married woman? This is not the marriage of the Balkhan Tribes that you can break off with words. They aren't contracts. Vedan marriages are solemnized across seven births, a bond solemnized in vows, not signatures.'

Duryodhan said, 'And that is why I need to know from her if her wedding rituals chimed to the tune of Vedan rites. The Empire still officially falls under the patronage of the Seven, no matter what the Eyeless Ehtrals keep cawing. If a dispute arises, well, we are all headed to the Conclave. What better place to resolve an inter-kingdom dispute?'

'Hold your arrows! What dispute?' Karna asked.

'I would have to wed Mati to rescue her from Magadh, and for it to be lawful, the first marriage needs to be nullified. Magadh would contest it. This dispute.'

'Oh, *this* dispute. I must be mad for not grasping it in the first go.' Karna took a breath to calm himself down. He could not let this happen. He just could not. 'There will not be any *dispute* or debate, Prince. There will be war,' Karna said. 'Not to forget you will never be able to wash away your crime, and Yudhistir will seize upon it to wrestle your throne away. The world will know your shame, and your name will be taken alongside a disgraced company.'

'And that is assuming Princess Mati is willing to be garlanded by you,' Marzana said, 'and leave Magadh with the knowledge she might be leaving it without a head on her body.'

'And! And that is assuming the Princess does not herself imprison you to turn you into a doll to fulfil a lost childhood fantasy of plucking off its limbs one by one,' Karna said, exasperated.

Duryodhan's face flushed red. The royal blood in him rose to his eye. 'Enough,' he said. It was a different voice, a king's voice, deep and commanding, and rich with royalty. Karna knew it. Karna knew it well, better than he cared to remember. 'Perhaps my reason is burdened with my passions but there is nothing wrong and undignified with emotions. Sometimes to even trust your instinct over your mind is an act of courage. I believe in myself and I have no need to convince others. I won't break any law and I will go to Magadh.

I know you both cannot comprehend how these two can coexist because you have bitter gourds for brains, but this is my will.'

Karna just stared at him, doing his best not to commit treason by grabbing his friend's lapels. Not that it would help. Duryodhan's walls were up, and his stubbornness was legendary. That infamous iron jaw hadn't been forged by yielding to others' will and wisdom. That was how Duryodhan had installed Karna as the Highmaster of Anga, pushed through the Resht Reforms, and filed a case of murder against his own cousin, Arjun. It was one thing Karna had always admired about his friend but he had no idea how it would feel to be on the receiving end of his stubbornness. He had to reach out to Duryodhan before he dug a moat around those walls. He glanced at Marzana, and nodded at her solemnly.

Marzana took her rain cloak. 'I will return now to the Temple. With the favour the Prince's patronage has sown, I look forward to reaping the harvest,' she said as she rose and tucked her skirts about her waist, 'you both can now celebrate your joyful reunion in peace.'

She got as far as the nearest vine before hesitating, then looked back. First at Duryodhan, who had already shifted his attention towards Karna, then to Karna himself. He understood what he saw in her eyes. A sorrow, defeated and resigned, as though she already knew what was coming, as inevitable as the Ganga's winding course to the Kalingan Sea. A chill rainy wind blew in from outside. Marzana shivered despite her cloak, and then climbed down.

'My Prince, I—' Karna started but Duryodhan interrupted him.

'There is nothing you can say, Karna. We are going after her,' Duryodhan said, with fire in his eyes.

'No.' It was not, apparently, the answer his only friend in the world was expecting. Or at least not as curtly as Karna put it. Duryodhan blinked, the fire inside him snuffed out as quickly as it appeared. He looked confused more than anything. Disbelieving.

'But Karna—'

'I said no. She is a murderer, Prince. Forget Kalinga. Look what she did in Panchal. So many innocents crushed under the stampede. So many innocents burned alive. If it were not for her assassins and arson, maybe... maybe Sudama would be alive.'

'You cannot blame—' said Duryodhan, but Karna spoke over him.

'I know I am the only one to be blamed for his death. But that does not mean I do not see her for the evil she is, Prince. As Highmaster of Hastina Union, I cannot support your decision in sparking a war between Hastina and the Empire. I cannot stand by you as you plan to make a murderer the Queen of the Union and the mother of your children. I just cannot.'

The chirp of frogs grew into a chorus in the silence that followed. Karna took in deep lungfuls of the fresh smell of the forest after rain. Summoning the last bits of his courage, he looked across at Duryodhan and saw the terrible expression of defeat on his face.

'I'm sorry, Prince.'

Duryodhan just sat there. Frowning at first, and then smiling that strange, broken smile. His friend tilted his head slightly, and said, after what seemed like forever, 'I know you are.'

He stood.

'Prince,' Karna began, intending to explain... he didn't know what, exactly. That he couldn't risk Duryodhan committing a crime, or leave the Reshts without a future if he went off south and the worst were to happen (and it would happen). Or that deep down the thought of meeting a vengeful Mati scared him shitless. What if she told Duryodhan of Karna's unwitting betrayal in bedding her just to hurt Duryodhan? He was afraid, he wanted to say, but could not.

Duryodhan, mercifully, cut him short. 'Tell Lady Divine the food was delicious,' he said. 'Or maybe she will see through that lie. Say nothing, then.' He laughed.

Offer him sympathy, some part of Karna's mind insisted. *A shoulder, at least*. Karna said nothing, just sat there alone as Duryodhan followed the curve of the stupa to the nearest vine.

Duryodhan stopped, looking back, the same way Marzana had but with steel in his eyes. Would he command Karna as his liege lord now? Would he remind him of the murder trial against Arjun he had mounted at great personal cost only for Karna's nephew?

All Duryodhan said, though, before descending into the depths below, was, 'You're a good friend, Karna but you owe me nothing.

You earned everything on your own, you deserve what you were awarded, and now, you deserve to be happy. Farewell, friend.'

Karna nodded. It was not the dagger Karna had anticipated. But what else should he have expected from the Prince of Morals? Then again, men with morals only make for good martyrs.

THE INKSPELLER

I

others have martyred themselves in their children's names
since the beginning of time, and so there was nothing particularly novel about Marzana betraying her love to save her children.
But now, she was finally liberated. It did soften the blow that Karna
was the one who chose to abandon her rather than the other way
around. Given that this was the second time it had happened, the
first when she had kissed him, Marzana reckoned she was becoming quite the adept at piecing her heart back together.

When he had not returned from the stupa to throw a pebble at
her window, she had understood. Karna must have fallen into the
old trap of obedience by blindly following Duryodhan into Magadh.
Well, if Karna insisted on dying on a fool's errand, so be it. His lure
had distracted her from where she ought to have been, letting a
few lively moments ruin her livelihood. No more. She willed a sob
back lest it ruin her efforts to paint her face. She would be calm,
composed—

*Why did Duryodhan have to return! He ruined everything, that con-
descending, arrogant dunglark!*

Breathe, Marzana. Breathe. Duryodhan was not a bad man, that
was certain, but the world judged foolishness far more harshly than
foul morals. Still, she would drop flowers at the feet of Kaamah and
pray that he died a peaceful death.

Yes, she would pray for Duryodhan. It was, after all, a consequence of Duryodhan's grace that Marzana found herself again
looking down the food chain in the Temple of Kaamah. She did

not even have to search far for its evidence. Barely a day had passed since Duryodhan had requested Marzana's favour in front of the whole world, and Old Khai had already sent word he would be visiting her tonight. That was all the Devadasis of the Temple were gossiping about. Just like old times.

And so, rather than weep for Karna, Marzana prepared for battle.

One girl rubbed the ends of her hair with a henna paste to lend a sapphire sheen to the black and only then did Marzana wash it with dried lime rinds. She limned her long eyes with a kajal, extending the black line at the corners with a dramatic sweep. Marzana had already plucked her brows with iron tweezers to curve them like swords. For the moment, she lay with her hair spread out like a peacock's tail on a woven basket. Inside the basket, frankincense burned on a brazier. When Old Khai pulled her diamond hairpin later that night, he would be intoxicated by the scent of her strands. Hopefully he would knock on her door later rather than earlier, for she still had to have the girls braid her hair and arrange it into a bun. If it sounded exhausting, it is because it was. But then again, if seduction were easy, the world would not have birthed jealousy.

She knew the thought to be self-serving but today of all days was not a day to toe the line of politeness. It was going to be a day of power and privilege. She had already set the toymaker to fashion toy horses to anonymously send them later to her son, Dhanush. Maybe if Old Khai lavished her with enough gifts tonight, she could even buy him back. That very thought of union with her son scoured away the remnants of woe.

Just then a knock brought with it a scroll that announced Old Khai would be reaching her house within the hour and hoped his change in schedule would not deprive him of Lady Divine Meenakshi's blessings.

'Wind up all of this nonsense before the hour of the elephant,' Marzana urf Lady Divine Meenakshi ordered after she dismissed the messenger with a wave and had her girls tie her hair in a bun. 'My house reeks of incompetence, and Old Khai will smell it from a distance. Labang, see to it that it is done.'

She had no intention of letting Old Khai claim her tonight. Oh, she would punish him. Tease him, yes, but he would find no release in her fist. It would take a while to dethrone Badi Dee and her daughter but Marzana knew her way on that tightrope.

These thoughts churned in her mind when in walked Damaya, one hand clutching her shabby skirt, the other firmly held by Duryodhan.

II

'I dined at Prince Viren's table, his cook has a detestable hand with the paan, and Prince Viren had not the tongue to taste it.' Duryodhan heaved a sigh once he was seated. 'But refusing the hospitality of the host is a sin, and alongside politeness, another duty owed to the host is manners.'

Pompous arse. But from what she had gauged of the Prince, he was not one to waste words. Was he going to ask to pay the bride price for Damaya? Was stealing Karna from her life not enough? 'I will have Damaya prepare a glass of summerwine to smoothen your palate,' she said stiffly and made to rise, hoping Karna was waiting outside the door, but Duryodhan held a hand out.

'On my way out to my carriage from Prince Viren's mansion, your sister, Lady Damaya ambushed me.'

'The girl. Ambush. You?' Marzana heard the edge in her tone, and coughed softly, as if it had been the result of dryness. 'Pray, explain.'

'Ambush with...' Duryodhan shifted, 'with kisses. Her words, which were many, could be summarized best as her wish to be the Queen of Hastina. I had not known she was your sister till she spoke of how...' he hesitated.

'How, what?' Marzana asked, bluntly.

'Of how old goods have a shelf life, and I should vie for freshly grown flowers.'

Marzana laughed out loud much to the surprise of Duryodhan. 'Children, these days. Tarry a moment.' A waft of wind had blown through the open window reminding her to close the shutters before the mosquitoes made their presence felt. One end of her sea green saree slipped as she reached through the grills to close the door. Her blouse was cut low enough in the back for Duryodhan to see intricate patterns of the whispering aetherwing etched into her skin by the former Inkspeller's needle. Sensing the absence of a burning stare, Marzana turned to find Duryodhan's eyes lost in a sea of thoughts.

Were all the men from the North so strange? Take any gent from Malengar, and either they would have returned Damaya's kisses with their one-eyed serpents or they would have paraded her through the streets for indecency. Either would have ruined Damaya's future as a Devadasi, which now Marzana could see was perhaps Badi Dee's last stab at Marzana before Old Khai restored Marzana to her position of power. *Well played, Badi Dee.* Unfortunately for Badi Dee's plan, Northern honour was as thick as their accents.

'I hope you will not be overly harsh in your punishment, Lady Divine.'

'She has done nothing to earn my ire, Your Grace, given how it was your fault that made her act a peasant.' Duryodhan's face was not built for expressions and so she felt pleased at seeing the skin on his face shift to accommodate surprise. 'Forgive me for saying this, Prince, but just as a bard's confidence falters when his jape does not fetch a laugh from the crowd, so is the case with a Devadasi when her dance doesn't earn a gasp from her patrons. We may be married to the Gods but we are still mortals, still afflicted by the need for respect. Is it that Hastina princes are not trained in the vocabulary of Sign to understand our steps? When Damaya danced in your honour, you said not a word in her's.'

'You must excuse my distraction for my eyes were less on the gestures of Lady Damaya and more on the woman who was last seen with my friend before he disappeared.'

Marzana did not rise to the bait. 'Your reasons matter not in matters of respect. She is a fragile thing and your lack of attention smoothened the calluses of confidence we Devadasis build on our feet through years of training. Is it any surprise she slipped?'

Duryodhan clenched his fists. A man clearly not unaccustomed to being wrong. And Marzana had held the upper hand on him ever since they had met. 'I understand your meaning, Lady Divine,' he said slowly. 'I hope you will convey my regrets to your sister and my reasons along with it, if you can.'

Marzana shrugged as she smiled, sparing a glance at the door, wishing Old Khai to turn up now. If he saw Duryodhan leaving her house, it would dramatically inflate the value of gifts he would part with.

'I see the smile on your face is devoid of pride, Lady Divine,' Duryodhan said. 'Impressive, given how you first won Karna from me, and now you have admonished me for a fault I did not know I had committed. You must meet my uncle. He will be quick to take a liking to you.'

'What do you mean? How did I win Karna?' Marzana paused, and then her eyes widened. 'He refused to go with you?' Marzana gushed excitedly, immediately regretting it.

'No. I asked him to not come with me. It would not be right of me as a prince to command his service for something that does not serve the Union. And, as a friend, I know his heart is indisposed to it. I could see it in his desperate bid to discourage my plans. Karna is not subtle at politics... yet.'

'Well... I... I am just surprised. I imagined Karna would have keeled over to your side.'

'Karna,' Duryodhan's eyes hardened, 'will always be on my side. Alright then, Lady Divine,' he said as he drew himself up to his full height and unobtrusively straightened his shirt. 'I leave at midnight. Please make an offering to Blessed Kaamah in Sudama's name and... take care of my friend.'

Marzana nodded, and escorted him to the door, prepared to see him off, but Duryodhan hastened away without waiting for her, heading straight for the carriage. He did lift one hand in farewell but then perhaps thinking better of it, withdrew it and vanished behind the curtains inside. She watched the carriage as it trundled out of her life before lifting her eyes to look over Malengar.

Gurumaa had always told her, proudly, that Malengar might be a small city state but it stood as regally as any kingdom within the Union. Now with the Devadasis scurrying for her favour again, with Karna returning to her side as her dirty secret and with the Temple Key, no doubt itching to feel her waist, it was time for Malengar to bow down to Marzana. The palmist and the parrot had been right: this was going to be the day when the sun shone highest on her life. But little did she realize such a noon only marked the beginning of a long descent into the shadows.

III

The rustic sounds of a walking cane disturbed her nap. Marzana's ears responded like a dog to the sound. She blinked her eyes open and, suddenly realizing how long she had slept, stormed out of her room to the verandah outside. There was a man walking in front of her house singing in a slow voice. 'Little lamps, buy clay lamps for the long nights.' Above him, the moon had emerged as a toenail clipping in the sky.

'Daeva take me! How long was I asleep?'

'Not long,' Old Khai's cracked voice rang behind her. Somewhere Marzana found the manners bred into her to turn and smile back at him and she pulled her hair softly and tied it behind her. 'I thought I would let you sleep. You deserve the rest. I dismissed Damaya and the rest of your servants as well.'

Hearing this, Marzana set aside her irritation at his casual assumption of welcome in her house.

'How fares Gurumaa?' Old Khai asked. Old Khai had never asked after Gurumaa in the last years she had been ill. Why now? Marzana even sensed a change in his manner though she could not put a finger on it.

'As she looks, My Lord,' Marzana replied quietly.

Old Khai shocked Marzana when he bent low by Gurumaa's face and opened her eyelids. 'The Abyss seems to be keeping her happy through the rot. That is good, Marzana.'

'I... I beg your pardon, My Lord.' How did Old Khai discover her name! 'There is no... no Abyss—'

Her words were cut off as the wrinkles on Old Khai's face seemed to blur and shift as if they were illusions. His back straightened and his shoulders broadened. A wig fell off, turning white hair to black and the mark of scales on his neck melted away to reveal a spade.

In the blink of an eye, Old Khai was gone, and the Inkspeller stood in his stead.

Broad-shouldered, a head taller than she was, with deep brown skin and a cold northern inflection, the Inkspeller's skin was unlined though threads of grey rippled through the greasy curls of his hair. To anyone who did not know him, he would have seemed a sober lad, sensible, if not for his face being neatly divided into two halves by a scar. It had never been a face to make a Devadasi weak in her knees but it did make this Devadasi tremble in her sandals.

'Sire!' Marzana bowed, and then hastily looked at the door. 'May I request you to attend another time? I am already stocked on the supply of Abyss, and I am expecting someone.'

'Regrettably, Old Khai shan't grace your doorstep this eve, Lady Divine, giving us ample time to talk about your debt.'

'I... I already paid it!'

His strong brows arched over his green eyes. 'By agreeing to spy on Karna for a throne's ransom worth of Abyss? Surely, Lady Divine, you do not seek to embarrass me. Not to forget you seem to have gained much in that bargain? That kiss of yours nearly ruined all our plans. But I forgave you that, did I not?'

Marzana took three steps back, crashing against the bedpost, feeling the familiar wood for support. How did he know? It was a stupid question she had vowed not to ask. She knew he practised the Dark Arts or was employed by one who knew it. How else could he change his skin so? Or how could he never run out of Abyss? Or how did he know exactly the manner in which Marzana should approach Karna to earn his trust?

You are a Devadasi! Malengar is yours, remember! Fight back!

'I have told you all his secrets, I memorized his journal, I drugged him on Abyss and I even saved him from certain death after he murdered those Vishkanyas!'

'Good. You have paid the interest. Now to pay the principal. I hear the Prince is bound to Magadh alone. We cannot have that. Karna needs to accompany him. We need Karna and Duryodhan to abduct Bhanumati.'

'I had no hand in his refusal! The Prince himself told Karna not to accompany him.'

'Well, convince Karna otherwise.'

'How will I convince him to go where his closest friend could not convince him to?'

'I hazard he will need a reason. Perhaps we should commence work on giving him one.'

'What do you mean?'

She did not even see his hand. Black stars danced in her vision. Blood flooded her mouth. He picked her up and slammed her into the wall, one hand around the back of her neck. Each word of his was punctuated by a crack of her face on the wall.

'Will.' *Crack.* 'This.' *Crack.* 'Be.' *Crack.* 'Reason.' *Crack.* 'Enough?'

'I doubt it,' he answered his own question. 'You were waiting for Old Khai, weren't you? Seeing how he could not make it, perhaps I can fill his void.'

There was no music in what passed between them. Given free reign by her bond and his rage, there was only the veena of violence that played the music. By the time she saw herself in the mirror, midnight had passed. Blood spilled through the gap in her teeth but she knew it wasn't over. Leather uncoiled from around his waist.

When the belt first lashed on her back, training turned its sting into a kiss but it did not last long in the face of his fury. Pain broke the ankles of pleasure, and overwhelmed it in her head, making her beg for a release she had never had to plead for before. After he was done, he stood above her crumpled figure. 'You know what you have to do.'

'But... I can't,' Marzana pleaded. 'I can't...'

'I have trusted you with my plan. While you're away, I vow Gurumaa and your children, both of them, will live with nothing to want for, and will live to a ripe old age.' The Inkspeller crouched near Marzana's face. 'Timing is everything. We can't have him break his chains yet. Anger now, rage later.'

Marzana coughed the last spit out. She was rage now. Her eyes searched for something sharp and found the sharp tears on Gurumaa's eyes instead. Her mother's eyes were open, and they were flooded with regret and desperation. Gurumaa shook her head as if willing Marzana to abandon care for her and defy this beast.

'By the way, I saw how you responded to the first belt on your back. Does Damaya know of these ways? Or is she too young to find pleasure in pain? Maybe I can teach her.'

'I will lose everything... please...'

'There is a demand for young boys in the pleasure houses beyond the Kalingan Sea, you know, and they are the real demons on earth, if you know what I mean. I forget who I am talking to. I am certain you do.'

Marzana closed her eyes and felt the ties of motherhood turn into a noose round her neck. She sighed. 'If I don't make it back, Damaya can never know I was her mother. Nor can my son.' She was not going to pass that terrible burden to her children, the knowledge that they were the reason their mother sacrificed everything good in her. What a horrible weight, especially for a daughter to bear, to know if she chose to bear a child, this would be her fate as well.

'As long as you stick to the plan, I will stick to my promise. Tonight, Karna and you leave for Magadh.'

IV

Marzana could not guess at her appearance as she entered Karna's workshop. It must have looked worse than she felt, for Karna's eyes widened in shock and he covered the distance between them in three long strides, hands just away from holding her.

'Marz...' he breathed.

She would later credit it to the pain but sometimes she wondered whether it was the way she heard him say her name that made her knees surrender. Without a word, he scooped her into his arms and headed for the door.

'Karna.' True fear cleared her head. 'I can walk. Put me down.'

As stubborn as his friend, Karna shook his head. 'I'm setting you down only before a healer.'

'Will you listen to the calling that led to this or do you intend on taking me to the perpetrator of this painting.'

Karna glared at her. 'I plan to heed your words once you heal. And then I intend to pay this man a visit.'

'You will do no such thing. You owe me your life for rescuing you from Vasuki's Nest and you shall repay the debt by not taking another.'

'I will not stand idly by—'

'Old Khai knows of... us.'

That silenced him. She stammered forth lies of her plight. Of how Old Khai discovered her friendship with Karna, the bargain he struck with her to hold his tongue, the men he had in mind who would parade her naked on the streets and the abominable ways he planned to let those men use her before hanging her. She spoke of Old Khai still with love and admiration, sure that his anger would abate, of how time would calm the tempers. Her voice was as Gurumaa had taught her, bold and trembling at the same time.

When the fountain of her voice ran dry, Karna reached across and did something he had never done before. Touch her by taking her palms in his. He could not have known he was comforting a tree already struck by lightning.

She unravelled a pouch to show what she had bagged before Old Khai had thrown her out. On the table where Karna built his bows were now scattered earrings in the shape of peacocks, bangles thin and wide, rings with emeralds as big as her fingernail and even a forbidden toe ring, for, other than royals, women were not allowed to wear precious metal below the waist. There was another pouch of green-coloured powder which Karna, despite himself, stared at hungrily.

Karna closed his eyes, guilt drawing lines on his face before its time. He clenched his fists, and for a moment, Marzana was scared she would hear that guttural voice again. That would spoil all her plans. Anger, not rage, the Inkspeller had warned. But when Karna's eyes opened, the flicker of her hope stood fast in the darkness. Marzana manufactured a smile. 'So, I can hope your Abyss-addled mind can see why you riding into the town with me would not make for a poem of romance but a ballad of tragedy.'

He said little as he gently gathered her into his arms once more and carried her to his table. He bade her use the salve he offered, unstintingly, which she did without protest.

'What now?' Karna asked.

'It is my good fortune that it was Old Khai who discovered us, and not the head priest. He is a Ksharjan, and they take life debts seriously. He enjoyed dressing as a woman in the secrecy of our time, and I helped him. I even accompanied him when he walked to his plantations in his disguise. It helped him with his impotence, and he sired a child not soon after. It wasn't alchemy but he believed it was and I let him. He owes me a debt no more.'

Realization dawned on Karna.

'Aye,' Marzana said, with a sad smile. 'But worry not. Damaya will not be harmed, he has promised.'

'You?'

'With a face so decorated, it is not as if I am returning to the world of dance soon. Old Khai tells me he will inform Badi Dee I am on a pilgrimage to the mountain temples to pray for his wellbeing. I doubt Badi Dee will purchase it but I also doubt she would shed any tears. She is more like to think he killed me in a fit of rage and dumped my body in the lake. I came here to say farewell, Karna. You have my word he will not harm you, though if I were you, I would try and not be seen around the temple for a few weeks.'

The Inkspeller's terrible future finally opened its palms before them when Karna asked the question, 'Will you come with me?'

The words of the Inkspeller about Karna whispered in her ears in a phantom voice. *It was a kindness in him, a strange kind I had seen as a boy. There are those who flinch at the sight of sorrow, fearful of saying the wrong word or doing the wrong thing. All they lend is their ear, and pray the victim of the sorrow rights himself. But not Karna...*

'Where?' Marzana asked, a touch of panic edging into her voice. She had been tasked to coax Karna into heading into Magadh but now she found herself on the brink of having to sew another tapestry of lies to steer clear of wherever he intended to suggest.

'Magadh,' Karna said.

Marzana was taken aback. 'Prince Duryodhan told me you had refused.'

'When did you meet?' Karna raised his brows. 'It matters not. Duryodhan is far dimmer than I am if he even thought I would let him go alone into the Empire. I have embarrassed myself far enough before him. It is my turn to see him make a fool of himself, and no way was I going to let go of that chance,' he said with a disarming grin. 'I was just winding up my clothes, preparing to meet you before I surprised him at midnight. Though now that you will be at my side, we would be toeing the line between surprise and shock, if I am being honest.'

'Karna...' Marzana's voice broke as she whispered his name, 'I will come with you.'

'Good.' Karna smiled, and then hesitated. 'Do you... have *any* on you? Sudama haunts my daydreams now.'

'You mean *in addition* to the pouches I already sent your way last week?'

'I packed them.' Karna looked down sheepishly and Marzana laughed.

They sat in the workshop moments after, forgetting their pain, his eyes green with Abyss and hers red with her life's eclipse. She could see the certainties of reality leeching out of Karna's eyes like calcium from a bone. Soon he would be exactly where he wanted himself to be – his reminiscences passing like torches passing a bat in a cavern, sweeping past him, illuming some dark memory here and there, only to swiftly fade and leave him in blissful darkness again.

Once more, the Inkspeller's voice echoed softly in her mind, resuming from where it had left off. *But not Karna... He lent relief. Not by way of a consoling arm or a gentle word... even though most would welcome it, but by doing what was needed even if it brought him grief. Even Maa warned Karna that it would just bring him endless pain but he still took another man's son as his own, raised him only to lose him to Arjun. Maa was right again. Kindness was Karna's bane.*

When Marzana had asked the Inkspeller how his mother could have known Karna so intimately, he had not hesitated. He spoke of how Karna, too, had called his mother by that sacred name. And of how the Inkspeller's own son had once looked to Karna as a father, before his life was cruelly taken. And in that moment, Marzana finally knew the Inkspeller's true name. She had read it in Karna's diary.

Shon... Karna's younger brother, Sudama's father and the leader of the Resht rebel group, the Red Blades.

INTERLUDE

VAHURA'S ADVENTURES

I

Vahura found herself incapable of properly gauging the reaction of the Rose Coterie to her greeting as she was preoccupied with the rather uncomfortable sensation of being pinned to the wall like a butterfly specimen. She could only see Asshaye, the wielder of the spear, her eyes blazing with bright fury. How had Asshaye moved so fast? Just moments ago, she had stood armed with a crossbow along with the rest at a safe remove, and now in a blink, she had acquainted Vahura with the wall.

'Three questions,' Asshaye warned as she pressed the cold end of the spear to Vahura's navel. 'Will slice you for every second you delay, and stab you for every untruth. Savvy? Give a nod if you grasp the concept, my dear.'

Savvy? Asshaye was a Kalingan, Vahura realized. She shelved that fact for the moment and tried valiantly to push back one last time but all she managed was a wiggle. How did this decrepit woman possess so much strength? Relenting, Vahura nodded.

'How?' Asshaye asked.

A half-strangled gulp escaped Vahura as Asshaye pressed the speartip in her navel with a force that did more than tickle. 'Your handwriting! The Rose Coterie's trademark you left on the Ayodhyan banner – pinched by a bard – Nar Ad! Ow!'

With a step back, Asshaye granted Vahura the liberty to express herself in full sentences. Panting slightly, Vahura continued, 'Nar

Ad allowed me to examine the banner for a fee. The loops and swirls on your rose sigil matched the writing in the false letter you sent, posing as a tavern woman, to Meru. In that letter, you had demanded recompense from Meru for something stolen by the supposed Rose Coterie.'

'We wrote several such letters, all of us,'Toshad said from behind, 'to confuse Meru by flooding them with false leads so that they'd disregard any real evidence that some fool sent their way.'

'Yes, but none of these letters ever spoke of a treasure that was actually stolen. This one, which I reckon Acharya Asshaye wrote, spoke of a "parchment born of a light that did not illuminate" – a reference to the Daevic Scrolls, no doubt.'

Light that did not illuminate – it had been rather elementary, a glaring nod to the Children of Light by Asshaye, a more than common error the wickedly sharp murderers make in every tale. The almost crippling need for acknowledgement was the tragedy of the truly terrific, and those in the world of heists were no different. Or rather, Asshaye was no different. Leaving breadcrumbs to trace their path was not just born out of conceit, but also out of fear – a fear that they would not find their way back to the bakery to claim the credit for the recipe.

Beside Asshaye Kalay fumed. 'I warned you, Asshaye! I warned you someone would catch it! I told you, your arrogance would be our undoing, I knew it!'

'Decades passed without a sniff, Kalay. Stick your underpants where the sun don't shine and gag yourself, will you?' Asshaye loosened her spearhold, and opened her eyes to look at Vahura. 'Still doesn't explain how you knew where we were.'

'I had written to all the libraries in the realm requesting books on Astras. The response by the Eastern Library had been in your writing. When later I had seen the tavern woman's writing in the false letter, and then the mark of the Rose on the banner, I remembered your writing in that response, and I was able to draw the connection. Upon comparing all three, I figured the tavern woman was a Rose. You have remarkable penmanship, by the way. Anyway, it all fell into place. The East is a place where the Seven held no sway. So it was from Nar Ad's place itself I sought an audience from the Eastern Library in return for a donation to get the Rose Coterie to meet me.'

'Storms!' Asshaye cursed.

'I can't believe Asshaye got hustled.' Ailmar laughed. 'Oh, this is gold.'

'So we aren't getting any real gold?' Orym sagged to his chair. 'I was looking forward to spending some. I say kill her.'

'Hold your sails, Orym,' Asshaye said. 'Sell one of your piercings, and that should keep you sated for centuries. Now, little princess, you said you remembered my writing from my letter to you denying we have any books on Astras – but that letter was sent seasons ago and the ink I used fades after a fortnight, and your letter wishing to make a donation to the Eastern Library came a few weeks past. I am assuming you met that fool of a bard somewhere in between. How could you...'

Vahura closed her eyes, regretting that slip. 'I... well, I don't, or rather...' Vahura exhaled. There was no point in lying. 'I can't forget things I read.'

The spear immediately fell away, and the expressions of distrust, of suspicions, of cold fury, were replaced by... what was it? Was it concern? Asshaye kept a hand on Vahura's shoulder. 'Oh, you poor thing.' So it was concern. That was unexpected.

And not just because Asshaye was a hardened criminal, but because those who were aware of her memory's clutches always considered it as a sign of the witch, as a thing to be afraid of, or worse, a gift that somehow diminished all her efforts, making her undeserving of any reward. She remembered what she read, but for that, she had to *read*. Spend hours flipping pages. And remembering without understanding has availed naught to anyone, and she was no different.

It had not, however, mattered to the world around her. Her brother always said it was an innate instinct in mankind to deny their own limitations by imagining none in their betters. Perhaps he wasn't wrong, for her scores were waved off with a shrug, her grasp of complex thoughts dismissed with a wave, and her ideas swatted away with a dismissal.

'Is it just what you read, or... everything?' Orym asked.

'Just what I read.'

'Thank the Spirits,' Toshad said, eyes glistening.

'I think I am missing something,' Vahura said.

The Coterie exchanged a terse look before Asshaye responded. 'Our sixth member was cursed with your affliction, but his case was worse. He absorbed everything, without wanting to, and then it trespassed onto his memory forever. Can you fathom how much appallingly useless information we had to scoop and sift through before a heist – well, they stayed with him, and he could not assign these... memories priority. The date he met his love was as important or useless as the date of the local headsman's appointment with the healer. With him, we realized the value of mystery, the unknown, the forgotten.'

'Aye,' Ailmar said. 'His burdens killed him.'

'Oh... I am sorry.' Vahura shivered at the thought of her potential future.

'Don't fret,' Asshaye said, gesturing her back to the table. 'He was a special nutcase,' she said, suddenly turning to the others. 'We know he was. He had his demons which he could not purge. And that is not a bad thing.' She shrugged. 'It is what it is.'

'Well, then, Princess Vahura,' Ailmar said, 'why did you go through so much trouble to seek us out?'

Vahura who had been massaging her belly, clawed her fingers in and out till she clenched them into a fist. 'Well, you know how I found you out by your reference to the Daevic Scrolls,' she looked at the faces of the Rose Coterie, 'I seek those very Daevic Scrolls.'

They all stood looking at her, and then Toshad became the first one to respond, and by response, he started laughing.

'Why are you laughing?' Vahura asked, the laughter gnawing at her last hope.

'Oh, there's plenty of reasons. We just don't know which one. For now, why don't you wait outside while we decide whether to kill you.'

II

As she twiddled her thumbs outside the door, waiting for the Coterie to decide, her head felt fit to burst with overthinking. What if they killed her? But she was outside their room, alone – she could still run. And then, what? Would that magically place the Daevic Scrolls in her hand? Purge the Marigold Mold? No, she needed to stay steady. But what should she do if the Rose Coterie refused? Plea? Barter? Blackmail? She was a Princess of Balkh – could she threaten them? Tell them that if she did not return before moonfall with the Daevic Scrolls, her cohorts would bring down the Balkhan soldiers on them? Would they see through her lie? Would they already know that she had come alone, only with an old governess for an ally? Her eyes flitted around the place again. Were the Daevic Scrolls here? Could she start hunting for them now while the Roses deliberated her fate?

By the end of the minute, not even a map could help her navigate the chaos inside her mind, a maze where the consequence of each possibility flooded her wounded heart with glacial water. Plans spiralled, the merits of each plot vanishing into thin air after she found loopholes with every idea. Anxiety sped up her heart and threatened to stop it altogether.

Stop! Vahura pinched herself under the arm to put an end to her self-interrogation or else she knew any clarity would be put to flight by her fatal questions. Exhausted but finally able to inhale stillness with the air she breathed, she massaged her temples. She only wished the Rose Coterie had asked her something, anything, rather than summarily dismiss her to wait outside.

Be careful what you wish for.

'Vahura?'

Vahura almost said 'Yes?' but caught herself. *Right.* She had to walk up to them, present her case and return with the Daevic Scrolls.

All members of the Rose Coterie stood tall, their pretence at being silkspined abandoned. Asshaye had swapped her slippers for block heels, bringing her nearly level with Vahura. No words left Asshaye's straight face for a while, leaving Vahura's back to sweat under the scrutiny. *Shake it off.* Vahura was absolutely not going to faint or scream or shout 'Marigold' or dissolve into hysterical laughter. *I won't. I won't. I won't.*

Fortunately, Kalay spoke before Vahura could. 'Before we begin, perhaps we owe you an honest audience. We are indeed Acharyas, all of us except Asshaye and Orym. I handle poisons. Being the Acharya of Human Sciences allows me to gift the guards with a bad case of flatulence that requires them to be away from their posts for long, uncomfortable durations.'

'Weapons.' Asshaye shrugged.

'Toshad here,' Ailmar kept an arm around the withered Acharya, 'handles Lore. He usually found us the treasures we needed to steal, engaging in as little leg work as he could manage. Works the least but is always up there to divide the booty down to the last decimal.'

'If I had to scurry around like little shits, I would have joined the Blue Order.'

'I am the locksmith,' Orym spoke, 'and a Grey Shaman.'

Vahura turned to look at Asshaye, who was waiting no doubt for compliments from the company rather than introduce herself.

'She... gets us out of sticky situations,' Ailmar said as Asshaye nodded towards Vahura. 'She's the Spider. The planner.'

'Planner is another word for leader,' she whispered to Vahura. 'Mastermind.'

'We have considered your request,' Ailmar said, ignoring Asshaye as he returned to his chair, 'and we are inclined to consider.' Vahura's heart leaped. *Touchwood! Touchwood.*

'Before we unfurl that sail, however,' Asshaye said, 'you must pass a test.'

'Acharyas... I thought that... uncovering, well, your where-abouts...'

Asshaye fixed her with a look. 'Is it not fair for us to expect a certain level of prowess from the person who seeks to be entrusted with our secrets, secrets gathered over reckless and life-endangering missions? Surely you did not think it was going to be that easy?'

Vahura's instruction as a princess kicked in, prompting her to shield her grimace with a feigned cough. 'I am yours to command, Acharyas.'

'No more tantrums?' Asshaye smirked. 'A promising start.'

Vahura reminded herself how she'd aced every test the world had thrown at her without missing a single answer. After all, this was why she had made no friends. She suppressed that thought, and stacked the arsenal of books she had read on a shelf in her mind palace.

'Good. Do bear in mind that you showed your sleeves when you revealed the floor plans of your mind palace. So, I do hope you can respect our intelligence by casting aside any plans of retching out what you have memorized.'

Vahura gulped as the stack fell from the shelf in her mind palace, crushing her optimism beneath. It was going to be practicals, she realized with dread.

Asshaye cleared her throat. 'I was there above, watching you, when that young priestess was talking your ears off about their past, a past in which the world was ruled by women. Your surprise at what you learned is understandable as no books talk about the Saptamatrikas: the Seven Horny Women. Your test lies here – answer whether you believe if it is even plausible to have a world ruled by women. A world unlike ours where history is not just reserved for the princes, for the kings and for the priests but for the princesses, the queens and the priestesses. We,' she gestured on either side of her at her companions, 'believe it is not possible. Debate us.'

'I'm weary and I'm sitting.' Toshad sat to the side of Asshaye, panting. 'Saptamatrika is just a fable fancy. Given how men are stronger than women, women could have never ruled over all.'

'The question isn't for you, you bat,' Asshaye said.

Despite the warning not to, Vahura could not help but flip through the pages of the books in her mind hastily, chewing through the table of contents like a beaver. Nothing. This question had never been addressed, and well, no surprise there, considering each and every book she'd read was written by a man, a Namin man at that. Panic laid siege to her mind again but Vahura, who had crossed her hands, was already pinching the underside of her arm to hold back the wave of despair.

Drawing a deep breath, she planted the words of the question in her mind, and let her thoughts grow into a theory and blossom naturally into wildflowers. 'That depends, Acharya,' she said slowly, piecing her words on the trot, 'on how you see strength. Women are stronger than men against the pox, against starvation and even maladies. No man can stand against the War Mistress in a sword duel.'

'The War Mistress is an exception, a singular one at that.' Orym cleared his throat. 'However, from a vantage point, history shows how the realm is the shore and wars are the waves of a sea. The waves will never cease, never waver, never slow in their assault on our realm, and in doing so, they shape our civilization. The strength you speak of in a woman won't win battles, and the ones who win battles rule. Men,' he shrugged, 'are just instinctively more aggressive, and suited to win.'

'Then the Seven should have been an assembly of warriors, not priests,' Vahura said, and then she quieted as a fresh set of thoughts began to frame themselves into a ladder she had to climb down. 'Battles are not brawls, Acharya. War formations demand strategy over muscles, and strategies rely on how fast you can think, not just how fast you can run. We no longer live in a world of savages where skirmishes are fought to the bitter end. There is surrender, and then there are terms, and for both, appeasement is the key. The antithesis of appeasement is aggression. So, if it were true that men are inherently more aggressive, these aggressive men are even now used, manipulated, forced or coerced by, well, less aggressive men, to go on the field and... perish.'

The Rose Coterie made no comment either way. Vahura began to grow nervous, and in her nervousness, continued unscrambling her thoughts to fill the silence. 'To solidify my hypothesis with an example, take my own kingdom, where the army stands second to the royalty. Even now, my father, who has never held a bow, plans our conquests. The casualties in conquests are never the rulers, they are the poor, the desperate and the powerless... the most aggressive of them, at least. And there is nothing wrong in it. It is a symptom of a healthy civilization where good rope is not wasted to make a fishing net.'

Orym narrowed his eyes, a faint smile playing on his lips, a subtle nod conveyed through his neck.

'But women can't control the brutes who would work under them!' Toshad shouted, making Vahura jump. 'They would never listen to someone who cannot beat them into submission.'

'Respectfully, Acharya, just because the men tilling our fields are low-born Reshts doesn't mean their field owners need to be Reshts as well. If what you say is true, it should not make sense that these landowners exploit men who are stronger than them but they do. So no, I agree not that women cannot or do not rule because of their bones or sinews or temper. If that were indeed the case, kingdoms would be ruled by young princes and not old emperors. Muscled Reshts working in mines would've brought thousand-year-old kingdoms to their knees. Wrestling duels would be played between the Acharyas of Meru to see who ascends to be the Seven.'

'I would barter my left kidney to watch that.' Ailmar laughed.

Asshaye chimed in, shutting Ailmar off. 'Then why do you think the women no longer rule? You have answers to quash our theories, well and good. But what is the answer to the question we asked?'

Vahura stopped pinching herself, allowing her shoulders to relax. 'Your answer lies within your question, Acharya. *We believe it is not possible.* Belief is the true kingmaker. Our bodies may enable but it is our culture that forbids, the same civilization where a vast majority were led to *believe* they deserved lesser, be it Reshts or Rakshasas or Mlecchas, the same civilization now *believes* that women are not fit to rule. So yes, I can imagine an Age where it was *believed* that women as rulers was the way forward, and seeing how belief is the most fickle of emotions, I can also see how that view could have changed, and how it might change again in the future.'

The Rose Coterie exchanged mischievous looks till Asshaye stepped forward. 'What do we say gents?'

'Flying colours!' Ailmar applauded. Kalay nodded, Orym grinned and Toshad grunted, which Vahura assumed was a compliment.

'Well done, Princess.' Asshaye turned to her again. 'We'll help you.'

After escaping her father, hiring bandits to abduct the Balkhan ambassador to the Conclave, crossing the span of the world to reach the East, swimming through a tar pit, sleeping under the stars and depleting her entire inheritance on bribes and donations, Asshaye's sudden kindness caused her to stumble. Not only because a band of thieves was not expected to trade gifts away without a soul-bartering deal in exchange, but because it felt too easy... even the test, it was... was that all? Had she actually... won?

'What is it, child?' Ailmar asked.

'I...' Vahura rubbed her arms. 'Is there a catch? Am I being played? This... why did you agree to help me so suddenly?'

'Are you so accustomed to the desert that you now quail at the sight of a river?' Asshaye scoffed. 'Never mind our motivations, tell us why do you *believe* you need the Daevic Scrolls?'

III

After stretching out a tarnished version of her quest before them, she waited, her mind – a bundle of past nightmares and future hopes – tangled beneath voluminous braided red hair that hid her skin, which bore wounds of her own doing. She remembered what her wrists had gone through because of her quest, and then shuddered at what they may go through if her fears came true. *Not if... when.*

Her revelation had fallen on the Rose Coterie like a reaper's scythe, the gap between their jaws a symbol of the horror about to be unleashed on the world. While the guillotine of law might have lost its grip of terror on the Rose Coterie, the Marigold Mold was an entirely different matter, even if the plague was almost as mythical as the Daevas. The last outbreak, six thousand years ago, razed the Ikshwaku Empire of Kosala. Acharya Sankara, chronicler of Sravast, documented those grim days.

By the end, half the city had beaten, clawed or eaten the other half in the rage that consumed an afflicted till his heart gave out. It had taken three neighbouring kings to quarantine the City of Sravast, trapping its citizens inside with arrows and fire, letting it burn itself. Acharya Sankara was found on his chair with a quill in his hand, his neck eaten by his plagued wife while he was still alive.

It was from his tomes that the world learned much about this dread plague. It spread from eye to eye, the afflicted maddening with rage in moments if they were older, and in minutes if they were children. The Green Order of Meru prescribed only two cures for the Marigold Mold: the axe and the torch. Decapitation without thought and burning to stop the rot. Stabbing the eye with a sharp pin did sometimes halt the spread of the plague, Vahura had read, but not always. It may save the afflicted but for stabbing it so, a man had to look in the eye of the Marigold, and no record of such a man existed. Seeing the eyes of a victim of this plague was the end of all hope. And now Vahura had told the Rose Coterie that the Marigold Mold was all set to be let loose in the Kingdom of Balkh. Marigold was the war Balkh could never win without needles. There would be no one left to rise from its ashes, no one left to make peace with the broken pieces. She did not even have to explain the rest, that if released in Balkh, it would sweep across borders, devouring men, women and children without distinction. The infected would desecrate their own faces, become their own devastating gods as they destroyed the world, especially now that the highroads had the realm a smaller place.

But to their credit, the Roses did not squirm at the threat of Marigold. Perhaps at the twilight of their lives, they felt pity, and yes, perhaps compassion for the realm that would soon find itself trapped in a nightmare from which there was no waking up, drowning beneath the torrent of a plague from which there was no rising up.

'And you're saying there is someone out there in Balkh wilfully infected with Open-Me-Not, breathing as we speak?' Orym asked.

She stealthily pinched herself to banish all memories of her sister. 'Aye,' Vahura managed to lie, 'we do not know who the infected is or, for that matter, who the scoundrels are who did this, but they... killed my Queen Mother with the plague to prove their point and are now holding our kingdom at ransom. Father believes that is all there is but I doubt that is where their villainy will stop. So far, the plague has been reasonably well contained till—'

'In the case of a plague that spreads through sight,' Asshaye interrupted, '*reasonably well contained* means *not contained at all.*'

'Let her speak,' Ailmar said. 'And you believe there is a conspiracy to use him... this infected as a weapon on Balkh?'

Vahura nodded nervously.

'Just when you think the human race couldn't stoop any lower, they astound you with bending on all their fours,' Kalay grunted.

Ailmar ignored him. 'And the Daevic Scrolls have the answers you seek? It has the way to protect the innocent from the miasma?'

'Yes,' Vahura lied again with conviction, wondering whether the Roses knew she wasn't being entirely forthcoming. That she had no inkling if the Daevic Scrolls had even asked the question about the Marigold let alone held the answers to it. But she could not confess that detail to the Roses. Even a shadow of a doubt would taint their resolve. They had to *believe* that the Daevic Scrolls were the only way out. She grappled with the guilt for concealing the truth but she had already misled them about why she truly needed the Daevic Scrolls – why change course now? It was not as if she had any choice. The truth was not an option. If they even caught the whiff of her sister being the infected, they would kick Vahura out, armed with a sword, and command her to sever her sister's head from her torso and burn it. That was the only spear recommended by history. Annihilate the carrier. The only spear. There was no shield against it. No cure.

'Each race on this world,' Vahura started, 'animal or otherwise, is trapped in its own unique sensory cage, perceiving a tiny sliver of the immense world. We just have the five senses. Our sailors cannot trace the currents of the sea the way sharks can. The Blue Order is not privy to the magnetic fields that robins use. We cannot hear the loud calls of hummingbirds or the deep screams of whales. We can't even imagine a new colour. But the bees can... The Children of Light could. I do not know what I speak of but I only gathered it from a ruined extract from the Daevic Scrolls. I do not know how the Daevas knew this but they wove meaning from miscellany, and they were particularly obsessed with diseases amongst us mortals, and so they must have a way to shield the world from the Marigold Mold.'

Orym sat on his chair with a resigned thud, startling her, and then he leaned forward on the table, as if just realizing something. 'You are a Princess. Why are you on foot... getting dirty for this? Shouldn't you have a bunch of yes-men doing your bidding?'

'She wants to play a god in her own small way,' Asshaye said, shaking her head. 'The little princess wants to play hero.'

Toshad made a gagging sound. 'There is no one more doomed than someone out to do the world a favour. Is that why you are doing this alone? Shouldn't your father be mustering armies to help you with this?'

If only... Vahura thought. Her father had asked unsettling questions. Of the many theories he had, his favourite pinned the blame for the plague on her Mura, her mother. After all, why would the villain take pains to slip into the palace, and especially into the heavily guarded Sapphire Spires, only to infect the royal women, when infecting even a maidservant outside would have done the trick? The question had hung in the air between Vahura and her father like a whiff of spoiled cabbage, refusing to disperse. How did Mura know of the Marigold Mold, and how did she know the alchemical blindfold to use to slow death's march on Vahura's sister? Questions had swirled like vultures over her brain's battlefield, but her father's suggestion had stood out like a lone, severed head on a pike. The so-called assassin had not truly been an assassin at all, but a thief, her father claimed. A thief who had come to steal a sample of the Marigold Mold from Vahura's mother. Vahura's sister must have stumbled into the room, her curiosity leading her straight into the heart of chaos. In the struggle with the thief and his loot, her sister must have gotten infected. Vahura's mother must have slain the thief, saved her daughter with what she knew of the plague, and in her final moments, blinded herself before writing Vahura the letter. The thief might as well have been a hero sent to destroy the last sample of such a dangerous plague. Why else had the plague not been unleashed in Balkh if they had more of it to spare? Her father's theory had been as twisted and tragic as it had been logical, leaving more questions than answers in its wake. It did not matter. Vahura refused to implicate Mura simply because it was convenient. Vahura would unearth the dark legacy left behind later. For now, the weight of her mother's sacrifice bore down on her like an iron chain, which she was going to use to cloak her truths.

'A man with hopes and dreams will not be swayed to abandon them in the face of annihilation. This is the doomsday paradox. Be it the mighty Saptarishis or the boldest king, the thing that can threaten them the most is what they believe they can defeat. Any danger that lies beyond the realm of this hope – like a marigold on the loose – it ignites their fear and burns their courage into cinders, leaving only denial in its wake. It is not a weakness but just human instinct to choose to fight a battle in the light of today rather than prepare for a war in the darkness of the future.

'They who hold power,' Vahura continued, 'will cling to their arrogance, not out of pride, but as a way to deny that they do not have the courage to sacrifice what is needed to save the world.'

Asshaye asked, 'And what is this sacrifice you think is needed?'

'Time and resources,' Vahura answered. 'Time to search for clues. Resources diverted from armies and spent in finding a shield. You think I have not tried knocking on my father's doors, chasing the Acharyas of Court or flooding Meru with panicked letters disguised as academic curiosities? They think of it as the ramblings of a woman unbedded beyond her childbearing age. Some have even taken to calling me the Harlot of Hysteria.'

Toshad laughed. 'Good name.'

The rest said nothing for a long while, each one content with just staring at her. Vahura's heart splashed about in the shallow waters of her insecurities. *Why won't they say any—*

'Doomsday paradox.' Toshad allowed himself a bitter smile. 'Well put, Princess. We cannot deny the hard truth of your words for we have seen for ourselves the poison that is denial. A denial of how we needed to stop, and that we had grown old. We perceived well the threat, and so marched down to steal, robbing the greatest loot, to live happily ever after. Or so we'd thought.' He sighed.

'We don't have to—' Asshaye started but Ailmar cut her off.

'It devoured us,' Ailmar said. 'We lost two of our brothers, and well, we hung up our cape then. Do you know what our last heist was?'

Vahura shook her head.

'The theft of the Daevic Scrolls.'

Vahura's eyes widened as she instinctively turned to Asshaye for confirmation, as if Vahura had any reason to disbelieve Ailmar. Asshaye nodded. 'And that is why we agreed to aid you. As to Fate's funny sense of humour, tell me what is the limitation period for even the most heinous crimes in Manu's Codes?'

'Thirty-five years.'

'The limitation period for theft of the Daevic Scrolls according to the Codes expires today, meaning yesterday was our last day as the Rose Coterie.' Ailmar gestured with his thumb towards the table behind. *That explains the feast.* 'We had a conversation while you waited outside. And we believe it was the Goddess Lavannai who brought you to us, little Princess.'

Asshaye snorted, ruining the magic of Ailmar's words. 'And the other reason we agreed so *easily* to help you,' she said, the grey steel of her eyes plunging into the blue sea of her own, 'is because we don't have anything to lose. We don't have the Daevic Scrolls. We gave them away three decades ago.'

IV

The revelation robbed all her words from her. It landed like a blow but it took time to bruise. Till then she stared at the table as though the secret to saving her sister was hidden in the patterns on the wood.

So, it had all been for nothing. All the work, all the sweat, all the gold. She had crossed the world to find the Scrolls. And for all the Forge damned good it had done, she might as well have plucked her sister's eyes with pincers than let her rot in the damn tower all alone.

'Calm, my dear. Calm,' Asshaye said in a voice that did not belong to a pompous mastermind. It sounded like a grandmother or a regular at the library. It was comforting but not calming.

While calm looked like it would elude Vahura for the foreseeable future, clarity stood within arm's reach. She reached for the skin on her wrist, and twisted. The searing pain shoved her panic to the sidelines. *I will not weep. I will not weaken. I will not waver.* If you pretend to be brave in a battle, that itself is bravery. She still felt like cursing and screaming though, something she had never been able to bring herself to do in her life. *No.* Tomorrow she would hurl curses at the dawn, but today, she had to hold on to her hope, mutilated though it may be. She used that hope to force words past her lips. 'Where are they now?'

'You gave us a fright, girl,' Asshaye said, her voice returning to her old self. 'Here we are celebrating freedom from the clutches of law and you, a Princess of Balkh, were about to descend to death at our doorstep. Who you do think they would've blamed for your unheroic demise?'

'Will you hold your spear, Asshaye!' Ailmar said. 'Poor thing. You have our empathy, Princess. And yes, before you ask, we do know where they are. They're with the current Tusk of the Tree Cities. We…' Ailmar hesitated. 'We handed them to his father to allow us safe haven in the East when we retired. We did not want to sell our last prize out of tribute to our fallen ones.'

Before Vahura could respond, she heard someone knock on the door.

'It is probably that dreadful little Yogini Rambha, likely seeking refuge to escape her punishments. I regret handing her the spare key.' As Asshaye moved towards the door, it swung open on its own. To her surprise, it was Zubeia, the Mistress of Ravens herself.

'Lady Asshaye,' was all the Yogini said, entering with a courteous nod in the direction of the Roses. Zubeia moved past them to the wall on the opposite end, resembling a mother on an errand, her eyes roaming over the walls in search of mischief.

'You!' Asshaye said, feigning a cough and waggling her finger like decrepit old people are wont to do. 'What are you doing here? How did you get the key? This is breach of—'

'Privacy, yes.' Zubeia's voice was so deep, so stately that Vahura wished Zubeia would burst into a song. 'I know not if you have seen our rituals, but privacy doesn't feature high on our priority list. The Iron Order is marching up the path to the temple. Now, they are either here for us, in which case I will handle them. Or they are here for you.' When Asshaye exchanged a look with Ailmar, Zubeia clarified, 'Not you, Rose Coterie; you, Princess. The Iron Order is many things, but lawless it is not. The Rose Coterie are now immune from prosecution, and not to forget, only the Tusk, you and I know them for who they are but you…'

The Iron Order, the personal arbiters of justice for the Seven, rumoured to be cursed with the Taint of the Voice, were capable of compelling truth from the tongue. They were the *Angrakshaks*, the Bloodguard of the Saptarishis, tasked with protecting them but also occasionally playing the role of Marshals to bring offenders of the realm – not just a kingdom, but the whole realm – to justice. What were they doing out here on the fringes? Of course, the Conclave. *What a dumb question to ask, Vahura.* No, it was not dumb. Why were they coming here to the temple?

If the Iron Order even caught wind of her quest... the Rose Coterie could easily defy their powers with their strong will but Vahura would spill her secrets like broken wineskin, and then... it did not bear thinking about.

'Why me?' Vahura asked.

'Leave that. How did you know we are the Roses, you sex-witch!' Asshaye's voice snapped her out of her reverie.

'The swarmsense is no myth, old hag,' Zubeia said. 'I have always known.' She opened a drawer and began sifting through the clothes inside. 'No, not this one.'

'I urge that you answer us at once,' Asshaye said, brandishing her spear. 'Oi! Why are you rifling through our drawers? And that drawer has been locked even before we were here.'

'Those are filled with iron spiders,' Kalay said. 'I daresay they are still alive in there.'

Zubeia prised open that supposed locked drawer without a trifle. Plunging her hand inside, she pulled out an orb. *Good faith!* It was no orb. It was a fleshy skull with a fragment of the neck still attached. Too frightened to scream, Vahura studied it instead to distract herself. The skull was rounded and the brow ridges on it were smoother. A female. *Top marks, Vahura.* Her eyes were rolled back, leaving behind milky orbs. The skin was mostly decayed and what remained was shrivelled and leathery. A horde of red spiders wriggled in the gaping mouth, coiling over each other to make it appear as if the skull's tongue was trying to speak.

'She molested one of the young girls when she joined our sister-hood, and as punishment was denied her funeral rites. But no death

ever goes wasted, and being part of our swarm, her skull was still...
helpful.'

Asshaye's body shook heavily as if an earthquake had been set
loose inside her. 'You have been eavesdropping on us for years
through a blasted skull! Storms! That's! That is—'

'Brilliant!' Toshad laughed.

Asshaye shot him a sharp look, and then sighed. 'Yes,' she con-
ceded. 'Brilliant. First a librarian uncovers our identity, then I learn
a sex priestess has been playing us for a fool. My appetite for this
affair has certainly waned.'

'We have no time,' Zubeia said. 'Whether it was her father who
sent the Iron Order to bring her home, or maybe the Princess's
nosing into the Daevic Scrolls reached the Seven, it does not matter.
Considering the Princess is out to save the world on her own, she
is our kindred sister, and she needs to leave the temple before it is
too late.'

'Sister.' Asshaye chuckled softly. 'More like, daughter.'

Zubeia ignored Asshaye, and approached the wall behind the
table, toppling a pyramid of books to the ground to clear the space.

'Oi, what do you think you are doing?' Asshaye said, hand on the
wall. 'We need to find a way to hide the Princess if the Iron Boots
are marching up to the front gate.'

Tracing her hand on the stone, Zubeia found what she was
looking for and inserted a key. 'Acharya Oram was wrong. Just
because you have tried every road does not mean you cannot carve
a new path.'

For a moment, nothing happened. Then Vahura's eyes flashed
as the wall beneath Asshaye's fingers creaked open in a small ava-
lanche of dust and debris.

'Damn me to the depths!'

Zubeia gripped Vahura's shoulders. 'The tunnel on the other side
of this door leads to the Underfall. There are passages within the
roots of the Umbrasils three hundred steps ahead. Once you reach
there, you can then climb to the surface using their trunks and vines.
Three hundred steps, remember.'

Anyone who had ever visited the Tree Cities from the outside world had been warned of the Underfall. 'Aren't the Umbrasils inhabited by Nagas?' Vahura asked, shivering.

'They left to join their kin in a place far deeper,' Zubeia said. 'Now hurry, Princess. Consequences find only those who stay behind to wait for them.'

ADHYAYA I:C

SHADES OF SCARS

SOMEWHERE IN THE NORTH

6 MONTHS BEFORE THE BATTLE OF MATHURA

'I never wonder to see men wicked, but I often wonder to see them not ashamed.'
—**Jonathan Swift**

NALA

I

'Did she say what I think she did?' Nala asked, as if she had heard a nightingale hiss, her hand coming to a dramatic halt over the scroll inked with Masha's mutterings. With no preliminary warning to soften the shock, Masha's words had momentarily unmanned her. It was not often that one was confronted with certain death on such a majestic scale. Given that a contingent of guards around a chest was about the usual fare that one read of in books on high-value treasure hunting, this... felt excessive. 'How can a *D'rahi...*' Nala could not even say the word out loud and clear in High Sanskrit, '...be guarding the Prophecy! Aren't... aren't they extinct?'

From her peripheral vision, Nala was aware of Masha clawing at the ground, gouging furrows on the soft carpet. Fortunately, they were in a room for a change and not on a cart. That left enough space for Masha to spasm on the floor like a wingless butterfly without giving Nala's quillmanship a bad name.

'Dreams are nothing but untethered thoughts,' Parshuram replied without answering. 'Divinations are nothing but untethered intuitions. That is why both feel real while we sleep. It is only when we wake, we feel trapped between worlds. That is how our mind decides that it will be easier just to forget dreams rather than confront them. And that is why Masha forgets her visions when she awakens. How do you capture an oracle's dreams in a cage then?' Parshuram asked as he casually stuffed a dowel between Masha's jaws to prevent her from accidentally severing her tongue. Built like a jaguar, a comparison made firm by the fur of the beast riding his broad shoulders, Parshuram's action in wiping the sweat on Masha's brow seemed as commonplace as a comet. Funny how that kindness never stretched to Nala.

'By jotting down her whispers the moment she is woken up,' Nala answered sullenly, wetting her quill again.

The Acharya raised an eyebrow.

'By not talking while tallying,' Nala said.

The Acharya nodded, satisfied, then returned to rest against the wall, lost in thought. Absently, he stroked the handle of his double-bladed axe, much like a recently sober man would the neck of a wine glass. As he gazed out the window of their rented cottage, his face was bathed in the sinking sun's light, a glow as thick as blood.

A while lapsed before Masha stopped divining and a long while before Nala shuffled the contents of her latest journal entry into the scroll to be sent to the Seven. Ever since they had set out on this quest to stop the destruction of the world at the hands of the Son of Darkness, they were obligated to send fortnightly reports on any useful insights on the future Masha came up with.

Nala did justifiably feel that having not apprenticed in the Black Order, she did not have the requisite qualifications to star as an Oracle's Matron, especially the Oracle tasked with finding the era's most feared villain. But Parshuram, true to his trusting nature in human capabilities, was all for teaching one to swim by tossing the newborn into the ocean. So here Nala was, an unofficial Matron, sifting through the husk of useful prophecies from the rice of visions. A far cry from her days as an assassin's apprentice mastering the Dance of Shadows.

Parshuram said nothing as he took the scroll from Nala and began to read it as though on a quest for spelling errors. 'I will seek out a raven in the town square to dispatch this.'

Nala wondered if Parshuram truly believed Nala would buy into his lie. *Find a raven, it seems,* Nala scowled. Parshuram had been vanishing come evenfall in every town they had halted in. She had no clue about his whereabouts at night but if pressed to guess, she would say he was off pursuing the same subject of interest who he'd tracked and stalked during the day. It was a bit like a summer fling, really – just the subjects varied from town to town.

In the first town, it was a courtesan Parshuram had tracked. It had also been the first time Nala had seen Parshuram as a *man* man. And why not? Immortality does not mean deadening of desires. But then, there had been that old charioteer in the next town, then that Unni Ehtral priest in the next, the poxed healer in Sajda and even that soldieress with the wolf cloak near Mathura, all subjects of Parshuram's curious pursuit across different towns. Either Parshuram had a rather diverse palate when it came to the carnal or he was building a strange army to fight those who were hiding the Prophecy.

Today it must be that moustached trader with those telltale blue eyes and the uneasy smile of a Southerner that marked him a foreigner around these parts. The trader had his boy with him as well, the one with the breathless laughter, fiddling away with a cube while the trader sold his wares at double the standard price. Parshuram had kept his sights on the trader all week since they had arrived in town, the same pattern he'd repeated in different towns. But what could a trader do to ward off danger? Haggle with it?

As Parshuram was heading out the door, Nala ran up to him. 'Acharya,' she bowed, 'may I accompany you, Acharya? Or are there any assignments I could help with? Infiltrate a temple? Steal maps? Spy on the town head? Brew a new poison?' Nala's manner, as she finished the query, suggested that she had little hope that business would result.

'Help Sister Masha when she comes about, and feed her the duskberries.' Settling his jaguar cloak firmly on his shoulders, he disappeared into the evening outside, leaving Nala alone.

Nala could not believe there was a time when she'd complained about Parshuram subjecting her to hours of mastering complex recipes, deciphering dead languages, learning the art of disguise and sending her on excursions to tamper with wine barrels. As old men were wont to say… *Those were the days.*

But that chapter had ground to a halt ever since Masha was unceremoniously thrust on their merry troupe of two by the Seven in their quest to find the Son of Darkness. Parshuram had resolved to stay aloof from Masha, deeming her a burden, but on their first day together, Masha had divined and let slip the word 'Iyran Machil'. Ever since, Masha had become the favourite child and Parshuram instructed Nala only in Nala's nostalgia.

Nala turned to look at Masha with the hospitality of a slaver. It was not as if Masha was painful company. She'd even agreed to Nala's plea to not dwell on her moments spent with Upavi, Nala's former friend at Meru, when Upavi had to summer-apprentice in the Black Order. For memories of Nala's last day at Meru loitered whenever Masha brought Upavi up – especially the gang's parody funeral for Upavi when he was horsed off to learn a skill at the House of Oracles. Oh, how much had they laughed at Upavi's pale-as-death face when they had met Sister Mercy. At that time, Nala had no clue the funeral had foretold her own grim fate. Masha, now mindful of past horrors, showed respectful silence on this subject, for which Nala was grateful.

The only thing in the nature of a flaw that Nala found in Masha was the fact that she didn't seem to be ideally unhappy in her wretched life as Nala was. Given Masha's history – witnessing her father burn alive, enduring torture, drugs and isolation all her life, and now thrust with an assassin and his surly apprentice – no one would have blamed Masha for being cross with life. But that girl was all sunshine and happiness as if she was living the life of her dreams. Nala hated the way Masha made her feel as if she was being melodramatic about her tragedies.

Nala wanted frowning faces about her, so to speak, and it looked to her as if not just Masha but everybody around her were bringing flowers to the poor, playing in the rain and taking their wives for a walk instead of cutting them up and hiding them in sacks in the marshes. Three times that week Nala had chased bored-looking cats minding their business up the trees and forced them to contemplate mortality. She had even clubbed a small boy on the head who had asked her if she wanted to play, and asked him if he knew that one day he was going to die, and then no one would remember him.

Masha groaned on the floor. That was Nala's prompt. She wiped clean the twin trails of blood meandering from Masha's nostrils and, not for the first time, gawked at Masha's scars that spread on her face like rivers on a map. Nala had tried to persuade Masha to use paints to dim them but Masha kept peddling some Black Order nonsense about how light could purify the soul only by entering through open wounds. Nala glanced at the craters running across her own body. Scars were nothing but a memory of how she had been hurt. It was little use explaining this to Masha for she took scars as a memory of how she had healed.

What else could be expected of a child? 'The river isn't as blue as the artists show in their drawings! The grasses grow so tall here!' 'Look at the way the horses gallop! How fascinating!' Masha, when sober, squirmed like a puppy at everyday sights with annoying enthusiasm.

Nala knew she had no choice but to tolerate Masha. Nala had always known, having read so many of these stories in the libraries of Meru, that when you are accompanying a great man on a great quest, you have to take the rough with the smooth. And there appeared to be no doubt that, despite all the urgency of the world ending around her, Masha was indisputably in the pink. Nala knew of the symptoms first-hand, having experienced them when she first entered the Citadel of Meru in the disguise of a boy. Every day had felt like she had been floating on a blue-white cloud, high in the air, only touching the ground at odd spots. Of course, that was before Prince Bheem of Hastina burned her mother and her brothers alive in Varnavrat.

Her chest began to feel heavy. Oh, not that again. Nala was like a baby who had not cried ever since coming to the world. It was important those tears come out. She knew it. She forced it. But she could not. Her tears stayed clogged inside her, turning green like the layer of algae over a pond, shielding the monsters lurking underneath from the naked eye. When she had Parshuram's endless chores and routines to follow, her mind did not have a moment's rest to grieve. But now that she had free time, she used it all to see Bheem breaking her spine and tossing her over the terrace, repainting the scene in different hues, styles and angles in her mind, till she felt she could have directed a play on it for the village fair.

She needed to meditate for inner peace.

II

Meditation was worst. Parshuram made it look so easy, the way he slipped into playing a statue, so still, so tranquil. It always seemed as if his soul had detached from his body and travelled elsewhere for a snack. The way he cleared his mind made old monks look like they were drunk. Nala, on the other hand, had never been able to meditate beyond thirty heartbeats. Whenever she meditated, her random inner thoughts about violence and revenge argued about the seating arrangement. But what else was there to do when Parshuram had abandoned her instruction altogether. Maybe if she could awaken one of her Chakras on her own, Parshuram would be impressed enough to resume her education on the side.

In theory, each mortal had the potential to rouse all seven prime Chakras along their spiritual spine, yet in practice, they were oft attuned to but one or two, known as Affinity Chakras by the wise healers. Once these Affinity Chakras were made manifest by giving them form, they could be *Turned* to stoke a mystical kiln that transmuted latent prowess into mighty powers. But here was the hitch: so far the shapes Nala had manifested were best left to vague metaphors.

Every meditation, a failure. Seven flaming Chakras, and she hadn't been able to awaken one, let alone *Turn* one. No matter how many times she balanced herself on one leg, hands outstretched, eyes closed, her thoughts soon dissolved into images of arson and assassination.

Masha advocated patience and Parshuram roared persistence but neither of these two keys fit the locks of Nala's soul energy. Their personal experience had been of no assistance, either. Masha remembered naught of how her own Crown Chakra had awakened to flex her power of foresight and Parshuram was as eloquent as a Resht on a stake when it came to sharing his stories from his days of struggle. Granted they were centuries past, but the least he could've done was make an attempt to remember. But Parshuram, for all intents and purposes, had abandoned Nala's instruction.

Nala, not ungrateful, did try her best at first to be understanding. Parshuram had a mission to save the world. She understood that.

Nala's family was gone. Parshuram was all she had now, and he had never asked her for much in return for helping her. So if Nala had to wait patiently until Parshuram was done saving the world, she would do so without complaint. And she would have, had she not uncovered a secret door.

Nala had come to understand that Parshuram had not idled away his immortal life. Rather, he was a hoarder – a hoarder of knowledge on the different hues of power. Not just the different levels of murder. He knew how to brew herbs to open the Chakras without ever meditating though he never shared that with Nala, despite seeing her struggle. He had once cursed at Nala that he would freeze a part of her body in a moment of eternal pain – which only meant he knew how to do that. Even lions and panthers bowed to him in the jungle to let him pass as if he knew their language. At first Nala had credited such vistas to Parshuram's secret powers as a Chiranjeevi, an immortal. That was until she had stumbled upon his almanacs.

She did not know if it was Parshuram or someone more ancient, but some luminary had catalogued the theory, the tricks and the practice of all that is arcane into eight almanacs. Nala had only heard two of them when she had first started training under Parshuram – the Art of the Sun, the Red Almanac of the Warrior; and the Dance of Shadows, the Grey Almanac of the Assassin.

Nala's first clue as to the existence of other almanacs came later when Masha, in her first week with them, had sprinted out from her room, blood trailing down her nose. She had been shrieking, trembling, her tears streaked with blood. Nala had hissed questions at her, and Masha had confessed how tormented she was with the task of divining their future. *Sisters never walk back the path of the Oracle*, she had cried. When Parshuram had pulled Masha back to her room, she had cried that she could not open her Chakras on her own, and had wet herself. But after that day, Nala had never witnessed Masha cry again, and Nala had known then. There were shortcuts to success.

Shortcuts denied to her.

So, what can one do when the test is rigged for you to fail? Better to win with dishonesty than fail with honour.

Nala shut the door to the room behind her. Then with a small smile, she pounced on the White Almanac: the Song of the Stars she had stolen, or rather borrowed, from Masha's bag. Nala was only cheating a little bit – she did not care about future or divinations – all she wanted was to know the recipe of the wonder elixir that helped Masha open her Chakras. Turned out what was difficult to achieve in the Dance of Shadows had an easier route in the Song of the Stars.

Nala wished Masha had shared this with her before but she did not bear the Oracle any grudge. Talking about their almanacs was the one thing Parshuram had passionately forbidden Nala and Masha. Masha thought it was to preserve the sanctity of the process. Nala felt it was because Parshuram didn't want any of his students growing too powerful. Not that any one ever dared to ask. Nala only dared to borrow.

It was not as if it was that easy, either. The sheer difficulty in translating, deciphering and understanding the words in the almanac was its own insurance against theft. Rolls of crumpled scrolls lay hidden – secret evidence of Nala's disgust at her incompetence in understanding what she had transcribed.

It was not until her crippling curiosity had her sniffing Masha's pipe did Nala see a new colour for the first time, a colour that did not exist in the rainbow. A colour that was key to understanding the code of the White Almanac. A colour invisible to her till she took a noseful of those horrible fumes of the Hashayne of Hastar. She thought the Hashayne was sustenance that the Oracles were weaned on to erode their will, make them pliant. Nala had been wrong. It was only when she smoked the Hashayne, it revealed its secrets to her. It showed her the coin had a third side. Meru had always spoken of sages who experienced this other reality, children too, until training and conditioning turned them blind. Somehow, the Hashayne had opened these ancient curtains. The fumes that helped Masha see her visions now helped Nala read those words and ascend. And so began Nala's tryst with destiny and drugs and the Dance of Shadows, a journey not without its cost.

There was a sound of shuffling feet. Nala turned, alarmed, to find Masha was walking around the room like a courtly mustang, eyes closed. *Shit on a stick.* Nala stuffed back the White Almanac where she'd found it and half jumped across the room to hold Masha and help her sit on a chair. Masha fluttered her eyelids open, her pupils trapped albino moths in her sockets.

Once Masha settled down, Nala soaked a cloth with water and laid it across Masha's forehead. 'Is that you, Nala?' Masha breathed. 'Did it help?'

'Same thing about monkey-tailed humans, giant scaled eggs and flying ships, and of course, Iyran Machil,' Nala passed her notes to Masha, 'the name that has him making the horses rue their fate. Oh, you also mentioned who is guarding the Prophecy.'

'How wonderful!' Masha said as she slouched back into her, squeezing her eyes shut. She clutched the seven-star totem around her neck till her knuckles were white. *Wonderful? You didn't even ask who is guarding it!*

'How long have I been...?' Masha asked.

'A week.'

Masha stared at her clean clothes and spotless ankles. No trace of piss remained. 'Forgive me, Nala. I know how horrid it is to play a Matron to an Oracle.'

Nala shrugged. It was the only task Parshuram gave her these days, to clean up after Masha while he peeled away Masha's last dreams and hunted the prophecies in them until no refuge remained. Cleaning, and climbing. For reasons unknown, Parshuram had Nala swinging from one rafter of the ceiling to the other, sometimes with weights on the wrists, sometimes with a heavy sack. Nala did try and remind Parshuram that she was born a Valkan – their preferred method of transportation from one neighbourhood to another was by swinging on vines – and that Nala would rather learn swinging a knife instead but Parshuram had taken his insults of calling Nala a 'monkey' rather too literally for Nala's comfort.

'Weren't you an Oracle once? Shouldn't this be easy for you?' Nala asked.

'A period of which I thankfully remember nothing,' Masha said, smiling. 'But even if I did, this is different. Oracles never divine their own future for it holds no surprises. They never leave the House of Oracles so their road to death is linear. They just see events of the world, sometimes past, sometimes future. And seeing how they are drugged all the time, the days go by smoothly till one day they either succumb or get summonned. I might be the first Sister in ages who has been asked to return to divination beyond the confines of our home.'

'Congratulations, I suppose,' Nala said, a touch uncertain.

'Thank you, Nala.' Masha hugged Nala again much to Nala's chagrin. 'Your words mean so much. I have read so much of you. Oh, it is so so good to meet you in person!'

'So you said the last week, and the week before.'

'Oh, I did? I... I mean I know I did but I did not know if it happened for real. I confess it has been difficult. I know I said it before but Oracles should never see their own futures. Can you imagine seeing the countless lives you did not lead as a consequence of every step you took, or every step you did not take? I am sure I saw countless variations where I did not tell you this. It is all such a blur. Because it would not stop at one step, would it?'

'I do not understand.'

'Let me illustrate. You see you eat that apple. Great. You then see it causes a flux in your stomach. Horrible. So, you decide not to eat that apple. And then you see, since you did not eat that apple, you went hungry, and fainted on horseback, and fell to your death in a ravine. Now multiply this with thousands and thousands of options... It corrodes your mind.'

Nala nodded nonchalantly, not having the time for Masha's complaints about a suffering that Masha had volunteered for, especially not now when Nala knew her own debt of inhaling the Hashayne was about to accrue in moments.

'Don't you ever feel what the Acharya is doing to you is wrong?' Nala asked. Parshuram had instructed Nala to ask Masha deep questions to dust off the different Mashas in Masha's head and help bring her back to shore.

Masha frowned. 'In the House of Oracles, we are taught that the judgment of what is right against what is wrong depends on the scale of comparison. What is one girl's broken mind compared to the fate of the world?'

It was as Varcin said, Nala thought of her old friend from Meru, *Oracles are as mad as wolves howling at a moonless sky.* Nala couldn't take Masha's sunny optimism any longer. The effects of the drug Nala had stolen and sniffed was coming. *Stop...* She clutched her hands together, but the shivers simply migrated to her arms. *Stop!* But it didn't. It was as crippling as a cramp.

'Forgive me, Sister,' Nala managed. 'If you're well, I have some groceries to buy before we leave for wherever you have divined us to go.'

'Oh, oh, can I come? I have never shopped for groceries before.'

'No,' Nala said, flatly. 'Forgive me, but you are too important to be let out without the Acharya. But I'll be back in a jiff. Will you manage alright?'

Masha smiled, her scars contorting around her lips grotesquely. 'Let the light enter through *them*,' Masha said, passing over a stack of bandages to her. 'Happy purge.'

III

Nala took refuge under the Bridge of Daisies though there was not a sign any daisy had ever grown within the five-mile radius of the bridge. All she could smell was chamber pots and sweat. She walked, hood raised, amongst the drug addicts lurking in their own company, searching for an empty spot on the wall to rest her back against. The sharp, cold comfort of the blades inside her pocket was reassuring. Finally finding an empty space against the wall, she inspected her would-be neighbour to confirm he wasn't a skinpeddler. The man was sobbing, fevered like that of a trapped dog. When he noticed Nala staring, he raised his hands to bury his face. Satisfied, Nala slumped against the wall, seeking the release she had been pining for ever since she had inhaled the fumes from Masha's bowl.

Unlike Masha, who danced like a fish out of water the moment the fumes touched her nostrils – a dance that lasted as long as Masha's divination – Nala's fits knocked on her a lot later with a lot lesser force. It probably had to do with the tiny doses Nala took which, in comparison, made Masha's intake a deluge. The worst

Nala had seen of her body's reply to the fumes was when half her body had turned stiff and unmoving if only for a few seconds, for it was a paralysis she had learned an easy cure for in her own Almanac. Bloodletting.

Too bad that this cure had now become a disease.

Her fingers shuffled inside her pocket to retrieve her release. The benefit of holding off a Hashayne fit did not even matter any longer – for those fits, one tiny cut was enough. For her own self, however... that took time. What Nala wanted most, wanted desperately, more than vengeance, was to cry. It was not as if Nala had not wept before in Meru, or even back in the forests when she was a Valkan. But perhaps when Bheem broke her body and spirit, he also broke the part of her which let people scream their anguish. Parshuram was supposed to help mend it. *That bastard!*

Now the thing about Parshuram was that history would dismiss him without a stain on his character. Tasked by the Seven to find the Prophecy of Desolation, and prove that Prophecy wrong by seeing to it that the Son of Darkness never saw a blue sky, he was a man on a mission, his motive pure to the last drop.

But one of the things that must be remembered is that Parshuram did not have anything better to do. Nala did. She had to murder – brutally – the five princes of Hastina to avenge her family, and so, she could be excused if the quest to save the world did not fill her to the gills with a sort of heroic chivalry. Every day she woke up with the painful realization that she was motherless, that she had no family, and that it was because of her they had died the most painful death. Day after day, she tried to hone her skills on her own – drugged – with the grim awareness that the friends she left behind in Meru were learning the arcane arts, together. But there was only so much she could do all by herself, especially when Parshuram had no time for her now, and so Nala went about the place like a rabid dog, doing such acts of cruelty with her expressions that the strangers she met would sooner talk to a lamp post than her.

Not that many people approached her in the first place. Even before the burn marks scorched the side of her face or the fall left a twist to her hand, Nala had been distinctly plain. The only thing about her that caught the eye were the faint white lines of vitiligo spread across her face.

Cries bottled up, dreams on hold, no longer the apple of Parshuram's eye, just a footnote on this journey with an over-optimistic oracle and an indifferent tyrant – what does a girl do then? Since she cannot scream her lungs out, she lets her skin scream instead.

She cut. A tingle across her arm just below her wrist. Tiny bubbles of blood erupted across the line on her hand, till they burst and trickled down her arm. Satisfied that there was something more inside her than nothingness, Nala smiled. It hurt, yes. But that was the point. Not just because it helped with the Hashayne fits. She had so many words to shout, and since she could not, she cut her words out instead. She cut out her mother. Cut out her brothers. Cut out Varcin. Cut out her friends, cut out her teachers, cut out her scars, cut out Meru and cut out being sad and angry and being ugly and unloved, she cut it all out till that patch of arm became a fine mirror of hell.

'Can I have one of that?' the man beside her interrupted, pointing at the now-reddened blade.

'Don't have the time to search it from your corpse,' Nala said, her release ruined, as she tended to the arm using the bandages Masha had lent her. 'Bastard.' She left the man to cry and took to the streets to find some ointment from a healer.

Cutpurses stalked these streets on this night where the pickings were easy, given how deep the pedestrians were in wine. Her blade at the ready, she sorely hoped someone would try to make a pass at her. But suddenly a few of these low-lifes ahead edged back to let a man walk past, a movement loud enough in its action to catch Nala's eye. In the light spilling through a window, Nala saw that man who had caused the commotion was a broad, muscular man, wearing a jaguar cloak, and none of these cutpurses wanted to risk his size or his axe.

Now, although the impulse to not court death by following her immortal master was intense, wasn't Nala supposed to train in the Dance of Shadows? Surely that included matters of stealth and stalk. And if Parshuram was indeed assembling an army, she needed to at least take stock of her potential new companions, didn't she? Convinced in her suicidal plan, Nala set out to stalk the stalker.

IV

Parshuram's second shack was in an alley not nearly as shadowed as Nala would have liked. The shack, a run-down one-storey building, looked like it was owned by a landlord who cared not for the general hygiene of its renters.

This is exciting, Nala thought as she finished bandaging her wounds. Did Parshuram have a mistress? It had to be that, no? He hadn't rented a different house in any of the towns they had passed. Ignoring the train of such thoughts, Nala waited. After a while, she squinted at the door of the shack from which Parshuram had just emerged. He carried a bag in one hand, furiously rubbing the back of his neck with the other. *Maybe the position was difficult,* Nala chuckled. If a position was difficult for Parshuram, the master of yoga, she could not begin to imagine what kind of debauchery Parshuram was into. Ahead, Parshuram's eyes searched the scant stalls set up along the alley, and not finding what he wanted, he strode off to the main thoroughfare.

With Parshuram out of sight, fuelled by a bout of foolishness and thrill, Nala scampered to the shack. Nala had been trained by Parshuram himself to crack locks open, and while this was a difficult one, she managed after three tries. Nala gingerly stepped in, all set to pretend to be a thief when caught by Parshuram's keep.

Though what Nala found did not match the décors of a sex-room. It seemed more like a hastily assembled makeshift alchemy chamber. The small bottles the Acharya had bought in the morning were now brimming on the shelves with potions. Beside the alchemy shelf, there was another rack of bottled tinctures and herbs. In the centre of the room, there was a big chair. Or so she called it, though it seemed more like a stretcher with its numerous straps. Had it been just the stretcher, Nala would have laughed and quipped that straps just seemed to be the sort of thing Parshuram would be into.

But, unfortunately, the stretcher's occupant obliterated the dirty thoughts in Nala's head.

Nala had been wrong. Parshuram had not been tracking the trader in the market. He had been tracking the trader's son, who now was strapped naked to the chair.

But the boy of the night looked nothing like the boy from the day. His limbs had atrophied. There were things – pipes and tubes and things, she had no words to describe them – leaving the nape of his neck to empty into an alchemical globe. The boy was still breathing, heaving into a transparent bag, which was attached to his chin somehow, and it was full of— *Spirits roast me! What is happening?* She sank on her knees and gagged. When she looked up, Parshuram was standing over her.

'Always keep an eye on the door of the house after you break in.'

V

The Acharya's face was still. No regret. No anger. Just a mask. 'Boy is a Tainted. He could never have served the realm in life, but at least he can suffer for the greater good.'

Nala was no expert in history. That had been Varcin. But she was aware of how the greatest crimes of antiquity always preceded the phrase 'for the greater good'.

'Are you… torturing a child?' Nala could not believe the words that came out of her mouth.

Parshuram considered Nala, paused briefly, fingering a scroll hidden in the folds of his robe and then grudgingly handed it to her. It wasn't a letter. It was a ballad inked in blood, a list of men and women. The same men and women Nala had caught Parshuram tracking in their journey to build his army. But he wasn't building any army. He was assassinating them.

'The scroll is a list of unnecessary heroes. Men and women who the House of Oracles foresaw as obstacles to the Wheel of Time, the path set out by the Seven for the realm. So, naturally, we could not abide their presence. For the Seven bring peace to this world…

by paving the road for that Wheel, keeping it dull and smooth as a butcher's block.'

Nala read the scroll again, her eyes narrowing with each line. The courtesan would have discovered herself to be a legendary archer, her arrow destined for a king's heart. The old charioteer in the Resht hamlet would have talked his gifted son out of joining the looming great war, altering its course. The Unni Ehtral priest would have reformed his religion. The wolf-soldieress would have saved a mighty swordswoman from a much-needed death. And the little boy moaning beside them – he would have gone on to invent a game. A game that did not involve any wagers, a game that would have gone ahead to replace *Chausar* as the royal pastime of the realm. And Parshuram had slain them all. All but the boy. Yet.

'But...' Nala's heart began to hurt again as she looked at the trader's boy again, 'how could a *game* trouble the Seven? That's a big leap.'

'A butterfly's flap now, a hurricane in the future. Someday you'll see it for yourself.'

'But...' Nala asked, more confused now than she was earlier, 'do the Seven also need you to torture and kill them so?'

'I am not killing him but I am removing what makes him a threat. A Tainted can never learn control of its powers,' Parshuram said. Was use of the slur *Tainted* intentional? A word designed to see the Tainted as things. No doubt it helped his conscience when he maimed them from the inside. 'They are agents of chaos that upset the scales of balance.' There was no inflection in Parshuram's voice, no emotion. 'So, the Tainted need to be purged but... I found another use for them so their worthless lives could find meaning. Once I'm done, it will be returned to his father. It will not grow up to join the Citadel but at least it will live. Not to forget, it doesn't feel pain. It had been numbed all the way to its soul before I started carving it.'

Parshuram approached the trader's boy, sliding a hand under his neck. He lifted his head, turning it cruelly as if he was just a carcass. 'Do you see its nape?' he asked as he pulled the tube out of the boy's neck. Nala didn't want to, but she looked anyway. There, across the back of the boy's head, was a wide cut embellished with congealed blood. It was at the juncture of the spine and the skull. 'Know what this is?' Parshuram asked.

The Eye of Horus, the pituitary gland, the organ responsible for growth. But in the boy, it looked different. Grotesquely different. 'The Horus's Eye in the Tainted are larger,' Parshuram explained as the boy's head thumped back into the chair with a weightfulness that set Nala's bones to quaking. 'You thought the route to immortality was a prayer? No. It lies within a libation.'

'Somras exists!' Nala gasped. The elixir promising immortality remained the most disparaged myth in the realm. 'The Citadel had ever called it a poor metaphor for laced wine.'

'Question your tenets, Nala, the way you questioned mine by barging into this house.'

Nala gulped but pressed on. 'And the way to create somras is... through the neck of the Tainted?' she asked, trying hard not to think who could be so twisted to discover this method the first time.

Parshuram turned to the boy, reattaching the tube into his neck. The boy spasmed a little, before settling into his open-eyed sleep again. 'This is spurious somras. I call it Amrit. Somras binds your flesh to the very age it touches. Amrit grants a fleeting glimpse of youth.'

'Like a fountain of youth from the fables? How did you...?'

Were it in his nature, Parshuram would then have smiled. 'With chemicals, gold and time, an alchemist can make a God beg.'

Spirits forfend. 'Do the Seven know of this?'

'You may have noticed when we were there, I do not get along with all of them. Some used to dangle somras as antidote for the poison of life in front of my eyes. They wanted me to grovel.'

Fat chance of *that* happening. 'So... the courtesan, the charioteer, were they all...'

'No, they were not *Tainted*. And even if they were, they would've served no purpose. The potential in a child's mind is infinite for that is when the Horus's Eye is strongest. It is why the House of Oracles plucks diviners when they're but sprouts. And this is what I need,' he concluded, very softly, 'to stop the Son of Darkness.'

'But you are... Parshuram, the Bane of the Ksharjans. Why do *you* need anything?'

Parshuram offered nothing.

'Alright, last question, Acharya. I am already Vachan bound to obey you. Then why did you not just command me to still my tongue? Why share this secret with me?'

'Because you're my apprentice,' Parshuram said.

'I... I am?' Nala asked, eyes moistening without notice.

'Everyone, even killers, needs someone to trust, don't they? Maybe it is time for me to put my faith in one who managed to track me. I have seen you change in the last weeks, Nala.'

Nala shuddered at that. If Parshuram found out what she was up to...

'The Dance of Shadows is a journey of the self through the self to the self, and on this road, you have gone from howling wind to still mountain. You could not meditate beyond minutes. I found you meditating for hours last morning. You hold your asanas, the grip on your feet is now as strong as your palm, your Chakras are ebbing within you. I left you to fend for yourself, let you wander around unhinged, and you used it to find the freedom in chaos. Free to act, you used your actions to mean something. A mind busy can be a pillar of power, but it is what a mind does when it is idle that builds a roof over the pillars. You, Nala of Valka, deserve to be my student. And who knows? Maybe... just maybe, even a dolt like you can even make my life easier.'

'That is all I want to do, Acharya,' Nala said, eagerly. 'What can I do? Anything!'

'You guard me when I am under. Drinking this reduces me to a catatonic state for hours, hours where I am most vulnerable. An immortal might not age, but he very well can be killed. And... I suspect that is why the Seven do not interfere with this method. I suspect it offers them the window to get rid of rogue Chiranjeevis.'

'Chiranjeevis? Other immortals like you? The Seven assassinate them?'

'Where do you think the rest have disappeared?' Parshuram said. 'The Saptarishis are necessary for the realm, Nala; the Chiranjeevis aren't.'

Nala nodded, absorbing the deluge of secrets. Then she looked up. 'So, if I choose, I can refuse to make myself complicit in this and you won't Vachan me?'

When Parshuram did not answer, Nala knew he meant for her to frame the answer herself. It had been so long since he had done that... Nala was, understandably, giddy. Let's see – a Vachan wasn't a contract to be abused. While it bound her soul to his through obedience, it roped his to hers through the hoops of duty. Repeated use of such a binding would dull the senses. Nala nodded in understanding

'A man might ride his horse from dawn till dusk but he doesn't, does he?' Parshuram said. 'Maybe the terrain is steep and the steed is naught but a husk. Then there is the ache on the cosmic spine, the stalking predators and the worn out chakras. So, no, a man bound by a Vachan doesn't ride all day, for wise men halt along the way.'

The comparison to the horse notwithstanding, Nala was genuinely pleased to be needed again. But she did not let happiness dull the opportunity she had. Parshuram was in the rarest of rare moods of giving answers. Perhaps torture brought out the conversationalist in him – Nala did not care – she was not going to let slip this chance of milking that elusive tonsil. Her fatal mistake, however, lay in the next question she asked.

'Do you truly think the Seven, I mean the Saptarishis, might try to kill you?'

'No,' Parshuram said, his expression darkening. 'But the ones pretending to be the Saptarishis might.'

'What do you mean, Acharya?'

Parshuram's eyes gauged the steel in Nala's nerves, the scrutiny so intimate that she flushed. But Nala squared her shoulders in answer.

'You've given me reason to believe,' Parshuram said, 'that the Saptarishis are all dead.'

'Save me... please,' the boy on the stretcher croaked, spasming again, but Nala found it a lot easier to ignore him this time around, a bone-deep chill awakened in her heart like a gust of surprised breath, her voice brittle with fear.

'The Saptarishis are *what* now?'

TAKSHA

Each year Taksha spent in the cramped cage, he kept his spirits up by imagining it as his childhood nest. The heat from the skinning knives became the comforting warmth of his father's belly keeping him and his siblings alive. The bits of Taksha's scales the slavers neglected to collect became his father's entrails, sheltering them from the cold. If only the bars of the cage had been as rich in marrow as his father's ribs, or better, if only they cracked as delicately in his mouth, he would have freed himself years ago. But all that would change today.

Taksha hadn't quite managed to kill his slaver but he'd certainly aged the bastard by playing dead. The slaver pulled off his mask. Seeing the wrinkled face of his tormentor for the first time in five years, Taksha was disappointed. It was too bland, too ordinary to belong to the man who had flayed him week after week. An irresistible urge to take the slaver down surged. His face was close enough. All he had to do was touch the slaver's face and send him to a world of fire. But by now Taksha was wise enough to know feelings were for fools. *Stick to the plan.* It was his own idea to, as they say in this world, 'play possum' in this little escape scheme. A dangerous idea but an idea can burst through a cage's door only when the fear of death grips its reins. And Taksha felt fear aplenty when the thralls' mitts hauled him out to the floor. Even when they thought him dead, they clung to their gloves lest his 'corpse' illuse them by accident.

He heard the slaver order his thralls to stoke the fire, knowing all too well what would unfold next. But that did not stop his scales from turning to stone. Growing used to being skinned alive was not something practice made perfect.

Taksha's will to live held back his screams at the hot, thick drip of oil against his naked chest. The new thrall's untrimmed nails pricked as he daubed the oil over the green patterns on either side of Taksha's neck and over the iridescent glyphs on Taksha's cheek. By the time the thrall had finished lathering him up, Taksha's scales and skin sizzled with the oil. It smelled vile but it helped in slicing Naga scales from their flesh with surgical precision.

To distract himself, Taksha wondered if he still appeared alien to his new torturer. Nagas did look like Softskins for the most part, only they stood taller than Softskins, with not a single ounce of surplus fat on their bones. Perhaps his emerald skin aglow with the Gehan on his forehead – Taksha's was gold – served as a stark reminder of the chasm between their races. After all, in comparison, Softskins' foreheads were so plain and mundane. And then there were his eyes. To the boring, foolish, round eyes of Softskins, a pair of twin crescent moons could understandably be intimidating. Though not intimidating enough to shake their resolve while skinning him. *Them*, he corrected himself.

Taksha looked at Isshahagezen's lifeless body at the corner for a long time, the scales overgrown at the edges of her eyes. Her blue hair still shone. Taksha remembered she had washed it in the Lake of Glints because she wanted to look nice after sleeping for weeks on their journey to the Surface. It was still the same length it had been when they had left Pataal Lok. As if she had never aged, had never been caged, had never died. As the Stonefang of the Mind, Isshahagezen was to help them all adjust to the Surface World. If something went wrong, if they felt homesick, if they felt the sickness of realm travel, it would have been her duty to talk to them about it and out of it. If only she could have talked herself out of slitting her own throat last night.

A crash and a rattle of iron filled the air. The slaver who had headed over to the far end of the hall to pray to his preferred deity before commencing Taksha's mutilation summoned his thralls over to get their tools blessed by the idol. Taksha had not quite got his head around that. The Softskins fancied their Gods were everywhere and in everything but apparently, they could only be disturbed for a conversation through these manmade contraptions of gold and clay.

In a nearby cage, the bars rattled as Eiccasasthee, one of the older Nagas, shook it, screaming at the slaver to release Taksha. Eiccasasthee's arms, legs and face were all a glistening mass of green muscle, not a single scale or shred of skin left to cover them. After so many skinnings, her skin had stopped moulting, stopped regenerating. The Nagin had been there for nearly ten earth years, twice as long as Taksha. Taksha could barely imagine what that was like but he was determined not to find out. One way or the other.

'Look what you did to him! You got your jackets, your purses, your talismans! And now you have his life, you murderers!' The old Nagin's screams echoed around the cavern, like something trapped. Taksha wondered if the slaver even understood what Eiccasasthee's screams of anguish were about. Eiccasasthee had spent time in Kamrup, a forest-city far to the east that Taksha had never seen, and spoke their oddly seductive tongue. Because Naga refugees leaving their underground realm of Pataal Lok could crawl out of anywhere, in any kingdom, the slave cages were full of Nagas from the Riverlands, from the Forests of the East and even from the Deserts of the West. Over the last five years of his captivity, Taksha had come to know something of all their languages. Eiccasasthee screamed again with zest to keep their attention divided between their God and her screams. Well done, Eiccasasthee!

Though in Eiccasasthee's words of calling Taksha a boy, lay a shard that pierced through, letting loose memories of when he truly was one in spirit and age. Long before the slaver's snare, long before he had burrowed out into this realm, he had served as an apprentice with Ere-Nuruk – the Truthsayer of Pataal Lok – destined to eventually succeed her when he came of age, a fate he had fled with much vigour.

He still remembered the day as if it were yesterday. The Truthsayer, a full head shorter than him, had been chewing her lip in some chagrin. Like Taksha, the glyphs on her cheeks were the colour of copper hued with golden. But they had blazed red then when she had learned Taksha was leaving home. Of motherly love, no traces remained. Though given

*how Taksha had spent the year before training for the mission, studying
Softskin maps, learning the common Sign and saying goodbyes, he had
been surprised that she was surprised. If she had perhaps ever bothered
to listen to his daydreams at the dining table, she might have known of
how Taksha hungered to cross the Arteries, the bridges that swayed like
spidersilk between the two realms, the underground realm of Pataal Lok
and the surface world of Prithvi. Of how Taksha hungered to see the
rumoured blue skies of the Surface World with their one giant Sun, of
seeing Softskin towers that touched those skies. Of how Taksha believed
that his friends and he would be the ones to find the Messiah and bring
him back to save their dying realm.*

*'You are running away,' she had hissed. 'Abandoning us all here to go
on your merryride while we all melt away to grotesque shells of what we
were. You're supposed to help!'*

*When his mother had accused him so, he had seethed, he had taken
offence, as if the accusation from his mother had somehow tainted his
resolve. Did she not understand? It was only a matter of time before the
last Sol died and Pataal froze.*

*'Pataal Lok is dead, Aayi,' Taksha had said, 'we don't even have
enough Softskins for our spawns to grow in. Only chance we have is to
find the Messiah...'*

*'Not that prophecy foolishness, again. The star-touched Messiah who
is supposed to end the dominion of mankind with his gilded gaze, the
D'rahi-slayer who will return the Nagas to the Surface! Redblood fantasies! Prophecies are the drug of the commons. You are a Zephyr! Do
you truly believe that some Messiah, wearing the charred skull of a baby
D'rahi around his neck, will come to our rescue? How can he be drenched
in D'rahi blood if they are charred, eh? Ask yourself these questions!
Where will he find baby D'rahis if they're extinct, Taksha? How will one
mortal ever slay a grown D'rahi?'*

'Maybe some D'rahis survived on the Surface.'

'If they had, Softskins would not be the ones ruling the Surface.'

*Taksha had remained defiant. 'The Messiah was to rise when the last
light winked out.' Taksha pointed at the flickering Sol in the rock ceiling
that was their sky. 'Last light?'*

*'I wish your brother had been executed before he sowed your mind
with such foolishness.'*

Taksha, a veteran at ignoring his mother's acid tongue, tried another tact. 'Listen, Ere-Nuruk, I vow to wind my quest and return in a week. I told you we have the number—'

'A week on the Surface World equals a year here! You know how time marches to a different beat...'

'And Nagas slither on for centuries. Your point?' Taksha remembered how he had dramatically swept his hand toward the desolate road and the ruined houses, their windows like eyes in a skull. 'See what Pataal Lok's become, Truthsayer...' he gentled his voice, not wanting to hurt her, not when this was already so hard, 'it is a memory, and memories of the past do not ever turn into visions of the future, not if we just bask here in darkness while the last Sol dies. And there are so many commons who left Pataal in the centuries past who must be living there. Now you know those commons can't find their way back without the guidance of a Gehan. If they could, I am sure they would have told us of the riches to be found there. For all I know they have already found the Messiah and are biding their time for a Zephyr to lead them back home. And it is high time a Zephyr answered this call. And have the number!'

'Takshaimai the Oathless,' she had spat, taking a step away from him. 'That's what you will be now known as. Just like your brother. I care not for your vow or your number. Don't come back. Begone.'

Taksha had just shaken his head. In training for this mission, Taksha and the other Zephyrs had gone over the possibility of them finding the Messiah on the Surface World. It was as close to nil a number as one can get without it being futile but it was still a high enough number that a few hopeful Nagas and Nagins joined forces to find the Messiah. That tiny number used to fill them with the Tangle, the aching eagerness, the pulsing hope, the hope that they would be the ones to save their dying world.

His vow to his mother lay unfulfilled, of course. And he doubted she cared any longer given how a Naga captured by the slaver last night confessed to them that Pataal Lok had suffocated in darkness and ice after its sole surviving Sol had shimmered for the last time. His mother was heard to have been torn apart by disgruntled devout in the days leading to the doom, and the rest of the Zephyrs had simply disappeared. Isshahagezen had not taken the news well and had taken her life shortly after while Taksha had slept. How she managed to get her hands on a glass shard was something neither the slaver nor Taksha had been able to figure out.

While Isshahagezen had been busy slitting her throat, Taksha had been dreaming violently of a life wasted, which was keenly similar to what he had felt awake when he had heard the news of his mother's death. It had felt like he'd spent his whole time on the Surface in exile in this cage, away from the hero he was supposed to be. And to think he was now homesick. Homesick for what? Homesick for a home he'd deliberately left, homesick for a home that had mummified.

No. Taksha was not going to let this be the end.

There was something about the death of loved ones, the grief for the lost places of your past, that slipped reckless courage into your resolve, and if there was one thing Taksha knew, it was how to devise suicidal escape plans. It was this courage that made him bear the scald of the hot oil. It would be this courage that would help him escape.

He cracked his eyes open just enough to check. The slaver and his lackeys were still clustered around their idols, backs turned and hopefully oblivious. The prayers had reached a crescendo, loud and deafening with bells and chants. This was Taksha's cue to escape. No one truly bothers about the deceased slithering about, and any faint noises he made would surely be swallowed by the chants.

The key was patience. Taksha finally opened the pockets in his flesh and took in the first breath of the day. The air stank with the smell of the skinning oil but the same oil on his scales made it easier to slither on the cave floor, silent and unseen. All he had to do was get to the other side of the door and lock the slaver inside. He knew the guards outside did not wear gloves or wear masks. Illusing them would come easy. What he'd do after? Well, that could wait until he was out. After a subjective week and an objective thirty seconds, his head bumped against wood.

The door!

Taksha climbed slowly and cast one last glance back at the cages of Nagas stacked in rows that disappeared into the darkness where the slaver was still praying. He was just turning to open the door, ready to be the hero the Nagas needed, when the door burst open, slamming his nose and sending him flying. Stunned, breath driven from his lungs, Taksha collapsed in a heap. He could not think, just blinked, his hands on his face, his fingers wet with the blood leaking from his nostrils, his plan in ruins.

Once caught by the slaver, Taksha would no longer need to pretend to be a corpse given he would be turned into one expeditiously. Taksha was not good with weapons but even if he were, he wouldn't stand a chance in a duel against the slaver. Taksha had witnessed first-hand the slaver cut down five Naga guards when they had tried to protect their reservation in the Khandava Jungles. If only Taksha could touch the bare skin of the slaver, he wished for the thousandth time, his illusions might buy him time. But that was wishful thinking. To let a Naga touch their bare skin would be an open invitation to madness, and so, the slaver and his staff dressed appropriately for office. Long gloves and long sleeves and long masks with narrow openings for their eyes and mouths. But who was it who ruined his plans?

He looked up to see an armoured figure of a half-giantess at the door. Deep red dripped from the woman's aura and Taksha could almost smell the coppery tang of blood from her. Certainly not one of the guards. The slaver only hired men, and Taksha noted the lumps on her chest armour and the short seat of her trousers. Her face caught the subdued light of the cell. A few wisps of long silver hair that had escaped from her raised hood snaked across her face. To Taksha, the face within that cowl was as brown as dried blood, like a corpse dragged from a cinnabar mine. Two baldrics criss-crossed her chest, each supporting a sword. Well, one sword now. The other, unsheathed, was in her hand, its blade dripping with gore. She flicked that sword, and a neat line of crimson splattered against the wall, leaving the blade spotless.

'Manners maketh murderers,' the slaver said from beyond as he inched closer. Taksha heard the sounds of more swords being unsheathed.

The woman grinned, revealing teeth dyed black, making it look like she had bitten off a D'rahi. Taksha hadn't met many humans but he was sure none of them had painted teeth. She clapped her hands and made a guttural sound, causing the slaver to chuckle.

'You're a mute,' the slaver scoffed. 'Sorry, lass, I don't speak clown. And the one who did is dead.' He turned his gaze to where Taksha should have been, and then at the door where Taksha was. 'Apologies. I meant he will be dead. For now, he would help translate, wouldn't he?'

Taksha nodded, shaking. Sign was the first human language he had learned for the mission before even entering this realm. The woman did not even look at Taksha and signed again at the slaver. Taksha was chilled as he turned those vicious signs in the air into words.

'Rahath Al Verna, for the crimes of raping my sisters and choking their children to death, I sentence you to torment. You have the right to draw your sword. But…' Taksha trailed off.

The slaver barked. 'But what, reptile?'

'It won't help,' Taksha translated.

The slaver turned to the woman. 'Which sisters? Which children? You will have to be specific,' the slaver raised his sword, laughing as he waved his thralls forward, 'but… it won't help. I won't remember them.' He scoffed.

The left thrall's eyes were on the unsheathed sword of the woman. His weapon was halfway out of its scabbard when the woman's sheathed sword flashed clear with a keening sound and opened the thrall's throat. Taksha watched the thrall crumple to the ground, a big red hole in his trachea spurting blood like a case of bad shits.

But the woman pressed forward. Parried a thrust from the slaver with one sword only to trap his blade between her two swords, sliding her swords on his blade, drawing it leftward, before a flick of her wrist tore the slaver's sword from his hand. Taksha gasped.

The new thrall buckled back in fear against the cages but a leg kicked out, tripping the thralls, and the chains of imprisonment rattled. Eiccasasthee's hand snaked between the bars, her long elbow wrapping around the boy's neck and pulling it against the bars. Legs thrashed, hands clawed and arms thrashed but Eiccasasthee did not relent till she tore off his mask and touched his bare face. The thrall's struggles ceased, his mind lost in an illusion of pain.

As for the slaver, he turned, perhaps to pick up another weapon but the woman almost lazily severed his spine at the base. He fell to his knees, screaming, stopping only when the woman came in front of him, her face inches away from his until recognition finally seeped in the slaver's eyes. 'I know them! I know them! I see your face in them! But I did not even touch them! I was just the lookout, there to steal things and—'

The woman made another series of signs, and glanced once at Taksha. Taksha nodded. 'You choked their babies from crying and alerting the guards. Your friend, Badran Swarup, confessed before he met justice.'

'Badran? He... he is lying! He!' The slaver whimpered. 'They asked me to—'

Before he could even finish his words, the woman punched him in the gut. The man coughed out when the woman entered her hand, knuckle deep in his mouth. Using the slain thrall's blood on her wrist as lubrication, the woman's fingers slithered deep. Taksha gulped at seeing the impression of her hand on his throat. The slaver's arms flailed wildly, punching at the woman's legs, biting her hand but it did not help. The woman drove her hand deeper, applying more pressure even as the flesh in the corners of the slaver's mouth tore. The slaver tried to punch upwards now but with his spine severed, there was no strength left in his bones. The skin on his face continued to rip until the woman's hand was wrist-deep inside.

The slaver's body spasmed. Puke began to trickle out of his nose when the woman, lifting her other hand, took her thumb and index finger to grab the nose. She twisted it sideways, breaking the bone in it to clog his nostrils with blood and pain, and block any release for

the vomit in him. Taksha could almost imagine the woman's fingernails scraping past the slaver's uvula and dipping into the sloshing
vomit in the back of his throat. The slaver gagged and choked on
the woman's fist and his own vomit for a long time before falling
limp. The woman pulled her bile- and blood-drenched fist out of
the slaver's mouth and wiped it on his robes.

'Are you quite done, Lady Ajath?' Another man stepped into
view, a floating orb of light hovering over his hand. A man the
Softskins would call old, by looking at the colour of his beard and
the lines on his face, stood at the doorway. Old he may be, but
he looked well built for someone with that white a beard. Elegant
strands of grey twisted through the black hair on his head which he
wore long, matted and tied in an Acharya's bun. Clad in loose grey
robes over which he wore a one-shouldered orange shawl, his attire
lacked embroidery or jewels but the conceit of modesty was belied
by the topaz rings on his fingers.

As if sensing his scrutiny, the old man looked down from his
conversation with the mute warrior and let the orb float over to
wash Taksha in light. His gaze met Taksha's, and he smiled. The
half-giantess suddenly clapped her hands and jerked her thumb to
the cage where even now Eiccasasthee was freeing herself using the
key she had pilfered from the thrall she had illused.

'We can't free you all, alas,' the old man said. The primary colour
of the wisps around his aura was a beautiful saffron that spoke only
of a sense of duty. 'The economy run here is worth a mansion of
sovereigns, and it will attract too much attention. A dead slaver can
be written off by the Sindh Guild. Not a contingent.'

The old man spoke in Sanskrit and so Eiccasasthee did not
understand. Taksha did. 'Please,' Taksha said, sparing a glance at
the cages. 'The Nagas deserve freedom. Your mercy. Their miracle.'

'Miracles have nothing to do with mercy or merit, young snakeling.' The old man surprised Taksha by speaking in fluent Angami,
the Naga language. 'And we are on a quest where distractions simply
won't do.' He looked at the dead slaver. 'Apart from the occasional
bout of vengeance, I suppose.'

The half-giantess gestured in Sign. '*Can we just take the one you
want to use and make off?*' she said, staring at the spasming young

thrall on the floor. '*What about this old woman? She looks pureborn, a Zephyr.*'

'*Can you refrain from sabotaging my schemes?*' the old man signed back. '*The woman is good but look at her. A Naga catches eyes but a skinned Naga like her will definitely paint a target on our backs. We can't afford distractions. So no, she won't serve.*'

'*I hope you know this one understands Sign,*' Ajath said, unanimated, pointing her finger at Taksha.

The old man cut his gaze to Taksha. For a moment he stared, his eyes widening. 'Impressive for just a spawn,' he spoke in Angami as he brought himself down to Taksha's level, offering him a kerchief to wipe the blood off his nose. He lifted a hand to gesture in Sign to explain. '*This is the Silent Tongue. An ancient art, mandatory to learn in the First Two Ages, now a dead language. Who cares about conversations with mutes after all. And other races can do well to learn our language if they wish to speak to us. Tch. Tch. Such arrogance will be our downfall.*' The old man sighed, as if burdened. He switched to Sanskrit. 'So, pardon my assumption that you did not know the language. I have a proposition for you, snakeling.'

'But first, illuse me,' he said, as he touched Taksha's bare hand. 'Have to confirm whether you are truly a Zephyr from the Underworld? You know how to illuse, don't you?'

At last, a word from Taksha's own tongue.

A word that only made him sad for his brood.

Taksha's ancestors could change their shapes, gift dreams, weave illusions – even their spit had temporary healing powers – such was their power, but no longer. Most of these powers had rusted over generations.

Taksha knew how to illuse though, knew the way to channel paintings into the eyes of Softskins. He had learned it in training but he was never supposed to be the one using it. Isshahagezen was both the defender and illuser of their company. The rest of them were only trained in the art of Illuse in case she… Isshahagezen should have been the one. The thought stammered in his head till he closed his eyes. He was here now. There was no turning back. And hadn't he planned to illuse the guards in the first place? Surely this was simpler. The thought to blind the old man and make a run for it did cross his mind but he had a feeling the size of his female companion was no obstacle to her speed. So, grudgingly, he obliged the old man by touching his face.

'Bless the miracle of stumbling upon a Naga fluent in both Sanskrit and the Silent Tongue and the illuse,' the old man said, beaming once Taksha had withdrawn his hand. The old man had a pleasant melodic voice and he said the words as if genuinely meaning it. 'Perhaps merit has something do with miracles.'

'What is that ball of light you entered with?'

'Oh, this old thing,' he said as he drew a rune in the air and conjured an orb of light in the air. Gasps from the cages. 'I am good with Light. Though all it is useful for now is acting as lanterns, given how Elementals are extinct. Enough about me. Come, let us help free your snake-friends.'

'You'll help, yourself? Where slaves?' Taksha asked, in broken Sanskrit.

'Slaves?'

'You know, to carry palanquin. I think you orange-robed men didn't have feet.' Taksha remembered the manual well. He was supposed to be respectful towards high-caste humans, especially the ones who called themselves male, as they were by nature primed towards overreaction. But Taksha was past caring.

The old man laughed. 'I fancy walking. It is good for the constitution. Almost a Blue in that manner,' he said and chuckled at his own jape. 'And I do not like a crowd. The lady by my side is pleasant company enough.' It was a lie. Taksha reckoned the old man was travelling alone because he didn't want anyone to know he was here. Well, that made sense given his silent companion was fond of choking people to death with her fist.

'You not say who you are,' Taksha said.

'I am Acharya Vyas of the Orange Order, Teacher of Lore in the Citadel of Meru and Keeper of the Light for the Saptarishis.' They all used titles like that, and his title meant as little as the ones he'd heard before.

'I supposed to understand all that?'

'Well, if I managed to impress you with my credentials,' Vyas said dryly, 'it would have saved us so much time.' He flashed that smile again. Taksha wasn't used to nice Softskins and he was having a hard time trusting this man out of sheer instinct. 'But to simplify it, I am a man who is well read,' he paused to stare into Taksha's eye so his meaning couldn't be missed, '... quite well read about *what you are.*'

'What you want from me, old man?'

'Perhaps we could start with respect,' Vyas said, teasingly, 'but that does seem unlikely.'

'Highly. What do you want from me?'

'No scales, no skins, no gems,' Vyas said with a theatrical shudder. 'I have a task for you with a reward at the end. In addition to, of course, releasing all your friends and dropping them off in the Naga Reservations. It falls on the way. All I need from you is your company on a noble quest.' When Vyas saw Taksha exchange a look with Myrrhan, who shook her head, he hastily added, 'Just you. Too many Nagas would—'

'Paint a target on your back. Yes, I heard. But what noble quest this?'

Vyas wagged a finger. 'The first question should've been: *what do I get in return?*'

'What do I get in return?'

'The Messiah.'

Taksha's blood chilled despite the heat of the scalping oil on his scales. 'You know the Messiah!?'

'We too hold such a prophecy among the race of Men. Only we call our Messiah the Son of Darkness. He is *our* saviour as well.'

The half-giantess flinched behind Vyas but Taksha ignored her. He bowed deeply instead. He had found his Tangle back.

'My will, yours to sharpen. Who we fight?'

'Your mortal enemy. The ancestor of Jatayus. A D'rahi.'

Taksha wanted to jump in the air! He knew the D'rahis were still alive. His mother had been wrong! The slaver had been wrong! Taksha had come to this realm with hope, in search of the light at the end of the tunnel, but what no one had told him was someone had to be there to hold up that light for you to see the path. After years of darkness, someone was finally holding a lantern.

'I speak now,' Taksha said once he had recovered from his fantasies, 'I help but I doubt swords she wields or my illusions will be of any help 'gainst a D'rahi. Legends say tribes lost, entire, in slaying a D'rahi—'

'Which is why our next stop is to assemble us an army,' Vyas cut in. 'Oh, don't look at me like that. A small one,' Vyas hastily added. 'Don't be so dramatic. By the way, am I pronouncing it right? My Angami is rusty. *Dhi-ra-hi*, correct?'

'You can use Sanskrit, Acharya. I understand it,' Taksha said, and then blinked in embarrassment. 'But I... not know word for D'rahi in the soft tongue.'

'They bear many names. The Matriarchs of Manipur worship them as *Kanglā shā*, the Meitei of the East hail them as *Taoro Inai*, but in the common tongue, they are called,' Vyas pronounced it slowly for Taksha to remember, 'Dragons.'

NALA

I

By now, they had bid farewell to three pairs of horses, two carts and a score of caravanserais. The map marked them at the border of the Khandava Woods, the grandest uncharted jungles of the Riverlands. A highway traced along the edge of these treacherous woods. It was peppered with safe zones courtesy of the Blind King. A popular highway. So, naturally, Parshuram steered clear of it in favour of the mule path through the jungle, shaving hours off their journey at the cost of their safety.

'This used to be the home of Valkans, didn't it, Nala?' Masha asked.

Nala nodded. 'Once, our ancestors thrived in these cold lands before we became people of the humid South. But now, the Khandava exists only in our memories. They've become the refuge for the Shedskin, sent by the Hastina Union to settle in our territory. How did the Union phrase it when they relocated these Shedskins here? *"A home without a people for a people without a home."* Little did anyone realize when the refugees turned into rulers.'

Masha hugged Nala from the back on their horse. 'I'm sorry to hear that, Nala. My father once told me a similar tale of our people. But I barely remember it now.'

Nala found herself turning away but her memory still migrated to her ancestors, wondering how no one had intervened when the Shedskins victimized the Valkans simply because they themselves were victims once. Just then the sounds of movement through the bushes distracted her. Just unseen animals fleeing their onward march, she concluded. *Much like the rest of humanity now, without the Seven Saptarishis to shepherd them.*

Nala dismissed the goosebumps with a brisk shiver. No sense in fretting over a suspicion she could barely comprehend. Denial seemed so much more comfortable. At least until Parshuram fleshed his suspicion with bones and blood. The man might have begun to trust her but that did not mean he was comfortable in gossiping with her. *Parshuram gossiping*, Nala chuckled at the thought. But how in the world did Nala give Parshuram any cause to believe the Seven were dead? What did she do? *No.* She wouldn't get lost in these murky waters again to no avail. He would tell her soon. *Bide your time.* She returned her mind to the jungles.

The only silver lining to the ill-advised jungle trek was Nala's escape from Masha's chatter. Masha was too occupied with quaking at the slightest rustle, of which there was no dearth in the forest. For this blessed silence, Nala owed a debt to the mendicants who had passed them in the caravanserais earlier. When questioned about the Khandava, each of them had plied Masha with myths of malevolent spirits. Thanks to them, the shrill trill of cicadas became the screams of trapped children and the hoots of owls took on the howls of wolfmen. Tales meant for nursery frights, but unfortunately, from a maturity standpoint, Masha was still a child.

So, it was completely understandable when three days into the forest, when a big brown beast suddenly appeared before Masha, she promptly fainted. Nala burst out laughing, an unkind act that reaped the seeds it sowed. For, the shadow of the hound's master grew on her, and a man from Nala's past emerged from the thicket, clad in the shawl of the Orange Order. Something unravelled in her, something that shouldn't have. A stitch come undone.

'No longer masquerading as a boy, splendid, splendid,' the man said, stroking his chest-long greyish white beard. A low whistle called the hound back to his side. 'Though I daresay Meru's library does miss your unsanctioned shuffling in the afterhours,' he said, giving the hound's ears a friendly scratch.

A statuesque, armoured woman with black-dyed teeth sauntered past. She gently propped Masha up and used her waterskin to sprinkle water on Masha's face.

'And of course, the youngest Sister in the history of Meru,' the old man spoke as Masha came around. 'It is my honour to meet you, Sister Masha. I am Acharya Vyas of the First Order,' he flashed a grin in Nala's direction, 'Nala's former teacher from the Citadel of Meru.'

II

Reluctantly, Nala trailed Parshuram, Vyas and Masha as they made their way to Vyas's camp. In a picturesque clearing filled with the smell of campfires and wood smoke, box wagons were arranged in a half-circle to form a cosy picnic. The sight of her old teacher had unnerved her. Nala's mind — against her will — went to her friends. She wondered if Varcin ever grew the moustache he wanted to or if Upavi's fear of turning bald ever came true. She remembered some of their last words to her, their smile of promise. They would be all apprentices now, and if they were to ever meet again, if she was granted that grace, she was sure she would meet them in chains, caged as a murderer. There was nothing Nala could do to fight the emotion that threatened to drown her in a swell. So Nala took a deep breath and packed it away, setting it aside for later. *I can't right now. I don't have the strength.* She looked around instead to distract herself with Vyas's entourage.

The men-at-arms around the wagons uncoiled a supply of neck in their direction, wary at first, amused later given how Masha cheerfully waved at them as if they had shared dormitories just the week before. A plump woman, her hair tied in a bun, hobbled over to them and offered two bowls of soup, though not before first sampling the contents herself.

'Good, still hot! Don't give their stares no mind, Holy Sister. They all are good men and women on the inside, even if it be a little too inside to make it out to the sun. Have this. It is Acharya Vyas's recipe, made of bloodraven seeds and is absolutely divine. Pity the Acharya has a case of the squats and can't sip his own wonder.'

Vyas and Parshuram stepped away to talk, while the woman led Masha into the camp to sit by the fire. Just as Nala was preparing to make her excuses to sit elsewhere, a shimmer of light caught her eye.

The green armour beneath their tattered cloaks looked strangely reptilian. Scales seemed to be drawn on their emaciated forearms and on their bony faces. Strange patterned tattoos ran down the lengths of their weathered cheeks except... they were not tattoos. When Nala recognized what they were, she bolted out like a horrified hen to warn Parshuram.

Nala heard the Acharya before she saw him. Curiosity turned her legs to lead and her ears to an elephant's. She had always been able to listen to the winds, and hear the words they carried, a secret she had not let slip to the Acharya. Not yet. It was, after all, his own lesson: never reveal the hidden dagger until your arms are twisted. So, with reckless abandon, Nala used the 'dagger' to prise open the wind and eavesdrop.

'You have what we need?' she heard Parshuram ask.

'Someone from the Third Order waits for us and has secured the pathway to Iyran Machil.'

Third Order. That meant the Blue Order of Pathfinders who draw map routes across the realm. Acharya Irum from Meru often scoffed that Acharyas who trained to be Pathfinders were more interested in intoxication than insights.

Nala peeped from behind a cart and saw Parshuram frowning. 'I have need of only a Pathfinder. You and your companions will burden me.'

'Respectfully, Acharya,' Vyas bowed again, 'it was not a suggestion but a direction I received from the Saptarishis.' Nala was in awe of how the expression on Parshuram did not falter an inch at the mention of his possibly dead employers. 'And if I may add, only prudent. It was your letter which informed us a dragon guards the Manusruti and the Prophecy in Iyran Machil. We need all the shields we can muster without causing a stir. More bodies also mean more legs to trot about and cover ground.'

Manusruti? What were these two talking about? She knew the Manu-smriti were the Codes of Law that were followed by the Riverlands but what was Manu-sruti? *Bide your time, Nala.*

'Fine,' Parshuram growled. 'Have you told them of who I am and what are we here for?'

'You were the bait I used to lure them,' Vyas said, smirking.

'Good. Saves me from the hassle of pretence.'

'You should be grateful I ran into Lord Chalakkha. Minor Eastern Lord serving as an envoy in the Empire's Court. Sent as a decoy to the Conclave on land while the Crown Prince travels to the Tree Cities on sea. I manipulated him into convincing me that he would serve the Emperor better by bringing him dragon eggs to challenge the griffin in Mathura. He volunteered his soldiers, and I did this without spending a single copper of the Seven.'

'I'm proud of you,' Parshuram said, not meaning a word of it.

Vyas scowled. 'But I did not reveal what is the charge of our quest. They seem to believe it is ancient records, and I have let them content themselves with that. What? It isn't as if I lied. The Prophecy is "ancient" and technically a "record". I am a man of morals, unlike your pupil who seems to think eavesdropping on an Acharya of the Red Order is wise. Oh, Nala, old habits die hard, eh?'

Spirits take me! Turning to Parshuram, Vyas continued, 'He, I mean, she and her friend, Varcin, were notorious students of their batch. Come here, Nala.'

Nala was not going to lie to herself. She did not want to. Over the last few months, Nala felt she had grown into the skin of Parshuram's apprentice but the sudden encounter with Vyas had flayed it off her flesh as if she were a fraud. You can never fully be comfortable as an adult before someone who'd seen you grow as a child. Only by scratching her healing arm bloody did Nala muster the resolve to walk again.

'Come, come, Nala. Look at you. Your muscles would make your Valkan tribesmen proud. Look at your arm! Bandaged just like in the days of Irum. How many Chakras has the revered Acharya coaxed Awake in you? Or are you already harnessing power from your Affinity Chakra to Turn?' Vyas shot a glance at Parshuram as if to impart, *I have heard unproven theories that women find it simpler to Attune than men.*

Nala, feeling a touch bashful, cast her eyes downwards. While Nala was grateful to Vyas for not bringing up her dead family, she still felt embarrassed about having not much to show for the last few months in terms of Chakra and Awakening.

'Oh,' Vyas said when he understood and then, perhaps remembering the devastating weight of an 'Oh', amended hastily, 'Not to worry, child. Look at the forest around us. So dense, filled with dangers of all kinds. There seems no way out. But with the right guide, we will emerge into civilization soon enough. In the same vein, you have the finest guide the world has ever witnessed when it comes to the forest inside you. The only one I know who can Turn three Chakras.'

'The only one?' Nala asked.

'Well, not the only one,' Vyas said. 'Mrytun Jay…'

Parshuram's jaw stiffened.

Vyas, unmindful, continued. 'Mrytun Jay, a name in the Old Tongue. Roughly translates to He Who Enslaved Death or, as the Seven called him, the Reaper. Mrytun Jay was a title bestowed by your dear old teacher on his favourite student, a name well deserved and regrettably, well earned. Before he profaned his bow with the blood of innocents, Mrytun Jay had been a warrior without peer. That was no man to jape with. You only had to look at him to know he had more cruelty in his eyes than all the Ksharjans combined. Perhaps no Paladin other than the Acharya here could have stood against him at his full strength, and it was the Acharya himself who brought Mrytun Jay to heel. And—' Vyas stopped, finally aware of the doors he had opened when Parshuram's silence turned solid. 'Forgive me, Acharya, if I spoke of things best left unsaid. I know how memories can be slippery slopes to despair.'

Parshuram shrugged.

'I digress, of course,' Vyas said in a sad attempt to change the course of the flood. 'Acharya Parshuram is notorious for his Third Eye. The manner in which he's Attuned it affords him kinetic vision, um, the ability to see energy currents and foresee the attacks of his adversaries.'

'Is *that* what the Third Eye does?' Nala asked Parshuram, her two eyes wide.

'Different ascetics have reported different experiences,' Vyas answered when Parshuram didn't. 'Seeing new colours, identifying the horns of a rainbow, and those like Parshuram can see the ebb and flow of energy itself. He simply bent it to the craft of war and I daresay, it served him well in the first wave of the pogrom he wrought against the Ksharjans.'

Nala now desperately wanted to steal the Hashayne and then pore over the White Almanac to find a way to explode her Third Eye open. The urge was intense, but she fought it. She could ill afford a Hashayne fit now, not with so many around in close quarters, and especially not with Vyas, who somehow always seemed to know in Meru when Nala was up to some mischief. Later at night, then? Perhaps. Her fits always came deferred and delayed making it impossible for her to predict their timing but when everyone was asleep, a few frantic twitches and some bloodletting would not disturb anyone's dreams.

'It was not a pogrom,' Parshuram said.

'Your entire Red Order was built on the dead bodies you piled up in that war.'

'The Red Order was built to defend, not... destroy.' Parshuram cocked an eye at Vyas. 'You speak as if you have not killed in the past?'

'Well... not *directly*. And I bathed in the Ganga river to ritually cleanse myself of my sins. The Seven took me in then. And they will do the same with you, Acharya. You should have been one of the Seven like your father before you.'

Parshuram spat on the side to show what he thought of that. 'The ritual is hogwash.'

'So? A religion without rituals is a book without margins,' Vyas said, and then gave up with an exasperated sigh. 'Why am I wasting my breath?'

'I was wondering the same thing,' Parshuram replied, looking condescendingly at Vyas's orange shawl. 'Along with wondering why are you accompanying us on this quest. Sometimes I think you belong in the Blue Order, Vyas. You like walking around way too much for a Namin.'

Vyas shrugged. 'To define is to limit, Acharya.'

'I apologize, Nala,' Vyas said, turning to her. 'We are old friends, and if allowed to bicker, even the stars will grow weary of us. Did you have something to say?'

Nala nodded as she stepped on the other side of Parshuram and whispered, 'Acharya, there is a Shedskin, I mean, Naga in their group. Nagas, rather. A small legion of Nagas!'

'So?' Parshuram asked.

Now that it was asked this way, Nala did not have an answer that did not seem laced with prejudice. 'I don't think they can be trusted.'

'The Bane of Ksharjas, as I live and breathe,' wheezed a puffing figure who staggered into view, 'I am Lord Chalakkha, Eastern Envoy of the Empire, sponsor of this noble quest. And I, for one, am entirely in accord with the sentiment of your pupil.' The years, clearly spent in the lap of luxury, had not been kind to the girth of the Eastern Envoy of the Empire. His black hair streaked with grey seemed to have retreated at an alarming pace, while his whiskers were salted white on a jowly chin.

Parshuram did not merit that with a response but Chalakkha continued. 'A travesty, I say, with respect of course. There is one of those snakelings in want of alms every way you turn in the woods, and blast it, even outside. Now with these many new scales to throw into their mix, they will only add to the woes of the realm. Half of those Acharya Vyas freed congregated at dusk, not dawn like civilized people, but dusk to sing prayers to the earth, and the way they were crying and talking to the soil, I wasn't sure if they were thanking their God for their freedom or complaining at the plight of what their freedom entails.'

'Unbound necks feel the chafe of shackles long after they are gone, Lord Chalakkha,' Vyas said. 'They need time.'

'Oh, it is easy to be so pious when you retire to your home in the peaks while commonfolk like us have to contend with them in our streets and sleep with one eye open.' But even as Chalakkha lodged that protest, Vyas called out.

'Taksha, come here. There is someone I would like you to meet.'

The Naga followed by Masha approached them warily as if it was Nala who was the one with the poisonous fangs for teeth. Nala felt a surge of hate rise in her. She had never lived in Khandava but the sheer presence of an outsider sparked an inherent sense of certainty in her that she belonged to this land. Nala had never been patriotic growing up but maybe because Matre believed in it so passionately or maybe because she was tired of how the Hastina Union ripped what they wanted from her, she saw Taksha as nothing but a trespasser.

Nala couldn't stop staring at him. The scales, a burst of brilliant gold, made her skin crawl.

'Acharya!' Masha beamed as fresh as a cut watermelon. 'A real Naga! Look! Don't you think he looks beautiful, Acharya?' Masha traced her fingers on his scales and Taksha so tickled, chuckled.

Acharya Parshuram appeared hesitant to set himself as a judge of male beauty. He made a noise like a horse choking on a cauliflower but refused to commit himself further. Nala on the other hand felt… angry.

Taksha bowed and raised his hand to Nala in a shake. 'I'm Taksha.' He smiled.

'Is that your real name?' Masha asked. 'It is a Sanskrit name!'

'I am not certain you would be able to pronounce my Naga name.'

'Oh, I would! Tell us!' Masha asked, unable to stop herself, eager to hear the Naga tongue.

Taksha nodded, and spoke. At least Nala thought he spoke.

It was a deep and guttural word that wormed its way into her ears and made her almost gasp. Masha held her chest and took short, quick breaths. 'That is your name!'

'Yes,' Taksha said. 'Apologies. Our language… is not the same as yours.'

'On second thoughts, Taksha is a wonderful name!'

'I'm a Valkan,' Nala introduced herself by interrupting Masha.

'Nice meet you, Valkan,' Taksha said, with a strange accent.

'I am called Nala. I *am* a Valkan. You know, the nation of Valkans – born when the rot of Nagas disfigured our society in the very jungle where you stand.'

Taksha exchanged a confused look with Vyas but Nala pressed on, all that frustration within her finally finding an outlet. 'Oh, you don't understand, do you? Do I need to enlighten you on how you spawns left your home in swarms, pushing into ours, till the largest forest in the realm became too small for the Valkans to stay. Do you remember now?'

'Nala, that is not—' Vyas began to explain but Vyas was her teacher no longer. She spoke over him.

'What is worse is you turned our tragic memory of being forced out of our home into some noble crusade. No, Masha, don't stop me!'

'But I will! We saw humans amongst them in the Naga camps up north, did we not?' Masha shrieked. By now the other Nagas had begun to emerge out of the carriages behind. 'See, they could live together, couldn't they? There must have been reasons why the Valkans and the Nagas could not stay together. There— What? Why is everyone staring at me?'

None said a word. Nala only smiled viciously.

Vyas finally spoke.

'The humans in those Naga Reservations are condemned criminals from Hastina, Sister Masha,' Vyas said, 'condemned to serve as hosts for the Nagas to breed their spawns.'

'Not hosts,' Taksha said sharply. 'Fathers. I forget not how my father made a nest out of himself. A nice parent. My father's remains fed me and gave me strength to emerge into the world. It was his remains I used to fight my siblings in his body. I survived on his carcass. Those Softskins are fathers. Not hosts.'

There went Masha's dream.

'You see now, Masha,' Nala said. 'Even today, we Valkans are expected to be happy with our exile to the fringe forests outside the Empire. We are to smile at being outcasts while these Nagas show no remorse for their trespass. Look at him! This one even pretends he does not know what I speak of! I am so weary of Hastina!'

'I think you are digressing a little, Nala,' Parshuram said, amused.

'No, I am not! The plays, the scrolls all exalt the Hastina Union for finding the displaced Nagas a home. What about the people the Nagas displaced? The very people these Nagas pillaged were the first ones who had welcomed them with nothing but a smile.' Nala scoffed. 'Mark my words, Taksha! Beware Hastina hospitality! They burn all who they invite to their hearth, and it will be no different for you, you homeless Shedskins.'

Taksha glanced back at the crestfallen faces of his kin lining up behind him. 'Lady Nala,' Taksha said, drawing a deep breath. 'You understand Sign?'

Nala said nothing, but with his fingers Taksha still exploded, *'You speak of claims and losses but my reality was of chains and longing. I know not much of what you say, given I was captured by your kind the moment I arrived and was then held in a cage for half a decade. Do you have any inkling what your kind did to my kin all these years? They skinned us alive, over and over, year after year. So forgive me if I cannot weep for the loss of your Tangle. But if your people did not fight for your home when it was overrun, maybe you deserved to lose it.'*

'Curious thing to be said by a *refugee* with no home left behind to speak of—'

Nala was probably on the point of explaining her insult when Taksha, injudiciously, got Nala in the right eye with a rather nice blow. After that, things got a bit mixed. Nala remembered putting what she had learned into practice. And while she valued her blackened eye as the prize of a good showdown, Nala realized she must have received the worse of the exchange, because when she woke up later, she woke with bees swarming in her head from a five-hour dream of walking upside down on a ceiling. *Scoundrel illused me to steal my hours!*

It was only later that Nala realized the Snake stole Masha from her as well.

III

The first intimation Nala had that their quest to find the prophecy was going to be run on lines other than dread and doom was when Masha, at Taksha's bidding, picked off a passing ponyrider with a well-aimed tomato, causing the poor rider to fall sideways into a ditch. Upon which, most of the twenty members of their fellowship had laughed like fiends in hell.

Of course, if Nala were in a state of peace, she would have realized that it wasn't that Masha had abandoned Nala. But it was that both these pimples on the face of peace had been shut up for years in cages with nothing to do but see futures and be skinned respectively. Only natural for them to let loose under the open sky.

But at that moment, Nala did not think of this, and her spiritual torment was all sharp edges. Nala did hope Parshuram would put an end to all this nonsense of Masha and Taksha. If there was one thing Parshuram hated, it was being noticeable. Noticeable was precisely what an immortal assassin could not be when he's in an entourage with a Naga and an Oracle and a couple of soldiers whose idea of passing time was singing ribald songs and hurling volleys of compliments at unmarried passers-by.

It was the latter that finally led Nala to lodge a protest with Masha days later. 'Do you truly have to? I mean, can you all just, I mean, just shut it, will you?' Nala said, feeling even as she spoke that her frustration had not been phrased as eloquently as she would have liked. Still, grammatically erroneous it may have been, it caused a stirring amongst the fellowship.

Soldier looked at soldier. Naga looked at Oracle. Breath drawn in furiously, eyebrows raised.

'And what have we here – the bickering couple?' said the bald mercenary named Gorin, who seemed to have elected himself foreman. He wore an army of golden rings on his ears. Exposing his rotting teeth, he asked, 'What happened to your face, lass? At least what Sister Masha has can be called scars. Seems like the moon took a piss on your face,' Gorin said, and there was a laugh as if the assembly considered that the remark had been well made.

'Ask your mother,' Nala responded.

Gorin was taken aback. Recovering his wits, he raised his hand. 'I will have you sold to a brothel for that, you bitch.'

'Quiet, Gorin,' Jaah, a soldier with a twirling moustache on a leathery face, warned. 'The girl is with Acharya Parshuram.'

'I ain't afraid of any old shits who chant prayers by the pyre,' Gorin said, his voice no longer as sure as it was a while back. 'And I wouldn't want to be around a girl who can spread their scars by touch,' saying which, Gorin turned tail, stepping out of the carriage to ride a horse instead. His words had an effect as alarm gripped the rest of them. *Great. There goes a good night's sleep.*

Nearby, the half-giantess grunted, silver hair streaming on her makeshift pillow, a sheathed sword in one hand. The half-giantess was called Ajath, a guard of Acharya Vyas, making Nala wonder how many other teachers of Meru employed women guards when they specifically barred women from studying in the Meru. Two other women shared Ajath's bedroll. Both were called strange names. Whisper was a scrawny Mathuran soldier with greying sandy hair and eyes the colour of iron who wore a whip around her waist. And the other woman, short with red hair and the whorls of a wolf tattooed on her cheeks, was Sidestep. Word has it that both Whisper and Sidestep were prisoners of war in Magadh until Chalakkha secured their services in exchange for their bail.

Ajath scowled at the men, and then nudged Whisper awake. She signed to her, making her the translator. 'Vitiligo is harmless. It is merely the sun not taking a shine on every part of your skin with the same love,' Whisper translated wearily, her eyes barely open, one hand over Ajath. The rest breathed easy after that and the Whisper pulled Ajath down to sleep again.

'What ails you so, Nala?' Masha asked later that night, nudging her elbow. 'Did I do something wrong?'

'He is a snake! Did you not see the scales on his face? It sheds! Worse, you were tickling it!' Nala buried her head in her lap, squeezing her temples with her knees.

'I care not for his face.'

'Makes sense. Scarred girls who can spy the future can hardly be picky choosers.'

Too far. That was too far.

Nala wished Masha would have slapped her then. Told her off. Broken their friendship. It would have made things easier, better. But she didn't do anything like that. When Nala looked up, Masha was still there, looking to the stars, one hand absently tracing the scars on her face.

How was she so calm? Nala could not be calm! Did Masha not know that? Even when that kind old woman serving Vyas's soup passed away in her sleep because of a flu three days past, they had remained calm. Yes, they put on guards, spoke about the dangers to come, but they spoke the same way about the fruits they traded, or the nuts they found in the woods. They had not a care in the world but the world would soon remind them what it was made of. Suffering. *Let's see who sings ribald songs then.*

'You ought to be a shade more kind to Taksha, Nala,' Masha said, smiling through glistening eyes, 'especially 'cause Taksha's the bearer of juicy gossip. Unlike Acharya Parshuram, Acharya Vyas spills all to his companions. When we reach Hastina, apparently, we are going to meet a famous Acharya of the Blue Order. Blue Order!' Masha repeated it slowly as if to wedge the point between Nala's eyes. 'How exciting, no?'

'Wait, what do you mean by *Hastina*?' Nala pricked up her ears, like an academic whose particular subject of expertise had come up in the course of conversation. It was as if doomsday was mentioned in the presence of Parshuram. 'We are headed to... Iyran Machil.'

'No, Hastina,' Masha said. 'Taksha showed it to me on a map. It is amazing how well a Naga from Pataal knows earth maps. He is trying to learn our cities. Charming, isn't it?'

Iyran Machil. A place Masha had often uttered in her divinations but Nala had not been able to make sense of it on the map. Parshuram had known it but had refused to part with any answers. Nala had just assumed it was a forgotten hamlet south beyond the Vindhyas. Retrieving her own map from her satchel, she unfurled it and demanded, 'Show me. Where is it?' When Masha, with a furrowed brow, pointed at the map, Nala's chest knotted. 'This is Hastina... But how can it be Iyran Machil?'

Masha chuckled. 'Iyran Machil is the hidden city under Hastina, stupid.'

Nala's eyes turned as desiccated as a rotten corpse, her hate of Taksha forgotten. At long last, she was bound for Hastina... the city whose princes had burned her family alive.

TAKSHA

I

The Naga Reservations had been easy to find in the forests. One only needed to follow the gaunt camps barely clinging to life. The tents grew in number as they wound deeper in the darkness, a few covered by the leaves of banyan trees, others by discarded rubbish stolen from town – a tribe of Nagas and Nagins sleeping off a lifetime of exile in one afternoon. It almost looked like a village. A village with no name, no buildings and no markings. A village that rose to find long-lost brethren return, greeting them with songs of yearning and gestures of sorrow.

No one came to Taksha.

No one came for Taksha.

The faces were unknown to him. He thought of calling out some names, the names of the commons he had met first with shock and disgust when he'd crossed over realms, but he didn't. Taksha was not one of them, after all. He was not born of this world. He was a Zephyr. He didn't even know half the time what they were talking about, and their laughs seem to be birthed from stories in the past that everyone but him shared. He was an outsider in this world. He might know their language but he wished he had their accent.

How he missed home! A home where the sky was stone and crystals. A home crowded with birdcages for blind birds, a home where you felt the caress of rock on your soles. Home was where he was safe.

Home was what he fled.

When Taksha bid farewell to the Nagas he had shared cages with, he could not help but wince at how ungodly they looked in daylight. Did he look like them too? His Gehan skin, scarred and dulled from years of chains and cutting instruments, lustreless under the sun's glare? Had hunger stripped him to near shreds? Sure, they might wear better skins now, stripped from those slain by Ajath or salvaged from the slaver's trunks, but many still had the blinking, confused gaze of birds caged long in the dark and suddenly thrust into light. He had seen some of them wave their hands absently around them as if to promise themselves the bars were gone. Freed from their cages, they looked if they could not yet recall how to slither freely or coil as they wished. They had not even shared their joy of freedom once throughout the journey, and looked at each other only with the dull recognition that slaughter cattle have for one another. The Tangle had been stolen from them. It would take time to reclaim it.

But would they find it in these camps?

The Valkan girl was right. These camps were not home. No inch of this world, or even this forest, was truly theirs. It grew clear that the only path to a life worth living for his kin would be found at the heels of their Messiah, who would lead them to a life where the Nagas might not have more but could not possibly have less.

And just as he was filled with hope at that thought, a horrible human experience arrived to mar his spirits.

Rain.

II

So far it had only rained once, and Taksha did not wish it even on the worst of his enemies. It was a terror of almost mythological proportions. Somehow the tales back home singing glories of the sky of the Surface World conveniently left out the part where the sky pissed on you when you least expected it. Of how it made your boots squishy. It even invaded the sanctity of carts with the smell of clothes on the verge of water-soaked death.

When they could trudge on no longer, the barterbows attached
to Chalakkha went about setting picket-lines for the horses, though
they might as well be planting flags in a swamp. Others struggled
with getting fires started while Ajath posted six guards, in pairs,
for the first watch. Taksha was given the task of tossing the goat
Nala had hunted a day earlier. He did not know why but Ajath
was behaving more and more like his mother by the day, something
he gratefully resented. He obliged Ajath silently, marvelling at the
grace of the half-giantess, the hum of sympathy behind her distant
state, the parts of her others no doubt failed to notice when she was
busy choking them with her knuckle. Her fingers were especially
delicate, slender things, the kind his mother would say were fit for
playing a box of music. A sharp contrast to most of Chalakkha's
barterbows who behaved like a lost tribe recently discovered.
Surrounded by this jolly crew of mercenaries, Ajath and Taksha
were an island of unshed tears. He remembered her silent words of
loss as she had earned her revenge on the slaver. They spoke naught
of it but their quietness fitted together like stacked wooden spoons.
They might not have had happiness in common but at least they did
share hideous grief.

Ajath slapped her palm and signed, *'You're no sage contemplating
the mysteries of life here. You're a servant in this kitchen. Stir your
feet!'*

Parshuram was served first, and then Vyas and Chalakkha, but
everyone else was served in the order of the line they stood in.
Somehow the Softskins had claimed the right to change the goat's
name to 'mutton' while cooking it. Now Taksha had no love for the
goat, he wanted to make that rather clear. He would gladly kill one
if it brought him a step closer to finding the Messiah. But his indifference to the goat did not translate into a desire for eating it. Rats,
pigeons, lizards, eggs, all wonderful. But not goat urf mutton. So he
settled for drinking just the broth, ignoring the chunks floating in it
as he sat around the fire and listened in to the conversation between
Vyas and Parshuram.

'For trust me when I tell you this – the board of kingdoms rests
on a wobbly table with now this Mati of Kalinga being the future
Queen of the Empire. Wild and full of mischief, she is an oracle's

nightmare.' Vyas leaned in conspiratorially. 'Perhaps it's time the Black Swan learned a little fear.'

'I have bigger fish to bait than scare a truant swan,' Parshuram said.

'You shirk away your duties, Acharya. Just look at the past decade,' Vyas said. 'A Republic run by Drachmas. Reshts putting Princes on trials. Kings popping up like mushrooms after rain. Heirs chosen without any of us having a hint of it until the proclamation. Mathuran defiance. The Conclave being hosted by a Rakshasa. Show me an Acharya who does not think that the Saptarishis are losing their grip on the future of the realm,' Vyas said, 'and if he is not a brother from my order, lost in books, he is likely dead.'

Parshuram cut him short. 'Masha told me that there was talk of Daevas stalking the woods?'

'Now that is truly a rumour, Acharya,' Vyas said, smiling. 'A few whispers in the Black Order but as I said, the whispers were faint, not enough to forge a thread. If the Children of Light were indeed walking beside us again, I doubt we would need the Oracles to tell us.'

The sound of a name Taksha finally understood seemed to affect him powerfully. Sister Masha the Oracle. He did not believe that she could actually see the future the way these Softskins believed. Too many soothsayers in Pataal Lok had claimed to see many a future in palms of others but interestingly could never predict their own. Lines on palms don't a destiny make, calluses on hands do. But Masha was not in the business to profit from the fears of others. The poor girl genuinely believed her hallucinations were horoscopes.

Taksha's slit eyes flicked to the neighbouring fire where Masha sat in the company of Nala. Her colours were full of yellow and pink. The aura pulsed with life. It should've been dizzying but instead was calming. Soothing. Comforting. Curiously, Nala's flames mirrored Masha's in the way they danced, only Nala's were a dark red colour that held flecks of blue and a great amount of sadness. They both looked the same age. He wondered if he was the same age as them. How many of his thirty-nine moults translated into years on the Softskin calendar? And why should that matter? Yet it did. Perhaps it was because he wanted to be Masha's friend. Experience urged hate against these half-ape heathens but he found himself incapable of such a sentiment, especially when he saw her. She offered her elbow over ditches. Translated words for him without being asked. Paused by the wounded dog.

Seeing the scars on her face, the fact that something so tender, so unbearably soft of heart had been mauled, and then permitted to exist, and existing so, had held on to her kindness, struck him as a miracle.

Seeing Masha so, Taksha had even tried to mimic her. Last week, while standing in queue for Vyas's tasty soup, he had witnessed the old lady's face fall after she received unusually rude customers from Chalakkha's barterbows who blamed her for their flu. So Taksha had channelled his inner Masha as he had thanked her and compli-mented her for her skills with the ladle. The effect was magical. The old lady had called him *love* first, *child* second and smiled when she thought Taksha had turned away. Too bad she was dead now.

And in sharp contrast to Masha was Nala. Though Taksha found he did not quite loathe the Valkan the way he thought he would. He understood how she felt. *Why did I have to say all that to her?* But that is what negligent words do. They make people like you less: a thought he was fool enough to share with Masha when she settled beside him. The next thing Taksha knew, he was dragged by the elbow to Nala to play a game.

III

'Nonsense, Nala,' Masha chirped up and snatched the jalebi from Nala's hand. 'You are playing. I have spoken. Now this last circular heaven of beautiful—'

'—deep-fried flour batter,' Nala offered.

'Right. This last circular heaven of beautiful deep-fried flour batter soaked in sugar,' Masha pressed on, 'will be awarded to the saddest act here. Someone with the finest troubles they can do nothing about! Nala? Are you ready to lose it all in the,' Masha leaned in with dramatic pause, 'Game. Of. Despair?'

Masha beamed as if she considered her suggestion one of her brightest and best, as if nothing could ease the tension amongst broken souls like an anecdotal story on the origins of those fractures. Taksha suddenly realized that he might have warmed a little too soon to a girl of her temperament. Masha was a menace! But he was even more taken aback when Nala answered first.

'Obviously, it is me, isn't it? Lost my father when I was a child. Didn't know him that well. Mother and brothers, well, I knew them. My trust in princes got them burned alive, and me thrown off a cliff to land straight in an immortal assassin's lap. So here I am, a servant to a madman, while my friends back in Meru – who think me dead, or worse, a runaway – stroll ahead to their bright future. A future that could've been mine.'

Masha nudged him, laughing. 'A future I doubt would have resulted anything 'cause Nala had to hide the fact from Meru that she was a girl.'

'Right, I forgot that.' Nala smiled. 'It wouldn't have been so bad to be honest,' Nala said, leaning forward, 'if I were able to wring the necks of the men who destroyed my life, but turns out killing princes needs work. Work that is now put on hold to save the world. Work for which I have to sit five paces away from Vyas – a daily reminder of my joyful past in school that was snatched from me. Can do nothing about it all now, can I? So *may I*,' Nala said to the laughs of Masha, 'have my jalebi back?'

'Well, now, hold on,' Masha hid the jalebi in her robes, 'at least you have Acharya Parshuram to help you find your heart's desire. Once this business with the Son of Darkness is behind us, it will be back to your quest: revenge. Taksha, if I am not mistaken,' Masha turned to Taksha, 'your home world is dead, isn't it? There is nowhere for you to return. You don't even have a grand villain in your life to keep you motivated, do you?'

This was such a strange, strange game but there was something… oddly uplifting about it. A contest of griefs. Well, not to be outdone in sportsmanship, Taksha opened his heart.

'My world just…' Taksha made a sign of explosion.

'Faded out,' Masha helped.

'Yes.' Taksha smiled, baring his fangs. 'I left Pataal Lok. Swim to your world in search of help. Surfaced in a cage where – oh, oh, I did have a – what did you say, Masha? Grand…?'

'Villain.'

'Aye, grand villain – the slaver who skinned me alive with hot knives, each season, since scales grew back. He did that for half a decade but… well, Ajath killed him.'

'That was heartless of her to deny you the pleasure,' Nala protested.

'*We did not know each other, then,*' Taksha shrugged as he signed instead, tired of losing thoughts in translation. It was painful to be conscious of two worlds when speaking from the heart. '*I can't even cry about it because I could have never done justice to the slaver's death the way Ajath did. It was… mastery over murder! So yes, a pointless life for most,*' Taksha switched to Sanskrit, 'unless Vyas's promise yields warmth, and I save future of my civilization in the moiri of my mother – erm – moiri is memory.'

'See, you have now something to look forward to as well, and unlike me, both of you mourn a family you remember,' Masha said. 'The only thing I remember of my father is him burning after they were done doing this with glass shards,' she pointed at a map of scars on her face, 'to awaken my powers. The rest of my life went away drugged. I have little memory of it all. One day, I just woke up and found that I was a Matron.'

'A girl in a room of old hags.' Nala winked.

Masha made a face at Nala. 'Yes, I did not have a childhood but I have been lucky in my own way. I found you all now, didn't I?' Masha's eyes by now were glistening with tears. 'I am helping save people. But surely that story merits a jalebi?'

'What about your Master, Parshuram…?' Taksha said, stretching his legs audibly to disguise his own tears.

'I'm sorry,' Nala stiffened, 'you think Parshuram deserves the jalebi? The immortal assassin?'

'From what Vyas told me,' Taksha said, 'he deserves a shot, doesn't he? His father on a rage, kills Parshuram's brothers, commands to kill his own mother, and then later in life, his father is khalassed by...' Taksha trailed off, looking at Masha and Nala's faces. They both looked troubled, like Vyas had been when he had bitten into a bad acorn. 'You didn't know, did you? I... I know not when to close mouth.'

'I reckon no one can claim ownership on suffering,' Masha said at last.

'Suppose not,' Nala said gravely. 'The world is full of weeping.'

'Good! Then the jalebi is mine!' Masha said, and took a big bite of the sweet. 'What! It was a tie, wasn't it?'

'Didn't you say you did not have a childhood? Well, clearly, you lied! You're having it now!' Nala scowled at Masha, turning to Taksha for support. 'I am glad now you are here. She can bother you with all her nonsense.'

'Happy to serve,' Taksha said, much to the look of feigned annoy- ance on Masha.

Masha chirped, 'See! I told you, Taksha is so pleasant *and* useful to be around. And this is how we three will help Parshuram slay the Son of Darkness.'

Taksha froze where he stood. 'Doesn't *slay* in your tongue mean *kill?*'

Masha nodded.

'What do you mean by *slay* then? Isn't the Son of Darkness who you call Messiah? Saviour?'

'Son of Darkness?' Masha chuckled. 'A Saviour? That's like appointing a fox as head of the henhouse. No, you silly snake. The Son of Darkness is who we are out to destroy.'

IV

A few moments later, seated cross-legged under an enormous banyan tree, the Bane of Ksharjas blinked his eyes at the growing glare of the golden scales approaching him.

'What?' Parshuram said, packing the one word with so much hauteur that a lesser man might well have keeled over backwards as if hit by an arrow. But Taksha was no man, and there was a sort of disregard for rules and conventions that not being from this realm allowed him. He could only hope Parshuram would empathize instead of eviscerate.

'Are you going to *slay* the Son of Darkness?' Taksha was screaming by now, the shimmer from his scales having attracted a sizeable audience.

'Acharya, it seems Taksha has been wrongly told that the Son of Darkness is a hero who is destined to save us, a Messiah who will save his home,' Masha said, panting, as she held Taksha's shoulder to balance herself after her sprint. 'I am certain there has been a misunderstanding. Perhaps if you could shed some light?'

'Break from work has fouled your head,' Parshuram told Masha. 'An idle mind is a demon's workshop.' And then he turned to Nala, who had approached by then. 'And a restless mind is a demon's harem. Why are *you* here, Nala?'

'I came to stop Taksha from being murdered but now even I want to hear this story,' Nala said, coughing. 'Especially about this hidden city under Hastina where we're headed.'

The other men-at-arms gathered nodded in agreement, most of them sitting down with Vyas's famous bloodraven soup in their hands. Parshuram turned to the approaching Vyas, hoping he would put a stop to this ambush. Instead, Vyas just walked over and sat on the ground, as if settling in.

'Tell them, Acharya, tell them about the Son of Darkness. It is time we gift them the motivation to climb that mountain. Tell them about Iyran Machil. Tell them about Manu.'

V

'"*In a Land Dead will the Last War be fought, in the Land Drying will the Army of Despair be wrought, in the Land Reborn will the hope of wraiths be for naught, in the Land Chained will the Son of Darkness be sought.*" This is a fragment recovered from the Manusruti. We are now headed to the Land Chained. Iyran Machil.'

'The city buried under Hastina?' Nala asked, almost accusingly.

Parshuram nodded. 'In the twilight of despair, just before the Great Tears, the floods that set off the current cycle of Ages, Matsya called upon Manu's court.'

'Matsya? The giant fish?' Jaah, one of Lord Chalakkha's soldiers, scowled. 'I know of the legend. When the world drowned, the man named Manu built an ark to be drawn around the world by the Matsya Fish to ride out the fury of waters. The Nagas helped Manu—'

'Pardons, Acharya!' Chalakkha interrupted in a voice thick with phlegm as he took a warm sip of the hot milk. Yet another victim of the flu that had gripped the camp. 'It is your tale, and from your lips should it be told! Jaah, stay shut or I dock your wages.'

Parshuram, frowning, started.

And so, the tale of the Dawn and Dusk of Iyran Machil came out splendidly. Parshuram was not a great conversationalist by any stretch of the imagination but after a couple of hiccupped starts, his impassioned prose gushed up like a geyser. Taksha did not interrupt him once, not even when the truth about the Orb of Agan Mian, which was the Orb of Naag Mani, was distorted to claim it was gifted to Manu by the Nagas instead of stolen by Manu from the Nagas. Taksha knew how easy it was to break a chain of thought and shatter a story, to fracture a fragment of memory being passed around carefully like a clay cup of tea.

And who truly knew whether it was the Orb of Agan Mian or Naag Mani? Powers hold on to their thrones with the tales they tell but just as important are the pages they tear out, the dark silences after the broken sentences in history, the stories they don't tell, the memories they burn away. The Zephyrs of Nagas were no doubt the same. They all wanted their race to emerge as the heroes of histories, allowing them to live with what they had done – or couldn't do.

'Iyran Machil is buried under Hastina?' Sidestep asked, scratching the wolfhead tattoo on her cheek. 'But it is not the same as the home of these Nagas? Are Iyran Machil and Pataal Lok neighbours?'

Vyas answered this time. 'Pataal Lok is a realm beneath our realm, not under our surface,' he explained, tapping the soil under his feet for emphasis. 'Taksha's home isn't buried underground like a

potato sapling, but rather exists beneath our world in the same way
the realm of Daevas floats above our world. Iyran Machil, on the
other hand, was built inside the Velas Kalein, or as you may know
it, the Veins.'

'Right, Veins, of course.' Sidestep nodded, clearly not understanding a word.

'Yes, yes,' Taksha said, abandoning civility, 'so Iyran Machil was
strong in Veins world. And then something bad happened and
big First Empire ate itself, till the Satpaweeshis, like Naga's Many
Mothers, tied up Iyran Machil and shut gates. What of Son of
Darkness? Or Messiah? They are same?'

'*And what are these… Veins?*' Ajath signed.

'And where did the dragon come from?' Gorin added. 'How can
we best get its eggs?'

'And what is this Orb of Agan Mian?' Chalakkha asked, eyes
glinting. 'To think it could stop ageing, stop death… Is it still there
in this Iyran Machil?'

'Are we done now, Vyas?'

'Perhaps another time, My Lord,' Vyas said. 'Acharya Parshuram
has other things to do.'

'Of course.' Chalakkha bowed again to Parshuram and turned to
Vyas. 'Killers of such repute can hardly be of a loquacious disposition. Isn't that right, Whisper?' Whisper merely fingered her whip
in reply.

Once Chalakkha and his armed entourage were gone, only
Taksha, Ajath, Masha, Nala, Vyas and Parshuram remained.

'The things you missed could fill a library,' Vyas addressed
Parshuram. Parshuram simply scowled. In the meantime, Vyas
turned to an agitated Taksha. 'Hold your scales, Taksha. Yes, you're
not wrong. We believe the Naga Prophecy of the Messiah speaks of
the same man as the Prophecy called Desolation. The Messiah and
the Son of Darkness are one and the same.'

'But you *kill* your Son of Darkness,' Taksha said, hoping the
emphasis he placed on 'kill' was not lost on Vyas. 'Nagas *need*
Messiah. I do not understand.'

'The Son of Darkness is the Promised One, my friend,' Vyas
interrupted, 'promised to destroy this Age. Whether he ushers in

a new Age of Peace or an Age of Ash depends on who is around him when he ascends to power. No one is born evil. The same man can be the Son of Darkness, the Prince of Phantoms, who will plant our severed heads and birth terrible things from our soils. Or he will be the Messiah, the Prince of Dawn who would sing to the river to let it meander into deserts and bring light back to Pataal Lok.'

'So... you only mean to stop the Son of Darkness *before* he turns evil?' Masha asked.

'When you dance with desolation, lead,' Vyas said. 'As you can testify, Sister, a prophecy is not written in stone. Even a prophecy can fail if the prophesied one is slain, falls sick or, worse, falls in love. And that is our task, Taksha. To make sure the Prophecy of the Messiah comes true so that the Prophecy of the Son of Darkness can be unmade.'

'And... we go to Iyran Machil to...?' Taksha asked.

'Find the Prophecy,' Vyas said. 'Manu, in his last hours, divined the fate of the world, past and future, and used the city as his canvas. Before the Chaining, the surviving tribes were able to chronicle a few of the stanzas, the few that helped the Saptarishis steer the world from the chaos that unfolded with Manu's fall. One of those prophecies spoke of the Son of Darkness, one of many fragments rather like the one you heard Acharya Parshuram cite earlier.'

'There are other fragments?' Masha asked. 'I was not shown them in the House.'

'No Matron is permitted to see them and you had only just turned Sister, Sister Masha,' Vyas said, apologetically. 'Most of them are just throwaway lines that made no sense. Some the Sisters deciphered but they were about what the Son of Darkness was going to be rather than where he was going to rise.'

'But what was this fellow going to be? What can the Son of Darkness do that would be so terrible?' Nala asked. 'Innocent men will fall? Hardly a novelty. Valleys will spawn demons? Look around us. Will the Son of Darkness just be a despot, a tyrant going about, uncaring for lives and lies? Ksharjan warlords are already tussling for that throne,' Nala said. 'Does anyone truly know what the Son of Darkness might do that is not expressed as a verse from a bad sonnet?'

Vyas smiled sadly. *'When The One Who Lived Two Lives touches the blood of Gods, thus will the final days be known.* Do you know what I mean by the blood of Gods?'

'Elementals,' Nala whispered. 'Oh.'

'What are Elementals?' Taksha asked, confused again at how swiftly Nala surrendered.

'The Nagas call it *Furies.*'

'Oh.'

'I am certain even your records speak in beautiful detail of those times,' Vyas said. 'Wars were apocalyptic episodes. The riversingers monopolized water by diverting waters to irrigate their crops, leaving downstream kingdoms to die. A sunwalker ignited a forest to threaten the enemy but the fire turned the fertile soil into a wasteland that no irrigation could heal. The wind cried out death howls, the mountains trembled like earthquakes and their rocks bled red. The gift Prakioni, the Goddess of Earth, had gifted the mortals was used by the mortals to wound her. Should the Channeliers rise again, Astras will rise again, and the realm will fall to tyranny without a whisper and with many a wail,' Vyas said. 'What do the sages call Astras, Nala?'

'Antiseed,' Nala answered solemnly. 'Plant one and watch something die.'

'And if the Elementals resurrect, the Ksharjan Royals will be the first to grab the Astras. No, it cannot be. Mortals were not destined to inherit weapons that could hurt many from a distance. An arrow may have your name on it but an astra is addressed to cities. The only reason our world hobbles ahead on three legs is because the Elementals stay dead,' Vyas said. 'And should the Son of Darkness resurrect them, these Elementals,' Vyas shook his head, 'Order will finally be slain by Chaos. And there is no such thing for either side as enough Antiseeds. If Astras return, our world will dupe itself into believing the threat of an Astra will go away only if each and every king is armed with them. But here is the truth we at the Meru know from the histories: the threat will never go. And before we know it, the kingdoms would have chased each other into oblivion in an arms race.'

Vyas paused, and took another sip of the tea in his hand. He was experiencing the quiet satisfaction of a fine storyteller. It also helped that Nala, Masha and Taksha made for a good audience with just the right hushed silence and the protruding eyes.

He continued, 'Of the fragments of Manusruti we have back in Meru, none speak of *when* the Son of Darkness would rise or *where* he would rise. But we now know that the part on *where* he will rise is in Iyran Machil. My dear Sister, it was you who divined and set us on the path.'

'But Iyran Machil is a City... even with Chalakkha's men and even without the threat of a dragon, it would take eternities to scour the whole city in search of the words,' Nala said, suddenly stopping as if remembering something. 'I remember Masha's gibberish I wrote. But that would mean... no, it can't be. The *where* does not just mean Iyran Machil, does it?'

'I feel... not happy... left out,' Taksha complained.

Nala turned to Taksha. 'The Prophecy called Desolation was written by Manu on... his own body before he fell,' Nala said, numbly, before turning to Taksha. 'It is on his corpse.'

'But... how this can be?' Taksha asked. 'If he wrote so, body rotted centuries ago.'

Vyas quoted Parshuram. 'Free from disease, free from sickness, free from...'

'Putrefaction,' Nala completed. 'The Orb of Agan Mian is not destroyed, is it?'

Masha rose to her feet. 'So, does that mean all those people who are dead in Iyran...'

'Lie unrotting and piled up,' Vyas said.

'That is... so tragic. I wish they had an oracle to warn them of their future.'

'You all are causing me grave discomforts, little leeches.' Parshuram finally rose from his meditative stance. 'Begone before I feel inclined to return the hospitality. Masha, you stay. I need you for one last divination before we enter Hastina. No, Nala. You rest. I will manage her fits on this one.'

'Last one question, Parshuram,' Taksha folded his palms in the Softskin gesture of mercy, 'if we pull back the Messiah from falling into the shadows, you not chop head, will you? You give chance, see if he good, correct?'

'He won't kill your Messiah,' Vyas said, pressing his shoulder lightly. 'He will save your Messiah.'

Taksha looked up, smiling at Vyas, tears in his eyes as he nodded gratefully and turned away. He had seen how strong Vyas's tangerine aura was at its solid core but as Vyas spoke the last sentence, the wisps, they had begun to fray and unravel, like the sinew of clouds torn apart by a storm.

And that only meant one thing. Vyas had lied to him. Taksha had trusted him but Vyas had betrayed him. No more.

Now only time would tell who would win this Game of the Chosen One: Serpent or Man, little knowing that no matter who won, the world would lose.

ADHYAYA II:A

A FAIRY TALE

RAJGRIH, MAGADH

3 MONTHS BEFORE THE BATTLE OF MATHURA

।। न हि सुप्तस्य सिंहस्य प्रविशन्ति मुखे मृगाः ।।

Translation:

'No prey willingly walks into a sleeping lion's jaws.'
—*Panchatantra,* 200 BCE

KARNA

I

The name Magadh inspired majesty, and like everything majestic in this world, it seemed to have fallen prey to vandalism. Painted murals of beautiful women stared at him sadly as he passed under a stone overpass, their faces smothered behind dog-eared yellowed bills pasted over each other. Similar bills were plastered on every street corner, proclaiming the Unni Ehtral as a saviour of humanity and restorer of order.

'Persistent echoes can turn any lie into a truth,' Duryodhan remarked when he saw Karna's eyes glaze over the badly drawn posters. 'After the arson at Varnavrat, they'd shouted and repeated *Duryodhan is a murderer* over and over enough for even me to believe it.'

Karna nodded, doing his best to avoid meeting his friend's eyes. Dressed in a well-fitted dark tunic adorned with an emblem of arrows crossed with fire, Duryodhan looked every bit a Ksharjan barterbow employed by the Empire to protect Ehtral priests on highways. Hidden gauntlets housed daggers and climbing hooks, and if anyone ever accosted them, he would have perfect reason to possess them. The only problem in this meticulous disguise was Duryodhan's face. Having never glimpsed Duryodhan's cheeks and chin behind the neatly groomed royal beard for the years he had known him, Karna was having trouble strangling his laughter on seeing him clean-shaven. When Karna had first seen Duryodhan emerge from behind the tree where the razor man plied his trade, Karna had just gazed, wide-eyed at Duryodhan's scheme to evade any looks of familiarity from the Emperor or anyone else in his retinue who might've split a word with Duryodhan at the Panchalan Swayamvar. It was not until Marzana had called him 'Prince Shaven-Face' and asked whether he was planning to pillage the palace or the nursery, that Karna's resolve had finally shattered into peals of laughter.

So, to avoid repeating that treason, Karna just nodded solemnly, turning to face the road ahead. *Huge*, he thought as he stared at the buildings that should've had no right to stare at the stars up so close, or at the arenas that might've fitted a dozen Resht colonies and still had room for a dozen more.

This was why he was morbidly glad when he found that while beautiful from a distance, the city stank like any other up close. Beside the finest villas of cream-coloured stone, squatted crumbling huts with rotten roofs. Through glinting windows of temple towers, one could almost see the sheets of plaster cracking from the ghetto walls. Every fine building – and there were many – was a lotus surrounded by the filth and muck of poorly plumbed shacks. Highbred horses dragged carriages on cobbled roads only to be obstructed by starving cows and water buffaloes. Beside a stall selling marigolds and chillies and lemons to be hung in doorways of the pious, was a hawker selling cow dung and, apparently, complimentary flies.

Oil and water don't mix. Poor planning is as harmful as a plague for a city, Duryodhan had said. No wonder the doors to these rich buildings were now guarded by night guards the size of a small army. This was... foolish. Rajgrih was a munition waiting to explode.

'There is nothing more poetic than a battle between a skytower and the slums that cower in its shadow,' Marzana said, uncomfortably encased in layers of black, adorned with a black turban over her head to hide the fact she was not bald as Ehtral priestesses were wont to be. Her priestly disguise billowed about her, making her look absurdly stout.

It had been Karna's design to sneak into the palace wearing clothes that did not draw attention. And the best way to avoid attention to detail was by overwhelming the senses with attention to the whole. His stomach still lurched with guilt at remembering the first time he'd tried this scheme to betray the friend walking beside him by rescuing Savitre Lios. It had been a victim of Ravana's Curse then. It was the guard of an Unni Ehtral priestess now. Unfortunately for them, they had discovered too late that private guards of Ehtrals or otherwise were not permitted into the Imperial Castle. And Karna guessed the disguise of a victim of Ravana's Curse would not receive a welcome carpet either.

So here was Marzana, a priestess of the Ehtral Cult, with Duryodhan in tow, a barterbow to protect her, and Karna, a Resht supplicant. Karna hadn't worried much about his disguise. He barely recognized his own face. In the same way that Duryodhan had suddenly sprouted a clean-shaven chin to shield himself from overly observant eyes, Karna's false longbeard became a bastion against recognition. The lone reminder of the Karna the world once knew remained in his sad, golden eyes.

A noblewoman in a light saree, white flowers on blue, accosted Marzana, whispering and pleading close to her ears. Marzana responded, 'Mustard oil to massage your locks. It will then sprout as thick and plentiful as the rain in the East. Xath watch over you.' The woman thanked her profusely and withered away.

Karna's heart was pounding. Every time someone bowed before Marzana in passing, he anticipated an attack, and without a bow on his shoulder, he felt naked to the storm. After all, daggers seemed more likely than devotion, and far more deserved. Hell, had he been in the crowd, aware that someone was planning to abduct a married woman from her house, he'd have wounded them on general principle.

And what was worse, it was not just any married woman, it was the blasted Queen of the Empire, and not just any Queen of the Empire, it was the blasted Black Swan. More than any Magadhan Claw, he expected Mati to stab them when they arrived.

Karna stared up at the walls of the Imperial Castle in the distance where Mati was surely plotting the downfall of a civilization. He imagined what he had heard of it: of its domes and its bronze and golden gates, and its palaces and gardens and public halls, its bazaars, bathhouses and barracks, its temples, shops and theatres, its statues, fountains and frescoes, its walls and ramparts that had never yet been attacked, and its shadow over the mighty Ganga river that kissed its east walls. None of this he could see with his own eyes but he knew all the same that they stood there. Magnificence shaped by human hands that gave Jarasandh a name – a name now lost in the debris of the Yamuna Wars – Jarasandh the Builder. Now... the world could hardly imagine Jarasandh as a builder, the same way Karna could hardly conceive of a plan to slip into the Imperial Castle.

'That was an easy one,' Marzana said as she blessed another person seeking advice on the appropriate time of the day for a goat-sacrifice. 'Can we rush this along before someone asks me if they have free will?'

'How do *you* know of that philosophical question?' Duryodhan asked.

'It is a common question that plagues the minds of Devadasis,' Marzana said. 'How do *you* know philosophy?'

'I had to read it on my own. Must have been nice for a patron to whisper it to you.'

'If only you knew how to whisper to a woman's ears, you would not need to stalk her husband's home.'

Facing a Valkan horde sounded more appealing than enduring another one of their pecking contests. Both Duryodhan and Marzana were ill-equipped for travel as the poor, and unfortunately, found a way to vent their frustrations by nipping at each other like baboons fighting over the last chunk of a banana. To Duryodhan, Marzana was a liability, someone who had no place on their quest in Magadh. To Marzana, Duryodhan was a condescending stiffjaw. Both were right but unfortunately utterly convinced the other was wrong, leaving no stone unturned to one-up each other. Karna, a seasoned expert in selective hearing, was good at turning deaf to these debates but given how the last argument had ended, he knew he had little time to distract them before they appointed him judge.

'Rajgrih looks so different from the Crowns and Crows in Hastina,' Karna said, hastily. 'I am not sure whether this is a sign of progress or bad planning.'

Duryodhan scowled at Marzana from the side, and then nodded. 'Resentment festers in a place where the unfortunate are forced to ogle at the wonderful lives of the other side. But this is what the

Unni Ehtral desired. To garden a place where these unfortunates simmer in hate, and the fortunate marinate in fear.'

'I have never understood their cult?' Karna said, this time the query genuine. 'The little I have heard of Jhestal's flock does not inspire confidence. They're into torture and starvation and ceremonial flaying and enemas. What did they do that made them so popular in the Empire?'

'They gave them a villain,' Duryodhan answered. 'No cult can rise without creating a race of the unrighteous to hang. For most decades, it was the Nagas. Before that it was the Vedans against the Mlecchas, the foreigners. Before that, it was the Rakshasas. The Nagas are holed up in their reservations in the forests, the Mlecchas running tribes in the hinterlands and the Rakshasas isolated in the East. The Ehtrals have tried their hand at something new. Language. Linguistic identity. It was the self-immolation by the first Ehtral priests that stopped adding the Empire from the languages of its vassal states to its administration. And so, anyone who does not speak the mother tongue of the Empire, Maghi, or the language of the Gods, High Sanskrit, is a foreigner and can forget the idea of enjoying the Empire's grace. Rajgrih is the most populous city in the world. Many came here for a better life, to grow with the Empire's power. And now they find themselves excluded simply because a language has transformed from a medium of emotion to a basis for the reorganization of everyday practices, knowledge, historical narratives and even plays.'

'It is as if every time speak you,' Marzana chimed in, 'you are parroting the unnecessarily complicated words of a Namin priest. The Temple gave sanctuary to many refugees over the last few years and so I know. Truth is, Karna, that the poor and the unemployed of Magadh make up the majority of the devout to the Black Cult. The Ehtrals have lent them a place to vent, a place where they think they have a voice, and that the words uttered by that voice are echoed by others even if those words are vile and pathetic. These poor Magadhans feel that the businesses the rich outsiders operate should have been their own, unaware of the darkness engulfing them in this cavern of echoes. The Magadhans were here first, and they want that privilege. First to eat, last on the street.'

'I said the same thing!' Duryodhan grumbled. 'And I would've thought a Devadasi would be trained in grammar and philosophy to find it easy to understand my words. I still do not understand, why is *she* here with us, Karna? She offers nothing to our cause.'

Karna groaned, 'Now that we have established you both are great at philosophies of the world, can we shift our attention to a slightly pressing matter? Something about how do we slip into the Imperial Castle?'

'Well, I, for one, am glad my disguise is to date.' Marzana smiled, the bruise on her face from Old Khai's knuckles having faded to green from purple.

'Of course you're glad,' Duryodhan remarked sarcastically, 'given how you enjoyed the *ordeal* of acquiring your vestments, Marzana.'

'It is still Lady Divine to you, Prince. And no one asked you to watch,' Marzana said. Karna shook his head to shut the door on that memory but it knocked nonetheless.

Earlier that day, when they were still pretending to be tourists to Rajgrih, the three had been scratching their heads in a tavern to find a way to rescue Mati. And rescue it was, given what they had heard about Mati not being seen outside the Imperial Castle ever since she had been wed and given the expression of general displeasure by everyone they had met over having a Kalingan as their future queen. To Duryodhan's credit, he had refrained from telling Karna 'I told you so', but Karna was sure it was only a temporary respite. The Prince was going to be smug for a long, long time, if they succeeded. But just as the first ideas were being struck down, an Ehtral priestess named Sarai had interrupted them, talking their ears off about joining their cult, until Marzana had held her hand.

With an evil, erotic wink that threatened to undo Sarai, Marzana had whispered words to her. Karna had heard Marzana tease him before but never in that tone of voice. This had been her Devadasi voice that completely caught him, and for that matter, Sarai, off-guard. Marzana had then run a finger up Sarai's arm till she had flushed a vibrant red even as she whispered more nothings to Sarai's ears. Karna sympathized with Sarai. He knew what it felt like to be out of your depth when Marzana teased.

Later Sarai had only been too pleased to follow when Marzana had taken her outside.

Duryodhan's brows had shown off their limberness when he and Karna had followed the women into the alley only to find Sarai drawn taut, shivering and glazed with sweat. Their tongues were dancing the same nritya as their hips. Marzana then pushed Sarai against the wall and touched her lip to each emaciated bone visible below Sarai's neck till she reached the rosebuds at the tip of Sarai's small breasts. Marzana had smiled when she had noticed the two of them from the corner of her eyes, which only made Duryodhan and Karna awkwardly glance at each other before stumbling back into the tavern, refusing to talk about what they'd witnessed.

'She was warmer than a forge, and I would wager her netherlips were wetter than Prakioni's tears. Kaamah's fire burns the brightest in priestesses who bank their desires. So I think I did her a service. And it fetched us the robes, didn't it?' Marzana said, breaking into Karna's reverie of the past.

'It fetched *you* the robe. May I remind you that it is us who have to slip into the castle, not you,' Duryodhan said. 'Not to forget, you could've jeopardized the entire plan with your reckless gambit. You are certain she won't tell on us?'

Marzana did not answer. Instead, she leaned in abruptly and whispered to Karna to wipe the Abyss dust from his eyelids. Embarrassed, Karna slowed down to let the two walk a little ahead. That had been the last of Abyss, which Marzana had told him to save for a rainy day... but Karna had seen a man with a boy on his shoulders near the fountain, and the rage had returned.

Before Duryodhan could turn to see what Karna was up to, Marzana spoke out loud. 'I used my finest twirls and tricks on her spots but I did not rub her. She is young, mostly an acolyte, still new to the ways of the Ehtral, no doubt joining it to escape a marriage with a gender she does not find titillating – as is the case with most priestesses. Even now, she will be pining for a release, and I doubt the Ehtral boys will be up for it. There is nothing more crippling than an almost-release,' Marzana said. 'Not to forget, I told her that I want her robe to scare my rich, stupid Ksharjan husband into releasing me from my marriage. Works every time. So yes, I'm certain she will keep her lips sealed in the hope I unseal them later.'

Around the next corner, a small square opened to unfurl its charms. Beside a fountain, citizens thronged around a small dais. Marzana told them to pause by the sweetseller's stall while she hurried over to the fountain.

'Could you be warmer to her, my Prince?' Karna asked when Marzana was out of earshot.

'Warm? Are you certain she won't melt given how cold she is?'

'That is rich coming from you, Prince of Expressions.'

'I do not understand why she had to accompany us,' Duryodhan complained. Again. 'I could have very well arranged for her to be safely taken back to Hastina.'

'She's keen to lend a hand. And you must admit, she has been plenty helpful. That thing with the priestess was genius, wasn't it? You think we could have come up with it?'

'We could have come up with a far more honourable way that did not involve abusing a girl's innocence.'

'The thing with honourable methods in an *abduction* is that they take time, time which we perhaps may not have.'

'The Karna I once knew wouldn't speak so. And can you cease calling it an abduction,' Duryodhan grumbled. 'I can only hope the Princess is in good health. Mati, locked in a tower, haunts my mind with the image of a sunflower hidden in the shadows.'

More like a demonic witch locked in to save the city. 'Indeed.' Karna smirked.

'I saw that,' Duryodhan said.

Karna let out a light laugh just as Marzana returned with a smile on her face that strangely was reminiscent of Mati's. Probably his mind playing tricks on him. She beckoned Karna to her side, away from Duryodhan, and said, 'There is a troupe out by the house named Gaur and Grapes, only a short distance down the street. They are all set to perform tomorrow in the Imperial Castle for guests from Chedi. It would seem their singer had a bit of mishap with a combination of ice and a wet towel – the details are unclear – but they are in need of a singer.'

Karna bore the expression which would make sense if Marzana was talking in Maghi. He squinted, till Marzana's idea translated in his head into a language he understood. 'And we think it might be a judicious move—'

'If we were to lend them aid by offering them someone who would put a bit of custom in their way.'

Karna smiled as he turned to Duryodhan. If Duryodhan had not been too pleased with the woman who had hitched her wagon to the adventures of two friends, wait till he heard this idea.

'What is it?' Duryodhan, the man of the hour, asked.

'Lady Divine found a way for us both to sneak into the Palace.'

'Good,' Duryodhan said, without nodding at Marzana.

'The thing is,' Karna said. 'You will have to sing.'

II

A silence, unexperienced by Duryodhan before, followed Marzana's read of her cheery plan. The effect on Karna's friend was rather remarkable. Practically every known emotion came and went on his face followed by a gulp, and then another. To Karna's lively imagination his friend's eyes appeared to crawl slowly out of their sockets, like a snail's head.

'Did you not tell me that princes are tutored in the musical arts since childhood? I can't sing for I am their saint. Karna's singing paints the picture of a rooster with a sore throat.'

'I am the Prince of Hastina Union. Not a common tavern bard.'

Karna intervened. 'I have heard you sing while I stood guard behind the doors and you took a dip in the marble pools. I know you can manage a bar or two.'

'He was also humming in his sleep the other night in my room. There's a singer in you.'

Duryodhan raised his voice discordantly to object but Karna shushed him. 'And even if there isn't, when the love of your life has been deprived of her voice, should you be worried for yours?'

The silence stretched. It was all Karna could do to not break character. He kept his face as neutral as possible till Duryodhan mouthed to Marzana, '*Well played*'.

'Do you know of the "Washerwoman's Bane"?' Marzana asked, doing her best to not gloat at her secret plan.

Duryodhan nodded solemnly.

'It is a crowd favourite from what I heard from the troupe master but no one has sung it yet,' Marzana said. 'His name is Runaan. Go out there, carol that song like a songbird, and find us a way into the lion's den.'

Duryodhan narrowed his eyes, and then stalked off in the direction of the troupe without a word.

'If we're going to die, we will at least die laughing,' Karna said.

'I thought you said he could croon a bar or two,' Marzana said.

'He can sing it,' Karna said. 'But I found his enthusiasm far more charming than his talent.'

'Marvellous!' Marzana chirruped.

Unaware of these eulogies, Duryodhan wandered onto the stage.

III

The auditions had been in full swing as Karna and Marzana pushed through the crowd, and somebody, who looked as if he might be the local executioner, was reciting 'Aag Ka Dariya'. The crowd, though not actually making that horrible booing sound, had a dark frown.

When Duryodhan had faced horrible monsters, be it a wild mob in Hastina or the giant Bheem in a mace fight, he had always steeled himself for the challenges ahead. So, he set out as he always had with a steely gaze that is a hallmark of men who are about to commit desperate follies in the name of love. But when Karna's eye ran over the audience, he realized only the montage of memories Duryodhan shared with Mati must have kept the Prince from calling it a day and boarding a carriage bound to the Union.

Through the buzzing sound of the crowd, Karna heard the sound of a veena starting to strum. Duryodhan must have heard it too for he commended his soul to Saraswati, the Patron Goddess of Music, took a good, long breath and hit the refrain in his larynx.

Soon came from Duryodhan the sound of a nervous, melodious voice singing, to the accompaniment of tabla and flute, words which exhibited all the symptoms of being from the 'Old Washerwoman's Bane'. Karna hadn't heard the song before and now his ear detected a lot of 'her husband did this and that' in the lyrics.

Marzana frowned. 'Karna, Duryodhan... Duryodhan isn't bad,' she admitted grudgingly.

Karna gleamed. 'He isn't. Too bad your plan to embarrass him failed.'

'You knew he sings well?' Marzana complained. When Karna shrugged, Marzana raised a finger. 'You are a liar, Resht! Good thing I had taken countermeasures. We might have taken a more scenic route but we did manage to reach there. Now see your Prince fall.'

Karna's smirk vanished as he felt knuckles crack all around him in the crowd. *What did you do, Marz?*

MARZANA

I

Marzana had only heard of such tales of public action from the South by fleeing refugees but now that she saw it for herself, she could not deny it: there was something sensational in the stirred. It gave one some idea of what it must have been like during the Years of Blood brought about by the Bane of Ksharjas when the kings were drawn from the pulpits and quartered on open streets.

But if Marzana had imagined it would be a cabbage that would be first thrown at Duryodhan, she could not have been more wrong. She did not take the shame too seriously. For the ladies and gents, used to regular hangings and decapitations, had honed an instinct for dramatic effect when it came to stage play. The moment Marzana saw a tomato splash on Duryodhan's chest, she realized how magnificently more aesthetic it was than any cabbage shower. Though, in all fairness, the cabbage school of thought and, for that matter, the egg school of thought were not left far behind.

What was particularly redeeming about the whole affair was that it took a while for Duryodhan to realize the volleys were not expressions of cheer. The last they saw of the Prince who ruined her life by arriving in Malengar was when he ducked behind the stage, chased by a particularly insistent banana.

When Marzana and Karna rounded to meet Duryodhan behind the stage, holding a beaker of water for him to clean himself with, it had felt like justice.

'That was a heroic effort, Prince,' Karna said through clenched teeth.

'I will have Uncle throw you into Narak if this ever reaches another ear,' Duryodhan said.

'Suffice to say our lips along with our ears are all sealed for now,' Marzana said.

Duryodhan's stubborn jaw twitched. 'Now what? I have bathed in tomatoes and bananas, and we are no closer to entering the Imperial Castle.'

A cough announced his intrusion. It was the troupe leader, the man who had asked her to call him Runaan. 'Quite unfortunate, I must say.' Runaan wore flowing robes, red flowers on blue, but it was his large red nose that demanded all the attention, a nose that could easily be concealed in a bowl of strawberries. He bowed before Marzana. 'Maekhela,' he said in a wonderful voice, and then turned to Duryodhan again. 'Quite unfortunate. But you sang well and with heart, lad. What did you say your name was?'

'I didn't,' Duryodhan said, gruffly.

'Ramdas,' Karna said, swiftly.

'Ah, Ramdas. As the Maekhela might've told you, I am Runaan, the Revelmaster of this humble troupe of vagabonds that the Lord of Misrule has engaged for tomorrow's festivities at the Imperial Castle. Yes, yes, even I am as surprised as you are that Magadh still has one Lord of Misrule but supposedly he does awaken in the Festival of Lights. And my singer-mummer betrayed me by allowing himself to be poached by another band travelling to the Conclave. Seems like all anyone cares about these days is the Conclave, im-agining themselves to be the next Nar Ad—'

Duryodhan stopped him midway. 'What does that have to do with me?'

Runaan used a towel to remove the make-up that still greased his face. 'You won't move women to stampede but as long as you don't cause ears to bleed, I think you can suffice for tomorrow, Ramdas. You do know songs other than the "Old Washerwoman's Bane", don't you?'

'I do. But… was I the only witness to the reception I received?' Duryodhan asked, confused.

'*This* crowd,' Runaan gah-ed contemptuously, 'they are fiends who dote on seeing the high brought low. Don't be fooled by their kind faces that disarm an artist with specious promises like a sunny day, and like that deceitful sun, deliver him into the hands of the cold wind. None of these rabble rousers will be there in the palace. Moreover, you have the blessing of the revered Maekhela, what better omen be there?' He bowed again in the direction of Marzana, who nodded solemnly. 'I would be honoured for you to grace our troupe with your voice. Also,' he leaned to whisper, 'it helps to have a barterbow in our midst. Keeps the company's spirits safe, you know, in these troubled times.' Runaan rose to his height again and boomed, 'Fifteen coppers, not a pence more.'

'That...' Duryodhan exchanged a glance with Karna. 'That is generous. Of course, it would be an honour. My servant will accompany me, of course,' he pointed at Karna, 'he is Surdas.'

'Of course, of course, artists are nothing without assistants, I am aware. But his pay will be taken from your share.'

Duryodhan nodded.

Runaan beamed. 'I must confess I expected a feisty negotiation but your openness of heart has moved me. If there is anything I can do for you, do not hesitate. Maybe hesitate a little. Come, meet the other musicians and singers. Revered One,' he turned to Marzana, 'if you could come too, your blessings would greatly motivate my frail fellowship.'

They followed the troupe leader to his caravan, Duryodhan still confused, Karna surprised and Marzana shocked.

'What is a Maekhela?' Karna asked.

Marzana shrugged. 'Must be the honourific rank for the priestesses of the Cult. Could you ask your friend to unknot his nerves? He'll draw suspicion.'

'Look alive, Prince!' Karna said. 'Time to save your princess.'

Before Duryodhan could answer, Runaan paused and beckoned Duryodhan closer. Runaan whispered but they all heard it. 'But here is the one thing I did not understand. If you do know other songs, why did you still sing "Old Washerwoman's Bane" when I had told the Maekhela the song had already been sung seven times today, and needs to be avoided at all costs. If you had chosen a different tune, you might have been spared that rain of tomatoes.'

II

Somewhere in the Imperial Castle, the shadow hands of the sundial were fading to signal sunset. Within the castle, the Palace of Creation was brimming full for the visit of Vishwakarman the Ninth, the infamous architect of Aryavrat who had designed the Virangavat, the Three Sisters of Mathura and the Lighthouse at Golabai Sassan.

The curtains had been drawn to let in a rose-scented breeze though it did little to flush out the heat. Feather fans waved everywhere so that it seemed as if a cage of exotic fluttering birds had been opened in the hall. Marzana stood with the other priestesses of the Ehtrals, face hooded. The other Ehtrals faced them across the carpet dressed in identical black robes.

You're almost done, Marzana reminded herself. Karna and Duryodhan had not suspected Marzana once. And she did not know what the Inkspeller had on Runaan but the stageman had played his part splendidly. Even Marzana would've fallen prey to Runaan's performance if he hadn't been wearing the flower jacket, the same jacket that the Inkspeller had asked her to be on the lookout for when she reached Rajgrih. And while the Inkspeller had assured her Runaan would find a way to smuggle them in, Marzana had seduced that young priestess into giving her robes just as a countermeasure. And that was a good thing too. Devadasis looked down on street performers, and Marzana, even when disguised, would rather be an Ehtral priestess than a performer-for-hire. *You're almost done.*

But as she realized she was nearing the end, she trembled like a butterfly at the coming rain. She cared for him, didn't she? *Tell him, Marzana. Just tell him. It is not too late.* But she stilled her heart of wind-blown flame by remembering the Inkspeller's words, remembering Damaya's future, Dhanush's finger and her mother's face. He was his brother. He would do him no harm.

It was only when the trumpet heralded Vishwakarman's entrance that Marzana's thoughts stopped tormenting her. The famous Balkhan architect, First Stone of the Brotherhood of Brass, briskly walked into the chamber, accompanied by the head of Ehtrals, Narag Jhestal. Vishwakarman, lean with a beard and hair as brown as the pupils of his eyes, wore a turban of gold cloth bedecked with a dazzling aigrette. He gleamed with the lustre of the sun, in sharp contrast to the robes of Narag Jhestal which exhibited the glow of the new moon.

'Your Majesty,' Vishwakarman said as he treated the Emperor to a low bow. One of his legs wandered off behind him and the rest of him arced politely till his turban was level with the Emperor's knees. It was less an obeisance, more a dance. 'What an honour it is to be received once more at your court.'

'The honour is mine, First Stone, that you chose to skip the Conclave for the Empire.' Jarasandh's voice was heavy with baritone, rich with authority and soft with familiarity. Of everything she had seen in Rajgrih, the Emperor was the biggest disappointment to Marzana. His frame might still proclaim him the peerless Conqueror, a giant among kings, the strongest bull on a field, but his face, lost in the past behind his great beard, spoke of a man forced to sit on the throne against his will. Lowly merchants in Malengar had brighter auras than the Emperor of Magadh.

'I must confess though, Your Majesty, it was not a particularly difficult choice. Mosquitoes and leeches deter creativity,' Vishwakarman said to a chorus of laughs from the courtiers.

'I look forward to your plans for the Imperial Contest,' Jarasandh said. 'You must have heard of the surprise Lord Chalakkha has planned for Virangavat on winter solstice.'

The word 'surprise' sent ripples through the assembled, whose shoulders leaned in the general direction of Vishwakarman as one, though the architect was not one to be loose with words.

'Indeed, Your Majesty. His Worship tipped me off on my way here, and I have never been more tickled. Virangavat stands at last, and now I have the honour of crafting a tournament unlike any before it. It was already destined to be a spectacle – the first contest to the death – but now I shall dedicate myself to shaping it into a worthy tomb for the fallen.' Vishwakarman bowed once more.

'Splendid.' Jarasandh smiled, then hesitated, and finally added, 'I had... a few designs, in case they can assist you.'

'Indeed—' Vishwakarman started with a reverent smile but was interrupted.

'I will ensure those designs reach Lord Vishwakarman, Your Majesty,' Jhestal interrupted, turning to Vishwakarman. 'With the Armistice ending, the Emperor will finally bring justice to the Usurper – from what we hear, he is your former employer – so I hope you can understand if His Majesty will not be able to grant you a private audience.'

Vishwakarman looked awkwardly from Jarasandh to Jhestal, and then nodded. 'Of course, Your Majesty. I would be honoured even to simply cast an eye on your designs, and will do my utmost to bring them to shape.'

But this time Jarasandh did not smile. Marzana could see how just a mention of Armistice stirred memories he had perhaps hoped to settle at the bottom for a night. Vengeance is but a sword that needs to be constantly turned in the forge lest it cool before its time. Jhestal understood that. Jarasandh only nodded and then stood to leave.

With Jarasandh's departure, many of the Ehtral priests and priestesses also left through the palace lawns, and with their exit, entered the joy Jarasandh had perhaps been searching for.

Most of the courtiers retired to the palace lawns. Marzana was seated with the few remaining Ehtrals at their own table. Fortunately for her, the Ehtrals did not believe in conversation as a way to pass time. They did not even look at each other, a tradition for which Marzana was grateful given the cowl only hid so much of her face. She only had to worry about not drinking deep the clear, bright cordial in her goblet that made the torches burn brighter. But it gleamed greedily in the goblets. *Kaamah, forgive me*, she drank, and drank deep, *Karna... forgive me.*

By now Runaan's troupe had struck up its chords in earnest, and the courtiers gathered danced uneasily on the green lawn amidst a heady scent of flowers, wondering if they were being marked for purification by the Ehtrals. She stole a quick glance over her left shoulder and found Karna watching the ground in the corner as he shuffled after Runaan around the stage, as if he were chain-snapped. The Karna she knew was lost in the luxuriant red cloak of a bard, hanging in velvet folds from his purple-whorled shoulders. His ruffled shirt, a mix of pastel pinks, lavenders and creams, made her want to gobble his cheeks. Duryodhan, to his credit, looked rather comfortable in a jacket which was a patchwork of rich fabrics. But it was the skirts that billowed and swirled around each of them in a whirlwind of colour, shades of indigo blending into emerald green surrendering to deep burgundy and then shimmering gold, that had Marzana pretending to cough each time she burst into laughter.

A smattering of tentative applause broke out once Duryodhan's bawling subsided. Many of the attendees caught Duryodhan with requests for answers, requests for dances or requests for something far more salacious, if Duryodhan's expression was anything to go by. The way he fidgeted, smoothing out his robes and adjusting his belt each time a woman accosted him, it was a wonder he hadn't been caught yet.

Marzana could wager her remaining jewels that Karna and Duryodhan hadn't yet slipped off to find Mati because they did not know where to go. There were just too many buildings and palaces within the Castle. She could imagine Duryodhan complaining for the hundredth time that he wished they had the sketches of the castle's outline.

A jury would have unanimously passed judgment that when it came to abduction, Karna and Duryodhan could be at best described as rank amateurs. Or so Marzana kept reminding them whenever she asked them to employ a professional from the Magadhan underworld to help them out. Surely there must be someone who had stolen a golden chalice or two from the Imperial Castle. But no. These dolts fancied themselves as students of siege tactics. In their heads, rescuing a woman in the room was in effect laying a siege to a room. All they had to do once they got their hands on maps of the city and of the palace was spotting the exits, clocking guard rotations and arranging a quick getaway should things turn sour. Considering Marzana, a Devadasi, could have come up with the same list if asked, she had been certain they were missing out on something keener.

She had been right.

Seems a city map is easy to procure but ask for a castle map and you'll invite suspicion like a homely innkeeper. The Imperial Castle, a city in itself with countless buildings, made guessing the Prince's quarters futile. Guard rotations couldn't be observed from outside, so the only option was to loosen guards' tongues with ale and bribes. Duryodhan had tried and got thrown out of the tavern – small talk with smallfolk wasn't exactly his strength. Karna fared no better, barred entry due to the Resht mark, and that was all fine given that when it came to charm, he had the social grace of something long rotted. And after one look inside the tavern, both refused to let Marzana try. As for escape plans, they needed local agents – ones Duryodhan couldn't contact, what with Shakuni being blissfully unaware of the grand plan, and Duryodhan supposedly halfway to the Conclave by now.

Rank amateurs.

And rather than take a step back and realize how out of their depth they were, Duryodhan had opted for a *'we will think of crossing the bridge when we come to it'* approach. An approach that usually ended with people drowning in the river under that bridge. Fortunately, the Inkspeller had predicted his brother's lack of skills at stealth and planted a backup in Runaan but now they were on their own. And given that Mati was nowhere to be spotted amongst the attendees on the lawn, that metaphorical bridge was collapsing fast.

'Meenakshi?' A woman's voice, low and rich, with a hint of fear in it like a foul spice added to soup, called her. It was a voice she was not like to forget, given how she had heard it in high octaves when Marzana had traced her areolas with her fingers just earlier that day. Marzana's head turned like it was on a string but if she was overwhelmed by the sudden appearance of the woman whose clothes she was wearing, she didn't let it show.

Marzana approached Sarai at her beckon. Even in the new robe, it was not difficult to discern Sarai's emaciated body whose exposed hands and cheeks were puckered like a plucked chicken corpse. Embedded into her forehead, worked into open wounds, nestled tiny shards of obsidian to frame a river pattern over her brows.

'What brings you here, Meenakshi?' Sarai asked in a hushed tone, worry creasing her forehead.

Marzana reached out to stroke the purple bruise her teeth had scored on Sarai's throat.

'Not here, Meenakshi,' Sarai said, struggling for reserve. 'If anyone were to see you...'

'None of you talk to each other enough to know each other.' Marzana ran a fold of Sarai's Ehtral robe through her fingers. She watched the effect it had on Sarai with amusement. 'I do apologize if I quickened the pulse in your veins, Maekhela, but you already know of my household's misfortune. I, however, have found a way out of it. It turns out the Queen-in-Waiting, Princess Bhanumati of Kalinga, is known to my brother from a voyage of old. Yes, yes, I know she is vile,' Marzana said when she saw Sarai frown, 'but in a world where husbands turn into gaolers, a helping hand from even heathens cannot be scorned.'

'But she is not here.'

'I can see that,' Marzana said, eyes not leaving Sarai's. 'Just my misfortune. I will leave now. I do not wish to cause you any more grief.'

'But you can't leave now. Before they depart tonight, the women have to gather in the Sheesh Mahal to sew a shroud for Yama and a flower garland for Xath. It is a ritual cast on every woman in the Castle on this night, be it high birth or low.'

Marzana sighed. 'Would you take me there?'

Footsteps sounded behind them, quick and sure. Marzana saw Sarai's brows arch and turned to see Karna approach, frowning. Karna made a swift bow, and rose with hands resting on his belt which Marzana knew hid two daggers.

'Maekhela, the troupe will retire soon, and would be honoured if you could part with your blessings for their next sojourn,' Karna said with a terrible Maghi accent.

Sarai clutched Marzana's robes. 'Maekhelas don't bless musicians, Meenakshi,' she gritted through her teeth.

Marzana turned to Karna and told him that there would be no more blessings for the night, and that she was headed to bless the royal women in the Sheesh Mahal. She made sure Sarai heard when she said out loud that she would take more time given how she had to discuss matters of great import with Sarai. Sarai's green eyes sparkled in the aftermath of that disclosure.

When Karna's eyes still begged her for a moment, Marzana scowled and turned to Sarai. 'A heartbeat, Your Worship.' She accompanied Karna to the side. 'What is it?' she hissed. 'Just—'

'Runaan guided Duryodhan to the palace of the Crown Prince,' Karna said. Runaan told them? Karna cleared his throat, 'Marz, you are not listening! Listen. Mati's palace is that sandstone one by the fort walls. Runaan thinks Duryodhan intends to use it to seduce the princess, a feat he claims he has accomplished a few times across the realm. Luckily for us, his heart is soft for skirtchasers. Scandal aside, Duryodhan suggests we climb the palace using the gear we have smuggled in.'

Take the name of the demon… Duryodhan appeared beside Karna, his multi-coloured skirt swishing behind him. 'Like Krishna did when he rescued Rukmini from marrying Shishupal.'

'You fool,' she told Karna but made sure Duryodhan knew it was aimed at him. 'Krishna knew where Rukmini's room was because *she* was helping him. His swan doesn't even know he is here. Did you notice that tiny difference, Builder of Bridges?'

'We'll then have to think outside the box,' Duryodhan decided solemnly without having produced any evidence that he'd done any thinking inside it.

'Uh, yes,' Karna said. 'All the royal women are gathering in the Sheesh Mahal for something.'

'The Princess might be in there sewing shawls, shrouds, something.'

'Mati would never agree to sew a shawl unless it is to throttle someone in their sleep.'

'Trust me, women change after marriage, or rather are changed in their husband's house.'

'And how would you know about marriage?' Duryodhan asked. Marzana grudgingly surrendered a smile to let him know that that was well played. 'Not to forget, she wasn't in attendance here, was she? She might be well done with the sewing long back,' Duryodhan said, pressing the rare advantage. 'She will be in her room.'

'We are running short on time, and we can't risk excluding either option. As I see it, I will head to the Sheesh Mahal while you both head to wherever Runaan has pointed you, and whoever finds her, does the needful.'

'Excellent idea,' Duryodhan said, making Marzana happy that he had returned to his dim ways. It took Karna to point out the obvious flaw in their plan of how Marzana had never seen Mati. Minutes later, Marzana left their august gathering following at the heels of Sarai, armed with the worst description of a woman she had ever heard from a lover: dark-skinned woman with short hair and murderous eyes. It was as if the local Marshal was describing the perpetrator of a murder. Not that it mattered. It was not as if Marzana truly expected to find Mati. She had smuggled Karna and Duryodhan inside the Castle. Her debt to the Inkspeller was paid. All she needed to do now was be done with this sewing ritual and quietly escape.

Before she left, however, Karna called out. 'Marz, you'll take care, won't you?' he said with his words carrying the soft of autumn, words of a love lingering between light and shadows. *Your light. My shadows.*

KARNA

I

A quartet played a romantic tune that the wind carried on its shoulders. A carriage went past them at a good clip. Its curtains were drawn but the Resht charioteer did cast the two a wandering glance. Surely if they did not disappear, they would become conspicuous soon. Two men in ridiculous skirts and ribbons streaming off their jackets playing hide and seek behind bushes was not something you saw often.

Why did the Prince's Tower have to be so far away from the rest? They had walked past a crowd of palaces and official buildings, three small temples, the Rajgrih Gold Guild's hall, the silksmiths' workshops, the floating gardens and even the ornate Baths of Elaria but the Prince's Tower was still ahead. The sounds of the river had turned into a mighty hum as they approached the east end of the castle, finally spying Saham Dev's palace built against the rear wall, its windows facing the river Ganga outside. Karna could only imagine the views the rooms offered. It was as if Jarasandh had wanted to make amends to his son for creating as much distance between their residences as possible.

Once they reached the palace, Karna and Duryodhan watched the pace of the guards' routine and peeked from behind bushes at the rooms on the different floors for the better part of an hour, and then began spying on the women instead. It was not difficult to imagine why they were here. The sudden pious makeover of Magadh had turned the harlots of the City into refugees. Those who had stayed back, he had heard from Marzana, had been pushed by the

Ehtrals to the straggling slums by the river. Given how no one could truly bring an end to the world's oldest profession, it seemed hidden exits from the castle had been established for the guards to find the women and boys they sought.

In that way, it was not much different from Hastina where the Reshts used the catacombs under the City to escape to the Crowns. No city could ever truly seal itself from its citizens.

With the guards half-distracted by their needs into fucking, and the rest distracted by the hour of the night into yawning, it had been almost too easy for Duryodhan and Karna to slip past them.

Karna would curse himself later for even thinking the word 'easy'.

For it seemed in an Empire every room was important, and worse, different. They had lost count of the doors they had opened and yet they were nowhere closer to finding Mati or her husband. Curiously, every room was empty on the first two floors. Not even a guard. Just a lazing servant here and there.

It wasn't until desperation took hold that they finally revealed themselves to a passing maid, who, without much prodding, informed them that the Princess's quarters were on the Imperial Floor – three floors above, no less, with the staircase guarded by an entire battalion of Rakhjais. However, by the Prince's decree, only the servants he had personally selected were permitted to ascend the staircase even to that floor. No threat of bodily harm seemed to deter the maid from her opinion.

After discreetly delivering the maid's unconscious body to a mop room, Karna turned to Duryodhan. 'Now what?' Karna asked with futile hope that Duryodhan might decide to abandon the plan. 'Kill the guards?' he asked, sarcastically.

Duryodhan frowned, scratching his moustache. 'We're doing this wrong. Marzana was right.'

Marzana's name distracted him. He did not know if it was his imagination but he felt the stars of her eyes turn into plumes of smoke when they had last spoken. *Definitely my imagination.* A few weeks with a Devadasi, and his inner thoughts had turned to using strange descriptions for eyes.

'Don't let her hear that.' Karna winked.

'We are taking this on as warriors. We need to think of this as what it is. A robbery. So... we have to think like Mati.'

Karna's humour vanished. He stared wide-eyed at Duryodhan. *Think like Mati* was possibly the worst advice you could give someone in the world. *Think like Mati* was probably the affirmation oath of serial killers, or at least the name of an asylum in the East.

And then Duryodhan's eyes glinted in a fashion that made Karna take a step back. 'I told you we'll have to climb,' he said as he broke the lute he had carried to reveal the smuggled climbing equipment.

So much for a law-abiding prince.

II

The tower's walls, ivy-clad but un-weathered, stood as silent witnesses to the ascent of these men in colourful dresses, their skirts billowing like a flying squirrel in the wind. Moonlight flickered in fragments, gleaming off the metallic hooks. These hooks found purchase in the crevices of the tower's stone, and with a shared breath, they climbed.

Karna thought of the guards huddled on the different floors, backs turned against the window and the strange cold-humid wind behind it. Duryodhan did not spare them more than a passing glance as he climbed. But Karna felt a stab of pity for them. Jarasandh's wrath would bury them alive when he learned his prized daughter by law was gone, and what he would do to the Prince did not bear thinking about.

What also did not bear thinking about was the fall below. They had climbed diagonally first to the side of the tower which had the balconies facing the Ganga and away from the soldiers on the grounds, and then climbed up vertically. One slip, and it was a fall. A very deep fall into the angry Ganga, her white frothing waters hissing away below. He was careful not to look down but turned out looking up did not present an inviting option, either.

'Oh, my eyes!' Karna complained as he wrenched his face away. 'Why aren't you wearing pants inside?'

Duryodhan paused. 'Why would a singer wear pants inside a skirt!'

'You're not a singer! You think the guards at the gate check for inners when musicians enter a palace?'

'I tutored under a teacher who knew the theatre arts. You have to slip into the skin of the character to pull off a character.'

'Too much skin, if you ask me.' Karna winced even as Duryodhan drove a small ringed spike into the seam between two blocks. Karna handed him the strap harness from his satchel, and Duryodhan fastened it to the eyelet of the spike's ring.

'You're a prude,' Duryodhan said.

'Can you ease up on the spikes? Too much noise, and we'll be caught before we can say *Hello murderer.*'

'I know what I am doing,' Duryodhan replied.

'Will you rush?'

'Stop rushing me!'

It took them a good deal of huffing and puffing before they managed to scramble over the parapet onto the tiny balcony to a room. Turning back, Karna took his time to admire the view of the river now that he was at no risk of falling into it.

'Come, Karna.'

He followed Duryodhan into the room. There was no one inside. Was this even the right room? The bedchamber was high-ceilinged, with rose-decorated walls, a marble floor and a vast canopy bed at its heart. The bolsters were brocaded ivory silk, the sheets were finest Hehayan linen, and there were two sets of drapes, one heavy and one light, no doubt there to control how much of the light the sleeper wanted to let in on her sins. A wicker basket waited at the foot of the bed and a mirror stared at a score of combs and face paints on the table. *Definitely not Mati's room.*

Boots were thrown near the door and a cloak thrown across the chair, and the sofa covers were full of wrinkles. A rich tapestry of a swan hunting a shark covered much of the opposite wall. Ships in tiny bottles decorated the niches carved into the walls on the right. *Could be Mati's room.*

Why am I troubling myself over this? Let Duryodhan decide whether it was his lover's room. Remembering his duty as a guard,

Karna moved back to the balcony to close the door, when a sudden intake of breath pulled him back. He turned to find Duryodhan had frozen mid-step. Karna, frowning, ambled to where Duryodhan stood opposite the bed and traced his eyes to the fluffy white bed-sheets between the folds of which Mati was hidden, fast asleep.

'Are you waiting for her to wake up?'

'She isn't asleep,' he spoke without emotion as he drew back the bedsheet.

Mati, Black Swan and Empress-in-Waiting, lay abed face down, her hair still impolitely short, her once-toned frame turned a little portly and soft – no doubt by the indulgence accorded to a future Queen. Beside her, dressed in a maid's clothes, slumbered a little girl whose cheeks were etched with dried drool and neck cursed with the caste mark of Resht.

The little girl was stabbed, and from what he could make out from the side of her face, Mati had been defaced by a dagger. They looked comfortably asleep in a pool of freshly spilled blood. But both were as dead as dreams.

MARZANA

Twelve chairs sat cheek by jowl. Most of the women were fooling about with the shrouds they had sewn, laughing, but they stopped at once when Marzana entered with Sarai. But Marzana barely spared them a glance as would befit her status as a Maekhela. As she saw it, it was not very different from being the prime lotus in the House of Devadasis. But it was the palace's interiors that had her gawking as a… rank amateur.

The Sheesh Mahal was a glittering jewel box. The ornate white marble pavilion was exquisitely embellished with parchin kari and convex glasses and mirror mosaics. Even the ceilings and panels were wounded with thousands of small mirrors, each mirror designed with a coloured foil and paint to transform night into shimmering day within the Sheesh Mahal by reflecting the candles inside.

'This was personally designed by His Majesty,' Sarai explained. 'Let its temptation not be the tempest that draws your ship aground, Meenakshi. Sew what they seek, and let us make haste on our way out.'

Marzana nodded absently. She just had to continue the charade for a little longer. Just a little longer before she left, found the next carriage out and made straight to Hastina to warn them of what was to come. Only they could save the man she loved and had betrayed. And then all would be good. Her debt to the Inkspeller paid, she and Karna could finally be together. He would forgive her, she knew, and she could spend the rest of her days painting his neck with the colour of her breath. Sighing, she looked around. It was only then she noticed that there were stands at one end over which stretched in piles the dried, hairless skins of animals. Most were stretched out on those iron frames but there were some soaked in tubs. A cluster of pumice stones, needles, thread, and folded sheets of vellum filled tiny baskets around the spiral shape on the floor. On the chairs, women huddled in their tiny islands, shivering silently as they made shrouds out of the hide. It was a hide of a strange colour she had never seen before. But then again, no clothing made of animal skin had ever been permitted inside the temple, so what would she know.

Sarai beckoned her to a chair and, not knowing what to do now, she obliged and absently took a chunk of hide from the basket along with sewing implements while swivelling her head from one woman to another. She claimed a quiet corner not far from the fire. No sooner had Marzana settled there and crossed her legs than something brushed up against her thigh.

'Can't keep away, can you?' Marzana said as Sarai brushed her sharp bony shoulders against hers by taking a chair right beside. 'Ow!' Marzana had pricked her hand on the needle, which had slipped through a hole in the hide. The shape of the hole looked strange, yet familiar. And there were two of them – Marzana shrieked as she dropped the hide and scrambled backwards, her chair toppling. It was a hide skinned off the face of a human.

Eyes widened. She turned to find each of the women in the chamber was staring at her blankly, sewing forgotten. The hair on the back of her nape stood straight.

'Waste not, want not, I always say.' A man, dressed in black robes, walked in. He was the same man who had been beside the architect in the Hall of Creation. 'The skin of the sinners is used to create comforting clothes for our prisoners below, to keep them warm in our winters lest they succumb before meeting the punishment deigned fit for their crimes.'

The night yawned and wrapped its arms around Marzana, the heat suddenly gone, replaced with a cold that made her want to cry.

'Oh, how rude of me to not introduce myself, child. I am Narag Jhestal, the *Lahawk*, Lightkeeper in your language. I must confess the robes of a Maekhela suit you.'

'Kaamah…' she breathed.

'Ah, yes,' Jhestal chuckled. 'That false god, indeed. You are from Malengar then. Good, good. Your plan was good but a little knowledge is a dangerous thing, you see.' He took the seat Sarai gave up for him like an old friend, carefully plucking the skinned human face from Marzana's hand to begin sewing on it. He did not say anything for a while as he sewed one of the eyes shut. The silence crawled on her back like a summer of locusts. 'You tried to use your wiles on one of my children to your vile end,' he made a *tut tut* sound, 'not knowing that the Ehtrals suffer no pleasure and enjoy no pain. The feeling of want has been purged from them, and in doing so they stand liberated. Sarai.'

Sarai nodded and pulled a chair in front of Marzana. Sitting on it, she lifted her black skirt and slowly parted her legs until Marzana was staring at a mutilated door where a tiny shaving blade was sewn to her hinges like a ring. *Kaamah protect! How can such evil exist in this world!*

'When your fingers were circling around her, I suppose you did not know all it was doing was strengthening her resolve.'

Shaking, Marzana turned to the priest and found her words, 'So, you knew we were coming.'

'Of course we knew. We keep a stern eye on Northern scum. The moment our devouts informed us of two poor men and a woman riding into Magadh on horses with saddles crafted of rich leather, we knew we had spies in our midst. Ill ones at that. So, we sent this young girl to find what you were up to. And Yama save me, you wasted no time, did you? Was this Runaan with you on this as well? Too bad. The smallfolk did love him. To be certain, we will be asking questions of him intimately.'

Marzana scratched her knee to still herself. 'Since when did priests concern themselves with spies? The godfolk running out of goodfolk to lynch?'

His grin was hard with malice. 'The Claws can see foul deeds, the Ehtrals can smell foul souls – ah, my breath is wasted, isn't it? What would a harlot know about a pure civilized society?'

'Considering the purest of your civilized society lurks in the shadows of my world, I say I might know a fair bit. Seeing how they are more honest on my bed than in front of a God, I might say I know a lot more.'

'You are an interesting person,' Jhestal said thoughtfully. 'It has been far too long since I've had an honest conversation with someone. It is refreshing but I'm afraid duty beckons. I thought there were two other spies with her,' he asked Sarai.

'Your Worship, the spies left for the Prince's tower,' Sarai said.

'Is that so? I did leave them a little surprise should they find their way around our able guards,' he said as he admired the flap of face on his hand as if it were an exquisite tapestry. Marzana flinched at the way he said surprise. 'If I were you, I would be more worried about your fate. You are trapped, and your God of Sin holds no sway in the South.' He turned to Sarai. '*Prepare* her.'

KARNA

'She isn't Mati,' Duryodhan said, flatly.

Karna felt uncomfortable. Despite the hurt the woman had caused, Mati was the first highborn woman to have shown Karna kindness, the first woman to... take his essence. He shook his head to find more appropriate reasons to mourn her.

She was Duryodhan's love. *Much better.* He knew he should comfort Duryodhan but found he was enormously ill-equipped for such a task. *Should I utter words of comfort, or hold his hand... or leave him be.* Wait. These were his options? Wisdom. Touch. Abandonment.

These are lousy options. Duryodhan turned to him again. 'She isn't Mati.'

'Don't be a fool,' Karna said and cursed inwardly. *Great. So I went with the option of cruel indifference. Well done, Karna.*

'Look, I know Mati's...' Duryodhan flushed red before continuing, '– this isn't her body.' He walked over to the side of the bed in response and pulled the blankets down from the corpses. The dead were naked from the waist below.

Surprised by Duryodhan's action, Karna's eyes inadvertently swept over the waist, the thighs and the legs of Mati before he turned away sheepishly. The sight of the corpse had lodged itself in his mind, and loathe as he was to admit *how* he knew this, but Duryodhan was right. Mati's lower body belonged to an acrobat, her skin as dark as a thief's pocket. And Mati definitely did not have a birthspot in the shape of Hastina on her buttocks. She definitely did not have stretch marks on the waist. The body... belonged to an aged woman, a woman who had birthed a child.

Karna could imagine Mati being offended at his mistaking this corpse to be hers.

Karna turned to Duryodhan again, who was now busy checking the other girl for signs of life. 'So, where is she? And... who are they?' But even as he said the words out aloud, the full weight of the situation descended on his neck.

'We need to leave,' Karna said, and Duryodhan nodded after confirming the girl was, indeed, dead. As they headed for the balcony, the door to the room burst open at the seams.

'Halt in the name of the Emperor!' a man in copper-plated armour and red cloak shouted. Curiously, none of the Claws even glanced at the bed. *Vayu's beard.* This was a trap. 'You are both under arrest for treason and espionage,' the soldier announced with stiff courtesy.

Karna turned to Duryodhan, 'It is a trap.'

'Really? What gave it away?' Duryodhan asked, hands stopping Karna from drawing the knives from his belt. He began to turn, announcing, 'Stay your weapons. I'm Prince Duryodhan of—' Then he grunted and grabbed his stomach. An arrow sprouted from his gut. When he wrapped a hand around it, blood leaked through his fingers.

Karna felt the bones behind his cheek harden and blaze. He shielded Duryodhan from the next quarrel that bounced off Karna's chestplate. Karna looked at his friend, and then the Claws pushing into the room. It did not look like they were intent on taking hostages.

Finally, the sweet promise of death. He smiled as he grabbed Duryodhan by the scruff of his neck and turned, twisting to throw him off the balcony. 'You better back your high claims of being a swimmer.'

'Karna, no!' The last words Karna heard Duryodhan say.

'You!' a Claw shouted. 'Go order the men below to shout a warning to the river guards—' He stopped short when a knife thudded deep into the wooden frame next to his face, its hilt shivering with the force with which it had been thrown.

'No one is going anywhere.' Karna grinned as he saw Arjun's face in each of the guards. *No...* he clenched his fist. *They are just guards doing their duty. Just following orders.*

'Ashes!' Karna cursed. He saw the crossbowman reloading. Instinctively, he dodged a bolt as it passed within a foot of his neck, shattering plaster on the wall behind.

Karna almost moaned with pleasure. Fighting was the one time he could be himself. Even while trying not to kill the guards, he at least had the liberty to maim and cripple. After all, he was doing his duty too.

So, he let the Claws come at him. Some he wounded, some he pushed, and some ran away, but there were more. He knew he had to hold the guards' attention to spare Duryodhan as much time as he could. Time for thought was scarce – so he abandoned the attempt. He took a deep breath and opened his Chakras to make maiming as graceful as a dance even in the packed mix of confusion and chaos. He stabbed one man in the thigh, and twisted gracefully to grab another by the neck and smash his head on the breast of the apsara carved onto the bedpost. A quarrel would have nicked his neck but his awareness was high and he dodged it with a simple flick of his gauntlet.

'Karna, forgive me...'

The voice entered low in Karna's ear and he felt it grate along his skull. His senses rang in horror like a tuning fork. A priest was holding the priestess Marzana had seduced in the alleyway in his grip, a knife to her throat. Sarai was crying. There was another priest beside them, standing tall, his face shrouded, his robe secured by a crocodile-skin belt, grinning as if Karna had been putting on a show for them, his eyes unhealthily occupied with Karna's chest.

You owe this woman nothing! a voice growled inside him. But Karna's shoulders sagged as he nodded back to the priest, and then let go. He heard the priest chuckle, 'She was right. He is honourable.'

But he was left no time to dwell on the thought. He let himself be tackled to the ground. His entire world reduced to glimpses of heavy-booted feet. And so, it came to be that Karna, loyal to the last, became a prisoner of the Empire and was sentenced to death before the sun even breached the horizon.

INTERLUDE

VAHURA'S ADVENTURES

I

It wasn't as if the word Underfall failed in conveying how dark the aesthetics were going to be. But the black leaves of the Umbrasils that blossomed in the absence of light cast the distinct impression that ghouls hid behind them. Gulping, Vahura held the mothlamp and shouted mentally every prayer known to mankind as she trotted through the woods, and whispered softly the number of steps she had left behind.

The Iron Order, the disciplinary army of the Seven spread across the continent to curb crimes of chaos, were chasing her. If her palms did not feel like spiders were crawling on them, she might have even felt flattered. But who sent them? The gears of memory clicked in her head again as she remembered sharing her findings and doubts with the librarian of the Citadel of Taxila. No doubt that librarian blabbered it on to his superiors in jealousy or fear, and the superiors whispered it to the Seven. Oh, if she found that librarian again, she would, she would – she would turn his library into a haven of un-pushed-in chairs and misshelved books. Vahura chuckled quietly, wondering how she even entertained such diabolical thoughts. But was that why the Seven were after her? Did they suspect the source of Vahura's new 'academic' interest to be tainted with infection? Or had her inquiries uncomfortably breached the line of Daevic Lore, forbidden to anyone who did not bear the title of an Acharya, especially not a woman?

Or could it be, as Zubeia feared, that the Ambassador of Balkh, bound for the Conclave, had turned back, his conscience awakened on the long road, or perchance realizing that the Princess's bribe was too meagre to risk the grim fate of quartering upon his return to Balkh? Did he, then, pen a missive to his grandfather, who, being so far away, summoned the Iron Order instead to retrieve her? Yet, more likely still, it could be the Sindh Guild that called upon the Iron Order, seeking to reclaim a defaulter, having learned that the bridal jewels Vahura pledged to them might have been appraised far above their true worth.

By the time she reached the three-hundredth step, she had thirty potential suspects who could have sent the Iron Order after her. A lone shaft of dimming light set her copper hair on muted fire to interrupt her interrogation, and the suspects got out on bail while she figured her way out. She climbed the vine ladder and emerged into a twisty little alley of the Tree City of Kamrup.

Vahura had toured Kamrup enough times to maintain career prospects as a travel guide (or as they called it here, Curator) yet the sight of Kamrup's Green Dome never failed to evoke a moan. The Everwood Trees, or as her kind crudely called them in their books – the Ribs, rose hundreds of feet into the ruddy heavens till they branched into each other, their foliage criss-crossing the sky like webs of deranged spiders – leaving the city eternally draped in long shadows. This was the Tree City of Kamrup. The books back in the Riverlands claimed there were scores of these Tree Cities scattered across the East but Kamrup was the mightiest. Or perhaps this was a lie as well, in the same way the books lied about the East being a land of barbarians and blooddrinkers who had not dipped their feet into the lake of civilization.

If there was any truth to be found in these books, it was in the paragraph on how the City never saw day. The Green Dome shielded the Kamrupans like an overprotective mother, allowing only slants of light to pierce through its bald spots. These were the Light Pillars around which the greenhouses of the City had been built. The rest of the City remained shrouded in their version of diluted morning called shadowmorn. And into this shadowmorn Vahura walked, pulling her hood about her red hair with a flick.

If her guess was right, she had emerged out of the Underfall on the western part of the district. The shortest route to her accommodations in Leafsong would be to take a flat swing to ferry over the swamps in the Boughs. It would also be the easiest way of standing out in the crowd. Her best wager had to be through Canopy Market.

As Vahura ventured deeper into the City, she kept the panic at bay by perching herself on academic musings. The City itself presented as an attractive subject. The City she had heard so much of from her mother.

Her mother did not rob her lullabies of their sharp edges. She did not drape tales of the world in a satin sheet. Her stories had fallen on Vahura's ears like a guillotine: of women hanging upside down from banyan trees to snatch wandering children, of the ten-horned queen of death, of men lured to their ends by beautiful women with fintails for legs, of boar-headed widows who slept with djinns and fornicated with the dead. It was as if she had always known that Vahura would one day travel through the worlds whispered by these lullabies.

But Vahura had always imagined the city of Kamrup in these stories, where civilization grew without watching the sky and the stars, as a humid cauldron of suicidal tendencies, short tempers and hostile social interactions. She had been a little miffed to see her forecast had been amiss. Little mothlanterns lit the streets of branches not by the hundreds, but by the thousands, to turn Kamrup, a city that never saw the sun, into a city where it was never night. The lanterns were not of the traditional Riverland-make either, and the alchemy inside the wick trapped moths and kept them alive while burning them slowly. Leaning into the horizon, these mausoleums of moths lit her way forward.

Suddenly, distant shouts travelled to her ears, followed swiftly by sounds of the crowd parting and cursing. She did not know if it was the Iron Order who had magically caught up with her or merely strangers shouting at each other, or perhaps she had accidentally stumbled upon a patrol, or worse, was it an ambush? *Rot it, Vahura! Stop overpondering!* But Vahura knew she could not pause to find out who was coming her way and she knew she did not have time to play it subtle. Her scattered thoughts shaped themselves into a single instruction: run.

II

The branches of the Everwood had been flattened in many places to connect the inner districts but they still zig-zagged over each other from one alley to another within a district. It was as if the entire roadway of branches was built by a woman to eliminate the very idea of heeled boots. Vahura still ran, blouse soaked, stomach empty, a satchel of the world's secrets bumping on her back and the realm's fiercest soldiers behind her back.

When Vahura had heard poets put music to their words on the Everwood, she had imagined herself as a sad Rakshasa princess running around in the forest singing, pining and yearning.

'I run with my hands full of Earth and eyes full of Rainfall. How many hearts can I keep secret before they pour out and you just pass me by, mistaking me for a broken dam.'

Perhaps she should have been more specific in her fantasies about the circumstances that found her running. The complaints in her mind against Fate did little to aid her lungs and legs in the effort they were currently engaged in. Incensed, they began to rebel.

Half-shadowed faces of Asurs with rainwarders across their heads, who were fighting over a public transport cart, scowled at her as she knifed through them. Naga girls who held their shoes by their heels as they waded through the riverine streets giggled at her when she tripped and her feet went ankle-deep in the space between two branches.

She had probably run the shortest distance possible for a race between children but she was done for. Panting, she held a tree trunk on the side and pulled her feet out of the ditch, and dragged herself out of the way. Propping her back against the trunk, she slunk down and stretched her legs. Water and mud squelched around her rump but she was past caring. She slipped out of her shoes and stretched the soles of her feet as she waited to be arrested.

She would be caught. It was inevitable. Best they catch a Balkhan who they did not have to carry on a stretcher. At the sounds of screaming and pleading of a Rakshasa from above, she startled to her feet. She strained her neck to the green ceiling. Amidst the network of rope webs, complicated swing mechanics and intricate netting, swayed a man-sized pod from a sixty-foot branch. It dangled precariously and swayed like a spider caught in its own web upside down, threatening to plunge down any moment.

The Seed Dungeon.

Vahura gulped like a pelican swallowing a brass doorknob. In the light from the mothlamps, she could see the inmate's silhouette against his light green prison. The Seed Dungeon rocked incessantly, ceaselessly with the wind, not lending its current occupant a moment of peace. The Rakshasas did not believe in capital punishment by their own hand but let their Ancestors decide instead. The Rakshasa in the Seed Dungeon would sway till the day the Ancestors sent a storm to liberate him from his captivity by blowing the dungeon loose and letting him fall to his death. The sight of the Rakshasa struggling inside that giant-but-not-giant-enough-for-him pod inspired Vahura to lash a mental whip on her lungs, and command her feet to stop misbehaving.

Inevitability is often the mother of surrender but with the right dosage of circumstances and will, can be the step-mother of defiance.

This time, her legs complied.

III

The best way to picture the Tree City of Kamrup would be to imagine the Everwood Dome as the shell, Kamrup as the oyster and the Rakshasas as the pearls. Despite being closed off from the sides and the skies, the river Brahmaputra still criss-crossed through the City with its multiple streamlets on its way to kiss the Kalingan Sea, making swamps as common here as potholes are in the Riverlands. To dodge them and their toothy fauna, one had no option but to use one of the Living Bridges.

The Living Bridges, birthed from the aerial roots of the Everwood Trees, were scattered all across Kamrup and the other Tree Cities, and in some places, they were double-decker bridges shaped from the roots of the same tree which helped the Tree Folk to cross rain-soaked rivers and streamlets. The world remembered Rakshasas as brutal tyrants of the past which, while true, did obscure their contribution to the field of gardening. Their 'earth magic' brought a holy matrimony of nature and civilization in a way Men have been struggling for centuries to achieve, or rather, destroy.

It was one of such bridges called the Bridge of the Drenched Veil that Vahura was running on for her life – barefoot. Beyond the bridge, she could see the Path of Thanks stretch the great span that the Rakshasas had built at the height of their glory. The rail line, supported by a constant barrage of Grey Shamans attuned to the Earth Elemental, was wide enough for a ship to be placed end to end but since there was only a single track, whenever an earth-ship set sail for the Kalingan Sea, it blocked the entire rail. So, daylight was reserved for earthships heading into Kamrup, night was for earthships heading out, making the whole affair incom-prehensibly beautiful no matter when you chose to walk out into the City.

Though the earthships on the rail faded in comparison to the Narka Rath – the Royal Earthship resting under Leafsong. Unlike the ordinary earthships which had ships tethered to each other by ropes and hooks, the Narka Rath had the bows and prows of three galleys moulded to each other to make a single earthship. Vahura had seen a caricature painting of the Royal Earthship as a giant sea centipede, and she had dropped a copper into the artist's pouch for accuracy. But all said and done, from Nar Ad's list, the earthships of the East gliding on the Path of Thanks were the most magnificent manmade wonders. She shook her head to return her attention to her own path.

Only a few mothlamps burned this evening on either side of the Bridge of the Drenched Veil, the light flickering like fallen stars. It was well she was afoot. Ahead, a wagon laden with mangoes had gotten its wheel tangled with one piled high with ostrich feather mattresses, and brought all the traffic on it to a halt. Many of the pedestrians had stopped as well to derive perverse pleasure from watching the drivers curse at each other. No one noticed a tall human girl squeezing through the throng. In the middle of the press, a ragpicker, however, tried to grope her breasts, but a hard stab from her hairpin put an end to that.

Buildings carved into the trunks of Everwood Trees rose on either side of her once she descended the bridge: *Chausar* parlours and brothels, temples and shops, taverns and inns. Most of them started at a manheight of three, each floor hanging over the one under it. By her estimation, she was now in Grove's Kiss. So named because the top floors of the buildings carved into trees on either side of the street almost kissed each other because of the way the trunks inclined towards each other. Passing underneath, it felt like she was passing through a tunnel made of just leaves. Squeezed between the buildings and perched on the mighty lateral branches were night shops of all sorts, selling all kinds of items that could never be found in the Riverlands. You couldn't throw a rock in the street without hitting a Naga dreamweaver, or a Rakshashi blood-swain, or an Asura armourer or a Centaur hoofsmith or or even a Yogini astrologer – all folks who would have been chased off or lynched in the Riverlands. No Namins in the City meant no sacred order, and no sacred order meant there was no one to encourage violence against other races. Turns out when the holy leaders of a city do not interfere with the life of a city to create order, chaos finds a way to behave splendidly.

The only thing more valuable than spice here were Scarlets – the name divine courtesans of the Tree Cities were called. The Scarlets were all Asuras, and each seductively eccentric in her own way. Even now an airavat lumbered past with Shadow Apsara, a courtesan who was waving from the castle on its back, and who was famous for teasing passers-by with glimpses of her obsidian breasts. She looked so enchanting that Vahura waddled almost right into what she hoped was mud but turned out to be a steaming pile of dung the airavat had left to mark its passage.

'Rust and sparks! What the—'

A commotion ahead turned her expressions of disgust to dread. Bulling through the throng of drunken merrymakers ahead, were the Iron Order, yanking caps and veils off women on the street. Only human women. *They are searching for me.* How did they get ahead of her?

She instinctively turned right into an alley that opened out onto a plaza where a controlled bonfire threw spokes of light through the legs of dozens of Tree Folk who were dancing around the flames, jumping over them, singing, as drums throbbed in the air in a rhythmic chant.

An old Rakshashi with a jackal mask threw a garland of mari-golds over her neck and smudged her forehead with a tilak of sandalwood paste and vermillion, all the while chanting tuneful blessings. When the Rakshashi turned, Vahura crushed the garland and threw it aside, the anger bubbling in her at the sight of the garland doing much to subdue her fears.

The common room inside was larger than the great halls of half the castles in Aryavrat, a dim-lit labyrinth of a hundred private alcoves, shady grottoes and hidden nooks whose blackened beams and cracked ceiling oversaw nights of debauchery and decadence. A trellis of flowering firevines threw orange-hued patterns across the flagstones where green moss grew between the stones. Tattooed Rakshashis scurried through, bearing flagons of winterwine that smelled of gingerbread. The Hashayne-pink misted air was filled with the babble of shippers and slavers, fencers and courtesans, money counters and captains, all cursing and cheating each other in half a hundred different tongues. No different from a human tavern, save perhaps for being a hundred times more exotic when it came to interiors and patrons.

'Have you spotted a red-haired girl?' she heard a boy ask the old Rakshashi with garlands behind her. The guard was a younger lad with brown hair and a kind face who wore the white colours of the Iron Order. Surely a boy of his age could not be a member of the most feared squad of soldiers in the continent. Tiny pages of ice slapped on to the pit of her stomach. Why were they so hell bent on looking for her? And how were there so many of them?

'Lad,' the Rakshashi drawled, 'look around you, will ya? There be scores of women in scores of colours. If that be your only description for your catch, then... good luck fishing.' She laughed and was joined by others.

'By order of the Seven, the Angrakshaks will search around the place – we are looking for a red-haired princess...'

Vahura wrapped the headscarf around her hair tighter.

'Oh, take that cock out first, and then we will see if you deserve a princess,' the old woman hooted, and the dancers at the door chimed in. 'Cock out, cock out, cock out!'

Biting down on her lip, Vahura pulled away from where she stood before her cheeks caught fire.

She hid behind a leafy potted plant of lavaberry whose flowers were rimmed with a golden light that all but sheathed anyone behind under its golden glare. What should she do now? She could not possibly stand like a mannequin behind a plant all night. Could she? Maybe they would think her part of the furniture, the way the Balkhans showed off their home slaves. Maybe she could join a card game on the table or strike up a conversation with the few humans who lingered around the gambling tables. But who could she trust? How would she know that? And what if she blurted out something bizarre or let them in on her secret, or worse, asked a question that would insult their dim minds. She had innocently done it before, and her detentions had not been a student's ideal dream of how to spend a picnic.

A strange sensation swept over her. It took birth as a tingling sensation on the back of her neck that blossomed to burn a brand on her. *I am being watched.* She stepped out of the comfort of the lavaberry, her eyes sweeping the floor, but she could see no one staring at her. She looked to the floor that circled the common hall above. Gauzy, blood-red curtains swayed gently before every door on that floor. *Maybe there is someone behind them.*

A hand on her shoulder made her jolt like a kitten before a cucumber, her hand seamlessly unsheathing her hairpin on instinct. 'Pardon me for startling you... girl.' A Rakshashi stood before her, wearing a green blouse over a three-flounced skirt spangled all about with tiny emeralds, sewn with exquisite care onto the sheer fabric. The skirt's cut on the sides left little to imagination but still clung to her body like a hug. She wore no pallu over her blouse.

The smoky grey skin of her navel did wonders to set off the green in her dress. 'Are you well? You seem out of place here, more so for a descendant of Manu.'

Vahura considered her mind a curious thing for the way it over-thought every decision but when it came to lying now, let words flow out of her lips like liquid. It was as if the little time spent with the Rose Coterie had infected her with a bad case of mischief.

'I fear you are mistaken, Mistress. I am quite content where I was, which was waiting for my paramours to arrive and escort me... to dance,' Vahura said as she nervously gestured towards the group of dancers behind the Rakshashi, who were gyrating their hips against the crotch of their partners. 'Is that even a dance!' Vahura blurted out, before courtesy could cage those words.

'It is the gramand,' the Rakshashi said, her voice as cool and liquid as flowing water Her deep black, almond-shaped eyes betrayed no humiliation at Vahura's poorly chosen words. 'Why wait for a partner who is committing the grave folly of letting you wait? Take any lass or lad on the floor. They will fight over each other to take your hand, or rather, arse for dancing, I assume. You do have a for-midable backside.'

Vahura doubted it but she did not begrudge the Rakshashi for being charitable with her compliments. 'It is an intimate dance. It would feel wrong to dance with someone else who I do not bear affection for in my heart.'

'It is just a form of dance, what they are doing. You Riverlanders lend way too much importance to your sacral Chakras,' she said, with a smile that made Vahura's sacral Chakras tingle. 'Would you begrudge a man if while dancing he were to clasp your hand tightly, or say, hold your bare waist in a Panchalan dance?'

'I... don't think so. They are part of the...'

'Dance ritual?'

'Yes,' she said after a while.

'My thoughts exactly,' the Rakshashi replied, pointing to an Asuran woman whose rear was making rather industrious circular motions against her partner's crotch. 'This too,' she continued with a casual wave, 'is a form of dance. The dancers grind their bodies together, matching each other's rhythm as they would in any other dance. Once the song passes, so does their partner.'

That was an interesting thought. Dances in the Balkh were intricate but, when it came to touch, did not stretch beyond a palm-on-palm. There was a lot of hopping around like rabbits though. What she was seeing right now in front of her did seem more enticing… even if it made her feel uncomfortable. 'But… doesn't it look vulgar?'

She smiled as if seeing through Vahura's act of propriety. 'Perceptions are a product of the world we live in. One woman's vulgar is another woman's vision. But, as Tree Folk, there is one guiding lantern in these Everwoods we call home: we do not judge.'

Reading thousands of books did not prepare you for fear but it definitely armed you with barbed comebacks. 'Shouldn't that include not judging a woman who finds the dance… tawdry?'

The Rakshashi smiled. Smacking a passer-by's hand away with a wicked grin, she guided Vahura on a walk, her body forming a serpentine curve as it stalked towards the staircase. The Rakshashi's thick, black hair spilled across coins on the tables as she passed them.

'My name is Arakha,' she said. 'I own this humble establishment along with a few others. You're a smart little thing. I do, however, apologize for startling you, Balkhan but when I see a lass doing a bad job of hiding behind a lavaberry, I err on the side of caution. Would you like to share a goblet of wine with me?' There was a rude sound of doors slamming open below, and Arakha's grin fell as she gazed over her shoulder at the door. 'The Iron Order. I have just had it with this grim white menace. I will find you soon,' saying which the Rakshashi floated down the staircase.

Sparks! Vahura knew that young guard must have returned with an entire regiment to accost her. And now Arakha would identify her immediately. Should she confide in her? She seemed nice. And then what? Arakha would risk her establishment to save a girl who looked down upon their culture of the crotch-dance? *Don't be a lamb.* Vahura, instinctively, scratched the nape of her neck as she felt the stare stab her again. This time, from a lot closer.

'Don't talk, Princess,' a voice hard as leather and polite as lace whispered in her ear. 'And sheathe that pin. I mean no harm but I cannot say the same for the White Rats. Now, onto the staircase, slowly.'

What choice did she have?

She climbed the stairs, her steps stately and measured even though every inch of her spirit was screaming at her to sprint. The man stayed behind her all the way to the floor above. They passed wooden doors curtained with drooping vines behind which voices moaned and sighed, the pitch no doubt proportional to the purse of the custom.

'Did you say something?' the man asked. He betrayed a glimmer in his red eyes, like a lone lamp in the library in the afterhours, that irrationally made her trust him.

'Nothing.'

Once they reached the third door, he stepped in front of her and produced a key. 'I am sorry for asking you to trust me blindly and follow me into a, well, a room you are right to suspect. But choices aplenty are a luxury we do not currently enjoy.'

We? How had they become a *we?* Who was he? Why was he helping her? And why was she trusting him? She was a librarian. She was a princess. Yet here she was skulking around a night inn blindly following a stranger into a room. *Pray, Caution, come up with what I should do then? Maybe you can conspire with Conscience while you ponder.*

Heart pounding, she looked behind. The shadow of his hood cowled his face. But behind him, she could see the patrons on the staircase edge closer to the railing as more patrons huddled into them, no doubt to let the Iron Order pass through.

Vahura nodded but stayed still, as if frozen. *If you want to wake up in your room instead of a Seed Pod, walk, woman.* She entered the room, one hand on the hairpin. There were no alchemical lamps, just a tree of candles on a mantel to the left and an empty fireplace to the right. She made a mental note to understand how the Tree Folk lit a fireplace in a city made of trees. Without even looking across, Vahura knew the only other piece of furniture had to be a bed. She had been taken to such a room before against her will. Vahura drew in a deep breath, expelling the memory but accidentally catching the scent of the man behind her. Cinnamon? But there was something else, something that reminded her of minerals and honey. She stepped back to turn, and at the same time he pressed ahead.

'Apologies!' 'Pardon!' they both said at the same time, and then backed away from each other.

She realized she had nudged against his body, a very hard body. She groaned. *Another gamesman.* She had not had fond experiences with their kind. But the distance allowed her to see his face in the soft glow of the candlelight, and she froze for the second time that day. She did not know who he was but she definitely knew *what* he was. Skin the shade of hammered iron. Only a hint of his curving horns was visible behind his long, straight hair. Features sharp, as if cut from onyx. And such interesting eyes – vertical pupiled with not just one shade of red, but many, with hints of black that glimmered in the blood sea. She pushed against the useless part of her mind, the librarian that had her thinking of eyes, their shapes and their light, but it was futile. As he prowled to the edge of the room to peer down through the only window, she turned the pages of the books she had read on extinct races. Pragjyotisha was no doubt founded by Rakshasas fleeing the Vanaras beyond the Vindhyas but they were long gone. Breeding with humans had flooded the Lakelands with Rakshasas of muddied bloodlines, or in some cases hastened the rise of a new race of Asuras causing the ancient line of Diti to wane.

But the creature making sure the room was safe from surprises matched every description of a pure-blood Rakshasa she'd read. There must hardly be a dozen left. The rumour that they were inhumanly beautiful with obsidian skin was clearly not just a rumour. Were the other rumours true then? That the Rakshasas delved deep into the earth for secrets best left buried. That they twisted the flesh of men and beasts to fashion unnatural creatures using blood magic or that they strongly believed that the Gods in their wrath struck them down and burned their homeland for their sins.

Vahura wondered if now would be a good time to ask the Rakshasa about these rumours. It would be nice to finally have some answers, for of late, gossip rather than sources had become the glaciers to the river of knowledge. She pinched herself to stay on track. '*He is like to be an assassin, or worse, if those same rumours are true, a Rakshasa starving for my blood.*'

'I trust the right to decadence so cherished by the Tree Folk should protect you here, Princess,' he spoke, still looking at the street below from the window. 'They don't open closed doors on this floor. And I doubt they would let even the Iron Order march through. The scenes would be too, let's say expressive, for their taste.'

Vahura could not help but laugh but just as she was about to relax her mind knocked hard at her skull. *Right. Questions.* 'How did you know who I was?' she asked as she backed up on the settee before the fireplace.

'In a land of grey-skinned, red-eyed creatures, a red-haired, white-faced girl with that satchel has a way of leaving a mark on the memory,' and then the Rakshasa stiffened, as if embarrassed at having said something impolite. 'I... apologize, Princess. I meant no offence when I used the word *girl*,' he said, abashed.

Vahura had not even noticed the slip in the etiquette. She had finally traced the missing note in the Rakshasa's smell when he'd opened the window to let the wind in: cinnamon, tea leaves, honey and a touch of vanillin from wood-based books. She could mark the smell of vanillin anywhere... for she herself smelled the same way. Her sister had often called her a vanilla stick in skirts. Realizing now she *should* have been affronted at his slip in decorum, she puffed her cheeks to breathe out a royal rebuke but the sound of a door knock snatched the Rakshasa's attention.

'We have a problem,' the Rakshasa said, massaging his temples. 'I should've touched wood when I said that thing about privacy. I jinxed it,' he said to himself.

Vahura's eyes widened. This cold-blooded, literally cold-blooded, assassin-like figure was lamenting about... touchwood. That super-stition was so... charming. No, no. *I mean it is so curious.* Curious. That was the word.

He turned to her, eyes determined. 'We can jump from the window. It is not too high a jump.' Vahura raised an eyebrow and walked to the window where the Rakshasa stood. Staring down, she laughed in her head as she pictured it, her skirts flying around her, as she jumped from the sparks-damned first floor of a building.

'I am not jumping from here.' She crossed her hands.

'Are you afraid?' he asked.

The Rakshasa might be trying to save her but that did not entitle him to a confession about her fear of heights. *Not fear of heights*, she chastised herself. That did not quite accurately paint the picture. She feared her own self. The overwhelming feeling that if she got too close to the edge of a cliffside or a terrace, the monster within would take over and step off into the space. She clearly had trust issues with herself, and that scared her more than the naïve fear of heights ever could. 'I'm never afraid,' answered Vahura. 'But it does not bode well for a Princess to be seen leaping from building windows.'

'I heard the Panchalan Princess jumped from the fourth floor of a building in her swayamvar.'

Of course. Because she is perfect. I am not. 'Well, I would expect such athleticism from a woman who decided to marry five husbands.'

The Rakshasa laughed, and Vahura's scowl melted. She pinched herself again, and her mind turned keen like a razor as she remembered Arakha. When in Kamrup, do as the Kamrupans do. 'You said the Iron Order would be embarrassed about anything too… liberal. Is that a correct generalization?'

The Raksasha looked at her quizzically before nodding. Boots thudded on the corridor outside as men gathered outside it. Vahura had no time. 'In that case, I am sorry.'

She leaped at him.

IV

Moments later, the Iron Order barged in through the door. Their long cloaks, pristine white and embroidered on the right breast with a circle of seven stars, trailed behind them. 'Oi!' called one of the guards. 'Could you not hear the knock? Did you see a woman around here?'

The Rakshasa, who was lying with his chest to the ceiling, raised his head from the pillow to stare at the door, giving the man a lecherous smile. 'I am under one right now!' he called back, and thrust his hips a few times, making Vahura almost jump in the air, causing her blanket to almost slide off her shoulders. '*I am really sorry, Princess,*' he said under his breath.

'*Don't be,*' she whispered. '*It was my idea.*' Vahura was definitely being consigned to the Seventh Circle of Hell for this. She let out a moan to match his thrust, taking him by surprise. 'Oh yes, harder! So hard!'

Clumsy as she was, instead of matching it, she moved against the grain of his thrust... and ended up... feeling him. Hard. Too hard. Fire licked her navel. Was she seriously deluding herself into believing she was the reason? She pinched herself to sober up but this time it did not work.

Behind her, the bald men of the Iron Order wore expressions of disgust. One actually whispered a prayer and averted his eyes. 'Try the Hall of Moans down the alley,' the Rakshasa called. 'This is a private room.'

'Oh, let them watch!' said Vahura, blaming Asshaye for her bad influence. The Rakshasa's eyes widened. 'I don't mind!' She started jumping on his breeches like a jack-in-the-box. The Rakshasa suddenly rose to reach for her. She was taken aback as his hand went around her waist.

'You are so dirty, you filthy... cunt!' he said out loud. '*Sorry for the language, Princess,*' he whispered as he deftly pulled a pillow under her so that it was a soft cushion against which she put up her performance, and not his... pants, which suddenly felt uneven.

Now that she had a better view of the Rakshasa, she saw he wasn't so frightening for one. Weren't they supposed to have fangs? He looked like the Rakshasa all the others made fun of for being so humanlike. The one that would be a reformist and ask the others to drink from animals when they all sat down to consume human blood.

'Then choke me!'

'*Are you sure?*' he whispered. 'You are such a harlot!' he cried loudly.

'*Perhaps not*,' she whispered. It brought back too many ill memories. Instead, she pushed him back and rode the pillow. She had never ridden any man before but it could not have been very different from riding a horse, she reckoned. The posture was the same. The pages of *Kama Shashtra: The Treatise on 79 Poses of Sex* turned before her memory's eyes, and none of the seventy-nine poses seemed to suit Vahura's infamous inflexibility. Vahura bet Draupadi could do it all. *Focus!* She leaned back on the Rakshasa's body, her hands reaching for his ankle. She caught a glimpse of the door, and the Iron Order still stood there. She groaned but disguised it with a moan. Just her luck to be chased by voyeuristic perverts. She needed to shock them into leaving.

She bent down, her face close to his neck, breathing in the scents of tea leaves now. 'Oh, yes!' To the Rakshasa's horror, she feigned a series of ecstatic cries. '*I am incredibly sorry for this,*' she whispered. 'Oh yes! You like that! Like that? You want a finger up your arse! Fine!' The Rakshasa's face widened in sheer horror but Vahura did not notice. 'You are so filthy, you want it deep in your arse, don't you?' She saw the reflection of their cloaks on the window glass inch back to the door and then she whispered, '*Sorry for the language.*'

'Oh, you are making me so damp!' She turned up the volume of her cries of ecstasy. 'You are going to die while eating me out! I want your last breath to be on my—'

'*Please, Princess,*' the Rakshasa whispered. '*My ears!*'

'*Sorry, sorry,*' she pleaded as she held his palms to hoist herself up. She knew it was a myth but the long fingers of her unexpected accomplice in this deception made her blush inwardly. From the momentary time they spent together before a cushion came in between them, her body had a sense of his, and she knew he had a front to match his fingers. *Vahura! What is wrong with you!*

'Princess.'

'Yes, yes!' She hopped on the cushion again like a little girl excited for the solstice gifts. She was not going to lie to herself. The rough embroidery on the cushion did much to make this less of an ordeal. 'Oh, are you close!'

'*Princess,*' he whispered, urgently.

She bent down next to his neck, the smell of tea leaves making her heady. *Am I doing it wrong? I am sorry. I have only read about it, and heard shouts from my brother's room...*'

'Ehm,' the Rakshasa responded but a laugh played on his lips. 'Princess, they are gone.'

'Oh. *Oh.*' She realized she was still rubbing against the pillow. 'Sparks! I am sorry!' She awkwardly took off the blanket that had hid her hair and frame, and slid off the Rakshasa. He, on the other hand, rose slowly, still holding on to the cushion.

After a bit of awkward silence, the Rakshasa asked, 'What have you done that has turned the Iron Order so brave?'

'Ehm, spices...'

'The Iron Order, the soldiers of Seven, are after you... for spices. That is... interesting.'

'I've heard so much about the chillies of the Tree Cities," Vahura said, the lie slipping from her lips as easily as a clown pulling an endless cloth from their mouth. 'In the Riverlands, we grow the finest spices – turmeric, fenugreek, fennel, you name it. But there's something special about how the Free Tree Folk use sun-roasted asafoetida and fennel paste in their famous Chutney of Doom. At first, I thought it was the King Chilli, which grows only under the Living Bridges. But then I realized the secret lies in the Sanjeevani root that the Asurs use. It blends all the flavours together, creating waves of smoky tastes, each more intense than the last. The Sanjeevani root connects everything, but it's been nearly wiped out, thanks to the Vanaras mining it and taking it to Lanka. Only one patch still grows in our realm, hidden here in the Temple of Prakioni in Kamrup.'

This was clearly more than the Rakshasa had ever contemplated on the trade secrets of preparing chutneys. 'All right,' he said, finally. 'I think I grasped some of that. So, you were picking up herbs in the garden of their temple, and they sent the Iron Order after you for this?'

'Well, it is their only temple this side of the East where the Iron Order have encamped for the Conclave. It is possible that I was picking them after hours, and I suppose it could be said, it was without their knowledge.'

He raised an eyebrow.

'I wasn't stealing. It just grows here, without helping anyone. Sanjeevani has great... healing properties,' her eyes grew alarmed, 'ehm... You're not going to call the Iron Order back on me, are you?'

'You are clearly a hardened bandit,' said the Rakshasa, trying not to laugh. 'But perhaps a warning this time might suffice.'

Vahura scowled at him. 'And you would presume to warn a Princess.'

'A Princess who is a chutney criminal, yes, I would think so,' he corrected. She glared at him, and then broke into a laugh.

He laughed as well, drawing nearer to the bed's edge, his knees mere inches from hers. Vahura's stomach lurched. *What is wrong with me?* She tried to change the topic.

'You are a ranger, then?'

'I am responsible for the peace in Kamrup, yes,' he said. 'May I ask you a question of a more private, perhaps delicate nature?'

'Depends,' Vahura said, 'on the question.'

'Why did you run?'

Vahura had been prepared.

'I did not want to cause an international scandal that might lend Balkh a bad name for such a trifle. What is worse is I did not even succeed! I broke the jar on my way through the Bridge of the Drenched Veil. And well, you know the rest. Glad you were here,' she said, smiling, and suddenly re-realizing the room they were in. 'Oh, I hope I did not... interrupt your evening,' she said leaning away from him.

'Uhm, I don't...' said the Rakshasa, embarrassed.

'Of course. Sorry. I should have known... I mean, a Rakshasa wouldn't...' *Stop. Talking.*

'Well, there's no reason a Rakshasa wouldn't... but this one,' said the Rakshasa jerking a thumb to his chest, 'prefers not to pay for intimacy. No ill will towards those who do, though.'

This time Vahura smiled at him. Why was she smiling at him? Was she glad he did not pay a visit to Scarlets? Why? There was nothing wrong with the flesh trade. Why was she such a prude? Did he think that she was a prude? *Stop smiling.*

'You must think I'm a lecherous fiend after what I did to you?' asked Vahura.

'Could you speak louder? I have grown deaf in my right ear,' the Rakshasa said.

'We will have to make do with the left for next time,' quipped Vahura.

The Rakshasa burst out laughing, a laugh that reminded her of butterflies escaping a cave. How long had it been since she had made someone laugh?

The Rakshasa and Vahura laughed again as they spoke of chutneys several times as they waited for the commotion outside to cease.

After what seemed hours, there was a loud knock on the door. The Rakshasa shielded her behind the door, and opened it slowly. At the door loomed a grotesque fat Asura with a forked black beard, holding a wooden baton. His robe was large enough to serve as riding vestments for a ceremonial horse but its loosely knotted belt had come undone, exposing an unflattering belly and a pair of breasts that sagged like the teats of a cow that had miscarried.

'Your time is up here. Pay the fee and then fuck off from here, or I will find others to fuck you to make up for lost time.'

'How courteous of you,' Vahura said, emerging from behind the Rakshasa. 'Have the Iron Order left?'

'Eh?' the cow-man asked, scratching his head upon seeing a human with a Rakshasa. 'The White Rats. Aye, they be long gone. Who are you? Are you new? Eh, don't matter,' he looked at the Rakshasa, 'you, Baggy Pants, pay up!'

Vahura thanked him and then turned towards the Rakshasa. 'I know you have already helped me immensely but—'

'I will pay the coin for the room.'

Vahura flushed. 'I can pay my way in life, thank you,' she said curtly as she dug inside her satchel for her purse. 'I just need to find directions to Leafsong.'

'I axed my own foot there, didn't I?' the Rakshasa said.

'No, no. I overreacted. I have a certain disposition against being paid for,' she said.

'I did not mean any offence,' he said. 'You are a Princess, after all, and could buy me ten times over,' he whispered. *Could she?* He straightened. 'But, of course, I would guide you to the Palace. Would you allow me to act as your escort till the Palace Gates? Please – I insist.'

'Insist elsewhere, maggots,' the Asur boomed.

She was the Princess of Balkh, and knew her courtesies. This Rakshasa had certainly saved her time, if not her life. And clearly, he was someone who was acquainted with courtly etiquette, and so she could not be the one remiss in hers. 'Of course,' she took his arm, 'what should I call you?'

The Rakshasa hesitated for a moment. 'Baggy would be fine.'

'You are using the name rather *loosely*,' Vahura said, and then slapped her mouth shut, instantly regretting it. Baggy only smiled, and the left side of his lip curved up to reveal a dimple. *Why did I have to say that? Oh, you are so pathetic, Vahura.* But it was the Asur who came to her rescue as he boomed into a hiccup of laughter.

'Baggy and Loosely.' He laughed, patting his belly as if it were the source of that joke. 'A fitting name for a song on old whores,' he panted. Slapping his baton on his open palm, his laugh all gone, he grunted, 'Now fuck off.'

ADHYAYA II:B

A LAMENT OF LOYALTY

KALINGAN SEA

3 MONTHS BEFORE THE BATTLE OF MATHURA

'A lover's eyes will gaze an eagle blind.'
—**Shakespeare**

DANTAVAKRA

I

Fields of passionfruit ripening in the sun, fisherfolk hauling in exotic crabs in their nets, sweet wines and sweeter women on the menus of resthouses with hot springs in the backyard to scrub away the grease. Dantavakra would personally advise the Emperor that the bards who painted the ports so, be hanged. He sniffed gingerly at the air and wrinkled his nose in exaggerated distaste as he took in the run-down island around him. Mati had called Tamra Lipta, an island off the coast of Kalinga, a museum of sin. But the island was so thoroughly disenchanted with hygiene, beauty and class that it seemed more of a mausoleum of shit. Dantavakra, his gamble having failed, now waved his hand in front of his nose, as if that would ward away the smell.

'This is Tamra Lipta,' Mati tossed over her shoulder. 'City of Acquired Senses.'

'Oi, oi! Oi!' Dantavakra jumped on one leg like a dance monkey. 'What is that?' He began to pull at the shiny crawling bug on his calf but it didn't let go. 'It has me! It is killing me!' He started to unsheathe his sword before Mati held his wrist.

'Scrape, don't pull,' Mati said, picking the leech off her own neck to show him how it was done. With one fingernail, she removed it, and then flicked it at Dantavakra's face.

'Princess!' Dantavakra waved his hands frantically but when he did not feel the squish of the pest against his palm-wall, he panicked. 'Is it on me?'

'Such a child.' Mati squished the leech under her boot, twisting her waist left and right to stamp it out of existence. The tenant in her stomach must not have liked that as she let out a groan of cramp a moment later. 'Storms forbid, if only the Crown Prince's foes knew that all they have to do is approach his room with a bowl of leeches to find the room unguarded. Come, *Rakhjai*. The sun teases our time.'

Darkness was on its way to dawn as they made their way along the shorefront of Tamra Lipta. But even at this hour, the streets were ablaze with light and crowd. They passed the scratch dens, the seedy taverns, the brightly coloured brothels and even an open theatre where the actors, twice more drunk than the crowd, staggered around on the stage. The crowds in the back were hooting, not out of applause for their acting skills, but for the chance to throw rotten tomatoes at them. The only time Dantavakra smiled was when he spied true soldiers wearing Kalingan blue wandering in and out of what had to be a brothel. The scenery would have made Shishupal pass out.

Mati wasn't wrong. The Island of Tamra Lipta was another realm in itself. High nobles in Rajgrih with Kalingan investments often spoke of the common ancestry shared by Kalingans and Magadhans but if this were so, Kalinga was definitely a step-cousin of Magadh.

'Princess,' Dantavakra tried. 'Are you certain the bag is not heavy? Please allow me.'

Mati rolled her eyes. 'I miss the olden times when no one cared. Don't fret, Rakhjai. Asanka spent so much time fussing over the contents of my bag, she could have outfitted an entire crew for a raid in that hour.'

Dantavakra thought the dwarf had done a splendid job, what with Mati dropping nearly everything she picked up on deck because of her shifting Chakras. Not to forget Mati could not even bend without adorning the air with a garland of curses. Asanka may have been a dwarf from Kalinga but she had grit and grace. And it wasn't just about aiding her captain. Asanka stood as the lone bastion of kindness to Dantavakra on deck, even going so far as to offer him sweets when the ship discovered the Princess was in a delicate condition. Dantavakra still suspected that the Princess had known she was expectant but had kept it from the Empire just to get a stab at steering a ship again. He sympathized with the feeling, but given how she was carrying the Heir of the Empire, she should have been home, resting, and not here, representing.

'Oh, blessed Mother! You are with child!' someone cried.

Dantavakra's hand went to his sword. He could not trace where that voice came from till it cried again.

'Oh, a child!' The culprit, a priest in brown-orange robes who stood on the balcony, called out, hands outstretched as if aiming to scoop Mati up from the ground. 'Oh, creation! Prakioni made all the delicate, inner parts of his body and knit it together in your womb with the aid of Agni!'

'Funny. I thought I had something to do with it,' Mati hollered back.

'We are all but Prakioni's handiwork, created by Xath, nourished by Indra, fuelled by Agni, lifted by Vayu, shielded by—'

'Yes, yes,' Dantavakra said. 'Heard enough. We should head on, Princess.'

'– to do the good works, for which they prepared us in advance,' the priest continued as if Dantavakra did not exist. 'But in this godless place, in this land of heathens, your unborn is not safe. I have been blessed by the Far Eye, you see, and I see your unborn.' He rolled his eyes up dramatically, exposing the yellowed whites as he stared up at the sky. *'Beware the twin stars, for when you think they have faded, they are just twinkling, churning darkness from light once again.'* An ungainly cough from his throat interrupted his performance. His eyes were a human's again as he pleaded through his coughs. 'Come, come repent your sins at the shrine to the Earth Goddess, and—'

'Come repent your sins here,' cried a man with bejewelled ears from the balcony of the building next to the Temple, 'and why repent before her priest when you can repent before Prakioni herself. She would spread her legs and redeem your sins for a gold sovereign.' On cue, a woman with folds for a stomach, emerged from his side, dressed in voluminous, sequined green fishnet tights that had seen better days. They might have covered her entire body but much to the ire of onlookers, left little to imagination. Her eyes and lips were painted green while a garland of leaves dangled around her neck. A crownlet of strawberries adorned her forehead though it miserably failed to hide the lines behind. The hag's eyes found Dantavakra's, and she licked her lips seductively.

'Father forfend,' Dantavakra said. 'This is blasphemy!'

Mati laughed, blowing a kiss at the harlot dressed in a lewd re-imagination of the Goddess Prakioni. 'This is Tamra Lipta. City of Sacrilege. City of the Godless. Come.'

They passed more gambling houses and more fencing dens, and even two inns, called 'Please Hop' Inn and 'Only Rabbits Hop' Inn, built side by side. Dantavakra grudgingly admitted that was funny. Alchemical lamps above stalls ahead threw pools of coloured light upon their path, turning Dantavakra's face red, then green, then purple as he scowled suspiciously at the goods on offer. Of whores, there was a generous supply, which was a given considering whores and sailors were symbiotic creatures. Oh, how he'd yearned to visit such lands of sex and abandon when he'd heard the tales but the tales had left out how the wares here were greasy as tar, and stood as advertisements of the cockrot instead of coitus. He felt their eyes on him as he walked past, heard them giggling between themselves, revealing sundried teeth. While definitely not wanting to indulge them, Dantavakra felt miffed that he wasn't even propositioned. Surely he was handsomer, or at least more hygienic, than any piece of wood they had wedged between their legs in their lifetime.

Frustrated, he walked right into a sturdy woman, taller than him by a finger with a face painted with such enthusiasm that he could see the colours even in the dark. She grabbed his balls, her face smeared with a drunken smile. 'Suck your cock for a copper?' she asked in the deepest voice he'd ever heard.

'Bastard!' hissed Dantavakra as he peeled himself away from their grab, and rushed after Mati. 'Their kind do not have the gall to walk the streets openly in Magadh.'

'Magadh's loss.' Mati turned in her hooded cloak, smiling at Dantavakra, who had shed his armour for something drab and grey. 'Get used to it. This is Tamra Lipta. City of No Judgment. City of Freedom.'

Dantavakra scowled, finding himself wishing the Prince had come with them. Painful as he was, at least he would share Dantavakra's opinion of the place. But Mati had shifted the *Gilded Lion* to a position off one of the long stone piers in the anchorage, and had the two of them ferried here on a small shoreboat to avoid eyes. For a change, Dantavakra did not stumble around blind as to the *why*. Lions were not welcome in this nest of viperous Swans. That did make him wonder now what they thought of Mati for wedding into the Empire. But before he could pry Mati for answers, a pungent stream of blood and piss trickling down the left side of the path had Dantavakra do a dancing jig to dodge it only to trip and fall knee first on a corpse – the wellspring of said stream.

Disgusting! This was the worst day of his life. Mati walked past without commentary as if passing a jasmine stall. A flock of pipe smokers squatting on the side, eyes flimsy with grey, stared at him from their nooks, sniggering as if he were next. Dantavakra rose, wiping his knees, hurrying to stay closer to Mati, all the while scraping the soles of his boot along the street to rid them of the grime.

'Don't worry about it,' Mati said, turning right at muddy crossroad. 'Just a sign of booming business around these parts.'

'Holy teats of the Ocean,' exclaimed a voice from the shadows ahead. 'The Black Swan in the flesh, isn't it? Bigger flesh, for sure.'

'Who speaks?' Mati asked, hands on the dagger on her belt.

'Did I really not leave an impression that night?' a bald man in leathers with iron studs emerged from the shadows carrying a dim lantern in one hand and a spiked club in the other, followed by scruffily dressed thugs.

'I think you answered the question yourself, Handsome Haram.' Mati nodded. 'How are you walking around free? Did someone leave your cage open?' With a belly to rival a stew pot and an ear whose hair bristles reached long to disappear in his beard, the man smiled genially as he stepped into the glow of the stall lanterns. Only a sparse collection of teeth remained in his mouth, less on top, more below. 'The Ocean have mercy, you grow uglier every time I see you, Haram. You're as ugly as a salad.'

'The Storm taketh its toll but,' he held his crotch, 'the Storm also giveth its gifts. Who this maiden behind you?

'What did you say?' Dantavakra's hand went to his sword.

'Hard of hearing too, is she?' Handsome Haram said without so much as a flinch. 'Is that why you have settled for cockless beauties in steels to give you company so he don't have to hear your secrets.'

'Haven't we all?' Mati responded, silencing Dantavakra before he could seethe. Handsome Haram laughed, shaking her arm in a tight grip. 'Good to see you, Captain.' Mati nodded, and with a sleight of hand, passed a pouch full of coins to Handsome Haram, who pocketed it eagerly.

'As ever your generosity remains legendary, Captain. It'll keep this belly in shape.' He patted his stomach vigorously. If Haram had noticed a belly on Mati, he did a fine job of keeping his eyes level on hers.

'Heading for the dice down below?' Mati asked.

'Aye,' he grumbled. 'All we ask is for the peace to be maintained, and for murders to be sanitary and shadowed. Leaving a dice out on the open near the harbour is a shitty way of welcoming guests. But woes of our paradise shall keep. On to you – Should I pass the word?'

'No. Here on a toehold, Haram, to fetch a pass 'round the Three Eyes from the High Table. Best not mention that I was here.' Dantavakra still could not digest that the Three Eyes of Elusa was a triplet of whirlpools that disappeared under a new moon only to appear somewhere else entirely. *How can a whirlpool, let alone three, shift so?* But whatever the cause of these sentient maelstroms, it was the only reason the Emperor had chosen the Princess to command. It was also the only reason they had disembarked at Tamra Lipta – to find the latest map around these whirlpools – though Dantavakra hardly cared for the reason as long as he got the chance to walk on land.

'Fine idea, Captain,' he glanced around briefly, and then his voice grew serious, 'but Matakshara Harran has claimed the High Table at Mourning Wood, and she knows there is a Lion ship shorebound. She has sent men strolling to escort any disembarkers from the ship. I thought it be best for you to walk in the door looking all-knowing.'

'Obliged. Onwards, then. May the waves carry you.'

'May the current bring you back, Captain.'

'These are Kalingan soldiers?' Dantavakra asked incredulously when he had lost sight of the men behind them. He had drunk with Kalingan soldiers back in the Magadhan camps and while they did not have class, they were certainly princes before Handsome Haram.

Mati laughed. 'Enforcers to keep the soldiers away, and public nuisance down. In this land of the lawless, you need the finest law-breakers to stop revellers from burning the place down or waking the place up during the day. Captains pay them a little of the load they bring in so that they can do their *enforcing* on a full belly.'

'And who is Matak?'

'Matakshara Harran, the Wraith of Storms, and thought lost to the pleasures of the Golden Islands, is back now on the High Table. Hm. That is a problem.'

'Why? You steal from her?'

Mati did not answer, face placid, lips pursed.

'Oh, Yama, you stole from someone who those enforcers feared. I told you we should've fetched more men. But worry not, Princess, if things turn difficult, you can count on me.' Dantavakra straightened. 'I have been known to diffuse many a fight back in the Capital. I can finally be of assistance here.'

'Let us not wet our swords just yet, Rakhjai. See what she has to say before we start slitting throats.'

He nodded excitedly as he followed her, half hoping he did get a chance to punch a throat at least. If the rumours around Mati were anything to be believed, things usually did get bloody around her but Dantavakra had reckoned a baby in the stomach would change that. Apparently not. 'Am I then permitted to use my sword freely?'

'This island is a temple to business and free trade, a Drachma's wet fantasy. A haven where fences can shortchange you, harlots can catch the rot, gamblers can lose and pirates can stretch their legs without trivialities like the law. The Wraith will exact a charge for lending us the path around the Three Eyes, perhaps a heavy one, and if it be too heavy, the custom demands we either bow or we cut.' She winked as she stopped. 'This is…'

'Yes, yes,' Dantavakra said, exasperated. 'This is fucking Tamra Lipta, the Land of No-One-Cares. How many times will you say it, Princess?'

'Actually, this is it. We are here at the Mourning Wood.'

II

Mourning Wood was heavy with the sounds of several dozen patrons cursing and laughing and shouting, all at once. Scull-boys and serving wenches rushed about with more panic than purpose while muscled minders prowled the tables as they passed, as if their livelihood depended on how many drunkards they tossed outside. Perhaps it did. Fragrances of blood, puke, burnt meat, bad ale, sex and sweat – the markings of civilized nightlife – were all available in plenty. Broken bottles and splintered carcasses of chairs spoke tales of epic brawls. On the other side, a section of the tavern was fortified behind iron panels through which ale and food could be served. That section resembled less a bar and more a murder-hole in a fortress wall.

As a tavern, it was far bigger than any Dantavakra had frequented in Rajgrih. Lights only came from the dim candles. The windows were draped with boards that seemed scavenged from the shipwreck of Manu's Ark. Stairs ascended dramatically high on either side of the communal area to the first floor that was less a floor, more a broad path wrapped around the perimeter of the tavern. But it was the bouquet of affairs he could partake of inside the tavern that made his head giddy. Back home, he would have to visit a different tavern to arm wrestle, to heel-dance on tables and to gamble. But here it seemed he could do all of it at once! *Finally! Tamra Lipta, the City of Revels.* So excited was Dantavakra that he did not even notice the cockroaches crawling over his boots, drawn to the blood and piss under them.

But Mati dragged him to the stairs before he could crack his knuckles. As she passed the tables, someone raised his glass hollering 'Black Swan' to which Mati curtly nodded. There was a sudden current of excitement in the air for too many conversations were hushed then, too many whispers were birthed, and almost every eye began to trail their passage. Gambling forgotten, Dantavakra gripped his sword hilt, making sure he made a scowling eye contact with each man he passed. He hoped he would win a chance to do some kingsguarding and finally let word travel of how accomplished a swordsman he was. His hope was thwarted when a sharp voice called out from the first floor.

'If you don't return to your business by the time I finish my next sip,' a woman peered over the railing of the first floor, wearing a four-cornered hat over the most dazzling silver hair Dantavakra had ever seen, 'I will come down and sculpt an arse out of your face.'

The entire tavern as a whole returned to their plates of grease-soaked parathas and scrambled crocodile eggs as if they had never seen Mati in the first place.

Dantavakra congealed in his tracks as he saw the woman up close. This had to be the Wraith. She was dark, with skin just a few shades lighter than charcoal, and she was striking even though not young. Lines about her eyes and mouth proclaimed her somewhere around fifty. Her eyes were ice as she spanned the gentry sitting on the floor waiting for someone to rise to her challenge. None did. Disappointed, she returned to her conversation with someone on her side, her silver white braids threaded with red ribbons turning with a flair behind her. Despite the winter, she wore only a weather-stained half-jacket, revealing muscled, tattooed arms. Dantavakra felt himself uncomfortable behind his breeches, having no idea why an old woman was causing him to stir awake or why he was walking now like a courtly mustang.

Dantavakra let duty take over instinct as he looked around to see how much of a fighting space was there for him to swing a sword. Gods, he missed his trident but even he had to admit it was not a convenient weapon to sheathe. Not that there was enough space to wield a sword, either, though there were plenty to wield the sword on.

Former patrons of the chairs had vacated them to stand clear before Mati and Dantavakra arrived. 'Mati of Magadh, the Empress-in-Waiting,' said the silver-haired woman at the head of the table, 'welcome to my humble establishment.'

'Wraith,' said Mati, taking a seat on the opposite head of the table, a full three chairs away from Matakshara.

After a searching glance that took in Mati's expanding shelves of her breasts and belly, Matakshara spoke. 'You are with child.'

'Old age has not dulled your eyes.'

Matakshara's arm was a blur as she dashed the contents of her cup into Mati's face. Before Dantavakra could even react, Mati held his wrist, wiping away the rum with her free hand. 'You still have a good throwing arm. Don't tell me you are still sore for losing the last wager.'

Dantavakra cursed inwardly. It would have been the finest moment in history had he seen Matakshara's attack and coldly swatted away the cup from her hand before she flung it. Dash it. He frowned, and looked up sullenly only to spot a woman on the other side of the table offering him a wicked yellowed grin. She was small, lithe, hair so bleached as to be almost white. Not his usual flavour but he hadn't charmed a blonde before. He shot out his flirtiest smirk, chest swelling, body angling to show off the fine swordsheath. The woman pursed her lips to show she was impressed. *Finally, someone with fine taste.*

'Pray that your child gives you less trouble than you gave me. Now will you behave or do I need to punch some manners to your mouth?'

Mati clenched her fists. 'Not unless you've grown tired of your own teeth, given how few are left. Lest you forget, Harran, you never won the High Table. You claimed a seat I abandoned.'

'Abandoned the Kalingans for the Greens, aye. The Storm God must be gushing in joy.'

'Peace, Harran,' Mati raised her hand, 'I will behave.'

Dantavakra was still using his smouldering-eyes-look on the woman. She tilted her neck as if to subtly gesture him to follow her into a private room. His manner, as he made a sad face, suggested he had little hope that business would result. He jerked his head towards Mati to convey he was oathsworn to serve but just then Matakshara banged the table, authoritatively, with her tree trunk of an arm. Dantavakra had never been with so muscled a woman before, and wondered what feats she was capable of in the boudoir.

'I will behave... *what?*' Matakshara asked, her beautiful jaw hardening.

'I will behave...' Mati swallowed as if in utter spiritual agony, '... Mother.'

Wait, Mother, what?

MATI

I

The floor emptied of Matakshara's crew of seven, and Mati's crew of one. Dantavakra shot a confused look her way as he was whisked away by Zuri to table-dance below. The yellow-toothed sneer on Zuri's face hinted at less than noble intentions. Well, Dantavakra had wanted attention, and now he would drown in it.

While the commotion of emptying the floor was underway, Mati diluted her enigma by excusing herself to the privy. She was sure by the time she reached the Conclave, she'd have seen the inside of every privy in the Tree Cities. Perhaps, she should be put in charge of Magadh's sanitation, a role which would benefit richly from her personal experience. When she returned, she found Matakshara leaning over the railing.

'You hiding in there, Red Hat?'

A booming voice answered from behind the bar fortifications. 'You know me, Captain. As cowardly as a mob.'

'Wisdom in that. If you've got a cask of anything that doesn't stink like hogpiss, send it up. My daughter is here, so send something light. Not sure if Lions can handle their liquor.'

One of Matakshara's heavies laughed as he passed them by to take the stairs, when Mati caught him by the scruff of his collar from behind. Mati cracked her hand against his face, and then held his hair, slamming his face on the table top, rattling the glasses. Then she pulled him to his feet, brushing dust off his jacket and adjusting his collar. 'You good?'

The man smiled a confused red smile till Mati shook him by his collar again to shake away the stars. 'Aye, sorry Captain,' he managed to say. All the other laughs at Matakshara's jape had a stillbirth.

'No harm done,' Mati said as she pulled her hand, her palm holding a purse that seconds before had been at his belt. 'We all have been clumsy from time to time, haven't we? I am always clumsy,' saying which she pretended to fumble, tossing the bag over to the patrons below where it was swallowed before it even touched the floorboard. 'Red Hat! A strong glass of ale for my friend here, and tab it on me. It is perfectly understandable that he will not be able to carry his weight around here any longer.'

'Your will, Captain. Sending the drinks in a huff.'

Matakshara nodded at Mati, and Mati rolled her eyes. She knew her mother had taunted Mati to give her a chance to remind everyone who the Black Swan was. But Mati had not needed her mother's help to do it. She could be so infuriating, always interfering.

'I hate to sting your feelings but I did not—' Mati started.

'Come, let us have drinks and pretend to talk like a mother would to her daughter.'

Mati narrowed her eyes. She had a nagging feeling that her mother had somehow known she was coming, and that was never a good thing.

II

Now that she was back again at the High Table, her memory was doing a grand job of wounding her. She had occupied the High Table many a time in her prime, but nothing had changed since then. Banners she had claimed from looted ships hung in niches with alchemical lanterns behind them, giving off an ominous dim, flower-tinted cast to the room. The wall behind one of the banners was still cracked from the Kasmiran brawler's head she had bashed in when he had spilled his ale on Mati's sleeve. She was sure if she were to flick the carpet from under the table, she would find it etched on the blackboard: 'Permanent Mati Table', which her boatswain had scratched in a dare in her absence. The strongmen had broken his arm for defacement of property when he had not been able to bribe them when caught. She had had the strongmen thrown to jadesharks in response. Always an even trade in Mourning Wood.

'So, you are turning a grandmother. Must make you happy,' Mati decided to open, considering she had to rush if she had any intention to catch the tide back.

'Oh, yes, I am as cheerful as a maiden on a pony's back. Though it does warm my heart to see you in a world of pain.' She smiled.

'Wish I could deny it,' Mati said, and then suddenly alarmed at the tears dancing behind her eyes, chugged the horrible rum from the clay in one chug.

'Is that happening too often?'

Mati shrugged. 'The uncalled tears are bearable. But this,' she lifted her shirt to show a dark stretch of skin curving down from her swollen navel to her hip, 'better be temporary.'

'No,' Matakshara said. 'But maybe it will bearable if you think of the stretch mark less as vandalism of your body and more as a badge of motherhood.' She burst into laughter at Mati's expression, and managed to add a choked amendment, 'It was just a jest.'

Mati found no humour in it. Motherhood was for lovers of misery. For four moons, she had retched on all fours, and now, when the sickness had passed, it seemed she could scarce keep from relieving herself. And now, her tears flowed as freely as her bladder's burdens But she would bear it all if it meant being back on sea.

Only after hoisting the sails did she realize how being kept away from the Ocean Goddess had shrivelled her like a plant starved of sunlight. And now that she had become heavier, especially on the hips, she had found the crew far more obliging. She wondered if other captains knew this trade secret: hips were far more persuasive than whips. A bard could weave a a song out of that line.

The sea also brought with it a clarity of mind. Her thoughts wandered to matters she had long avoided, chief among them, her unborn child. What was she going to do with it? What would it expect of her? She needed the child, that was true. It was her investment. A return on nine months of misery and years of discomfort till the child grew to wield a sword. But what would she do until then? What did her other pirate friends do? Sell their

whelps, mostly. To slavers, to temples, to begging guilds and sometimes even to harems, if the babe was a boy.

'Lost in the glories of your past?' Matakshara asked.

Mati nodded.

'It isn't entertaining when you surrender to my barbs.' Matakshara
frowned. 'You look like a jadeshark without a pod. All okay, dolphin?'

'Aye.'

'Alright, so that was a lie. Now I know I do not have to worry
about any man treating you ill,' she sniggered, 'especially after the
way you paid back your debts in Panchal, but you seem… different.
You dress… different. The gold ring on your ear seems as expensive
as having children.'

'It probably is.'

'And what are you doing wearing a gold circle on your ear instead
of copper? What use is that to Stormborns?'

'A gift from the husband.' Mati shrugged and then leaned closer,
her elbows now on the table. 'Tell me, what is Zuri doing here? She
was *my* handmaiden.'

'What do you mean? After you refused to take her, your father
had her sent to me. You know he does not know how to deal well
with young maidservants. So, I am training her to be a shipwench.'

After I refused? Huh. 'The husband seems a keeper then if he gifts
you so.'

What did Matakshara mean by *Mati had refused Zuri?* Wasn't
it her father who had refused to let any Kalingan from her household accompany her to Magadh? *Maybe Father lied to Matakshara.
Wouldn't be the first time.*

'A keeper, indeed,' Mati said. 'We overlook each other's faults,
and often.' A little too often, perhaps.

'Ah, the early ecstasy of a marriage.' Matakshara nodded, under-
standingly. 'You are fortunate. Forgiving *you* is an all-day all-seasons
job.'

Fortunate? Perhaps. The perception of what is forgiveness could,
however, be prejudiced. The memory of Amala and Amala's mother
in silent embrace as they were imprisoned on Saham Dev's orders
returned like a winged demon. She clipped the memory's wings in a
distracted way, torn as Mati was by disgust at having watched them

be tortured, and the understanding that it had been a necessary lesson for Mati to learn from Saham Dev's point of view.

'What would you know about it?' Mati snapped.

'Not me, of course. I meant your father. The dolt keeps complaining you have flown too close to the sun. That you don't respond to his letters.'

Mati blinked in confusion, her lids heavy. What letters?

Matakshara continued, 'I understand not letting him meet you at the wedding but don't give the poor man a regret that did he not sire another child, will you? Write to him.'

Mati forced herself to remain expressionless, although a tightness gripped her chest. The smell of something rotten filled her nose but she could not figure out the guilty ingredient. Her father had refused to meet Mati, not the other way around. Had he simply lied to her mother to stay in her good books? Oblivious of it, or perhaps ignoring it, Matakshara continued.

'We digress, however. Though, if someone asks after your ring, claim you looted it off a merchant's corpse. I have a reputation to hold,' Matakshara said as she took a sip from her tumbler. 'But I do understand the madness in the first few months of marriage, little one. The things I had ignored, drunk on the sweet lie of eternal matrimony,' she raised her voice instead of lowering it, 'especially on the bed, if you know what I mean.'

'My ears will pop off along with the golden ring if you press on.'

Matakshara frowned. 'You are a lot of things, Mati, a prude is not one of them.'

If only she knew that Mati was none of those things any more.

Matakshara groaned. 'Since you insist on spoiling the fun, I would say don't worry, dolphin. There are certain perks to carrying a slug in the belly. Winning trade deals is akin to throwing a net on the Sun Lake. You can haggle tough with a corsair, but not with a woman making life. More strangers smiled at me in those wretched months than all my lovers but that was perhaps because I was fatter than them. Not to forget no one expects a woman with child to suck their cock.'

'I like sucking cock.' Mati tapped her clay cup, and the serving wench obliged.

'As do I,' she winked at Mati. 'Why fight a sword when you can swallow one to rule the world. To your sharp tongue, then,' Matakshara emptied her clay cup, and slammed it on the floor, a sign for more. 'Enough about my experience,' Matakshara leaned across the table as she drained her refilled cup. 'I'm sure you must be deeply craving meat.'

'The thing I crave most is for men to be saddled with the task of bearing a child.'

'Well said. More!' Matakshara slammed the cup on the table again, and Mati realized that her mother was trying to get her drunk. Oh, this was going to be good. Her mother had an agenda which meant Mati was definitely earning the pass. At what cost though?

'Who was the meat you carried with you? Looked as lost as a river disappearing into an unknown sea.'

'He is Dantavakra of Chedi – Imperial Blood. Rakhjai to the Prince.'

'A Rakhjai that young?' Matakshara shook her head. 'Shame. Though it does now make sense why he was that eager to reach for the hilt. Only fledglings would pledge away their life to protect kings. The wise have finer things to squander their lives on.'

'I can hazard a guess that family is not a thing that features on that list,' Mati said.

'Scab that wound, will you? You're going to push out a melon of your own. Let's see how you stop yourself from chasing the finer things in life when you have someone else's shit to clean.'

'From where I stand now the only fine thing in the world worth chasing is a clean privy.'

'How did you let this happen to you so early?'

'He had not finished so I had assumed there was no danger. But alas! The early extracts of his essence sufficed, and I found it only when I had retched my way through three full moons. I wish you had taught me about the symptoms I need to keep an eye for,' Mati sighed.

Matakshara frowned. 'I can wager my ship you knew of Widow's Boon.'

'I skipped Widow's Boon as I was too busy fleeing Panchal.'

Matakshara chuckled. 'Your handprint at the Yellow Wedding always brings about a laugh. Truly, the realm would be a lot more populated if the Riverlanders did away with swayamvars,' and suddenly Matakshara's eyes stretched wider. 'Stay that oar! Panchal?' And then Matakshara smiled. 'The one inside you isn't going to resemble the Prince of the Empire, is it?'

'Unlikely.'

'Dangerous.'

Mati nodded.

'Why didn't you take care of it?' Matakshara asked, drawing a finger across her throat. 'You know there are other alchemies to scour the seed out of you.'

'Perhaps if I were in the Golden Islands, yes, but to find a healer to carve out the future heir of the fucking Empire while stuck in Rajgrih was impossible even for the likes of Black Swan.' She slammed her cup this time. 'Damn his driblets!'

Matakshara laughed. 'The Driblets of Duryodhan. Fine title for a song. Don't blame him though. You should have known better about how a seed works. It takes just a traitor to open the gates to our womb, not an army,' she said as she chugged from her cup, humming a tune to match the lyrics of a bawdy song that she was no doubt composing on the go.

Mati looked at Matakshara, a woman she had always thought she would end up being. Why didn't she tell her mother the truth? Surely Matakshara 'the Wraith' Harran would have appreciated the heinousness of how Mati truly got with child. Of how she wanted to plunge the dagger of revenge so deep into Duryodhan that neither could he die nor could he pull the blade out. She held her cup and saw in the black rum the scenery of Panchal burning from the window when Duryodhan, ignorant of the chaos, had been ploughing her. Saham Dev's footsteps had interrupted them and denied her her ending. She had been as mad as a hornet and as horny as a rabbit. In the rage of an unfinished ending to her plan, she had forced his seed into her by her own hand to impregnate herself with Duryodhan's child. Why else had she let him live? No doubt the fool thought out of some vestige of love. No. It was so that Duryodhan could know that his firstborn would never be his.

Duryodhan was obsessed with the idea of firstborns. His own father, a firstborn, denied rule for being blind in favour of his younger brother Pandu till Pandu fell to cockrot. Even Duryodhan's own right to rule hinged on his being born before Yudhistir. That Duryodhan's own firstborn would be the one who would one day carry the banner of the Lion, clip the Eagle's wings and place the Hastina Union's crown at her feet made any sacrifice worth the trouble.

Mati had thought her plan had gone awry, believing she would have to resort to siring a child with Saham Dev instead. But Duryodhan's trickles proved to carry a punch, leaving her with a swelling she discovered only three months later.

Matakshara would have appreciated the ingenious plan, wouldn't she? Then why didn't she tell her? Was it because of the unforeseen cost of her dignity that Mati had had to pay for her plan? She clenched the cup, closing her eyes shut in anger. Stupid, stupid, stupid! She took a deep breath and let it out in a long exhale, her eyes opening to find peace from the familiar surroundings.

'Why not… take care of it after?' Matakshara's question, thankfully, interrupted another bout of self-pity.

'You mean wounding it dead,' Mati said coolly, though she uncharacteristically flinched on the inside at the thought and absently stroked her belly under the table. 'I'm forever shadowed by handmaidens, and now Rakhjais. How I wish I could break their sniffling noses! In all these months, this is my first time alone,' she lied, and then she looked at Dantavakra dancing on the floor below, 'relatively speaking. It is too late. I don't want to hurt it now. So, I have decided to bear it, if not for anything else, to arm myself for a game of the Nevers. Once I push the baby out, I will wash my hands of this motherhood business.'

Matakshara mock gasped. 'Is that empathy for me I see?'

'You planned to have me. This is different.'

'Plans change.'

'Not after the child was born! Storms!'

Smile unwavering, Matakshara raised her own goblet. 'Shall we raise our glasses to old times? Granted, they weren't too many, and the ones that were, weren't particularly fond; nonetheless, we are here, hale and hearty, are we not?'

'I suppose.' Mati emptied her drink.

'So, tell me, does Duryodhan know? Are you planning on surprising him with the news at the Conclave?'

'I do look forward to seeing his expression when he sees this,' Mati pointed to her belly. 'But no, no one knows.' Mati straightened. 'And I intend for it to stay that way. At least until it is old enough.'

Matakshara made a sign of sealing her lips. 'Scandals like these make a woman popular in Chilika but the Magadhans are so prejudiced. One should never make a debut in Magadh with a scandal, not with one's firstborn at the very least. The audience is usually able to swallow the infidelity if it were the second or the third.'

Mati shrugged. If her plan worked, she would not have to worry about Magadhans in the future.

'But then I have other tidings you'd best hear about the father of your unborn,' Matakshara said. 'Duryodhan's name is on every tongue in the South. They say he wanders around the North, doesn't sit in Hastina no longer. If the talk in the markets can be believed, Yudhistir will soon start a campaign against him.'

'The rumours of lettucemongers are not to be relied on, Mother. Still, I suppose it was about time that wretched stepling raised his serpent's head. Duryodhan saw it coming years ago, and will no doubt be armed. You don't think it will come to war now, will it?'

Matakshara shrugged. 'Perhaps the Eagles might be content with just pecking at each other but the Lion wouldn't have it so. The Saptarishis are called the wisest of us all. Of their wisdom, I cannot testify, but they do not lack for cunning. They sent two of their Orange Order fucks – the Order that studies scriptures, does the holy fires and gives all the bad advice to Kings – so two of theirs, I call them Twins, with a chest of gold for carrying a cargo to the Tree Cities. I heard gossip that they don't like your former lover.'

'Makes the three of us. But tarry a moment. The Seven reached out to *you?*' Mati was far too bewildered to play it coy. Not only was it unorthodox for the Holy Masters to send for the wiliest of corsairs, but also a twisted way for them to reach the Tree Cities. Kalinga was long leagues across the rivers. A far longer route from the icy Mai Layas where the Seven squat, even if an easier one.

'I may take time to moisten but I am still the Wraith. Or perhaps they think I bear a grouse towards the man that hurt my little dolphin and seek to find common cause.'

'Don't call me that,' Mati said. 'How has Duryodhan offended the Old Saints? He is righteous as redemption.'

'Righteous?' Matakshara laughed. 'If even half the stories coming from Hastina are true, Duryodhan has turned a monster. They say he is soft of the mind, taken in by a jaundice-eyed sorcerer from the Reshts who forfeited his soul for skill with the bow. They say those who speak against him are roasted alive in houses made of lac to die lingering deaths. They say they both feed on the flesh of Namins, mock the gods, threaten the caste order and that they mate with each other, spending hours locked till they satisfy each other.'

Oh, they both satisfy all right, Mati smirked. 'By *they* say, you mean the Namins and the Ksharjans who stand to lose from the idea of justice Duryodhan wants to bring in. Mere slander.'

Matakshara chugged her drink, and turned the mouth of the clay cup towards Mati. 'The finest slander,' she said as she showed the berry-seed sediments left behind in the cup, 'is always spiced with truth. I care not for his adventures behind closed doors. And who I am to preach against murder? But the boy's original sin is not knowing that the profits of the caste system were never confined to the bald fools in the Riverlands. Reshts in search of opportunities form the thread of the slave trade that spans the world, Mati, and your prince has set a moth loose on that thread. Even on land, merchants who would be out and about for us to loot, sleep poorly, listening with fear as their servants sharpen their sickles.'

'Since when did Kalingans care about the castes?'

'Kalingans may think they are above them but look beyond the curtain, and see the neck of our thralls. Yes, we do not bar them from our temples but that is because we have none. We do not bar them from our wells because we are as dirty as they are. We do not forbid them from changing their trade because we know they can't survive the trade of the sea. We allow them to take up arms to be the first chargers when we board a merchant ship for someone has to be the first to die. Reshts, everywhere, clean our streets, put our dead to rest and grow our food. They plough the fields, row our galleys and unclog our latrines. And now they look north, they see this young prince gleaming from afar, this *Curse of Castes* and become inspired to rebel. The so-called noble blood cannot suffer that. Even the poorest soldier in the army or a destitute priest seeking alms stands higher than a Resht. The grim prince would rob them even of that consolation. I still can't see what you find in him. You are as opposite as the—'

'Rain and red earth,' Mati said, moodily. A bard by the harbour had once serenaded them as rain and red earth. Duryodhan was not an admirer of the arts but he had tipped the bard a gold sovereign. 'Why?' Mati had asked him later, confused, to which Duryodhan had simply smiled, and she had been content in that. Weeks later, a raven had brought her a message, 'You and I are the song where the rain meets the red earth. You soak the leaves with joy while I tend to its roots. I wish I had the words when you had asked me before but know I am drunk on the nectar of its fruits.'

Mati should have known better than to grin like a fool at that. Rain might lose itself in the red earth but it only takes a day of cloudless sun to separate them.

'By the Tide, Mother,' Mati said, 'can we shift the sails before you force me to defend the man I detest most? On to the to the matter at hand, I have left the pirate life behind.'

'You know what they say about resolutions?'

Mati groaned. 'That they are always made too late, I know.'

'Alright. On topic, then. You must bear the cargo to the Tree Cities.'

So this is what she wants from me. 'Why can't *you* deliver them?'

'For one, they came here seeking you, not me.'

Mati suppressed a smile but did a poor job of it.

'Oh, I am going to enjoy the next part when I wipe that smirk off your face,' Matakshara said. 'The other reason is, with my weak hips, I am uncomfortable with carrying such contraband across borders. I'm afraid the appetite for risk is not a blessing gifted to the aged.' Matakshara milked the moment out for as long as she could before she languidly fell back on her chair, stretching a leg under the table.

Mati sighed. 'What is it? Heretic scriptures, Vanara heirlooms looted from tombs, Mathuran munitions, idols of sex gods the

Vedans no longer honour Daevic relics, or wait, queens who have been inconveniently impregnated? No, it can't be any of those, for you have smuggled them all in the past.'

'Perhaps the Twins who brought the proposal in question would be better poised to answer the question.' Matakshara cleared her throat to hide it but Mati saw Matakshara flinch. Whoever these two gents were, they... well, they bothered Matakshara, and that was no mean feat. 'The Twins, those two envoys from the Orange Order, are here, sitting on the far end by the Alcove. Leaving them down with the hooligans seemed fraught with risk.' Risk for who, she failed to mention. Before Mati could ask her more questions, Matakshara whistled.

III

The priestly Namins, other than the one who was allowed to preach from his Temple of Prakioni to be mocked at leisure, were always in mortal danger of being burned on the stake or buried alive in Tamra Lipta. But in strolled Tamasa and Tapasa, two Acharyas of the Orange Order, sauntering to the table as calmly as Magadhan high nobility visiting the Unni Ehtral House for the Destitute.

Misunderstanding Matakshara's whistle, however, the scullies on the floor brought forth plates of food. Without even waiting to hear from the Twins, Mati pounced on the plates. Her appetite had swelled enormously in the last few weeks. She tore a big chunk off the unleavened flatbread of wholewheat dough baked on a *tava* and finished off with shallow frying. The stuffing of minced lamb within the flatbread and the generous pat of butter lathered on the outside elevated it a thousand times above an ordinary paratha. She rolled the flaming hot, stuffed flatbread into a roll. It was so hot it singed her fingers but it was so good she could not resist another bite. She washed it down with cold white buttermilk laced with spice, fruit and, Mati suspected, cannabis. When she looked up, mouth full, she found the two brothers staring at her, the food on their plates untouched, while Matakshara gently sipped her own drink.

There were a few simple ways for Mati to tell the Twins apart. First, Tamasa was three and half hands shorter than Tapasa. Second, Tapasa wore a grin like jewellery and Tamasa wore a scowl like one. Third, Tapasa looked like he enjoyed words while Tamasa looked always too hungry for them. Also, the Twins looked nothing alike.

Mati wiped the white creamy moustache from her upper lip with her sleeve. 'So, what is this cargo you holy gentlemen need me to smuggle to the East?'

'A girl carrying the Marigold Mold.'

Mati pushed her tongue hard at her lower teeth behind her closed mouth to temper her face. She was not going to give her mother the satisfaction, difficult though it was. There were so many questions she had, starting with: *the Marigold Mold is real?* It was a popular yarn, spun to coax children into closing their eyes and drifting off to sleep. Now, Mati found herself pondering just how much truth lay behind the other horror tales she had grown up on.

'Secured?' Mati asked.

'Impressive,' the grinning one said.

'My daughter,' Matakshara said, proudly.

'Secured,' the scowling one answered.

'By an alchemy blindfold filled with, well some – some huhab-ruha powder that holds it back,' Matakshara explained. 'Tis good.'

'In a cage?'

'She hasn't turned rabid yet,' Matakshara said.

'The alchemy blindfold?' Mati asked. Matakshara nodded. 'Is it a cure?'

'No,' the scowling one said. 'Just a cracking dam.'

'Why do they need her to be sent to the East?'

'Since when did your ilk start asking questions?' Tamasa asked. 'Losing touch, *Black Swan?*'

'For not asking questions, I charge more.'

'*Charge more?*' Matakshara asked. 'I thought you would agree to it for the heck of an adventure. You are the future Queen of the Empire. You cannot possibly be in need of gold,' and then she stared at Mati's belly, half protruding over the table. 'They always make you soft, don't they?'

'If you think I need a baby in my belly to know what to charge for smuggling a carrier of a dangerous plague you are the one growing soft, Mother.'

'Well, what we have to offer should keep you sated,' the smiling one said. 'We need you—'

'To evade the barriers that a Royal Galley from the Magadh Empire would not have to bother with at the port of the Tree Cities.'

'Brilliant.' Tapasa's lips creased in a smile. 'Isn't her grasp of things just brilliant?'

Tamasa grunted.

'Here is this month's map around the Three Eyes. Those damn whirlpools shifted again, twice this year,' Matakshara chimed in, pushing a long, rolled scroll on the table.

'Is the map dependent on me doing this for them?'

'No. It is my wedding gift. Do as you please with it, dolphin.'

Tapasa gave a handsome grin as he adjusted his chair. Too bad they were celibates. Not that she was interested in Tapasa's brother. Tamasa stared at the space behind Mati with a hunger in his eyes that meant Mati had to use all her will to not turn back and see what he was staring at. The last time she had failed to keep her gaze steady had not yielded rich dividends.

Tapasa's smile widened momentarily, a flicker. 'Have we a bargain?'

Suddenly Tamasa's dagger shone in his hand, and then it was no longer in his hand, and it was quaking almost ten feet away. He walked over to his dagger and picked it up by the hilt. He examined the white rat impaled on the blade, its tiny legs still struggling feebly. He crushed its skull between his molars.

'You will be a useful passenger to have on board.' Mati, who hadn't even flinched, smiled as she stretched her legs under the table.

IV

The Marigold Mold. Like love, old age and nightmares, the Marigold Mold began in the eyes, an itch, a tingling, a loss of control over blinking, and then the mind. Mati had never seen it, obviously, but it was a ghost tale the sailors loved sharing over bonfires and mothers loved scaring their children with. As the rage stole past the mind into the heart, the body stiffened and strengthened, and when it completely took over, the poor sick person clawed, killed and destroyed everything in sight. All hearsay, of course, but a good story. But even if a chapter of that story read true, no matter the sorcery in that blindfold, it was still courting certain death to even be in the same building as an afflicted. To carry one on a ship over weeks on choppy seas with nowhere to turn was madness. It was a good thing Mati was beginning to find herself again, the mad woman inside her who torched harbours to escape patrolmen and burned down swayamvars to settle debts.

As they sailed back on two shoreboats, Dantavakra kept staring at the two priests and the blindfolded girl with confusion.

'And she is blind from birth?'

Mati rolled her eyes. 'How does that matter?'

'Of course it does. Born-blind children won't be able to tell colours or shapes, and would have a harder time navigating the deck.'

'I am sure she will do a finer job than you do, Rakhjai,' Mati said. 'And not to worry on her count. She will be resigned to her quarters till we reach port.'

'Oh, oh,' Dantavakra nodded thoughtfully, 'that is good. And it really is inauspicious in her culture to open the blindfold – what if she feels sweaty or itchy behind?'

'Dantavakra,' Mati said.

'Yes, Princess?'

'I swear by the Storm God if you ask me another question today, I will issue a royal command that you will personally pull *this* out of me.' She pointed at her stomach that seemed to have grown by a finger in one day. Dantavakra shut up.

'Captain, with your permission, the crew won't mind a living cargo. But clergymen on board are as much of an ill omen as a rainbow,' Asanka whispered as she rowed, her eyes on the Twins, her knuckles tattooed with the words 'HOLD FAST' clenched tight on the oars. 'Why do we have to take them?'

'You want to be my midwife, Asanka?'

'I think I would rather clean a kraken's arse, Captain. Understood, Captain.'

Mati eased back on her seat and counted the coin in the box. It was a king's ransom. Enough for her to escape to the Golden Islands with Saham Dev before whatever the plan was to do with a Marigold Mold unfolded. She traced the curve of her stomach with her fingertips. Everything had fallen into place. The fate of the people of the Tree Cities and this plague on the boat drifted through Mati's mind for a moment, but then it passed on, leaving scarce a ripple. The world was always destined to burn. At least now she will make a fortune from the flames.

DANTAVAKRA

I

He had been glad when he had seen his friends off, fed himself fat on their envy that he and only he had been chosen to protect the future Emperor and Empress on a quest to the Hem of the Realm. Let them jest now how his already married brother was chosen over him for the Swayamvar. Shishupal could gloat over the glory of a contest where any skull priest or lowborn horsefeeder could stroll in to claim the hand of a princess. The Conclave, where the true powers that be met, was worth a thousand swayamvars.

Was it though?

Maybe they could have sent at least one of his friends along with him, as an underling of course. It was a long journey to the edge of the known world, a long and lonely journey. The discomforts of ship life had in no way diminished with repetition, and he wasn't going to lie, he missed listening to bathhouse-gossips.

He had tried asking Dimvak. The idea of sending just one Rakhjai with the Prince on a mission to the East seemed reckless by even Dantavakra's standards. Even if Chitragandh, the King of Kalinga, had assured the finest and most loyal officers of his navy to be the crew of the *Gilded Lion* and even if Dantavakra was worth ten soldiers, it seemed the Empire was playing fast and loose with Saham Dev's life. It was not until Dimvak, exhausted by his badgering, let him know that a royal decoy led by Chalakkha had already been sent through the land route to the East to keep Krishna occupied if he misbehaved in the Armistice, that Dantavakra had understood. Another large Magadhan routine on sea would foil that play.

Dantavakra now suspected the true reason was because ships were lousy and everyone else had refused. The *Gilded Lion* should have been called the *Gelded Lion*. It was slow, cramped, and there was nothing to watch but the sea. The initial excitement over spotting the shiny fin of a bullserpent had faded away like a lover's letters. There was just the sea, and the sea and the blue fucking sea. It wasn't as though they were cruising on a river through the ruins of a First City or skirting an exotic land with primitive tribes. Out here on the ocean, the view lacked diversity. How many sunsets could he stare at dramatically with hands outstretched?

It did not help that the crew on the ship had nothing more interesting going on in their lives other than talking about their last seascapades. *Good grief! You are already on the blasted sea. Perhaps you could talk about something else, anything else?* Dantavakra had always been the life of a conversation, always making everyone feel included, steering their talks through wild avenues that left men impressed and women seduced. Here, they did not even bother to explain the silly maritime terms they used as punctuations. What else could he expect from these pirates? The blasted sea's answer to cave dwellers!

But Dantavakra of Chedi was nothing if not a charmer. He knew the tricks. To win them he would cook them savoury compliments and pretend to take interest in their lives. When one is, however, the only civilized person in a group, one begins to look like a barbarian. All his compliments earned him was a nickname. Flower, they called him, and the worst of it was, it had taken him quite a while to understand that it was an insult.

Dantavakra was not one of those weak-spirited loons who needed to be cherished by all the people around them. He was just... used to being cherished. And if these pirates hated his guts – he assumed most of them did – the important question was whether they could do anything about it. As if these backstabbing mermaids could ever take a swing at a Kingsguard. Yes. That was it. He was a Kingsguard. A Rakhjai. He had no need for courteous attempts to get in the good books of sulky, vile shits.

So, he spent his time on the afterdeck, huddled in a blanket on a chair, deluding himself that he was sniffing because of a cold. The jogging and the training and the endless lessons that had seemed so unbearable in Rajgrih beckoned to him like a siren, calling him to soft women and softer beds, to simmer in the pleasure of doing nothing. He thought of Lady Milani. Her cousin, Mair, had assured him that she'd returned home that very evening from the Temple but inexplicably had left for her country the next day to take care of her ailing father. Such a shame. She had been so bold, so carefree and the way she had tugged him was something she should have charged lessons for. He thought of that arrogant Page he had planned to torment, the Page who had suspiciously come down with the pox a day before their voyage, leaving Dantavakra to lug his own bags.

He sighed, and wondered if he had sighed more than he had talked in the last few days. People did not sigh in real life but here he had turned dramatic exhaling into a sport. There was, however, something more on the back of that sigh than just the loneliness of the now. It was the awareness of the loneliness of the future. His friends back home were no longer his friends, *could* no longer be his friends. His elevation had curiously left them behind in the sunny valleys of youth and pushed him into the grey seas of responsibility. A Rakhjai could not fraternize with soldiers under his rank, especially those who weren't even knighted. And he wasn't even sure if his friends would want to fraternize. Knowing how he himself would have behaved at the out-of-turn knighting of any of his friends soured his stomach. But he argued with himself that this was different. He was the finest warrior of his group, his ascension was not a matter of *if* but of *when*.

Ah, my head hurts. He did not care about realities. All he knew was that the small world on this ship would have been more bearable to live in if he had had a friend to laugh at his jokes and share his criticisms about their present company.

Mati spent most of her time in the privy, and when she was not inside, she scowled at everyone, and at him most of all as if he were responsible for her being with child and for her cramps. In these hours, she was usually content with cursing at someone she called the Storm God. It was blasphemy but there were no Ehtral priests on deck to keep her virtuous. The only time Mati took a break from cursing and captaining, things not mutually exclusive of each other, was after lunch. There was an unsaid understanding amongst the crew that disturbing her noon naps was an invitation to walk the plank. She spoke rarely, and then only to her crew, to snarl about sails, or maps, or the possibilities of being stalked on sea.

Mati reminded him of Shishupal. No day was good enough for their men and women to earn a rest. She had shockingly arranged her crew into the sacred Orders of the Namins. If the Red Watch was busy swabbing the deck, the Blue Watch played dice, told tales and carved drawings on pebbles. If the Green Watch was busy singing sea jingles as they hauled on ropes, the Yellow Watch played their banjos in closed rooms. Dantavakra wondered, where was the dancing on the yardarms, the rolling barrels of rum and the drinking from sunset to sunrise? There was just greasing the wheels, inspecting the seams and slushing the masts from top to bottom. Everything was endless repetition, the knots had to be opened and reknotted, the rigs had to be loosened and then tensioned, the capstans had to be polished and repolished, the clean that became soiled was made clean again, over and over, day after day. Size did not matter, be it of the tiniest leak on the ship, the faintest fray on a rigging or the smallest smidge of rust on a wheel. Mati captained as if she were fighting a prophecy that her ship would come apart due to ill repair. Even things as small as pins demanded inspection akin to an interrogation and the word 'dirty' would send terror through the spine of the burliest sailor on board. By the end, even Dantavakra had become immune to the stench of vinegar.

He was denied comfort even in the world of dreams, for the sailors seemed to engage in a contest of whose snore was the loudest. A game in which Dantavakra, being the only one who could not sleep, found himself as judge and audience, both. Amongst the night growls of these beasts were the loud moans of crew members whose turn it was to use the sleeping cabin. Dantavakra was no prude but the way the sailors swore while being intimate made it rather difficult for him to sleep on his front. And if by the grace of Varuna, he did find sleep between the swears and the snores, the meows of cats woke him with the passion of a nightmare. He had been aghast at the presence of the vile creatures on the ship but turned out Mati's passion for a ship free of rats was symbolic of her desire to have a world free of mainlanders.

If he thought rum would soften his discomforts, he could not have been more wrong. Rum was horrid, for the quartermaster added pinches of white salt to supposedly strengthen his belly against rupture. And there had been no bribe strong enough to dissuade him. Dantavakra had already parted with a gold sovereign to stop him from piercing his ear with copper to ward off cataracts. A lone ship journey did not warrant marring his earlobes which his lovers so loved to nibble.

Maybe if he had been busy, he would not have felt like plunging a sword through someone and everyone. He could not believe the conclusion he had come to: he would rather bite his fingernails bloody in fear in Tamra Lipta than stay on deck guarding the Prince from seagulls and the occasional lightning strike. Dantavakra of Chedi was made for ambushes and attacks, and not prancing outside doors of arrogant royal bloods.

For Saham Dev spent his time in his room busy giving lectures to the blind girl on every subject Dantavakra had hated growing up. To be honest, Dantavakra was surprised at how warmly Saham Dev had received Vauri on deck. Known to throw a fit at the slightest of provocation, he had somehow become more accommodating than a mattress. Perhaps it was because the girl gave him a chance to chase his dream of teaching. At least it kept the Prince busy. To make himself feel like an arm on the quest instead of an appendix, Dantavakra had started patrolling the deck outside the Prince's room till Saham Dev had come and dismissed him from even that.

So, here he was, leaning on the ship's railing, pretending to look for dangers on the horizon while steadfastly refusing to look at the sea. All in all, it was safe to conclude, the charms of being a Rakhjai had diminished in the last week.

'Still seasick?' a smiling voice asked. Dantavakra jumped, startled. What was his name? Ugh. He did not understand why the Twins had to be named so similarly. 'Or are you homesick? Homesickness tears the heart far faster than seasickness can puncture the gut.'

Before Dantavakra could answer, the Acharya stepped behind and held his shoulders, squeezing and massaging. 'The knots on your shoulders are large as tumours, Ser.'

'He looks dehydrated,' a heavyset voice spoke on his other side, making Dantavakra jump again. It was the other Twin. What was it with these brothers and their silent steps on a creaking deck? He wasn't wrong though. Dantavakra was always thirsty but he didn't like drinking the water on deck. It had an unfamiliar feeling of other living things in it.

'Though I wonder if water does come, should he drink first or bathe first?' the beaming Acharya chuckled. That was an arrow to his pride. Dantavakra pulled his shirt and let the smell reach him. *Mother of Worms!* In light of freshwater rations to take in the additional three passengers and the fact that he was always in armour, he had begun to stink almost as foul as Mati's crew. The fact that an Acharya had insulted him for having a bad odour was enough on its own to make any decent man run mad but, on a ship, where does a man run to?

'Just seasick, Revered One,' he managed to get a word in before they observed anything else unsavoury about him. 'Cursing that healer who sold me shellflower herbs, claiming they'll keep the headaches at bay. If I return home, I will use my hands to give him a good demonstration of how the ship sways in a storm.'

The Acharya on his right grinned, making his skin crawl. Dantavakra had cracked a joke. It would have fetched either a true laugh or, in the likely case the Acharya did not have a sense of humour, an awkward chortle at least. But the Acharya's grin never left him. It was plastered to the Acharya's face as Dantavakra's linen shirt was plastered on the space between his shoulders or the blind girl's blindfold around her eyes.

'Good.' The Acharya smiled. 'I enjoy talking to people who are in the shadow of death, their unique perspectives on life always makes me appreciate my life a lot more.'

'Death's shadow.' Dantavakra awkwardly chortled. 'Could not have put it better myself. Every time the ship takes a dip, my lungs reach my balls. Oh, forgive me, Acharya.'

'The Scriptures of the Seven say we are all on a wheel of time. We may be falling now, but without a doubt we will rise.' The Acharya grinned back.

'Honestly, Acharya, the Meru should do something about these charlatans who sell herbs and charms in the name of the Seven. This damn mendicant I was telling you about also sold me a charm of Varuna, the God of Sea, to keep the rashes at bay.' Dantavakra pointed at the band of totems around his wrist. 'Turns out this band itself was the first to give me a rash.' Dantavakra laughed, knowing how self-deprecatory jests always made it easy for people around to trust him.

'Personally, I don't think that a charm of Varuna protects anyone from seasickness or,' the stern Acharya paused and turned to him coldly, 'a shipwreck. From a kraken, yes.'

'Forgive my brother,' the other Acharya grinned, 'he doesn't understand the notion of japes.'

'Sail ho!' They all turned in the direction of the wheel, where Mati had shouted fresh orders.

'What a remarkable woman,' the smiling Acharya said. 'So unpredictable. When we were tasked to engage her services, our employers knew not she was with child. I would imagine any woman would steer clear of danger, especially in that delicate condition.'

'Any woman who seeks to carve her own destiny will always find herself in danger,' the scowling Acharya said ominously.

'She seems a fine captain though,' Dantavakra said.

'You fancy her,' the other Acharya grinned back at Dantavakra. 'Remarkable. I would definitely peg you as far better suited as her companion than than His Grace.'

Dantavakra blinked his eyes rapidly, blushing, and realizing he was committing treason, raised his objections. But before he could speak, the scowling Acharya spoke, 'Aye, a prince of glass, the heir to the Realm. Pity. But we deal with the cards fate deals us. Can't change the future now, can we?' Suddenly he exchanged an unsettling look with his twin, and the grinning Acharya laughed, this time a true laugh, a laugh that deeply unsettled Dantavakra.

'I take back my remark about the japes, brother,' the grinning Acharya said.

And just then he heard the voice that comforted his heart like cool waters of a pool on the hottest day of summers, the voice of a friend he cherished like a seed he had never sown, of hands that wrapped around his little finger, of laughter that felt like home. Little did he know he had found his safe place on this deck in the hands of a plague.

II

Dantavakra finally felt alive as he unsheathed his sword and raised it above his head in a battle-ready stance. She came at him, sword swinging wildly without any direction or rhyme. He responded by chuckling and lunging forward, slashing through the air to disarm her. She fell back on the deck and squealed in delight. Using the help of one of the sailors, she rose and sprinted away, her hair and imagination running wild. The other sailors who had built a human wall to protect her cheered her on madly as if in a bloodlust. The boatswain, a frowning man, stepped from the throng and placed in her hand an improvised shield, crafted from cardboard and pieces of fabric. Her face, whatever remained of it outside the blindfold, shone with joy as she gripped it.

The sailors turned her around in the right direction and egged her on. She took across the deck like a fluttering butterfly as Dantavakra braced for impact.

'You wish to challenge the mighty Raavan,' said Dantavakra pointing his sword at Vauri with a fury as though he truly were that mythical Rakshasa demon of old. Then, belatedly realizing that Vauri could not actually see it, nudged her little stomach with the blade.

Vauri laughed and ran at him with her shield. The shield crashed against his wooden sword, and Dantavakra fell back on the deck. Even the sailors who were busy working smiled at the two of them. After a struggle on the deck, Dantavakra ended up on his back, the tiny shield's edge hovering over his neck. 'Do – you – surrender?' asked Vauri between laughs.

'Never,' cried Dantavakra and kicked at Vauri's ankles, knocking her onto her back and tickling her till she surrendered.

Vauri laughed. 'Stop tickling me!' Her laugh was everything that was soothing in the world.

'There is a thin line of difference between tickling and torturing. This is the latter. Gahhhh!' Dantavakra renewed his attacks till they fell beside each other, laughing. Vauri's laughter filled the deck with a joy few treasures could have matched. Dantavakra was just about to crack another joke to make her laugh harder when a royal voice startled him to his feet.

'Vauri,' Saham Dev said with Mati behind him. Vauri stepped behind Dantavakra's trousers as if to be shielded. 'This is not becoming of a woman of high birth, Vauri. Come, attend your classes.'

'No, I do not want to,' Vauri protested.

'Ser?' Saham Dev said.

Dantavakra bent on one knee. 'I promise we will play afterwards, again.'

'But he—'

'Ser.' This time Saham Dev's voice held the command of a King's own to his Rakhjai.

'Later, I promise. Come,' Dantavakra said. Vauri nodded solemnly, clouds of red hair bobbing in waves. Dantavakra held her little finger and escorted her to Saham Dev's chambers.

Vauri was the only balm in the rotting wound of this journey. She had been confined by Mati to her quarters for days, not even permitted to take a leak on the deck, her circumstances always an anchor point for Dantavakra to compare his life to, and feel better.

When Saham Dev had forced Mati to let Vauri outside her confinement so that he could teach her sums, Dantavakra had not thought much of the girl. With her skin the colour of cedarwood, her auburn hair might have been nice to look at if it were not so tightly bounded behind her ears by the blindfold.

Her blindness posed a problem, for sure. Doors were never where they should be. A railing was too near, or too far. Swinging hatches often tripped her, earning her bruises plenty. The poor girl never even knew if it was day or night, leaving him to wonder just how tight her blindfold was. Her only sanctuary was in her bunk but she shunned it, following ropes and railing to map the deck instead, impressing the crew in the process.

The blindfold itself was not ordinary. Strange symbols were stitched on the red cloth, and the cloth itself seemed as if it was clamped on her eyes rather than tied around them. No doubt she came from a wealthy family but seeing how her feet had grown too big for her sandals, he reckoned they had fallen on hard times.

But there was something about Vauri that was disarming. And it was not just because she was the only one kind to him. It was because she could see magic even through her blindfold. Maybe it was because she looked for it, he knew not. But she did let him know, in vain though, that a day spent feeling refreshing breezes and having nothing to do could not be bettered.

So Dantavakra of Chedi spent his time against the railing opposite the Prince's cabin, waiting for his new friend while simultaneously avoiding any attempts at friendship by the Twins. With Vauri, it felt easy. She always came out with fresh demands, a demand for a joke, a demand for a stroll, a demand for the description of dolphins, for a neatly wrapped gift or a make-believe game with straw dolls. Luminous memories of his time spent with this girl were what Dantavakra was going to remember every time he wished he had a sister. That was why when she came out today, her brows furrowed, Dantavakra obliged her when she leaned in to ask of him a request: 'You need to make new friends, Ser.'

III

Waves pounded white against the bow and spray rose to splash the back of his bare arse. Dantavakra knew he would never get used to this but he was grateful that there was no one else on the craplines at this hour. It was bad enough he had to pull his breeches down in front of strangers and bad enough that he had to wait till Vauri went for her lessons but hanging his arse outside the ship's railing filled his eyes with images of a red-bum baboon.

He almost felt envious of the Crown Prince whose chamber pot had to be emptied by his servants. Even Mati was whispered to have a urinal attached to a lead tube that emptied into the sea but she kept the secrets of its workings closely guarded as if an effective public sewage system on a ship would sink it. Well, would it? He did not know.

Amidst his philosophical musings on poop-management devices, he heard a soft whistle as the dwarf ambled on over to the railing, nodded at him and pulled her breeches down. Dantavakra almost lost his footing before he grabbed the craplines for dear life, swaying around like a pendulum before coming to a halt. 'What do you think you are doing?'

Asanka stared at him confused. 'Here to drop some brown on blue. This be the craplines, ain't it? Now makes me wonder what you is doin'?' She laughed as she climbed the railing and turned her butt to the sea. 'Just yanking your rigging. Peace, mainlander.'

Peace, Dantavakra scoffed. Peace and privacy on a ship were rarer than pleasure in an Unni Ehtral temple. *Make friends,* Vauri's request made her way to his ears again. As if he had not tried with the officers on the ship before. A nefarious idea took birth in his mind. What if he could appropriate naval knowledge, not a whole lot, but just enough to impress in a room of sailors? What if he loaned the information from someone low in the hierarchy of ships who would not even be allowed in the room?

He winced initially at the idea of having a conversation with Asanka while they were balancing half-naked on the railing but how different was it really from gossiping in bathhouses. Only the half-bare arse was different. And what was the saying? When in Balkh, do as Balkhans do. And he needed the dwarf. After all, he would not have shied from asking a stableboy his opinion on raising of foals. Why not consult a hardened deckhand on the subject of, ehm, what should he even ask her so that he could understand it enough to faff later?

A smell gripped his neck and turned it in Asanka's direction. Asanka had raised her head to the heavens, letting out a grievous moan. *Dup dup dup.* 'Ah, that is much better. Bastard fish had been building an empire in my insides for a while now.'

Alright. This was nowhere close to a gossip in a bathhouse but it was too late now.

'My gratitude for that information.'

At the sound of Mati's voice, Dantavakra leaned back from the ship's railing to squint at her in the distance. She wore a black jacket today covered in tarnished brass buckles and her wind-weathered face made her look like a delicious villain. She lifted a whistle that hung around her neck on a leather cord where ideally her *mangal-sutra*, the sanctified necklace worn by a wife, should have been, and she then blew it three times. The Green Watch assembled hastily in an unkempt crescent.

'Properly inspected?' Mati asked.

'Properly interrogated!' the ship mate answered.

'That is the way with sailors!'

'And with all things!' the crew bellowed.

'See how stern she is,' Asanka said, pulling out the chutta. 'No damage to ship on account of the crew is the Captain's one rule. What you heard now is the oath every crew of the Black Swan swears to. Clear?'

'Savvy,' Dantavakra responded.

'Ai, look at you speaking our language. There be hope for you yet.'

'So you must have spent a lot of time on the sea,' Dantavakra asked and then affected a sailor's drawl to add, 'eh?'

'Aye, the things I have seen,' she said dreamily.

'You know I have even been to the drowned city. Walls and towers and domes under water, glimmering in a blue ethereal light of our ancient enslavers. Waters that the captain's charts put at a thousand fathoms. Many a lad on deck heard the tale and fancied diving for treasure till they leaned over the railing, their mind changing. The place was... wrong, somehow. The city was... even I had trouble believing... but it felt like it rose in the time we gawked on it. As if it was climbing towards us... You don't believe me? I swear on the Ocean Goddess the island rose to the surface. Had me shiverin'. Not long after we'd returned to the warm currents of the Kalingan Sea, the tales came to us from the old crooks—the story of Amravati and Alantris, the cursed islands of the false gods. They called them twin islands, said to be the last refuge of the Children of Light before they vanished.'

Dantavakra climbed down from the railing as the waves completed their cleaning assignment, and pulled up his breeches. 'You mean before they were defeated.'

Asanka only smiled sadly as if Dantavakra was too naïve to be taught life. 'A pirate or two poked around for treasures after it happened. They found nothing apart from hungry jadesharks. Years later they found a ship bearing the colours of Alantris floating aimless on the sea. It was frozen in a block of ice. Several pirate crews towed the frozen ship to a coast and many a merchant crew worked hard to melt it for treasures. It took a while but when ice turned into water, they found the crew on the deck, all turned into marble statues.'

Dantavakra gulped.

'So pay attention, Ser Vakra,' Asanka said, gesturing at the circle of rowdy sailors who had all given Dantavakra a hard time, 'they have all sailed the sea where shit worse than this happens all the time, but they deal with it because their ship is their home. I know why you are talkin' to me.' She pulled her breeches up but continued to stand on the railing. 'Now these are the sort o' folk who earn respect, not request it. To them, the sea does not pose any danger. Even crawling with Nagas with their siren calls and krakens that can devour a ship whole in moments, the sea is their home. The danger on a ship is a Green. A Green is unpredictable. A man on the ship who doesn't know his business can be worse than ten leviathans. But your duties insist on you roaming the deck, and for them, that is an unearned privilege.'

'So, what can I do to... earn it?'

'Why do you need it? You are a knight. Enjoy the journey and get paid for doing nothing. You got a life worth envy.'

'The grass looks greener on the other side,' Dantavakra grumbled.

'The grass is green where you stand if you fucking water it. But fine. I will help you.' She scratched her beard that was no doubt a sanctuary for fleas. 'Take my broom and sweep all this sand back into its bucket. Start small, eh?'

'You want a Rakhjai, a decorated winner of the Imperial Tournament, to sweep?'

'Ship maintenance is what nobody values unless attacked. Nothing inspires—'

'Alright, alright.' Dantavakra stared at the broom. His idea of sweeping was to sweep the room with a glance and beckon his servant. *Make new friends.* He took the broom and started. The task had seemed easy enough at the start, till it turned out to be as tedious as a drunkard's sermon. Sweeping is the most enjoyable thing ever, said almost no one.

Dantavakra complained to Asanka after three minutes. 'Is there nothing else?'

Asanka hummed to herself. 'If you want to work sitting on your arse, hm, then you could help the top watch up there. Just climb the rig and enjoy the horizon.' Dantavakra stared up where the canvas rolled and snapped, where ropes creaked as their length was added or adjusted, and the mast watch spoke to each other as they worked with nothing but blank space for dozens of yards beneath them.

He returned to the broom, grumbling. After what seemed an eternity, he he raised his broom like a warrior. 'Done!' The deck was scrubbed clean and immaculate, the ropes glistened, the sand wiped. It did not matter to him that the rope he cleaned was frayed now and the sand just moved to another part of the deck.

'Well, you can't get one place clean without getting another dirty.' Asanka looked up at him, shaking her head. 'You are absolutely useless, Vakra. How about this? I will help you win over the crew and get you a friend.' Asanka traced a finger on her palm. 'I scratch your back and you scratch mine.'

Dantavakra fumed. 'Why wasn't this your first idea?'

'I needed you to truly know your options. So... have you ever tried a dwarf? Don't look so confused. You can lift them like a ball, or like a sloth, and just move around, y'know. If I curl me under a blanky, I'll look like a pillow on your balls. No one will even know. Eh? What?' Asanka asked when she saw Dantavakra's face. 'You're not my first choice, either. But you know how difficult it is for Asanka to come across another dwarf on sea? And the fools who had wanted to claim they did something wild, they tried me already and they stink. You smell fresh and I am lonely.'

Yama's teats! Asanka meant the back-scratching quite literally. Dantavakra simply walked away numb to his hammock. In hindsight, he had only himself to blame for Asanka interpreting it as an acceptance of her offer.

IV

So, between weird priests who made his skin crawl and a weird dwarf who wanted to crawl beneath him, Dantavakra was again left sulking alone, waiting for Vauri to come out.

The door to the Prince's cabin finally opened. Dantavakra rose so quickly to his feet that his head transcended space and time. When the stars before his eyes dimmed, he massaged his head and saw Vauri skulk out of the room where Saham Dev stood with a book in his hand. She limped to her cabin, her hand on the wall, along the memorized trail to the room. The Prince watched her leave. He was a small man, built in the shape of his mother rather than his father. He had always been awkward growing up, alternating between cruelty and chivalry, with Dantavakra having seen only one side and having heard only rumours of the other. Though seeing him worried about the education of a blind girl, and for that matter, all those orphaned children back in Rajgrih, made it difficult to hate him with a vengeance.

If only that could be said for Vauri. Dantavakra did not know how Vauri figured it out but the moment Saham Dev's back turned to retire to his room, she turned grumpily to him, a middle finger raised defiantly.

It took all of Dantavakra's will to hold back his laugh as he caught up with her. 'You don't show the crude sign to your elders, lass,' he said, mindful that Dantavakra, the Duke of Bad Manners, chastising a child to mind her courtesies was funnier than the finger. 'Had he seen it you would have had to apologize to him,' he said insincerely.

'But, why should I?' Vauri's cheeks reddened below her blindfold. 'I am not sorry. And if I apologize, that would be lying.'

'That is your line in the sand?' Dantavakra asked, amused. 'You just flipped the Crown Prince. He is just trying to teach you. Take it from me,' he said, 'you don't want to ignore your sums or you will end up waiting at a Prince's door in the world's most boring pirate ship.'

'What?' Vauri asked, confused.

'You will get used to Ser Dantavakra's grumbling,' Mati said as she passed them by. 'And remember, kid, you don't have to mean the sorry. You just have to look it.'

'That is lying. I was just being honest when I showed him the bird.'

'And look where that got you,' Mati said.

'Ah…' She nodded and then bowed, smiling.

Dantavakra looked at Mati in horror. 'I think she just lost her innocence.'

'About time.' Mati smiled and patted the hair on Vauri's head. 'C'mon now. Why did you flip him off though?'

'He hurts me,' Vauri said, head bowed, as she followed her with Dantavakra in trail. 'He hurts me, tells me that everyone's days are numbered, so I should learn it while I can.'

'You should listen to whatever he says,' Dantavakra said. 'Every teacher hits. It is only normal. Be a good girl, and he won't hurt you.'

'I am a good girl! But the cane hurts. He tells me if I don't learn, I won't find a gallant knight to love me. That if I don't impress him he will tell my secrets to the crew.'

'An effective incentive.' Dantavakra nodded, impressed.

'He forces me to drink, and forces me to drink it highborn fashion,' Vauri sobbed.

'Wine? A little too early for it to be taught to her, no?' Dantavakra asked Mati.

'I was taught when I had seen only eight summers,' Mati answered. 'He does the same to me. Just… sip your draught and be a good soldier, Vauri. Far less vexing that way. My father was the same. Whips and canes every time I misread the charts or mistook the stars.'

'For me, it was my mentor, Dimvak,' Dantavakra grumbled. 'Ever did he spout his motivational quotes while he used his mace to alter my nose.'

'Vauri, between you and me,' Mati whispered to Vauri, 'the Crown Prince is an absolute waste of breath on land but he does care for you. He cares for children.'

'Aye, you should have heard the tales of how his own father treated him,' Dantavakra said.

Mati raised her hands in the air thanking the Storm Gods. 'Finally, some gossip. Knew I should have come to you when I was bored. Jarasandh isn't fond of Saham Dev, is he?'

'The Emperor,' Dantavakra corrected, 'doesn't care anymore. I recall well the day when we saw Dimvak bear young Saham Dev to the healer. We were just boys then. So Shishupal and I, curious and unseen, gave chase. When we reached the healer, we saw Saham Dev had bloody holes all over the arms. He had been stabbed repeatedly by the sharp end of a quill. He kept crying "*it doesn't hurt, I'm alright, it was my fault, I was stupid*" over and over again. I learned a lot later that Saham Dev has difficulty learning the letters, and, well, the Emperor was not a man famed for his patience and – and from your expressions, I understand, this is no way an appropriate tale for a child and a woman with a child. My... I haven't had a real conversation with anyone in weeks, alright! Go easy on me!'

Mati shook her head and held Vauri's shoulders. 'You seem to have given the Crown Prince purpose, and no, you do not have to apologize to him but you will go to your room and repent by doing his lessons and listening to whatever he asks of you, okay?'

Vauri nodded and left sullenly.

'I cannot believe I told that story to a child.' Dantavakra stepped closer to Mati to whisper but froze. He felt cold air crawl up his neck and he knew Tapasa had arrived.

'She is made of tougher bark than you think, Ser,' Tapasa said, grinning again. 'Princess Mati, if I may have a word.'

Before Tamasa arrived on Tapasa's heels, as he was wont to do, Dantavakra excused himself without hearing what was said after, chasing instead after Vauri.

He knocked on her door. 'Pardon for disturbing you, Princess. Can I hide in your room? Princess Mati does look rather intent on having me for breakfast.'

'Oh, that is so silly,' she giggled as she opened the door, one hand wiping her tears away, 'I will command her to not eat you.'

'So, tell me, did the Crown Prince hurt you bad?'

Vauri nodded.

Dantavakra felt a great urge to loom threateningly over the Crown Prince. 'As I said, forget him,' Dantavakra said, remembering his own oath. 'I mean, His Grace only has the best intentions. How about I tell you about things His Grace doesn't teach you about. Remember I told you about an arena for warriors to fight—'

'Yes, where you won the Imperial Contest!'

Dantavakra coloured at that lie but, in his defence, only a little. 'Yes, it is smaller than the arena in Balkh but more exalted for it only allows the trueborn warriors to fight: the Ksharjans. Battles are messy, a place where you survive because of how feral you are, how many brothers and sisters you have on either side, and most importantly, how lucky you are. A battleground is no place for skill, not of the one holding a weapon at least. But an arena...' he was almost giddy at talking about his favourite place, 'an arena is a place where patience breeds perfection. A perfection born out of scars and failures, a dance of disorder and demons. A place where warriors burn a taper before entering, a symbol of burning their luck away, the symbol of their surrender to their skill, and skill alone.'

Vauri gasped.

'Gasp, indeed.'

'Then why do they allow only Ksharjans to fight? Don't the Reshts or Namins have skill?'

Dantavakra scoffed. 'Warriorhood runs in the blood of Ksharjas. Heroism runs in our veins.'

'Are all Ksharjans good warriors?'

'Of course not.' He was embarrassed by how it was Saham Dev's face that came to his mind.

'Then skill doesn't depend on blood.'

'Uh, yes. It depends on practice...'

'And you said the arena tests just skill, and skill alone.'

'Yes. So?'

'So is it possible that a Namin or Drachma may be skilled with a bow and arrow?'

Dantavakra could not believe it but at this point he truly empathized with the Crown Prince. He shook his head, irritated. 'It is just the way the Seven have made us, Princess, and it is not for us to question them. Why do you think Virangavat sentences a lowborn who spoils the fighting pits with his feet to be eaten by animals, cursed to never achieve salvation? No one has ever been sentenced really,' Dantavakra said quickly, realizing that he may have breached every etiquette in the rulebook of 'What to Say to Children', 'it is just to deter adventurers from entering to harass the ladies present.' He tried to forget the mass sacrifice of the Kosalans in the last tournament, glad he was at the healer's when they crucified those poor children.

'Women are allowed to witness the duels? How exciting! Do you name a beautiful maiden the Lotus of Grace in the Contest?'

He remembered calling many beautiful maidens queen in the mornings after the Contest, but nothing that could be told to a little girl. 'Lotus of Grace? What is that?'

'In the Balkhan Arena, contestants race on chariots. Gallant riders often gift a flower to a woman who they crown as the Lotus of Grace, and if he wins, they end up marrying, and everything is perfectly splendid,' she said, her voice sounding melodious.

Dantavakra publicly acknowledging a lover? He might as well sign his own death warrant. But he couldn't help but feel warm at her words. They were so innocent. 'Why, I will remember it the next time, so that I can crown you as my Lotus of Grace.'

'You will? Yes!' As she embraced him, his arms protruded on either side of her back like the tusks of an airavat, caught halfway between hugging her to death and pushing her away. And suddenly, much to his disappointment, she stopped. 'When is the Imperial Contest due, Ser?'

'When autumn breaks.' Dantavakra felt sad at the thought he would never enter the arena as a contestant again.

'Ah, I am honoured to be your choice, Ser,' Vauri said, distracting him from his melancholy, 'but I am afraid I will be long dead by then. Why else do you think I asked you to make more friends?'

His stomach rolled. 'Dead? What do you mean?'

There are some words that are best left to languish in silence, words that ruin the story, but not the word uttered by Vauri, a word which here meant that the story was over.

Marigold.

MATI

I

Sometimes, to secure what you want the most, you have to do what you like the least. Lunch with her husband fell in the latter. With a crisp rap, Mati announced her presence at his door.

'Come in.'

Mati entered and leaned against the doorframe nonchalantly. Seated at the head of her large circular table, Saham Dev surveyed her with smiling eyes. Beside him, Dantavakra shifted uncomfortably in his polished armour, his hand wound tightly on the hilt of his sheathed sword. She shook her head in dismay. Had Dantavakra now taken his complaints about Asanka's wandering hands to the Prince himself? Woe betide the poor drawf.

'Come, butterfly.' Saham Dev beckoned her to the chair. 'The cook that Father lent us has at last overcome his seasickness. He does sorcery with a goat.' He twirled a fork around between his fingers. 'He's more mage than cook, even on a ship like this.' Saham Dev turned to Dantavakra. 'Ser, let us not stand anymore on ceremony. We are friends now, you and I. Sit.'

And then there was silence, for Mati did not deign this worthy of a response as she took her chair, but for some reason her eyes began to tear up. Again.

'How are you feeling, Princess?' Dantavakra asked.

'Livin' the dream,' Mati snapped.

Dantavakra, ever chasing to fill an awkward silence, turned to Saham Dev and offered stupidly, 'Congratulations, Your Grace.'

'Even the bones are cooked so tender that it just,' Saham Dev said, closing his eyes and kissing the tips of his fingers before fluttering them gently away, 'dissolves into nothing. You know,' he opened his eyes and smiled at Mati, 'like lies against the Empire.'

When the food did come, the pleasant smell made Mati's stomach rumble but the meat was cooked rare. She was just able to nudge the mutton around the plate with the fork. A rope had sliced her fingertips as she had tried to pay the debts of her ego even with her strength mortgaged to her belly. Now, even holding the damn fork between her fingers hurt. Could she eat with her hand instead? No. She could not handle another sermon from her spouse. So, she picked up the fork and stabbed at the meat before her as if it were Duryodhan.

Saham Dev groaned. 'Princess, we have discussed this a thousand times.' He held his tine and said softly, 'The small cutlery is for fish. Please, we have company. And the tine in the left hand, if you will,' he said.

'I know my table etiquettes—' Mati started.

'Not on a table where I would want to eat.'

Dantavakra gulped, and acted as if his world was defined by the circumference of his plate, refusing to look up even once. Mati swallowed her pride and simply prodded at the mutton, a little blood seeping onto the gravy around it. She now imagined it to be Saham Dev's.

Saham Dev smiled, pivoting his attention to Dantavakra now. 'It appears we both have become men from boys since the last Contest. How shallow were we back in the past?'

Dantavakra nodded solemnly while his right leg fidgeted nonstop under the table.

'Honour has a way of holding our heads under the river of duty until the child in us is drowned,' Saham Dev carried on. 'Tell me. I have seen over the past few weeks you have grown close to the girl. Why did you still rat her out to me?'

The meat lost all flavour in Mati's mouth.

'Rat?' Dantavakra's tine stopped midway to his mouth. He clearly did not like this perspective at all. 'Your Grace, Vauri only confessed to me moments ago. She is a danger to your good self, a danger to everyone on the ship. How could I keep this from you? It… would be treason!'

Mati massaged her temples. Mati knew she should never have let Vauri out of that cabin. Should've kept the door barred and damn the whining. But the Twins had assured her that Vauri understood. That Vauri would keep her secret if she had any hope of reaching the East and finding the cure. That and pity were the only reasons she'd let the plague loose on deck. *Softness has wormed its way in, Mati and it'd be the death of you, sure as steel.*

Saham Dev smiled at her and then turned to face Dantavakra. '*Treason?* That is interesting. You go far, Ser. It is not as if you would be lying to me. You would have just been mum.'

'Your Grace, with respect, I disagree. Keeping things from your liege, especially one of such import, is not just treason but high treason.' He looked at Mati if to back him up. Mati just looked down at her plate.

Saham Dev wiped his mouth delicately with a cloth. 'Glad we agree.' *Here it comes.*

'You already knew, didn't you?' Mati asked.

'I did,' Saham Dev said.

'The Twins?'

'The Acharyas,' he corrected. 'And yes. On the first day. I had been hoping over the weeks you would do the right thing and come clean. But alas, my trusted knight here beat you to it.'

'You knew?' Dantavakra stared at her, aghast. 'You both did?'

'See how you embarrassed me again, my butterfly. That is all that I had asked for in our deal. Do not embarrass me. Look at him. He cannot believe his ears. What say you, Ser?'

'I…' Dantavakra turned his attention to his plate. 'I… do not know what to say.'

Saham Dev smiled. 'Do not worry, Ser. The girl is safe. The blindfold is alchemically secured to her eyes. Not to forget, Princess Mati here did observe her for days before the Twins asked her to let the girl out at my behest. The crew doesn't know and I would prefer it so. Superstitions have slain more innocents than swords. I want the girl protected, given she is Eastbound to receive aid.'

Dantavakra's eyes brightened with joy. 'I thought there was none. No cure, no shield.'

'The Acharyas seem to think otherwise.'

'Oh, that is capital! Just splendid news!' Dantavakra beamed at Mati. 'Vauri is a noble human. This is just...' Dantavakra positively gushed over the news but Mati knew better. The conversation was not over. She unsheathed the dagger strapped to her thigh.

'I am certain we are glad the future Queen won't be hanged for, as you said, treason, aren't we?'

'We certainly are.' Dantavakra smiled sweetly at Mati.

'Break her nose.'

The moonlight from the window turned Dantavakra's eyes to the colour of leaves in shadow. 'I beg your pardon, Your Grace.'

'I know you heard me, Ser. And I know you remember your Vachan.'

Dantavakra kept staring at Saham Dev as if time would suddenly make him recall his ruling. 'Your Grace... the Scriptures say something about forgiveness,' Dantavakra said, hoping that it did, as he looked up to stare at Mati.

'If you do not punch her face, then I will ask you to punch her belly instead. Your call.'

The chair's legs scraped loudly as it was pushed back. 'But... Your Grace.'

'I have spoken.' Saham Dev returned to covering his mouth as he picked the mutton chunks out of the gap between his teeth. 'Don't take off your armour or your gauntlets. Mati has been known to take advantage of it.'

Mati was breathing hard. She had gone through this before. More times than she wanted to count. *Just kill him. Fuck vengeance. Have some pride! Where is the Black Swa*— Mati cut off the voices in her head. She was too far in the game to fold. And Saham Dev hadn't been wrong. That had been the part of the deal. She had planned to tell him as well but had no idea why she hadn't. She turned her chair to face Dantavakra as he approached her.

Dantavakra stood before Mati, resplendent in his shining armour, hair tied neatly behind him, chin quavering, cheeks crunching, as he held back a cry. His shivering arm rose in the air.

'Now, obey!'

Mati crossed her legs, eyes dry by now, face lifted high for Dantavakra to get the best angle. But he just stood still as a statue. Unable to move. She could see anger bubble behind his eyes. Torn between loyalty to the Prince and loyalty to whatever code humanity had about not hitting a pregnant woman. She decided to put him out of his misery. He was different after all. The last Rakhjai had come to relish these moments but Dantavakra was on the verge of crying. Mati relaxed her grip on the dagger, abandoned her plan to slice his throat and just nodded, mouthing 'Do it.'

Dantavakra kept flexing and unflexing his fingers, breathing heavily. Saham Dev looked at Dantavakra with the hate of an ox who saw red. 'As you will. On your Vachan, I command you to punch her stoma—' Dantavakra must have seen the word 'stomach' form on Saham Dev's lips, for before the words could finish carrying the sound out, Dantavakra punched Mati on the face. The sickening thud echoed in her ears as the gauntleted fist connected.

Mati blinked her eyes open, dry as dust, and there was Saham Dev. Her head rested in his lap, and he was dabbing at her nose with a ragged scrap of muslin, trying to stop the gush of blood and set the break right. 'You are incorrigible,' Saham Dev said, shaking his head before planting a kiss on her forehead. 'And, Ser, I trust you'll spend less time fooling around with the infected and more time actually keeping an eye on her.'

Dantavakra nodded silently. Mati blinked her eyes open and saw tears glittering on his wind-chafed cheeks. Mati hated the maternal feeling she again felt. 'Don't worry about it,' Mati said. 'I am used to crimson snots. My gratitude for not punching my womb.'

Poor Dantavakra, Mati mused. He had held back his punch. Too bad a soft punch in a mailed fist still hurt. He reminded her so much of Karna. Mati was glad she did not kill him. She suddenly felt dizzy. Opening her eyes became too much of a chore.

'It is a concussion,' Dantavakra said. 'I'll go and call the healer!'

'No, help her to her bed and then fetch Vauri to my chambers. It is time I added secret keeping to one of her lessons, you know.' He laughed and spared a friendly punch on the shoulder to Dantavakra, who feigned a poor chuckle in response.

As Mati felt herself rise in the air on Dantavakra's arms, blackness hit her like a cloak thrown over a flame.

When Mati stirred from the depths of her unconsciousness a day later, coughing, her eyes opened to smoke and soot.

Head hurting with the force with which she woke up, she looked out the window. *Damn me to the depths!* The Mathurans were here and her ship was on fire.

II

The Mathurans, forbidden from trading with the East under the Armistice on land, must have deployed their own smugglers on sea to twist out of their obligations. Or worse, the trap that the Magadhans had feared the Mathurans would set on land for any Imperial delegation to the Conclave, stretched to the oceans as well. Either way, for the Mathuran galley to stumble on a lone Magadhan ship on the sea was like an army of ants discovering an abandoned sweet.

Mati shuddered to think how motivated her pursuers would turn if they discovered that the Magadhan ship was playing host to the Crown Prince... well, who doesn't like their sweetmeats bathed in honey pastes. Yet, the *Gilded Lion* was a fast beauty, and keeping the fire aside, had a crew seasoned in the timeless pirate tradition: run.

So she was rather confused and understandably livid when she burst forth out of her cabin to find her ship unmoving.

The deck on the ship was all chaos, as expected, but unexpectedly none of it was appropriate for a ship being pursued. Sailors should've been struggling to pitch razor nets, archers should've been jostling each other for the bigger quiver barrels, watch should've been arguing about whether swords or polearms are better to greet unwanted guests. But all she saw was her crew running around like rats on the deck, without direction, without purpose.

'Why is no one preparing to repel the boarders, you scabrous dogs? Why did no one rouse their Captain?'

A crewman skidded through the deck and slammed into Mati. Mati kneed him first, making sure he had no air to answer her questions. 'Give me one reason why I shouldn't tie your balls round the mast, you bilge rat!'

Her First Mate, Sada, chased after her, holding his hat. 'Let him go, Cap'n. Think I didn't callin' for ya first light. Clergymen on board invites poor fortune, I warned ya. They told me to let you rest. That you was havin'... women problems. What's gone and happened to your nose, Cap'n?'

'Belay that!' she shouted. 'And you listened?' She unsheathed her sabre and placed it at his shoulder. 'To two green idollickers? Are you a landlubber! What are they goin' to do? Pray?'

'Orange, Cap'n.'

'I swear by the Storm God I am but a second away from lopping off my First Mate's head if he does not speak plain.'

'Beggin' your pardon, Cap'n! But them scallywags threatened to Shrap me. Shrap, Cap'n! They could give me piles, infect me daughter with syphilis or doom my descendants with a cow's brain! I'd sooner be a coward and die by the sabre at your hand than face whatever twisted things those perverted priests be plannin'.'

Mati shook her head. 'They drink rum, they eat salted beef. Do you think they are the ones who have that kind of power?' she seethed, but she sheathed her sabre. 'Whatever ate your brain must be suffering something fierce. I promise you, Sada, if we make out of this alive, everyone on Tamra Lipta will know what you did. Now, if you'll excuse me, I have a ship to save and priests to hang.'

'Foe in sight!' Mati hollered in an impossibly loud unwavering voice as she crossed the deck. 'Stand by to raise anchor, you bloomin' cockroaches! Mast men, eyes wide awake! Aft and fore watches, at the rails! Archers to the waist, as able! Await instructions.'

As she hobbled across the deck, one hand on her belly, and the other on the railing, she saw the purple-blue colours and the cow flying on the ship approaching them from west. Javan soldiers-for-hire on a Mathuran ship. Storms. She doubted her reputation as Black Swan would chill their spirits when they saw her girth. Ugh. She could kill someone. And she found the two most likely candidates standing at the railing, staring at the horizon with an even smile.

'Tell me why should I not toss you both overboard right now?'

The grinning one turned. 'Because it would be ill advised to lift heavy weight at your stage.'

Mati's eyes darkened.

'I jest, I jest,' Tapasa said, 'the Scriptures say nothing of the sort.'

'Are you out of your goddamned minds telling *my* crew not to wake me up when a ship – a ship with a cow on its banner – is on our tail. That Mathuran cruiser, look at it, it is a beast compared to this belle,' she spread her arms around, her left hand sharply pulling back to her stomach at an ache, 'but we're sleeker. We could have outrun them in a straight stern chase but they have made the gain on us. Not to forget that those girls look freshly careened, and we are way, way past due. We've already lost the damn race.'

'Maybe they just want to talk?' the scowling one, Tamasa, said.

'Oh, oh, is it?' Mati said. 'Maybe you both can swap holy tales with those heathens over supper.'

'Is this one of those moodswings we have heard so much of? A sign of a healthy raging baby inside.' Tapasa grinned at her, but it was the way he said the word *baby* as if he knew something about her that she didn't that irked Mati.

She removed her hat and ran her other hand through her hair to pull it back. 'Listen, Acharyas. The Mathurans and Javans on it would have seen the Magadhan flag flying on this ship. Lions can't swim, it is known. Now this school of tuna is coming for it. How many?' Mati hollered.

'Hundred fathoms under us, Captain!' Sada yelled back.

Kraken's arse! 'Listen, you two. The sea isn't going to be friendly today. They have more bite in the water than the *Gilded Lion* does. If we're going to settle this at coupling distance, I intend to impregnate her in a position I prefer. Please stay out of my way. So, all ye maggots!' She turned around. 'Spears and halberds get behind the swords and the shields, and don't take your blasted sweet time about it or you'll meet the rope's end for that. If you can't stab someone, knock them into the sea. At a hundred fathoms, there will be plenty jadesharks in the water. So let us give them a feast they'll remember. Now, Asanka, choose your best arms-and-eyes, and send them aloft with the wood to do their worst. Three per mast. Where is the girl?'

'We sent her to the Prince. Poor thing better worry about numbers than pirates.'

'Good.' She raised her hand. 'I need every steel on deck we can get. Someone reload my crossbow. And – what!' She turned to see what Asanka was staring at.

Dantavakra appeared, completely decked in armour, eyes shining with joy like a child at a fair. He stopped short when he saw Mati, his joy sapped at the memory. 'You have nothing to worry about, Princess Mati. I'm here.' He stared at the Mathurans as if they would provide him redemption. 'Aye,' he said, his teeth clattering against each other. 'Come on, you cows!'

I can't deal with this. Mati did the breathing exercises that Amala had taught her.

'Can't wait to save the day, is it, Ser Vakra?' the sombre Twin said.

'Aye, Acharya!'

'But you aren't oathsworn to save the day. You are oathsworn to save the Emperor's blood. So I suggest you return to the door you are never meant to leave.' He turned to the horizon. 'And everyone else, no one will move,' his command rang out clearly. 'I speak with the authority of the Crown Prince on the ship, the true commander, and I hereby command you all to stand down. I'm sure the Mathurans mean no harm.'

III

By the time the Mathuran ship, *Veritas,* had crept up to hailing distance, its men were already hauling on the grappling lines to draw the two ships closer while their archers kept bows on the ready for any who might try to pluck the grapples out. Even from this distance, Mati guessed the *Veritas* crew outnumbered that of the *Gilded Lion* at least three times over. A Mathuran climbed the railing of *Veritas* to face where Mati stood, hands down, behind the Acharyas.

She held her own crossbow, palms sweating, half wanting to shoot the quarrel into them. But a captain must hold her pleasures at bay at the pleasure of the commander, and Saham Dev had indeed signed off the authority to these two. That was the one rule even she could not disobey. 'Moment of truth, gents,' she whispered.

The armoured Mathuran frowned at the standing pattern when she realized the Acharyas were leading the ship. When understanding dawned, she bowed a fraction before the Acharyas. 'Revered ones,' the Mathuran said. 'I am here just to escort Prince Saham Dev to our ship. Our Lord Krishna had foreseen an attempt to reach the East on sea. We appreciate you for striking your colours and in view of this—'

The Twins each took off the shawl from around their chest, their hands moving in symphony as if they had the Yogini swarmsense. Mati forgot weeks of indifference in the fear of a moment when she saw the *janeu*, the sacred thread, on their backs.

Namins around the realm wind eight sacred white threads around their bare upper torso when they are initiated into their respective orders. These threads are said to be made of aethair – the strands of hair left behind by the Old Gods before they abandoned the realm. Mati reckoned the Old Gods must have been very old when they began suffering from hair loss for the threads were all silver white, and reckoned they must have been very strong, for the threads could not be burned, could not be dampened, could not be frayed. They could just be cut into shorter pieces. Many a sailor had wished that the Old Gods had thicker hairs for building rigging in a ship. An invincible white rope, even if it might have been the ear hair of an Old God, could have been the difference between ship and shipwreck. But, as it was, the Old Gods only left behind thin, white, threadline hairs, good only to make janeus.

Only one of the Old Gods, however, had red hair. The Twins wore eight sacred threads of this God around their muscled torso, the hair as thick as ropes, and as red as murder.

They had lied. They were not priests of the Orange Order. The only offerings these two burned in their fires were lives. Now the fear in Matakshara's eyes began to make sense. The Twins were of the Red, the mythical order founded by Parshuram on the foundation of massacres and pyres. Mad, immortal, and worse, they knew nothing of moderation. Here, however, was the itch. The last Ravager of the Red Order was sighted decades ago when a man with a red thread had obliterated the last of the centaurs in the Riverlands.

But here there were two. And both of them were looking very, very intently at the Mathuran captain.

The fear was so far beyond anything in that Mathuran's experience, that she stammered her next lines. 'It will be like we never saw you, Acharya. Ahoy! Return to your positions!' The other Javans on deck stopped laughing, stopped hooting. The Javans cawed in disgust but they had picked up on the fear of the Mathurans. The Mathuran captain was the last to leave but not before bowing all the way to the deck before the looming shape of the Twins.

They waited for a long while till the *Veritas* turned around and reached the horizon. Only after, did Tapasa turn to Mati, grinning. 'You were right, they didn't want to swap tales.'

Mati felt fear ebb through her bones but kept her gaze level. She wiped a tiny smidge of blood trickling down her nose. Holding a kerchief to it, she mumbled, 'The deck isn't your closet. Pick up your shawls before you return to your cabin.' She turned to head back to her cabin, hackles raised, passing the terrified mass of Kalingans. 'And you, maggots! The fires better be quenched and the mast be star-looking by the time I wake from my nap.' But if Mati had been hoping for a bout of quiet sleep to settle her nerves now that trouble had turned tail, she was wrong.

For no sooner had she touched the door of her cabin than a door burst open on the other side and a chain of events unfolded like a string of Mathuran munitions, altering the very course of the Realm's destiny.

DANTAVAKRA

I

Dantavakra, lowered spiritually by the snide remarks of the Twins, had stomped his way to Saham Dev's cabin. *Who do those damn godlickers think they are? Telling a Ksharjan what to do? Did he tell them how to squat their arse around a fire?* Jhestal was right. Things had gone to shit because people had started trespassing onto their neighbour's domain. You don't hold your finest warrior behind in the trenches. You put him in the vanguard. And what was the worst wound of it all? The Javans behind the Mathurans had looked so easy to beat. Small pieces of shite that made the sailors on the *Gilded Lion* look like paragons of cleanliness. He could have finally saved someone, not a woman, not an old man, but a whole ship carrying the two heirs to the Empire. This had been his chance to finally face a foe and silence gossip that he had never seen battle.

Blast the Twins! He was going to ask Saham Dev himself for permission to draw his longsword. The Prince didn't give a rat's arse about what Dantavakra did with his time. The Prince would be only too delighted to allow his Rakhjai to play the hero, especially now that Dantavakra had found his way into the Prince's good graces. Deluded so, Dantavakra hoisted his hand to knock confidently on the door but, alas, the tip of that very longsword by his belt caught the deck at an awkward angle, and seeing how his luck was on sabbatical this season, naturally he got tangled with it and careened into the door.

The door wasn't locked.

It swung open with gusto, and he fell on the floor face first in all his clumsy glory.

'Thousand pardons, Your Grace. It is the… Oh, it is so dark.'

The curtains were closed, draping the enormous cabin in blackness. The light from the lantern by the door was set on low burn. There was a familiar smell of sweat and seed. A sobbing sound. He picked up the fallen sword behind him and unsheathed it softly. Had the savages found their way in already? He picked the lantern off its hook and rolled the frame on the floor like an offering. The moving globe of light illumed bits and pieces of furniture in its passage. He could see discarded books, then the legs of the table and eventually the bed against which the lantern thudded to a stop and rolled back a palm's length.

Another sob. This time he caught the sound. It was Vauri's voice. Remembering her plague, he instinctively shielded his eyes, feeling rather foolish. *She is blindfolded, you idiot.* Guilt washed over him again as he recalled how he had shunned her the past day despite the Prince's reassurance that her plague posed no danger to anyone on deck as long as they did not get too friendly with her.

And so Dantavakra, with the grace of a jittery fox, had shifted positions every time he had spotted her bobbing red curls attempting to navigate her way to him. His manoeuvres had done much to diminish his reputation with the ignorant crew, even earning disapproval from Asanka when she caught him cowering behind a barrel while Vauri searched for him. If only they knew the reason behind his actions.

But he wasn't thinking of all that any longer. The room was too dark, too silent for good news. His sword unsheathed, Dantavakra called out, 'Your Grace… Vauri… ?' He kept his eyes peeled for any assailants who might jump out at him from the shadows, half-hoping they did. It was then he saw Vauri.

Fires lashed, a whisper of pain. 'No…'

There she lay on the bed, making that wheezing sob, still securely blindfolded. Spit around a dowel in her mouth had turned to froth but otherwise she looked unhurt. Bastard Javans must have tied her up to stop her from screaming! *Fuck! Where is the Prince?*

'Your Grace?' whispered Dantavakra, kneeling by the bed, placing a reassuring hand on Vauri's shoulder. With the same hand he then wiped away the froth and gently smoothed her hair back. 'It'll be fine. I'm here. I will protect you, little brat,' Dantavakra said, finding it difficult to pull out the dowel with just one hand while his two eyes searched for shadows in the room.

Vauri only gave a feeble grunt, a flurry of twitches rippling down from her neck to her sides. It was only then Dantavakra realized that… Vauri was unclothed.

Any disbelief over his eyes was dispelled when the door to the privy creaked open, light from the lanterns inside bringing day to the bed. Dantavakra rose in a flash, sword out. 'Halt in the name of the Emperor!'

The Emperor's son halted, stark naked, a drying rag in his hand, silhouetted black against the light from his privy. Dantavakra lowered his sword, not understanding.

He glanced at the specks of blood and filth on the sheet, not understanding.

He saw the naked Prince… refusing to understand.

It was only later Dantavakra realized he was still gripping Vauri's hand tight even though her sobs had ceased. He let go absently, seeing the marks of his fingers pink on her frail arm, his mind lost in the echoes until Saham Dev's voice rang out sharply.

'How dare you enter my room?' Saham Dev started and then he must have seen something in Dantavakra's eyes for he inched backed into his privy. 'Now hold on, Ser. She still has her maidenhood, if you must know. I would never spoil her for her future husband, if she ever lives long enough to have one,' Saham Dev said casually, as he stepped out of the room to walk to the other side of the bed and lit his cigarillo. 'Now, go outside and do your duty.'

Dantavakra left, numbly, mind lost in a red mist of questions. How could she still be a maiden? Dantavakra frowned, not quite understanding. Not immediately, at least.

II

He hurts me, tells me that everyone's days are numbered, so I should learn it while I can. Dantavakra calmly took the dowel he had gently pulled out of Vauri's mouth and pushed it between Saham Dev's teeth. Saham Dev was never a warrior, a weakling. In an act of desperation, Saham Dev used the lit cigarillo in his hand and pressed the hot ember against the side of Dantavakra's neck. It singed. Dantavakra wished the scald hurt more.

You should listen to whatever he says. Be a good girl.

'Shhhh,' Dantavakra whispered as Saham Dev struggled. Sang it, almost. 'Shhhh.' Ever so softly, Dantavakra sobbed as Saham Dev punched him. His punches hurt no more than a mosquito's sting. He let them fall on his face for a bit as he worked on methodically spreading the fingers of Saham Dev's right hand. He snapped each of them into two, one by one. Dantavakra had thought, or rather hoped, Saham Dev's muffled cries would be music to his ears but he felt nothing. Maybe the melody wasn't loud enough.

He tells me if I don't learn, I won't find a gallant knight to love me. Dantavakra broke into tears as he took the other hand, gripping the fingers in contemplation, and then deciding against it. He went for his arm, and broke it instead. Not a simple snap of bones. He threw him to the floor and began stomping on the rapidly bruising spot with the heel of his boots. Again and again and again, till he heard the satisfying sound of bones being pulverized. When he looked down, he saw what remained of the bone gleaming red amidst torn flesh.

That if I don't impress him he will tell my secrets to the crew. Dantavakra smashed his face into the mirror now. The shards stabbed into the Prince's face, opening up his cheek. Dantavakra's hand gripped Saham Dev's hair with all of his might as he turned the Prince around to face him. This was what an Oracle from the Black Order must look like at her initiation.

I will crown you my Lotus of Grace. He remembered that hug, the tears Vauri had left on his shoulders, and now his own sobs turned into a growl. The world dissolved around him. He made sure he dragged the naked Crown Prince by his broken arm as he kicked open the door, hauling him across the deck. Saham Dev shrieked, the dowel in his mouth slipping out, momentarily distracting Dantavakra.

'You're a Rakhjai! You have taken a Vachan to protect me! Cease in the name of Yama!' Dantavakra's steps paced uncertainly for a moment. 'Yes, remember your Vachan, Dantavakra! Remember it! The Vachan will burn you if you break your oath! Remember!'

His Vachan as a Rakhjai, his life in Magadh, his dreams, his hopes were a distant tune in his head but the other promise he made rang louder in his ears. *I will crown you my Lotus of Grace.*

'I remember,' Dantavakra said calmly as he tossed over to the sea the Prince he was oathsworn to protect.

III

A blur of movement caught his attention. Two tangerine shapes blurred past him. The Twins must have witnessed Dantavakra break his Vachan from the other side of the deck. Wordlessly the Acharyas leaped into the waters like dolphins returning to the deep.

Mati came running to Dantavakra's side, almost crashing against the railing as she looked over, down at the sea. She turned to stare at Dantavakra with calm but puzzled eyes. Some of the crew members had already turned their polearms in his direction. 'You will be hanged for this, Danta. Or worse. Why? He can swim back you know.'

Dantavakra lowered his hands. 'Not with broken arms he cannot.'

He didn't answer her unasked question as he continued to see the bobbing head of Saham Dev with great pleasure, hoping the Twins didn't reach him in time but they did.

'Well, that's about it, I reckon. Now you—' she stopped short. The silence hung, an unstruck bell. Dantavakra, frowning, turned towards the suddenly silenced Mati, and spied a hand clasp Mati's on the other side. He shut his eyes again the moment he realized who it was. Not because of fear. But because of shame. He didn't have the courage to see the child, not now, not ever.

But Mati did see her.

She saw the blood trailing down Vauri's skirts, the trail that followed her all the way from the Prince's room.

I will crown you my Lotus of Grace.

Grief and guilt had stung him when Mati had lifted her gaze to meet Dantavakra's, but he had known, from that fleeting moment of flared eyes and parted lips, that Mati too was now irrevocably poisoned.

Even the sailors understood. The ones holding out the swords and poleaxes returned them to the weapon's locker. Asanka approached Vauri and offered to take her to be cleaned.

'Your will, Cap'n?' her First Mate asked.

'Turn the ship around, and put wings in those sails,' Mati hollered.

The First Mate whispered to Mati, 'What of the Red Order, Cap'n?'

'They have many powers, Sada, but wings don't count in them.'

'Marvellous, Cap'n.'

Mati turned to the railing, staring at the Twins, who had swum over and now held a shrieking Saham Dev in their grasp, all three of them afloat. Mati must have seen something else in the sea for she suddenly raised her hand, turning to her crew.

'Too much ill will has been spread on my deck, and that is all we are ever going to speak of it. Your true journey begins now, a journey under the aegis of the Storm God, and not of the false heathen gods the Green worship. The Storm God is an unkind God but a predictable one. You can see him. You can feel him within your bones. But not the Sleeping Mistress of the Corals, the Ocean Goddess. She is an unseeing, unhearing power that cares for us even as she sleeps, and for that we are grateful. And to her, let me make a tribute.' She leaned on the railing and slowly drew a dagger against her palm. Blood welled up and dripped to the sea as a dark offering.

Sailors, each and every one, be it the scrub watch or the boatswain or the carpenter or even the ship boy who'd climbed down for the ceremony, went to the railing, stretched their palms and gifted their blood to the Ocean Goddess. Or rather the prophets of the Goddess – the jadesharks whose emerald fins cut through the grey sea to their ship even now, their noses addled by the scarlet feast the crew of the *Gilded Lion* had so graciously set out for them.

'Let's bring a spring upon the ship, you brine-breaths!' Mati commanded. Shouts of the Twins to send a rowing boat to fetch them floated in the winds as the *Gilded Lion* turned its back to them. Mati climbed a barrel and hollered. 'Tanal, roll out that cask of ale with the Lion stamp on it, and I want it to be bleeding dry by tonight. We begin anew!' The sailors cheered and hooted. 'Sail ahoy! Three points off the larboard bow!'

'Aye, Captain! Where are we bound?'

'The Tree Cities. There is a Conclave to attend, after all.'

Dantavakra, his hands outstretched, was still staring at the sea, where the *Gilded Lion* had left three of its passengers. He caught glimpses of frantic human forms alternating with copper-green hide as they turned over and over in the sea a few times, orange then copper, orange then copper. Before the ship completely turned, the last thing he saw was the sea bubbling with a pink foam that turned dark crimson as the panicking shadows sank into the depths. *And here it comes.*

The faint halo of the lost sun dipped behind the *Gilded Lion* as if she were sailing out of an unearthly portal. The heavens darkened to a bruised purple with only a thin gold seam clinging to the horizon. Wind unsettled his hair, and Dantavakra looked up to see a sea-bird's silhouette against the moon. Yet the fire that Dantavakra had steeled himself to endure - heart pounding, muscles tense, ready for the searing blaze to char his veins - never came to pass.

'What in the bloody depths are you doing?' Mati asked. 'Aren't you tired of posing so?'

'I... I did not burn.' Dantavakra massaged his arms, suddenly cold. 'I had taken a Vachan to protect the Prince, and I sent him to his death. But I did not burn.' He turned to Mati. 'Why? I broke the Vachan. Break the Vachan, and you burn. It is known. I do not understand. Surely, the Prince could not have survived.'

Mati's expression changed as if she remembered something, and she burst out laughing. 'So you were *that* Rakhjai.'

'Probably. But what do you mean by that?'

'You never took a Vachan, Danta. They tricked you into thinking you did. The Namin who was to administer your oath was... otherwise occupied with me. Look at that. Fortune favours the fools, eh?'

Releasing a breath he couldn't remember holding, Dantavakra pivoted in her direction. 'You mean I will not die! I will not die!' he gasped. 'Oh, Yama! Wait. You took a Vachan? I do not understand.'

'Does not matter,' Mati murmured, then leaned forward, edging over the railing to gaze out at the sea beyond. 'All those plans are now roaming in a jadeshark's belly. So...' Mati pursed her lips, 'you tossed over Saham Dev despite knowing that the Vachan would char you from the inside.'

Dantavakra shook his head, as if confused. 'I... I guess I did.'

'Oh, cursed tides!'

'What? What is wrong? Did they save him?' Dantavakra jerked his head across the horizon and back.

'The whelp just stretched out its tiny little toes and kicked me under the ribs. Looks like the baby seconds what I was thinking. What I am certain this whole ship knows.'

'And what is that?' Dantavakra asked, eyes still shying away from turning to where Asanka had disappeared with Vauri.

Mati smiled, patting his back. 'That you have what it takes to be a pirate. Welcome to my crew, Ser Dantavakra of Chedi.'

MATI

The sun chiselled its way into every single pore on Mati's face. Behind her, the deckhand grumbled as he swept up the shattered shards of her bangles, each one crunching beneath his broom. Without so much as cracking an eyelid, she held out her hand, and he was quick to relieve her fingers of the mangalsutra. And just like that, the last evidence of her wedding was gone, swept away like so much broken glass.

The deckhand left Mati alone at the bow of the ship with her thoughts to join his mates in pilfering Saham Dev's room for treasures. He was the last one to enter Saham Dev's cabin, which Mati had been the first to exit. The 'loot' she had stolen from his room now swirled and spun like delicate pinwheels in the air, carrying Saham Dev's betrayals to the winds.

One letter bore the earnest plea of her father, imploring his daughter to meet him in the Capital. Another brimmed with the ire of a loyal servant, Zuri, so humiliatingly ousted from service as her handmaiden. Other letters cradled crude jokes from her old crew, replete with a menagerie of lion puns. None of which she had ever read. None of which she ever knew existed. The rest of the letters were in Mati's own hand, letters she had written to loved ones, to old captains, to friends, to her father, letters that had never touched the claw of a raven to be winged away to their recipients.

Soon the letters on the railing dwindled in number leaving just the one which Mati had crunched in her wrist. Its envelope wore a broken eagle seal and was dated a week before her wedding. Duryodhan's words in it carried his care, his concern and his confession of the scars he deserved and the scars he was collecting. His revelation that he had asked Karna to compete in his place for

Draupadi moments before Mati had abducted him filled her with a fire that did not warm.

The deckhands only saw a wisp of smoke rising and knew to keep their distance. When that last letter finally burned to ash in her palm, she blew it away with a whisper of her breath. She felt a strange feeling at the pit of her stomach. It was as if the visor was all of a sudden lifted from Mati's eyes but she was blinded by the discovery. She had become so used to manipulating others that she had never bothered to build walls to stop someone else from doing it to her. Laughter rose but did not touch her lips. *Saham Dev, you brilliant swine.*

Had the Emperor trusted him and appointed him General of the Empire, the Yamuna Wars would have ended a decade ago. The way Saham Dev had carefully isolated Mati, the manner in which he had fingered her insecurities, the methods of gifts and praise, the way he let her think she was manipulating him – he had tied brick blocks to her ankles without her knowledge and then taken her swimming in his poisoned pool.

Ingenious! Had she discovered Saham Dev's deceit in his lifetime, Mati did believe she would have come to respect him. Maybe they would have joined their diabolical minds and used them against the world. Their friendship would have been a fire and the kingdoms of the realm would have been those little things that hide in the highest trees. Respect him that is till she discovered Saham Dev was a filthy fiend even by Mati's low standards. *Vauri...*

Suddenly chilled in a place far deeper than the ocean's winds could reach, she cursed. Rage twisted her features. He had turned little girls into women before their time. Was there any greater crime than that? Amala, Vauri, the dozens of girls in his school... Why had Amala not confided to her? They had planned to poison Saham Dev for storm's sake! Yet she had not said a word. Had Amala been like Vauri, oblivious to the fact that she did not deserve the pain? But Amala was street-smart. How could she have not known?

How did you not know? came the thought in Duryodhan's voice.

I am not going to do that. Introspection was a tunnel that never made a person smile when they came out the other end. No point in mulling over what could have been. Saham Dev had met his fate and now slept with the carcasses of mermaids.

Mati finally opened her eyes, running her hand over her freshly cropped hair, as she looked down to see how far the bump in her belly had come along. She shuddered at her proportions. But resting a hand on her stomach, she felt a rush of calm fill her body. The baby would live in a world without a father, without a mother, in a world far away from the world she was born in, in a world where she might learn of pain, for there was no avoiding that, but never abuse. She would never be abandoned. She would just be loaned to the blue skies of curiosity, and the tinted hues of wonder, and every night she would be brought back from those shores to be hugged till she gasped for breath. Mati would leave her at the doors of the Monastery of the Bear in the Golden Islands. They were good people. Her new family would cherish her, would love her, would fill her with magical stories, and well, do everything for her Mati could not. She was not giving up her baby but rather gifting her to someone who deserved her... and who *she* deserved. And after that, Mati would disappear.

You called her a she. Duryodhan's voice spoke in her mind as Mati climbed down to stretch herself. *An improvement from a whelp. So, you think your baby will be a girl?*

Shut up, Mati snapped but couldn't keep her thoughts from drifting to what lay ahead.

It wasn't going to be the usual chaos of Mati's life, but it'd be a damn sight more peaceful than the mess she was in now. A life without vengeance. A life without a baby. A life without Duryodhan. She had no other choice after all. With Saham Dev slipping away to his Ehtral God, the noose around Duryodhan's neck had also slipped from her hands. Now who will fund the army her baby would have led, who will put her in a position of power higher than the future King of the Union?

Of course, she could always return to Rajgrih, claiming she had sired the heir of the Empire and that the Prince fell to the attacking Mathuran convoy. Too many leaks in that plan. Not to forget the Unni Ehtral she would have to deal with, but maybe she could manage them.

But... after what she had seen be done to Vauri and after what she had read in Duryodhan's letter, she was left with no appetite for games. She blamed her, the tyrant who was making Mati soft, making her abandon all her plans so that her baby never had to go through what Vauri did. 'You better appreciate this, little girl,' she cooed to her stomach.

But before that, she needed her gold-raising plan to work.

Her plan was set. She ran it over again on her fingers to see if there were any leaks.

– First, she'll collect the shipment of giant airavats on behalf of the Empire, all proper and official.

– Then she'd sell them off in the Golden Islands and split the coin between her and Dantavakra. Dantavakra would drop Vauri back home assuming she was not skull and bone by then while Mati will slip into whatever life a wealthy fugitive can find.

– She'd keep the useless Rakshasan Relic that Saham Dev had been carrying—meant as some grand gift for the Tusk of the Tree Cities. She'd keep that key for herself, just in case she needed a bit of extra coin in a pinch.

The sun, its shine stolen by a passing cloud, peeped out, seemingly amused by the futility of human plans.

INTERLUDE

VAHURA'S ADVENTURES

The world was going to die in two weeks but Vahura decided she deserved at least one dinner that she did not pick from a scroll-strewn table. She could not lie in bed another night with thoughts of her failures haunting her, of knowing that sleep would solve all her problems if she were to not wake. So, when they reached the front of the queue, and the vendor already had two cups of cocoa tea in dotted cups waiting for them, Vahura grinned, forgetting all about the apocalypse she was supposed to prevent. Baggy handed a cup to Vahura and took the other two for himself. They spoke little of the Conclave, but spent most of their walk discussing culture and paintings, lost relics and favourite legends.

She had thoroughly wondered how a mere Ranger of the East could know so much of art, before deciding not to ask. Perhaps it was because, for a change, she did not wish to know the answers. For a change, she wanted to walk around the stage taking in the delights without having to discover the pockets in the magician's sleeve. Perhaps this was why she was happy calling the Ranger, Baggy. Of course, by then he had taken to calling her Loosely.

Vahura flushed at the memory the name opened, her cheeks colouring as she remembered the episode from last week when she had assaulted the poor Rakshasa. She still could not come to terms with what had possessed her to act so out of her skin. She had never been good when exposed to society. They emptied her. After all, nothing irritated society like a woman, well read. Her natural state was nervous and weird, an outcast pressed into the wall, shrinking in the corner, not slithering on a stranger in a brothel on the other side of the world. And that was what scared her. Had her quest changed her? It was hard to put into words the change she felt but it was as if when she had been asleep, someone had come and pulled her apart like books from a shelf, and then hurriedly put them back again. Same books. Not in the same order. That sort of feeling. Of the woman who would drink tea and read her books and cross the street to avoid conversations with acquaintances, there was little evidence. Perhaps this was what men who wrote of deaththrill in the throes of war meant. The knowledge that death was a step away wrenched your fingers away from the part of you you were doing your best to hide.

The pair soon passed a horde of Grey Shamans. Chanting and muttering strange prayers, the Grey Shamans danced in a row on the street kerb, eyes closed, lost in the drug of their own song, own tune. Their cymbals, manjeeras and drums beat out tunes that in no way met to form music but it was still mesmerizing. In her hunt for the Daevic Scrolls, Vahura had consulted many of them but they had known naught. Even the secrets of the earthsong the first Grey Shamans had used to lattice the roots of the relatively tinier Everwood Trees to build the mighty Living Bridges and the bigger trees to build the Green Dome was lost to them.

'Their song must be chaos to your ears, perhaps?' the Ranger asked as he plunged his thumb into the peel of the orange he had flicked from a stall. The tangerine skin surrendered its hold, peeling away in one undulating ribbon dance. The burst of childlike glee on the Ranger's face distracted her despite having seen him so more than a few times since they had first met. Shaking it off, she tried hard to remember the Ranger's question.

'The chaos of its lyrics is the secret to its serenity, I believe,' Vahura answered.

'Either the Curators assigned to the Conclave are doing a grand job,' he remarked, 'or... Miss Loosely has studied them before?'

Vahura nodded, sniffling back through a nose that was competing with her hair in a contest of being the reddest. 'They are in the search of the earthsong, picking from the thousands of words they found in the Broken Lament, singing different words, combining them in a thousand different ways, in a thousand different tunes, till they believe they will find the song to awaken Bhumi, the First Ancestor who tilled the Earth.'

'Top marks. I'm impressed with your knowledge and your respect for our culture. Redbloods often love what they are while hating who they are not. It pleases me it is not a general rule.'

Vahura rolled her eyes. 'How archetypal of a Rakshasa to look down on humans. The symbol of your barbarity is walking on the other side of the street.'

Women with full-body rainshields made from bamboo and banana leaves strapped to their backs were headed the opposite way, looking like upright beetles from behind. Baggy flushed.

'Contracted workers whose job is to carry away excess water from the city to dump it outside.'

'Contracted workers? Aren't they the sex slaves the Tusk freed after his father's death?'

'No.' Baggy's face darkened. *Please, don't let your mother or sister be one of them. Oh, Vahura, your mouth is loose-ly!* 'They... went away. These are lowlanders who do the same work on the other side of the borders but...'

'They are Reshts who came here to escape the oppressing wheel of caste, only to find the oppressing wheel of poverty,' Vahura hastily added. 'Well, I am sure they are compensated in *respect*, which perhaps is more valuable to them than any coppers in the Riverlands. I did not mean to cause offence, Baggy, but it is just the structures of shackles, much like cultures, differ from place to place, united in intent even with different skeletons. The system your world employs is no different from what is done in Balkh.'

Baggy nodded. For a Ranger, he nodded solemnly a lot. But Vahura felt unease crawl between her fingers as she felt she had offended him with her lip that she knew was an acquired taste.

'How about I contribute some gold to the Grey Shamans dedicated to bettering the lives of the raindiggers?'

'We don't trade for gold, Princess,' he said as he looked behind again. Baggy had looked behind them frequently as they made way through the crowded city streets. There were Asuran men-at-arms posted at regular intervals on the route they had taken but the shadow of the Iron Order had the Ranger fretting like an apprentice

with an overdue book. Vahura imagined if the Iron Order were
that persistent in finding her, they would have simply knocked on
Leafsong but they hadn't been seen or heard of in the three days
Vahura had holed herself in her quarters. Either they did not know
the red-haired woman they were hunting was Vahura or they had
been called back by the Seven to chase some other chaosbringer.

'How about dry wood?'

Baggy, despite himself, laughed. 'You know your trade,' he said,
running a hand through his long hair, shaking off the pollen from
the hearts of graveblooms that were growing on a leafy roof above.

'It wasn't that hard to guess. Sure, you have all the wood in the
world around but they are wet, and worse, you can't chop them.'
The Everwood served not only as the giant pillars, the walls and
the ceiling of the City but also as temples of the City's natives. It
was blasphemy to hew the Everwood for lumber. The Rakshasas
held no devotion to any God but their own ancestors. They believed
that when they died, the leaves of their homes held their memories,
and that the entire Rakshasa consciousness of their ancestors stood
united in the Everwood to protect their descendants.

'I pity your opponents in the meetings leading to the Conclave,'
Baggy said.

'His Grace Bhagadatt's Conclave must keep you working day
and night, right?' Vahura asked, ignoring the remark, and hoping
her refusal to accept invitation to any of these meetings would not
go to harm Balkh in the long run. So far most of the rejected diplomats had chalked it to Vahura being a girl playing at a woman's
game, and Vahura was fine with the prejudiced assumption. Too bad
the Tusk of the Tree Cities, Bhagadatt, had conveyed to her that he
would grant an audience to her only after the Pre-Conclave Feast at
the Gilded Table of Giving, held weeks before the Conlcave began.
Now she had to play the game she hated the most: the waiting
game.

'It is the Realm's Conclave,' Baggy corrected. 'I assure you, the
Tusk wants no part of it. I hear tales he bid for hosting the Conclave
along with the other royals at the Panchalan Swayamvar, bidding
low, little knowing that the lowest bid would turn out to be the only
bid.'

'But you are not wrong, Loosely,' Baggy said. 'It does keep me awake. Last night, we had a tavern riot, a lady of the night beaten to near death, two rapes, thievery beyond count, and a drunken airavat race down the Street of Suras. Just this morning, the Grey Shamans found two human heads floating in the spring pool. No one seems to know whose bodies they belonged to or how they found their way there. Kamrup is now an unsafe place.'

'How would a drunk man even climb an airavat?'

Baggy raised his eyes.

Stupid Vahura. Of all the horrible incidents he set out, why did she have to remark on the mystique of how airavat-riding worked? He must think Vahura absent of any empathy. She could already hear her mother's words. They had stood on the balcony then, watching her cousins show off their archery skills in the training grounds.

While Arjun sees only the eye of the bird he is meant to kill, you watch its feathers to mark its breed, the hue of the sky to note the time, the patterns on the branch to know the tree. All well and good but by now the bird has flown, and you have starved yourself to death.

Vahura, instinctively driven to justify the priority she had assigned to the news, prattled on. 'I heard the airavat are keen to the senses of their mahouts, and are not kind on disrespect.'

'That is… well, correctly summarised.' Baggy stopped himself from laughing when he saw through Vahura's measly attempt at a coverup. 'But here the fools got the airavats drunk, and not themselves. So, a race with a drunk airavat, while not dangerous to the rider, is immensely harmful to the architecture around him.'

Vahura laughed, and for a stretch, they strolled in comfortable silence till Vahura cleared her throat. 'Your regretful tone about the Conclave has begun to vex me and I am inept at keeping frustrations bottled up so I hope you will pardon my candour.' Don't do it. Just don't lecture yet another man. *I am weak, okay.*

'By all means,' Baggy offered.

'Every coin has two sides. Kingdoms who have hosted the Conclave prosper from such events. And to be hosting a Conclave to celebrate peace instead of problems carries a comet's worth. I was young then but I remember how a Conclave brought conversations of merit to the table, allowing women and men from across the realm to share their ideas, their culture, and their way of approaching a subject. A free flow of thoughts, my father called it. And while Royals, as is custom with their ego, did more chest thumping than ear opening, I am sure somewhere these ideas travelled to their minds, marinating there and turning into a well-cooked empathy for others when they returned to their homes. Even if one mind was moulded, the Conclave was a success.' Vahura continued, 'You see inn riots, I see full inns; you see a woman beaten, I see a woman walking bow-legged, burdening under the sack of coins on her back. That is the thing about perspective, a tilt and it can kill wars in the womb.'

'Now it is your turn to forgive my candour, Princess, but your mind is… fascinating. Why aren't you speaking at the Conclave?'

'I'm out of cocoa tea,' Vahura complained, holding out her cup, and eyeing Baggy's extra cup with envy. 'Apologies, I did not hear you. You said something about speaking?'

'I have no knowledge of how the Royals from the Western Frontier, the Riverlands, the North or the Southern Plains are, but I would gamble my savings, meagre as they are, that you are the brightest star of them all. Knowledge is commonplace, but stitched with sensitivity, it is gold. And you are a bright star, someone who should have been addressing the Hall as the keynote speaker, and not Lord Shalya of Madra, no offence.'

'Even the brightest stars,' Vahura pointed at the Green Dome that blotted out the sky, 'need a willing sky to shine, Baggy.'

He nodded solemnly. The conversation reached its natural end when they came face to face with the gates of Leafsong. It rose above the Green Dome, above even the clouds, hidden in the skies from where she stood, making it impregnable to any attack from land. Vahura could not help but admire the sad poetry in that fact.

For that is the thing about strengths, they are just as moody as wealth, just as disloyal as people. Trust them too much, and they betray you, the way they betrayed the current Tusk's father, Narkasur, when Krishna and Satyabhama had attacked him from the sky.

'Oh, we are here, already? Splendid!' She said the last word, hoping to have suppressed the sarcasm at the last minute. All she wanted to do was meet the Tusk and convince him to part with his secrets. But she had to endure the traditional banquet in the Gilded Table of Giving tonight before earning that opportunity. Her task of the day was to simply stand with shoulders held back, accept the occasional greetings and smile at a compliment even though she was sure none would come her way.

As they inched forward in the queue at the gates of Leafsong to hitch a ride on a guest-carriage to the residences atop the peak, they came upon a score of Asuran guards lazing beneath the portcullis. They wore the traditional garb of the royal guards in the East with their belts woven from living vines and cloaks fashioned from enchanted leaves. The guards suddenly became alert and ushered Vahura, Baggy and the rest of the queue aside to clear the way for a column of royal riders.

Vahura turned to see the first rider through the gate, carrying a long red banner. The silk rippled in the wind like something alive, and across the fabric was blazoned the sigil of an olive wreath against a red sky.

The sigil of the Yavanas. The sigil of the Greeks.

'Make way for Archon Kalyavan!' the rider shouted. 'Make way for Archon Kalyavan the Undefeated!' And close behind rode the young Archon himself, a boy on a white horse, his black satin cloak dusted with two-headed eagles.

'We heard you joined the Emperor against the Mathurans, My Lord?' one of the guards of the Matsya contingent waiting in the queue asked Kalyavan. 'Is it true?' he shouted.

'Well, someone has to teach the Emperor how to win,' Kalyavan shouted back as the queue cheered. Even from where she stood, she could see Kalyavan basking in the applause. As a Mleccha, despite his war exploits, he would have earned little to no admirers in the Riverlands but in the Tree Cities, Vahura reckoned, he was a veritable hero.

'God's Tears, if his head turns any bigger, people will mistake it to be pregnant!' Vahura muttered.

'You are learning our curses.' Baggy laughed.

'Curses are the shortest route to understanding a culture.'

'Though perhaps for an expletive, you utter it too elegantly. What else have you learned?'

'*May the mosquitoes bite your mother.* Oh, *May your spear rot!* Then there is *Flood you, and your whole flooding family!* if I am feeling particularly feisty.'

'Loosely!' Baggy mock gasped. 'Such uncouth language is unbecoming of a Princess of Balkh.

'But… suits a fugitive from the Iron Order.'

Baggy laughed. 'It has been an honour and, to be honest, a true pleasure to escort you here, Princess.' He bowed.

'You're leaving?' Vahura asked, wondering why she was upset.

'Aye, I see a woman hurrying towards us from the other side of the gates, and by her look, I would rather take my chances with the Iron Order,' saying which, Baggy bowed deep. 'I will see you again soon,' he said as he rushed away. Vahura did not even notice when the empty cup had disappeared from her hands.

What? Any thoughts of questioning him, or asking him whether he was going to be at the Gilded Table of Giving, or a word of thanks, or a query on what *soon* meant, or perhaps even a hug, were all melted by the sound she heard next.

'Little Princess,' Old Ella spoke politely as befitted a governess as she took in the sight of the retreating figure of Baggy, no doubt wondering when the Cult of Yoginis had started admitting young Rakshasan Rangers in their sisterhood. Well… it was not as if Vahura had lied. Old Ella had just assumed Vahura was dining with the Yoginis.

As ever, words were not needed in any further conversation between governess and ward. Vahura looked at Old Ella. Old Ella stared at her. And their passionate conversation, expressed through expressions, needed no translator.

'!'

'__'

'?'

'.'

'.'

ADHYAYA II:C

THE SAGE OF BLACK DOORS

HASTINA

3 MONTHS BEFORE THE BATTLE OF MATHURA

*'We do not describe the world we see, we see the
world we can describe.'*
—**René Descartes**

NALA

I

Songs of seasoned bards made it clear that the finest time to first see the Rose City of Hastina was from the deck of a wherry cruising along the river Yamuna at sunrise. As the wherry glided into the harbour, the rising sun peeled away the shadows draped over the pink-quartz roofs of the Crowns and the sapphire dome of the Crest. All the bards sang that it would take a heart harder than a miser's vault to remain unmoved by Hastina's majesty. Why else had Chalakkha spared no expense to enter Hastina through the riverside at dawn?

So, understandably, Masha was in a foul mood when informed that the three of them would be entering Hastina on land when the sky above had darkened to a gangrenous bruise. No bards sang about this route, for all this route witnessed was a sea of hovels stretching from the Crows to be framed on the horizon by a sweep of what the songs called the Rose Wall. A wall that guarded the rich from the stench of the Reshts.

And Nala could see why. The place was like a dream, and not the pleasant kind. The Crows was a chaos of colonies, hemmed in stalls and shops, none selling anything Nala could trust. Women out of nowhere thrust wares at her face, making her stomach lurch with the rotten fragrances of fish and rotten milk. Men, gaunt and filthy, stared at them angrily. Ragged and dirty children played on the streets, choking the roads with their bodies and rubbish. The Union must not be doing well, Nala thought, if so many were rich in naught but misery. *Like prince, like city.*

Ahead, there was a great press before the gate in the Rose Wall. Nala could see speartips glinting over the heads of the crowd. Soldiers keeping the people of the city out of the city. But the crowd still pushed in, some pushed out, one falling on his haunches in the mud, all desperate to get inside the Crowns.

'I'm a Namin and not a Resht! Just because my house is here...'

'But I have the pass!'

'Me is an important witness! Me saw what happened to Sudama's head!'

'I'm Karna's wife! I need to be there!'

Everyone was shouting of how special they were, and why they deserved to be let in. All wanting to climb onto the other side of the wall. Nala would be lying if she said she was not one of them. To have the chance to let Prince Bheem know she had survived and that she was coming for him. *With what? Will you meditate him to death?* She shook her head as their cart turned to avoid the traffic. Power can never blossom in poverty, be it of skill or circumstances.

'Sire,' the man holding the reins of the cart called out, 'this is as far as we will go. The roads ahead are too narrow. I could take you to the Crowns through the main thoroughfare but I daresay you will have to bribe your lass's dowry away to find your way in this month.'

'That is alright,' Parshuram said, 'our business lies in the Crows.'

'Why, what's so special about this month?' Masha asked as Parshuram climbed down.

'Lass, haven't you heard,' the driver chirped, feeling as important as the news he had to share, 'the trial of Prince Arjun will begin any day now. That is why those mad fools are clutching for the gate as if it were their mother's tit. The Hundred are here in attendance with all their livery, but bah, who cares about them? Everyone wants to see the Princess of Panchal who seduced five brothers into marrying her.' He lowered his voice, 'I have heard tales that even those five can't quench her ravenous thirst, and that she has taken to sleeping with the horses when her husbands aren't around...' Parshuram cleared his throat. The man stopped short and blathered a series of apologies first to the Acharya, and then to Masha. 'My bad, my bad. Poor manners to speak of matters of the room before a girl.' The cart-man nodded his thanks and snapped the reins before he was Shrapped in two.

'I know of the matters of the room,' Masha called out but the cart-man resolutely did not turn back. She turned in the direction of the Rose Wall, and sighed. Of the Crest, they could only spy the outline of towers around a dome but moonlight did not do half as good a job as sunlight might have in bouncing off from their tips in pretty patterns that would've made silly girls giggle. 'We even missed the sapphire that glistens only at sunset,' she grumbled. 'I'm going to take this up with the Pathfinder.'

In his wisdom, the Pathfinder that Meru had assigned to them had chosen the Crows as the place in which to meet, and he must have had his reasons. But now that Nala saw it for herself, she too wished she could have seen the Crest under the sun. That way she could spend her nights imagining walking in it one day as she left a bloody trail on the marble floor below. She pictured the red splatter across the white statues – the blood of Bheem and his cursed brothers and his bitch mother. *If not today, then some day in the future, there will be a reckoning, Bheem. There will be a reckoning.*

'Why are you so quiet?' Masha nudged Nala.

'Just lost in how beautiful it must look on the other side.'

II

A musical note, wispy as a cloud across the moon, drifted into her ears. Awoken from her scarlet musings, Nala realized that they had ventured deeper into the Crows. This part of the colony seemed lifeless. Crumbling houses with rotten shutters jostled on either side, the plaster parting ways with the bricks. Rats scurried from their path, and a two-legged stray dog paused in its scavenging assignment to watch them pass. All in all, the streets, if they could be called that, were hushed save for the notes. The notes floated through the air like glistening dust trapped inside a sliver of sunlight in a dark room.

Nala had always had a good sense of hearing which had never given her cause to complain. But now she wished the bard, whoever he was, would stop playing. The notes stabbed her body with pinpricks of peace. She tried, desperately so, to cling on to the painful ecstasy of her serrated daydreams but the notes knew no rest. They raced ahead of her, stabbing her with melodious blows in the passing, destroying all thoughts of violence while replacing them with something akin to… contentment. *Is this what it means to relax?*

Parshuram wrinkled his face on her side. 'Not him,' Parshuram pleaded in a whisper no louder than a sword leaving its sheath. 'Not *him*,' he repeated, the words like a prayer, burying his face in his palms. Did Parshuram look… afraid? He certainly clenched his fists as if he were reconsidering giving up on the quest and letting the world fend for itself.

'Is everything alright, Acharya?' Masha asked.

'Why would they send him?' Answering his own question, he said, 'A pain in my arse. A master of mischief, trickster of the foulest kind that relishes in horseplay. His shenanigans have more often derailed us from our quest rather than aided us in it,' Parshuram lamented as he picked up his pace. 'Be wary of him, the both of you. This tune he plays is evil. The Raag of Bhairavi, he calls it. A disarming song. Deadens your senses and calms your anger.'

'Why would a Pathfinder want to disarm us?' Nala asked.

'Not us,' Parshuram said. 'Me. He knows I'm here. No wonder Vyas decided to stay back with the others. I should wrench the sage's neck for this.'

'At least she looks finally peaceful.' Nala pointed to Masha, whose grin had stretched from east to west, and who was circling on the spot with her arms stretched like a scarecrow.

Masha opened her eyes with a sigh when she realized they were staring at her. 'Isn't it just wonderful,' she chirped. 'The music has smothered all the disquiet in my stomach.'

Parshuram picked his ear vigorously as if that would somehow cause the music to fall off his ears. 'This is a Resht colony. They see a pretty unclaimed bird like you, and they won't spare a second in pawning you off to the next butcher for a day's meal.'

'You think I'm pretty?' Masha's eyes almost welled up.

'That girl needs to set her priorities straight,' Nala mumbled.

They followed the trail of the music and stopped by a one-storey building, which looked like it was built centuries ago in some serious haste. It was no bigger than the sheep pen at Meru. Shards of light spilled out into the night here and there from around the ill-fitting door which suddenly flung open, and a bald man emerged carrying a large pot. He cast the pot's contents, the skeletons of several stewed pigeons, into the street. Immediately, a dozen crows set upon the scraps. Ragged Reshts shooed them away, throwing their stones to scatter the scavengers, and divvied up what the birds had left behind to stuff it into their mouths while thanking the tavern for their generosity.

The keeper came to them when they entered, mopping his face with a rose. 'I suppose you're on your way to see the False Eagle like every other fool in the North. Well, it's five to a room and three to a bed, and if that doesn't fit well with you, I've nothing for you.'

'We've come to meet the Pathfinder,' Parshuram said politely.

'Oh, oh,' the keeper wiped sweat from his brow, 'the bard sits by the corner under the alcove. Pray, don't disturb him for long. His songs have kept these fools' minds off Prince Arjun. There's been five fights already over whether or not the Prince murdered Karna's whelp.' He shook his head as he muttered a few curses under his breath. 'Stow your things in the corner and I will fetch you some ale and bread if you have the coin.' When Parshuram nodded his thanks, the keeper breathed easily and guided him to the alcove.

Parshuram fumed as he stalked off. Nala sidestepped a drunken customer to see who it was that had incensed the Acharya so.

Her jaw dropped.

Nala had seen the Pathfinder's likeness more times than she cared to count on numerous scrolls in Meru. Plucking a pear-shaped lute on his chair that rocked back on its rear legs was Nar Ad Muni, famed traveller, navigator of routes and author of *Wonders of the Realm*.

To say he was flamboyant would be to undersell his efforts. His deep-purple beard, no doubt meant to be cut like the prongs of a trident, flopped lifeless under his chin. Purple flowers circled the man-bun on the top of his head. He wore a blue stole around his neck instead of the Meru-commanded blue robe for his Order. The buttons on his open half-jacket were carved ruby beavers but he was missing more than a few. His garish belt could have fetched him a cow once but the gilt on the buckles had flaked away. The long-necked lute in his hand was the sole thing that looked whole.

Nar Ad welcomed Parshuram with the warmest of smiles as if he were his brother returned from years of duty on the borders. Parshuram grunted. 'You planned this, you wretched—'

'Uh, uh, not yet.' Nar Ad raised his finger to silence Parshuram, and Nala's heart skipped a beat. 'It is about to end,' Nar Ad said as his dirt-crusted nails glided over the seven strings across twenty-four fixed frets. 'Girl, continue.'

Nala had not even seen the girl in the flimsy dress who was hidden under the shadows of the barred window. The girl, as if woken up from a trance, emerged into the faint light from the lanterns on the ceiling. She had a doll's face under a forehead fringed with black curls. Her lips were coated deep blue from drinking the nectar of the night. A rat was perched on the girl's shoulders. Unbelievably, the rat had a tiny hat strapped to the top of its head. 'Yes, master,' she spoke slowly.

Nar Ad's left hand pressed, pulled and glided on the frets of the lute while his right hand plucked the strings. The girl cleared her throat and then she sang. It wasn't so much a song as an incantation of arcane strolling out of her throat. Nala felt herself shed worries like Taksha shed his skin as the melody ascended. The girl's voice was exquisite as she flexed the fingers of her right hand in the air too as if weaving on an invisible spinning wheel. Goosebumps erupted over Nala's arms and she felt… happy, till… Nar Ad joined in the singing.

And the castle of glass where the floors had brimmed with hope and happiness, shattered. Men and women around them began to blink their eyes open, frowning. The rat scampered back with a squeak to hide on the nape of the girl. Nar Ad had barely dived into another stanza when Parshuram banged the table.

Nar Ad preened. 'That good, eh?'

'That appalling,' Parshuram seethed. Nala could not agree more. 'Why, why you would ever open your mouth and push words into a rhythm is beyond me. I told you this the last time as well. When you sang then, the local chickens migrated to another town, and chickens are not a migratory race.'

'Oh, you exaggerate,' Nar Ad scoffed, despite the sight of groaning patrons exhibiting their irrefutable evidence. 'I know singing isn't one of the blessings I was born with, but a sword isn't sharpened by one swipe of a whetstone. Isn't that right, Shree?'

'The whetstone told the sword it doesn't believe in love at first grind,' Shree said, without expression. Nar Ad burst out laughing while Parshuram threatened to burst into lava.

'No, it is not that you aren't *blessed* with singing, you are *cursed* with it. Cease this blasphemy or you will find how effective unsharpened swords can be at slitting throats.'

'Fine, fine,' Nar Ad said. 'Sometimes you just need the right light for a work of art to be truly appreciated. Isn't that right, Shree?' Nar Ad gave her a sad look.

'Without light, not much difference between a wolf and a dog,' Shree intoned. The rat, invisible amongst her tresses, squeaked a dissenting opinion from its safe haven.

Parshuram grunted after Nar Ad kept his lute aside but no trace of anger survived in his voice. Nala half suspected that Nar Ad had knowingly subjected them to the torture of his voice to soothe their spirits. Nothing like a sprinkle of harmless aggravation right after a meditative trance to unsettle the best laid plans of the mind. 'Still up to little tricks with your lute, bard?' Parshuram asked after easing into the chair.

'And I see you are still a barbarian despite living through the fall of three civilizations. It is a veena, you dolt.' Turning towards Masha, he said, 'Your grumpy friend here is such a savage. Much like the old philistines that sit in the House of Saptarishis.'

'Leave your woes to your whore and her vermin. I need a guide, not a prattling fool for this quest.' Parshuram shook his head again. 'Why would the Order send you?'

'First, she is not my whore. She is my apprentice. You think you are the only one who can pass their skills to a new generation to carry on their legacy. If the Meru won't grant me my Order of Music, I'll make my own. Meet Shree, the first student to be blessed with my tutelage. And her lovely friend here is named Mister Nomnom.'

Masha went up to the rat and handed it the tiniest piece of cheese from the folds of her robes. 'Greetings, Mister Nomnom.' The rat found the tribute wholly acceptable.

'As to the assignment at hand,' Nar Ad continued, 'the Seven were not very forthcoming to my request to be sent to guide you in your path. As a gift, I swore to not make any further request for an Order for Music, and in return, they gladly gifted me... well, you.'

'You joined this voluntarily!' Parshuram said, aghast. 'What about the Conclave?'

'*The* Parshuram out on a quest to the buried Land of Memories, to find the missing half of the Prophecy of this Son of Darkness, the man the Seven have been barfing on about for years. Armed with an Oracle-Sister, and from what I hear from Vyas, a Naga, a small battalion and,' Nar Ad finally turned to acknowledge Nala, 'and whoever you are. I honestly expected you would bring Mrytun Jay back to the fray for this, old man. He was your finest pupil. Regardless, a bard would be a fool to give up on this chance to shape the course of history. The song of this quest will echo through ages, and with that echo, my name will be rendered immune to the ravages of time. Not all of us are immortals, you know. Come, come, Vyas must have used my map from the riverside to smuggle his vast retinue into the catacombs without notice.' He rose with a whistle. The keeper approached their table with a worried look, and was handed the veena along with a gold sovereign. 'Keep it polished for me, my good man, and I'll reward you with a song when I'm back.'

The keeper nodded faintly, one hand groping the veena's neck like a lover and the other biting the gold coin as he hurried away.

'Time and prophecies wait for none.' He turned to Parshuram. 'Hurry along, Parshuram. As fast as a Raksha, as they say. We have a world to save. Isn't that right, Shree?'

'It isn't going to save itself, Master.'

THE TUNNELLERS

I

Nala watched as Chalakkha's men took positions around the second catacomb gate with crowbars, arranging themselves haphazardly so as not to get in each other's way like the last time. They grunted, they pushed, they heaved. Mortar crumbled from the edges. A tremendous gust of air from the outside got sucked in as if in a prolonged moan. Her lantern flickered while men around coughed from the swirling dust. But the iron plate was dislodged enough to reveal a river of blackness in yet another catacomb under the City of Hastina.

As the dust settled, Nar Ad took the lead and strode confidently into the tunnel. Following in his wake were the motley crew of Shree, Mister Nomnom, Masha, Chalakkha, Vyas, Taksha, Ajath and Chalakkha's other barterbows, each burdened with an assortment of drums, lanterns, airavat traps, hooks, diamond nets and rope. As Nala hefted her own gear, Parshuram raised his hand in a gesture of polite refusal.

'You will stay here with Jaffa, and keep an eye out for any stragglers who might have followed us,' Parshuram ordered, his eyes hard. 'If we do not return before your hunger gets the better of you, fend for yourself and return to the surface. Use the coin to send a raven to the Seven. If I do not return to you in a year, you will find the vial behind that absurd painting you drew for me when I took you in. Do with it as you please.'

But why? Why was *she* being left behind? Nala felt as though

she might weep blood. 'Acharya, no...' She gulped down thorns.
'Please... I am ready...'

'You're lost in your vengeance, Nala, so focused on it that you
will miss what lies on the edges of your eyes. A wandering mind is
a liability where we are headed. Now I am trusting you to guard our
rear. It isn't an empty title so I expect to see you do it well.'

That made no sense at all! If Nala was too distracted to be reliable on the mission, then she sure as hell wasn't reliable as a rear
guard either! *Reason. Make him listen to reason. He does not trust me.
Give evidence.* 'Acharya, my thoughts of revenge *sharpen* my focus.
It does not dull it. I am the best climber in this group. My arms are
so strong from being suspended that I am now an ape, an asset!'
Seeing Parshuram's face remain gloriously indifferent, the ice of
reason cracked and Nala slipped into despair. 'I am alert and agile!
Bheem, who is he? I am your apprentice! Your pupil! I know you do
not trust me, you do not have faith in me but I will prove myself as
I have over the last few weeks! I am useful, Acharya! Taking me out
just... doesn't make sense! Please don't kick me off the group!'

'No, Nala, listen to me carefully. If you come in here, you will die,'
he declared in a manner indicating this was what he knew rather
than this was what he thought.

Nar Ad's voice echoed from inside, 'Our untimely ends aren't
going to meet us by themselves. Hurry.'

Before Nala could muster another protest, armed as she was with
a hundred objections, Parshuram entered the tunnel. He singlehandedly pulled the iron plate shut behind him from the other side
of the black river, leaving Nala stranded with an unsoothable thirst.

'You know if I was interested in women,' Jaffa slurred, drunk, 'we
could have passed time here easily. You look almost pretty in the
dark, you know.'

II

Taksha looked ahead to take in the rest of their company, a sorry
assortment of soldiers and scoundrels, all clad in dark clothes,

haphazardly armed and lightly armoured. In comparison, his newly bared scales shone brilliantly in the torchlight though no one admired it. If only they knew what a grand deal moulting was in Pataal. He could not wait to ask Masha her view on his scales but for now they'd been ordered to stick in pairs in the darkness of the tunnels. Taksha was Ajath's shoulder, and behind Ajath trudged Parshuram, bringing up the rear. Taksha still had a hard time believing Nala had been left behind. That girl would not take kindly to being abandoned but hopefully they'd be back by evening before she did anything reckless.

Evening?

Taksha would later laugh at his stupidity. Downwards they'd gone, round and round in the dark for hours, then a day, then two, Taksha the only one comfortable with the weight of the city above them and the cushioning darkness. It reminded him of home. The rest seemed like they were doing their best to ignore the panic crawling up their back. The descent was clearly demanding its toll. Already, two of Chalakkha's men had experienced hallucinations. Some took refuge in fantasies or memories, depending on how honest they were, to keep the ghosts away.

It wasn't all rock and stone though. In the flickering light, Taksha spied the pillars flanking their path, sculpted rather than formed. He could even make out the swollen tops of buried domes in the vast, shadowed space beneath the stone bridges they walked on. Vyas had not been exaggerating then – there indeed was a city buried under Hastina. A forsaken city now emptied of life. Seeing this world brought a wave of homesickness up his throat.

Nar Ad's voice swept over him from ahead. 'Double check the muzzles on those hounds. Keep them quiet now.'

To Taksha's eye, hounds were wolves enslaved. One day some wolf must have made a mistake of helping out a Softskin, and these Softskins rewarded him by taking away his dignity and making him beg for biscuits. He would not let the Nagas in this realm suffer the same fate as hounds. Never. That was why when Gorin shouldered Taksha rudely to pass him by, Taksha held back his anger and smiled at his new partner.

'I best walk ahead, snake. Don't want 'em getting wet, do we?' Gorin tugged the right side of his jacket to show a Mathuran munition strapped to his belt.

Taksha looked away to focus on his chalk, wishing he did not have to partner with Gorin out of all the Softskins. But what choice did he have after discovering Vyas's betrayal? His mother had the right of it. One race's prophesized hero is another race's doom. Vyas wanted to stop the Son of Darkness. But Taksha was going to stop Vyas.

So now, in a strange way, in this fellowship of liars, Taksha could only trust the most dastardly liar of all to keep his lips sealed. It was not as if Taksha did not trust Masha, who treated Taksha as one of her own, or find Ajath dependable, who singlehandedly fended off Gorin's men from picking on him.

But it was hardly a secret that Masha had a history of making decisions rather quickly about people. She fell in love fast, and without any shred of caution. It was only a matter of time before she became a victim of her own faith. Even when they had started descending into the catacombs, she had spent the first hour weeping and begging Parshuram to bring Nala back until Parshuram had threatened to torture the hound if she did not seal her pleas. It was only by chance that Taksha overheard Parshuram confiding in Vyas about Masha's visions from the day he told them the story of Iyran Machil. Visions which revealed that Nala would meet her death if she entered the tomb of a city. While Parshuram did not hold divinations in high regard, he had said he wasn't going to risk Nala's life on future's fickleness. But the fact that Parshuram could not trust even Masha with this knowledge only confirmed how sensitive Masha was. Her humanity would be her ruin. And it was the same humanity that made requesting Masha to divine a future to save the Son of Darkness, instead of stopping him, a fool's quest. So, Masha was out of the picture.

And Ajath... Taksha had banished the notion without thought. The manner in which Ajath had choked the slaver to death left little doubt that the giantess hungered to settle a debt. Unlike Nala who carried her rage on her back, Ajath carried it inside her pockets. Ajath's vengeance to her was what finding the Messiah was to

Taksha – the rat dangled by Vyas in front of them to keep them on his path. The same way Taksha would not forsake his quest for salvation for Ajath, he did not expect her to abandon her path to redemption for him either.

Parshuram asked curtly when they had stopped to rest, 'How much longer, bard?'

'The Gate will remain where it is, Parshuram. It is only our pace that is in our control, and our opinion on the use of caution. Unless, of course, your Oracle can divine a shortcut which the greatest Pathfinder of the world could not decipher. No? I thought not. Now, speaking of oracles, how is that you found two Tainted? Do you know how difficult it was for me to find a Tainted who Masha's sisters had not burned alive in their hunt for diviners?' Nar Ad looked accusingly at Masha, and continued. 'Fortunately for us, Shree's father was a man of commerce and had sold her young. The blue nectar they force feed their girls dulled her powers enough for her to go unnoticed by bounty hunters. Isn't that true, Shree?'

'As dull as a monk's haircut, Master.'

III

Nala refused to count how long it had been since Jaffa helped her slip into the catacombs below in exchange for an evening with the Naga. She had heard Nar Ad whisper to Parshuram about the gaps in his map: *'The ritual of parikrama, Parshuram – ours is the land of clockwise circumambulation around temples. So, when in doubt, veer left.'*

So Nala had. She had spiralled downwards, descending through countless left turns. But she was still alone, the world still dark, the third torch in her hand dangerously close to its last life. Nala might have had no idea of the passage of time but it felt like days had passed, which meant she was desperately lost. She was hurt. Tired. Blood rush, long gone. The smell of darkness made it difficult to keep her wits about her, especially when the chalk marks on the wall had disappeared. She was beginning to feel that she could neither find her group nor find her way out again.

More than anything, she longed simply to roll up in the corner and close her eyes, but closing her eyes in such darkness would only invite dread. *Not you, Mrytun Jay, whoever you are. You aren't his finest pupil. I am.* Drawing strength from that thought, she climbed to her feet, replenished her torch and set out again. But where were they? Sometimes she found the food they had carelessly discarded. Sometimes she even sniffed out their piss and shit, all markers to let her know she was on the right path but they still remained hidden while her fears were being slowly peeled apart.

Nala was used to climbing mountains. They were dangerous, they were horrifying but they gifted freedoms to those who dared to climb them. Caves stole away that freedom. The darkness of the tunnels and the weight of the world above them were tyrants. They flattened her vision and bent low her soul. But Nala was going to hold fast to her resolution of completing seventy turns today. She would find them. Surely they did not have such a headstart.

If only optimism alone could make her a Pathfinder.

By the ninth time she rekindled her torch, her determination had wallowed down into despair. Then she had even lost that in the dread of the darkness in front of her, until she came across hope. Hope in the form of a corpse.

IV

Masha was from the Black Order of Sisters, Matrons and Oracles. Darkness was comfort there but there was something grasping about the black colour around her eyes, especially the way light from the torches did little to push it away. Her mind did tell her it was rocks, and that they could not be pushed but something inside Masha told her that was not it.

Hundreds of bat eyes looked down on them from the ceiling of the temple. Taksha reached out to her, letting her hold his arm as waves of bat sound rippled across the ceiling, making a sound like many small doors being opened on dry hinges.

Suddenly they slowed, and Masha almost ran right into Sidestep's back. She wasn't sure what was unravelling ahead, but Sidestep, and Whisper ahead of her, were now moving with caution, backs crouched. Turned out the floor of the catacomb dipped downwards in a series of shelves coated with dark slime, eroding the distinction between walking and sliding.

'Black guano,' Nar Ad explained from ahead of the line, 'the ooze of digested insects left behind by the velvety mass of bats around us.'

Sidestep stopped short, and looked at Whisper and then at Masha. 'Did he just say—'

'Let it go,' Whisper said. 'Guests don't grumble about what the hosts do with their faeces.'

'Quiet, girls!' Nar Ad said. 'Now these lower levels are homes of the imprisoned Robber King's descendants,' Nar Ad warned before entering the next tunnel, 'who over centuries of in-breeding have not earned a reputation for their hospitality. They stay in their crevices and fear fire so they shall not disturb us... if we do not disturb them. So, unless you fancy being boiled in their cooking pots, I suggest a long stretch of silence.'

Farther on, Nar Ad's tunnel reached a wall with a large slot at forehead height. He turned to face them. 'Since the next bit is a rather cosy passageway, we need nimble volunteers to scout ahead and see if there is anything we need to keep in mind while crawling through with our gear. Lord Chalakkha?'

He nodded. 'A gold sovereign to the first, and a silver to the second hand.'

Sidestep almost jumped behind Masha. 'I will take that gold!'

'Then I will take that silver,' Masha chirped.

'No, not you Sister Masha,' Whisper declared. 'We don't send a queen in the opening move. I will head in and keep your shoulder safe, Sister Masha. Nothing will go wrong.'

V

Nala's heart hammered but to her credit, she did not flinch. The man stood crucified at the right instead of the left, frozen mid-scream, with fluorescent writing trickling around him like a luxurious barbed wire. Taking a moment to ease her breathing, she lashed her torch across the macabre milestone marker. He was not one of theirs. He was too meticulously preserved to be fresh. She did not quite understand the writing on him but her hope let her imagine the corpse as a navigational checkpost.

She plonked herself down on the turf, diary in hand, to inspect the trail she had been charting to track her descent. On the page, was a tangle of zigzags. Maybe... this time, it was a right turn instead of a left. She glanced up and was jolted, her hands frantically scrabbling at the ground to pull her all the way back.

For the corpse was now smiling.

Nala was sure the corpse's open mouth had been frozen in a silent scream, but now she saw his teeth exposed in a smile. *Flee, Nala! Take your chances with Bheem on your own!* No! It had to be the light playing tricks, that or perhaps her memory had failed her. But she distinctly remembered a look of torment on his face, nothing like this wild smile. Her joints locked in rebellion, and she had to push herself, limb by limb, as she hurried into the left tunnel.

She looked over her shoulder at the corpse one last time. She was lucky this time. Getting lost here would be a death sentence. Lost she was in these thoughts but a muffled voice from ahead still reached her. The tunnels did share common, porous walls after all. Nala abandoned all thoughts of smiling corpses, and put her head against the stone. It was bitterly cold but she felt warmth surge through her when she heard the voice calling out.

It was Masha. Masha was calling for Whisper.

VI

Whisper found a foothold and pulled herself in the slot after Sidestep. The slot was just enough to squeeze through. Gear would have to be rappelled.

'Just another day in Satyabhama's training camp, eh, Whisper?' Sidestep said, coughing. 'This damn flu!'

'Satyabhama was worse.'

'I don't know, I think the darkness all around is giving her a stiff contest. But, Gods, I can't wait to pay the Fat Lord his due and rescue the other two. Life as a prisoner of war did not suit me. It definitely does not suit them.'

'I was made for it,' Whisper said dryly, almost stepping into something hard and bulbous. It was the same shiny thing they had spied while crawling through the slot. It had shone like a tiny coin. The same dull gleam. But turned out, it was a skull. A polished skull of a rat perhaps. There were no cracks on it, just burn marks on the back as if it had been tortured by a precise fire. A tiny voice told Whisper not to pick it up but there was no way she was not going to. The skull was almost sensuous, its eyes narrow, its ears…

Whisper dropped it.

It wasn't a rat skull. It was a deformed baby's.

Ahead of her, Sidestep lit another torch, and Whisper saw another skull winking in the black of the passage ahead, and yet another beyond it, barely visible from here.

Whisper frowned. The skulls… they were too neatly appointed against each other. She swallowed hard, forcing herself to think it through while ignoring Masha's repeated questions from the other side of the wall. She examined the skull again. Cold as ice. With one fingernail, she scraped away a thick coating of tunnel dust. It had been perhaps lying here for decades, or centuries. The more she thought it, the more her horror rose.

What if these skulls had been placed, not left? Like crumbs of sweet to…

'Side, stop! The skulls are a trap. Out! We need to get out!'

Time was not a consideration for whoever set this trap. Patience had nothing to do with it, either. It was just as her mother used to do, set traps at random outside the fences, and maybe a fawn came, and maybe it didn't. But then who came here? In the belly of the earth? That was easy. People like her: spirits of greed wanting to unlock something the ancients had specifically warned not to.

They climbed back through the slot, Sidestep cursing her jacket, cursing the rocks that shifted underfoot, cursing her greed. Maybe it was because of Sidestep's scampering, Whisper felt she heard sounds that didn't exist. No, not now. She could not afford to jump at shadows. The despair would never let go then, not here.

They got back to the main chamber out of breath. Nar Ad stood with his arms crossed, face scowling while the others were busy lighting a smoke, or talking, or finding a place to piss. Only Masha was by a plunging shaft, shivering and praying.

'Well?'

While Sidestep explained what happened to Nar Ad, Whisper strode to Masha. Even from a distance, she could feel the column of cold freezing air streaming past from reaches too high even for a lantern light to reach. She joined the praying Masha, held her hand out, and let the freezing wind pour through her fingers. An invisible waterfall. Slowly, so as not to startle her, Whisper kept a hand on the Oracle's shoulder. 'We are safe, girl,' she said.

Masha looked at her with a grin, and then down the edge of the shaft. Before Whisper could stop her, Masha cried out loud, 'Thank you, Seven!'

Bat cries… and human howls answered back.

VII

Nala could no longer hear Masha's voice but that did not stop her from running headlong into where the tunnel led. She realized that if not for Masha, she would have talked herself out of further descent.

It seemed funny that until just a few days ago, she would go to bed and Masha's face would be the last thing she would see before closing her eyes. But that was a while ago. Their silences had grown longer than their arguments. Taksha's readily available arm did not help. Nala did not blame Masha. It was perhaps possible to stay with someone who was grim, say like Parshuram, but not with someone who was not content until they painted the rainbows around them with their dull patch of grey.

Nala pictured their reunion again, playing it out in her mind over and over until she'd almost worn a groove in her absent thinking. Anticipation was a gift, a child of hope that kept her sane. But it was the same anticipation that blinded her to a stumble. Torqued forward, the momentum whirled her into a shaft in the wall, slick with guano, a shaft whose dead end was filled to the brim with... live bats.

She crashed into them, Nala shrieking, the bats screeching. She felt the leathery wings and soft, wet noses kiss every inch of her nape, her arms, her hair. Felt their sounds to the marrow of her bones. Her hands tried to find the wall to climb out, but everywhere her fingers grasped, they only clutched more fluttering bats. Bile threatened to tear out of her pores.

But before madness claimed her, something solid gave way on the other side as bats tore through the slim dead end and dived down into a hole like an army of suicidal birds.

It took a while for the storm of black panic to settle down. The sensation of bats on her body had gone through her mind like a devoted mother, closing, one by one, her mind's hundred torches of sanity. For a while her only thought was *Aaaaggghhhhh*. Once she had rubbed her arms, her neck and her face to scrape away the phantom touch of the bats, she leaned over and peered down the hole her tormentors had slithered off.

Deep, deep below something blue shone. Maybe this was the luminous lake Masha had seen in her vision. *Oh, Spirits, is this a shortcut to Iyran Machil!*

Nala took out the climbing gear from her bag. She lodged the hooks, clipped onto the rope and began her descent, waiting until she passed the second bolt and was comfortable on the hole. Cutting through the darkness, Nala rappelled down in smooth, even leaps. The bolts held. Nala made good time by trusting them, shoving out any thoughts of falling. *It won't happen*. It couldn't.

The bolts held.

And she descended deeper into the earth's belly.

She covered the first descent in a little under two hours, found a small ledge, took a break to drink from her bag, and then swung down again to descend deeper. Hallucinations of someone singing grew louder in her ears but the newfound open space around her freed her lungs from deeper breaths and her heart from its deeper beats. Still... the floor could not come fast enough. The hours passed like kidney stones. Her limbs grew tired, her eyes blurry.

The luminescent lake was not far. She could do this. Just find the floor, and then she'd be good. She'd be safe. Wouldn't she?

Suddenly Bheem's face stared back at her.

Nala shouted in panic, fumbling with the rope, desperately trying to clip in. She had to get away. She had to...

Not real.

Shaking her head, Nala descended at a reckless speed. By the time she landed on the luminous 'lake', her mind had become dizzy. Cracks spreading under boots on the ice looked like a spider web to her. When had she fallen on a glacier? She couldn't remember, couldn't tell if she'd tripped, or if her legs had buckled.

It took a while to reassemble her wits which she had lost from the sudden descent. But now that she was herself, she saw nothing in itself to fear. The something blue she had seen had been the luminous lichen growing underwater, which conjured up in her mind the image of paralysed aquatic fireflies. And there was nothing else in the cavern apart from this radiant lake. But Iyran Machil wasn't through the ice, was it? Masha had seen a body of water but there was nothing in her visions about ice. No, this wasn't it. The lake was shallow enough to see the bottom. A glorified frozen puddle, really. There were also supposed to be two giant statues flanking the crossing. Those statues were the markers. She could not spy any statue around. The wall had to have the holy symbol of *Om* on it. The fractured limestone walls around here were identical to the ones she had already crossed. No *Om*s in sight. The only thing different about the place was the air... it felt inhuman. There! She heard singing again. *Find a way to it. Focus on that. Focus on the details. Focus on the wall.* The walls were poked with nest-shaped tubular holes. Surely, one of them led out to Iyran Machil.

She chose the largest hole.

It would still be a tight fit. She had to imagine herself as a lizard, pressed flat to cold stone and only then did she slither in. The internal walls of the tube with their grasping edges tore at her clothing and hooked her cuffs as she dragged herself through it. The rock cut her arms and the low ceiling knocked her head. *At least there are no bats. I should be thankful for that.*

Nala tried to keep the fear of being wedged in this tube alive out of her mind. Trapped alive awakened bile in her brain. *No. Don't think on it. Just hope that the tube leads straight to a large, open space.*

Yes, just picture that. Large and open space.

She breathed deep, and crawled, and then cursed again as another jutting rock snagged her trouser around her ankle. Nala yanked angrily to free herself but the rock did not let go. She tried to crane her neck and see behind her but her own body filled the opening to block any sight of the tube. *Fantastic.*

And then she felt the rock on her ankle move.

To her calf.

But Nala hadn't moved a muscle.

Another tug at her ankle. And then a taloned hand suddenly began dragging her back.

VIII

'Please, Ajath, I want to see,' saying which Taksha made his way to the edge of the shaft where Gorin was still staring down. He was about to sess their auras when he was startled out of his scales by Gorin.

'Bitch woke them up. They are coming!'

Down the shaft, dark shapes swarmed into a chamber at the bottom, the shadows bristling with horns and barbed points. The bowelmen. They resembled horned demons from tales his mother used to scare him with. When they looked up to see Taksha staring down, their faces made Taksha retch and drench them with his bile before he could turn away.

Oh Sweet Mother of Moults!

Ajath yanked Taksha away from any attempt at apologizing to them and set him on course to follow Nar Ad. Their pace was brisk, their weapons at the ready, their fingertips shivering. In the deeper catacombs, they found still deeper tunnels, and at the bottom of those, they found more passageways.

'When the fuck will this end?' Salam complained. 'Ants descending the belly of an airavat!' From somewhere Mister Nomnom squeaked his assent from Shree's pocket.

'I want the sky, too, my love. Soon, soon,' Shree answered.

In their rush, there were injuries. Yes, it was bound to happen in such tight spaces. Salam's leg was badly wounded by a twist, a twist he blamed on Vyas. Chalakkha himself saw darting shadows in places without light. Taksha did not quite understand but it seemed darkness threw Softskins into a freefall. But this was about to grow worse.

For when the catacombs forked for the hundredth time and plunged still lower into a limestone corridor, they came on horrifying taloned prints on the walls that were neither animal, nor man. But there was no time to settle on them for their way ahead was blocked by a circular plate.

And beyond this plate, some creature was singing.

IX

Nala's whole body spasmed. The tube suddenly became too tight, no space to breathe. Images of her future, her body crushed to a slime, crashed against her eyes, and she was blind from them, breathing too fast, trying to raise her head against the low ceiling on instinct. If the taloned hand managed to drag her back, she knew she'd be dead. Parshuram would never even know she had tried.

She kicked, she screamed, she cursed while her abductor sang. Fucking sang! Nala kicked again, and her feet found face. And then, without realizing, Nala crawled ahead at a frantic pace till her head popped free, and in the next moment, her body and legs cleared the tube like a baby from a womb. Only to roll down a dune of black sand all the way to the bottom.

Slimy, dazed, disoriented. She knew she should run. She could not wait for her relieved sobs to pass. With difficulty, she found a way to win the duel with unconsciousness this time. Hands bare, she plucked out a candle and a pair of flints from her bag. Her last source of light. As she fumbled to light it up, there was a sound, distant or near, she couldn't tell.

'Masha?' she challenged. She paused, listened, heard nothing more. *Bloody hallucinations.*

By now her blade was out in one, her eyes squinting through the candlelight. She might finally be in an open space where she could breathe but breath did not come easily to her. For on her way, she had to cross dozens, maybe hundreds of suits of ancient armour hung from rawhide thongs knotted to knobs and outcrops. It looked like a small army of ghosts. A vanquished army. As she made her way through the army of empty armour, her fevered mind conjured eyes under the helms, staring at her, shining in the blackness.

Hundreds of other physical details clamoured for her attention as she ran blindly. Some she absorbed, most she simply passed between. The trick was to see simply. She realized she had rolled down the dune into a colossal cavern. And while darkness still reigned supreme down there, there was a thin, biscuit-thin stretch of light on top of the wall on the cavern's west side, just between the wall and the ceiling. From where she stood, the crevice of light resembled a glowing cut inflicted to decapitate the hill. Illuminated in the light was the mark of *Om* painted on the cliffside's face with the same fluorescent colour she had seen on the corpse scarecrow.

Her discovery made her sigh in relief, her breath blowing her candle out.

Just then, there was a scratching sound that now joined the song from the other direction. She caught it loud and clear this time.

Nails scratching slate? Bats?

This damn candle! Why was it misbehaving now? *Drink the spark, fucker!*

The scratching sound and the singing grew louder. Nala wanted to run, any direction, just run. *Remember your training. Be the shadows.* She repeated it like a mantra till she found her will. Clenching her teeth, she tried again, and the spark caught.

Light, sweet light.

The scenery of murder lasted one instant. Then the candle flickered.

No! Nala kept her fist in her mouth to choke her screams. When she subdued them, she cupped a hand around the flame to let it live. The candle flickered in its death throes but the light was more than enough, and Nala took her eyes from it to look up again.

They hung before her from the wall, strange humanoid shapes, pale to the point of white, eyes the grey of blindness, jaws protruded. Their pubic patches were a wild rush of snow-dressed bushes. Some of them bore scars of weapons, some had inscriptions on their waistline while some were overrun by an army of warts. They all had strange symbols drawn on them in fluorescent paint like that corpse she had run into... but judging by their wounds, the lacerations, too deep, strangely massed on their neck, they all had been mauled to death by jaws! Was that how Nala would meet her fate?

In the area conquered by the light of the candle, stepped a crea-ture as if in answer. Whiter than ivory, her long hair was matted into horns. She wore a half-mask but her eyes were misty as if they were blind. She was muttering something. Nala could see flashes of her tongue, coated in black fungus. There were even black threads at the corner of her mouth. But it was her head... her head bent over at a horrifying angle, neck terribly askew, that stilled Nala. The way the bowelwoman had to turn her whole body to face Nala, even as her head flopped sideways, was so dreadful that Nala silently blew out her light.

Blackness rose like a wave around her even as the weight of the cities crashed from above. But it was still better than watching her death roam around blind. Nala collapsed to the floor.

With what were her last acts of will, she pulled out a quill and the diary where she wrote Masha's visions, the older ones. 'I... tried, Masha. I tried. I'm going to try to make it to that *Om* cliff. I was caught by a bowelwoman but I managed to escape. I do not know where she is now. I just wanted to tell you, in case I don't get to speak to you again.'

That what? I'm sorry for being rude to you. When you were not there in my life, I had no reminders of what my life had once been. I could simply go day to day doing what I needed to do to learn how to be a killer. I could give my attention to being an apprentice and think no further than my revenge. But your face, your eyes, they were crueller than any mirror. You pitied me. You could not look at me without betraying what you had seen of me in your visions. You remembered me as the joy-chasing, spoilt pupil of Meru, doing no more than playing at disturbing a class, and that was the bitterest of all. You saw me as I was. It made me so angry, I'm so sorry, I wish we'd met some other way, I wish you weren't mad, I wish I wasn't a fool.

She did not write it. She wrote nothing. Because the thought of farewell somehow steeled her nerves for a brief moment. As if right on cue, the scratching sound of nails on stone returned as well as the song, and this time there was no question. They were coming from opposite directions.

So, fight or flight?

Neither. Both were useless. She tore the sides of her clothes and smeared her arms with ochre grease from the corpses on the hook. With the blood, she stiffened her hair into a circle on the top to match their fashion. If the bowelwoman was looking at her pathetic attempts to disguise herself, Nala was dead anyway. But if she was blind as Nala suspected, there might just be a chance. So, like the Kiratas pulling themselves into the womb of a dead horse to hide in a storm, Nala pulled down the bodies and dragged the dead upon her.

'Forest Spirits, help me,' she whispered.

The scratching sounds became loud. The song grew louder.

She only had one real choice left to make. Whether to keep her eyes open or close them to her death. She kept them open as she held the dagger close to her heart.

X

Whisper blamed Parshuram for trusting these trigger-friendly morons with reason in the face of danger. The moment the door had been rolled to the side, bolts had flown into the darkness from crossbows without command. But no one screamed on the other side. The only thing that ceased was the song.

Once the first volley of bolts was exhausted without effect, she watched Parshuram stride into the darkness. Chalakkha's barterbows spread out behind him, planting their torches in the ground. Light soon revealed carefully stacked urns, chests undoubtedly filled with treasures, an army of empty armours and sacks overflowing with gold coins. Salam and Sidestep wasted no time with ceremony quickly emptying their rucksacks to make room for the gleaming haul. 'These seem to be some offerings by the bowelmen to their deities,' Nar Ad said. 'Though I see no idols.'

'Maybe that light, Master.' Shree pointed to the light slipping through the crack on the other side.

'We got dead bellies, here!' Jaah called out. 'But it ain't our bolts that did the job. They seem bitten and beaten to death, Lords – oh, Yama's beard!' His voice broke with terror as he stepped back, watching a bloodied hand rise through the corpses. 'A belly! A live belly!'

Parshuram silenced the poor old mercenary with a swift blow to the ears, then threw aside the first two bodies to reveal Nala buried beneath them. She lay there, grim-sheathed, dagger in hand, her hair twisted into a feral shape, and murder gleaming in her dry eyes.

XI

Nala could not believe it. Parshuram had come for her. Tears burned in her eyes, and suddenly she could feel every ache and pain in perfect clarity, perfect detail. She paused, closing her eyes at the swell of tangled emotion in her throat. She wanted to scream at Parshuram, wanted to hug him, wanted to lie down in his arms until her life slipped out.

'What have you… done,' Parshuram said, without anger. 'You shouldn't have come, Nala.'

'You… did this?' Chalakkha suddenly exclaimed from behind Parshuram. 'Oh, you… you not only came here before us on your own, you actually slew four of them!'

Gasps rippled through the group like a bit of scandal as most of them formed a semicircle behind Chalakkha. Masha rushed to Nala's side while Taksha offered her his waterskin, his slit eyes staring at her with pity. The other soldiers and cutthroats burst into open applause. Nala, confused at first, saw the awe in their eyes and swiftly understood. They believed she had killed the four bowelmen.

She had been uncomfortable at first. She could not sort out how she felt about their misunderstanding. It stirred her pride that so many came to her to congratulate her but seemed uncouth that she was taking credit for something she had not done. Though she did deserve credit for what she had. Nala had impregnated the catacombs alone. That was worth a statue. So she rose in the half-light, a tiny Goddess of Wrath, to stare at Parshuram.

Before Parshuram could say anything, Nar Ad spoke, 'Now we have evidence of how even immortals can be wrong. For if Sister Masha was the most important of us all, then Nala *Undergod* is the most deserving of us all. Oh, come now, Parshuram. Diamonds are forged in nature's disobedience. And you honestly can't send her back even if you wanted to.'

'Undergod! Undergod!' The cheer was picked up by the men and women who stepped in to pat Nala in the back. The applause had threatened to go on indefinitely if not for one of the hounds whose canine intuition sniffed out another dead bowelwoman.

The same bowelwoman who had chased Nala through the tube. The singer.

The bowelwoman had been only moments away from Nala before one of the crossbow bolts had taken her in the neck. Nala limped over to her. Nala stared dispassionately at the alabaster skin over the woman's flat stomach, curved hips and ruined full breasts. The bolts in her neck had missed their mark, Nala now noted in the light, but the bowelwoman would still be dead soon. She heard her trying to say something, whispering, gurgling. Gorin excitedly tipped her half-mask and frowned at the horribly disfigured face that was at complete odds with her luscious body. But despite the disfigurement, the bowelwoman's eyes held pride in them. Not pride. Victory. She coughed out blood, still trying to say something. Was she laughing at them?

'Fucking bellies!' Gorin muttered, kicking her ribs with his boot. 'Why is she still chattering!'

Nala read the movement of her lips, and realized she wasn't chattering. She was chanting.

'She is summoning someone,' Nar Ad's voice dripped with dread, and then he turned around. Even Nala heard it. 'Something's coming. We need to run.'

XII

Whisper ran through the maze of armour to the cliffside. At first, she thought she was a fool to be running blindly simply because someone said so. No one was behind them. But the air, which had been still so far, now shivered with an ill wind. Whisper did not know if someone was summoned or not but she was not going to stay to find out.

'Men and women, it is each one for themselves. Use your gear. Climb like you had snakes biting your arse!' Nar Ad shouted.

Whisper scaled the summit first. The other side of the cliff was an icy slide down into an eerily lit chamber. Bathed in that light, she stopped there at the summit, carefully planting her torch on the side, as she helped the others climb over the perch. Taksha was the second to reach the summit. 'In here? It is so cold!' he asked uncertainly, shielding his eyes. Ajath, who came after, simply pushed Taksha to slide down the icy slope and followed suit.

'At least and at last we are here,' Nar Ad said, one of the last to climb, beaming as he followed after Chalakkha. 'Here, boy,' he handed his bag to a young spearman, Orrhan, 'carry this for me, won't you?'

Once even Gorin and his lackeys had climbed over with their muzzled hounds and gear, Whisper called out, her chest hammering. 'Sidestep!'

'Coming, coming!' Sidestep slammed into the base of the hill, bag clinking with coins. *She was lugging treasure! Is she mad?* Behind her, Salam's wounded leg made running difficult. Sidestep looked down and saw Salam and Vyas were having trouble climbing, and cursed silently. Sidestep slowly climbed down.

'Don't wait for me, Whisper!' she shouted, and dropped back down the cliff. Whisper saw her grab Vyas's hand and haul him up a few ledges. And then Sidestep climbed down to help Salam.

Vyas watched this for a moment, helplessly, and Whisper whistled at him.

'Acharya,' Whisper said, 'you have to keep climbing. Now.'

Vyas nodded, and in a matter of moments reached the top where Whisper helped pull him up and, in one smooth motion, let him slide down the slope on the other side to safety. Hopefully. The absence of screams left her optimistic though.

As if in answer, the torches in the cavern below, the ones they had left near the door they had entered through, started to flicker and then went out. Something dark spread in the room.

Not completely dark.

Whisper could see the glistening oil on spikes and horns as it squeezed its way through the narrow door. The stench that hit Whisper was the smell of stale semen rolled with fresh shit and boiling sulphur. Sidestep abandoned her plans of helping Salam and sprang up the cliffside.

'Faster, Side!' Whisper urged gravely.

'What do you think I am doing?'.

Whisper looked down to see the darkness reach the base of the cliff. It began to climb. Slowly but surely it swallowed Salam as he was trying to find purchase on the rock. The moment the darkness rose to his stomach, Salam retched and let out an inhuman scream. She could see Salam no longer in the dark and was grateful for it.

She stretched her hand down as Sidestep reached the perch of the hill and started to climb up the last rock. By now the darkness below her was complete and full. Sidestep strained, and then their hands finally met. 'Remind me never to play hero again,' Sidestep huffed.

Whisper rolled her eyes as she pulled, but suddenly Sidestep's expression changed. The grasp went soft. Sidestep's eyes went glassy and her lips let out the softest gasp that was barely audible in the wet, chewing, tearing sound that came from below her. Perhaps the most agonizing sound Whisper had ever heard.

Sidestep's eyes watered with tears, and with the last bit of will, she focused them on Whisper. 'Promise me, Whiz!' she hissed. 'You will save the girls! Promise me! Fucking swear it!'

Whisper nodded, cold.

Sidestep nodded, smiling, and then opened her mouth to say something. She was yanked right out of Whisper's grasp and down into the darkness. Whisper almost fell herself before she caught a rock, turned and leaped to the other side to slide down the slope even as the torch she had left above guttered out.

XIII

Gorin cursed under his breath as he landed hard on the narrow corridor, his slide down the steep slope not exactly graceful. The landing area was dotted with broken urns and chests filled with coins, gems, skeletons and broken figurines. And as for the ghastly light, it was coming from a blasted lichen that stretched all the way to the corridor's end into a lake.

'Why is it not following us down there, whatever that was?' Chalakkha asked, his breath misting in the cold air down here.

'Maybe its stomach is full,' Gorin remarked darkly, earning a withering look from Whisper. He blew her back a kiss.

'Or maybe this area is sacred,' Nar Ad said, pulling a shawl out from his bag. 'Look at the urns and chests. They were rolled down from the crevice to whatever God the bowelmen venerate here. It does not look like they themselves ever descended here, at least not while they were alive, and I daresay, neither did their ghastly pets.'

But what was this pet? Demon? Poisonous air? Swarm of maneating locusts? Even the bard did not know and Gorin did not care. He had finally found some reward to justify this trek. He and his gang of ruffians laughed as they sifted the tribute-treasure with their hands, picking up handfuls of coins to let them rain.

Nar Ad moved past him with a worried frown. Gorin didn't like the sight of the bard all bent out of shape. He left his gold for a moment, and trailed after him, soon realizing what was eating at him. Apart from the holy tributes of the bowelmen, the chamber was as empty as his purse after a night on the dockside. The corridor on which they stood ended a little above the lake. And that was it. There was nothing but the glimpse of a wall on the other side. 'What in Yama's arse is going on? Shouldn't there be a grand gate, or at least a damn door?'

And suddenly, even in the humbling mass of natural, almost glacial architecture around him, Gorin felt as if he was trapped in a cold coffin, for there was no exit. They couldn't climb the slide. Was this a fucking one-way route?

'Found it!' Nar Ad shouted as he pointed at a bronze plate carved onto the floor scarcely distinguishable from the surrounding stone corridor. 'Gents, here with your tools, please!'

Gorin's men eagerly took their crowbars and went to town on the mortar that held the bronze plate in place. Small gaps cracked and unhinged the plate a bit. Before long, three more lads joined the fray. It took bloody ages before they finally shifted the massive thing. But bugger all else happened. There was just thick black water in there.

Black oil, he corrected himself when Parshuram plunged his torch into it. The chamber burst to life as twin lines of fire wove on either side of the oilpit, flowing through narrow gouges carved for them in the walls. The fire lines danced entrancingly as they painted the ancient walls with their light all the way to the other side of the lake, unveiling the star attractions of the chamber.

Its ceiling.

All eyes were glued to the cave's low ceiling, hidden behind twisting stalactites. The contours of these structures were bathed in the glow of fire-reflecting crystal spurs, dangling the stalactites like flowers nestled within a bouquet of leaves. Unlike their fragile limestone neighbours, the crystals did not look like they were in immediate danger of causing a cave-in.

The toothed ceiling soon lost the staring contest to the far wall where the firelines unveiled towering statues of two swordswomen, standing like they owned the place, flanking an ancient-looking gate.

'Behold!' Nar Ad beamed. 'The gate to the cradle and graveyard of human civilization!'

Only two problems.

One: only the bloody heads of those statues were peeking out, the rest of 'em were submerged in the lake. And judging by the size of those heads, it was one deep-fucking-lake.

Two: Something moved *inside* the lake, and it weren't fish.

XIV

Shree was called an odd thing, a lunatic who liked to talk to birds, to bees, to trees and to everything that was not man and that was free, be it the rats, rainbows or seas. And Shree relished it. But suddenly, given charge of feeding Nala who was only slightly younger than her, she felt... so good. She had always felt jealous of the girls in brothels who were sold by their parents along with their sisters. Jealous of how those sisters knew when they were smiling, even without light. She had seen them, overheard their sweet, mad conversations full of half-formed sentences and delicious misunderstandings. And she had learned that between any two sisters, one is always the guardian, one the garden. Now Shree could be the guardian, something she had always wanted to be, and as usual, she only had her protector to thank. Nar Ad the Bard. She would have thanked him too if the man ever let anyone else talk.

'Veins can be gates under water, in air and on land. Is this one under water?' the Orange man asked.

'No, this one seems to be just submerged,' Nar Ad said.

The mute Blackteeth stepped forward to create a dance out of her fingers.

'Considering the cavern is not fully drowned,' Orange translated, 'the waters must be exiting somewhere. She wagers that the stone pommels jutting out behind those statues are levers – levers to turn a mechanism to release the water completely. Possible.'

The Snake spoke, 'I am used to swimming in the lakes of Pataal with not a light to see and with currents you would think sentient. I can get to the other side.'

'Are we forgetting that something is moving under the waters?' Gorin asked.

'We could kill it,' Whisper said. She had not said anything since they had landed here, and out of experience, Shree could see the silence was one of tears.

'You're assuming you can harm it, let alone slay it,' Gorin said as he stepped towards the edge of the platform. 'If only there was a way to find out what it is. A crocodile? A fish? Hello, beautiful! Care to show Papa your lovely face, eh!'

Shree, keeping a firm hold on Nala's shoulder, leaned over to see what Gorin was looking for while Mister Nomnom sauntered along the edge of the platform, his whiskers twitching.

Nar Ad scoffed. 'Only one way to find out.' He casually kicked Mister Nomnom into the water below.

XV

Nala held Shree back with all her strength before Shree could dive. Why was no one trying to help her? Did they assume Nala was strong enough to hold this screaming girl back? *Damn that Undergod title! Now I definitely cannot let her go,* Nala thought as she held on to Shree for dear life.

'What did you do, you cactus-throated fucker?!' Shree screeched.

'Well, at least now I know your true opinion of my singing. Don't fret, darling. Rats are excellent swimmers. They can even tread a sea for days.'

'Do you expect Nomnom to climb the statues and pull the lever as well? Let me go, Nala!'

'Shree, just breathe!' Masha said when Shree scratched her across the face with her nails.

'Nala,' Parshuram commanded, and Nala twitched the nerve under Shree's ear to end her struggles. For now.

'Acharya Nar Ad,' Masha said, tracing the fresh cut on her face, 'why would you do that to Mister Nomnom?'

'The one thing I have learned from these dear rodents is that it is always the second rat that wins the cheese. See! We did not have to even wait. Time for our sentry to meet our adversary.'

The waters of the lake stirred, the blue-hued blackish water frothing as a body rolled beneath the surface. The length of a rowing boat, it sent ripples spreading, swimming closer and closer until at last something like an oily, glistening black tentacle peeped over the waters. The water rolled over it in hypnotic waves as it slithered in their direction, its body making an obscene and obscenely long S pattern on the surface. Each member of their troupe uttered some variant of 'Gods' when the creature's head finally broke the lake's surface to swallow Nomnom.

Red eyes without any pupils, like a love child of an eel and a chameleon, two long tongues slipped out of its eyes as it neared Nomnom. So strange, so exotic, so beautiful... Nala kept one eye on it even as she took advantage of the distraction and stole a pinch of Hashayne of Hastar from Masha's bag. She was weak from the descent, and she needed the clarity of her Chakras. Nala barely even noticed as Mister Nomnom was pulled down the lake by the creature's twin tongues, its squeaks disappearing in the inky darkness.

'Men, fire!' Chalakkha commanded, and a flurry of bolts either disappeared in the water or bounced harmlessly off its skin. 'Munitions, then!' he relented.

'We can't use a munition here. It would have the ceiling coming down faster than you can say dragon.'

But Taksha did not miss the dark look Parshuram exchanged with Vyas and Nar Ad. The bard turned. 'We can't kill it,' Nar Ad said. 'Not when it is surrounded by water.' Nar Ad's surprisingly sombre tone stilled all protests from dissenters. 'This creature predates the Ages. I was truly hoping the records had been wrong about this.'

'Predates the Ages?' Masha said. 'Older than even Acharya Parshuram?'

'There are worlds out there, my dear diviner,' Nar Ad whispered, 'which are shaped by memories, and in such a manner, defy death and even time.'

'You cannot defy time,' Masha said even as Nala slipped to the side to snort the drug, though Nala wondered why Masha did not add 'death' to 'time' as well, but the presence of an immortal in front of her undercut that point.

'Men mistake time to be this unending tide, forward, constant and continuous,' Nar Ad said. 'They aren't wrong. But the Orange Order knows how half-truths are more popular than facts, aren't they, Vyas? The thing is, time is like water. In our realm, it may act like a river, always going forward, in others like a whirlpool, and in some, like Iyran Machil, time... is a glacier. Frozen. Unmoving. The ancient records all perished in the Time of Great Sorrow but from what we do know, there are seven realms in the cosmos. We only know the names of three. Our realm, of course. There is the Svarg, the abode of the Children of Light and Darkness. Some say, it is above our realm. And there is Pataal, home of our dear friend Taksha, below our realm. Sometime in the world's history, the Children of Light figured out a pathway to travel up and down across these realms through...'

'Arteries,' Nala said, despite believing that it was a rather inappropriate time to be giving sermons on history. Or was Nala the only one who remembered a monster eel lurking in the neighbourhood?

'Top marks, Nala. But the mortals weren't to be left behind. For every vertical rise casts a horizontal shadow. If there was a road to travel across realms, there had to be a pathway to travel across different points on the same realm, and so the Veins came to be discovered. Velas Kalein. A Pathfinder's dream. The Veins are passageways that you enter through a Dvār – a Divine Gate – much like this drowned gate you see on the other side of the lake. You trot an hour in the Veins, and you venture out through another Dvār and find yourself a hundred leagues away from where you started on the map. The Veins form a labyrinth of different turns leading to different places, or so the ancient Pathfinders claimed. Imagine the Veins as the catacombs we descended, only each tunnel led to a different city on earth. You see many novices mistake Manu to have used these Veins to build Iyran Machil in some alien realm to shelter his people during the Great Tears. But that is false.' Nar Ad smiled mischievously. 'Manu built Iyran Machil *within* the Veins, within the highway that serves as a shortcut to different points across our world.'

'What happened to these Veins?' Chalakkha asked, coughing from that persistent flu. 'I mean, imagine if we could move armies through these Veins – it would make the world such a smaller place. Mathura would bow down to the Empire in the span of a day.'

'Exciting prospects of tyranny aside,' Nar Ad scoffed, 'the Seven believe the Veins are actual veins of the Sha or Purusha, the First God, the creator of the primordial waters which he used to sow the seed of all creation. The cosmos is nothing but the sleeping body of Sha. Don't look at me with those incredulous eyes. I am just parroting the scriptures. I personally find God is the most dull answer to the most delightful questions.'

'So, what? Did the God just wake up and leave?' Chalakkha asked.

'Oh no.' Nar Ad laughed again. 'The God died. There are Dvārs still inside Iyran Machil… but they were chained shut by our ancestors. This – what we see ahead of us – is the only entrance to the Veins and to Iyran Machil.'

'Unfortunately, we are still in a place where time flows like a river, bard,' Parshuram growled. 'Masha, you ready?'

Taksha asked, defensively, 'She isn't going to swim through that now, is she?'

'She is going to divine our future here and now,' Nala answered, 'and chart the path for Acharya Parshuram to take through that lake of death. This was already foreseen.'

Unfortunately, as Nala was talking, the future changed.

XVI

Masha was used to inhaling the fumes to enter her trance but to be able to divine her own immediate future, something oracles were specifically warned not to do, Parshuram had her snorting the Hashayne infused with powdered Abyss. The Abyss would help Masha detach from herself and see Masha as another person, as another subject.

It was a white pain, shooting up her nose, travelling swift and hot through her sinuses and into her brain. Blood flowed freely now from her nostrils, puddling over lips, and then trickling down.

She broke herself apart into consequences of hundreds of decisions. Holding to the memory of every future she saw every fall, every slip, every moment across the ceiling that ended in a catastrophe, and she scribbled them all in her illegible hand on a scroll. Death. Death. Drowned. Eaten. Buried. Shot. Eaten. Eaten. Death. Light.

Stop! This was it. This was the future. She found it. Still in a trance, Masha drew lines and circles on a piece of paper. A full-fledged map of the stalactites of the ceiling. She had found a way to swing through that barbed ceiling. But she could not speak it out loud. For breaking herself into different futures was the easy part. Pulling back to the true reality was the problem.

Having witnessed hundreds of futures, she had no idea which path to take back. She knew if she lost her way, she would be lost in that life, leading it only in her head, while her body rotted on that platform in the madness. Not to forget, rotting alongside her friends who would be trapped there forever. She analysed every vision of the passage across the lake. She tried to see the expressions on people's faces, how those expressions changed in every future she saw, what those expressions meant, whether what they said changed across visions, making the path back a sham, an illusion, a trap. But there was so much to balance on the way back, so many edges to inspect in every vision to identify false truths. She fought against the migraine and against the chaos, struggling for control from her alternate selves. All Masha wanted was to bang her head against the floor to divert the ache from her mind to somewhere she had control over. *Wait. Is that why Nala cut her hand?*

The sudden memory of Nala made Masha hear her voice. Nala was the most familiar place Masha could think of. Using Nala as her north star, slowly, agonizingly slowly, Masha pulled herself back together from her visions, and it was only then she realized something had changed.

'And?' Parshuram asked.

'Something happened, Acharya. Something changed,' Masha said, her voice shaking. 'I know you wanted me to divine you a path through the lake but I am afraid, it won't be you who will open that door. It has to be you, Nala.'

XVII

Nala could do this. With her senses heightened with the Hashayne she had snorted when they had been distracted by the elephant-eel, Nala's memory turned into a spider web, catching and memorizing the patterns of the crystal spurs Masha had set out on the scroll. The more she saw the spurs to avoid and the holds to catch, the better she became at understanding the ceiling. The better she became at understanding the ceiling, the more she could remember it.

Nala slipped out of all her baggage to shed any weight that could bring her death. Suddenly uncertain, she looked at her arm and then went on to carefully unwind the gauze over her wrists. The wrapping stood the risk of being trapped in those nasty holes in the ceiling, and she could not afford that. Once the gauze came off, Nala took a moment to admire her handiwork. She would have to cut new lines over them once she was across the lake to stifle any potential fits from Hashayne. The thought of the pleasure about to come made her squirm in delight as she stepped into the lake.

The first minute was troublesome. The water was dark and unnaturally cold. Vyas's orb floating above her didn't pierce far into the gloom either. All she needed was to get to the stalagmite ahead, and use it to climb to the stalactites on the ceiling. She made her way slowly, fingers trailing along the wall of the lake. Her toes struck one of the rocks below, and she spasmed away from the sudden contact, twisting in the blackness to find only her dull, tired, bluish reflection. *Please, eel, be deaf! Ignore me!* She finally found the stalagmite, pulling herself tight against it as she climbed it.

'This is going to be torture,' Nala said as she readied herself to jump to the nearest crystal spur on the ceiling.

You think that is torture?

Breath catching, she whirled around. None showed any sign of having heard that. Great. More delusions.

To be hungry for eternity, unable to die, unable to live, all alone. That is torture.

Nala suddenly realized… these weren't her thoughts. They were the… eel's. Her face darkened. 'It is all in my head,' she whispered.

But today, one way or another… my thirst will be quenched.

'I'm ready,' Nala said, eyeing the crystal spur again.

So am I, the delusion whispered.

Nala cursed as she leaped and grabbed the crystal spur blindly, felt it crack a little as she pulled herself into the next jump. Through her mind's eye, she saw Masha's drawing of the future. Remembering that memorized path, she reached out, swinging on the spur to the left. With another one-handed pull up, she caught hold of the next crystal, and then swung back and forth before launching herself through the air as she made her way across the ceiling. All the training Parshuram had put her arms through was finally yielding fruit.

Just then one of the crystal spurs she left behind cracked, distracting her from her fantasies. It cracked some more, and then fell into the water… right into the tentacled mouth of the monster-eel.

About time.

Nala could see the sickly pink insides of its enormous mouth, the rows of teeth like half-broken prison bars. Her pulse quickened. With a swift, desperate movement, she pulled her head to her knees in a crunch, wedging herself between two low-hanging stalactite formations.

'I hope you aren't growing weary, lass,' Nar Ad shouted.

'I am fine!' Nala panted. 'Just 'bout fine!'

'That is good to know because it would be awful if you grew weary and lost your hold and fell into its jaws.'

'While I appreciate your faith in me,' shouted Nala, who was busy timing her crunches to dodge its vicious bite, 'actual assistance would be…' she dodged its bite again, '… much more welcome,' she managed to complete.

Ajath snatched a shield from Gorin and started slapping it with his sword. Others picked up the trend. It did nothing to hurt the beast, but it distracted it enough for Nala to flex the arch of her foot and switch to a hand grip on the crystal spur instead. And, just then, an untimely cough from the mild flu she had caught, rose, and Nala instinctively covered her mouth.

She fell.

The cold numbed her mind but as if out of sheer instinct she knew the eel had heard the splash, and was no doubt swerving for a quick lunch. Turning under the water, she saw the lichen glow growing brighter to her north, and so she swam in that direction. There were small living things in the water, toothed fish and crawling arthropods, and they all scattered away from her path.

Here!

This was a different voice, a softer voice than that of the eel. A hallucination? No, she definitely heard the voice though it was more of a squeak. She swam in its direction, powerful strokes she had learned not from Parshuram but from her mother in the harshest rivers of the forest.

Underwater, she saw a swarm of the glowing lichen growing around a… was that a small ice peak? *Later, you wretched druggard!* Right. She swam up and, finally, broke the surface of the water to haul herself onto the stone bank next to the sentinel statue's half-submerged nipples.

Now what? How would she climb this? Behind her, the waters sizzled in dark anticipation as the eel rushed at her, the hunger of eternity no doubt fanning its resolve.

Here!

That same voice again. 'Nomnom!' Nala cheered as she rushed to the rat who was on top of the statue's shoulder. He jumped onto Nala's back, and Nala stroked his little head. Nomnom bit her back. 'Oh, you little thing – ow! Damn you, cheese-stealing curse!' Whiskered nose twitching, Nomnom's glittering eyes seemed to be pointing. She set him down, and he swam under the water to emerge from behind the statue's shoulder again.

'Of course,' Nala realized. 'The sword! Good job!' Nala applauded, not registering the fact that she just had a conversation with a rodent. She swam behind the statue to its side and used the edge of the sword's crossguard to climb it to safety. Nala's heart slowed its wild run, and she used the remnants of Hashayne to channel her strength to her arms and push against the pommel to lower it. It took three almighty pushes for the pommel to finally press down.

Frozen hinges protested, and unseen mechanisms turned. There were loud muffled sounds of things moving from their place, and the gate began to open outward, and as if sucked into a whirlpool, the water of the lake began to drain out of the cavern while Nala held on to the pommel for her dear life.

Thank you, little girl.

Nala peered down from the pommel to see the enormous eel flapping like a fish on the bleached lakebottom by the statue's feet. Even from the huge height, she could see life draining from its eyes, white, blind eyes, but... happy eyes. Nala knew it was a trick of the adulterated Hashayne but she could not help herself. 'What is your name?' Nala asked, feeling incredibly foolish.

Matsya.

Matsya? *The* Matsya who saved Manu and his race in the Great Tears by steering his ark? *No. It cannot be.* Could it? If there were other questions, Nala did not get to ask them for by the time she climbed down to meet Matsya, Chalakkha's men were upon it. As everyone congratulated her again the second time, calling her a hero, the Undergod, the saviour and every other name she had hungered to hear for so long, Gorin leaned into his spear, driving it through Matysa until he felt the point bite the ground on the other side. Odious fluid poured out of Matsya's body as it thrashed violently. Gorin flashed his rotting teeth at Nala in a respectful grin as he pulled his spear out and changed his angle to drive it across the eel's head again in an effort to sever it, no doubt to bag it as a souvenir. It did not do the job, and worse, the thrashing did not stop.

'That will be enough,' Vyas said. 'The head will still be here when we return.'

'Oh, Nomnom!' Shree sang two stanzas in pure happiness as she put Mister Nomnom inside her blouse, making not just the rat but all of them happy with the magic in her voice. Momentarily. For the sound of ice slowly splitting, cracking, echoed in the cavern.

'Now what?' Old Jaah groaned.

'What... is that?' Chalakkha pointed at the ice peak Nala had passed underwater, now exposed.

The hounds stood stock-still in their leashes. Parshuram's eyes narrowed to slits. Nala spun on hearing swords slide from scabbards. The big block of ice on the ledge above began to crack through the middle. Light from the blue lichen was dim but the silhouette of the sculpture inside was not. And then, in a blink, the entire slab of ice cracked, like a mirror breaking from the inside till it shattered into a thousand shards, and out came the silhouette.

'Is that the dragon?' Chalakkha asked, greed and worry writ large on his face. 'We aren't ready! Whisper! The traps! The nets! Take them out! Is that the dragon, Acharya?!'

'Worse,' Parshuram said.

If not for the tail, Nala would have thought the silhouette was Bheem. Enormously tall, shaped like a man, ghastly muscles, veins ribboning from his arms to his shoulders like snakes. His white hair was smooth, long, flowing to his shoulders. His face belonged to an ancient statue lining a colonnade, his fur the shade of snow, his sapphire eyes staring at them with the same indifference of all such statues. Ice sparkles swirled around him, landing on his fingers, his shoulders, his face. His face twisted as he bared his tusk-like incisors. Nala couldn't tell if it was a sneer, smile or snarl. Nala's recollection of histories – fraught with pained memories of Meru – returned to her with a jolt that shortened her breath. Of course, the ceiling! Nala could only assume for the Vanaras, the extinct race of giant monkeys, swinging from the stalactites would be as commonplace to them as strolling on the street was for her.

Vanara. This was what Masha had seen when she had muttered things about a monkey and a dragon's eggs… Spirits! Parshuram had known this all along. Nala still could not digest she was gawking at an actual Vanara. A name of past triumphs, of a race of warriors who had stood alongside Men against the Rakshasas of Lanka. A name now found only in footnotes of forgotten texts. Though Nala reckoned this Vanara's name was known to all.

'Welcome,' the Vanara's voice was low but hard, as fitting the God of Monkeys, 'I am Hanuman. Steerseraph of Iyran Machil.'

XVIII

Even if Nala had been able to speak in more than whimpers, she would not have known what to say in the presence of Hanuman. The Son of Wind. The Hanuman. He would easily have been thousands of years old. Nala knew she ought to be pissing herself with fear and awe but all she could think was how close she was to where Hanuman and Parshuram stood. Nala closed her eyes and stilled to eavesdrop on them. '… the Vanaras are gone…' Parshuram answered a question Nala hadn't heard.

'How long has it been?' Hanuman asked.

'Constellations have been changed.'

'Outlived stars? Shame,' Hanuman said. A frozen moment passed between them before he asked, 'Was it you? Did you slay the Vanaras?'

Parshuram shook his head, and finally, Hanuman nodded. If the news of his race's extinction unnerved him, Hanuman showed no emotion to mirror it.

'You were frozen?'

Hanuman nodded. 'Meditating for… I don't know. Decades, centuries perhaps. Ice likes me.' He turned towards Nala and waved a hand, and Nala could not hear them after. Their talk was now a secret ceremony, the details only known to the two immortals. After a while, Hanuman nodded as he left Parshuram to stand in the centre of the hall and address them.

'Don't take my warning lightly. The Vanaras are immune to the poison of Veins. You aren't. Evil crawls in Iyran Machil after dark. Time flows differently inside. An hour you spend there may easily be a week or longer here. From what I sense, it is day right now which means you have ten hours before darkfall. If you stay beyond the twilight inside, you will not find your way back for I will be gone. So, I would recommend not stopping to admire the scenery.

'Son of Wind, Burner of Lanka, Lord Hanuman,' Chalakkha prostrated himself to the ground, his belly keeping his buttocks in the air, 'forgive me but your blessings will be the difference between life and death. Please come with us.'

'I think it is time we leave the world to rise again from its ashes, son of Manu. But for there to be ashes, we need to let the world burn first. So, no, I won't come with you inside that cursed city.' Hanuman turned to Parshuram. 'You shouldn't, either. Come with me. We will speak of memories where you lost against my Master.'

'It was a tie,' Parshuram growled. 'And the world, although it deserves only anguish, is dear to me and I will defend it as would have your Master.'

Nala's skin crawled at the idea of Parshuram finding anything dear let alone calling it so. Vyas emerged through the human circle around Hanuman. 'My Lord, you said you will be gone. You won't... guard this Gate any longer?'

'The Vanaras are gone, learned one of the First. When Janai, the last Steerseraph, handed me her burden, it was to protect the world outside but the world I wanted to protect no longer exists. The Age of Sin is upon us. And no matter what the Saptarishis do, the daggers of Chaos will always find a way to dig into Order's armour.' Hanuman sighed. It held the chill of high winter. 'My watch is at its eclipse,' saying which Hanuman turned, dragging his mace along the ice and then raising it over his head. 'Come, Acharya Parshuram,' Hanuman said. 'The past awaits.'

INTERLUDE

VAHURA'S ADVENTURES

I

'Remember, breathing is given far more importance than it deserves, Princess,' Old Ella said as she pushed a knee into Vahura's back and pulled at the laces of her corset, no doubt to cut her in half. 'The present with the tightest knots invites the most enthusiasm from a child.'

Vahura wasn't listening. As her lungs scampered around to hunt the treasure of air, she whispered a prayer to let her bodice hold back her breasts this time. Three attempts, and each of the three times, one of her twins had mutinied to pop out. The designer of corsets clearly nursed a vendetta against the big-breasted woman. At least now she knew if her coquettishness didn't work in charming Bhagadatt to part with his greatest treasure, she could always resort to flashing him. Vahura chuckled at the scene, immediately regretting the painful constrictions the action brought around her belly.

'Good. The laces around your waist will remind you that a lady holds loud laughter in disdain. A coy smile, at best. Now let out the air, Princess.'

Vahura exhaled everything she had in her as Ella pulled back on her laces as if she were trying to hold back a rabid bull. Something unseen ripped through the fabric, and Ella let go. The recoil should have forced Vahura forward but she stayed painfully erect. A bard, hard pressed to come up with a simile, would have cited a tuning fork.

'It fits. Now keep your posture upright.'

As if she had any choice. She hated wearing clothes which showed skin but hated the assumption that women who did not were not fashionable. But she had too much at stake to question the foundations of genteel society. She turned to look at the mirror.

A red-haired woman wearing something like a midnight-blue blouse reincarnated as a corset suffered in the reflection. At least she looked regal in her suffering. Her unruly red hair was piled above her head and held together by a jewelled cage adorned with sprays of cobalt feathers. Her eyes, rimmed in a striking blue, matched the colour of the hand-embroidered skirt which shifted colours between cobalt and forest green. Barring a choker of perfectly cut sapphires circling her neck that somehow drew the gaze to her cleavage, she wore no other jewellery. Ella adjusted a lightweight black organza dupatta with a scalloped border to rest 'casually' over one shoulder. 'I resemble a peahen. How did I let you talk me into this?'

'Just the faint touch of morbid with a dollop of elegance. The Grey Ones would love this.'

'But why the choker? It looks like my throat has been slit.'

'He has something you need, yes. So you must have something he should want.'

'My cleavage?'

'I do not think any book that you may have read encourages crassness in a woman as a virtue.'

'But they were all written by men.'

Old Ella crinkled her nose, which was the closest she came to a groan. 'Very well. Then the answer is yes. Of all the curves in the body, the cleavage is the coyest, holding promises of great adventure, a valley immune even to the siege of sweat; on the contrary, it amplifies it. A cleavage tempts but never seduces, a cleavage distracts but never demands, a cleavage is the poisonous dart of body parts, holding within it the power of gravity.'

'You speak as if from a book written by a man but... I won't deny it. There is something very wrong and very seductive in that thought.'

'Precisely. Morality is the refuge of those blessed with an ordinary life.'

'And not of an outlaw princess attempting to wrangle out a treasure from a Rakshasa Princess.'

'Indeed. Sorry, Princess. Now I have to apply paint on your face.'

'You just applied it before I put this thing on.'

'Yes. Now I have to paint it to look as if it hasn't been painted on.' Ella leaned in, different shades of paints and powders smeared on her arm like an easel, and set to work on her with the tip of her finger. While Ella was busy so, she began humming a sonnet, a sonnet Vahura realized with dread was something Ella had herself composed.

'A plague knocks at my door, the hourglass empties and demands its due, thorns emerge from the floor, but she no longer plays as well as she used to, no longer a woman of virtue.'

Vahura's cheeks began to colour. 'Ella… please.'

'So little time to figure it all out, so many bogeymen to best, and now she wanders in the woods with neither path nor route while the marigold blooms with no rest.'

'Ella… I know what is at stake. Please,' Vahura almost pleaded, tears threatening to undo Ella's work. 'Just because I took a break does not mean my resolve is broken. I will save her!'

She unclasped the locket around her neck and wiped it down the front of her dry scarf. Satisfied, she numbly worked the tiny catch. Two sides popped open. Rainwater had penetrated the locket but behind the glass case, the miniature charcoal painting of a freckled girl still smiled up at her, her eyes hidden behind her mother's tiny silk scroll.

They didn't look much like sisters. Her sister was so beautiful that it made Vahura want to weep. And especially when she saw Vahura, the way her face used to light up… Vahura realized all over again why she would never give up on her. 'I will save her,' she repeated.

'Fair. As long as you know you are just treating yourself, and not cheating yourself,' Ella said as she returned to drawing on her eyelids. 'Bhagadatt is not going to be easy to seduce or manipulate. Even Draupadi's beauty failed to sway him into bidding for her at the Panchalan Swayamvar.'

'As if Drupad would have ever permitted a Rakshasa to bid for his daughter. And he was seduced into bidding for the Conclave now, wasn't he? He could not possibly be that sharp.'

'Are you certain you are willing to risk the fate of your charge on this assumption?'

'What could I do, Ella?' Vahura rose in a tantrum but Ella used a firm grip to settle her back on her seat. Vahura surrendered. 'There is nothing I can do but wait. Wait for him to give me an audience. He sent a message, didn't he, that he would meet me after the feast at the Gilded Table of Giving? You know I cannot rush it. All I can do is wait...'

'Then wait. We're already at their pompous charity dinner. The Conclave itself is but a few weeks hence which means your world will end in a few weeks hence when the time your Father gifted you finally runs its course. And that is assuming he has not yet discovered your little ruse and already sent soldiers to escort you back to Balkh in full wedding regalia. I do not mean to alarm you but you are, as it stands, the only one who can save your sister. But your chances only diminish if you dine with distractions. You need to keep your eyes on the prize: you need the Daevic Scrolls. Men will come and go, some men will come to support you, some to unsettle you. You need to know the difference, especially when one is out being charmed by a soldier of a lowly rank.' Seeing Vahura's expression, Old Ella simply shook her head. 'Do you truly believe I did not take note of the shabby clothes and mud-splattered boots of a ranger on your new friend?'

'Do you truly believe, Ella, that I will take my eyes off the Daevic Scrolls even for a breath? You have seen me – from the Seven to the Rose Coterie – I have left no stone unturned. I am only a step away... how can you think I am distracted? You know... what it means for me. You know I was the first to see Mother with her eyes clawed out by her own hands. You know...'

'That is all I needed to hear,' Ella said, satisfied that Vahura, having won in her mind, would now win in reality. She bent low in

front of her ward. 'Now, do not ruin my efforts. It is fortunate that
the realm values a bust more than a foot,' Ella said as she wielded
a brush over her cleavage as if dusting a rack. 'The Cinas present in
the Conclave hunger for small feet, and their women wear binds to
deform them into tiny shapes.'

Vahura took a moment to settle her nerves now that Ella, having
angered her, had segued into a harmless path. Vahura should have
been used to these slimy tactics of her governess but somehow the
truth she had sensed in her warnings had riled her up. Regaining
her composure, she spoke again.

'Comparison of pain would have made me feel a little better but
I am increasingly feeling the difference between a noose around the
neck and a lace around the waist diminish.'

'Strangulations can be erotic, you know. It was my favourite thing
in the Temple of—'

'I do not need my ears to turn a shade darker than my cheeks.'

'With due respect, Princess, you are prone to be a prude.'

'A *quality* normal governesses value.'

II

'One burp, and this corset will rip. Why did you have to feed me
before a dinner, Ella?'

'Dinners are not meant to be dined at but danced at. I am confident the Princess would not appreciate a conversation with the
Tusk with meat between her teeth or accidentally blowing a gust of
garlic on his face?'

'What would I do without you, Ella?'

Ella did not answer the question, which answered plenty. 'Now
that the Princess has washed her mouth with salt powder and sage,
might I suggest restricting your diet to the drinks and, if you feel the
irresistible need to chew, grapes or orange slices.'

'I will settle for air to be honest.'

'The hospitality at the Conclave shows the Tusk intended to
impress, which means he has ambition, the greatest weakness in a
man. So, you already have something to exploit.'

'Oh, joy,' Vahura remarked dryly.

'We are here.'

Vahura, for all her anxiousness, loved grand events. The bigger the crowd, the more opportunities there were for her to learn something new. Knowledge was, after all, an endless, slippery cliffside of complacence that one was always in danger of sliding down unless one kept clawing at it with hooks and ropes, always fighting to climb higher... A cliff made of not just books, but of everyone else's culture, experiences and, most importantly, viewpoints. From that perspective, events came no grander than the events leading to the Conclave.

Hundreds of candles burned in the darkness, filling the grand hall with creeping shadows, making the jewels glitter, the crowns glimmer and the rosaries shimmer. Sweat was already beading on the forehead of guests like little diamonds, each impatient to play their game, win their prize and return to a place where winter humidity is a myth. From her vantage, she could already make out three sneers, two forced smiles and an outright heaving of chest. Vahura wondered how long it would take for these proud lords and ladies to tire of a peaceful meeting and turn it into a fitting sequel for the swayamvar.

Talking about women, there were not as many as she would have liked and far more than she expected. Her eye was trapped like a cheese bait by the woman who sat on a high stool by the bar, the skin of her thigh on full display. She was young, almond eyed and thin but in a muscled way. A silver-laced sun veil stretched from ear to ear, shielding her smile behind a thin gauze.. Dressed in a scarlet jacket and skirts trimmed with emerald lace, she had the air of someone used to seeing unspoken wishes fulfilled. Men around the woman confirmed her suspicion by hastily offering their kerchiefs when the woman crinkled her face to sneeze. Even that, she did with the grace of a tigress, though Vahura had to admit she had never seen a tigress sneeze. The sneeze half-abandoned, the woman settled for a sniff, smiling courteously at the kerchief offerings of the dejected hands.

'I don't think I want to head... there. She does not seem to want for company, Ella.'

'Of course she doesn't.' Ella narrowed her eyes. 'She is Matriarch Chitran.'

'Manipur?'

'The very one, Princess.'

'Isn't that the kingdom where—'

'Yes, the one where the queens find it much easier to change husbands than to change their last names. The Riverlanders often call her a princess instead of her august title so be wary of that. The last man who blasphemed so lost a finger.'

'How fascinating! They rule like bonobos while we squabble like chimpanzees. Maybe I can ask her about how they view patrilineal societies. Are they indeed that—'

'It is my duty to remind you of your duty to keep your eye on the prize. I fully trust you to get lost in a conversation with her while the Tusk meets the rest of the dignitaries on the other side of the hall. Perhaps this one – oh – never mind.'

Vahura traced her eyeline and spied Lady Sokarro, the Tusk's right hand. She wore a blue winter saree that cleverly unconcealed her curves. The saree was dotted with tiny sparkling crystals as if fashioned out of the night sky. Her hair was bound together by luminous green vines, her curving horns curling elegantly through the foliage. Sokarro scowled at Vahura as she found her eyes, though Vahura could swear she was not staring at Sokarro's nose, or searching for the ears, which rumours said had been ripped off by men. The nose she wore was made of solid steel, its edge crafted to a point like a needle.

'Perhaps we can take a different path.'

'Agreed.'

Vahura and Old Ella were not the only ones who navigated a route that would put them at a maximum possible distance from Sokarro. The area around her was visibly empty like a killing field. But the empty area around her seemed a tiny strip compared to the space around Lady Asmai of Mathura. Mathurans were unwelcome in the Tree City, and Vahura had to commend Lady Asmai's courage in attending the Conclave even if she had no interest in meeting her. Talking to a Mathuran would brand Vahura a social pariah.

Not for the first time in the evening, Vahura found herself wishing her Ranger had been present. It had been so long since she had had a riveting conversation with anyone that she had forgotten they existed. He had been so charming, so witty, so respectful, traits she had not found in unity in any of her cousins. He would have definitely entertained her with choice quips or philosophical musings on the fashion choices of the august gathering. Perhaps she could talk to the other Tree Folk but of the Tree Folk, there were only a few she could see around. Far fewer than the famous entertainers, painters and poets that the human ambassadors had brought with them from their kingdoms to write about the Conclave, ensuring generous glory would be shed on their employers in their portraits of the grand event.

Speaking of humans, there were a disquieting number of Ksharjans present, all looking eager for some chaos to uncoil. Their hands itched to set arrows to string, to brandish axes, and to tear scimitars from scabbards. Having missed their moment at the Yellow Wedding to brandish their brutish warrior blood, these Ksharjans did not intend to let a second chance pass by if it presented itself. Yet more than the presence of Ksharjans, it was the absence of the Iron Order that was unsettling, even if it did make breathing in this infernal corset easier.

Apart from Ksharjans, Drachma merchants from across the land made up the bulk of the audience. There were ship captains of Kalinga with feathered hats and copper hoops through their ears, heavy-bearded merchants from Kasmira and even almond-eyed Drachmas from beyond the Mai Layas, all eyeing profitable deals to be made.

But God refused to be outdone by gold. A pair of priestesses from the Seventh Order, heads shaved to black stubble, a Grey Shaman from Kamrup, neck heavy with leaves in place of necklaces, and an Unni Ehtral priest clad in sober black were engaged in a spirited debate. Even the Vedan priests of the Orange Order had shed any pretence at humility, and swapped their rough-spun orange cloth for saffron silk, fur and sparkling rubies. Seven rings were the symbol of the Saptarishis, and so she had no idea what the additional jewelled rings on their fingers stood for. The priests were the only ones at the moment not accompanied by any of the local Curators who were busy acting as guides, translators or annoying pests to other guests. Vahura had quizzed her assigned Curator on her second day here, and he had not shown his face to her ever since.

'How is my favourite Eagle doing?'

Vahura turned, and saw Lord Shalya of Madra walk towards her. Soft, balding and grandfatherly, Shalya had grown an absurd white puff of beard to hide his triple chins. The sigil of Madra was worked across the front of his plush topaz doubled in beads of lapis. Over that he wore a mantle of grey velvet decorated with a hundred silver airavats.

'Lord Shalya,' Vahura bowed, 'as always, the most luxuriously dressed.'

'This little nugget – I just threw on the first thing I found,' he said nonchalantly, and then boomed into loud laughter. 'I do what I can to feel young, if not look young.'

'Sages would claim you have found the secret to life.'

'Though I do not like this grey robe I had to forcibly add.' Now that Shalya pointed to it, Vahura saw that Keechak of Matsya wore cream, Susharma of Trigarta purple, Sudakshin of Kamboja russet and green, but each prince wore a cloak of dark grey in honour of their host. Vahura wondered if she should have kept something grey on her self as well.

'I do apologize for missing your speech, my Lord. I was late...'

'Rubbish. Women are never late. The rest are early. I must confess I just modified what Lady Rasha said in Magadh about Emperors. Have you met her? No? A fascinating woman. Right, coming back to the speech. Dry is the throat that ushers the Conclave, my precious. The list of things I could not say was longer than this blasted robe. It was the same gibberish about unity and peace. You missed nothing scandalous. Even the Crown Prince and his Swan wife were rumoured to make an appearance but there is no sign of any Magadhan envoys.'

'After all you did to secure their alliance between the Empire and the East, the least the Magadhans could have been is be respectful.'

Shalya chuckled. 'Do secret pacts ever stay secret?'

'No way of knowing, I suppose,' Vahura said. 'But if that be the case, why is Magadh absent? I did hope to take a measure of the Young Lion.'

'I hear their ship ran into trouble and is delayed. Fair tidings, I daresay. Saham Dev is a worthless son much like my own, a sheep born in a cave. The Emperor no doubt sent him to keep him away.'

'He is of his body.'

'So are the contents of his chamber pot. Doesn't make it fit to place it on the Empire's throne. Too bad his daughters took their lives. They were of an age to be re-wed, and could've birthed an heir worthy of Jarasandh. Still, I hope Prince Saham will turn up at the Conclave in time. And as for Eagles... you won't believe who they sent as their representative! No, never mind that. Enough politics! You tell me. How did the old scorpion send you so far away from his shadow? All the way to the East! I daresay you are the youngest ambassador here, barring that dolt Kalyavan. Did you see how he was dressed?'

Vahura had, indeed. He had not bothered to change and had walked in wearing mail and boiled leather and a breastplate of grey steel, the ruby-studded hilt of a longsword poking above his right shoulder.

Shalya continued. 'Kalyavan is as obsessed with being ratified as a warrior as I am with looking fashionable. Alas, little boys wielding swords skilfully is the second most vexing thing in my life after the incessant sounds of rain in this damn City.'

Vahura was glad Shalya enjoyed the sound of his own voice, layering questions over questions, allowing her to cherry pick ones that didn't need her to lie. 'Kalyavan does have a high opinion of himself. Defeating minor tribes does not mean you can call yourself undefeated. Wins over your lessers do not an unvanquished make.'

'I daresay he knows that, Princess. Hope he wins his chance at glory by fighting the Mathurans under the Emperor.'

Vahura had her doubts. No matter how skilled the soldier, it was the king who laurels for a battle won.

'Oh, Seven Hells!' Shalya cast a dark scowl at the fairest boy Vahura had ever laid her eyes on, incidentally, her cousin. Nakul, the youngest son of Pandu and twin of Sahadev, and blood of Shalya through Madri, Pandu's second wife, the one who jumped into or was pushed into Pandu's pyre (depending on whether you were a Black or a Red), walked in with unbound dark hair that gleamed with jewelled braids interwoven with it. His cloak, however, was red with a black eagle on it, the bastard sigil of Yudhistir. Vahura shook her head. The tussle between her cousins was turning downright childish. If the Blind King were to know of how Nakul had swapped the colour of the royal sigil, he would mar his flawless skin.

'Look at that imbecile! I tell you he is as stupid as he is beautiful. This is too brazen.' Shalya swept the murmuring crowd with rheumy eyes. 'Winning Panchal must have gone to Yudhistir's head. Talking about head, here goes the biggest head in all of Aryavrat.'

Kalyavan was strolling towards Nakul, smiling the way the winner of a game of poker smiled at his ruined opponents. A song in a blood-rousing tune serenaded him as he passed, pressing reluctant hands in his, laying generous hands on unlucky shoulders he passed.

'Let me go and put the fear of God in Kalyavan before he spoils my blood.'

Left alone, Vahura turned in a circle to see where Ella had disappeared to, only to see a door open on the side of the hall.

The Tusk had finally walked in.

Dressed in devices that set him apart, a long robe of night-black overlaid with ornate gulmohar leaves, the Tusk truly had not needed his clothes to stand out with his long, braided black hair, face as grey as a storm cloud, set with ruby pupils in eyes as black as the darkness between stars. But then again, what the Tusk wore was truly magnificent. His shirt was not brown cotton but vines, the material woven so fine one could barely see the whorls, and what Vahura had taken for a black cloak with red leaves was made of a single wing of some giant, certainly extinct bird, perhaps a Jatayu. Vahura wished she could see his face clearly but he wore a silver half-mask of royalty, most of the features of his face hidden behind the mask's forbidding beauty.

The Tusk made a swift pass round the first greeters, pressing the hands of a few choice ambassadors. By now, the entire hall as one had turned in his direction.

Finally, the Tusk mounted the ornate chair reserved for the host of the Conclave, behind the half-mask, the way Draupadi must have when she was forced to wed five husbands after the swayamvar.

Venerable, his manner seemed fit for a Tusk who had been on the throne for many winters, yet his shoulders spoke of fullness, of the strength of a young warrior. The Remnant Monarch of Kamrup and the Tusk of Tree Cities, Bhagadatt was known to be mighty amongst both Rakshasas and Men. Vahura supposed it was time to introduce herself to him, bow a bit, and then whisk him away for a spirited conversation about plagues when the time was right.

She did not have to wait long in the queue. Upon reaching the dais, she passed her palm over his without touching, in the traditional royal Eastern greeting. Bhagadatt's skin was dark grey like the Ranger's, having the same consistency of bark and the same smell of apples. She decided to make these observations known to the Tusk as her opening remarks, and see where the conversation took them. When she looked up, she found his eyes, the scarlet of blood in sunset seas, holding her own, deep and steady as he took off his mask.

Vahura then wished with all her heart that she had the valour of Satyabhama to rise to the dais and slap him bloody. Unable to find a way to vent, she stuck her tongue out at him and half screamed in the middle of a gathering of the most powerful men and women of the realm.

'May the mosquito bite your mother!'

MANUSRUTI

PART I

THE DRAGON'S PATH

OUTSKIRTS OF IYRAN MACHIL

'The cry of the cicada
Gives us no sign
That presently it will die.'
—**Matsuo Basho**

 WHISPER approved the broad, general principle of distracting a dragon to let the bard and his friends slip past to find their poem inside the City. But she couldn't help but have doubts at the prospect of putting it into practical effect. After Sidestep's death, however, Whisper trudged without a care through the petrified forest in the first row, doing her best to ignore the heavens above.

For nomatter where she looked in the sky, she saw her face, some true, some a mirage in the large stretches of the silvered clouds. Spotting a Whisper weep in one of them, she felt her own eyes well up with the same question. Had Sidestep died because Whisper had not pulled her to safety swiftly enough? *No. Not now.* But the guilt still gnawed at her, leaving little room to marvel at the path beneath her feet – a road so unnaturally plain and smooth, it seemed to be carved from a single, vast stone. Pieces of burnt buildings lay here and there, remnants of enormous glass statues of ancient kings and apostles, their faces and limbs spattered with red. The glass itself was sapphire hued with a suppressed glow in it. But the most haunting sight was the stone arch gate they crossed on the path. Scrawled atop it, in what disturbingly looked like blood, were the words: 'Who killed the world?!'

Many of these glass statues held smaller statues on their outstretched arms, and as they drew closer, Whisper felt a wave of nausea. The smaller statues were not statues but dead, blinded children, their bodies trapped in a half-stage of decay for centuries, perhaps longer. It was as Vyas had said: nothing decomposed in Iyran Machil.

'Heaven's arse,' Gorin whispered before a statue of someone Vyas claimed to be Manu. Its blood-mouthed glass statue stood at the stern of a wooden boat, gripping a map in one hand. From the other hand, before his belt, dangled a boy's corpse, his hair clutched by its glass fingers. 'Looks like Manu was getting head,' Gorin snickered, even as the boy's legs swung gently in the air like someone executed.

'Iyran Machil,' Chalakkha moaned as he gawked at the outline of ruined spires rising in the distance like broken stubs of glass fangs. 'A beauty, isn't it, Whisper?'

Whisper said nothing. The familiar weight of her bladed whip, coiled around her waist, no longer made her feel as cosy as it had in skirmishes past. Her discomfort had less to with the desolation she saw in front of her and more with the man leading them through it.

She wouldn't have gone so far as to say Chalakkha didn't look like a hunter but his commands so far were of a bent calculated to excite suspicions. When a man who was loaned a war wagon and two pet airavats (by an immortal Vanara in exchange for a gold pouch and a list of the new wonders of this Age) decides to leave them in the reserve instead of helping in the hunt, one begins to think a bit. Especially when the misgivings were birthed not just from the incompetence of her employer but also from the climate of the ruins.

Despite all the giant marigold trees to shade their journey, no birds called. The only sounds came from the flu when it reared its ugly head in the shape of coughs and the sound of drums being beaten by the two boys to attract a forgotten beast. She was grateful for the marigolds though. Tangerine flowers, warring against the darkness of the forest, seemed to be the only ones on the side of life here. What else did one expect? Unholy magic wielded here had poisoned God himself. Worse, Vyas claimed he could sense the faint presence of Elementals in the air. Just traces... memories of an ancient power, he called it. The worst of all omens.

Focus on why you are here. All Whisper had to do was keep Chalakkha safe, and use his gratitude to rescue Fidget and Itch from the Magadhan prisons. Just keep Chalakkha safe. The same man who was behaving as if this was the best day of his life.

Chalakkha patted his belly as he called out over the sound of pounding drums to boost the morale. 'If we dilly, Lord Hanuman would leave us stranded. So, no time for sightseeing, lads. Oh, no answer? Let us not be like that. Don't let fear soil your hearts, my friends. All we have to do is make certain the dragon opts for a fight instead of flight. Crucial that we keep it invested in us to buy our friends the time to carry out the Seven's command.'

As if Chalakkha gave a rat's arse about the charge of the Seven's command. All he wanted was to ride back in the Emperor's good books with a basket of dragon eggs.

'Does what you told me about this place having one entrance but several exits still hold true, Acharya? I am afraid I have lost my taste for the catacombs,' Chalakkha said.

Vyas smiled. 'While the Dvārs are lost to the corrosion of this place, Lord Hanuman has assured me that he would personally escort us out of the realm on his ship. Far more comfortable than a trek through those tunnels, I wager.'

'Capital,' Chalakkha said. 'Still can't believe it! Lord Hanuman! Even in the East, we have heard stories of him! What a fascinating being, eh, Whisper?'

Whisper nodded. She thought of Hanuman waiting on his gigantic eight-mast ship anchored in the cove that led to this realm. The orange tides of that strange ocean had still been rising when he had put them all ashore on a beach of black sand. Glancing back, Whisper had marvelled at Hanuman's ship. And then she had marvelled at Hanuman himself, its lone crew, all eager to return to the world he had left centuries earlier to guard this wretched place. She wondered what that kind of waiting did to a—

A sharp whistle found everyone with a weapon in hand beside Chalakkha. The two scouts came running back with Taksha behind, lances erect against the sky, faces grim as if they were being chased by the Daevas themselves. 'The Naga found it! And I saw it!' the man at the head shouted all the way from the crest till he reached the war wagon.

'No, my Lord!' the scout said, coughing. '*I* saw it enter the lair, my Lord. It lies directly in our line of march. It cares not for our drums but it is here! Largest thing we ever seen, My Lord.'

Chalakkha grinned as if the man had been describing the breasts of his would-be bride. 'A fine job, Naga!' Just then, a flare of light exhaled over the sky as Parshuram's firework took flight over the city. That was the first signal they had decided on before splitting up.

'Parshuram found it!' Vyas said, a smile writ large on his heavily bearded, wrinkled face. 'He found Manu's corpse! Bless that bard, Nar Ad!'

'Now, now, Acharya,' Chalakkha said, 'he has not sent the second arrow yet which means the quest is not at an end. And surely we are not the only ones who saw the sky burn.'

Vyas nodded. 'Then we must hurry before the dragon moves for them. Time is of the essence. But remember, we do not have long till Acharya Parshuram sends us the second signal to return to the beach. If you have to steal those eggs, the time is now!'

'You see, lads,' Chalakkha's voice boomed. 'Fortune smiles on us, and there in the sky is proof. Now let us down the dragon and find what we came here for so that I can be home for dinner.'

The barterbows cheered and hooted as they looked up. Fiery dandelions and starbursts left from Parshuram's arrow brightened both the sky and their faces on the clouds.

'My Lord,' Vyas said, 'Our task is to draw the dragon's wrath to buy Acharya Parshuram the time he needs on the prophet's path, and only if we can, steal the dragon's eggs. But *kill* the dragon? Such a deed is beyond us, not without an army at our backs.'

'Kill?' Chalakkha mock-gasped, with a peculiar squeaky tone. 'Who said anything about kill, my old friend. We're going to capture that dragon. Alive.'

 TAKSHA, in his stint as the enslaved, had learned how Man was singularly unique in his obsession with caging other races for show and he was glad he had managed to nudge Chalakkha into seeing the undeniable benefits of a live dragon behind bars on the night of Vyas's betrayal. Why else had he turned down Masha to join the Fate Squad under Parshuram, choosing instead to remain with the Fire Squad?

'This was not our accord, My Lord,' Vyas said, frowning. 'You can have those eggs.'

'Acharya, please don't get in a stew.' Chalakkha bowed. 'We do not even know if there will be dragon eggs to be found. And how long would they take to hatch? By the time we manage to raise a fully grown dragon to attack Mathura, Krishna would be dandling his great-grandchildren on his knee. But why submit to the whims of adolescence when we already have a fully grown dragon? Please, could you bless my quest? I would owe you *plenty*.' When Vyas nodded grudgingly, Chalakkha beamed. 'Taksha, whenever you're ready, son! Is it still in its lair?'

Closing his eyes, the Gehan upon his brow aglow, Taksha sessed out to sense the aura of the D'rahi. His inner sight, drifting through the sprawling forest of the city before him, fixed upon the lair, where the pale, shimmering light of the God whom the Nagas had long prayed to keep away danced. But... whatever God lurked there, did not lurk alone. *Mother of Moults!*

Taksha opened his eyes, half-panting.

'What happened?' Chalakkha asked, worried. 'The dragon is still there, is it not?'

Taksha measured his words. 'You're right, my Lord. No eggs. D'rahi... male. We will have to hurry, else it will fly out of its lair. It will trouble Masha and the others.'

'Gorin, time to ready your Mathuran munitions!'

'Sire,' Gorin said, crestfallen, 'they are damp now! The air here! There is something wrong with the Frostwater in them!'

But Chalakkha's optimism was a wall that no dragon could scale, explosives or not. 'Never you mind, friend. The fire in our blood will be enough!'

Ajath came up to Taksha while the others geared up, and signed calmly, *'Why are you wearing so much armour?'*

'I was asking myself the same question.' Taksha had difficulty signing in the heavy vambraces. *'I would rather be swift there than stew.'*

'You're not going to be there.' Ajath shook her head.

A little later, Taksha scratched his elbows mindlessly as he settled onto the branch. A gnawing feeling that the yellow flowers would spit out a tongue and infect him kept him distracted. There were so many trees here, he could not even see the lair. The idea of hiding in one of the marigold trees while the others charged headlong beyond the trees seemed ridiculous to him! He was destined to find the Messiah! *Ow! What is that terrible smell?!* A loud sound of a carriage door opening made Taksha sneer and turn in disgust.

'Apologies!' Gorin grinned, showing his rotten teeth, and pointing to his rump. Disgusting Softskins! That decided it for him.

You can save a chalk from breaking apart by hiding it in a box but that's not what chalks are for. And Taksha meant for his name to be written in glory, not in farts.

 AJATH meant for Taksha's name to be left out of the eulogies much to Chalakkha's chagrin. Her sisters were raped and their children were butchered in her absence. No harm was going to befall the young Naga while Ajath stood. So Chalakkha relented and let Taksha be part of the forces stationed by the tree traps behind in the distance when Ajath volunteered to be the first to scale the lair.

Though it wasn't so much a lair but a giant pyramid, its summit sunbathed, fifty shoulders tall. There were no trees here. Just skeletal ruins of a towering building that flanked the pyramid. A tall, gaping hole yawned at the pyramid's mouth, making Ajath wonder why a dragon would nestle on the ground.

A beast, even a majestic one, is chained by its instinct to hunt. And like any beast, its will could be broken by making it understand it wasn't the most fearsome creature in the world.

'We don't have the time to wait for the dragon to nod off and sneak in to sever the tendons in its calves. Assuming it even sleeps. Though surely, even an immortal beast must slumber sometime,' Vyas said.

'Leaf-covered trapholes, then?' Whisper asked.

'*We've neither the tools nor the time to dig a pit deep enough, much less drag a dragon out of it should it be a miracle fall into it. Besides, those kinds of traps tend to kill the prey more often the cage it,*' Ajath signed.

'And I like my dragons hale and hearty,' Chalakkha saisd.

'That leaves only Diamond or Iron.'

'We'll try Diamond, first.'

Drums began pounding. The earth shuddered soon after. Sounds of hefty footfalls. Two of them. Ajath was confused. Didn't a dragon have a quartet of legs? The others had not noticed the tremor – they were still arguing – Chalakkha visibly shouting, Vyas replying too fast for Ajath's eyes to follow. Eyes that were briskly yanked back to the pyramid when a huge shadow emerged from the cave.

The dragon was here.

Except… it looked nothing like one.

Ajath, confused, turned to Vyas, whose mouth was wide open enough to catch butterflies.

'Lord Hanuman did not warn us of this,' Vyas said. When Ajath jerked her chin in inquiry, he muttered to himself. Remembering Ajath's deafness, he looked up at her and spoke slowly, surely, each word a drip of cold acid on each of their hearts. 'That sandalwood-coloured horned crown… that is not just any dragon. This is not good. We *need* Parshuram.'

'We are Ksharjans,' Chalakkha claimed. 'Warrior blood meant to be doing just this! We'll triumph! Surely someone must've bested it if its wings are chopped up so.'

'Yes, someone did,' Vyas turned angrily to Chalakkha. 'Thorin Drazeus, the King of the Children of Light. That is Vrita the Droughtbringer, the Monarch of Dragons.'

 Vyas realized in hindsight that he should not have brought these facts to light. If these men and women were to die in moments, they should die with courage in their hearts, not cowardice. And die they would. For Vrita was the dragon who had held the Rivers of the World hostage and led the draconic army against the Children of Light in the Lost Hope of Ages. *And we woke him up.*

Vrita appeared like a burnt hill, carrying several scars and burn marks on his abdomen – keepsakes no doubt from his tussle with the Daevas. He, however, no longer resembled his flattering paintings in Meru. Those wings strong enough to whip up a typhoon now resembled a rooster's. Even its front two arms had become puny things, twisted and malformed. A grey skull on a crocodilian horror thrust forward on a sinuous neck as it strolled out on its gigantic hind legs. But, despite a bad case of cosmetics, he looked every bit a

wyvern of woe, particularly with his two-horned sandalwood crown
perched atop his head.

Courage before this monster? Optimism had its limits. Some
of the barterbows had already let their arrows loose in fear. If only
they could have borrowed guts from Taksha, who had defied Ajath's
orders and was even now climbing the iron beams over the pyramid.
Rather, each and every hireling took a few steps back, waiting for
the first to run away.

And run someone did. But, towards the dragon.

Despite the gallantry, it wasn't Ajath's wisest manoeuvre.
Vyas assumed she had seen Taksha too, and was doing this in a
bid to keep the dragon invested in the ground. But the flamebreaker armour shielded a body from fire when it was just the
air that burned around you. It did not stop it from intruding
through the gaps in the armour. In mere moments Ajath would
burn to ashes and Vyas's plan would be undone. 'Chalakkha, save
her!'

But Vrita had already lowered his neck, opening his palatial jaws
in invitation, tremors rolling out of it. He gathered up his breath.
Agni, please... Vyas prayed to the God of Fire for the first time.
Protect Ajath! Vrita huffed out a mighty gust of... wind. Wind! *It
had no fire left! Oh, thank you, Agni!*

While Chalakkha looked disappointed with the absence of arson,
at least this made things easier for him. 'Diamond! ATTACK!'
Chalakkha screamed at the top of his voice.

 WHISPER could barely hear what Chalakkha was
screaming as she finished climbing the beams of
the unfinished metal building that spread like an
iron skeleton over the pyramid. Beside her, Khalad
Sike puked his breakfast onto his boots. Whisper
considered imitating him but shied away at the
thought of accidentally puking on the dragon's horned skull. That
would not bear well on her plans of longevity. She prodded the
soldier and unfurled the diamond net between them.

'Whisper, help me up!' She turned to find Taksha climbing the metal beam. 'Before you tell me to return, know my way lies through D'rahi's path.'

Whisper scoffed, certain Ajath would kill her later for permitting this folly. She returned to studying the dragon. Beyond the fanged grin, the claws with crescent-shaped talons were a cause for concern. They looked like they could punch through a breastplate as though it were made of eggshell. Its muscled tail was a worry and so were its height, weight and strength.

'Glad it came out to meet us,' Whisper said. 'Saves us the trouble of having to hunt it down.' Pretending to be brave on the battlefield when you're frightened is called bravery – just something Satyabhama had always said.

'You are the meanest bitch, aren't you?' Khalad asked even as he unwrapped the diamond net. 'Seven hells!'

Whisper shook her head, staring at the mute woman standing alone before the dragon.

 AJATH lowered her sword as she came within arm's length of the dragon, who had curiously remained inert so far, unfazed by her charge. She let its flared nostrils take in her scent. A hesitant look surfaced as Ajath's gloved fingertips grazed its snout, and then it cooed as Ajath increased the pressure on her fingertips. She wondered how Chalakkha would react at seeing his fearsome beast, who could not fly or breathe fire, coo when cuddled. Too bad she was not going to find out.

Someone shouted 'Seven Hells' and a diamond net, cascading from the beams above, expanded in the air above by alchemy. Badly aimed, it made things worse by not being large enough to snare it but robust enough to stir it. *Fuck.*

She whisked her hand away just in the nick of time before the dragon's jaws snapped shut. Rolling on the ground to dodge its claws, she unsheathed the sword that she then held sideways, carving a path through the dragon's right jaw, the blade only finding scale. Still, catching the dragon off guard with her pace gave Ajath a direct line of sight to thrust at its eye. Remember! Chalakkha, and that meant Vyas, had forbidden blinding or killing the dragon. *Just wound it enough that it can no longer walk for the day. Morons.*

For, while the dragon could not fly, it could hover, allowing it to pivot faster than it could have on just legs. Ajath had not been ready for it, and wielded her sword in the last moment to fling soil from the ground into the eyes of the dragon, which had stooped low to finish her off. The dragon staggered back from the assault but it was not a witless prey. It was the apex predator. Using its recoiling momentum, it swept back to deliver a swatting tail. Ajath, nimbly for her size, leaped back, her face and chin contorted skyward, just about evading that tail when she caught the sight of Taksha rope-walking on the beams above.

Was it any wonder she did not see the tail the second time? The tail catapulted Ajath into the air – a tossed rag doll – her bones saved by the bush in which she landed but only barely. Breath driven from her lungs, she struggled to prise her eyes open, desperate to dispel this unfamiliar feeling of uselessness. She managed to raise her head above the bush, to find the dragon pounding towards Chalakkha like a puppy racing towards its master, only Ajath very much doubted it was going to stop at just licking his face.

 VYAS'S conviction licked his fear away as he decided to take matters into his own hands. 'If you act like a prey, it will act like a predator,' Vyas shouted, knowing courage was two-thirds faith and one-third chance. 'The bloodraven seeds in the soup were blessed! God's vigour runs in your veins! You can't lose!'

'You heard the Acharya!' Chalakkha screamed. 'The God of Thunder himself has blessed our steel. Onwards, men! Archers! Do your thing! Rest, stick to your formation like wood but move like the wind!'

Gods always proved handy when glory seemed to falter. The devout formed a line of guard in front of Chalakkha, brandishing their lances aloft as they advanced. The man standing closest to Vrita screamed Indra's name and jabbed his lance at the dragon's face just as he opened his jaws to roar – the barbed head scratching Vrita's tongue, drawing forth a trickle of black blood. The men hooted and cheered.

Vrita's jaw opened wide in reply, lunging forward to snatch the lancer off the ground, the man's upper half disappearing in his mouth. With a powerful pivot, Vrita raised his head, shaking the helpless warrior like a hound worrying a rag doll, until the lancer's lower half tore away, flung aside like a broken toy. The dragon spat out the mangled remains, disgust curling his lips

Seven hells! He did not grab the bait! Even as Vyas worried, Vrita stomped on two other archers, flattening them like flagstones. Content with his handiwork, Vrita now turned to Chalakkha, his line of sight clear, given Chalakkha's guards had all scattered away in panic, bloodraven seeds be damned.

Not all guards.

Like a nefarious creeper, a bladed whip descended from above, producing a crisp slapping sound when it wrapped itself around Vrita's neck. Employing the dragon's neck as an axle, Whisper gracefully swung from the beams, acrobatically uncoiling her whip to cushion her landing while leaving a trail of lacerations on Vrita's hide.

Vrita roared in frustration, lunging forward, but Whisper sidestepped him with practiced ease. Her whip snapped out, slashing across Vrita's tail, the barbed tip coiling around it and drawing a line of dark, oozing blood. Vrita jerked violently, his tail lashing high and to the left, but Whisper held fast. She used the momentum from the yank to vault into the air, springing off a vertical beam as she flew over Vrita's massive head. His jaws snapped just inches away, teeth clashing with a bone-rattling force, but Whisper twisted mid-air and landed smoothly on Chalakkha's side, a goddess of feline grace. Her whip was now left behind, still wrapped tightly around Vrita's tail.

Two guards, seeing Whisper, found their courage and charged Vrita from the other side to buy Chalakkha more time. Vrita had not even seen them. He just turned, and the guards came below the hasty steps of his taloned feet. Whisper, ever resourceful, seized the chaos to drag Chalakkha away.

But two knights of Chalakkha – dead in a blink of an eye, and not a nibble did Vrita take from either of them. At this rate, they'd run through the entire roster of the hired help, and Vrita wouldn't be any closer to capture. *Is Vrita a… vegetarian?* Oh, dear.

Chalakkha's remaining men, who had been clutching another diamond net between them, melted away like butter from Vrita's path as he turned towards them. Did not matter. Each and every one of them was thrown into the air in fountains of blood, as his savage jaws crunched right and left, spitting all, swallowing nothing.

'Diamond has failed! Iron, now!' Chalakkha barked his command. Chalakkha's reserve forces relieved the weary lancers, each armed with long sticks blazing at one end. They waved the torches wildly, sending up thick, acrid smoke that drifted into Vrita's eyes, causing the dragon to flinch and blink in irritation. Hounds circled Vrita, barking incessantly like beggars harrying a lost princess, while drummers pounded their skins relentlessly. While still unscathed, signs of fatigue were beginning to creep in on Vrita. The backup plan was working. *Disorient and deplete.* Soon the stickholders would coax the weary Vrita onto the path that was specifically decorated by Chalakkha for him, and just maybe, just maybe they would have a chance.

But Vrita then did something very curious. In none of Vyas's forecasts could he have imagined a dragon running *away* from them. If the dragon ran away in the opposite direction, it would all be over. Vyas looked frantically around for any survivors in the direction in which Vrita had set off till his eyes met Taksha's. The Naga was perched on a far-off beam along with Khalad. Vyas nodded at him. The ridges on the Naga's neck flared as nodded back at Vyas, and uncaring, Taksha jumped onto the dragon.

 GORIN jumped each time the distant roars rolled along like thunder. The last one, however, had a distinct quality to it, a sound of a plight rather than fright. His head popped through the dense marigold foliage for the hundredth time, his hand precariously holding on to the trunk as he stood on the branch and saw the mirror clouds. Where was the dragon? Shouldn't it have taken to the sky already? He hoped they captured it soon so he wouldn't have to resort to drastic measures, like be killed, or worse, return empty handed.

He squinted at the mirror clouds again. *Indra have mercy.* Was the cloud magnified or was that a giant upright lizard being chased by Chalakkha's men? To call it just giant would be an opportunity missed to use the word 'leviathan'. Someone yelped from another tree of how the lizard was headed in a direction that would avoid the traps. The same traps he had broken his back laying around the trees where he was hiding. The hell! Well, that was a good thing, wasn't it? He didn't care much for the lizard in such close proximity, traps or not.

As if it had heard them, the lizard's head swerved left. It wobbled, shaking its head violently, as if attempting to dislodge a mosquito. Gorin frowned. He had seen this dance before. *Illusions.* But the Naga should not be able to do it without touching the lizard. *Daevas take me!*

In a shifting cloud, Gorin saw a wee, green, scaled creature clinging on to the lizard's head for dear life. The lizard jerked its head around like a dog smacked on the skull. *That is... spectacular!* The lizard finally prowled ahead in the direction Taksha wanted it to go.

In his direction. Traps. Right.

Ajath's idea had been that a flying dragon, unable to spot them from the sky through the foliage, would be forced to alight on the ground for a good old-fashioned chase on foot, unless of course it adopted a more dramatic approach of incinerating them from the sky. But Gorin supposed the traps, forged to trap airavats and procured at great cost by Chalakkha, worked just as splendidly for an upright lizard as they did for a flying dragon. And work, they did.

The lizard's wails of help could have made thunder blush. Its foot caught in one iron trap, triggering it, and the trap closed with such ferocity that the blades pierced its thick hide clear down to the bone. Stumbling back, a part of its tail, the middle part, met another trap. Metal clinked. Steel jaws snapped shut, and with a rattle, it closed on its tail. The tail looked to be made of pure muscle, and offered no resistance. The lizard swooned, tracing its steps back haphazardly till it crashed against a tree with concussing force.

Gorin's tree.

Now Gorin was either remarkably intelligent or incredibly foolish. He had secured himself to his branch with a rope. So instead of falling to the ground, Gorin found himself suspended upside down from the branch right on top of a leviathan lizard in distress. To compound his troubles, Gorin's head had hit Taksha's skull on his way down, and in a dark comedy of errors, Taksha fell off the lizard's head, unconscious.

Illusions shattered, the leviathan wrenched both the traps as it decided whether to make a meal of the human on top or the Naga at the bottom. Arrows from Gorin's colleagues in the trees didn't even bother the damn lizard.

Perhaps since it preferred omelettes to hanging grapes, it decided to squash Taksha under its taloned foot first. Gorin was grateful for the mutual reptilian love but because of the way Gorin was hanging upside down, swaying and swinging, he was perhaps the only one who saw a miracle take form.

Ajath charged the monstrous lizard from behind, hurtling with a pace and grace no man – let alone a woman – should have been able to manage. She ducked and skidded beneath its bloodied tail, then straightened, fighting against time as the foot descended on the Naga. Ajath roared soundlessly, diving, blacksword out, she skidded beneath the taloned foot to crash against Taksha's unmoving body – and slashed against the lizard foot right above her with a mighty strike, carving chunks of hide from its sole, black blood painting Ajath's face.

Multiple overlapping howls echoed as the lizard raised its leg again, ready to crush them with raw fury. In that sliver of space between Taksha and the descending foot, Ajath jabbed her blade like a frenzied woodpecker – stab after stab, relentless. It was fucking insane! Watching the woman he'd once mocked stand over Taksha, inches from getting flattened by a leviathan's weight, yet refusing to back down, refusing to break, made his heart pound like a war drum. She stabbed – again and again – until black blood poured over her in a deluge, soaking her from head to toe, turning her black-dyed teeth, her blood-drenched face, and her dark blade into one indistinguishable mass of nightmarish determination. It was hide and weight against pure will and steel, and in the end, Ajath fucking won. The lizard stumbled back, both its legs wounded, one by her sword, the other by the trap.

Ajath rose, still trying to relentlessly stab its foot, now from above, till she found an opening and rolled beneath its howling snout, darting between its legs to come up behind it. With a silent bellow, she slashed her grime-coated sword at the tail, just where the trap had pierced it, slicing the tail cleanly in half. *Chalakkha is not going to be happy.*

Ajath would have to never worry about that though. For, a moment later, the leviathan's skull swung back to collide against Ajath's ribs. She flew through the air to crash against another tree trunk nearby, with a sickening sound.

Ajath should've died. But Ajath rose.

 AJATH smiled as she rose, feeling the rush of battle red fade in her. Seizing Taksha by the scruff, she flung him to the side. Breath ragged, heart burning, Ajath limped ahead on one leg, the glittering hint of the afterlife turning brighter. Most of Chalakkha's henchmen and barterbows lay crushed or gasping. The stickholders had still not caught up, and even if they did, she did not imagine they could make much of a difference. There was no vanquishing this dragon, the dragon who was now upon her. *Forgive me, Father, but I go now to my Sisters.* Ajath smiled. *I hope.*

That bite should've torn her to shreds. But instead, a flash of light cut across the forest. Blindingly bright. It crashed into the dragon's flank, harmless as a feather, before shattering into a thousand shards. Shards that whipped back together, forming that same glowing orb over Vyas's outstretched palm, standing off to the left, his arm thrust out. Elementals, she realized, recalling Vyas's mention of sensing them in the air. Why hadn't he used them before now? A trickle of blood ran from Vyas's nose, his lips moving in a silent chant. *Ah, that'd be why.* Whisper stood behind him, drenched in sweat, whip gone, dagger in one hand, and the other gripping Vyas's shoulder, keeping him steady. Whisper shot a wink at Ajath, and Ajath vowed to kiss her later with such fire that the stars would tear the sky open just to watch.

Ajath saw Vyas turn slightly to Whisper, and lip read him, '*Do you trust me?*'

Whisper looked at Ajath as she contemplated the question, not knowing Vyas personally. She was from Chalakkha's side after all but Ajath nodded at her, and trusting Ajath, so did Whisper.

'Stand your ground then, Silver Wolf,' Vyas said.

The dragon did not care for such sentiments. Closing its eyes to foil any other trick, it charged with jaws agape. Vyas, with astonishing agility for an old man, stepped lightly to the left just at the last moment. His hand still clasping Whisper's arm, he yanked her forward – and shoved her straight into the dragon's open maw.

A lizard with a fly in its mouth. The dragon's tongue flicked, shifting Whisper's thrashing body to the right side of its jaw. Three times those jaws crunched. Three times, Ajath watched Whisper be pulverized to a pulp.

Just then, Vyas hurled his light orb at the dragon, harmless as ever but bright enough to startle it, causing it to accidentally swallow Whisper whole before it could spit her out as the dragon had in times past.

'*Finally,*' Vyas mouthed.

The dragon stumbled around as if drunk, careening clumsily into the trees, before pitching towards the ground. Chalakkha's stickholders who had been chasing after the dragon, armed with the diamond net, shot it out just in time as the dragon plummeted. Specks of dirt flew about it as the dragon slid across into the waiting net that Chalakkha's stickholders twisted around the incoherent dragon. It wriggled for a bit before realizing it was never going to walk free again. But Ajath did not care as she limped past and seized Vyas by the lapels of his robe.

'You murdered Whisper.' Ajath did not even sign it. Just screamed it soundlessly into the air, as memories tugged free in her head to make sense out of the chaos. Bloodraven seeds in Vyas's soup – poison. It had poison in it. Of course. That's why the damn flu had them all in its grip. Vyas had been poisoning them all along!

'The art of necessity may strike you as strange. Bless the sacrifice instead of cursing the price.'

Ajath left Vyas, and tried to sign with just the one hand. '*That old serving lady died!*'

'Ah, yes, regrettable,' Vyas lamented with a wistful sigh. 'Not meant for old constitutions. She insisted on tasting it to ensure it was hot every time she served it. Not that I could have forbidden her doing it. Don't be naïve. How else would we have won if a thing like that had been guarding Manu's corpse? Dragons are allergic to bloodraven seeds mixed with human blood. It is not as if we could have forcefed a dragon. It is just...' Vyas looked into the horizon. 'If only Vrita had swallowed the first man he killed, the celebrations tonight would have been more spirited. Vrita does not have a taste for human flesh, I reckon.'

'*But you do,*' Ajath mouthed instead of signing as she choked Vyas.

'Perhaps,' Vyas said in a hoarse voice, 'you should find out what happened to Taksha.'

 TAKSHA did not have time to tend to his wounds. Darkness was setting in and Ajath would be on her way to him. The rest by the traps were scampering to bind the D'rahi and tie it to the war wagon. Taksha handed Gorin the scales that he'd forcibly, bloodily and painfully skinned off its chest, waist, groin and thighs. Gorin admired the leathery trophies against the glow of golden rings on all his fingers as he absently delivered Taksha the stack of Mathuran munitions he'd shamelessly

flaunted about at the camp till Taksha promised to grease his palms in return for them.

'Mind you, they are the low kind,' Gorin said, his eyes still on Taksha's skinned scales. 'They will just go *pop* without a fuss but they will leave behind a dreadful mess. What do you need it for?'

Taksha's plan had always been a slippery scheme, but he had faith in it – faith that they would capture the D'rahi alive for when the time was ripe. And by ripe, he meant when the Messiah would rise from the ashes of a D'rahi he had slain. He just had to ensure that Chalakkha, or rather the Softskins, had no other choice but to bring the D'rahi out of this cursed world.

'Does it matter?' Taksha asked.

'Reckon not. A deal is a deal. I ought to attend to the dragon they are hauling to the wagon.' Gorin beamed. 'Good day, eh? Lord found his beast. Priest found his writing. I got to hang upside down and get front row seats to the play. Trust me, happy endings are rare amongst humans. Pleasure doin' business with you, lad.'

Taksha nodded, watching him scurrying back to the forest before Taksha turned to the pyramid. The rest did not know, hadn't noticed how the D'rahi had cast a mournful glance at the pyramid before running away. They hadn't even asked why he had ran away.

Taksha entered the cave with the munitions and a pair of flint stones. *I will find the Messiah.* The thing was, Taksha had not lied through his fangs when he told Chalakkha he hadn't sensed any dragon eggs. Oh, he'd sensed them all right. Sensed the one egg. But broken, shattered, the yolk having leaked away a long time ago.

Taksha's forked tongue flicked as he struck the flint, sparking the munition to life even as the faint cry of a hatchling rose to serenade him.

The little creature quivered, not with fear but with a trust that pierced through what remained of Taksha's scales. Its eyes, wide and shimmering pools of molten gold, gazed up at him with a silent plea for affection. Such promise of a future filled with soaring skies and fiery roars, so easily snuffed out. But he just could not let Vyas get his hands on it. Not if he wanted to save his home, and with the Messiah nowhere to be found here, Taksha had no choice. He had not hurt a single person in his life. And now he was going to start with extinction... *Happy endings are rare, indeed,* Taksha hissed as he lit the munition and stormed out of the cave, a shadow fleeing his sin on the mirrors above.

He returned only to collect the skull when the smell of a burning infant curled through the air.

In the chaos after the hunt, during the frantic scramble back to the beach, no one – not even the bloodied Ajath – paid any mind to the small pouch of infant dragonskull strapped to Taksha's belt. Nor did they notice that Parshuram's second arrow had never flown, never cut the sky to mark their triumph to those waiting in the City. It wasn't until they stumbled upon Hanuman by the shore, moments before the sun dipped below the horizon, that the truth sank in.

That Parshuram, Nar Ad, or rather, any soul from his company had not returned. That they had no choice but to abandon Masha and Nala in this cursed land. That... their fate was death – if death hadn't already claimed them.

MANUSRUTI

PART II

THE PROPHET'S WRATH

'A great Hope fell
You heard no noise
The Ruin was within.'
—Emily Dickinson

 MASHA chuckled through coughs, watching Acharya Nar Ad twitter like a goldfinch amongst sunflowers while Acharya Parshuram fidgeted like a carrion crow amidst corpses. The immortal man could find no beauty in the immortal city whose last memories were of death but clearly, no dust from Iyran Machil's violent past had settled on the Pathfinder's eyes.

Acharya Nar Ad had insisted that before entering Iyran, they climb the city walls. He claimed it was for deciphering the map from a vantage but given how short these walls were compared to the Rose Wall of Hastina, Masha suspected it was for the view, an indulgence for which she was deeply grateful.

The entire city was drained of colour but it only deepened the beauty of these ruins against the backdrop of the marigold trees that spread like scars on her face. Statues, some even higher than these trees, flanked the roads ahead, though most of them had toppled. Towers peeped over the tangerine foliage like eager fingers of Glass Gods trying to touch their reflections, but with their summits fractured, shattered knives came closer to describing them. Beached domes with broken roofs spread across the landscape like burst boils. Masha could scarcely believe the magic Manu must have wielded to turn mere stones into such a prayer, and then turn the prayer into a vile curse.

'Shree!' Nar Ad shook her shoulders, startling Mister Nomnom who had been staring at him with baleful eyes. 'Oh, how the Pathfinders will burn when they read my notes.'

'I cannot believe I was complaining about being forced to part from my pals,' said one of Chalakkha's hirelings, a man with scarce a hair on his face – named Orrhan she thought. He had taken to hovering behind Shree, a gesture Shree was rather enjoying.

Nar Ad stroked his purple beard. 'No longer will I dream of the charred golden palaces of Lanka, a golden tiger amongst cities, nor gaze in the Ash Sea at the reflection of the destroyed towers of Tripura whose shadow once cut across the three realms like a sword. This bard's songs will now forever sing of Iyran Machil, the frozen crack on the lips of time. Dare I even dream of how she must have dazzled in life when she is so resplendent in death?'

'Enough, bard. Find me Manu's corpse.'

 NALA wondered how a corpse qualified as a geographical landmark, though, to Manu's credit, he did make it a tad easier to find him. As they entered Iyran Machil, they found runes in the First Tongue, inked in blood that Time had petrified, on walls, pillars and even the base of statues. They twirled in intricate patterns all across the City in patterns of a *henna mehndi*. The blood writings grew denser as they waded deeper, eventually giving way to charcoal, perhaps marking the juncture where ordinary writing instruments must have failed Manu for him to resort to his own blood.

Many of the First Tongue writings had been marred and defaced. *Wonder what secrets of the future were lost to the past forever?* For whatever was said and done, this place was a heritage. The whole world knew Manu was a great scholar. His Manusmriti – *Manu's Memories* – that were carried out by Seven Tribes to the Surface made the Codes that still ruled the Riverlands as their Constitution. But these writings on the walls of Iyran Machil – Manusruti – *What Manu Heard* – was Manu's magnum opus.

'Could've used a lesson in metres though,' Nala muttered to herself, coughing, when she managed with ease to translate the writing on the breast of a toppled, headless statue, thanks to her Hashayne-fuelled mind, sharp as a freshly whetted blade.

'The golden shadow will circle the dark sun. Beautiful faces with eyes of ash and hearts, none. The earth will open its visor and trap the wheel of fate as death follows in a dishonoured state. It will either be a Humanity's new dawn or our Age will finally drown.'

'I would not blame Manu. The First Tongue has this peculiarity of rhyming whenever translated to Sanskrit,' Nar Ad remarked, smiling at the tattooed architecture of the city. Nala frowned. Watching Nar Ad walk as if he were in a museum instead of a mausoleum unsettled Nala, and clearly, even Parshuram. But it was nothing compared to the other sensation. That sensation in the catacombs, where she couldn't shake the feeling of being watched? Well, that feeling was a constant companion in Iyran Machil, where the goddamned mirror clouds above watched her every move. Worse, they seemed to mock her, reflecting fragmented versions of herself, some mirroring what she once was, some hinting at what she could be – playing tricks on her mind that twisted her gut with each step.

'We need to get back to the beach in time, which we won't if you don't cease your foolery, Nar Ad.'

'Shree,' Nar Ad called out wearily for his apprentice, who had been busy admiring the shield on Orrhan's back. 'Time to put on a show.'

Shree passed by with a smile that left Orrhan blushing in her wake. Nala would ordinarily have scowled at that but she sympathized. She doubted the other Chalakkhans in the Fire Squad made for titillating company for the soldier. Orrhan would have leaped at a porcupine for an erotic encounter if it had batted its eyelid at him for a second longer than what was considered—

Spirits save me!

Shree had let out a shrill cry without warning. A cry which rang out in spurts, echoing through the dead city. Shree wheeled in each direction, and repeated it like a lost kitten seeking its mother.

'If the records hold true, Manu must be buried with the Orb of Agan Mian for there has been nary a whisper of the gem by history since,' Nar Ad explained, unprompted. 'Many claim Iyran and all its treasures are cursed. Stands to reason why the Seven Tribes did not retrieve it. Descriptions that survive suggest the gem was fashioned from quartz crystals. Quartz buzz like bees when packed together, a buzzing sound our ears are not equipped to perceive. Shree's cry will bounce off quartz to let her know of the direction where he is buried.'

'Like a—' Masha realized.

'Like a bat, dear sister,' Nar Ad said, tying the flowers snugly around his bun, 'like a bat. Ingenious, isn't it? My plan.'

Nala was about to roll her eyes when she heard faint thrumming in the air come from the north. Like someone plucking a lone string of a veena repeatedly. Out of tune. But persistently. Glancing left to right, she saw none of the rest react to the sound. None apart from Shree, who pirouetted to Nala with a knowing smile. 'Follow us! I found Manu's tomb!'

 MASHA found it curious to find that Manu's tomb was in a temple. That this was the place they had been looking for, there was no doubt. A carpet of broken bones and dented armour spread out before the door in morbid welcome. Ahead, Nala carefully stepped around torn hands and legs that had been ripped from bodies rather than admire the temple's breathtaking interiors.

'For once, can you admire the beauty around you? You will never find the stars if you keep looking down to see where you are going, Nala,' Masha asked, coughing. Mister Nomnom seemed to agree as he nibbled at the cheese block on her palm. 'Good boy, aren't you?'

She did not know whether it was Nala's silence or the lingering effects of Hashayne, but a shiver made Masha jolt, prompting Mister Nomnom to scurry back to Shree. *No, wait!* Masha turned around to find Orrhan on Shree's arm. Nala had told Masha that Shree was putting the charade up to rile Nar Ad for what he did to her mouse yet an odd sense of unease gripped Masha. It bordered on hatred but she could never hate Shree. No, it was more of a longing. She just could not help thinking that Shree had something Masha ought to have herself, and since she did not have it, she had a strange urge to witness a block of stone fall on Shree's head. By Prakioni! Perhaps this was what jealousy was! Horrible but... so irresistible! Nar Ad had rescued Shree and made her feel important but Orrhan seemed to be making Shree feel something altogether different – making her feel nice. She wanted that kind of attention, that gaze that never left her, wanted to fill it into a flask and carry it back so that she could bathe in its warmth whenever she wanted. Parshuram had rescued Masha and made her feel important but no one had ever made her feel nice. Maybe Taksha. If only he were here, then she could also walk arm in arm with him. She did not care if it was petty, for only the truly blind souls would favour feeling important over feeling nice.

'The temple is dazzling, isn't it?' Nar Ad said. 'There is always beauty in the broken.'

'I know a lot of men who say that about horses as well as girls,' Shree said, her voice echoing all over the place in the vast inner sanctum. 'It is somewhere here.'

Sometime later, while Shree was still performing her oral magic to find the quartz gem, Nar Ad was busy translating inscriptions on the side to help figure out where Manu's corpse was, and Parshuram had stepped out to shoot off a flare arrow in the sky to let Vyas know they had found Manu's tomb, Masha lost herself in thought of the bygone souls who once filled this amphitheatre. She imagined everyone in the House of Oracles could have filled the benches. She turned to find Nala approaching her. 'Do you feel a tremble under boots? Or is that just me?'

'Tremble?' Masha lifted her feet to turn her sandals. 'No, I don't.'

'These… vibrations Shree is making, there is something different in the way they are buzzing here. Feels like they are shaking the very foundations of this place. I think we need to be careful about where we step.'

'You can ask her yourself if you can pull her away from him.' Masha nudged Nala and pointed her to Shree, who had placed a metal helm beside her own to pull comical faces and make Orrhan laugh. Satisfied with the results, Shree tossed it casually to the centre of the clearing.

Nala's warning cry came too late. Ancient stones shifted under the stress. The vibrations spread. The floor cracked open, and into the darkness they fell.

 SHREE cracked her eyes open to broken shards of light as she found herself rolling across the flagstones like a carpet. A thick blanket of detritus and dust descended on her. She reached out, groping to find purchase, till she grasped a platform's edge. Using it to support herself, she propped her back against a wooden pillar on the platform, coughing. On finding her bearings, she immediately tuned her ears to squeaks. She smiled as she heard them, knowing Mister Nomnom had survived another near-death experience. Luckiest rat in the world.

Light filtering through the broken roof over the floor through which they had crashed slowly illuminated the place around them. Pillars, charred and rust-dusted, held what remained of the room as they went off into the distant dark, perhaps extending for leagues.

As she wiped the grime from her face, she spotted Orrhan crawling towards her with Mister Nomnom on his shoulders. Shree could not help but laugh. 'My hero!' Her laugh cut off suddenly when she saw Orrhan was not looking at her, but at something behind her. Turning around slowly, she finally took measure of the wooden pillar against which she rested. *Guess no one will complain at me now for causing this mess.*

It wasn't a pillar but a cross in the shape of an X, as tall as three Ajaths. Built of polished black flint, the cross bore words in an unknown language. And pitted to the X was a corpse – hands splayed wide, legs impaled. A studded girdle was cinched painfully tight around his neck, the chain drawn through iron loops and pulled taut to force his face permanently upwards. Enormous nails driven through his palms and ankles gleamed – not under the dismal light from above – but in the blinding brilliance of a gem. A gem that dimpled the forehead of the man. A gem, made of quartz crystals, that was still buzzing in the hues of Shree's voice.

'Manu's corpse...' Shree whispered.

Manu's unrotting body was a shrunken shell of withered muscles and tendon. His skin was white, or rather a colour that is formed by an absence of all colours. His face was pale and sage, and, perhaps, a little lonely, made more so by the eyes that had been sewn shut. An arrow had pierced his mouth, exiting just below his right ear. The jaw bone gleamed crimson amidst torn muscle in a face that could never close its mouth. Feathers of deep-driven arrows crowded his chest. And on that chest, inscribed by clawed fingers, were words.

'We found it,' Shree said as she tip-toed to put her hand on his chest. She screamed. For beneath her palm, she felt Manu's faint heartbeat.

 MASHA felt her heart beat hope when Parshuram unlimbered his axe. He would release the poor man, she thought, but all Parshuram did was use the sharp end of his axe to flick away the long strands of Manu's hair lying limp on his chest. Parshuram nodded at Nala, who stepped behind them a few paces to squint at the prophecy through an eyeglass and write it down.

'You've finally found someone older than you,' Nar Ad said. 'Should you not have tea together, and grumble about your golden age and the decadence of this?'

Parshuram did not respond but Masha wished he'd considered it. She approached the living corpse, hands raised, trailing a serpentine path around the arrow heads jutting out of his sides. 'How is he alive? Is he, too, a Chiranjeevi?'

'Chiranjeevis are immortals but they can be killed, Sister Masha,' Nar Ad said. 'And they do age, say every hundred years or so. Either that or Parshuram here salts his hair.' Nar Ad moved right in front of Manu, his head reaching up till his breastbone, staring up at the man. 'But Manu, it seems… can't be killed. Between the air in the Veins that freezes time, his Taint, his own disease and the magic of the Orb embedded in his skull, he is truly immortal. Death and Manu are now two parallel strings on a veena. Always close, never meeting.'

'Then where are the others in the city?' Nala asked, pausing her quill.

'Dead. The Marigold Mold took them all. It took the sacrifice of the First Saptarishis to cleanse Iyran Machil of the plague though there have been three outbreaks in the last two Ages, three more than what should have been possible had *Manu* here,' Nar Ad uncharacteristically emphasized his name viciously, 'saved his people instead of pursuing personal glory to save some distant future. Oh, he is trying to speak. Acharya, keen to listen to some ancient wisdom?'

Parshuram shrugged. Masha hurriedly took the shears out of Nala's bag, and climbing on Orrhan's shoulder, snapped in two the arrow lodged in Manu's mouth. Then with both hands, she took out the two halves of the arrow gingerly, colourless blood trickling on her fingers.

'Wrong, ye are, bard,' Manu rasped in the oldest form of Sanskrit – a rough translation of the First Tongue, which was surprising given Sanskrit came after Manu's time. 'Killed they my sheep before eyes mine, so a shepherd loses his soul before his mind.'

'And then they so kindly left *you* alive?' Nar Ad asked.

Manu gave a short laugh. It was odd to see him speak, his head chained to stare upwards from a face with eyes sewn shut. 'Not graced me with its presence hast a jest in days, or years, or more since I have been so tied. Though difficult be it to determine passage of days here where time lied.'

'Do you remember the Son of Darkness, Realmseer?' Parshuram asked in the First Tongue, his tone eerily reverent.

'Many secrets were whispered to me in my day of madness, Son of Jamadagni,' Manu replied in broken Sanskrit, 'but only echoes remain. To be fair, I did have a large canvas to paint on, before I succumbed.'

'And then you killed everyone,' Nar Ad said.

'My deeds were born out of love. Knew I not, the Marigold Demon cared not for humanity or fear of gods above.'

Masha caressed Manu's crucified hands like a healer.

'Stop feeling sorry for him, Sister,' Nar Ad told her, his tone dripping with disgust. 'He destroyed his city, murdered his kin and kind, and obliterated our heritage.'

'It was a sickness, Acharya Nar Ad. Can you blame a fevered man for coughing even if his air sickens the ones around him to death? We should end his suffering.'

'Be at ease, children, for such is not the object of my desire,' Manu interjected. 'Released, I will burn you all. Suffer I must Time's hateful grip, till I am freed by the Daughter of Dawn.'

'At least he is not a liar,' Nar Ad quipped. 'And who is this Daughter of Dawn? And how in Seven Hells do you know how to speak Sanskrit?'

'Saw it in my visions, learned it then, a noble language, worthy of the race of men.'

Nar Ad snorted, turning away, while Parshuram turned to Nala. 'Are you practising calligraphy?'

'Pardon, Acharya,' Nala said, despair loud in her scratchy voice. 'The wounds have blotted out certain letters. But I am done.'

While Parshuram saw what Nala had written, Manu spoke again. 'Dost thee play the lyre, bard?' he asked. 'Pluck a tune before you discard.'

Masha, curious, turned. Nar Ad had been inspecting a lyre that he had picked from the artefacts strewn around Manu's cruciform. The lyre, made of glass, reflected the flames of their torches strangely, turning it into blue hues. The strings glowed as if made of light.

'Last of its kind this lyre ye holds. I was given one by the Gandharvas, scions of Vac, musicians great. They were generous to part with it as a welcome gift. This was I suppose almost a hundred years before I was imprisoned. Quite a while ago, at any rate.'

The Gandharvas are real? Nar Ad certainly thought so as he shivered, his fingers examining the lyre reverently.

'Use it well to sing of bygone sunlight, when you play outside in the world, bard.'

Masha turned as Nala read out loud the words on which the fate of the world hinged.

'The Breaker of Furies
The Emperor
Of no Empire
Rises from Coloured Fire
When one war ends
And another begins
On the longest night of grim greens

Between red lions and white snakes
In a wonder made by Ma■■■■an
Will rise the S■n of Darkness.'

'I knew I was a genius,' Nar Ad said, dramatically scratching his chin as he closed his eyes. 'We already knew he was destined to rise on the day of the winter solstice from the divinations which this,' he gestured towards Nala's translation, 'confirmed. *Lions.* Plainly obvious – Magadh. *In a wonder made by Ma something four letters and an...* I penned the book on wonders – it is Virangavat, a wonder made by a Magadhan. *When one war ends.* Armistice ends somewhere close to the winter solstice. It is also the day of the Imperial Contest. The Son of Darkness will rise in Virangavat in the Imperial Contest.'

A shock ripped through Masha and the others. A shock of respect. 'Brilliant!' Masha said, eyes widening, throat hoarse with cough. 'You would make such a good Matron, Acharya!'

'I will keep that in—' Nar Ad was just mid-boast when Manu shrieked, startling everyone out of their minds, except Parshuram.

'Leave before the sun descends for shadows dance where daylight ends.'

Masha stared at the sand glass Parshuram was holding in his hand. They had two hours before darkness set in. She looked back at Manu again.

'Is it the season of the dead in the world you came from?' Manu asked, face up. 'For surely you know that the days then be shorter in winters.'

Suddenly she saw Shree and Nala's heads snap to the west, both their eyes widening, as if they'd heard a sound which no one else seemed to have heard. But Masha paid them no attention. Manu was right. From here in this cavern, they had no view of the horizon but the way darkness was folding over the sunlight from the hole above left little reason to doubt him. They were late... and as if in agreement with this verdict, screams tore through the air.

This time, *everyone* heard them.

White breath fluttered from Manu's mouth. 'Run.'

Shree's joints screamed as she ran, breath short, heart heavy, Manu's last warning echoing in her mind. 'Remember, when you hear a mournful wailing, don't let it plague your ear.' Suddenly she felt herself lifted in the air, her hands clutching Mister Nomnom safely against her breasts. *I thought it was the dragon! Orrhan, my hero.* But the mournful wailing still chased them in hot pursuit, coming from behind them instead of from above them. Wasn't the dragon a beast of the sky? If the drawing Masha had shown Shree of a dragon was true, she wondered how it would look jogging through the streets and could not help but chuckle, returning to her old way of dealing with crippling fear.

Manu had told them to find a house with an intact roof and a door that closed. Here, that would be like finding a whore without a touch of Kaamah's Itch. She giggled, head thrown back, while her reflections spun above her like a bleak carnival. Her head jerked as Orrhan paused, and before she knew it, her face in the skies was replaced by the cracks of a ceiling.

Orrhan deposited her on the floor before darting to secure the windows while Nala shut the door to drape them all in darkness. Parshuram drew a symbol in the air and conjured a spherical orb of light over his palm. Masha, predictably, gasped even as the bard lit a pipe to calm the nerves. It was all Shree could do to not ask for a drag.

'Where is Jaah?' Masha asked but none replied.

Mister Nomnom emerged out of Shree's collar, and she stroked his head as she surveyed the shelves lined with dust-covered jars, many of them cracked, their contents dried to brittle husks or congealed into thick, unrecognizable sludge. Cobwebs draped over the containers, and a lengthy table dominated the rear of the room. Shree frowned, turning back to see the windows Orrhan had shut. Those were not windows but shutters. *This is an apothecary!* Was *an apothecary.* Shree turned at the sound of a howl.

'The dragon is close,' Nala said. Of course, Nala could hear them as she could. 'Does that mean Lord Chalakkha failed?'

'It is just a dragon. I will handle it.' Parshuram slithered into his flamebreaker hauberk while Nala unsheathed her daggers.

'*Just a dragon. Just?*' the coward bard asked. 'Surely not, Acharya?'

'We need to leave before nightfall. And not just because without the Vanara we would have to swim the chasm, but because every hour or two spent here is a week back in the real world. Can that world afford it if we miss the winter solstice, bard?'

Nar Ad sighed while Parshuram readied himself with Nala's aid. Masha chanted a prayer with Orrhan joining in, his hand intertwined with Shree's. They both stood at the back of the room where Shree had just perched herself on the long table for a good view. And just when Parshuram moved to the door to open it, a baby cried. A human baby.

 MASHA did not have any experience with human babies, having never seen one in her life, but she doubted they could knock. It had to be a dragon with the cry of a baby, didn't it? The thing now banged on the door, the force demanding. Masha squealed. The banging increased, angrier now. The sound was maddening. Parshuram made for the doorknob, ready to be done with it, when Nar Ad pulled him back, and shook his head. Parshuram scowled but just then the crying and the knocking stopped. Silence moved like a wraith amongst the frozen figures in the room till the soft mewling and coos left no doubt that it was actually a baby outside their door!

'Oh, the Seven have mercy,' Masha said, moving towards the door. Nala pulled her back again, too alert to speak. Masha looked on aghast. How could they stand unmoving in here when a crying baby suffered outside? The baby's only desire would be for someone to touch him, feed him. Masha understood that. She needed to go to that baby, show the baby that the world could be trusted, that he was in a kind universe.

A woman's voice shut off her protests.

'Oh, there you are. Did you find them? Did they have food?' the woman asked in the First Tongue, presumably to her infant.

'We have to help them!' Masha whispered urgently when Nala kept her palm over Masha's mouth to silence her. But Nala's hands were caked with marble dust, making Masha cough, and by then, it was too late.

'Someone there?' the woman's voice begged, knocking on the window. 'Please, we are trapped in this city. Have been. For so long that we have forgotten. We are so famished. For so long we have not eaten. Please!'

Shree asked in Sanskrit from behind, 'What did she say?' but none answered her.

'Could it be possible?' Nar Ad seemed to have lost the initial shivers. 'The Orb of Agan Mian can sustain mortals for centuries. Reckon these are Manu's people who the Tribes left behind – perhaps they were spared from the Mold, and simply forsaken.'

'In the name of mercy,' the woman outside begged, her voice breaking Masha's heart. 'My baby... Just take my baby.' The baby cried again, his cries tearing at them. *That's it!*

Nala cried out as Masha sank her teeth into Nala's wrist right on the bandaged part. 'The Gods do not sanction us to be so cruel!' Masha shrieked. Parshuram moved to block Masha by the door but she flung open the window shutter instead.

And then the mother... who wasn't a woman, entered.

 NALA felt terror enter her arms as she felt the bite of Masha on her wrist resurrect the memory of the fits. She had forgotten to blood-let after crossing over the lake, and now just the mere pinch of teeth on skin sent her vessels pulsing. Maybe if she had drawn blood from her hand then, things would have ended differently. As it was, she fell on the floor, spasming, helplessly watching the apparition enter through the window.

A seven-foot-tall woman stood still as a stone. The clouds must have shifted in the sky for the woman was made molten by the lurid streams of dusk's light, making Nala realize the woman was not still... as a stone.

She was stone.

Remnants of human flesh spread on her face in patches. Her one empty eye socket oozed out nothing but roaches that crawled across her face to take refuge inside her human lips.

The Stone Mother stooped to enter through the window, moving on all fours like some enormous, hairless spider. Bare from above the waist, fleshy breasts dangled like eggs from a bug's belly. Each movement from her made a sound like that of a millstone grinding. Fingernails scratched Nala's spine from the inside as she felt fear freeze her.

'HELP. MY. BABY,' the Stone Mother cried out, following it with a heart-rending wail. Her hand shot out. Masha choked in her grasp as her feet lifted off the ground.

'Nala! Fetch Masha back!' Parshuram shouted, hurling his axe, its gold inlay shimmering as it spun end over end. The woman's face turned left on its neck without her body turning to see Parshuram, and the axe struck her forehead... and fell back with a clang as if it'd struck a wall. The Stone Mother, momentarily startled, loosened her grip on Masha. Masha's feet touched the ground. Nala made to wring back Masha but Nala's legs stiffened. *No!* Nala's throat constricted. *Not now!* Nala's mind, severed from her hands. *No! No!* The fits grabbed the inside of her thoughts and squeezed till it felt as if they were twisting and turning her mind inside out. Nala's body spasmed even as she stood, her body shaking violently, her feet frozen.

Through the paralysing fit, Nala saw Parshuram make for the Stone Mother but just then, the door was ripped from its hinges to crash and pin Parshuram down. The *baby* stood on top of the door. Only that it was a baby the size of a three-year-old, his face bloated like a corpse dredged up from the bottom of a lake.

'Hungry,' the Stone Baby bawled.

The Stone Mother dangled Masha before her baby like a prize doll from some cruel fair, her legs kicking, thrashing, useless in the empty air. Masha's eyes locked on Nala's, wide, desperate, pleading for help. But Nala did not move. Could not move. The memories surged back – Bheem's brutal hands snapping her spine, the stench of her burning kin, her family's screams ringing in her ears. The same helplessness, the same horror, crushing her chest. Her mother's face twisted into Masha's, the two blurring together even as pain ripped through her body. Not again. Gods, please... not again. Just... let her go. A heartbeat passed in this prayer.

And in that heartbeat, Nala saw the Stone Mother stoop to pick Nala's fallen dagger, its blade winking in the dim light like a cat's eye. Humming a haunting lullaby, the Stone Mother, still looking at her baby, slit Masha's throat.

 NAR AD heard the sickening gurgle as blood poured from the slit in Masha's throat, soaking the seven-star locket of the Saptarishis hanging at her chest. It was deafening. The Stone Mother then threw Masha on the floor towards her spawn, who seized Masha, and with a gluttonous wet crunch, began chewing on her windpipe.

'Oh, but there was so much left to see.' Masha's last words would haunt Nar Ad for a long time but he was glad to see her death had done its bit to motivate Parshuram. Though Nar Ad did wish Parshuram had attacked the Stone Mother with a bit more strategy.

Nar Ad supposed an immortal terror who had been slammed to the floor like some amateur warrior by an undead baby and had, upon waking from that moment of failure, found one of his wards dead, and the other ineffective, could not be expected to retain an intelligent outlook. What Parshuram should have done, of course, was to aim for the fleshy parts of the Stone Mother so as to get the best wounds on that stout frame. Instead, Parshuram used his axe as he had used it on countless kings, like a madman in rage. And all he managed was to blunt his blade. In other words, Parshuram's strikes, which could have saved them all from this stony horror, turned out to be merely, what Nar Ad could call, a gesture.

It was in such a moment of idle speculation that the Stone Baby raised his head from Masha's butchered throat and turned his eyes in the general direction of Nar Ad. It was evident the glutton had discovered that in the general hierarchy of cuisine, a slightly portly bard who had sampled the wines and cheese of the world ranked significantly higher than a tortured Oracle weaned on rations. The Stone Baby crawled at an alarming pace to what he no doubt thought was his main course. The sheer look on the Stone Baby's face would have caused a lesser man to freeze, Nala's body a clear exhibit in evidence. But the whole point about Pathfinders is that they are not lesser men. They keep their heads around tolls and trolls. They act quickly.

Nar Ad had by now observed that the Stone Baby was more flesh, less stone. So, when the baby grabbed his ankle, a grip like a horse's bite, and made him fall, the bard deferred his screaming and pressed the glowing end of his smoke pipe on his rotted cheeks.

The results were satisfying. With a sharp wail, the Stone Baby released the ankle and disappeared into the darkness on the side. Unfortunately for Nar Ad, evolution has selectively mutated mothers to be sensitive to the cries of their children. The Stone Mother's left hand had been hacked by now but it still hung from a piece of stone to her shoulder. While the other hand handled Parshuram, her head turned an almost circle on its axis like an owl. She stared at Nar Ad intently, and he so wished she wouldn't do that. Her roar that followed was that of a puppy being boiled alive. Fortunately, it was then that Orrhan decided to impress Shree by stepping over Nala's body to join Parshuram's efforts.

Nar Ad was a man who knew when to and when not to be amongst those who chose to confront difficult situations head on. 'Shree, there comes a time when we must choose between bravery and practicality. The window might be our exit, eh Shree?' Shree said nothing. Nar Ad grunted. There was only so long you could hold to a grudge. Taken for granted, his kindness was. 'Shree, enough!' He turned around.

Shree lay on the long table. Her head lolled listlessly on the side, her eyes glazed over. Her tongue had been cut off by her own teeth. The big Stone Baby was above her, punching her, no, not punching. Pushing. *Oh...* The Stone Body was digging a hole in Shree's navel, pulling out her insides from it with one hand while Shree was still alive. Now the Stone Baby took his other hand, Mister Nomnom inside that palm. He then pushed the rat inside Shree's stomach through the navel, his arm plunging in up to the elbow. The Stone Baby growled and screamed at the hole in her navel, kept screaming, kept screaming until suddenly it began to clap.

'No!' Orrhan had finally seen it from wherever he was. He rushed past Nar Ad, screaming, his spear crossing the distance, neatly impaling the Stone Baby's head to the wall.

Nar Ad could only stare as he turned. Watching Stone Mother move past him was like seeing a statue in glimpses. It moved fast, faster than it was possible but... choppily, in jerks, as if she materialized on every spot. Orrhan jumped over the long table to retrieve his spear and turned to face her.

Well, devastating, of course, and one wouldn't be far wrong in assuming that a tear ached out of Nar Ad's eye. He doubted there was any soul in the whole of the wide world who was more moved. If he'd been closer, he would have attempted violence. But though there is that vengeful streak in the bards, they're not without a dash of realism, and it didn't take long for him to spot the other half of the half-empty glass.

One monster was dead.

The other monster was busy.

He held Parshuram's arm back for the second time that day. 'World or soldier?'

Parshuram grunted, and then agreeing, lifted the spasming Nala on his shoulders, climbed over Masha's corpse and ran out, Nar Ad following, pausing only for a moment at the threshold when he heard a squeak. Nar Ad, despite better intuition, succumbed to curiosity and turned. Mister Nomnom had clawed his way out of Shree's mouth, coated in his mistress's guts, barely alive, but alive.

 NALA felt barely alive, her mind fallen to pieces like moth-chewed silk. Throwing her arms across Parshuram, she let out a single devastated sob. Now every heartbeat felt like a hammer blow, every breath a swallowing gasp. Someone, probably Varcin, had once told her that you only realize you have made a true friend when you spend a day without them. The

horror of spending the rest of her miserable life without Masha's annoying questions soaked into her like acid.

Why had Nala not cut her hands on time?! Why had she not pulled her back?! How could a timid girl bite the palm of an assassin's apprentice and get the better of her?! She had been ready, had she not? 'Nala, it is not over,' Parshuram said gravely.

Self-pity came to a standstill as a mass of stone and skin poured from an alleyway and began spreading to fill the square before them. A Stone Girl emerged from the mass, the only one mounted on a horse, the horse emaciated and gaunt. She stabbed a long, slender arm in their direction, and shrieked. It wasn't a cry. It was a command. Hundreds of stone faces swung to look upon them. And before Nala knew it, Parshuram, one hand holding her on one shoulder, axe out in the free hand, ripped through that press of forgotten humanity.

 NAR AD could only hope Parshuram had forgotten Nar Ad's past transgressions and would not leave him behind, for the bard could scarcely keep up with his pace. He was panting and running, fear shaking his bones, wind and breath rushing, his reflections chasing him above, dark ghouls below. Ahead he saw Parshuram wield his axe to deadly effect with his free hand, killing none, but definitely dissuading any unwanted closeness.

They dashed ahead like deer fleeing a forestfire, with no thought for anything but nostalgia for home. Sparks and stones danced through the air as Parshuram carved a river through peaks of Stone Creatures. He did not escape unscathed, his ability for violence limited by the convulsing body of Nala on his shoulders. Hands, nails and swords had carved a new map on Parshuram's armour, and where they had torn some of it off, his arms leaked ancient blood.

But why were they being attacked? If they were survivors, why not simply ask for help? Nar Ad would gladly author a dozen more volumes to fund their rehabilitation but he doubted he would find an avenue to convey these thoughts to them especially when on a walkway he saw another Stone Woman atop Jaah, the sword of Chalakkha who had deserted them, taking a great bite out of his belly.

To imagine these poor souls trapped here, unable to die, unable to live – no wonder they harboured only hate for the outsiders who had abandoned them. *Song of Stone*, he smiled as a tune began to compose itself in his head. Ideas always chose the oddest time to germinate. Just as he was hanging on to that tune, Parshuram slashed wide at a Stone Girl's neck, spraying black blood into Nar Ad's eyes, which had already zoned out, blinding him to the Stone Girl's flailing body, which crashed into him. The world spun, full of guttural sounds of the city's tenants, as they rolled onto the hard floor like lovers till he came out on top.

Driven by instinct, Nar Ad smashed the Stone Girl in the head with the lyre, once, twice, three times, shoved her to the side, scrambling up and then stomping on the back of her head thrice for good measure. 'Vaikunshard lyre, this, bitch!' He shook the lyre defiantly and then realizing what he had done, apologized to the relic for the disrespect. When he looked up, he found a line of Stone Men between where Parshuram was running and where he knelt. *Fuck.*

Parshuram, on the other side of the line, Nala on his back, axe in another, just stared. For there were too many of them. *Too many.* Parshuram tried to double back but other Stone Men cordoned him off. *Parshuram is trying to come back for me. I knew he was custard on the inside.*

'Oi, old man!' Nar Ad shouted, as he took out the flower string holding his hair together. 'World or soldier?'

Parshuram's eyes revealed a world of pain. 'Run!' Parshuram shouted from the other side. *But why?* Running would buy him a few minutes of life only to fall to death in a mad rush. Nar Ad was not a runner. He was a lover. He was Nar Ad the Bard, and preferred to meet what was coming in style. Save the world with his song – that was his style.

'Give the Son of Darkness Nar Ad's *hello*.'

Parshuram only nodded, slashing two Stone Men who came at him, then turning to run towards the horizon to outrun the dipping sun. *Hope he reaches the beach on time.* As Nar Ad held the lyre, Manu's sly words, *sing of bygone sunlight*, came back to him. Nar Ad chuckled. Bastard had known all along, he realized as he put his fingers on the strings. Remembering the mandala for Earth Elemental, the only one he knew, he sang one last time.

The air around the lyre rippled and twisted. The ash on the ground lifted slowly and curled up around the strings. The Third Chakra in the solar plexus was now wide awake, and he was almost certain he was turning sound into an energy of a kind, a destructive energy that made the tortured earth around him groan. At least it had distracted a sizeable chunk of the Stone Men Army from chasing after Parshuram.

'Eternal life, spent all alone. We built a wall around you, we let you down.'

On the periphery of his hearing, the Stone Folk growled and grunted to each other, his audience applauding him perhaps. He opened his eyes to steal a glance.

Around him, cracks began to snake their way across edifices while the air echoed with crashes and anguished wails even as the ground quivered under his sandals. As for his audience, the Stone Children had scattered, screaming, some disappearing in their black alleys, but Stone Men and Women remained. As did his reflections on the sky.

'But we were cut from the same stone, brothers. Only we were made to sink, you were made to skip.'

The lyre's music soared, whipping geysers of tar and dust around him. The earth trembled with the screams of the Stone Men and the song of Nar Ad till the song stopped abruptly, leaving the song unfinished, the last line just floating in the air.

'Oh but how the old tyrant was right still, my singing did bring a city down, the immortal city of Iyran Machil.'

INTERLUDE
VAHURA'S ADVENTURES

I

It was reasonable to assume that the Princess of Balkh was not too well pleased. As the women closest to the podium would gossip later, she called Bhagadatt an impostor who should be in chains, an infinite and endless liar. And if one wonders whether that annoyed the Tusk of the Tree Cities, the answer remains shrouded in mystery, for the Princess was dragged away politely by her governess, who seemed to defy the old adage that had something to do with old age. It was within reason to conclude that the Tusk and the Princess had parted on distant terms, and that Vahura's plans of ingratiating herself with the Tusk to eventually ask, 'My dear friend, can you spare the Daevic Scrolls to save the world?' seemed rather bleak.

'I will step out to arrange for the carriage,' Old Ella said, having the look most geriatrics have when they judge the new generation poor on will. 'The boy assigned to us was told we would not be leaving before midnight. I doubt he will be dutiful enough to be waiting outside.'

Vahura nodded grumpily. Driven by a blend of anger and shame, Vahura sought refuge in the dark garden outside, hoping to be alone with her thoughts, but even in this she failed. The shadowed mothlamps flickered around a slender golden statue, revealing several others had already discovered the garden's charms. In a dim corner, a knot of people writhed in the half-light to the sound of

giggles, grunts and moans. Vahura tried to tally their number by
the dance of limbs. Three at least. Perhaps five. Oh! One of them
making himself feel right at home in the middle of it all was
Kalyavan himself! *By the Forge!* Vahura quickly turned away only
to find another couple engulfing each other beneath an ornamental
orange tree. Since she had no other place to look, she just absently
stared at the golden statue itself, her mind split at the seams, one
part pondering what she should do next, and the other wondering
how they had sculpted fiery gold eyelashes on the statue. Giving in
to her curiosity, she moved a step to the left to see what precisely
they had done with the statue's hair, when she felt the statue's eyes
follow her. *Bless my parchment heart!* It's no statue. The statue was
moving so slowly. So slowly that Vahura could not put a finger on
the exact motions of her body but a few seconds later, somehow,
the woman had slightly changed her posture. Soft flakes of gold
floating to the ground like leaves were the only evidence that she
had moved.

'You are marvellous,' Vahura gasped.

The golden woman's eyes seemed to acknowledge it, though the
gold-flecked lashes did not blink. Inspired by the woman's strength
of resolve, Vahura trudged on to the Room of the Feast, four hours
before dinner time. *Courtesies can go eat a sour gourd.* She might as
well storm out of the Conclave on a full stomach.

And was she glad she was the first to enter. With the absence of
a crowd, she was able to drink in the sights, relishing the effort that
had been poured into arranging the entire feast. The green darkness
of the leafy canopies above, the grey lustre of the Rakshasas at the
doors and the curious absence of a menu lent the entire affair a
nocturnal charm, reminding her of tales devoured illicitly long past
bedtime.

She forgot her woes with every flavour she could not identify and
every meat whose origin she could not trace. There were those from
the lesser nobles, who had followed her, soliciting the servers for a
glimpse beyond the veil but their inquiries about the ingredients
were only met with insincere regrets. Vahura was grateful for it – in
a world where the unknown was scarce, such ignorance lent the dish
a life of its own, a life greater than the sum of its individual parts.

But then again there were always those who wanted to upturn the minstrel's magic hat and tear his long sleeves.

She passed, stomach begging her to try the stalls serving honeyed frog legs or steamed hornet larvae or at least the spiced silkworm pupa decorated with fermented bamboo shoots, but Vahura was most intrigued by a plate of red rice which the server claimed was sprinkled with a powder made of burnt chicken feathers. It seemed evident that the theme of the Conclave must be: come for the battles but stay for the banquets. But just as she was about to take the plate, a horned Asuran passed by with a tray of something resembling doughlings alongside a bowl of red chutney – fresh, sharp and stunning. The doughlings were white clouds, pierce-with-a-pick soft and melted the moment she took one in her mouth. Vahura devoured it in three bites, masticating the soft white pulp after bloodying it with the pickle as orgasmically as possible between her molars. The succulent meat fillings inside tasted like flavoured broth in her mouth, the sweetness of the wrapping waging a war with the hotness of the pickle, the balance giving rise to an empire of flavours in her mouth. The Tree Folk hospitality shone in their thoughtful inclusion of alien ingredients like onion, mustard oil and coriander to appease the human palate.

Vahura was so stuffed by the end that she could not manage more than seven little doughlings, as much as she cherished them. She was wondering whether to attempt the eighth when a voice whispered.

'It is called a *momo*, in case you wanted to eat it again tomorrow. A Bhota dish.'

'A perfect name to celebrate this momo-entous occasion!' Vahura said as she turned, thoroughly amused with herself, when the empire of flavours in her mouth fell, leaving behind just the hot ashes of the pickle.

Baggy urf Bhagadatt stood facing her. In the light of the chandelier, she received the full brunt of his ghastly and ghostly beauty. His jaw had the sharpness of a fresh hardbound tome, and the glaze of his grey cheeks could put the newest blackboards to shame. The grime of the Ranger had been scrubbed away to let the Tusk shine in full grey glory.

'Before you storm away again, allow me to explain,' Baggy started, tracing the tiny pouch at the end of the locket around his neck. 'Rakshasas carry these seeds throughout their lives, so that after we pass away, our spirit carries on through the trees these seeds give rise to.' He plucked the pouch from his locket, took her palm, and gently placed the pouch on it. The effect was marred slightly by the traces of the chilli pickle on her fingertips but she barely noticed for she was too busy gasping.

She obviously knew of the legend. The Rakshasa refugees who had followed Shurpanakha carried a pouch of Everwood seeds from Lanka to rebuild civilization in the unhospitable land of the East. She knew of the custom, and of how unheard of it was for a Rakshasa to trust their sacred pouch to someone, let alone a stranger, and let alone a foreigner.

'Why are you handing these to me?'

'As a token of my faith and goodwill, to show you I meant no malice with my... deception, Princess. I know you are not here for the Conclave. Lord Fahamin, the ambassador from Balkh, reneged on your accord, and reached Kamrup. Worry not, Princess, for I have kept him as a guest of honour in a far away palace on the coast... away from any ravens. I want to aid you, Princess, if you will have me.'

Why was he being so nice to her? What did he want? Did he want something from Balkh? Did he plan to take her hostage? Vahura's mind was a flurry of conjectures so she settled for the least incensing thought. 'I do not like being deceived.'

'I...' He looked at his feet, and suddenly Vahura's heart warmed. Baggy appeared genuinely remorseful, and given that she was technically deceiving him by exploiting the Conclave, she could not rightfully claim the moral high ground. She would have forgiven him even if he hadn't said the next few words. 'It was unjust of me to coax you into talking so freely to me without you knowing who I was but I do not regret it. I did want you to talk to me without the shackles of pretence, but not out of ill intent... out of a curiosity to know you. Honourable as my destination was, it does not clean the taint my methods left on the path I took to reach there. For that I apologize. Is there anything I can do to make amends?'

Give me the Daevic Scrolls. She was about to utter it when she suddenly became very conscious of how her breath smelled. *Sparks! Ella was right. Why did I have to eat the pickle?* Who cares, Vahura? Remember why you are here. But what if he asks why do you need the Daevic Scrolls? *I will lie, like I have ever since.* Her mother's bleeding eye sockets stripped away all feelings of insecurity from her shoulders.

'There is one—'

'Cousin,' a deadpan voice called out. Lady Sokarro had joined them. 'You are desired at the Conclave. The Hearthside Talks would commence soon as is tradition. It would not bode well for the Ksharjans to be driven to an early dinner simply because of your presence here,' she said, eyeing Vahura politely. As politely as a tigress stalks a deer with a limp leg.

'Princess Vahura, Lady Sokarro Sinh, my Cousin and Chief of Thornwatch—'

Sokarro interrupted. 'Go, or else they will think we are trying to get them to leave.' Bhagadatt looked like he would protest but then Sokarro spoke over him. 'I will ensure the Balkhan comes to no harm in your absence,' her tone inspiring no confidence in her assurance.

'Of course,' Bhagadatt said. 'Thank you, Cousin. A pleasure, Princess.' He bowed and left.

'Are you alright, Princess?' Sokarro asked. Long hair hid the blobs of flesh on either side of her face but there was no hiding the burn marks around her steel nose. Leathery skin marred the area below her nostrils and spoke of a tortured legacy.

'I feel like an angry mouse trying to hold my own amongst airavats,' Vahura said, softly tucking the pouch inside a pocket, before absently wiping her hands on a kerchief.

Sokarro smiled but her upper lips failed to move, giving a perpetually sly cast to her face. 'I've tried airavat as it happens. Thoroughly bland meat once the hide is off. A mouse on the other hand is a delicacy. You're panting. I suspect it is 'cause of the momos. Might I interest you in a *sewaiyan* to douse the fire?' She scooped a small ceramic bowl with a cold pudding and offered it to her. 'But I would advise against it if you were concerned about your waist.'

Vahura remembered the seven momos she had already eaten, and then saw the bowl in her hands. Fine strands of wheat vermicelli danced in a lake of thick milk around almond slivers and golden raisins. Delicious. 'I reckon I am not.'

'Fortunate are the few.'

'*You* care about your waist? But you're perfect. Your allure gave me a panic when I saw you, and I can only imagine the effect it has on men.'

'I care not for men,' she said. 'I do care about slipping into narrow spaces to catch an assassin. The last one they sent was a one-and-ten-year-old boy.'

'Assassins? After the Tusk?'

'If a leader is not hunted by assassins, he isn't a good leader. Tree folk around here are rather unhappy about the bridges the Tusk is building with your kind across the Ganga. The burdens of our ancestral memories hang heavy on our eyelids, closing them to the prospects which our Tusk can see. We trust him. He is a good Tusk but there are some who enjoy expressing their disaffection with daggers.' By now they had walked to the edge of the hall, where they watched a sparkling blue bonfire that was breathing out cold flames instead of warm. 'You must be curious about why I chose to accompany you.'

The sudden detour from the topic stumbled her. Vahura honestly had not given it any thought amidst all the food. Her face said as much as she devoured the sewaiyan, half hoping that a simple nod would suffice. It did. 'I protect the Tusk, and so a human girl who seems to have fascinated him for the last week, distracting him from his duties, naturally piques my interest.'

Fascinated? With her? What did that mean? Did Bhagadatt know about the Daevic Scrolls as well? Oh, rot! No wonder he was being nice to her! Did he not have them? Or did he need her to understand them? Who knew what secrets lay under the text of the Daevic Scrolls? They were a treatise on the human body, not the Rakshasa morphology. Was he planning to use them to unravel some sick method to bring mankind under his thumb? Oh, did Sokarro think Vahura was an assassin? So many thoughts collided with each other in Vahura's mind that she should count herself fortunate she did not choke on the dessert. Before Vahura could conjure a reply that did not implicate her, a messenger approached Sokarro and whispered into her ears.

Assuming a practised smile, Sokarro turned to Vahura. 'The royals are heading for Hearthside Talks in the Courtyard of Dreams. It appears the Tusk has invited you personally,' Sokarro said, taking the bowl of sewaiyan from her hand and handing it over to her messenger.

'Me?' Hearthside Talks was a convention in such meets where the most powerful men and women of the Realm slipped away to talk politics and make themselves feel important. Vahura had not truly expected the granddaughter of a king to be invited.

Sokarro turned her eye lazily to her. 'I am as surprised. Now come, time to go back amidst the airavats. See you don't get trampled.'

II

'We stray from the point!' said Keechak of Matsya, dribbling wine on his cream-coloured doublet and staining the sigil of Matsya sewn on the breast: a fish supposedly in the image of the creature that the Father of Mankind had employed to save the world from the Great Tears.

'As I was saying, now with Mathura... on the brink of destruction, forgive my saying so, darling,' he bowed to Lady Asmai who nodded in curt acknowledgment, 'we find the world at the doorstep of another war between the Hastina Union and the Magadhan Empire.' Keechak reached for a triangular pastry filled with meat, potatoes and peas spiced in cumin, turmeric. 'These *samosas* are delightful!' He ate fastidiously, licking his fingers and wiping crumbs from his beard. 'What are we to do?' he asked after he was done. 'Do we sit out yet another war that shapes our realm?' he asked again, looking as though he were half wishing he could goad them all into one right now.

'If only talking about a war could make a war happen, then the Daevas are no doubt returning on the backs of flying lizards,' Vahura bit out. It had leaped from her tongue before she could catch it, like a slippery die rolling across a table. 'I... I apologize.'

Matriarch Chitran of Manipur turned to look at Vahura – possibly looking impressed – she couldn't really tell through the sun veil. Sokarro narrowed her eyes, folding her arms as if to see how she would hold her ground. Keechak stared at Vahura as if she were a Resht who had touched steel. Even seated, the brute's size was substantial, no doubt making expenses on tailors a formidable entry in Matsya's royal accounting.

'Trust a woman to arm herself with an opinion so opposite to logic that all it can do is awe,' Keechak said, eyebrows raised. 'That is why we never called in the younglings to these discussions in the past Conclaves,' he said, politely, the kind of politeness that is a curtain for condescension.

Bhagadatt cleared his throat. For a moment, Vahura thought, or was it hoped, that Bhagadatt would teach the brute some manners. Her hope suffered a terrible mishap on the road.

'I'm afraid I am inclined to agree with Prince Keechak,' Bhagadatt said. 'Our realm's woes seem far from over. Hastina and Magadh do seem to be on the warpath. I am afraid, Princess Vahura, you are mistaken.'

Mistaken? Mistaken! Now there was no turning back, especially not from him. The lies, the laughs, her guilt and her shame, they all came together violently, like bubbles in boiling water. Vahura could no longer hold it in. It was, however, Matriarch Chitran who spoke. 'Perhaps the Tusk may illustrate his point. Why does he think great war between the two most powerful factions is inevitable?'

'Economics,' Bhagadatt said, rising from his chair, his lean frame towering over all, his hair longer than all. 'If and when Mathura were to,' he shot an apologetic glance towards Lady Asmai, 'crumble under the Yamuna Wars, then who, I ask you, would take over the Queen of Trade Routes? Mathura is far too conveniently and closely located for Hastina to ignore the delightful prospect of tucking it snugly under its wings. But no, it would be Magadh who'd march in and lay claim if the Emperor wills it, making the whole affair a bothersome thorn in Hastina's side. So far, the Cow has served as the charming buffer between the Eagle and the Lion and should the Cow be dehorned, the goblet of peace shall be shaken viciously, and there will be no putting the blood spilled, back.'

Vahura dashed off before Bhagadatt had even completed uttering the final syllable, 'True. Mathura is placed in a fragile spot between two giants. But why should this be a problem if Mathura is gone? I daresay, if and when the Emperor does capture Mathura, his intention is to raze it to the ground. The City would be reduced to rubble, leaving the trade routes open to all. No taxes. No cess. Free flow of trade. As it should be, with due respect to Lady Asmai.'

'Please continue as if I am not there,' said Lady Asmai from Mathura before taking the tiniest of sips from her drink, 'the way you are anyway.'

'Of course, a Balkhan would say this,' Bhagadatt said, eliciting snorts from many. 'After all, your favourite method of war is free flow of your goods, is it not? Curiously followed by their unceremonious dumping on unsuspecting kingdoms. But even if I were to accept what you say, that does little to forestall the inevitable clash of powers between the Hastina Union in the North and the Empire in the South. What about naval rivalry?' He turned to a Unni Ehtral priest who had also been strangely invited to the discussion in the absence of Prince Saham Dev. 'Why is the Empire expanding its navy when to all intents and purposes it is landlocked?'

Vahura chimed in, 'You use the word *naval*, Tusk, but I use the word *mercantile*. Take the case of the three great maritime kingdoms – Kalinga, Hastina and the Tree Cities – for many summers they have been in agreement, informally of course, about the relative size of their fleets in the Kalingan Sea. Should Magadh join the maritime dance, they will come to a similar understanding. Vast is the sea, and contest is good for the market's wellbeing. I mean, simply because Balkh chooses to bolster its caravans with a few elephants, it hardly follows that you would send your airavats to quell us out of fear of losing their ivory supremacy, does it?'

By now, the entire room had turned into an audience to the fencing match between the Balkhan Princess, Vahura and the Tusk of Kamrup, Bhagadatt.

'What about Hastina then? It seems to be growing greedy for territories,' Bhagadatt parried.

'The ravens bringing you these tidings might be old, Tusk – understandable given the hassle it is to reach Kamrup,' Vahura said, earning chuckles from the assembled company, 'but Hastina has its hands full with its own civil strife.'

Shalya gave her a pointed eyebrow at that and Nakul straightened, but none rose.

'*Nonetheless*,' she pressed on, 'these squabbles have been lately decided without raising spears. Even recently, when Hastina found itself cut off from Anga to carry its trade, it reached an amicable agreement with Panchal about the thorny issue of access to the East Road. If people continue to go on about such civilized ways I divine – though I may be no oracle – but I divine no reason for any kingdom to return to the ways of war.'

'It's often the most *civilized* kingdoms that splurge the highest on war, Princess,' Bhagadatt said, turning to the Unni Ehtral priest again. 'Would you pardon me if I remind you what the Emperor is fondly called by the bards: Jarasandh the *Conqueror* for his conquests of kingdoms, not hearts. Magadh is and has always been aggressive when it comes to expansion. First, with swords. Now, with Gods.'

'Aye, that be right,' Kalyavan drawled from the gallery, smirking as he spun a goblet of wine in his hand. 'These pesky bats seem to be making themselves at home all over the realm, spouting calls for one kingdom under their Twin Gods. And wouldn't you know it, Magadh's already struck a cosy alliance with Hastina's neighbours by tossing around aid in exchange for a few shrines.'

'Quite the scheme they've got going, building their little chain of influence around Hastina, wouldn't you say?' Bhagadatt said, looking doubtful that she could ever return from this thrust.

'I would rather say,' Vahura smiled at the challenge, 'Magadhans may be the only ones in Aryavrat who aren't aggressive any longer.'

A symphony of patronizing chuckles gripped the room at the declaration. The idea that Magadh wasn't aggressive was akin to calling a jadeshark well mannered. Sounds good in poetry, not in practice.

Not unless they had Vahura on their side.

She caught Shalya smile at her as if he knew exactly what she was going to say.

'Yes, there is the Yamuna Wars, but that is being fought for personal rather than imperialistic reasons. Otherwise, the Magadhans are far more peaceful than their Ksharjan counterparts. How come, you may ask? Alright, let's start with the West. Archon Kalyavan, your Greek legions seem to have ambitions to take from Balkh the hamlets around Ice Lake.'

'Stolen from the Greeks a decade ago,' he said offhandedly with a practised nonchalance.

'I will not argue that,' Vahura said. 'Let us say, those regions west of the lake were annexed to Balkh after your predecessors defaulted on their loans. Regardless of whether it was stolen or liquidated, you have to allow that the Greeks want those lands back.'

'Obviously.'

'Even Trigarta would like to wrest from Matsya the territories of Ashadh and Selahilla.'

'In their dreams!' Keechak of Matsya guffawed.

'Most of the villagers there speak our language *Prakrit*,' said the Prince of Trigarta evenly. 'The Matsyas favour *Pali*—'

'And the fertile land near the Dvaita forest, which is full of Pali-speaking people who do not follow the Trigartan customs?'

The Trigartan Prince flushed. 'A strategic requirement.'

'Of course.' Vahura bowed with a smirk, and then turned to Shalya. 'Now, let us consider Hastina. Lord Shalya here wouldn't deny that the Eagle is already extending its wings beyond its borders along the Mai Layas in the North.'

'There is a perfectly good reason for that!' Nakul protested but Lord Shalya spoke over him.

'Those territories lay empty for the Union to claim. It is the Ksharjan way to expand borders, and in this realm of peace, possessing vacant lands offers no violence to the realm's peace especially when the Union offers these lands away as sanctuaries for displaced races. Or have you all forgotten that it was only the Union who took in the Naga refugees?'

'That may be so,' said Vahura. 'But Panchal, too, wants territory in the Mai Layas. So does Videha. And I'm sure, the Hill Kingdoms of Malla and Nepa there wouldn't want their suzerainty threatened by the sudden emergence of such powerful neighbours.'

While Videha, Malla and Nepa rulers were too small to be invited to Hearthside Talks, Prince Dhrishta, the new heir of Panchal after his elder brother was slain in Draupadi's swayamvar, sat stoic on his chair. When Vahura realized Dhrishta was not going to chime in his opinions, she turned to answer on his behalf.

'And I understand Panchal's sentiment – it cannot allow any other great power to dominate the mountainlands. It would give Hastina way too much power, even if they're now related. On the other hand,' Vahura said pointedly, 'all Magadh has fought in the last decade is a war for personal reasons, and has not shown any inclination to expand its borders even by an inch. It is not as if something stopped them. Their army is the largest standing army of the realm. Surely, they could spare a few soldiers to grab a few kingdoms. But still, they didn't. So, who is the more aggressive power of Aryavrat? The Magadhan Empire? Or one of your kingdoms who all covet what your neighbour has?'

The others glanced at each other, nodding, pondering and scratching their chins. She turned to Bhagadatt now, her blue eyes scowling against Bhagadatt's red in a clash of ice against fire. 'The truth is that the Yamuna War will be the last war fought with swords and shields,' she said, raising her glass. 'A new age is upon us, fellow Ksharjans, in which if you desire something from someone, you'll need to lay the path for them to walk over and deliver it to you.'

A silence of murmurs descended on the Ksharjans as Vahura's raised hand remained in the air. A silence shattered by Keechak's booming laugh. 'She has you beat, Tusk!' He gave his bark of laughter. He then devoured another samosa and held out his glass for the servants to refill. 'She has all of us beat! A pleasure to witness, this was! She is right! As long as we Ksharjans keep comparing cocks, no one will have the time to shoot.'

Shalya stood up to give a more polished toast, 'To the Age of Iron Fists in Silken Gloves!'

'Hear! Hear!' the other Ksharjans chimed in to applaud Vahura.

Bhagadatt himself approached Vahura, who was nodding at Shalya. He bowed. With a resigned shrug of the shoulders, Vahura did the same. And then she saw the smile hidden behind the Tusk's feigned frustration. *Damp on your pages!* Her diagnosis of the situation had been off the mark. Had she been baited by Bhagadatt to reveal her mind?

'Now the world will know your shine.' Bhagadatt smiled as he said it, recalling Vahura's words confided to him just a few days prior. She knew it! He had baited her. Again! Once with the disguise of a polite Ranger, and now with the garb of a short-sighted Tusk.

'I trust the Princess can grace me with her presence for evening tea tomorrow. I would like to split a word with you, and seeing your expressions, I gather you have a few choice words for me as well. I have left a message with my aide to stay in touch with your governess on how to find me should you be so inclined. Just one thing...' Baggy hesitated, 'I am fond of how you talk like a book,' saying which he left, leaving Vahura to drown in a deluge of frustration that deceptively felt like a flood of delight.

ADHYAYA III:A

CALM BEFORE THE STORM

A FEW DAYS BEFORE THE BATTLE OF MATHURA

'The hour of departure has arrived, and we go our ways, I to die, and you to live. Which is better God only knows.'
—Socrates

DANTAVAKRA

I

Boots thumped across the deck. Asanka came to stand beside Dantavakra, smelling him. Vauri trailed along, dressed too nicely for the muck that awaited them. All lace and ribbons, perfect as a shop-fresh doll. Dantavakra tucked back a stray curl that had escaped her braid.

'The East, at last,' Asanka said. 'Ready?'

'No.'

Vauri patted his back. 'You will be.'

'Right on, Sister.' Asanka kissed Vauri's hair, and adjusted the flower braid on it.

Dantavakra shuffled through his pockets and handed Asanka a gold sovereign. 'For… everything.'

Asanka pushed his hand away. 'I think I'm goin' to be squattin' my arse here in the East for a while. Don't want no Lions sniffing my trail, if you catch my meaning. And gold got no value in the East. In my journeys, we bought forestborn pigeons for letters aplenty and sold them off to merchants in Bali. So, unless you got a pigeon instead of a cock in your pants, you can keep your gold, city-boy.'

Vauri made a coo-coo pigeon's call, and they all laughed, the high-pitch delighted laughter of children. She then asked to perch on the railing and commanded Dantavakra to describe everything he saw. Before Dantavakra could start, Asanka poked him with her eyeglass.

'Give the lass a good show, won't you?'

He took the eyeglass, smiling, and peered at the horizon, and almost dropped it. *Fuck*. Asanka had not been yanking his chain. How on earth? He held the eyeglass so close to his eyes he was certain he would earn red circles around them. But it still did not change what he saw. The giant forest rode the horizon like the vanguard of an army warning him to turn back. Behind the horizon loomed trees that dwarfed even Virangavat, the colossal trunks standing shoulder to shoulder, like walls holding a secret the sun itself could scarcely pry open. How would he describe this? Would Vauri even believe him? Did he even believe it? How in the world could they not see this all the way from Magadh? It was enormous.

'Fuck...'

'Oi! We don't say that word!' Asanka said, surprising Dantavakra. Since when did Asanka became the gatekeeper of swear words.

Vauri giggled. 'You said *that* word, and now you'll have to drop a pence in the swear jar.'

This ship had a swear jar! They should call it a treasure chest then. When Asanka saw him looking at her quizzically, she crossed her hands. 'Because we love her and want to protect her, and a clueless child is a happy child,' she whispered.

'Tell you what,' Mati came on the other side of Asanka, 'here's fifty. That should cover me till lunch.'

'Are there no farms? My home has so many farms, no forests,' Vauri said.

Hm. That was right. Dantavakra looked again, scanning west to east, but found no evidence of farms. Maybe they too were hidden behind walls of trees.

'The Rakshasas of the East are different, lass,' Mati's voice snapped him to attention. She weaved like a cobra as she moved closer to the railing and feigned an eyeglass out of her two hands. 'They think of farming as eeevil, unnatural, a deed that butchers...' she repeated the word thrice, laughing, 'bucha bucha bucha! Funny word. Cattle buchas forests. So, they're content with the fruit, edible plants and,' Mati burped, flavouring the air around her with spiced rum, 'small poultry animals that make food bearable, you know.'

'That don't need no large expanse of grass,' Asanka added. 'But there are some, the wealthy ones, who import their millets. That is where we came in.'

'I was already explaining, Asanka!'

'My apologies, Captain. Found the rum, did you?'

'Aye, aye. I did.' Mati tried to hold Asanka's shoulder, perhaps forgetting Asanka was a dwarf, and almost stumbled. 'Someone had hidden it. Treason, I say.'

Dantavakra's mood soured as he smelled Mati's breath. She had been poisoning her liver ever since he had widowed her. *Fuck*. That brought that memory again before his eyes, and he had worked so hard to eclipse it. No, no, no.

'Is it really wise for you to drink so much, Princess Mati?'

'Ehm, well yes, there are things inside of me that I need to kill.'

Dantavakra's eyes widened like an owl.

'Not the brat, moron. A bad mood.'

'Mother said rum is the seed that germinates into scarecrows and not plants,' Vauri said.

'Oh, little girl, did she,' Mati burped again, which made him reel back a step, 'speak of how many people are born because of it. A lot more, I daresay.' She drew out her flask and drank down a mouthful. 'Ugh, someone take the lantern off my face.'

''Tis the sun, Captain.'

'Tell it to move, then.' She shielded her face and squinted at the horizon again. 'Beautiful, isn't it? The Wylds of the East. Perfect hiding spots for thezze races. Humans hate nothing more than humidity, and so they kept to their side.' She made a gagging sound.

'It is a... w-wonder how the human race was propagated by women when they suffered so much for propagating it. I feel like those servants melting at the harbour.'

'But who are they?' Dantavakra pointed at the harbour. 'I spied many humans amongst them.'

Mati beckoned Asanka to answer this time.

'They would be waitin' here all the while till their ladies and lords returned from Kamrup. The Grey Skins don't allow lowlanders inside Kamrup, even those of men and women who can afford the toll of this harbour. Not unless they are sanitized and sign declarations.'

'Afford?' Dantavakra squinted his eyes again. 'Afford what?'

Mati laughed. 'I'm a Kalingan but I am better read than you are, Ser..'

Dantavakra reddened. He had read everything a Lord's son needed to read about Pragjyotisha. He might not have enjoyed it but he'd crammed it nonetheless. Ladies of court cannot be wooed by muscles alone, after all. But just because he had not read whatever the Princess had read in some ragtag Acharya's book about a forgotten piece of land didn't mean he wasn't well read. He thought of all of this but in the journey of these thoughts, the time to conjure a comeback had lapsed. So he settled for a grunt instead.

'We are late, I think,' Dantavakra said, changing the subject.

'Gooddd,' Mati said. 'It would have been a chore to explain to each… and every ambassador waiting in the queue why a Kingsguard is there without a King and why I am with child without a Father. Take the airavats and slip away in the quiet. That is all what we are here to do. Savvy?'

Dantavakra shook off the gloom. 'Even then, it would take weeks to go in a cart through… all that mire. If we are that late, won't it make for more trouble?'

'Weeks? Seriously, Ser! What do you think those… those lines, ehm, rails are for?' Mati turned his chin westward and gestured with her pretend-eyeglass to squint at a passage that led between the trees. Asanka handed him the eyeglass again.

'Fu… Yama's horns,' muttered Dantavakra.

'Told you I hadn't been lying,' Asanka said. 'They finished the damn thing last season, thanks to your Emperor fork'n over gold at the Tusk in exchange for his precious airavats.'

The passageway was paved with hard limestone, etched with parallel iron grooves, stretching out in a vast cream-coloured crescent into the grey-green marshland. Three ships flying the airavat banner were pressed against each other on the grooves, head to tail, secured by mighty tethers fastened to the girdle of six airavats. The iron rails of the passageway glinted dully below the ships. His eye couldn't make sense of the scale. Ships treated as if they were naught but sledges to be drawn by airavats.

'The legends were true.'

'The Seventh Wonder in Acharya Nar Ad's List of Wonders,' Asanka said.

It was Vauri who raised her hand this time. 'I know this! The Path of Thanks.'

'Top marks,' Asanka said. 'See, the girl knows of it without even seeing it!'

Fucking hell.

II

For a Curator about to rest his taloned feet on the table, the sight of an imperial ship angling in towards the Airavat's Reach like a weary beast of burden was annoying to say the least. His day of chores at the harbour should have been behind him. The Gilded Table of Giving was over, and the Conclave almost on them. What were they coming here *now* for? He eyed its sailors readying the lines along the portal rail with malice, wondering who was the wretched captain that had delayed the ship so.

He would be answered when the Captain, a wretched pregnant woman, strode down the length of the gangway, followed by an armoured lowlander, a blind red-haired girl, a dwarf and half a dozen aides. The way the Captain weaved to and fro on the gangplank as if she were a cobra about to spit venom left little doubt as to why they were late. The Curator would have proceeded to spirit out a snarled opinion of the drunk lineage of Kalingans to add to his stream of profanities but his attention was sharpened by a shift in seismic energies. He would at once sense there was something fated about the Kalingan and even the armoured lowlander but the details would elude him.

The Shaman in him had often frowned – had been frustrated by the diminishing power of the Earth Elemental in the East. He would complain that all they were good for was riding the damn earthships. But he would have no doubt now that chaos was rolling towards the Tree Cities with the force of a tsunami. He would lament his Tusk's decision to let the foreigners in, knowing he would do nothing to warn him. He could do nothing. All he could do was to complete his duties on the earthship today and sail as far away as possible from the succession of ghastly events that awaited his country.

But these epiphanies would come in a moment.

For now, the damn wraith of guilt hovered over the armoured guard's shoulders again. Though Dantavakra was no longer certain whether it was guilt over having failed Vauri, or the fear of the future masquerading as guilt. For, increasingly, he had been daydreaming, and hopefully not divining, his future. A future where Jarasandh severed his head when he found out that the man he had anointed to protect his son had been the one to break his son's arms and toss him overboard to be eaten alive by sharks.

'What are you overthinking about? Your forehead looks like it is doing yoga. Cease it or your pretty face'll be marred with lines before 'tis time. Not to forget... you are depriving me of the dumb 'ook on your facce as you climb a wonder,' Mati slurred.

'Just...'

'T'll me one thing, Ser. If you had a chance to reverse what you did, would you?'

'No,' Dantavakra said without hesitation.

'There you have it.'

'But do we have to be fugitives, Princess? None from the ship would tell. We can simply claim he fell off into the sea. Or someone else killed him. Can't we just say the Mathurans abducted him the way they had planned to? The Emperor will easily believe it was Krishna who took his last living child as well.'

Mati frowned at the last line but said nothing for a while. 'You can but perhaps if you take the course o'action to its logical conclusion, you'll see the holes in the plan for yourself. Try,' she tapped her finger to the side of her numb head, 'close your eyes and try.'

Dantavakra obeyed, and shuddered. She was right. It was bad enough Mati was drunk but to be drunk and still be wiser than him, did not sit easy with him. The future was plain as day to him. The first thing the Crimson Guard would do was question the crew, a crew which miraculously survived without hurt in a Mathuran attack. Would they survive interrogation? Would he? What if they asked him to recount the deeds under a Vachan? *It is the murder of the Crown Prince: the heir to the Empire. No expense will be spared.* And... what would be his fate even if it was. A Rakhjai who let his future King get abducted, or worse, let him die. He would be worse than an untouchable. The Princess was right. His life was ruined.

Opening his eyes, he nodded at Mati. He did not tell her this but he had decided he would write a letter to the Emperor and Shishupal with his truth, but only once he was safe and sound in the place where Mati planned to take him. He would lie low for however long it took for Shishupal to sort things out with the Emperor. But to endure his exile and to take care of Vauri till she... he needed gold, and for that he needed the Tusk's airavats. He did not tell this to Mati either but he intended only to steal a few. The Emperor needed the beasts for his war and Dantavakra was many things but a traitor he was not. *You weren't a thief before, either.* Couldn't believe he was going to become a thief now. *Definitely a step down from kingslaying.*

He borrowed the bottle from Mati and took a mouthful himself. He might as well break all the rules. When it was finally time to board their designated ship, Mati, Vauri and Dantavakra flashed their Royal Triple Pass and trudged across the plank onto the earthship. As for the rest of the crew, they remained sprawled on the *Gilded Lion* waiting, one imagines, with all the enthusiasm of livestock at a dip, to be scrubbed down. After that, the crew could choose to wait for them to return or use Asuran-drawn carts to take a ride into the nearby Marsh Settlements to earn some trade copper.

Once aboard the earthship, Dantavakra shoved his worries aside and took Vauri on a tour of the deck. Hell, he was standing on a genuine Wonder, and he wasn't about to waste the chance to savour every bloody moment. And it wasn't just the Path of Thanks that deserved awe. No, even the earthship itself was a marvel. And Dantavakra was here, surrounded by wood that did not rot, on his way to a city whose walls lived, to steal giant tusked beasts from a bloodthirsty Rakshasa king. If this was not a heroic adventure, he didn't know what was!

The dark thought that this time he could not flaunt it to his friends swirled in the recesses of his mind. He drowned the thought. He would make new friends. He turned to Vauri, who was asking him one question after another, flushed gold with the excitement of it all, and Dantavakra was reminded of sunlight sliding along the side of a ship. He had already made one friend, hadn't he? And what were his petty troubles compared to this poor girl's suffering? A girl who had barely had time to live and even those precious hours had been filled with pain. The rage returned and brought with it a grin on his face. Mati was right. He had no regrets about breaking his oath to kill Saham Dev. *Fuck the Empire!*

If Vauri could make the most of her time left, he would do the same. He took Vauri to the railing to describe the Path of Thanks in as much detail as he could.

'I still cannot believe this is the Path of Thanks that ships in the East use to move overland across the riverlakes. They never describe it like it deserves to be in the puppet shows.'

'Because they lack belief, Ser,' an Asur said as he approached him from the other side, his face a swirl of terrifying arcane tattoos, like a shattered glass puzzle, that were etched even on his small curving horns. 'Some things, you need to see to believe. Tribes in Mai Layas refuse the idea of an ocean. South of Magadh, there are hamlets who do not believe in snow. Though rowdy bards prefer to call what you see before you the *Path that Sank*.'

'Why?' Vauri asked.

'The *Sank* is a metaphor, little lady. Know the conclusion of the Battle of Thunder, Ser?'

'Who doesn't? The War Mistress and Krishna flew over the armies fighting in the mires and bogs below on the borders to that,' Dantavakra said as he pointed at the Tree City Dome on the horizon, 'and to slay King Narkasur. The arrogant slaver was caught unprepared like a goat on sacrifice day.'

'*His Grace* Narkasur rescued me from a Javan pleasurehouse after torching it and all the overseers inside, and then placed me in the Temple of Ancestors to be initiated as a Curator.'

'I...' Dantavakra wiped the sweat from his brow, 'I...'

'You weren't wrong, however,' the Curator smiled, 'His Grace was indeed caught unawares, yes. But he wasn't unprepared. For some reason, he was always paranoid of ships descending from the clouds and dropping their armies at his doorstep.'

'Daevas?'

'Maybe. On land, the Tree Cities are impregnable owing to the land or lack of it surrounding them. But those same wetlands would have also prevented aid, should an attack come from the skies. So, His Grace built the Path of Thanks that cut across the wetlands and,' he grabbed a map from his waist, unrolling it on the railing, '... allow boats to move overland across the Isthmus of Bora here, Isthmus of Caraga there, and even the narrow strips of land here. A path that would allow the army to bypass the dangerous wetlands safely and swiftly to reach the palace in a jiffy should the need arise. If its construction had been completed by the time of the Battle of Thunder, the history books would be shorter.'

'Safely, perhaps,' Vauri said, 'swiftly, I am not sure. Men pulling the ships still take a long time, no?' Just then Dantavakra realized he had completely forgotten to describe the most important detail about the earthship to her.

'Airavats, not men, rule the Path of Thanks, My Lady,' Dantavakra said, eyes on the largest animals to walk on land pulling the largest ships built by man. In its essence, simple logic. Animals pulling a cart. In its magnificence, Yama's eyeballs dancing on a roast pit!

For the next hour, Dantavakra kept his mouth shut as the Curator spun his tales, his words painting scene after scene, like some master artist brushing life into every stroke, each earthship more magnificent than the last. Vauri did not need to move her blindfold any longer to see the earthship they were on. Even Dantavakra could barely contain himself – this Narka Rath the Curator spoke of, the Royal Earthship, sounded like it was born from the dreams of a thousand madmen. But soon enough, the Curator lost them. His words drifted into the wind as he droned on about the technicalities of Narka Rath – the galley decks fused into each other, the Grey Shamans and their control over Elementals and airavats, how it launched at the first hint of trouble with the Royal Blood and State Treasures from Leafsong to Airavat's Reach. All the intricate details, the brilliant design – none of it mattered anymore. The fool didn't realize that once you shine a light on the gears, you ruin the magic.

By the time the Curator was done, the earthship was secured to the stern of the ship ahead on the rail. Scores of other ropes from the ships ahead were now fastened to the hooks on their ship's bow. Platforms were placed, leading from one deck of the ship to another, allowing a flood of merchants, power brokers, reputed Acharyas and nobles to mingle with each other.

'Stay here, Ser,' the Curator said when ushers requested people on deck to move to the berths below. 'You should experience it on deck on your first time.'

'Experience what?'

'In addition to my duties as Curator, I also serve as this earthship's Shaman,' the Curator said, raising his hands with a flourish. Dantavakra noticed then that every ship tethered to this earthship had its own Shaman, each standing ready. He was just about to whisper a description of the scene to Vauri when the air shimmered, rippling with gusts of wind and a blast of heat, and the ships groaned to life, creaking forward along the rails.

Dantavakra panicked in despair while Vauri squealed in delight. 'What is happening, Danta? Tell me! Tell me!'

'Give your friend some time, My Lady,' the Curator-turned-Shaman remarked with a smile, casting a sympathetic glance at Dantavakra. 'I shan't hold it against you, Ser. I have come here often since I was a child. It's only overwhelming the first six or seven times you see it.'

As the airavats thundered along the track, Dantavakra held on to the railing for dear life. 'I shall have to take you for your word for I do not intend to climb an earthship ever again.'

Somehow the Shaman doubted it.

VAHURA

I

'**D**id you ever hear of such a thing, Ella?'

'I confess that in the circumstances of far more eye-pleasing and courtesy-minding women in the Conclave, his interest in you occasioned me surprise, Princess.'

'I should think it did,' Vahura said. Frowned a moment over what Ella said, and then asked again, 'What does he want from me? I wager he wants a loan from Balkh.'

'Perhaps you may be better suited to marshal your facts *after* you have heard what the Tusk has to say,' Ella said tonelessly.

'Quite right you are, Ella, as always,' Vahura said, and then looked down, 'but I cannot believe you talked me into wearing a boned corset even for tea. I should get a few ribs taken out if this is turning into a regular affair.'

'History shows evidence of many unions between Leeches and Humans.'

'That is not what I meant by affair! And please call him Rakshasa, Ella. Don't be rude.'

Ella shrugged. 'If I may be intrusive, Princess, what be your plan?'

'You're asking me now?' asked Vahura, peering outside the carriage window. 'Just when we're nearly at the doorstep of...' Her gaze fell on multiple barrels, bearing the double-headed eagle, being gingerly rolled down from parked wagons into a nearby shed. Before she could decipher why, Old Ella spoke.

'You will find a way to get him to part with his secrets with that mind of yours,' Ella said as if she were remarking on the weather.

Vahura nodded. In the brief respite she had had when Old Ella was rifling through the wardrobe to pick a corset best suited to asphyxiate her, Vahura had scoured her luggage and her mind palace to find books on negotiations, statecraft and even table manners, to arm herself for the evening that lay ahead. She even managed to sketch a rudimentary flowchart from the political prescriptions she had gleaned from her readings. Step one: Draw him in by asking questions about his life. Step two: Weaken his walls. Step three: Manoeuvre a visit to his treasury. And then what? Step four: Grab the Daevic Scrolls and make a run for it? *Rot! This is the stupidest plan in the world.*

Vahura found her thoughts drifting again to Bhagadatt. What to make of him? First, he rescues her, and then he takes her on long walks where he lies to her about his identity and, when caught, orchestrates a charade in front of an entire Conclave by feigning a debate. She had not liked that one bit in hindsight. Suddenly she found she empathized with the last woman she had offended by faking an orgasm. She could see it was dishonest and... humiliating, but then again if Bhagadatt's intentions had been as honourable as hers had been with her lover, should she still be offended? And it was not as if he had gone easy on her. He had made all the points Vahura might have from the other side. What game was he playing?

'Where exactly did he rescue you when he was pretending to be a Ranger?'

'What?' Vahura sat bolt upright, her mind flooded with carica-tures of two bodies humping on the bed. Oh, all those books she had read in the restricted section had turned her mind into a gutter. *A gutter of grinding bodies.* Stop!

Before Vahura could feign a tale, Ella looked up from knitting her socks. 'I only ask because saviours in shining armour often turn out to be men with an addiction to saving others. So, carve a path for him to trust you, and play the helpless girl, and he would want to save the world for you himself. Ah, his attendants are here to escort you. It is your time to shine, Princess,' Old Ella said, lifting her kerchief to conceal her grin. *Hilarious.* Vahura scowled.

II

Leafsong was a labyrinth of stone passageways and ominous doors darkly illuminated by wall sconces that were placed a little too far apart, leaving shadowy gaps for sentinels to stand guard in. She drank in the cool, dark interiors, feeling more comfortable than she ought to be as she waited outside a door on one of the high floors of the palace. But she need not have worried for she soon lost her composure when Bhagadatt opened the door to his terrace from the other side.

'Welcome to my Garden of Broken Things.'

The sheer beauty of the place gave her a chill, as if she had put a foot through a hidden patch of ice. Vahura quietly hyperventilated, feeling dizzy with delight, as she did her best to commit the museum-in-miniature around her to memory.

A chamber of glass cases like none she had ever witnessed before filled the room like plants in a nursery. While some of the cases had manuscripts displayed open to pages with illustrations on them, the rest exhibited a wild collection of bizarre objects: a set of ancient playing cards, a scarab of emeralds, a luminous finger whose decay had somehow been arrested, a pair of cylindrical dice, a crystal globe with a girl in a saree sculpted inside it, moving, ever moving in a hypnotic dance. There was even a framed footprint-map of Leafsong drawn in stone colour by the hand of a child.

There was no genre of artefacts, no sense to their arrangement, there was no categorization visible much to the horror of the librarian in her but there was one thing the collections of this museum in miniature shared. They were all… imperfect in some way. The emeralds in the scarab were chipped, the fingernail was half removed, the faces on the cards were defaced by red splatter, and the dancing girl's head was crushed from the top. *Ah*. Garden of *Broken* Things. Vahura closed her eyes to let the beauty of that name sink deep within her skin.

The sound of rhythmic scraping tickled her ear, letting her know they were not alone. A lone woman was absorbed in the gruelling process of scraping away centuries of varnish from an old painting. She bowed as Bhagadatt passed her, then returned to the painting without further fanfare. Enamel miniatures of Indra fighting off a winged serpent, of Sita entering a pyre so red it glistened, and of the World-Boar lifting the realm on its tusk were scattered around as paperweights on her table. Vahura choked her curiosity and refrained from glancing down to see precisely which painting she was working on. Personal experience had taught her that lone female wardens of intellectual nooks did not take kindly to being disturbed. Vahura took care to press her feet deeply on the ground to muffle the sound of her sandals. Amidst the scraping and the sandal shuffling, the only other sound in the Garden came from an imposing structure standing nearby. 'What... is this?'

Bhagadatt shrugged. 'My best guess is it is a Daevic Clock.'

'Clock? As in, timekeeper? That... is...' Vahura paused. There was no word to describe what she felt. She had witnessed many clocks, sundials, water clocks, incense clocks in her time but never had she beheld something so complicated and so magnificent. Baggy explained to her how the clock had three hands, perhaps to indicate the categories of time the Daevas used. The hands travelled across the face of the clock much like the shadow on a sundial but, in this case, different objects emerged from its different apertures to signify different times. A perfectly carved water vase from one, and a tiny pyre that actually ignited when it caught the light, emerged from another. A small queen on a birthing bed awaiting life to emerge pushed out from the left, and a colony of bats chasing each other from the right.

Behind the short hand, blue clouds floated across the face of the clock, disappearing when they reached the opposite side. Vahura was taken aback when the clock chimed at the hour of the possum, for then, from the centre of the clock, a woman emerged from a hole. Dressed in a silvery saree, she held a flute to her lips, and a tune played out of her tiny instrument. Accompanying this tune, an opal serpent curled around the rim of the circular face but it stopped midway against the number twelve, as if knocking against an invisible wall, endlessly till the tune ceased and the girl vanished into the clock's dark depths.

'Every sunrise, the gardeners wind the broken serpent back to where it was so that it can resume its endless strife to reach its destination that lies just beyond midnight.'

'How inspiring.'

'Most find the snake's fate sad.'

'On the contrary, when faced with an immovable wall, the snake turns into an unstoppable force. I would still say inspiring.'

'I suppose only *time* will tell.' He smiled at his joke, a coy smile that distracted her. 'I always fancied it as a broken representation of the Elementals. Your optimistic interpretation may just ruin the theme of my garden.'

Vahura stepped closer to the clock, hands behind her to chain the temptation of touching the relic, and answered without turning back. 'Broken in body does not mean broken in spirit. Why are there three hands?'

'I know not but I do know one of them moves an inch every ten years, and the other, every twenty.'

'The legend of realms.' Vahura's eyes brightened. 'There are tales from our lore about multiple realms and of how time moved differently through them.'

'The clockmaker must have been exceptionally skilled if he was recording the passage of time across realms.'

'So are you. That footprint of Leafsong was by your hand, wasn't it?' Vahura said, realizing in hindsight that she had made him almost blush.

'In defence of the hideous drawing, I will claim that it is accurate to a broom cupboard. Come, I have something to show you,' he said, after he was convinced Vahura was not going to leave the clock alone unless prodded.

She turned to find Bhagadatt by a table. He pulled out a shabby journal from the nearest glass case. Carefully placing it on a stone table, he pulled open the book with a pair of tongs with surgical stability. The book was a survivor of an arson. What was not blackened, was inlaid with gold-leaf and on it, hand-drawn with ink that time had eroded, were diagrams, or were they geometric shapes? Whatever they were, they were interspersed with squiggles in an ancient script. Her mind palace lent her no key to the secrets on the page. As every historian could testify, a good memory was about as useful in arithmetic as a glass hammer. But behind the diagrams were sketches of an army of black playing tug of war with an army of white, holding an uroboros instead of a rope, the snake body wrapped around a peak in the centre. 'Churning of the Ocean?'

'Good eye.'

He turned the page, and there was a ring suspended from a thread in between the pages like a makeshift bookmark. With a flourish, he shook out a kerchief with one hand before delicately extracting the ring with the other, placing the ring on his kerchief-covered palm. It was a small thing, the ring. Too small in its radius to fit any man. Engraved on its interior were the words *Aryun Nahath Kiman*. Old Melada, probably from the Second Age. *Only through death, is life imprisoned.*

'You know Melada?'

Vahura nodded, distractedly

'How many languages do you know?' he asked, eyes wide, the red growing in the black.

Vahura understood every language, almost every language, past and present. She could speak in most of them even though some required special piercings of the tongue or arcane equipment. But how many in all? Vahura had lost track of the count but her most humble guess would land her perhaps at seventy. How long to learn them? These days it took her a week at best to master a new one. 'Just a few,' she lied before being drawn like a moth to a flame to another glass case. She had heard of this one. The Rings of Aditi. Were they really as powerful as the Scriptures claimed? *By the Forge! Vahura, focus! The Daevic Scrolls might just be lying around here.*

She wanted to linger before each case, to touch the fabric of the books inside, then perch herself on cold mahogany tables at the side, and read them to find if they were the Daevic Scrolls, or read them even if they weren't. It was a curious thing, but lately, every time she found herself in a world of delicious riches where she would give anything to slow down time, time had a discourteous habit of picking up its pace. For Bhagadatt had already crossed the space, as if the treasures here were commonplace, and was now waiting for her by a pair of large glass doors, thrown open to perhaps the rarest treasure in Kamrup – the view of a sky.

III

The shelves, the corners, the spaces between shelves in the room she had just left had been all packed to the brim with pots of devil's ivy but out here, the terrace was a forest in miniature, ringed by stone walls invisible behind overgrown moss and ivy. Plants spilled over beds and out of pots around her. The beds themselves teemed with blue and white and pink flowers. She longed to close her eyes and breathe in the fragrance of frankincense and myrrh until it erased the scent of her worries but Bhagadatt was already moving.

She followed him up a cobblestone path that snaked through the terrace under a natural hallway of tumbling mahonia bushes whose prickly leaves and dark yellow berries snagged at her hair. She could even hear a fountain bubbling nearby and clamped down on her urge to turn down the now grass-covered path to find it, when she found that her robe was caught by a plant with glossy red leaves and bright green berries. She looked at it for a moment, and then up at Bhagadatt, incredulous. He shrugged.

'I grow a lot of poisons in my garden.' Now that she had noticed it, she could not believe they had not jumped out at her. The entire terrace was a forest of death, with beds overflowing with not just frankincense but belladonna, henbane, vervain, mandrake and other herbs that were perhaps not even catalogued by the Third Order. Even the giant stone urns at the corners of the terrace, full of waxy green leaves and light blue flowers, held oleander, an assassin's favourite in the right doses.

'Perhaps you could put up a warning sign, Tusk.'

'And ruin the fun of discovery for trespassers.'

'Are there any? Trespassers? Given that Your Grace has stationed a small army at every door I passed on my way here, and given how high we are if we have steered clear of the Green Dome, it would take perhaps Elementals to breach your Garden's defences.'

Bhagadatt only smiled at the joke, making Vahura wonder if it was that bad. Why did she have to open her mouth? She was horrid at the small jokes. Couldn't she just ask him? The Daeva Scrolls might just be another museum artefact for him. Though given the broken state of every exhibit in his Garden, Vahura hoped what she was looking for did not make the cut to be placed here. Lost in her thoughts, she had not been noticing where she was walking and she bumped into Bhagadatt, who turned without stepping back to create distance.

'Don't call me Your Grace, Princess,' he said, his breath smelling of cedar... and that smell which only rises after a truly cold snap of weather, early in the morning, an icy fresh smell which freezes everything around you. 'Can we return to Baggy?'

Being so close to Bhagadatt was like a holding a hand to caress a lightning eel. A sharp pulse she'd never had the courage to touch before. Now she yearned to put her hand inside the eel's mouth. *Charming.*

Vahura gulped, hating how her translucent, freckled cheeks coloured so easily. 'Why the fascination with poisonous herbs, B... bbaggy...?'

'Every poisonous plant is a poultice waiting to be discovered,' he said as he kneeled near a bed, deftly parting the leaves of the herb and attending to them with a pair of creaky shears he had picked from the side.

He sat back on his heels and wrapped a thread around a broken branch, the delicate way in which he was holding back the leaves at severe odds with the rest of him. It was the first time Vahura noticed the way his arms were sinewy without being too muscular. 'Here.' He offered her a pink-coloured flower from the branch. Before he could explain, Vahura had already rubbed the herbs between her fingers before dotting the oils on her neck.

'I appreciate it, Baggy, for the mosquitoes of your kingdom take hosting rather seriously.'

'The depth of your knowledge fascinates me,' he said as he rose, 'but it yet remains to be seen whether *you* are just a poison or a poultice waiting to be discovered, Princess. Come. Let us talk more by the edge there. It is a rare rainless night, and I have heard the views are best appreciated from the eyes of a tourist.'

The remark about poison had not gone unnoticed. It had been rude. She steeled her gaze, and decided to return his gesture in kind. 'And what would we talk about? Surely you have a list of topics at your disposal should you need to feign another debate.'

Guilt flickered on his face momentarily. 'I realize in hindsight my actions were... unwarranted. I just...' he uncharacteristically gulped and then said, 'I don't like it when prejudice doesn't realize that what it treats as weeds to be removed are instead wildflowers that help trees make fruit.'

For once, Vahura did not need to pinch herself. 'Weeds aren't bad, you know, for without them we would not have had mangoes.'

Bhagadatt's eyes brightened, turning to a vibrant red from the dusky rust they had been a moment before. *Forge it! He makes it difficult to want to destroy him.* She decided to not bleed him with her jabs. 'After you?'

IV

With night fast approaching, the entire terrace, which was neatly inlaid with jade tile, glowed faintly underfoot. There were mandala patterns strewn throughout the terrace which would be almost invisible under the sun but left little to doubt of their existence under the moonlight. She examined the carvings on the floor and the vines twining between the cracks in the floor but her gaze kept returning to Bhagadatt. Her attempt at stealth was ruined when he repeatedly caught her eyes with his own.

'Finally, moonlight.' Bhagadatt looked up at the sky, and beckoned her to the second floor of his Garden of Broken Things. She climbed a wide staircase that was cut into the rock and wound its way up to the second floor, spiralling along the curve of the peak. By now the moon, amused at the disappearance of her cloudy captors, refused to stop smiling on their path. Vahura had to occasionally step over slithering, leafy shapes that hung down from above, which she realized later were the dangling vines of the Garden, swaying in the winter wind. She tugged at one and found it to be as sturdy as a climbing rope.

'To give thieves a fighting chance,' Bhagadatt jested as they crested the top. 'And while I do not believe in them, I enjoy it when I interpret omens to suit what I want to do. The clouds clearing on the night of the Conclave might bode well for the realm but I would rather it meant the clouds clearing as a sign of truth and transparency.' He wasn't looking at her as he said it but Vahura felt something crawl on her skin. He then turned to her. 'You've perhaps had the privilege of seeing the horizon shrink inside a mariner's eyeglass.'

Vahura nodded, distracted by the sudden swerve in the conversation.

Bhagadatt gestured to the wooden scaffold that sat atop a round dais. Small wheels under the dais allowed it to rotate atop a track. Under the scaffold was a brass contraption that stood on an ornate rune-inscribed three-legged stand at the edge of the balcony. A pulley system lay suspended from the wooden scaffold that could control the angle of the massive brass tube. 'What if I were to tell you that, forget the horizon, you can now shrink the heavens itself? May I present the lightcatcher?'

'No...' Vahura saw the shape of the device, saw the optics at the end of the tube and saw the direction where it faced, and she knew instantly what the lightcatcher did. Without waiting for Bhagadatt's permission, she perched on her knees to peer through one end.

'Oh. Oh, what in the what? What...? My heart hurts.' Vahura gasped as she slowly withdrew herself from the eyeglass. 'The stars... are not all white. Son. Of. A. Motherless Hamster!'

Bhagadatt laughed and borrowed the lightcatcher to see what Vahura was looking at, smiling as his eyes squinted through the glass. He made a few adjustments on the screws of the brass tube and shifted it a fraction. 'Here, see this.' He handed it back to Vahura. 'That is Shurpanakha's star, and the white spiral band behind her, those are her people as they fled Lanka to come to the basilisk-infested rain-wylds that would one day become the Tree Cities of the East.'

'I had heard of the legendary tale in which she led many great ships crammed with Nagas, Rakshasas, Asuras and even Giants, all old, women or children, after the… genocide.'

'I must confess I am surprised you know of it. Didn't the Seven burn every book chronicling the history of the Rakshasas after the Fall of Lanka? What do you know of her? Tell me more. I want to know how the Meru presents her.'

The pages of *The Other Aryavrat: Speech from a Radical Princess* flipped open and she quoted the passage verbatim.

'She is a hero, a hero of the Other Races, of those pushed outside, those who have grey skins, who have wings, or horns, or glimmering scales, or long tails, of all those who drink blood to survive, of all those forged in the crucibles of differences. But her successive generations have been forged in the crucible of hate, not differences, of disdain, not fear. The East now practises what it abhorred: exclusion.'

She passed spit around her tongue to moisten it before she continued.

'Just see the way the humans are treated around there, their existence tainted under the shadow of memories thousands of years ago. Is that fair? Do we grudge them for eating us in the past? They distrust our traders, they send away our priests. They do not understand that the simplest cure to old wounds is a welcome carpet. So, it is up to the East to entertain or to exclude. But I do say this, dear readers. Builders of walls are usually imprisoned by them.'

Vahura stopped short with a nagging feeling she had over-quoted. Surely she could have omitted the sick nonsense about blood drinking and human eating.

'*Dear readers?*' Bhagadatt smirked. 'Your memory is remarkable,' he laughed as he said it, 'but I love the way you quote *everything*.'

Vahura crossed her hands in dramatic childish fashion.

Bhagadatt raised his hands in mock surrender. 'A fine strategy, of course. Nothing gets lost in translation in this manner. By the way, the author isn't entirely wrong.'

'Is that why you went to Panchal, Your Grace? To break down these walls?'

'Perhaps,' Bhagadatt said. 'I know not for what I went. I just know what I discovered. The world on the other side of Ganga is splitting at the seams, and no talk is going to change that. The only reason these high lords and ladies have come here is to open trade channels with the East after Mathura's fall but from what I have heard so far, they will sit, and listen, and nod. Scatter a little trail of hopes that free trade will flow soon and they will allow Eastlander merchants in, right up until their own merchants appear outside the walls of Kamrup with their wares and dump their goods on us. Well, they are in for acute disappointment.'

That was not far from the truth of why Balkh had sent its own emissaries to Kamrup. But Vahura did not want Bhagadatt angry. She needed to make him at ease. 'Why haven't we in the West heard of this contraption? This could change the way we think of the heavens. You could dangle it before them like a carrot and then see if anyone dares to dump their goods into the Tree Cities.'

'A lightcatcher is a torch in truth. The masters that be do not enjoy casting light on the void.' There was a creak in the lightcatcher and Vahura almost jumped back, hoping she had not sent civilization centuries behind because of her clumsy hands.

'Fret not, Princess. The brass tube often misbehaves. Let me take care of that.' He took off his jacket and rolled up his sleeves again but here the mothlamps were more in number so she could see him better. His arms were muscled for a king, and from behind, a few locks of his hair, wet with mist, lay plastered to his neck in oddly satisfying whorls, leaving horns gleaming sinfully in the moonlight. Seeing him so felt... intimate and illegal.

'I hope you enjoyed the view.'

'What – no – how dare—' The view. He meant the lightcatcher, of course. 'Oh, yes. Splendid. Stars, of course. A sequin glint of white on black velvet.' *Bravo, Vahura.*

'*Sequin glint on Black Velvet.* Isn't that how Acharya Nar Ad described his hairfrost in the *Seven Wonders?*'

Vahura looked down sheepishly. 'Guilty.'

'I found it to be an excellent metaphor.' He flashed that half-smirk grin again, and Vahura's heart lurched in response. *What the demons is wrong with me?* 'As to your question, it is not the traders that worry me. How do you think the Seven are going to treat a lightcatcher that gifts the smallfolk with the ability to see the stars better than their priests?'

'Assassinations, burning and lynching, aye,' Vahura sighed.

'The Seven aren't against alchemy as long as it furthers the fire of their ethos, and not extinguishes it. The lightcatcher is yet to reveal something that could further their cause. I'm trying but the cosmos is a safe with its key locked inside.'

Vahura nodded. 'If I may, how does it work?'

'Earth alchemy. By now you know the Grey Shamans are attuned with the Earth Elemental. None of those mythical earth-quake-inducing powers, of course.' Vahura had a sense he meant nonsensical when he said mythical. If he did not believe the myths, maybe it would be easier for him to part with the Scrolls, no? 'They found vast mines of vaikunshards in the swamps. As vaikunshards can't be cut or shaped, no one has ever found a piece small enough for an eyeglass but our miners chanced upon a perfect circular piece of the vaikunshard.'

Uh, what? 'A perfect shape? That is—'

'Unheard of, I know. It was the shape of the vaikunshard that gave me the idea of a lightcatcher, and as you know, vaikunshards trap light in a way we haven't understood but just marvelled at. We have long suspected the ethereal sapphire glow in the vaikunshard at twilight is trapped light, and using designs left behind in draw-ings of Daevas on ruins, our Shamans created this lightcatcher to destroy the distance between the eye and the heavens.'

'I know you do not worship Him, but Tvastr bless you,' Vahura chirped. 'Oh, I do want to see the moon and finally see if there indeed is a rabbit lurking there. May I?'

Bhagadatt laughed, making her stomach lurch. 'Do let me know of your findings, Princess.'

'But a moment, ugh, my unruly mop…' Vahura took out a band from her satchel and began to tie her hair back to corral her curls from annoying her eye. From the corner of her eye, she could see Bhagadatt's gaze lock on her, his mouth slightly parted, his red eyes slightly widened. It took her more than a moment to understand why. Oh. Uh. Tying her hair into a ponytail. Yes, she remembered. Men found it rather alluring, didn't they? It did make her breasts look better she supposed. Was this the time she teased him or should she try something else, given how she was out of knots to pull her hair into, and probably nobody found tying the drawstring of a skirt alluring. *I'm so bad at this.* She remembered Old Ella's advice – ask him something about his interests, stoke his fire.

'But Kamrup is perhaps the wettest place on earth with a sky that sees the clouds more often than the sun. Forgive me for saying so, but despite the height of Leafsong, it still isn't a suitable place to build a lightcatcher to see the stars.' *Wonderful job, Vahura. The award for the greatest flirt in the world goes to you. Arjun should come and learn from me!*

Bhagadatt's face held a smile that she somehow knew hid wounds. 'The lightcatcher wasn't built to spy on stars but the foe.'

Wha— I, oh, Embers! A sudden flood of history caught her unawares, drowning her eyes in horror. Turning to the horizon, she found herself swept away by a moving mural painted by her own imagination – of Krishna and Satyabhama flying over the swamps on their griffin, over the Everwoods, right over Leafsong, under the cover of a thunderstorm – Narkasur realizing that the tiniest army in the realm had tricked him, and recognizing that Satyabhama was better with a sword than he was. Surrender had flowed, as inevitable as a flood, especially when Narkasur had found Krishna caressing the hair of little Bhagadatt.

But there are no pacts between giants and ants. Narkasur would've known that there was no scenario in which Satyabhama could have let him go, for the ant can trick the giant by sneaking into his ear but just the one time. It had to either eat through its brain or face a good squishing when it crawled out. She wondered if Bhagadatt had seen Satyabhama decapitate his father in that duel. Rumours did claim that the darkness of that night never left his heart, and while he did not sully his tribute to Mathura in the years to come, he did close the borders of the Free City, earning the name of Bhagadatt the Brooding. Even her brother had spoken of how the Rakshasa was a joyless man who seldom smiled, who did not hawk or hunt or joust, but here he was, showing her the wonders of heavens, a smile of a boy on his lips that she had snatched away with her question. Stupid Vahura!

'The memory haunts me, Princess, but it is a nightmare I have grown familiar with. Familiarity dulls the poison...'

'... but it still corrodes,' Vahura said, knowing how it was to want to go back to a time before it was too late. After all, she had seen her own mother claw her eyes out. Some things you can't be cheered out of.

Bhagadatt blinked at her, and a little of the wounded look left his eyes. Vahura felt an irrational urge to put her arms around him, and that was absurdly stupid of her. He certainly wouldn't want her sympathy and who was she to comfort him? Just then tiny blue flashes zigzagged, leaving trails of sapphire dust around them as the night grew darker. Moonflies, illuminating their conversation, with the magic of earth she could almost touch.

'I'm certain the Curators have told you how Father always believed an assault would descend from the skies,' Bhagadatt said. 'Devoted a tidy sum shoring up his defences against the Daevas. In fact, right there under that golden canopy covered under the red-blue tarp is a relic of Ravan, a windkeeper that doesn't work, another beautiful broken thing in this garden.'

Vahura's heart skipped a beat. A real windkeeper! But no. She couldn't ask to see it now. Bhagadatt was talking about Daevas. This was it! She had to wait for the right time to ask.

'Father had commissioned artificers from around the realm to coax it to fly, and when they failed, he tossed them over the terrace but his will to make it work never waned, for his paranoia of the heavens never ceased. Strange how his fears of the sky manifested in a way he could've never fathomed. It is why I commissioned this lightcatcher to be built here, on the very spot my father breathed his last. Even the railing here is unchanged, weakened by the taloned grip of the griffin, a reminder of no matter how strong the airavats are, they can't fly.' Vahura suddenly felt very uncomfortable about her feet on top of a spot he no doubt considered sacred. 'He isn't buried here, Princess,' Bhagadatt laughed lightly, seeing Vahura's expression, 'I wanted something more than a statue to serve as a memorial, and this,' he traced the gilded surface of the brass tube, 'is special, but also—'

'Functional.'

'Yes. I want to protect my people by building a future rather than by brooding over the past. In my solitude, I spend my time here weighing the forlorn rays of dead stars with my eye on the river of moons in the sky and my mind's eye on the events of the realm. And I could not help but notice that the stars have deviated from their courses. This happened right after I returned from the Panchalan Swayamvar. I have an orrery in my study, an iron model of the planets that displays their current positions in the sky. The lapis and steel spheres in the orrery had moved to positions that are at odds with what the simplest of astrologers could plainly see even with their naked eye. The forces of chaos reign supreme now beyond our borders, be it the Yamuna Wars, the Hastina Civil War or even the rise of Unni Ehtral – which makes me believe we might be at the cusp of a change. Good change, bad change, I know not.'

'It is how we respond to change that determines the nature of the change,' Vahura said. *No. No! Keep on track, Vahura.* Politics was not the way for her to win what she sought. *Compliment him,* she remembered. But on astrology? Vahura felt like a fraud but she went on nonetheless. 'You know, Old Ella did wonder why you would host the Conclave after moonrise, knowing how the Riverlanders obsess over the holiness of ceremonies under the sun. Now I know. Astronomers, like poetesses, musicians and fireflies, work best after hours.'

'As do, thieves, death-priestesses and librarians.'

Vahura felt her compliment haemorrhage.

V

They were now close enough to touch though he kept his hands clasped behind his back. 'I noticed something about you. Each of the artefacts you paused before, each of the treasures that made your eyes twinkle, everything was related to the Children of Light. The Daevas seem to have made a settlement in your mind. A distraction no doubt, Princess?'

'A girl needs to keep busy with the fantastical to bear the fanatical.'

'Ah, another quote from Asshaye's *The Princess*.' Bhagadatt smiled, widely. 'I can only assume that the most wanted band of rogues must have had rather critical information about spices, considering the hours you spent with them.'

'Asshaye wrote *The Princess*!' she gasped, realizing too late she had given herself away.

As if reading her thoughts, he turned to her, his posture rigid and constrained. 'I have always known of the Rose Coterie, Princess. But I thought it best to let them be. Imprisoning them will only lead them to stage another successful escape, and I do not wish for my prisons to earn that reputation.' His words sounded so well-mannered, so polite, so soft.

'I'm afraid Your Grace has lost me, or confused me for someone else,' Vahura said.

Bhagadatt suddenly stiffened, warmth vanishing from his manner. 'I must apologize for causing you discomfort earlier with the sordid tale of my father. But I wanted you to understand my seriousness when I request you, while standing over this very spot, to tell me why you are chasing after the Children of Light in *my* city.'

And all at one she realized she had flown too close to the sun. The cloak of softness she had imagined around him melted away. It wasn't she who had come here to seduce knowledge out of him. It was the other way around.

'My father was disturbed but his paranoia of the Daevas was not unfounded. So, let me rephrase my question to incentivize a true answer. What would you say if I were to toss you over the railing,' he said as he took a step closer to block her way, 'and hold you by your index finger till you answer my questions truly?' asked Bhagadatt conversationally.

Vahura pinched her wrists to keep panic away, blinking at him. 'Err, "Please don't," probably. "Ow," most likely. Definitely, "Stop, stop, I have a fear of heights," something along those lines?' *How do I answer this?* she complained.

Despite her entire plan unravelling, Bhagadatt laughed. 'You... are funny, Princess!'

Vahura was unsure as to how to respond, backing away. 'Erm, thank you, I reckon.'

Once Bhagadatt stopped laughing, he confessed, 'I am terrible at threats, aren't I? Sokarro warned me against trying to look danger-ous. Apologies, Princess,' Bhagadatt said, the laugh reducing to a smile. 'Let me try honesty instead, and perhaps what better way to do it than with a story, given how many we have shared already. I hope you will indulge me.'

Rules of courtesy and fear of loss of life left little choice in the matter. Vahura nodded.

'Decades ago, long before my father became king, the Tribes of Kinnaras had returned with the carcasses of five airavats who had made a sport of chasing, raping and murdering rhinos. They had raped and murdered hordes of rhinos before the Kinnara hunters caught up with them. The Kinnara Chief had reached them just as one of the airavats had trampled a child to the ground with his leg while another had sodomized a horse with its tusk. The grey robe he wore today is of the cured hide of the same airavats.'

Vahura gasped. Airavats raping rhinos was a violent thought to even consider. Hordes of them! She crossed her heart. 'So the grey robe was a victory token.'

'Not a token. A reminder of their duty to protect the airavats. You see, each of the five members of the gang was a youngling. Just imagine. One of the most peaceful beasts of our time, and their younglings had committed crimes that had shocked our conscience.'

'I do not understand... why would they?'

'The airavats, like elephants, have always lived in a matriarchal society like the Manipuris. The younglings learn their good manners and embrace fraternity in societal rings of caregivers, birth mother, grandmothers, aunts, friends, bonds that usually lasted a lifetime. A young airavat, unless orphaned and unlike us, stays within fifteen feet of its mother for the first eight years of its life. And even if orphaned, its circle grieves the loss and mourns the departed ritually. The matrons of the airavat herd hold weeklong vigils by the corpse, shading it with leaves and grinding their trunks along the teeth of the dead, a gesture of greeting amongst the living.'

'That is… beautiful.'

'Aye, it is. But those were dark times, times of greed, when humans had crossed the eastern borders and murdered, mutilated and poached an entire generation of older airavats who would have blessed upon their children the familial traits required to handle fifty thousand pounds of power. Power which, if untamed, can wreak havoc. Which is what happened with that gang of airavats then.'

He continued. 'Rakshasas you see in the Tree Cities are these youngling airavats. There is arcana in us that make us stronger, more powerful than we understand, and worse than the humans understand. We are all each fifty pounds of bone and muscle forged in the anguish and wrath of our ancestors. Having lived in these swamplands we understood at heavy cost that innocent-looking humans often turn out to be poachers. And in a world of such a lost generation, a murderous airavat is born, which in the case of Rakshasas, was my father. He had no elders, no matrons to consult, no Acharya to teach him to bear pain, no matriarchs to twist his ear when he overreached, or show off their own long lives lived peacefully and lived well. His older generation died out of persecution: poached for their grey skin, hunted for sport or packed off on slave ships to the Golden Islands, and that is if they were lucky enough to be halfbreeds.'

Fear pounded in her ears, drums in the dark as Bhagadatt continued.

'The lost generation of Rakshasas left behind only the angry who sought to use the fragile shards of their identity to punish and retaliate against those who had ostracized them. Do not get me wrong. I am not justifying what my father did but I am justifying his fears. We can never know whether the ones who come to our lands to learn our secrets have come to preserve or to poach. The

Yoginis are under my protection, and they did not let you in without my consent. I have tracked your every movement ever since you stepped in the East illegally. I was the one who detained the Iron Order knights who were after you. So, knowing all this, I hope you can tell me: what is a princess, who has escaped her home with a dangerous governess, doing hunting for the forbidden? In the time I have spent with you, I know...' He took a step towards her.

Alarmed, Vahura ripped the poisoned pin that Old Ella always stitched to the folds of her dress in preparation for unsolicited adventures. 'Now listen, Your Grace. Back away.' But the pin, with a mind of its own, stumbled out of her hand, bounced on her palm once on the safe end, and then dived into her cleavage. She tried to reach it with a finger, leaning back on the railing that was there one moment, and not the next. A sound of wood cracking. The suddenness of waking up from a dream assaulted her. Her thoughts raced through her mind palace but it could not find a book that taught her how to stop gravity in its tracks.

Her world shifted slowly in her head, the gardens of poison shifting into the garden of stars, till a pair of red eyes swam into view. She had never seen anyone move so fast, though given her state, her perception of distance and time was not reliable.

Bhagadatt dived, grabbing her wrist and yanking it behind him. Vahura felt her arm shake out of her socket but the force was enough for her to find purchase on the balcony edge and stumble forward, only to fall face first on the balcony floor. *Ow!* She realized belatedly she had bruised her left breast. How? *I will kill you, Ella!* Her left tit was out and she had no idea how to return it to its holder. The poisoned pin rolled on the floor guiltily. Covering her breast with one hand, she rose to her knee. 'Your Grace, don't look! I am not in a fit state to negotiate. I urgently need the assistance of a handmaiden! We can discuss—'

The scenes of her rescue took the form of a play she had forgotten to appreciate the first time. The force taken to pull her must have required an equal and opposite reaction. Her fingers started trembling as she watched it again in her head. Shivering, she turned back and took unsteady steps to the edge of the balcony. *Please, no. Please, please. Just this one time, please. Tvastr, I will do anything you demand.* She peered over the balcony to find that unfortunately Tvastr wasn't interested in anything she had to offer. The body of Bhagadatt lay amongst a pile of sharp rocks below. She had pushed the Tusk of Kamrup below to his death.

VI

Vahura turned to see whether anyone had heard the sound but no guards came in to arrest her. No one shrieked below. What had she done? Damn this cursed balcony! What should she do? Should she run? Run where? The Tree Cities were a thousand leagues away from Balkh. She could run to the Rose Coterie for help. Would they help her? They were all thieves, not murderers. But surely they would understand. Or maybe they were in Bhagadatt's pocket like the Yoginis! No, he did not mention that. So, no.

And then what? She would run away? What of her quest for which she had sacrificed everything? No. There was no turning back. Sobbing back a sniff, she pinched the underside of her arm so hard she knew it bruised purple. 'Alright, perhaps Bhagadatt seemed to know a lot about me, and if he knew I was after the Daevas, he might have known what I was after.' Could she be so lucky? Could he be carrying the damn Daevic Scrolls on his self?

Only one way to find out.

She looked around helplessly, then saw the vines hanging below from the gardens. She had been a good climber. Staring down at her corset, she sighed. *After murder, public indecency seems a trifle.* Her fingers looped beneath the laces of her corset and pulled them through the hooks, one after another, and at last the corset fell. Air gushed into her lungs. Borrowing the jacket Bhagadatt had hung over a hook on the wooden scaffold, she walked to the nearest vine and tugged at it. Strong. Good. She looked down. The ladder led all the way down to the rocks. Fortunately, the cliffside was jagged, so he hadn't fallen all the way to the bottom.

She slowly turned over the railing, one hand at the vine. Her long skirt almost came below her feet. She took a deep breath and started climbing down. It would be rather comical if some guard saw a half-naked ghostly figure climb down and shot her with an arrow. The errant thought did nothing to calm her. She was sweating profusely even in the cold but she continued climbing down without looking. The vine swayed with her weight left and right, but Vahura closed her eyes and continued climbing down. No thoughts. One step at a time. Down. Down. Another. Down. After a long while, there were no more steps to climb down. She opened her eyes and saw the broken balcony far above her. She gulped, tears in her eyes. She willed herself up again.

A boot gazed out from behind the rocks. *Remember your purpose.* Chanting a prayer, she trudged closer and then started crying when she saw how his broken leg was stretched out across a rock, bent horribly. His head lay over another rock, limp and lifeless.

'I am sorry!' she sobbed. 'All I needed was to borrow the Daevic Scrolls. Why did you have to ambush me? Why did you have to save me? Why? I am sorry, Baggy! Sorry for pushing you down the hill. I didn't mean it! I just wanted to save...! To find a cure! I am not a murderer!' She touched his forehead and made the sign of Life on it. 'May the Forge temper your Soul on the Afterpath.' Her crying became hysterical as she looked at the dead Rakshasa again. *I have ruined everything, Mother.*

And then Bhagadatt's limp leg moved. The knee bone slid back into the thigh, making a sickening crunchy sound as it mended itself. His bent spine cracked, and with a loud sound, straightened out. The gash on his neck sealed shut as though he had never crashed into the sharp rock in the first place. His nose snapped back to its former glory. And just like that, Bhagadatt sprang to life, standing tall on his feet to look at Vahura with his usual wry grin that set her heart beating fast enough to outrun an earthship for all the wrong reasons.

'That was rude,' Bhagadatt said.

The attitude of princesses towards finding a mangled corpse healing itself varies. Most fancy it. Many might even worship it and herald the coming of a Prophet. A very few don't. Vahura didn't. She drew herself up at a dramatic, slow pace and stabbed him with a glance of pure horror. Absolutely wasted, of course, given how she was silhouetted against the moon.

Decapitation rituals. A skull that was alive. Fugitive of the Iron Order. Humping against a stranger. Wearing a corset. Debating politics at the Conclave. Multi-coloured stars. Pushing the Tusk off to his death. Climbing down a vine in a jacket with her breasts hanging loose and bare. As far as productivity went, this week had been as fertile as a turtle. But her mind drew the line at the dead returning to the land of the living.

Vahura, despite her aversion to clichés, fell unconscious. Understandable. After all, how often do you see the king you murdered rise to chastise you on your manners?

MATI

I

Mati had never been on an earthship with open windows. Their current conveyance was the oldest incarnation of the earthship, reserved for the poor, available at the port only because the grander earthships were already in Kamrup. She did not mind. Her freshly cropped hair – a return from being a damsel in distress to a damsel in finesse – had reunited her nape with the wind, and she did not mind the occasional reminder, especially in the land of humidity. As Mati gazed out at the menagerie of marshes unfolding beyond the open window, she clasped firm Vauri's pale hand which shifted weightlessly on Mati's own as she slept, her head resting on Mati's shoulder.

Mati settled in for a long, comfortable journey that would hopefully lure the baby inside her into a long sleep like the girl next to her. But sleep eluded the mother herself. And in this lull of the journey with no commanding and captaining to do, she found herself looking inside. Bad idea. Those who look outside, dream; those who look inside, awaken, and what she awakened to was a nightmare. The fingertips of her free hand brushed against the ends of her hair again as if to confirm her shackles were indeed sheared.

Now liberated, Mati could not understand how had she worn the shackles in the first place. Perhaps what they said about the Daevas applied squarely to Saham Dev as well. Darkness never lured. It is the stars they need to fear.

Maybe this was why Mati never saw Saham Dev for what he was.

Their first night together had left its phantoms behind. Saham had been hard as a rock but then he had kissed her, and then he had recoiled as if Mati's breath stank, which was impossible because Mati always chewed fennel seeds right before a planned kiss. But Saham Dev's face had twisted with disgust all the same, a face that turned into Duryodhan's in her head. Saham Dev had then turned Mati on her front violently, pushing her face into a pillow with his right hand as he finished on her back with the other, leaving Mati too surprised to turn and stab him to death. And that had been the first mistake. Forgiving him.

Again, it wasn't as if Mati did not find subjugation in bed thrilling but Saham Dev had not been interested in subjugation but in making her feel self-conscious. He humiliated her and not in an enjoyable way.

Mati had chuckled then as she turned from the pillow. Discarded by Duryodhan because she wasn't wife enough. Shelved by Saham Dev because she had pretended to be too much of a wife.

She had soon discovered the source of Saham Dev's mood swings. Since he could not turn hard for her on the bed, he became hard on her. Understandable. Love without value was impotent in the case of Duryodhan, as love with impotence had no value in the case of Saham Dev. If only she could have explained to him that diligence more than depth make a woman moaneth. Instead, Mati had cut off the source of Saham Dev's helplessness by not seeking to consummate her marriage again. Saham Dev had grown happier then, lavishing her with gifts and servants.

But, as she soon discovered, even if the world considers you a legend amongst stars, it doesn't mean you cannot be made to feel as common as dirt. Mati had initially found Saham Dev's relentless drive to mould her into 'queen material' charming. It was rare to find someone so invested in your betterment, someone devoted to witness the best version of you. So, she had swallowed her murderous impulses when he used to lock her in a luxurious study, forcing her to digest ten chapters of a book before she could eat dinner, or when he summoned renowned artists to explain to her the nuances in famous works. After all, she had to wait just till she birthed Duryodhan's spawn, or if his seed failed to take root within her, then some other man's with the same hue as Duryodhan (like Saham Dev). Once her child was secured as the Empire's heir apparent, she would smother Saham Dev in his sleep. But, over time, she strangely began looking forward to when she answered Saham Dev's quiz satisfactorily, for he used to reward her with treasures that in her past she would've led an entire pirate raid to steal.

To be fair, I did try to kill him once before. The first time Saham had his Rakhjai slap her for eating a ram's leg with her hand, Mati introduced a poison seed into his night milk. But, come the evening, she learned Saham had ordered his Rakhjai to gouge the eyes of a street artist who had scaled the tower on a dare to peek at Mati in her bathing tub. The subsequent day witnessed a wholescale relocation of every man in his palace, their positions assumed by eunuchs under Saham's decree. This public exhibition of the lunatic's possessiveness did something no amount of ale had achieved in the last few weeks. It made her smile, genuinely so, pleased at the violence of it all, violence for her sake.

She had settled for feeding the poisoned milk to Saham Dev's cat instead, and convinced herself it was revenge enough, and in that deception lay her downfall. By letting the first moment of defiance slip from her hands, she spent the rest of her months testing the threshold of her self-control. When a punishment should have included decapitation, she settled for a thousand cuts, tearing his favourite books, public insults or killing his Rakhjais, little acts of declaration that only granted Saham Dev the leash the same way wardens ignoring prison riots from time to time does – *Enough!*

This was a pointless exercise. Saham Dev's machinations were gossamer strands spanning months of their married life, a deadly web, a skein tethered to a thousand little acts of manipulation. And in this odyssey of abuse, he had turned her into the unsuspecting crab who realized too late that the water around her in the pot had soared beyond boiling point.

Charred and burned beyond recognition the crab may be, it had scuttled out of the cooking pot before the end. And now this self-same crab would ride on the back of tusked giants by stealing the airavats meant to be supplied to the Emperor of Magadh for his last onslaught on Mathura. How was that for a feat of resurrection? Unfortunately for Mati, someone else had the same idea first.

II

The first view she got of Myra was her prodigious backside. It was wide enough to disappear into permanently. Stippled with coarse, reddish hair, Myra's ruddy brown skin had the texture of pebbled granite. Others were arrayed around her formidable rump as well. Mati could not resist, so she reached over and gave her rump a rub. She had been warned against doing it but given how her life tenure was significantly shortened by Bhagadatt's revelation, she might as well dance on the edge. Completely worth it!

'What do you mean the airavats have already been collected?' Dantavakra asked, meeting the required quota for panic and chaos all by his lonesome.

Bhagadatt stood calmly, as a polar counter to Dantavakra, pulling a glove that stretched over his left forearm, past the elbow, almost to his shoulders. Three mahouts wrapped the airavat's tail in what looked like a jute wrap and held it off to the side. One mahout grabbed a pail and stood beside the mouth of Myra who herself was lying on her side. Mati could not see what was happening there but she could hear Myra chomping away at whatever she was being fed. While Myra was thus distracted, Bhagadatt delicately inserted his arm into the airavat's anus.

'Sanskrit isn't my first language, Ser, so I'm afraid I do not know how to make it clearer.' Bhagadatt dug his hand deeper into her rectum. 'The airavats have been collected.'

As though in response, her baby stretched, pushing hard with a knee or an elbow perhaps, almost eliciting an entirely non-maternal comment from Mati's lips.

'How can the Empire collect the airavats when we ourselves are the Empire come here to collect?' Dantavakra waved the useless piece of paper again. 'This bears the authority of Emperor Jarasandh to collect the shipment.' When Bhagadatt just twisted his arm inside the airavat in response, Dantavakra continued his mindless tirade. 'How could you hand it to someone else? How about you be a man of your word and hand us our shipment!'

'How about I crush your skull between a finger and thumb,' Sokarro said, 'and then I push your carcass down the Kalingan's throat, so she can defecate her baby and your pompous self at the same time as conjoined twins.'

Mati chuckled. She still found Sokarro's face beautiful – even if marred by a botched-up job of burning her nose and cutting off her ears. When she had spied Sokarro waiting beside Bhagadatt, she had been glad to have a familiar face around. However, the manner in which Sokarro had crushed Mati's hand in a feigned handshake had made her wonder if she still nursed old wounds. Sokarro's eloquent diplomatic skills on display here only con-firmed it.

'Why don't you try, Rakshashi?' Dantavakra's hand went to his pommel.

By this point, Bhagadatt's entire arm had disappeared inside the airavat. 'Myra is pregnant,' he announced but everyone drew gasps of shock. 'Twenty-two months in the Seed Pod for the mahout.' He softly took his arm out and settled his red gaze upon Dantavakra, who withered in the Rakshasa's attention. It was evident to even the dolt that Bhagadatt was in a sour mood. Luck had abandoned them for good.

Bhagadatt wiped the palm of his glove on Dantavakra's armoured plate. The Rakhjai, stunned into silence, settled for a scowl. The Rakshasa had just started his threat with a 'Ser—' when...

'You!' A hooded woman barged into the stable, ignoring the reception of raised spears. She was a striking tall thing, face full of freckles. A satchel hung across her shoulders. She narrowed her eyes at her audience till they rested on Bhagadatt. 'May I have a word with you, Tusk,' she hissed her request through gritted teeth.

'Have her taken away,' Sokarro announced to the guards, who did not need telling twice, 'and have the guards outside the door whipped in the barracks.'

Eyes widening, the hooded woman screamed. *'Where is your wrath, for now my land is overcome, bent and in beloved Lanka's soot skies, lately the banner of evil flies—'* One of the guard's hands clasped shut on her mouth before she could complete *Shurpanakha's Lament*. They dragged her outside the door while Bhagadatt just watched, looking torn.

The Lament was one of betrayal. Imagine that – *seems like the Tusk had a jilted human lover.* Bhagadatt had rebuked Mati's advances so strongly the last time she was here, she was sure he did not partake of humans.

'I must confess I am growing sick of Princesses,' Sokarro announced.

Bhagadatt was evidently unnerved. The horror he was about to inflict on Dantavakra would have to wait. 'Perhaps this conversation can be continued on a fuller stomach and between the representatives, given how the Crown Prince is not present, and you are representing him. I will let Lady Sokarro make the arrangements. I am afraid I have to leave. Princess.' He bowed at Mati, and ignored Dantavakra as he turned to his attendants.

'Ah, a drink to relive old times then, Lady Sokarro,' Mati said.

'Drink with the Black Swan, it's said, and you wake up on a riverbed. Drowning brings out an unhealthy pallor on my skin.'

'Just rumours, Sinh. Dinner, then?'

Sokarro scowled while the Tusk finished changing into a fresh shirt. He turned to the mahouts. 'Kill Myra. I will send the seeds.'

Dantavakra exchanged a frightened, clueless look with Mati. Mati, herself, stopped petting the airavat so sentenced. 'Honoured Tusk,' she said. No longer flexible enough to twist, she turned around to face his retreating figure. 'Could you at least tell us who tricked you into handing over the Magadhan shipment?'

'Say *tricked* again, you pregnant hamster!' Sokarro Sinh jerked her steel nose at her.

But Bhagadatt paused at the stable door, mulling her words. 'The Archon of the Yavanas,' he said, without turning back. 'Kalyavan.'

III

'I do apologize for my manners, Lady Sokarro,' Dantavakra said as he devoured the food on his plate. 'My guts have undergone trials I do not wish on my worst enemy.'

'Think nothing of it,' said Sokarro. 'Courtesies were never meant to be performed on a starving stomach. Let me call for reinforcements.'

In moments, the surviving sugar globes found support from strawberries coated in looping patterns of honey. Dantavakra looked at Sokarro as if he had fallen in love with her. He wouldn't have been the first on the table.

The server then glanced down at Mati's still-full glass with a searching look. Mati made a face. She hated goat milk, and she was tired of puking. And goat milk in the East was as strong as ale. She could already see in the server's eyes that he was going to say it was good for the baby. *Maybe, but I am the one who has to drink it.* The server instead simply shrugged and left without a word as if he knew Mati would make the right call.

Storms! She hated that assumption that she was responsible enough to do the right thing. Picking up the clay cup, she frowned, and then swallowed it as swiftly as she could.

'You better appreciate this, baby,' Sokarro spoke to her stomach even as Mati's body shuddered at the aftertaste. 'Your mother wouldn't do this for anyone else. Not a sacrificial bone in her.'

Well, she wasn't wrong. 'Sok, it would not bode well for the relations with the Empire to renege on your promises. You know of it, don't you?'

'The East will be in trouble. What is new in that?'

'It is unlike you to permit such a thing without any scroll from the Emperor.'

'Your suggestion that in case of redbloods, we should rather wait for a piece of paper or a raven than trust the general of your army, especially when no one turns up from the Empire's side, confounds me.'

'Envelopes are more trustworthy than people. Sealed ones, at least. This cannot be the first time you have learned of how red-bloods cheat.'

Sokarro was slapped, and the table was lulled to a silence splin-tered only by loud sounds of chewing. It was risky but there was no point in sheathing the knife when you have spent time forging it in the fires of your former lover's insecurities. It would be a shame if she did not put her lessons learned from Saham Dev to use.

'*You* left me,' Sokarro said.

Finally. 'I made no promises to stay.'

Dantavakra heard them both this time. A brief battle of wills raged before his eyes but his stomach won over his manners. He mildly pushed his chair back as if to give the two of them space and returned to his plate.

'I hunted you till the borders.'

'Is that when you were caught?' Mati pointed to her steel nose.

'Poached seems more appropriate than caught.'

'It is an improvement on your looks.'

'You are a tapeworm that lives off its hosts.'

'Got one of my own.' Mati pointed at her burgeoning belly.

'Heartburn?'

'So bad I turn blue. Screaming pains in the hip and butt. Nosebleeds every time I sniffle.'

'The circles under your eyes are an improvement.'

'Why, thank you, I hadn't noticed.'

'Karma.'

'Karma,' she agreed.

'Why did the Prince not come for the Conclave?'

'The Prince is dead. Killed for sodomizing a little girl.' Mati paused. 'Girls,' she corrected.

Dantavakra shifted tables this time, momentarily returning to take the spare plate from the table to his own. Sokarro tapped her knuckles. 'Is that the same girl in your accommodations?'

Mati nodded.

'I will ensure no one disturbs her, and send for a box of our choicest delicacies come morrow.' She paused. 'Your race needs to be exterminated.'

'Agreed.'

Sokarro sighed and settled on her chair, and Mati knew she had won. 'Kalyavan and Bhagadatt joined the Yamuna Wars together.

Kalyavan had fostered a good friendship with him since the Yellow Wedding. So, when no one from Magadh showed up—'

'Kalyavan took advantage of your hospitality, and you had no reason to doubt him.'

'The airavats we lent to the Empire…' Sokarro started before correcting herself, 'to the Archon, were terminally ill airavats, an illness that causes them to be infertile. Strong. Deadly. Most importantly, sick so that none could breed them.'

'Like Myra?'

Sokarro shook her head. 'That was different. The mahout sentenced to the Seed Pod was a drunkard. When he was out in a tavern, his airavat stumbled outside her stable, and she was found impregnated by an elephant. The elephant had been crushed by her weight.'

'A sentence of death for her indiscretion still seems harsh.'

'It was not a sentence but an act of mercy. A halfbreed foetus in an airavat does not eat food the way your bastard does. Being smaller than an airavat foetus, it slips out while still being tied to the cord and eats the organs of the mother airavat instead. Slowly. Steadily. Never too fast to kill the mother. Twenty months of unbearable pain. The airavat mother holds her screams back for she knows she will be put out of her misery, and its calf will die.'

'That makes no sense and does not sound believable at all…' Mati said nonchalantly, wondering if she could ever bear so much pain for her child, and was surprised her *no* was not as enthusiastic as she'd expected.

'Twins are often known to eat each other in men. The Nagas sting men, paralyzing them, and lay their eggs in their bellies for the larva to burrow into the man's insides, feeding on its organs in a specific order to keep the host alive until the larva is ready to pupate. Nature is beautiful, and like all beautiful things in the world, cruel.'

'What happens to the halfbreed if you let the mother live?'

'A halfbreed weaned on cannibalism. Can you imagine if these giant beasts ate meat? Or ate each other? The forests would not have survived.'

'What about castrated males?'

'Can't castrate – elephants and airavats have no scrotums – their testes are lodged deep inside the body.'

'And that is why you cannot reimburse us the airavats, for you have no sick ones left. Shame.'

'If I were you,' Sokarro said, 'I would be worried about why Kalyavan scooped the airavats out before your Emperor could.'

Mati shrugged. 'Maybe Krishna seduced him.'

'I hope you aren't right. It would prolong the War by ten years.' Sokarro stretched her leg under the table to lean against the table. 'Fie on years! I can't wait to get this month behind me. I am tired of redbloods and redheads.'

Mati raised an eyebrow at the last word. 'That girl who barged in? Jilted lover?'

'None of your business.' Sokarro straightened, realising she had slipped. 'The Conclave is two days later, after which the first Earthship leaves for the shore, and with it will leave your entire race from the East. In that time, might I suggest, given your condition, you rest so that even if you return to Magadh without a face, at least you have a stomach to show for it.' She stared at the space below Mati's breasts. Something Mati still had not grown used to.

'Maybe we can get reacquainted in that time,' Mati suggested.

Sokarro rose, a wry smile on her face. 'Even in this state?'

'Always.'

'Filthy Mati as always.' Sokarro smiled as she left, but Mati held her hand. She rose as if to whisper in her ear – ear whispers – the secret kingdom of women guarded by the cups of her hands around it. Nothing out of the ordinary. Only Mati plunged her tongue deep into Sokarro's ear. It was cold, at first, then very warm and very wet. Sokarro stiffened against her touch. She did not budge but her chin angled away from her, letting her ear press deep against Mati's lips. Her tongue traced circles, rough and urgent. Sokarro seized her wrists and let out a nervous laugh, whispering, 'Whoever's willing to fuck you is just too lazy to touch herself,' but Mati could see her ears. The grey had darkened so much it was as if Mati's tongue had flayed them.

'If not an airavat, maybe you can conjure one of these Curators for me?'

Sokarro nodded numbly, before turning away to leave.

'The ear-kiss trick.' Dantavakra smiled when Mati settled back on her chair. 'Often have they coaxed open closed doors. If done right, of course. So... will she hide us here till eternity?'

Mati cut him off. 'We are heading on a guided tour of the City.'

'Why?'

'Not sure.'

'Why didn't you just give that Rakshasan Relic?' Dantavakra said. 'That might have earned us goodwill.'

'If things come to bolt, we will sell that key. Might earn us a few months of luxury before the noose comes calling.'

'You are smiling.' Dantavakra stiffened. 'Your smile reminds me of a senior sapper I knew.'

'And?'

'He blew up his entire squad while juggling Mathuran munitions.'

The baby stirred inside her as though it was just waking. She smiled and traced the motion with her fingertips. 'I think the baby enjoyed that imagery.'

IV

High above the bustling Canopy Market, a shutter cracked open in the trunk of a massive tree, and out flew a wicker basket, arcing down towards the throng below. The basket spasmed on its rope, shuddering as it skimmed against the rough bark, shedding bits of moss and debris in its wake. It danced a precarious descent till the Curator, a leathery old Asur with one eye squinted against the glare, glanced up. He wiped the leaves from his brow, muttering a curse, then caught the basket with a deft snatch. Inside were special nectar cakes. He scooped the cakes, pocketed the change, and tugged thrice on the rope. The basket wobbled and then began its climb, bouncing along as it rose higher, the rope creaking with each sway. It startled a cluster of perched skylashes, sending them squawking into the air, and carved a zigzagging line up the ancient trunk until it vanished once more into the hidden window above.

'Where was I? Yes, ingenuity of our ancestors. The Elder Races had built ley lines, or what the Acharyas of Meru call the Godstrings. Streams of Elemental energies holding what is left of the world together after the Last Shattering. Poems that survive the Age of Satthhya speak of worlds hidden in these Godstrings, a port city between two islands...'

'Aren't Elementals extinct?' Dantavakra said as he took a squelchy bite out of nectar cake.

'Not at all,' the Curator said with his mouth full, 'for without them, we could cease to exist. No, what is extinct is our ability to tap into them for power. Elementals very much exist, as do the Godstrings. Our lore speaks of as many as fifteen Godstrings, each formed between two poles of power on earth, each devoted an Elemental. And while we cannot use them to abuse its power, we still unconsciously rely on them for our world.'

Mati wanted to slap the two men walking ahead of her. Had they forgotten that she was walking for two? But the silver lining of being slow was that Mati did not have to mum astonishment from time to time to keep the Curator busy. She had not been interested the first time the Acharak had brayed on about this, and she was not intrigued now.

'But you said Kamrup is built on a Godstring?' Dantavakra asked, mouth full.

The Curator grinned, excited at escorting an interested patron. They were the best tippers. 'Ser, we do not know where exactly the Eastern ley line is but what we do know is that the Godstring of Earth cuts through our wetlands with one of its poles hidden somewhere in Kamrup. The Godstring was discovered when the Marshmen Tribes saw that the rare plants, the ones used to brew potent alchemical herbs, grow alongside a definite pattern. Earthquakes and floods never seemed to touch the area around this line – all theories, of course, for the map of Godstrings did not survive the First Age.'

Mati needed a break, loath as she was to admit it. She disguised her need in the wrapping of a question, 'And so, you built the Path of Thanks along... this ley line?'

'Excellent, Princess,' the Curator paused to answer Mati. 'The earth energies on the Godstrings are more accessible to the Grey Shamans, who sense it to keep our shipways tethered, and our ships running on land. The Tusk believes that the Path of Thanks will one day outshine the Uttarapath, uniting the Tree Cities in a way that even His Grace Narkasur could not have dreamed of.' The Curator fidgeted around with his bag, and after finding what he was looking for, offered it to Mati. 'It will help with the walk, Princess.'

So much for the deception. Mati took the handful of coca leaves along with what the locals called laija - a sweet mixture of ash and flavour. Within moments of chewing it, her lips grew numb but her aches began to fade.

'That... is miraculous,' Dantavakra said. Mati nodded in agreement, nipping at the leaves ravenously though Dantavakra was talking about something else entirely. 'If there are two poles to each Godstring, and one of them is in Kamrup. The other is...?' Dantavakra trailed at the end of his question, brow raised, waiting for the Curator to fill in the blanks.

The Curator adjusted his optics. 'The delegation from Meru who had visited a decade ago returned with findings that the Godstring disappears after the seacoast. Does it curve along the coastline or does it head over into the Kalingan Sea? Our sailors have brought no welcome tidings in their search. Personally, I think it ends in the Three Eyes of Elusa.'

They soon reached the water-sodden, twisting streets of Hallow Marsh, the intellectual quarter of the Tree City of Kamrup. She could hear birds calling, but only rarely could she spot them. It was difficult to see the fauna behind the flora.

'Princess, I know you told me you seek to meet Princess Vahura...'

'That is the red woman with the freckles, isn't it?'

'Yes, the one and only. How is that you know her, again?'

'We grew side by side,' Mati said.

'Ah, and you branched apart in your older years with distance. Do you seek now to discover if your roots are still tangled? I must confess she is already quite popular in Kamrup.'

'Popular?' Mati asked.

'Infamous.' He leaned closer as if the three were long lost friends. 'It is rumoured that the Angrakshaks of the Iron Order sought an audience with the Princess of Balkh and, in return, the Tusk gave them the old kick-in-the-arse from his lands. They also whisper that Princess Vahura slapped the Tusk in the Day of the Feast in front of all the dignitaries. Or else how do you explain the Princess being shifted from her accommodations in Leafsong the very next day to Hallow Marsh? It's a ripe peach of scandal, and I am itching to sink my teeth into it. The East, alas, is a peaceful place, and peace often means boredom.'

'Relish it, friend,' Dantavakra said. The Curator smiled and nodded. Even in the East, the customer was always right.

But what he said was turning out to be interesting. The Iron Order sought an audience with this Princess, and the Tusk had the gall to banish them. But then the Princess and the Tusk had their own drama, which ended with the redhead reciting the *Lament of Shurpanakha*. The Curator was right. Their troubles aside, this had all the makings of a fine yarn of salacious.

'Ah, we are here, Princess and Ser,' the Curator said as Mati leaned her pack against the corner of a building, glad of the chance to rest. She spied the tower: a small, stubby one. An odd mist drifted lazily out of its chimney.

'Those are her new quarters up by the seventh branch – they are numbered. And between those two trees, that is the botanists' library where she spends most of her hours.'

'You have our gratitude, Curator,' Dantavakra said.

The Curator tried again to gain more coin from Mati. 'May I suggest a jaunt on the Floating Gardens to rekindle old friendships. I can as easily orchestrate a guided trip for three—'

'That will be all.' Mati raised her hand, unable to believe her eyes, as she stared at the window of the library, chewing her lips in some chagrin. She knew it! She fucking knew it!

'Oh, oh, of course,' the Curator said. 'I must say it was a sheer pleasure to be a guide to such distinguished guests.'

Mati wondered if the Curator's smile would disappear if he were to know he was serenading an oathsworn kingslayer and an immoral pirate who were hiding a girl ill with the Marigold Mold. Perhaps not. Her geniality waned and she drew herself up coldly, flicking a pouch of spice at him. The Curator weighed the pouch in his hands, bowed, and disappeared into the streets.

'Princess,' Dantavakra asked, 'why are we looking for this woman?'

Mati nipped at the leaves as she yanked Dantavakra by his arm sleeve and turned his chin rudely towards the library. Dantavakra dropped his pot, which shattered into pieces.

'Is it?' Dantavakra asked. 'It is her, isn't it? Yama's horns! Just, what? Fuck!'

'While you fumble about searching for words to compliment my sheer genius, I'm going to go find a privy inside and then we go meet her. And don't—' A sudden cramp threw Mati's head back as she slammed her open fist onto Dantavakra's shoulder. 'Fuck!'

'Princess! Are you alright? Oh God! Is it the baby?' She swatted at his hands trying to help her until he caught her wrists. 'Princess, take a deep breath and tell me what is wrong.' There was a tone of command in his voice she had never heard before. Mati tried to speak but her breath was caught on another cramp, and then, something that could have been predicted by the most useless of oracles happened – she started weeping.

'I'm taking you to a healer.'

'No. Just… let me sleep here.' She wiped her nose on her sleeve. 'Perhaps not in the middle of the street, though.'

Dantavakra slipped his arms around her and tenderly drew her close into the embrace of his arms. 'Rest, then. This Vahura can wait. We come here tomorrow.' After a moment, Mati felt her head lolling in the air as he lifted her up, and then grudgingly, she let her head nestle against the curve of his shoulder. She squeezed at his shirt when a third cramp twisted the muscles of her lower back, completely oblivious to the dusky old woman who had been staring at them from the corner of a shop, a malevolent grin writ large on her wrinkled face.

VAHURA

I

Vahura was wide awake before dawn but she remained abed at her desk, staring at the window framed by devil's ivy, watching the light creep between the curtains, oblivious to the thin, wet trail left by her drool on her journal. *I need to stop passing out at my table if I expect to stand upright after a decade.* There wouldn't be a decade to look forward to if she failed. Vahura begged the critical voice inside her to stop badgering her. She was trying, wasn't she? But how do you open a box which has no latch?

Vahura once more buried her face in the journal, pulling higher the blanket around her shoulder (no doubt left by Ella) as she read about Rakshasa morphology. Tried to read – for her thoughts were elsewhere. Why wouldn't Bhagadatt even speak to her? The other morning the errant thought that she'd loosed wind before Bhagadatt when she had swooned at finding him breathing or that he had found her repulsively vulgar when he found her crying next to his dead-not-so-dead body with her breasts out, had her burn her tea in the kettle. There were probably thirteen hundred possible ways Vahura could have mired her chances yet it still did not explain why he had not even granted her an audience since that night. It was as if… he was afraid of her. She was the one who should have been scared of him, not the other way around. For a person who death could not kiss, the Rakshasa had turned incredibly shy.

Of one thing she was certain, however. Bhagadatt had clearly devoured the Daevic Scrolls to usurp their secrets! How else does one resurrect these days? He wasn't a Chiranjeevi – they could be killed, and they did not return from death. The cure to Marigold Mold had to be tucked away in those Scrolls, and this had made her spirits soar higher than a kite in a gale.

Maybe there was a cunning way to sway him, to find his desire, to use some loophole to bypass whatever bound him to hiding the Daevic Scrolls. And if not some way, then someone... But what on earth could one use to entice an immortal? She supposed if he had spared her life for killing him, he couldn't be completely... wicked. Maybe she could trust him with the truth. Or maybe he had left her alive because he thought no one would believe the ramblings of a silly old woman in her twenties spurned by every suitor in the shire.

While she strained to force her mind to come up with a key, the lock on the house's door clicked open, and – *screech* and *thud*. She bolted upright to find a knight sprawled in a heap on the floor. The bucket, once poised to deliver a swift drenching to any intruder, now hung limply from its makeshift perch. At the sight of mailed armour, her first thought was the Iron Order had tracked her down. However, as the knight muttered curses at someone named Shishupal, Vahura saw it was the same knight who she had seen in Bhagadatt's stable.

'Tvastr on toast! What are you doing in my room? My brother's due back from the store any time now! So you'd best scarper!'

'Impossible as it may seem, I think I'm growing rather fatigued of the fairer sex!' he muttered, rising and dabbing the water off his face. He frowned at the dangling bucket. 'Your nanny told me to enter. Come to think of it, she was not keen on being called nanny.'

Vahura backed to the corner, her journal raised with the menace of a mass-murdering weapon, as a dusky woman entered behind the knight, and *she* looked dangerous. The way she was draped in black from head to toe – tunics, breeches, and a flowing, mantle-like coat – she deserved the title of Mistress of Ravens far more than Matrika Zubeia. But it was her hair that seized Vahura's attention and did not let go: cut short, and let loose over a wind-whipped face, a red scarf hanging in folds around her neck; the dusky woman was what Vahura would have submitted as her entry to a Bandit Painting Contest. Only later did Vahura note the swollen stomach hiding behind her coat. *Remarkable. A pregnant Bandit.* The bandit passed the knight with a disappointed look on her face.

'You truly make it difficult to stop underestimating you, Ser,' the bandit woman bit out.

'Says the woman dressed as if she goes to the park to punch pigeons,' he retorted, and turned to Vahura. 'You think a bit of water bucket will keep a Rakshasa from coming for you?' Vahura's blood went cold. How did he know?

'Worked on you, didn't it?'

'I like a woman with a sharp tongue,' the bandit woman said.

'Good to know,' Vahura said, pinching herself as her heart finally calmed. 'Mind your next words carefully if you don't want to get cut by it.'

The woman smiled suggestively. 'And what makes you think I would not like that?'

Vahura flushed crimson. 'Your Tusk assured me sanctuary here.' He had given no such assurance but she hoped he would still stand by it.

The woman strode over to the curtains and flung them wide, revealing a sky that was still a deep periwinkle, splashed with hues of pumpkin from the rising dawn. 'I bring a proposal for you that can help all of us, Princess.'

Vahura opened her mouth to speak but Old Ella entered, a breakfast tray in hand. She bid the uninvited guests a curt glance, set the tray on a small table by the window. 'I see you have finally risen, Princess. Need I remind you how our scriptures insist we spring from slumber an hour and thirty-six minutes before sunrise to keep the mind sharp. Saving the world is no excuse for being tardy in habits.'

'Ella!' Vahura said, exasperated. 'Forget the hour! Who are they?'

'I have been led to believe their intentions align with yours,' Old Ella said, pouring her a cup. 'Might I advise a sip of tea to steady your wits for the next part.'

'How can you put faith in the word of strangers? You don't even trust me on your good days.'

Ella coughed politely, a whip in the world of governesses, reminding Vahura to temper her voice and drink the tea. Vahura gritted her teeth and, sitting on the bed's edge, took a big sip. Calmness, if not clarity, found her. 'Now will you answer me, Ella.'

'They presented a convincing case,' Ella said, with the slightest of smiles tugging at her lips.

'Vahura,' a voice squeaked, and Vahura froze, her fingers on her locket. Her entire being shuddered under the weight of the memories the voice brought on her in a landslide, making her realize how one could be homesick for a person, too. For a change, there was no deluge of thoughts, no pinching, no panic. Just... the magic she felt in her bones.

She turned with hope, she turned with despair, and saw the straight nose she'd inherited from their mother that crinkled with laughter at jokes. Her soft mouth that made funny faces whenever she sang. Her red hair that was still neatly braided, just the way Vahura had taught her. Her clothes were neatly pressed, and neat was the blindfold around her eyes that held back the deadliest disease in the realm.

'Vauri...' Vahura said, hoping her sister could hear her heart.

II

Vahura had been always been careful as a child. Her mother never had to run after her. Rather, she kept her mother company, watching as she hoarded books from the library in her room or commissioned painters to draw Daevic relics based on bardic poems. Even when not shadowing her mother, Vahura spent her time helping her grandfather add quotes from Manu's Codes to his decrees. Even if her favourite moments were those stolen in solitude, reading her mother's books late into the night till dawnlight flickered like a restless robin on her wall, Vahura stayed in clear view of everyone, a beacon of manners. Not Vauri.

Vauri was always disappearing, hiding behind pillars or in antique rooms. She hid compulsively, under the bed, behind the shrubs and over armoured statues. She played this game without announcing it, on her own, sneaking into her hidden corners, forcing their mother, when she called and Vauri did not answer, to cease reading. Their mother never got irked; rather, she humoured her and looked for her, calling her name. Vahura, being the elder, had often wondered if her reserved nature had caused her family to be less fond of her. Because her family never had to worry about Vahura causing them problems and yet, she knew, they did not favour her. Her duty was to impress her parents with her obedience while Vauri's duty was to surprise them with her transgressions.

Perhaps it had been one such transgression that led her to where she should not have gone and to catch the marigold in her eye or was it, as her father suspected, Vauri tussling with the thief over her mother's dark secret leading to the accident? Vahura did not know for sure. No one did. Vahura had only discovered her mother's dying body, her eyes pierced by her own hand, her last act to put the alchemical blindfold around Vauri's eyes as she became sick herself, and her last words, to task Vahura with saving her sister. Her mother did not even get to tell Vahura how she knew how to save Vauri or... that she loved Vahura.

But Vahura had no time to mourn, for in the corner of the room, she had to save Vauri. Why else had Vahura travelled to the end of the world, spent her inheritance, had a Balkhan envoy abducted, lied to the Rose Coterie and pushed a Tusk to his death?

Vahura leaped awkwardly on the floor, and took her sister in a mighty embrace, smothering her cheeks and forehead with kisses, not caring for one bit how Vauri had escaped their father's prison.

'By the Forge! Sister, stop!' Vauri tried pushing her away, but not too strongly. 'You're embarrassing me before my friends.'

Vahura stopped, turning to the knight and the bandit. 'Friends?'

III

Vauri and the knight called Dantavakra were playing the Flying Carpet. They had climbed onto the divan and sat side by side. 'Where shall we dine tonight, young Nar Ad?'

Vauri chirped, 'Jungles! The Burnt Lakes of Lanka! No, the Arena of Magadh! I can't decide!'

'Then allow me,' Dantavakra said in an accent, smooth and velvety, a local Curator's drawl. 'That's the Kalingan Sea far below, shining under the moonlight. Can you hear the sound of krakens? Feel the wind in your hair?'

Vauri nodded excitedly. 'Where are we now, Pathfinder?'

'We're in the forests of Magadh. Can't you tell? There are sandal-wood trees over there. Smell them?' And Vauri inhaled deeply the rich, woody fragrance, whether because Dantavakra was discreetly passing sandalwood shavings beneath her blindfold, or because they truly were soaring over the sandalwood groves of Magadh, Vahura found it impossible to decide.

The cast on Vahura's face deepened through shades of despair as she grew acquainted with Vauri's biography from the time she was abducted from Balkh by the Twins to how her new friends found Vahura because of the red hair and how similar the sisters looked, even though Vauri and Vahura could never agree on that observation. Dantavakra had hesitated when Mati had insisted on being honest in the retelling, and Vahura had learned through soft whispers of how the depravity of humankind knew no bounds. The tale of malevolence took a bit out of her spirit. *My poor sister... I could have stopped this, I...* The poetries of helplessness inside her were not made for parchment to handle... She pulled the blanket now around her chest, and painted her wrists a beautiful red with her nails to silence her pain. This was the only way she could keep sane, but the Kalingan held her hand firmly.

'Don't,' Mati said. 'If you're feeling blue, cope with red. Red wine,' Mati added when she saw Vahura's wrist.

Vahura slipped back her tears, confused. 'Don't *what?*'

'Don't weaken your sails against the storm. Think Vauri a victim, and her ship sinks. Think of her as someone who refuses to be a victim, thank your Gods for her courage and gift her the present of treating her like a warrior.'

Vahura looked into Mati's bluish grey eyes. 'How... how do I do that?'

'By choosing to laugh with her, instead of weeping for her.'

Vahura felt Vauri's finger on her cheeks, melting the icicles of pain away.

'So, let me unknot this,' Mati said, perhaps in a bid to change the current of the conversation. 'You came here and told the Rose Coterie there was a threat – that someone was going to unleash the Marigold Mold in Balkh, and you needed a shield against the storm. You conveniently *forgot* to mention to them that your sister was that storm.'

Vahura nodded sheepishly. 'Or else I'd have been up the creek without a paddle. Marigolds are cut off, never contained. No one would've helped save Vauri if they had known she carried the plague. My own father did not. They would sooner pluck her eyes out and burn her.'

'But then those priests abducted her and brought her all the way here to the East, presumably, to unleash her in the Conclave.'

'Come, Vauri,' Dantavakra interjected, giving Mati a stern eye as he took Vauri's hand and guided her into the other room. Once they had left, Vahura nodded slowly.

Mati chuckled. 'Some twisted God wrote this reunion.'

'Listen, Princess Mati, I owe you my thanks for what you have done for my sister,' Vahura said, glancing into the room where the knight was playing a silly child's game with Vauri. 'I thank both of you.'

'Kalingans don't do charity, Red.'

'Old Ella told me. Thank you, then, for not holding her hostage to shake the gold off me, not that I have any left.'

'Count yourself lucky then that your unpaid governess ran into us and drew an unkind picture of your finances.'

'So…' Vahura said, 'now you seek to join hands in helping me.'

'I could have simply asked you to do it yourself while we held your sister captive but, thing is, I have taken a liking to the little clownfish. Blame it on my plague.' She pointed at her stomach. 'So, I'll lend a hand and make sure you don't botch the job. You repay the debt by handing over the Daevic Scrolls, after you are done saving her, of course, and we are good.'

'What will you do with them?'

'Lease them to the highest bidder.'

'The Empire running short on gold?'

'Punishing the man who wronged your sister has pushed the two of us out of prospects of a long life. Gold is the only magic that can renew the lease on it. Two broke Princesses and one sad excuse for a knight on a quest. Imagine that.'

'Pardon the rain, but how will we do that? Ella must have told you the Tusk has refused me, and Sokarro has asked me to leave on the Earthship after the Conclave. Vauri doesn't have a lot of time left though I can only guess. Another turn of the moon perhaps...'

'We will have to steal the Scrolls before we leave, then,' Mati said. 'You are the key, Red. From what I saw of the Rakshasa in the stable, he seems to have taken a shine to you. Maybe we hold you hostage and ransom the Scrolls out of the Tusk.'

'Sparks! That is such a... a...' Vahura did not know why was she smiling. The Kalingan was clearly mistaken. Shine, it seems. 'You do talk tripe sometimes, Princess.'

'Tell that to your cheeks, love,' Mati said, smirking as she leaned back on her sofa. 'But don't go swimming in the sea where you're soon going to piss. Remember Vauri.'

Vahura steeled. 'That lyrical metaphor aside, I think you are wrong. The Tusk has been kind to me. Past tense. It hardly amounts to whatever you are insinuating. And even if it were to be true, which it isn't, how would it help us? I did ask him for the Scrolls after... well, after we met, and he refused – he even taunted me by claiming that the Scrolls are on his bedside table for nightime reading. Jeering is hardly the way to start a courtship, no matter which part of the world.'

'It is called teasing. A man playfully pulls your leg with his japes to show you he is interested in courting you by challenging you instead of flattering you. See, I don't know what you mean to him. I just know you're his weakness, right now. He was left quite disturbed when you were so unceremoniously escorted out of the stable.'

The butterflies in her stomach went on a rampage. Vahura shot them down, 'So what do you propose?'

'I am good at robbing,' Mati said, 'not stealing.'

'Aren't they the same thing?'

'Stealing requires a plan. Robbing requires a sword. Honestly, Flames, I thought you would be the one to come up with the idea.

You managed a trek across the breadth of the known world. Your sister could not stop chirping about how intelligent you are, and considering your stakes are dug far deeper than mine, surely that skull of yours can come up with an idea.'

'Ehm,' Vahura said, eyes fluttering as she turned the pages of the books in her mind palace. If only she had a working windkeeper at her disposal, she thought on the side. Maybe they could have soared over Leafsong like Krishna had all those years ago, then slipped through the gardens, past the guards, rummaged through all his rooms and lockers, unearthed the Daevic Scrolls, and made their unnoticed escape the same way they came. Even as she thought of the plan, her heart sank at how impossible it all sounded even if they had a windkeeper, which they didn't, and even if the windkeeper could fly, which it didn't. 'I have read about the botched heist of the Talisman of Tahar in Sindh, I have studied the foiled robbery of Kosala's Crown Jewels. Then there was that detailed report of an attempt to steal the Chalice of Chitragupt two summers ago.'

'Did you happen to read about any *successful* expedition?' Mati asked.

'I did,' Vahura said. 'The ones by the Rose Coterie. They describe any such undertaking as a web of lies but... it needs a Spider to weave it. A crewmaster. A planner.'

'So, open that book in your mind, and see what you need to do to be a Spider.'

'How... how do you know about my memory – oh, Vauri, right. But... I cannot be a spider.'

'She's right,' a new voice said. 'Vahura is not qualified enough to be one.'

Vahura sprang to her feet. 'Acharya?' Her eyes twinkled with shock and shame as she glanced past Mati. The dusky old woman, who had been tracking Mati and Dantavakra before and who had introduced them to Old Ella, scowled at Vahura.

'So, this is what you meant by saving the world, eh? All those incredible lines about being a hero to stop the plague but, the truth is, you are incredibly selfish, Vahura of Balkh. Any sane ape would have killed Vauri then and there to arrest the spread of the plague but you're ready to risk plunging the world into desolation just for a slim chance at saving your sister? To save one person, you'd risk sacrificing thousands of families, sisters, mothers, children and,' she eyed Mati's stomach and added, 'babies.'

Vahura, chastened, did not know where a ready-to-move pyre would be available at short notice. But this time she chose to speak true. 'Yes.'

Asshaye then hobbled over to her side and kissed her forehead. 'I am proud of you.' Vahura, surprised, did not get a chance to react before Asshaye turned to Mati. 'Your plan to hold Vahura in a fake hostage to ransom Bhagadatt showed initiative, lass. But it has too many flaws and assumptions. He will see right through it.'

'How do we run this rig then?' Mati asked, uncaring about the identity of her guest. 'How do we steal the Scrolls?'

'Stealing is for amateurs. I have something better, lass,' Asshaye said.

'Pray, tell,' Mati said. 'What is better than stealing?'

'A heist.'

MATI

I

The slate board, resting on its easel, was wider than it was high,
in the manner of a landscape painting capturing some monumental vista of history in chalk. Flanking the board, votive candles
exuded a fragrance of rare Manipur spices. One of these candles
illumed a hand-drawn map of the skeleton of Leafsong. Behind the
board, a mural of winged women being torn apart by men made for
an appropriate backdrop.

After Mati chalked circles around the vulnerable points on
the board, she settled herself onto the largest chair within reach.
Dantavakra and Vahura sat on either side of a wooden table, flooded
with Vahura's journals. And Asshaye, a member of the bloody Rose
Coterie – hailed as the greatest planners in legend – lay sprawled on
a velvet chaise. They all stared at the board, that we-are-definitely-
suicidal expression on their faces intensified.

Ella leaned close to light Asshaye's pipe when Vauri caught a
whiff and raised her hands, finally disrupting the crematorium
silence. 'I want!'

'Now, now little Princess, it is the Acharya's pipe,' Mati said.

Vahura held Vauri's arms. 'More importantly, you are to never do
this. Pipe. Bad.'

'I'll crush ye barnacles,' Vauri hollered back at Vahura and then
began laughing. Horrified, Vahura turned to Mati with an accusatory look.

'Erm, as you can see, there are certain drawbacks,' Mati said as
the rest did their best to disguise their laughs as coughs, 'to children

spending time amongst sailors. Though *that* is not my contribution to her thesaurus.'

'The Storm God shit on your face,' Vauri yelled, immensely pleased with herself.

Mati shushed her. 'Alright, this one was mine.'

'*Curses are the shortest route to understanding a culture,*' Ella said without inflection. 'Isn't that what you said the last time you swore at the Tusk in public?'

'I... I...' Vahura's blew her cheeks. 'That was different, and you know it, Ella!'

'Mateey,' Vauri held out a cupped hand, and dropped a shock of pink on her lap, 'there were berries by Vahura's window. I picked some for you.'

Mati felt her eyes grow dangerously damp. *By the Tide! The Rose Coterie is here*, she warned herself. *Do not even think of crying, Mati!* 'Thank you, Vauri,' she managed.

'Come, Princess.' Ella took Vauri's hand. 'Let us pluck berries for all of them. You sure you don't need anything, Princess?' she asked Mati.

'Gold enough to build an empire?'

'Alas, I am the wrong old woman to ask.' Ella kept a hand on Mati's shoulder. A silent gratitude for returning Vauri, she supposed. Or a warning to not get Vahura in trouble. Either way, Mati nodded, and Ella left the room with Vauri in tow.

Asshaye strolled to the board. 'We have to assume Bhagadatt is the only one who knows of Vahura's quest? If he had to trust it to someone, it would have been Sokarro, and from what both of you have told me of your encounters with her, she doesn't know. And no, I don't believe he read the Scrolls for literature. If he had to, he would have read them long ago.'

'Pardon the interruption, Acharya,' Vahura said, 'but I'm confident he *has* read the Scrolls.' Vahura cleared her throat, exchanging a grave look with everyone before regaling them with the Night of the Living Dead: a tale of nerves, wonder, treasures and horror from her evening in Bhagadatt's gardens. When she paused for dramatic effect to let the shock sink in, she was disappointed that none drowned. Dantavakra looked at her sceptically, and Mati just nodded, insincerely.

'They drink blood, lass,' Mati said, 'maybe that makes them heal faster. They're called leeches for a reason.'

'I thought that was a racial slur!' Dantavakra gasped, and loath as she was to agree with him, even Vahura had thought the same.

'I am certain he doesn't drink blood!' Vahura protested, her own face paling to a rather alarming shade of white. 'There was a huge feast...'

'Did you see him eat?' Asshaye asked, smirking. 'I didn't think so. Though I'm not sure the blood is to their bones what the wind is to the ship, dear,' Asshaye said to Mati. 'I live with witches who drink blood and they only die if you deprive them of unnatural sex. Either way, the purebred Rakshasas are rumoured to be difficult to kill. Stake through the heart.'

'I still cannot believe Rakshasas actually drink blood,' Dantavakra said. 'That is disgusting!'

'You look like you've spotted a goblin in your garden, Princess. All wind in the topsails?' Mati asked Vahura.

Vahura managed a nod.

'I care not for what the Rakshasa feeds on but what the Rakshasas fear, and they fear everything Daevas,' Asshaye said. 'He must have locked it away in a chamber never to be seen again till the Librarian came along. If he is indeed fond of her, he was reading it to find what Vahura is after. Chances are the book is still on the bedside table, perhaps in a locker of his or inside the drawer of a side-table. Of course, we will need confirmation – which we have, thanks to a maid I had planted years ago in Leafsong – should we need to steal something from his damn Garden. Turns out, ever since the Librarian has come into his life, he has taken to reading a strange book that disappears into his Assyrian steel-backed mandala safe.'

Mati whistled. 'Assyrian steel and mandala? Leech knows his way around locks.'

'If he is fond of her, why not just tell him the truth?' Dantavakra asked, not understanding Mati's murdering looks. 'Men like to help women they care about.'

'He is *not* fond of me,' Vahura protested.

'I was just—' Dantavakra started but Mati interrupted him before that speech could take root. The boy was spectacularly dim. If Bhagadatt permitted Vahura to read the Scrolls out of love, how would Dantavakra and Mati – who needed to steal them to sustain a living – benefit?

'It won't work,' Asshaye said. 'One, he might not trust Vahura. He isn't even agreeing to meet her. Two, truth will not get Mati what she wants. So that route will end with Mati exposing Vauri's secret. A word of the Mold, and Vauri would be burned alive and so would we all, for good measure. For better or worse, your fates are irrevocably tangled.'

Vahura recovered herself soon enough, and for that, she earned Mati's respect, and so did Asshaye earn Mati's gratitude for rescuing her from deciding to say something unsavoury.

Asshaye asked Dantavakra now, 'When you entered their stable, how thorough were they?'

'Like a man suspecting his wife of an affair. Disrobed me of every piece of steel even down to a pouch of coins before permitting me inside. Good luck on robbing it from his bedroom.'

'An unsettling number of guards were posted along on my route to the Garden as well.'

'The guards are a problem but there are other hooks too,' Mati said. 'Leafsong itself is too deep in the city. The root roads, the bogs, the swamps, none of them complement a getaway. And then there is the other matter of our colour. Humans aren't exactly strolling around the corridors of Leafsong. We would stand out as conspicuous as Dantavakra on deck.'

'Hey!' Dantavakra said, and then sighed. 'But she speaks true,' he admitted sadly.

'Not to forget, we three are on Sokarro Sinh's blacklist. That is as good as having a bounty against our names. She will leave no stone unturned to see us to our berths on the earthship she has booked.' Mati chuckled. 'Stealing from Leafsong would be swimming wounded in shark territory, Asshaye.'

'We must then toss some blood to the sea to lure the shark to the surface,' Asshaye said. Sudden unease crossed Dantavakra's face at the imagery evoked as Asshaye walked over to the giant slate board, hands on her hips, before she turned. 'The boy, as much as it pains me to admit it, is not wrong. We can't steal it from Leafsong. It is their stomping grounds, too deep in the City, so even if we nick it, we can't slip away unnoticed. Plan B.' She flipped the board to reveal a crude sketch of a centipede-like creature drawn by airavats.

'This is Narka Rath – the Royal Earthship of Kamrup.'

On a closer look, Narka Rath was different from other earthships. Here, three galleys appeared to be fused into each other to form one giant earthship. 'As you can see, it is different from the tethered buggy you two arrived in. Rumour has it, it has stirred Nar Ad to write a sequel to his book – it is that magnificent. Boasts its own special rail line connecting Leafsong to the Reach. We are going to steal the Daevic Scrolls from the Narka Rath.'

Silence could be peaceful. Silence could be wild. In that room, it was both at the same time.

II

'But the Daevic Scrolls are, and we are guessing here, in Bhagadatt's room.'

'So we have established, Ser Repetition,' Asshaye said, turning to Mati with a judgmental stare as if she had expected her to bring a better escort. Hard to find fault with that assessment. '*Obviously*, we have to find a way for the Daevic Scrolls to walk over to the Earthship. Alright.' Asshaye clapped her hands, rubbing the palms together. 'Good news and a host of bad news. Bad news. First. Due to the threats to Bhagadatt's life and the banishment of the Iron Order, the security in Leafsong and in the Narka Rath now would rival that of the House of Seven.'

'And how would *you* know that?' Dantavakra sneered.

'I have robbed the House of Seven.'

Ignoring Dantavakra's gaping jaw, Mati nodded to the others. 'Sokarro is in charge of it. She is thorough.'

Asshaye continued, 'Getting to shift the Daevic Scrolls to the Narka Rath, unless you have sired secret babies with each of the guards, will be a little difficult to arrange. Even if it is successfully moved, the Daevic Scrolls will be snug in a locker in Bhagadatt's cabin inside the First Galley. The Librarian and the Pirate can get into the Narka Rath but they will be confined to the poor Third Galley under heavy guard, reserved for royal members of a low race like ours. Past the Third Galley, lies the Second. This is where it gets tricky. Here you'll encounter royal Kinnaras and Nagas and Asurs, all with a distaste for those of our kind, who will not make exceptions to your presence there. Then you have to stroll across the Second Galley into the First Galley, reserved for Bhagadatt and Sokarro, which anyone will tell you takes more than a smile to slip into.

'Once you enter the First Galley,' she tapped the head of the centipede ship on the board, 'you have to locate Bhagadatt's room. Unlike the other two Galleys, which are packed with seats and benches, the First Galley features cabins on both sides of a narrow corridor.'

Mati raised a hand. 'Outside entry, then?'

'The cabins have windows but Sokarro somehow found perfect vaikunshard shapes to fit them on it. Can't carve a hole in them from outside. Opens only from the inside.'

Mati nodded. 'What next?'

'Next, we hunt his locker down which, if the boasts of the Sindh Guild are true, is a mandala-forged masterpiece. It will be secured with a mandala maze—'

'Which we can't crack,' Mati finished, 'without a key to the puzzle.'

'And for all this, we also need Bhagadatt to not be on the Narka Rath,' Asshaye said.

'Fantastic,' Dantavakra finally said. 'So, once we somehow get the Tusk to *not* board his own Earthship—'

'—the Tusk who can't be hurt,' Vahura added, chipping her nails at the same time.

'Right… once we get the Invincible Tusk out of the picture, we have to get the Leeches to shift his locker to the Earthship and make sure we are on the Third Galley when it leaves—'

'—one which a Knight is not allowed to climb on,' Asshaye pointed out.

'*Splendid!*' Dantavakra's smile was a hard one as he pressed on, 'and then get past the Second Galley filled with guards and human-haters, and then into the First Galley where even other Rakshasas and Asurs aren't permitted, where we enter the room of Bhagadatt—'

'—which we wouldn't know, right?' Mati asked.

'Yes, yes. Pardon me. I forgot to mention: one room will be Sokarro's. One room will be for the Grey Shamans to rest in some garden of his, and the other will be for Bhagadatt. The fourth room will be filled with guards who are rotated out of duty to rest. We don't know which cabin would be his because they shift it every month on mock runs,' Asshaye said.

Dantavakra exchanged a harrowed look with each of them. 'Right, and then let's say our guess is right, given we only get one chance to guess, we then find his room, we open the safe which we can't open, and then we just – what – leave the same way we came back?'

'Aye. Succinct synopsis, lad. And this brings me to the sole good news. By the time this is done, the Earthship would already be there at Airavat's Reach. You can escape on the *Gilded Lion* before the Easterners find their Tusk is missing, and definitely long before the Tusk finds out his treasure is missing.'

'What? *This* is the good news!' Whole sections of Dantavakra's face had gone limp, as if no underlying thought could hold them to an expression.

'What is the first step?' Mati asked, smiling.

'I thought you would never ask.' Asshaye studied the array of grim faces before her, looking eminently satisfied. 'Vahura has to abduct the Tusk of the Tree Cities before the Conclave.'

VAHURA

I

Vahura groggily ran a comb through her hair before the mirror, content after the midday nap she had shared with Vauri after so long. Her journal lay sprawled on the table filled with scribbled notes outlining the different stages of Asshaye's plan, its pages doodled on the margins with runes and glyphs. She glanced over at it, hoping that she'd still be able to read her own handwriting given how fast Asshaye had spoken. Though, why bother? Her role was simple. Smile and seduce Bhagadatt on a stroll through the woods. *Smiles and seduction.* Just two of the gifts Vahura was born with. *Sparks!*

Had they not listened to her tale? He wasn't interested in her. He was intrigued by her quest of out patriotism not out of romance. The others seemed to have forgotten he had her thrown out of the castle, twice. And why did it have to be *seduce?* Why couldn't it be – entertain him with historical facts or lure him to a library? That was doable. Somewhat. Ugh. What a thing to involve yourself in. There was still time to escape, wasn't there? As if she would, Vahura thought as she turned to find Vauri sleeping peacefully, her destiny dancing on a razor's edge of her blindfold.

I need tea. Tea will fix this. Or it will do something, she thought as she headed to the kitchen, journal in hand. It was good to have the place to herself again. Old Ella was off running errands for the Magadhans, and the Magadhans were busy with the Rose Coterie, making preparations. Come evening, it would be Vahura's cue to take the stage. Hope Bhagadatt came alone to meet her in reply to her letter lying to him about her plans to leave tonight, and not with the daunting Sokarro.

Lost between her journal and her thoughts, she wandered into the kitchen already fragrant with the smell of tea leaves. Instinctively, her hands sought out the teapot with her free hand. Sleep leaped out of Vahura like rats from a burning ship when someone cleared his throat next to her. It was a soft sound, a cough that alerts of the cougher's intention of politely making their presence felt. Yet Vahura jumped, whirled around and hurled the journal directly at the intruder's face, missing it entirely.

Bhagadatt, standing near the kitchen slab, noted the fallen book with wry amusement and turned to the slab. He was dressed as a Ranger again, his face a shifting hue of grey in the sunlight, the colour of smoke and shadows. 'I'm sorry, Princess,' he said. 'I did not mean to startle you but given your rather fiery ultimatum in your last missive, I thought our meeting should not wait. So, I commanded Sokarro on oath to mind to her duties for the day so that I can spend your last day with you if you permit. Tea?'

What missive? Oh, the letter Mati wrote.

'How did you get in?' she demanded.

'There was no one at the door, and unlocked doors unsettle me, so I let myself in to make sure you are... you are okay.' *Door unlocked. The old hag needs her wages halved.* 'I hope you don't mind that I took liberties with your books. I grew bored.'

Vahura narrowed her eyes. 'How long have you been here?'

'A while,' Bhagadatt said. She stared at him. 'Well, it would have been impolite to wake you from your slumber,' he added sheepishly. 'I could hear you snoring, so... um... it's not like I could just go into your bedroom, especially when I heard someone else snore... you had company.' Vahura frowned at the way he had turned his face at the last remark.

Great. Now he thinks my sister and I are lovers. It was not as if Vahura could tell him why he was wrong. 'So, you've been sitting out there the whole time hearing me... breathe aggressively?'

'On my oath as a Tusk, I did not step within five steps of your room. I just heard you... While I waited, I read some of the books you brought with you,' Bhagadatt said. 'For a chutney maker, you are deeply interested in diseases.'

Vahura was no longer listening – *Good Gods* – the journal, or rather the heist manual, which she had thrown at him lay wide open on the floor near a potted rack.

'And then I began rummaging through your kitchen to brew tea for you when I sensed you had risen,' he added.

She paused mid-fret, momentarily forgetting all about her journal. 'Brew tea?' *A Tusk made tea? For me?*

'Tea,' he said. 'I brew tea. I am a warm-beverage person. Maker. Who brews. Mostly tea.'

They stared at each other, then both looked away again immediately. *Who would have thought? An unkillable blooddrinker... enjoys tea.*

'I can take the tea directly from the pot, thanks.'

'Just as there is a way to preserve books, turn their pages and stack them back in the right order, Librarian Loosely, there is an art to pouring the tea. I am no maestro but I do know that the make of the cup should be matched to the tea being served,' said Bhagadatt. 'Please allow me?' he asked.

'Fine,' she surrendered.

The recollection of her journal lying open on the floor returned to her as soon as Bhagadatt turned his back to her. Vahura could not decide whether to casually pick it up and move it, or would that arouse too much attention? Would he sense her fear? Could Rakshasas do that?

'Princess,' Bhagadatt called out and Vahura looked up to find him holding her journal, 'your book. You need to work on your throwing skills.' He smiled, and then using the smell of clay to guide him, he pulled out a tray and two clay teapots ahead.

'You need two?' Vahura asked, distracted again.

Bhagadatt smiled cheerfully and without condescension, something which as a librarian she was yet to master. 'One for steeping and one for resting.' She had no inkling what those two words meant. 'This is the last jar of the amethyst tea leaves. It is from the harvest I had helped my mother with before she passed away.'

'I am sorry,' Vahura said, genuinely sympathizing over a shared cup of grief.

'Don't be. She was not particularly fond of me,' he said, smiling. 'But she did know her steam. Here.' He opened the lid of the jar and held it for Vahura to take it all in. As Vahura inhaled the scent of the roasted leaves, the rich fragrance turned to guilt on the back of her tongue.

Bhagadatt plucked the tea leaves using wooden tongs and deposited them in a teapan with practised precision. 'Trouble you for that cup? That water seems boiled enough now.'

Vahura obliged, and then saw how, with a twist of the wrist, he slowly let the hot water cascade over the tea leaves inside the pan. The leaves began to uncurl leisurely, releasing their secrets into a steam that burned yellow.

'That is a strange hue for a steam?'

Bhagadatt sighed in pleasure as if it was the question he had been waiting for his entire life. 'The sheer kinds of tea that are grown in the East, Loosely! You have the Ginger Honey Black, you have the Tulsi Ginger. Masala Tea with cardamom, clove, pepper and cinnamon is popular in the Riverlands but I do not enjoy it one bit. Just Cinnamon Tea – now that is helpful in relieving a human from the effects of nausea. But they are the ordinary kind – the ones Drachma sellers sell long after the flavours have died a suffocating death. Here in the East, we enjoy tea made from the delicate tips of the amethyst bush,' he made the sign of a chef's kiss, 'full bodied with robust character.'

'Are you sure you are still describing tea?'

Bhagadatt smiled again. 'Next time – I will brew you a tea infused with fragrant jasmine. It will help you devour a book in a day. Not that you would need it but…'

'Do you think there will be a *next* time?'

Bhagadatt did not smile now. She felt stupid for asking the question. He was just being polite. Stupid, stupid Vahura. 'If the Fates will it, I would like that very much,' he finally said, without looking at her. Now that she thought of it, he had not looked at her once since she had entered, keeping his eyes downcast.

Wait, nightdress! She was still in her nightdress – oh, the impropriety of it all. Her mother's ashes must be stirring in the riverbed, no doubt sending a scathing message to Old Ella from the beyond. Ever so gingerly, Vahura sidled towards Old Ella's shawl hanging from the hook by the kitchen door and just about managed a manoeuvre to flick her journal onto the book stack on her bed.

'So, you still have not told me why are you here?' Vahura asked once she had restored some dignity to her arms with the shawl.

'I wanted to apologize for my behaviour the last time we met,' saying which Bhagadatt emptied the amber liquid from the steeping pot into the one for resting, the tea making a delightful sound as it filled the tiny cups. He handed them over to her, and softly raised his own. 'To a world where we finally find a cup of tea large enough along with a book just long enough to suit us.'

Vahura was still angry but that was a damn good toast. Especially the *us* bit.

'You still haven't apologized.' Vahura crossed her hands.

'My duty is to build scaffolds for the dreams of my people. I opened the borders to bring prosperity to my race, and I was doing well till I met you. For ever since our lives have become so entangled in my head that I don't know where mine ends and yours begins. That evening, I should have killed you for discovering our secret – that was the only way for me to dance through that thunderstorm without getting my people struck. But I couldn't... and it took me a few days to realize that I couldn't, that I couldn't deny how cradling your hope dictates the tides of my heart. So here I am, as a friend, to say I am sorry for being a mule! I might not be able to help you but I would love to make your trials my trials.'

A prince amongst apologies. She did not know what to say to that so she quickly took a sip of the tea, the flavours and warmth assaulting her throat with moans and aahs. 'I feel like I just received a new dispatch of rare scrolls from Meru.' She held the edge of the table to steer her through that switch in topics. 'Marvellous. Your tea may just be the solution to world peace.'

A smile spread across Bhagadatt's grey face, like a lake set off by a stone skipping across water, and her heart skipped too. 'Provided they trust a Rakshasa to pour it for them.'

'Hah, a woman might just turn an Acharya of Meru by that time.'

Her shoulders relaxed. She strolled to the balcony of the room half captured on the left by berry shrubs. The sun was still rising gently on the horizon, glimmering on the river under the Bridge of the Drenched Veil, painting it with orange and pink hues. Bhagadatt joined her with his own cup. Below, outside a spice shop that had not opened yet, a struggling vainika plucked the strings of his veena to a soothing raag, hoping to saw a few coppers from souls who felt like starting their day with charity. A blanket of peace swept over her as she took another sip.

'I think the reason you truly enjoy tea is because you enjoy witnessing the beauty in the little things,' Vahura said when he joined her.

'The same way you shrug at the earthship but that lone dandelion on the grass lawn brought a smile to your face.'

'The same way peeling the whole orange in one go brought a smile to yours.'

'I should peel my orange in secret. I am not an admirer of how bare my secrets are.'

'They are safe with me,' she said.

The vainika had switched to a flute, and the soft music singing of something lost lingered in the air. A couple walked, hand in hand, stopping only to drop a generous copper in the musician's basket. Birds chirped by in a nearby bough. Why was she noticing these things?

'I cherish the first minute in a hot bath on a cold day,' he broke the silence, his eyes almost challenging her.

'I enjoy drawing a perfect circle!'

'The sound of leaf crackling while walking in the autumn.'

'Finishing a book. Oh, wait. Hugs.'

Bhagadatt made a face as if he was contemplating giving her one, which made her stomach lurch. 'Still your turn,' Vahura prodded.

Bhagadatt thought. 'Finding an oddly shaped baby carrot.'

Vahura laughed. Their shoulders almost touched with only the warm smidge of Kamrupan sky between them.

'I... am glad we met, Princess.' He took his palm out in a handshake. Vahura obliged but regretted it instantly. They'd touched each other in far worse ways in the Scarlet house. But there was something different about this touch. Far more different. Bhagadatt's hand didn't just rest there. It squeezed, ever so lightly, and Vahura felt a strange need to blink rapidly without stopping. Her mind was begging her to take his hand, and pull him closer, to her face, to her mouth. Bhagadatt was now looking her right in the eyes, lips slightly parted.

'I want to confess...' Vahura started.

'I want to tell you something...'

They both spoke at the same time. Vahura's throat felt suddenly very tight. 'Yes?'

'I... need... to say—'

'Here you go!' Her governess blundered in to the flat through the door, neatly tossing the bag on the kitchen slab. Vahura and Bhagadatt sprang apart as if they were children caught stealing sweets from their mother's kitchen shelf.

'What smells so nice? Did you make tea?' She turned towards the balcony and stopped short. 'Oh, my, Your Grace,' she gasped, and Vahura knew Ella was feigning her surprise. 'I apologize for barging in. Princess, you wanted to tour the tea estates before you leave Kamrup – I have arranged a buggy but it can only go now.'

Below, the two lovers started an argument, pushing each other. A crow's cawing shooed away the robins, and the vainika, scowling at the disturbance to his music, left the place to play somewhere else.

'Right, yes. Oh.' Vahura frowned, completely dishevelled in the mind. 'Should get ready.'

'Pardon me for vaulting into your conversation like a mischievous jester, Your Grace,' Ella said. 'Perhaps... you might join the Princess in her tour. My knees are weak and I must confess your City has not been constructed with the aged in mind.'

Bhagadatt looked genuinely surprised (and pleased) with the request, and then slowly turned to Vahura. 'It is almost evenmorn. It would... also be safe for me to be your escort, Princess, if you will have me.' *I would like nothing more.* No. She could not do this. She had to tell him the truth. In the middle of that thought, Bhagadatt laughed. 'Unless you would prefer... someone else.' His eyes slipped to her room, as if suddenly remembering Vahura had a bedmate.

'Oh, that be an urchin girl I stumbled upon, caught in the clutches of one of your mischievous Asurs,' Old Ella elucidated. 'I deemed it wise to offer her solace within these walls. A tender sprout of seven summers, she will be asleep till apocalypse come. Go, sample the sights, Princess. All arrangements to leave will be made by the time you're back.'

The mention of Vauri shattered the spell that had lingered mere moments before. The awkward moment was gone, and she had to admit she was relieved.

Relieved and crestfallen, both at once.

II

When they arrived at the estate on the eastern outskirts of Kamrup, the sheer scale of the emerald plantations overawed her. Terraced gardens of luxuriant tea shrubs snaked parallel to each other. No marshes. No swamps. They stretched for miles, covering the hillsides as far as the eye could see until they disappeared into the tall trees of Kingswood. She wondered if this land had been cultivated so on the west of Kamrup on the side of the Riverlands; the humans would have grazed it down long back.

They rode on their horses along the tea garden path, the afternoon sun warming their backs and filling the glade to welcome them. In a matter of minutes, the gardens gave way to the mist-shrouded Kingswood, unnoticed by Vahura who was busy falling apart. She did not know whether it was the tea she had sipped or the knowledge that this was their last walk, but somewhere between letting go and holding on, impulse cast aside the chains of courtesy.

'You're a Rakshasa – an immortal Rakshasa,' Vahura said and wished she could have bitten off her tongue. So much for seduction. 'The kind the rumours claim drinks blood.'

Bhagadatt's eyes were ruby glints in pools of darkness. 'Yes, I'm afraid so,' he whispered in a low and soft voice, like the rustle of ancient parchment, a rare manuscript you kept in a drawer that you pulled out only on special occasions, just to feel the fragile pages between your fingers.

The honesty disarmed Vahura, and she could not think of a blasted thing to say. She compromised with, 'Interesting.' *Interesting? How eloquent? Silence would've been better!* But Vahura was not done. Hoping against hope, she asked, 'Do you drink animal blood then?'

'No. The idea of animal blood is as repulsive to me as dog meat is to you.'

'Oh.'

A faint sweet smile touched his black lips, its arc softening the strong, straight lines of his nose. 'I drink human blood, yes, but I do not murder.'

'I'm sorry... It must be difficult. To control that thirst, that is,' Vahura said, and he just gazed back, eyes unreadable.

For a moment, Vahura thought he might get angry, but he considered the query seriously. That was a thing that she was noticing, that he took all her questions seriously and considered them, and felt they were worthy of an answer. She wasn't used to that.

'From what I know, our thirst for blood is the same as your thirst for water,' he said, 'and given blood is scarcer than water, that is if you aren't a mass murderer, there have been episodes that have given flights to the fancy of humans who imagine us as monsters. You're the sharpest person I have met,' he said. Vahura perked, especially when he used the word person instead of woman. 'You can conjure ways for us to feed, can't you?'

Vahura pondered for a moment. The book of *Pricking the Vessels: Nadis, Arteries and Veins* by Acharya Sahai flipped its pages in her head. *Fits comes from an imbalance in body humours, and bloodletting is one of the oft-used method, though in my advice, an unwise method of curing seizures and fever.* 'Bloodletting?'

'Bloodbarters, blood prostitution, call it what you will, but it helps, especially for the ones offering their arteries for it is believed our saliva has anti-blood clots that lower their risk of a heart cataclysm or tiger nerves.'

'So... tea? Is that how you...'

'No. Tea brewing is something I enjoy. Just 'cause you need meat for sustenance does not mean you cannot enjoy tea. Rakshasas are not very different. I know it is a lot to take in,' Bhagadatt said. 'I had the same reaction when I heard you humans eat the flesh of other animals, even the ones you ride,' he said, pointing at their horses. 'You hunt them, kill them, skin them and boil them, sometimes not necessarily in that order, and then eat them, sometimes flesh, sometimes bones, sometimes even brains and liver. Worse, you even eat their unborn as eggs and steal their milk by squeezing out their udders, milk meant for their calves. To us Rakshasas, that is... difficult to digest.'

Vahura silently chuckled at that unintended pun but her eyes glinted at that fascinating perspective. Humans indulged in all kinds of carnivorous pursuits. Drinking blood, peculiar as it was, struck her as kinder and much more hygienic than flesh eating. Then why did it bother humans so? Was it the realization that Nature had never intended for humans to be the sovereign predator?

'I know you have more questions. I would be disappointed if you didn't. Ask away.'

'Are you an immortal?'

'Not like the Daevas of yore, if that is what you mean. We do live a lot longer than humans, and we also heal from bodily injuries of the kind I received when I fell from the balcony.'

'I'm so sorry for that.' Vahura turned red. She had wanted to breach the subject of the night for so long that she had forgotten what her part in that scene had been. 'But can you heal from anything and everything?'

'I recovered from drowning in a mire as a child. If I am well quenched, I heal swiftly from steel cuts. In my room is a shelf with acid vials that I test on my fingers just to see which acid burn would my fingers not recover from. I combine them, to burn me, to poison, to freeze, to even stab it with lightning sometimes. I have recovered from all of them at varying speeds.'

Vahura wondered... whether a Rakshasa could recover from Marigold Mold. She doubted it. She had read an instance of an outbreak in Lanka in the Second Age where the Rakshasas had rained down arrows on every villager in the infected hamlet.

'And with that I have laid open what I hide from the world, Princess. Could you place your faith in me as well?'

Vahura pinched her wrist. 'What is it that you seek of me?'

'The truth,' Bhagadatt said, reining his horse in. 'Why do you seek the Daevic Scrolls? I want to trust you. No,' he shook his head, 'I trust you. But is that enough to hand over a potential weapon that in the wrong hands can wreak destruction upon the world?'

'Is it?' Vahura responded without dropping a beat. 'Is it enough?'

Bhagadatt was startled by her question but then his red eyes steeled. 'It is...'

It was? A scream caught in her throat at those words, and she forced it back down. But her gullet still pulled tight as her knees shook. He trusted her. Her chest knotted with the sensation of having triggered a collapse, like a chain reaction of towering book-shelves down upon one another around the library.

No. She couldn't do this to him.

Ruby eyes met Vahura's blue.

'You're shaking,' Bhagadatt said as he took her head in his hands, forcing Vahura to face him. This time, Vahura couldn't look away. His thumb pressed softly to the muscle below her ears. Her breath-ing slowed without her having resorted to bleeding herself. 'Loosely,' he said, 'I am with you. Do you understand?'

Vahura nodded.

'Do you understand why?' Bhagadatt asked.

Vahura pulled her lips inward, biting at them, her chest tight again but this time with an unfamiliar sensation. 'Why?' she asked.

Bhagadatt turned sharply. Oh, Vahura did not even realize they were in the woods. But that was not why Bhagadatt stopped midway. A woman had sauntered onto the road ahead.

Half her face was webbed in an intricate set of tattoos, minute, black symbols in a strange pattern covering her skin like a scroll. Her long white streaked hair was left loose, and it was eerily breath-taking. Her hair rested on a cloak of boar hide. She wore a vest of armour that seemed to be made of giant skulls. The stone pommel of a bladed weapon jutted out from the side of her waist.

'Afternoon, lovebirds,' a voice called out. 'Come out here, girls. Looks like we've found our food for the day.'

III

Other Yoginis-who-didn't-look-like-Yoginis emerged from the woods, in their cloaks and hoods, revealing old leather armour with stitched iron scales. Weapons of all kinds flashed in their gloved hands. A few had their bows drawn, arrows at the ready. Dark, drugged eyes in tanned, tattooed Yogini faces held cold and firm on Bhagadatt and Vahura.

'I understand you know who I am,' Bhagadatt said, angling his horse to move in front of Vahura's, though even he must know it did not matter. The Yoginis had them surrounded. 'Matrika Zubeia and I are friends. And yet you have chosen to accost me in the presence of my... friend. Speak your piece, then.'

'I care not for Zubeia and her pious ragtags, Tusk.'

'You are Arahi,' Bhagadatt said, shaking his head as if realizing he had a real problem on his hands, 'the leader of White Crows and Black Doves.'

'Mother of Outcasts, aye.'

'Outcasts?' Vahura asked.

'Our intentions to reciprocate the human hospitality we'd been shown in the Riverlands was considered... aggressive by Zubeia's flock. You see we—'

'They are murderers,' Bhagadatt said, simply. 'Now what do you need, Arahi?'

'Look at the balls on the leech. You think our powers won't affect you 'cause you heal, little Rakshasa,' she asked with the lazy drawl of a Sindh Guild broker.

'I'm sure they will hurt me just fine. The question is not whether, but why? The Tusk Guard doesn't bother with your business. The townsfolk leave you alone. The villagefolk send you tributes in the form of fresh corpses. That is more than you can say about the Riverlands you fled.'

'Mind your tongue, bat,' another outcast said. 'We did not flee. We left. Can't meditate when we have horde of peasants wanting to burn us now, can we?

'Let him be, Gopali. He ain't wrong all the way. The Lakelands have been welcoming, aye. But that be the thing with a place filled with savages of all kinds – savages don't fear each other. Too many of them think Zubeia's temple is a tourist spot to come and awe and spit at. If Zubeia's parrots don't mind, we don't mind. But we made this neck of the woods our home, and we do think there be a toll to pay when you'a come visiting. And by heathen's balls, turns out it will be the Tusk himself who will inaugurate this tradition.'

'So, you're saying if I don't comply to paying the toll, you will kill the Tusk of Kamrup?' he asked with a mocking smile as if he could have taken them all down. Could he?

'You know we won't do that but we sure can maim that dainty little thing beside you.'

Bhagadatt stiffened on the horse. The Yoginis now stood on either side of them like haunting bookends. 'We have nothing you'd want.'

'We will be the judge of that. Now if you would be so kind as to introduce your weapons to the forest floor and take a step back.'

'Just…' Bhagadatt said through a stiff jaw, 'don't hurt her. Ease those bowarms.' A chorus of howls answered from the trees.

'Methinks the Tusk has taken a fancy for his new exotic pet.'

They complied. Bhagadatt flung his sword and upended his pack. Vahura kept her satchel on the ground. Arahi whistled, stepping close to examine the contents of the loot even as the other Yoginis poured out from where they had been hiding like a pack of hyenas. 'Yellow socks. Those should help in our war against the leeches. And there is a roll of parathas too! Were you two planning a romantic picnic?' *Wait. Was he?* 'Now, now, don't try anything funny, Tusk. Get back. All the way behind the horses.'

Bhagadatt touched Vahura, only the slightest touch to guide her back. He paused behind his horse, while she stood behind hers. Vahura shook her head. No. No. *I won't do this.* Remember Vauri. All she had had to endure… Vahura pinched herself so hard that she was sure it was going to scab but her mind found its compass.

She was no expert in horse care but she knew instinctively Bhagadatt was standing too close to the horse for the right angle. Vahura coughed, pretending to hobble. Bhagadatt reached out to help her but kept his hands to himself when he saw Vahura had steadied herself. But it was done. He had taken a step away from the horse.

Vahura turned to look at Arahi, and... sneezed.

Arahi flicked the nerve of Bhagadatt's horse, and the beast kicked its hind legs, straight at Bhagadatt's face. Bhagadatt collapsed like a pile of rocks, groaning, and dazed. Vahura leaped at Bhagadatt's fallen frame, cradling his head. He still smelled of vanillin. She pinched herself again. 'Your Grace,' she acted, 'are you alright? I think you are bleeding.' He wasn't. He probably couldn't.

'Are *you* alright, Princess?' Bhagadatt asked, eyes closed, lips trembling. He had a concussion.

'Here.' She took out the kerchief dabbed in alchemical ether used to make an airavat unconscious, and dabbed his forehead, making sure the end of the kerchief kissed his nose. 'Deep lungfuls...' and she herself demonstrated it by inhaling dramatically as if Bhagadatt were a little boy who had forgotten how to breathe.

Bhagadatt, as if surrendering to her, obliged, and within moments, proved that while a Rakshasa might heal from injuries, he faints like any other puny human. *Oh, it worked! I cannot believe it worked! Never distrust a Yogini.*

Zubeia emerged from the other side of the woods. 'Like clockwork, little princess. Shadowsin never fails.' She turned to Arahi. 'You have my gratitude, Sister.'

'Keep your gratitude,' Arahi said, 'I am happy with the debt you owe me.'

'Will he truly heal?' Vahura asked.

'He will,' Zubeia said, smiling. 'Shadowsin is harmless. Just a hypnosis draught. Do not worry. He won't suspect a thing. He will wake up, and thank us for taking him in. He will worry about you and we will tell him we escorted you safely to a ship. He will be indebted to us, especially after we return him those ugly socks. Though, about the sandwiches.' She looked regretfully at Arahi's Yoginis who had carved the sandwiches into many territories. 'Well, they do spoil fast.'

'Vauri?'

'Safely with us. We will take good care of her. The Roses have already—'

From beyond there came the distant sounds of thunder. Overlapping sounds. The birds rose suddenly, hundreds, voices a chorus of shrieks, and beneath their feet, the earth shifted with a groaning sound.

'What was that?'

'That was a Mathuran munition, a big one at that,' Arahi said. 'Nasty munitions created by men to kill. Rambha, get down here.'

The Yogini's descent from the tree was a little loud, a little fast. In a mess of snapped branches, leaves and one abandoned bee hive, the priestess landed heavy and hard on her rump. 'Ow, Mother! Ow!'

Ignoring her plight, Arahi asked, 'Rambha, what passes?'

'Blue smoke, Matrika, and plenty of it.'

Blue smoke. Vahura blessed her memory for being reliable again. The barrels she had seen on the Night of the Broken Gardens had indeed been blazebane barrels gifted, presumably gifted, as a token by Kalyavan to earn Bhagadatt's trust. It was a good thing she had memorized the outline of Leafsong drawn and framed by Bhagadatt in his gardens. She was almost doubtful if it had worked.

'Verdict?' Zubeia asked.

'Leafsong is on fire. Most beautiful fire I've ever seen.'

The Yoginis had done their bit. The Rose Coterie had done their bit. All at great risk to their lives. Vahura looked at Bhagadatt's face again and tucked his hair back behind his ear. Now it was time for them to play their part.

'I still can't believe this has been so easy so far,' Vahura said as she rose again.

'Don't. Say. That,' Arahi said, making a sign and spitting twice on the side to ward off ill luck. Vahura frowned in confusion till a page flipped open in her mind palace –

'To compliment a plan before its time displeases the Goddess of Crime.'

Silly superstition, surely. But when no one was looking, Vahura quickly whispered, 'Touchwood.' Unfortunately, it was too little, too late.

The Goddess of Crime was displeased. So displeased.

INTERLUDE

I

THE GRIM ONE

Heavy twin doors divided the strangely circular temple, made stranger by the absence of a roof. On all sides, the temple appeared rugged, primitive, resembling the bark of trees. Shapeless humps lay at the threshold of the door, their two killers silhouetted against the ember-cast grotesque dance of the naked, oiled priestesses in the temple's central plaza. One of them shuddered, the disgusting display tingling his sphincter. Merely standing here left him feeling impure.

As they stalked through the empty corridor, they crossed monstrous halfbreeds made of stone nestled in niches on the wall, the oil lamps behind the sculptures casting eerie shadows across them. He longed to take a sledgehammer to them all but his last effort centuries past had yielded only frustration. The statues then had cracked but not shattered, the animal heads bleeding from their eyes, haunting his dreams for nights to come. And as for these filthy witches, they'd managed to cross the continent to escape justice and practise their tantric rituals here, to take for themselves power they did not deserve to hold. Unnatural, all of them.

Backwards they went, all of them, weaving in and out of the firelight, drugged by the solemn notes of the pipes, moving like puppets on invisible strings. The tantric music jerked them around the poor bastards sprawled beneath them. Men forced to hold back, letting the women ride them, letting them exhale their ecstasy between their thighs, then drinking it from a tumbler mixed with the blood of a fresh corpse. Proper women didn't even know they could exhale like that, but here – here it was a damn carnival of feminine juices. Made his gut churn, though he'd grown a stronger stomach over the last three centuries. Unholy ritual, sure, but unholier still were the powers that bloomed inside those who practiced it.

His brother was not perturbed by the ritual as much as by the humid weather. He was still smiling. Always smiling. What was there to smile for here? The East's hot, moist air rife with the stench of decay? Or the smell of sex and corpse from the compound?

He scowled at him. 'Have you found the smell of the strain?'

II

THE GRINNING ONE

His brother always scowled and always asked questions, even when they were busy murdering. He simply grinned the way his father had asked him to as a child while breaking his jaw methodically. Effective strategy that. Centuries later, he still had not stopped grinning.

He glanced inside the room as he passed, centuries of consumption giving him the ability to see in the dark. A score of fresh corpses lined the walls inside like pigs, iron hooks jutting from tonsils, feet dangling an arm's length above the ground. Eyeless, tufted heads hung downward, their orange stoles dripping with blood and sweat. He reckoned these corpses would not be used in their rituals, no, but they would hang there to be used as grim warnings if other human guests of the East decided to feel morally righteous.

It was not difficult to trace the smell of the strain to the room where she was. He knitted his brows at the absence of guards by her door, his chance at sport robbed. Peering inside, in the dim light of reflected lanterns, he saw her languishing on the bed. He frowned again at the lack of chains around her. He was not a stickler to caution like his brother but there was a border beyond which care-free turned callus. Given what happened on the *Gilded Lion*, who knew that better than him.

His head throbbed again with the incessant chanting of mantras by the sixty-four witches around the central altar, drowning out the moans that had at least entertained him by stirring him between his legs. Squeezing his temple and then cock, he turned to his brother.

'She is here, and there is a Leech with her. Curiously, in shackles.'

'What of it? She should be in shackles.'

'*He* is in shackles. The Grey One. Not her.'

'Curious,' his brother said, turning behind to whisper a choice expletive in a lost language. 'Their damned mantras are twisting my head into knots.'

'We can't kill them without cause,' he said, genuinely sad. 'I was counting on at least one of them at her door here. I told you we should have taken our time with the ones at the gate.'

'I. Want. To. Kill. Them,' he said through gritted teeth, a finger on his temple to summon Dhyana to stop from him breaking loose.

'We can't be unprincipled.'

'Unprincipled.' His brother turned to him, his hand curling into a fist, which he slammed hard into the side of the closest sculpture of a beautiful Yogini with the head of a crocodile. There was no change in the tone of his voice. His brother would never pick a tone of anger with him. 'They will consider *us* unprincipled? Well, we will remind them it was we who burned down the City of Lanka for which Hanuman got blamed. Like that pious man would ever burn innocents alive. We spread the rumours of Sita's infidelity that drove Ram to exile her and led to the events that stopped Ram from turning more powerful than the Seven. We slipped into Pataal to hurt their Sols and kill their world. We assassinated a score of kings, two Chiranjeevis, half a hundred heroes of inhuman races and even a Daeva. On our last mission, it was we who whispered to that nine-fingered tribal boy our ways to win the War, and we did not even stop to bask in the glory of our work. We are utterly principled,' saying which his brother caught a crow that had landed, no doubt drawn by the smell of corpses, and put his hand round its little neck and squeezed till it stopped moving, before eating it raw. 'But we deserve to be happy from time to time!'

'I see.' The grinning brother stretched his arms around his back, eyes almost brightening when a Yogini in the throng ahead turned back to glance at the door behind them. But for the shadows that were their friends, he was sure she could not see them, and she did not as she turned back to chant her mantras while the two fresh practitioners in the centre prepared to join their bodies in the most bizarre of positions. How long had it been since he had yielded to the demands of his flesh, demands now weakened over the centuries. Could he pull off what the man was doing in the centre? *Sure I can*, he thought as he stretched. Was not he the one who had wrestled jadesharks and swum an entire ocean?

His brother was right. They deserved to be happy after what they had been through but what about principles? Well, what about priorities? What had their employer said? *Black Swan is first. Conclave, second.* An idea took birth in his head, and he turned to his brother, his companion of centuries. Seeing the glint in his eyes, his scowling brother's face perked up. That rare smile was enough for him to play around the rules. He could only hope their employer sympathized. 'There is a way we can be happy without killing anyone we can't.'

MARIGOLD WINTER

PART I

NARKA RATH EARTHSHIP, TREE CITY OF KAMRUP

FINAL DAY OF THE BATTLE OF MATHURA

'Beware the fury of a patient man.'
—John Dryden

 MATI opened her eyes to a familiar bounce on her bladder. There was still no sign of Sokarro or for that matter any sign that the damn Earthship would set off sailing. And while she had no objection to her baby being awake before time, why did she have to wake up as well?

She rubbed her groggy eyes, wondering if Sokarro had received her message. A flight of fancy entered her mind – that if she closed her eyes and sent out her thoughts along the Royal Earthship of Narka Rath, like a message along a wire between two houses, Sokarro might just turn up at the heavily guarded door that carved out the First Galley from the Second. *Sokarro.* The Earthship swayed gently beneath her, and she leaned against the window to feel the cold glass against her cheek, and hoped Sokarro had heard her. Though, given the chatter behind her, she doubted it.

Amidst the hubbub of other envoys on the Third Galley, each vying to outdo the other in a contest of panic, Mati struggled to stifle her amusement. Credit where it was due – some of the floating theories being bandied about the blue fires in Leafsong about deserved their own award for sheer imagination. Some were adamant that Bhagadatt was battling Krishna on the same terrace the latter's wife had slain the former's father. Others suspected that an alchemist had bungled a surprise affair planned for the Conclave. Another faction claimed it was a lightning strike gone wrong. Still others swore they saw five Daevas stand sentinel on the palace's walls. If only they knew the reason for all of it was just a simple heist to a steal a book. Asshaye was a genius.

'We burn Leafsong,' Asshaye said.

'I beg your pardon?' Dantavakra asked.

'You told me how the Curator had bored you with earthship technicalities. Didn't you mention something about the personal artefacts of the Tusk being State Treasure?' Asshaye asked.

'Right, I did.' Dantavakra scratched his head.

'Think faster, bonehead,' Asshaye said.

'I hope I get a chance to kill you, hag! And yes, he boasted about how Leafsong would never find itself again at the mercy of a cowardly air assault from Mathura, something about using the Narka Rath to shift the Tusk and his family and the State Treasures outside Leafsong in a matter of moments in the event of a griffin sighting, an earthquake or...' Dantavakra frowned as he tried to remember, '... a fire. He said he witnessed a drill or something – I do not remember.'

'I know Tree Folk ain't used to strangers in their lands, but I'll be keelhauled if it ain't strange for a guide to share evacuation plans with a soldier from another kingdom. Never mind that now though. If the Tusk's personal artefacts are considered treasure,' Asshaye said, 'his locker, his safe, any place where he might store the Daevic Scrolls, will be shifted to the Narka Rath.'

'How do we burn a stone palace in the wettest place on earth?' Mati asked.

Vahura's eyes brightened. 'Kalyavan.' She turned to them. 'You know what I think Kalyavan gifted Bhagadatt to earn his trust and steal the airavats?' Vahura said.

'Please don't say blazebane,' Dantavakra said.

'Blazebane!' Vahura chirped. 'I saw Greeks roll barrels into the barracks on my way to his tower. And in his Garden, I spied the footprint of Leafsong. Let me remember.' She closed her eyes as if searching through shelves in her mind. 'I know exactly where the barrels were rolled into.'

'Blazebane burns stone.' Asshaye had smiled, her face taking on a sinister cast in the orange pipe-light. 'Proud of you, lass. Point us on the map, and the Roses will take care of the fire. You take care of getting the Tusk outta the way. What's Step Three?'

She broke her attention away from the glass window and returned it to her comfortable chair. It had been easy to directly climb into the Second Galley instead of the Third. Racial prejudice simmered on the surface of hearts but empathy for expectant mothers burned deeper. No one wanted her to be jostled around in the Third Galley packed with kings, priests and merchantlords of the human race.

'Were you here for the Conclave, My Lady?' asked a well-dressed Asuran whose dark green horns peeked out of his black curly hair.

Mati frowned as she nodded politely.

'How splendid, dear sister,' the old Asuran said. 'I love earthships. You never know who you might run into. The Conclave hasn't even taken place, and already a scandal, aye?'

Ever since her belly had swollen, terms like 'sister' and 'daughter' flowed easily out of males when they had been such misers with these words. She touched her stomach. *You are diminishing my value on the market, little one.*

'Perhaps,' Mati said. 'As for the scandals, they may be just embers floating on the wind rather than the bonfire itself.'

'Oh, embers they are, but the kind that cause a forest to burn. The Night of the Feast, too, was rife with scandals – an indulgence I keep my legs away from, but not my ears. Salacious tales are food for the soul, especially of one whose children find him dull. And I am happy to share more with someone of your race – for you all are so rare on this side of the world. Peer Sood, at your service.' He joined his hands in the Vedan *namaste*.

'Charmed. You can call me, Lady Em.'

'Now, where was I? Yes. Conclave. My station has helped me glean much of what happened there behind the palace walls. But it is not what transpired during the Night of the Feast that was made into the gossip of midwives. No, it was what happened after, when the Black Swan turned up fuming, and you won't believe it, with child and without its father.' He broke out into a fit of laughter. 'Can you imagine – the Black Swan – a mother. I would rather trust my own child to a nest of vipers for caretaking than the pirate princess of Kalinga.'

You and me both. Suddenly, Mati heard her name from the side.

'Princess Mati.' Sokarro Sinh gave a curt nod.

Mati rose, letting the shawl around her drop for Sood to see her stomach. 'You were right, Peer Sood. These earthships do turn interesting. You never know who you can end up meeting.' She took his shivering, sweating hand, and kissed it lightly. It was only decades of fawning in courts which helped him quiver out a measly bow.

Mati passed before him, and followed Sokarro to the entrance door of the First Galley where she turned to face her, eyes and beak, all pointed in her direction.

'I heard you wanted to talk to me,' Sokarro said. 'Say your piece.'

'What do you know of the Sutra of Kaamah?'

DANTAVAKRA wondered if Vahura knew anything of balance and grip as they climbed the ratlines of the Third Galley. Vahura was not someone anyone would call sure-footed. Her frequent slips on the footholds had convinced him that she must be a terror in the dancing circles of Balkh. Why couldn't she just admit that years of steady exercise had given Dantavakra the wind to lead a task like this but she had resolutely refused to climb behind him.

And it was just the third step of the horrid plan. He stared up the mainmast, dwindling into the greenness of the ceiling above, and squinted as rain fell directly on his face.

Dantavakra had always cherished the rain. Memories plucked at him of how it cleaned the streets of ragpickers and priests, of how it made the world greener, of how it made women want to be courted, to be teased, of how it made their dress cling to their clammy skin making it easy for him to offer his jacket to them. His admirers, his friends and his lovers all clapped when he walked through a puddle instead of around them, and gasped when he danced with his mouth open, without a care for the fever or his clothes. That was Dantavakra of Chedi, a man who embraced the world for all its pleasures, who did not care if he caught a fever, who truly lived, who treated his women to hot, spiced toddy in his dry quarters even as he changed before them, letting them take in his glistening chest. The sound of rain for him was the delightful squeals of women he warmed beside a crackling hearth.

But that was before.

I mean, what is the point of having a ceiling over a city if it can't keep the damn rain out. It wasn't the tears of a cloud but the shit of a sky with an upset stomach. There was no predictability, it came daily, at all odd hours, in sheets that flooded the street gutters, in sounds that made conversation futile, and in strength that could leave a hole in a plank. And it felt even worse way up this high on an earthship.

They had already climbed the footholds from the deck to the one crossbeam that ran uninterrupted across and over the three galleys. They now had to tiptoe undetected across this infernally narrow beam all the way to the horn of the Earthship. The horn, a bit of architectural whimsy, was fashioned from a pair of airavat tusks constructed on either side of the crossbeam to create the illusion of a crown resting over the First Galley. Then they had to tie ropes to the horn and lower themselves before the window of Bhagadatt's room while the Earthship rolled on at breakneck speed. A horrible plan by all accounts, but the abduction of Bhagadatt and the explosions at Leafsong meant there was no turning back.

It would have been so much simpler to rely on the backup plan in which Mati sneaked into the First Galley and just picked up the Daevic Scrolls. If only she knew how to break open mandala locks. No. That was Lady Crankhead here.

The sole silver lining on this opaque fucking cloud was that Dantavakra got to play hero. How many knights had the fortune to save not one but three princesses? How many Riverlanders could claim to have ridden triumphant on the top of an earthship? Forget youngest Rakhjai, Dantavakra had now joined the ranks of the legendary King Ram in being a rescuer of damsels in distress. The man the pamphlets had once dubbed the loser in the Imperial Contest had risen like a splendid phoenix from the ashes of decay. And so what if he was kingslayer – did not even Krishna carry such a burden? Life often thrusts hard choices on heroes because only they have the will to sacrifice duty for the greater good.

Though he did wonder if any of these heroes had been ever as humiliated as he had been in their pursuit of being a legend.

Mati coughed loudly, tears streaming from her face. Vahura's cheek turned red as she hid behind a journal, her shoulders shaking. Asshaye, on the other hand, had burst out laughing hysterically.

Dantavakra had emerged from Vahura's room in a blue high-neck gown, his face hidden behind a sun veil, his stomach squished against a cushion behind the gown. He hated to admit it but he made for a rather fine woman.

'No,' he said, obstinately. 'Never.' Dantavakra flicked the sun veil overhead to reveal his painted face. 'This is... a dishonour and entirely inappropriate! How can I pass off as Princess Mati?'

'Well, considering you are going to be dressed as a pregnant woman,' Asshaye patted the pillow tucked into his pants behind the dress, 'I would say it is appropriate that you look so large and looming,' she said, wiping flecks of laugh spittle from her chin. 'Move those hips, wench!'

'I will slay you, you hag,' Dantavakra boomed. 'How can they allow two Matis on the ship?'

'There will be a fire. Mati will be in the Second Galley. They won't have time to ticket check across all the galleys in the first hour by which time you will be up in the skies.'

'Must say, Ser,' Vahura laughed, 'you are a sight to behold. The passengers will be smitten by you.'

'With respect, Princess Vahura,' Dantavakra said, 'this is a stupid idea, and I am not wearing this.'

Dantavakra's skirts swished around his boots as he climbed after Vahura. Vahura had spurned his gift of help with a spit on the wind that he wished landed back on her face. He never, not once, believed that women were inferior to men but he was growing awfully tired of women not letting him serve them. Take chivalry and charm away from a knight, and he was no better than a bodyguard. When he had said as much to Vahura, she had responded that a chivalrous knight was nothing but a patient crocodile. *She would not have survived one day in Rajgrih's royal circles.*

Though truth be told, he was not just offering to help her out of the goodness of his heart. It was also his politest bid in asking her to hasten. Not a lot of time had passed by her own personal reckoning, but when Dantavakra dared her to look up, she had finally seen how the clouds behind the leafy ceiling had vanished and the sky had been drained of all colour.

'Gods above!' Vahura hissed when her legs found wood that was blessedly firm. They were on the crossbeam that ran uninterrupted over the three galleys of the Earthship. 'It has been hours. Princess Mati's got to be having fits. She must already be in Baggy's room.'

'Baggy?' Dantavakra asked. 'Who is Baggy?'

'The wind ails your ears, Ser. I obviously said Bhagadatt,' Vahura said, though she looked like she did not believe a word that came out of her mouth. *The tangles in the words of a woman can shame a web.* His grand theories on women were, however, interrupted when Vahura decided on crossing the crossbeam by sliding on her arse rather than walking it.

'Oh, pardon me if I do not spend every day walking on a thin crossbeam on the top of an earthship wearing a heavy leather belt on the waist,' she shouted over Dantavakra's attempt to interrupt, '*while* the wind is conspiring to topple me down to my death.'

'But the belt is our salvation, Princess.' He pointed at his own belt studded with iron rings. The belts were custom climbing harnesses lent to them by Asshaye, who called them a burglar's dream. 'Just jerk your thumbs inside the iron rings on that belt and find your balance core. We, swordsmen—'

'Need to learn to feed their own ego because I am terribly busy. Listen, good ser, I know you'll go far in your life, but I do wish it can be now, and I hope it stays that way.' Vahura dragged ahead on the crossbeam with the grace of a rabbit paralysed from down below.

They lapsed into silence as they threaded their way through the little maze of netting, fendoffs and canvas. He saw Kamrup's archers, who kept watch from their perches on the yardarms, marvelling at how his time with Asanka had acquainted him with these exotic mariterms. He was also glad to know the old hag had not led them astray. Since this was not a ship on sea, they had never needed to use mastboys as lookout for rival ships, making their lives easier. The soldiers on deck, in absence of actual experience, had been drilled to keep their eyes peeled for trouble outside the Earthship, not inside. On the deck itself, he could see only a sparse crew, busy rolling barrels of ale or guiding guests who had escaped for clandestine escapades back to their seat downstairs.

'By the Forge... This is Daevic glass! Vaikunshard!' Vahura exclaimed.

'Vaikunwhat?'

'Glass used by Daevas, and some say, even the First Men, to build their giant cities,' Vahura said. Dantavakra could see she was talking to distract herself from what she was doing. 'The shards cannot be broken or chiselled by any instrument known to man. They are used as they are found. With the sun setting, you can see them shine. See...' She pointed below at the wires around them. Glittering like ringmail against the sharp glare of lamps over it, the bluish light spread like a map of veins around the walkway. 'No wonder. The vaikunshard wire-hooks let the entire earthship flex as it turns around corners at such high speed without a galley toppling over to the side. Oh my—'

'What is it?' Dantavakra's hand flashed to his sword hilt.

'I just remembered where I am and what I am doing.'

'That is just fear, Princess,' Dantavakra said. He wasn't even sure his words reached her, and right now, he found he couldn't care less. Chance had brought him here but he decided he was going to let his choice make his destiny, and his choice was to turn his walk across the Earthship in Vahura's skirts into the most roguish entry in the book on heroes.

After what felt like the endless drip of sand through an hourglass that measured seasons instead of seconds, they finally reached the First Galley. Glancing down, he could see they were perched directly above the aft which, as luck would have it, was stark and empty. The young Grey Shaman, who Dantavakra had met earlier that day, was fooling around with the steer that had no use on the Earthship, while five guards in their leafy cloaks were playing a round of cards beside a collection of crates and barrels. Just ahead of them, the silhouettes of the giant airavat humps bobbed in the air as they rampaged through on the rail, a mahout and a Grey Shaman on each of those airavats to oversee their progress.

'They managed to even get *that* on the Earthship. Brilliant,' Vahura suddenly said, catching his attention.

'What?' Dantavakra followed her eyes to something large, odd shaped, stacked in the middle of the crates on deck, hidden behind an enormous blue-red tarp drawn taut over it. 'What is that?'

'Nothing. One of the Tusk's treasures I had seen – they brought it on the Earthship as well. This is a good omen. If they can bring *that*, they would have definitely brought his locker. His suite is the second one on the left, correct?' Vahura asked.

'There's no one more trustworthy than a man in the throes of an orgasm,' Dantavakra murmured, a dreamy smile tugging at his lips as he recalled the Yogini wrangling the secret out of the Shaman. Gods, how he wished he'd been the one in the Shaman's place.

'Hand over the silk. I will take it to the right and tie it over the Right Horn,' Vahura interrupted Dantavakra's reverie.

'Why are you headed to the Right? I thought we had to go to the Left?'

'I will anchor it here so that the silk has a good tug and line when we make our way back.'

So complicated. It was a simple thing to hook a rope to an anchor and descend. Considering this time, he was in charge of their safety, he kept chivalry aside for a moment and ventured an opinion that might very well save the Princess's life.

'Why can't we just climb down using a normal rope knotted around the Horn?' Dantavakra said, carefully shrugging out of the dozen coils of spidersilk draped around his waist inside his dress. 'And then we could do that instead of... abseil, that's the word, right – yes, abseil down this scarlet cloth thing? This is too... convoluted.' That was the one thing he had learned from his time guarding the architects behind the Virangavat. Things need to be simple. The costliest part of building an arena is the mistakes.

'You mistake *intricate* for *convoluted*, Ser. Hand me the silk.'

Dantavakra scowled as he wondered how this Sanskrit-demon could be the sister to the kind Vauri. *Vahura must be adopted*, he concluded as he tossed a coil to Vahura, who, for all her still-footedness, plucked it deftly out of the air. She walked to the right side of the left-right crossbeam with her arms windmilling for balance like a bird. A few moments later, she arrested her pace by wrapping her arms around the right Horn of the Earthship. With a swift tug, she liberated a length of spidersilk and wound it around the Horn with practised efficiency.

'Now, why abseiling?' Vahura said. 'Because, I am not a rope-climber, I am a librarian. And this is not a descent from a terrace to a girl's window. It is a huge fall, from the mastbeam here down the deck, all the way down to the room. What if we run into complications? Consider the time taken to climb down using a hemp rope. Can you assure us we won't be spotted by someone on the deck? One stray eye, and our plan sinks. And what if we slip from the rope? And...' Vahura said as she hefted the knot of the spidersilk in a bight around the Horn. Satisfied, she jerked the spare coils of rope towards him.

From her satchel, she pulled out a heavy bit of iron, a figure of infinity with one side larger than the other, and a thick bar right down the middle. 'So, yes, where was I? Right, abseiling? Think of this rope as a road to the Prince's room, and this descender is like a horse whose speed can change as you descend the road. This harness is like the rein of a horse, allowing us to use the horse safely and securely. Do you see now how much better this is than just downward rope climbing?'

Yes, Mother. Thank you for spoonfeeding me. Chivalry! He reminded himself. *Chivalry!* 'Aye, Princess. How do you know this?'

'My mother used to take me abseiling on the off chance I had to run away from a forced marriage. Don't depend on anyone else, she had said. Be a Satyabhama, not a Rukmini. Now don't forget to get rigged up after you are done and remember, two lines. Main line, and then belay,' Vahura said as she clipped her descender into one of the harness rings on her belt, and threaded it through with one of the spidersilk lines leading back to the Horn. A second line was lashed tight to another harness for added safety. 'I am going to cross over to the right side now, alright? Be safe, Ser.'

Dantavakra grumbled as he rigged himself up in a similar fashion, struggling with the stopper knots. The Earthship turned around a bend, and shook like an inmate with fever. Dantavakra barely managed to hold the two rabbit ears he had made for the knot.

'Will a simple knot suffice, Princess?' he asked, realizing his words would have been lost on the wind again. Already, the wind was screaming through the lines and yards overhead. Sighing, he looked up to find Vahura. She was not there.

Vahura had fallen off the ship.

 MATI'S head reappeared but Sokarro slid her fingers into her hair, then pushed Mati's head somewhat painfully down. *Not that soon, Soks.* The easiest way for a gifted artist to diminish her value was by churning out paintings by the day. And... on the canvas of bed, Mati was the greatest artist alive.

She pushed aside Sokarro's hand, denying her slippery slope to gratification. Before Sokarro could protest, Mati stuffed her kerchief into Sokarro's mouth to shut her up, all the while holding her breath. With the Rakshasa silent, Mati took her time. She found the hooks of her drape, and then the laces of her blouse: beneath this, she saw, Sokarro's grey breasts were mottled scarlet from the hundred tiny pin-stabs of the humans that had chopped her nose and her ear off. Mati ignored the Key Relic she had handed to Sokarro to gain her trust – which Sokarro wore around her neck – and took her time to see these wounds, lending Sokarro's suppressed insecurities time to break through her tough exterior, and break they did when Sokarro's proud shoulders shrugged inwardly, self-consciously.

Mati laid siege to the memories of those wounds by kissing each scarlet scar, one hand gently stroking the side of her neck, pleasuring and reassuring her. Sokarro's hair fell over her face like a slice of night as Mati pushed her to lie back. The skin around her dark eyes was smooth, broken only by laugh lines which Mati knew to be scowl lines. She kissed those lines. Peeling her layers one by one, she felt Sokarro's back rise in an arch. Mati renewed her attacks. She dipped her fingers into Sokarro's hair. She touched her brow that was sharp, avoided her kerchief-stuffed mouth, kissed the dimpled cheeks around it instead. Her steel-beak pinched Mati's cheek, and Mati pressed against it, holding her breath, till it drew blood.

'Oh,' Sokarro gasped. 'Oh! Oh seeds and soil!' Her back curved, her fingers clutched desperately at the bed railing, she kicked a pile of stacked books onto the floor, smacked her head against the wall behind and sent a little shower of wood-flakes across her shoulders. Sokarro tried desperately to push Mati's face away, but Mati had Sokarro by... the ovaries. Avian liqueur-coloured skin met the calluses of Mati's fingers. Smooth and wet as ice melting in a velvet glove. Sokarro hissed one more desperate 'Mati!' through gritted teeth, then stiffened and fell back, heavy and slack, her legs shuddering weakly with aching after-spasms.

Mati rose like a swimmer rising from the pink depths of a black sea, a conqueror, to draw herself up until she lay along the length of Sokarro.

The Rakshasa's defences were down. Now all she had to do was wait for the shadowsin in the kerchief to do its magic. It had worked like a charm on Bhagadatt. She did not expect it to take time now. Till then, Mati granted her the courtesy of her silence as Sokarro lay, heaving.

Mati's hands scrambled blindly on the tray bearing pomegranate juice and sherbet in tall glasses alongside a basket of freshly plucked bananas on the bedside table. The cabin was richly lit by faceted alchemical lamps in jade frames. The walls were draped with layers of tapestries, and the corners hidden by silk pillows. Mati felt a pang when she saw a flag from a Kalingan ship pinned like a stag's skull on the wall opposite her. Several sea chests held up a tabletop piled with folded maps, half-filled inkpots and navigational instruments of fine quality. A chair lay empty beside the makeshift table.

'Here, take your kerchief back. Surprising that you carry one, and even more surprising it tastes like rose and myrrh, two tastes I would never associate with you.'

'Tastes change. Toss it to the side. If I want the essence of your mouth again, I know the path.'

Sokarro blushed. Flicking the poisoned kerchief on the floor, she said, 'You're swollen like a cow, and yet you're as raunchy as a chimpanzee.'

'I would hope not,' Mati said as her fingernails traced a line on her bare skin, 'as chimpanzees show no initiative. I would rather be a bonobo.'

'So, is that what you were doing?' Sokarro asked, teasingly. 'Showing initiative?'

'Well, a girl sometimes has to take matters in her own hands.' Mati sucked the dampness off her finger. 'Though I must confess, I was roused by how the presence of a third person in the same room does not bother you in the least.'

'I don't see what the racket is about. I find the glow, the sheen and the fullness of your body alluring,' Sokarro paused, 'as long I don't have to stay back for the morning sickness.'

'The nausea is fleeting. Only lasts the first four full moons. Now it is just the charming companionship of cramps and contractions. Oh, and of course, the trips to the privy.'

'The enlarged areolas are a welcome sight, though.' Sokarro laughed. 'I am most amused by where you find yourself now. Mati of Kalinga being treated like a vase to be protected rather than a farm to be ploughed. Life must have grown stale for you in the Empire while you were waiting for the second brain inside you to hatch.'

'You've no inkling of the horrors of boredom that surround me. A vase can be protected for all eternity but it loses its purpose without any flowers to choke its mouth.'

'You are a filthy pillow writer of the most common class, Kalingan! You must've been a treasure in the Magadhan court.'

'Speaking of treasures, you still haven't answered me. Is it here?'

Sokarro frowned. 'It is a useless piece of junk that the Tusk collects out of boredom. Why does that even interest you?'

'I am a sailor first, a princess next. Will you show it to me if I request?'

Sokarro smiled. 'It is upstairs on the deck, hidden amongst crates. But... only if you *request*.'

Mati licked Sokarro's ear as she held her belly in preparation for a second trip down south when a thud startled them both. But it did not come from outside the door. All Mati's work came undone when Sokarro stiffened with resolve, drawing a sabre from under her bed. She drew away the curtain from the stern vaikunshard window. Mati glanced from over Sokarro's shoulder to see what had cracked against the window.

You had one job, you imbeciles! The left side!

Sokarro turned to glower at Mati. Behind Sokarro, in the window, a red-haired princess hung upside down, waving awkwardly at them.

 VAHURA could not believe she waved at Mati and Sokarro. That ranked as by far the stupidest thing she could have done. Well, second stupidest. The first was when she had tried to lean against the Horn in some show of feigned nonchalance and bravado at the knight. Her pretentiousness came at a steep price. In the blink of an eye, her heart, her stomach and the night sky had turned a somersault in unison. She'd slipped, slid, and felt wood yield to empty air beneath her feet. She had flailed in a mad scramble, clipped a handhold with her boot, only to find herself hurtling headfirst over the ship's side. For one bright moment, she thought maybe she could arrest her fall by clutching the deck's handrail. Easier said than done. She fell belly first onto the rail, and that knocked the wind out of her, hands completely forgotten as she slipped onto the ship's side.

Her line finally decided to go taut, and the shipside rushed to greet her just a little too eagerly for her taste. Like a loose pendulum, she had swung in, tucking her knees to absorb the impact. It worked for the rest of her body but her face hit the window of a cabin, the glass's dampness sticky. Her cheeks squeaked against the glass, slowly, in abrupt, loud pauses like a braying donkey, her hand on the window, the diamond drill having slipped from her fingers – she had no idea when.

And while Vahura had hung precariously so, heart hammering and stomach hurting, she had looked down to find the moonlit iron tracks humming mere inches from her undone hair. It had taken her a while to grow self-aware and realize that a naked Rakshashi had drawn the curtains from the other side of the Earthship and was staring at her with her an unfriendly emotion. It took her longer to realize that not only had she rappelled onto the wrong side of the

Earthship, of all the room windows she could have cracked her face against, she had chosen the room where Mati had been working on neutralizing Sokarro. How neutralizing involved making a person naked remained a baffling enigma, one her books did not have an answer to. She couldn't even pinch herself in the upside position. So, when the upside figure of Mati glowered at her from behind Sokarro, despite all the blood rushing to her brain, Vahura waved. Like an idiot.

Slowly, Vahura began to re-orient herself to an upright stance so that at least she could remain suspended mid-air with dignity when she felt the lines tug at her. *Oh good.* Dantavakra was pulling her back. She could leave the naked Sokarro for Mati to handle. Just as peace began to find her, a faint whisper carried in the wind that sounded like: 'Hang on, I'm coming!'

'No, you imbecile! We won't be able to climb back up! Pull me! Pull me!'

The wind swallowed her words with an evil sound. And a heart-beat later, Dantavakra hit the side of the Earthship with a whoomp about a foot above her. 'Tvastr save us,' Vahura said, heart pound-ing in her ears, as she realized their plan to save Vauri had failed spectacularly.

'Whew!' Dantavakra said, holding on to his line with both hands. 'You were right, Princess. This descender is fantastic.' She saw him grip his taut main line and release a bit of tension on his descender. Slowly, smoothly, he slipped down to hang right beside her. 'Here to save you, my Princess. Jumped without a second thought,' he said, proudly.

'That… I can agree with,' Vahura groaned.

'You looked miffed. Are you hurt?' Finally, his instinct took charge as he turned his head to take note of their audience in nude. 'Fuck…'

Sokarro's face drew close to the glass and released a vapour of frost breath that fashioned itself into a delightful swirl of geometric patterns on the glass, until Sokarro took a finger and traced a few lines to outline a skull with two crossed bones behind it.

Dantavakra's next words echoed her sentiment.

'I miss my brother.'

 MATI'S eyes widened when Sokarro said she would beat her back into her mother's cunt. It was a good cuss. Mati admired a good cuss, especially from someone who should've passed out a while ago. Sokarro snarled as she came forward, her grey breasts drenched in sweat, her ego dented and her eyes blade red.

Mati tried lying. 'But, why do you think that I am—'

'A mouse would have better sense to trust a python than you,' Sokarro said, and drew her sabre at her in a flash. 'You are worse than a cunt, for you are even lower!' She was seething now, the blade shivering in her hand. 'You... you are an ankle!'

And here's where Mati made the folly of laughing. In Mati's defence, it was a mighty tumble from the last insult and Mati had already been building to a laugh, picturing how uncomfortable the sight of two unclothed women grappling in a room must have made Vahura, who was still suspended upside down outside.

In Sokarro's defence, Mati's cruel laugh toppled the pillar of peace that had already loosened at the foundations after being used, discarded, seduced again, only to be re-used. For Sokarro stopped screaming then, and whispered something far more cutting. 'You are worse than the men who did this to me.' She jabbed a finger at her steel beak.

Mati froze mid-laugh for she knew now Sokarro meant business. Had her betrayal really skinned so deep? *By the Tide*, Mati groaned. Sokarro didn't even know what game Mati was playing at, and to fill a vase of empty knowledge with such anger seemed unfair to Mati. *Oh, that vase metaphor again!*

Sokarro's sabre swung around, interrupting her thoughts on equity and fairness. Mati barely managed to catch it on the wooden tabletop she had dragged away from the top of the barrels, spilling the scrolls and instruments to the floor. But it still felt like a ship struck by a charging kraken. Sokarro wrenched the sabre free, tearing away a great sliver of wood, allowing light from the alchemical lantern to stream through from Sokarro's side.

Mati tossed the tabletop away. She had no weapons and she could not back away outside the room for that would be the end of this plan, end of her escape route.

'Sokarro,' Mati said as she now pulled a chair in between them, 'those two are lovers! They probably had a wishlist to fuck on top of an earthship. As if we didn't take things to the extreme when we were young.'

'Liar!' Sokarro screamed through tears in her eyes as her sabre fell again, and this time the chair's legs took the sabre well as a shield, but there wasn't enough space or strength for Mati to wield the chair. Mati staggered back, her hands wildly groping for something, anything. She found the sherbet glass on the bedside table.

'Where is my Tusk? He had gone to meet the red bitch! He had taken from me an oath to give him one night free of restraints. What did you do with him? Did you kill him, you liar?'

'What do you mean, liar?' Mati demanded, incensed as if she were a Monk of the Moon accused of lying. 'Sokarro, stop! Listen to me. The truth is rarely pure, and never that simple. Can you just listen to my tale?'

Sokarro responded by lunging with her sabre, which Mati dodged, stepping behind to put the bedside table between them. Mati was still smiling – and still clutching the sherbet with one hand, and cradling her belly with the other. *Baby, hang on.* With an almighty effort, she flicked her foot and sent the bedside table flying, slamming it into Sokarro.

Even as Sokarro recovered her bearings, Mati shoulder-rushed Sokarro into the glass window. *Ow, that hurt me more than her.* The Rakshasa groaned as she slid down to a seated position and Mati groaned, hunched over, one arm around her belly and the other arm still holding on to the slender glass.

'For someone just flooded, you are rather wound up over such a trifle.' She downed her sherbet in a single gulp and smashed the glass against the wall.

Mati flicked the glass stem out in an attempt to stab her side, but Sokarro was fast, snake fast, and she dodged under Mati to get behind her. Mati turned her wrist, one hand on her belly to help her pivot, and stabbed Sokarro clean.

Sokarro staggered as a hot fire spread through her breasts, and probably not the kind she fancied. She screamed, and Mati could only hope that anyone within earshot outside the door mistook it for cries of passion. The stem of the glass, sticking out of her left breast, made a fine fashion complement to her steel nose. Sokarro yanked the glass free, the wound in her breast already healing, the blood flow already staunched. Damn Rakshasan healing powers.

'Could I interest you in a sip of my blood perhaps to soothe your nerves?' Mati tried.

'Like I would ever drink your diseased filth.' Sokarro swung the sabre again. Mati leaped back just as the sabre swung where her legs had been a moment before. *Oh, that was not a good idea!* Bent over like an old woman and holding her stomach in pain, Mati put distance between herself and Sokarro. Mati's muscle memory was planting trees her body could not water. She could not fight the way she used to. Sokarro seemed to have arrived at the same conclusion.

'You're a slower, bigger target now,' Sokarro said, flicking a drop of blood from the tip of her sabre as she paused against the door, making no effort to leave.

Mati rolled out her shoulder. 'Even still, it is no fair fight.' She peeled a banana and took one enormous bite of the fruit, cleaving it at its base. 'For you,' Mati's voice came out muffled.

'Did he even write to you after the Swayamvar? I think not.'

Mati was about to chew the fruit but stiffened. She wanted to tell Sokarro to not do what she was going to. Mati liked Sokarro. She had been stalling to let the battle-rage in Sokarro fade but instead it had changed into something far more monstrous – battle-calm: where the fear and the rage sublimes in the air, to be replaced by the sinister joy of murder.

Mati rolled the banana to the side of her mouth. 'I woudth suggesth—'

'Shove the suggestion up your used hole, the public dumping yard of Kalinga. Duryodhan was smart to crawl out of you. You were wrong to call him a fool. When a prettier, younger woman turned up, he tossed you—'

Mati's extended foot snapped into the leg of the toppled chair and flipped it back onto Sokarro, catching her by surprise. Mati barrelled into it, pinning Sokarro to the wall with the chair's legs straddling her on either side of her breasts and stomach. But Sokarro managed to free her sabre hand from the hold in time. Sokarro twisted her wrist, ready to stab at Mati till Sokarro realized the blade was pointed at Mati's pregnant stomach. Sokarro hesitated.

'You were ready to kill me but you wouldn't stab my stomach for fear of killing the unborn child. What did you think? The child would have crawled out of my corpse to live a happy life forever, you hypocrite!'

Sokarro spat at her. 'Where is my Tusk, whore?'

'Always the temperamental person. That is why I did not tell you the child was Bhagadatt's.' Mati's voice was garbled but the seriousness of it registered with Sokarro.

Sokarro's eyes widened, and the lips of her mouth slammed open in shock.

'Just joking,' Mati said, as she swirled her tongue, and spat the huge chunk of banana right inside Sokarro's mouth, followed by a quick punch to her food pipe.

Sokarro mouth stayed open as if she were trying to scream, but only a sick gurgle escaped. *Ecchhh Accchhh.* It sounded like a cat choking on a hairball. Her hands clawed at Mati's arms for help as her eyes probably turned bloodshot. It was difficult to tell that on a Rakshasa.

Spit frothed at the sides of Sokarro's mouth, and the Rakshashi knew then, knew she would die. She tried to scratch Mati again with her sabre, blindly, her eyes turning glassy upwards. But a woman pregnant with a baby is still stronger than a woman choking on a banana.

Sokarro dug her fingernails into Mati's wrists. Small, ragged gasps escaped her throat. Mati felt Sokarro's life slip away, breath by breath, inch by inch. It was not until Sokarro's arms sagged that Mati let her down gently.

'Death by a banana in the throat,' Mati said, as she snatched the Key Relic from her neck and wore it around hers. 'As far as deaths go, you are now in the Hall of Fame, Soks.'

Afterwards, Mati opened the vaikunshard window and let the pair of idiots in. They gawked at the sight: a beautifully breasted Rakshashi who had choked to death on a banana and a dusky, heavily pregnant human heaving on the bed.

Dantavakra readied his sword. 'Are you alright?'

Mati nodded. 'Just give me a minute or two to catch up. Danta, go to the door and check what the weather is like outside and Vahura, turn around. Give me some privacy as I change.' Once they had turned, Mati sat on the floor beside the corpse of Sokarro Sinh, peeling another banana – still naked – all the while wondering why she hadn't told them about the blood between her legs.

 VAHURA discovered the blood between her lips – a souvenir from her fall. The cut in her lips helped keep her mind from the corpse in the room. No one was supposed to be hurt. No one. And because of her slip, Sokarro, Baggy's trusted friend, died a horrible death. Because of her. Because of her plan, her clumsy feet, her misguided belief that had led her to believe she could do this by herself.

'Did the poison not work?' Vahura asked, voice scarce more than a whisper. 'She should have been unconscious, right?'

Mati cleared her throat like a mother wishing to spare her son from news of the guilty verdict. 'We did not account for her... nose. The steel blocked it somehow. That was my stupidity.'

A shudder racked Vahura.

'No, it wasn't.' Vahura gripped her satchel bag tightly, her nails digging permanent creases on the strap as she sank on Sokarro's bed. 'It was mine.'

'Red, I will tell you this for the first and last time, she died because of an accident,' Mati said as she finished dressing up. 'Do not spend your salt on guilt. That is why I always encourage women to work on their gag reflex.'

Vahura nodded absently as she pressed the swelling behind her lips to increase the dosage of pain. She had no choice, for her conscience would dim her clarity, dull her senses and destroy any chance of saving Vauri. Clarity returned soon on a thing with black feathers. Sokarro had attacked first, tried to stab Mati's unborn child – she had seen it. Her sabre had been aimed at her stomach. It was only instinct that drove Mati to spit at her to distract her. Who could have known that the fruit would lodge so fatally in Sokarro's throat?

Mati clapped her hands strongly to bring Vahura back. 'Awaken that manticore, that griffin, whoever sleeps inside you, and remind the world what a monster looks like when it wears the skin of a sister. Okay? Must not allow pain to overstay. Now off with you.'

Vahura squinted at Mati's neck. 'That... does not look human-made.' Vahura delicately held the Key and turned the metal-forged relic in her hands, moonlight from the open window playing gently over the dragonfly wings on either side of the stem. 'This is remarkable craftsmanship. It is oddly familiar though...'

Dantavakra sidled up behind Vahura with news in tow. One, the room which was supposed to be filled with guards on rest was instead cluttered with all kinds of garbage – an enormous clock, some old books and weirdly shaped plants. The Garden of Broken Things? The bad news was that the reason he saw this was because the only two guards inside that room had opened the door and joined the other two who were standing outside Bhagadatt's room.

Mati did not respond but moved towards the door, cracking it open just a smidge. After a swift survey, she beckoned them over. Vahura trailed Mati's gaze to the door on the left, which led to the bridge between the Second Galley and the First. There was a standing area on the First Galley side of the door, stretching across the entire width of the Earthship, perhaps intended for stray luggage or fruit carts to be stashed. A staircase by it led to the deck above.

Mati turned to Vahura, undressing again. 'While you hide, I'll distract the guards. Do what you got to do after. If my gamble does not work, well, we will see each other in prison.'

'Wha... at?' Dantavakra said.

'A jest to calm the nerves,' Mati explained.

'Forgive my saying so but you should definitely hire a governess for your child, Princess,' Dantavakra said, rubbing his chest.

Mati, naked again, smirked as she slid the door of the cabin open, and then ushered them out. Vahura and Dantavakra huddled behind the cart in the standing area by the staircase. It struck Vahura she hadn't asked Mati how she would create the distractions.

DANTAVAKRA sailed into Bhagadatt's unlocked room as Mati distracted the guards by calling attention to murder. Even after he locked the room, he could still hear Mati's cries. 'Help! Lady Sokarro is choking! Guards!'

The room was splendid, and made the *Gilded Lion* look like a leper colony in comparison. Wall hangings of silk and carvings of alabaster decorated the room. He passed silver coffrets set with emeralds and crystal bottles of dark purple wine, jealous of the clean linens and plush pillows on the bed. There even lingered a hint of perfume in the air, despite the room being deserted. *Must be nice to have your room looked after even in your absence.* Dantavakra would settle for someone to simply fold his clothes and stack them in his wardrobe.

Vahura paid little heed to the décors, her eyes hunting for the safe. Admittedly, it turned out to be a task, given how Bhagadatt's artefacts and journals were scattered across the room by the packers and movers. Blazebane in the building was understandably not a rally cry to keep doing quality work. Mid-thought, Dantavakra's gaze was trapped by an array of weapons mounted on a polished wooden stand. A fearsome battle-axe, its heavy blade bearing marks of countless conflicts, stood alongside a pair of elegantly forged shortswords, gleaming with malice. But Dantavakra's heart was stolen by someone else. Someone whose prongs curved sharply, resembling the fangs of a serpent ready to strike. *I missed you, trident.*

'There,' Vahura whispered, pointing to a locker piled on a battered desk under an army of cushions, a knife-scarred dartboard and a deluge of vellum sheets. The safe was, according to Asshaye, of Balkhan make, straight from the smiths of Jerdog. Vahura paced towards the safe, delicately removed the garbage on it and ran her hands around it like a lover.

'This is most impressive, Princess,' Dantavakra said as he saw Vahura ease a lock of hair out of her braid, and yank the strand free to reveal a wire with tiny hooks. 'A Princess who is a librarian who abseils off earthships and who has cracked Indra-knows how many safes!'

'This is my maiden voyage with a safe,' Vahura explained, without turning to look at him.

'Oh, of course, naturally, why would a Princess have the need to peep into a safe? Dummy safes, then. Is it a rite of passage in Balkh then? You tinkers are mad.'

'No, uhm, no dummy safe,' Vahura laughed nervously, 'this is the first safe...'

The effect of that revelation was magical. That quiet sense of confidence left him, to be succeeded by the apprehensive feeling a fellow must have had facing the first apocalypse.

'Surely you do not mean you have never cracked a safe open in your life. Because our entire plan of stealing the Daevic Scrolls relied on you to crack this safe, apparently a rather difficult safe, open.'

'Rein your horses in, Ser,' Vahura said, irritated. 'I memorized the route to find the centre of a mandala lock in this Assyrian safe from a book. I know my way around it.'

'*Memorized. From. A. Book*,' Dantavakra said through gritted teeth. All that he had ever heard or read about the recklessness of the educated fairer race seemed to come back to him. 'If this is your idea of a jest, I am afraid you'd best steer clear of Princess Mati's company from now on.'

'You are vexing me greatly, Ser.'

His jubilation at finding a trident had waned. 'Vexing! *I* am vexing *you*? You proclaimed to us that you could crack the safe open. You think memorizing how to break open a lock in a safe it is enough to turn you into a master thief? Why don't you memorize how to swim, and let me hurl you into the sea and see how you fare? There are certain places in the world, Princess, where knowledge is no substitute for skill. The open sea is one, and a locked safe is another.'

'It is just a matter of turning the pressing wrench into the lock, and turning it slowly enough to catch the telltale click of the tumblers inside. You match the right clicks, you enter the next concentric circle of the mandala, and on and on, till the maze of mandala is breached and the door opens. Thievery, at the end of the day, is an illusion, just like the courage of a Kingsguard.'

Dantavakra wondered if he could stab her with that trident and later claim he was trying to stop her from robbing Bhagadatt.

They would even award him for his feat, crown him a hero. He wouldn't even do it for the laurels. Just for world peace. A world without Vahura would be a less condescending place. *Damn you, Vauri! Your sister is such a pain!*

He saw Vahura pull a chair to the table and pluck out a listening tube from her satchel. She set the tube to her ear and leaned against the safe door. Dantavakra squinted. Vahura did look confident. She sounded confident, too. Maybe his outburst was not needed, even if not unwarranted. He turned to the window of the room, the window through which they were supposed to enter by carving a hole into it with a diamond drill.

Two deaths.

Saham Dev. Sokarro.

All for one little girl.

Dantavakra smiled when he came empty-handed in a hunt for remorse. He would do it again. He suddenly found himself wishing he had a daughter like Vauri, someone whose cheeks he could kiss endlessly, who he could protect against men like Saham Dev, actually even men like himself, he grudgingly admitted. He still did not want to be married. If any such thoughts had lurked in the back of his mind, they had been stamped out when he had seen the makings of an *ideal wife* in Mati. But he would love to teach his daughter the ways of the sword, maybe even teach her the ways of cracking open a safe. He chuckled at the thought as he caressed his false womb. But why not? She would be a hero's daughter.

Through mounds, mines and mishaps, his journey was turning out to be the hero's quest he had dreamed of. Maybe the Emperor might actually be glad his worthless son was gone. Maybe he would raise Saham Dev's child, a worthy heir, who Dantavakra could train to be a knight of honour, and who knew, eventually wed his daughter. Dantavakra, father by law to the future king of the Magadhan Empire. He liked how that sounded. But the bird of his boundless imagination fell from the sky because of another sound.

'By da Forde!' Vahura snapped as she dropped a suspicious number of picks from her mouth. 'I can't open it!'

How he wished he was weak enough to just let go and topple Vahura on her arse.

VAHURA wished she had the strength to grab and topple Dantavakra on his arse. She had been stared at many a time in her life, which girl hasn't, but not one came within a league of the spectacle that Dantavakra was putting up. That look of shock, anguish and I-told-you-so on his face needed to be shaved with a razor.

But she truly thought she had it! The clicks... she heard them all, but... she could not distinguish them. *Don't give up. Try again.* She opened the door to her mind's library. The iron-smelling pages of *Safe Orgasm: A Master's Guide to Claiming Metal Maidenhoods* flipped open:

'Safelocks are like a woman's breasts. Pleasure is achieved by jiggling, with a key in the hands of an owner, and by a pick in the hands of a master. Jiggle the...'

Such rot! That author was such a degenerate! Vahura pinched herself. *Focus, Vahura.* She already knew the anonymous author's work manifested itself as a tawdry blend of erotica and training manual, all forcibly rolled into one. So there was no cause for shock. She shook her head, and turned the page.

'All a master has to do is to listen through the heart, or a steth of the safe, to the moans made when these discs rub each other in the right way. Timing is key. Hold them tight, circle them right, and their individual moans will tell you if you've hit the spot. With the key, of course, you can just slide in and each of the doors moans open. But those using hands have to paint to get the colours out.'

She turned the dial right three times to the first number, and felt the cold touch of metal as she pressed her ear flat against the safe. She could hear... some sounds. Must be the discs grabbing each other. She turned left – one full turn – then to the second number – repeated the routine for the third number.

'There you go!' Vahura chirped but the safe did not.

What was she doing wrong? She rotated the lock several times, taking notes of the dial position, but it made different noises at different positions, and she had no idea which sound was which. The sheer number of combinations felt infinite, and by now, the clicking sounds had all merged into one, clacking and clicking, taunting her like a crab from the other side of the door.

'Remember, like a charmer of night, disclocks can have "false" notches to feign moans.'

How would she distinguish between fake moans and true moans if she had never heard them in the first place? Which notes rang true? Which were echoes? Why couldn't sound be described in books like smells are?

She should have known this flaw in her plan.

Like she should have known that Sokarro with her metal nose would not have been able to sniff the shadowsin. Why was she playing the fool when she needed her wit the most? She was nothing but a fraud, and facts had finally caught up with her.

Wit, don't abandon me, please. She dragged the sharp point of the wire sharply over her skin to feel something other than shame. It helped. Her wit spread its tendrils through the crevices into which some memories might have slipped, to find them, to use them. What had Asshaye said? 'When you can't bully your way through the guards, blast through them instead,' she murmured and suddenly Baggy's words in Kingswood came back to her like a strayed sheep returned home.

'I recovered from drowning in a mire as a child. If I am well quenched, I heal swiftly from steel cuts. In my room is a shelf with acid vials that I test on my fingers just to see which acid burn would my fingers not recover from. I combine them, to burn me, to poison, to freeze, to even stab it with lightning sometimes.'

She rummaged through Bhagadatt's articles on the table. Nothing. She surveyed every shelf and rack around. Nothing. Exhausted, she fell back on the bed and felt a bite lance through her arse. Angry, she yanked the blanket away. The culprit was a brass frame carefully made to lie on the bed but carelessly concealed by the haphazardly thrown blanket. Its circular frames, seemingly designed to cradle candles, sheltered glass vials in each frame.

Fortune must have finally taken pity on her for these vials to not have broken because of the shift or because of her big butt. Flipping the pages of the alchemy books in her head, she drew out a little glass vial, capped with silver. Tore the stopper free with her teeth, unscrewed the cap and sniffed. Wincing but nodding, she murmured, 'Blackwood.' Plucked another one which held sapphire water that twinkled as if vaikunshard pieces were hidden inside it. The Mathurans called it Frostwater. The main ingredient behind the Mathuran munitions.

'What are you doing?' Dantavakra asked.

'This safe is Assyrian steel. Assyrians who were wiped out in their battle against the Frost Giants in the bowels of Mai Layas: the coldest place on earth, home to Rikshas...'

'Yes, yes, all fascinating. What has that got to do with... whatever you are doing?'

'Their impenetrable steel failed them there because it does not do well in the cold. Ice of Mai Layas trumped against the fire of Assyria.'

'Like Lord Dimvak's blade...' Dantavakra gasped. Ignoring him, Vahura sprinkled the Blackwood into the vial of Frostwater before sealing it. She shook the vial vigorously, and then using her picks as makeshift tongs, she held the vial against the safe's lock. The acidic cocktail first ate through the vial to spread over the lock like lava over rock. The safe's door hissed as it froze, and then cracked, and then blackened. In a matter of heartbeats, Vahura, using a pair of gloves, swung open the safe door in a cloud of cold smoke. 'Told you I could crack open the safe.'

'You melted the lock with acid which you had no idea would be here in the room.'

Vahura threw a cushion at Dantavakra, who caught it with both hands before it hit his face. 'Why can't the plans of my subconscious receive the same applause as my conscious mind? They work together, don't they? Just like a swordsman dodging an attack from behind. Would you not credit it to the fighter?'

Confident as she felt, the thick gloves on her hand did not disguise the shiver as her fingers groped for salvation within the locker. In the blindness, they grasped and clutched the secrets of Bhagadatt without distinction, and pulled them out from their safe haven. One by one, they were discarded. A faint sketch of a Rakshasa with his son, a carefully preserved griffin feather, a vial of blood and... a book.

This was it. Her last chance. Her last gambit. Once she opened the book, hope would open the window to reality and what season would greet her was anybody's guess.

This time she did not pinch herself. She touched the cover of the book... and dropped it when loud metal knocks startled her. Her other hand instinctively bid the unsheathe-friendly knight to hold steady. Moments later, Mati's scream reached them through the door. Too muted to be the cries of a woman in the throes of labour. Too high to be the feigned cry of a woman in the throes of a performance.

'That must have been Mati letting us know,' Dantavakra said as he shifted the cushion to one hand and clicked open the door with the other, only to find a sword plunge into his stomach.

An eager set of old eyes appraised Dantavakra's skirts and blouse. 'Pleased to meet a knight from the South anointed in the light of the Seven.' A man smiled sarcastically through a broad, downturned mouth that bore no lines of laughter as he shrugged out of a dark, hooded cloak. His head was shaved to denote the sundering from ego and vanity.

Upon seeing Vahura, the man bowed, hand still on the sword that had stabbed Dantavakra. When he bowed, Vahura spied the white cape now revealed – the cape of the Iron Order. They had never left. 'My name is Balthazar of the Angrakshaks,' he said, eyeing Vahura, as white knights on either side of him drew their swords. 'For what it is worth, I take no pleasure in what I have to do.'

 DANTAVAKRA would take no pleasure in crediting Asshaye for saving his life. He bled feathers as Balthazar, slightly confused, pulled out his sword, the cushion, that had been Dantavakra's supposed pregnant belly, clutching on to its tip like a hat. *Find your steelsong.* Dimvak's voice followed him like a spirit on his shoulder, the hard wood under his feet now feeling like the sands of Virangavat as his training flowed back into him. The same instinct that had driven him to leap at Eklavvya a year ago drove him now to leap at Balthazar, his sword unsheathed.

Balthazar calmly stepped back, dodging his sword. A capeless knight, wearing white enamel armour, caught Dantavakra's sword instead but Dantavakra drove the pair, both Balthazar and the capeless knight, back to his left, once, then twice, their boots sliding on the floor. Balthazar and his knight drew back, one behind the other, in the narrow hallway. *Fuck*, Dantavakra thought when he realized another capeless knight was still behind him. He could only hope they did not hand out capes to the lesser skilled swordsmen.

'That was whipsmart.' Balthazar nodded as he stepped further back at the end of the corridor, and motioned for the knight behind Dantavakra to stand down. 'Using the narrow hallway to nullify our numbers. Shows initiative. Wouldn't have mattered against us but, perhaps, you might last longer against unbled recruits.' Balthazar jerked his chin towards the capeless knight in front of him. 'We won't interfere.' He raised his hands as he leaned against the wall on the side.

Behind him, the knight stepped further back towards the Second Galley, passing the three dead Asuran guards, hacked apart and brains splattered near Sokarro's cabin. How did they manage to climb the First Galley? How did no one notice? Mati, clothed – thank the Gods – was propped against the door of Sokarro's room, her hands tied behind her. She nodded at him, unworried. Those unwavering eyes reminded him that he was a damn Rakhjai, the finalist of the Contest at Virangavat!

The capeless knight with a moustache in front of Dantavakra attacked when Dantavakra turned to face him. No warning, no flourish, just a furious set of swipes using every trick in the book to tease, to feint, or even bludgeon out an opening. Dantavakra's momentary panic turned into condescension like a marvellous butterfly rising from a putrid chrysalis. Realization that he was a better duellist made him parry like Vahura's barbs. It was all too easy. The Moustache Knight's breathing grew frantic, his feet slipping, blows turning to wild, desperate swings. And Dantavakra? He was smiling all the while, every misstep tightening the noose around the Moustache Knight.

'You are using wide arcs that are not suited to this alley, love.' Dantavakra blew a mocking kiss at him. But the Moustache Knight, stubborn and hopelessly proud, refused to see the wisdom for what it was – a man drowning too deep in his own ignorance to bother saving himself. So, when the Earthship rocked with a sudden jolt around a turn that sent a stumble through everyone's knees, Dantavakra lunged, more energy than elegance. His sword found that perfect spot between the shoulder plates, and sank into the collarbone with a sound Dantavakra had dreamed of Eklavvya making, a thousand times.

But Dantavakra shifted his stance so swiftly the sight before him swam. He lunged behind him at the burly caped knight with brown curls, but this one was no fool. Brown Curls parried it with contempt as he pushed Dantavakra to the side, kneed him in the groin, and then slipped away before Dantavakra could stab him. They pivoted in the cramped corridor and now stood facing opposite ends – Dantavakra's back to Mati, Brown Curls' back to Balthazar. A stalemate? Only for a heartbeat. Brown Curls feinted right and then stamped his boot on Dantavakra's, using the distraction to slice at Dantavakra's chest. Both Dantavakra and Brown Curls exchanged a confused, embarrassed look. For a moment, the sound of cleaved oranges falling from Dantavakra's blouse and rolling on the ground was the only sound on the Corridor of Death.

Brown Curls recovered first and stabbed him. Dantavakra avoided turning into a skewered kebab only with an undignified backward lunge. It did not help. Brown Curls' kick sent him arse over elbows on the hard wood across Sokarro's room and into Mati's legs. *Yama's balls.*

In the wine-coloured light of the mothlamps, the length of Brown Curls' grin was murderous scarlet. *No man smirks at me! You may be an Angrakshak! But I am a Rakhjai!* Dantavakra kicked sideways at the knight's left calf. 'Fucker!' Brown Curls stumbled and slipped on splattered brain to crash against the corridor wall – into the point of a wine-glass stem, which Mati had slipped just in time between the wall and Brown Curls' ear. 'Grotesque' did not quite do justice to this conclusion. Time slowed as Brown Curls' momentum carried him all the way against the wall, the stem piercing his ear, his eardrum, his brain, as red filled his right eye like a spherical wine glass.

'Just an advice for the afterlife,' Mati whispered to Brown Curls' other ear as he crumbled into a heap near her, shaking the weakness out of her wrists, 'if you want to tie a pirate down, don't use a grandmother knot.'

Dantavakra knew it was far from over. He turned around to see Balthazar lazily unsheathe his sword at end of the corridor, glimmering whorls floating in mystical patterns on his Assyrian blade. Balthazar did not attack. A paragon of politeness, he waited for Dantavakra to find his feet.

'Take Vahura and run, Princess. I will join you shortly.'

Mati tapped the back of his head. 'Don't under any circumstance waste time talking to him about killing him. Find you on the Third Galley.' She opened the door to Bhagadatt's cabin, and dragging a fearful Vahura out, rushed to the Second Galley even as Balthazar whistled.

'Shall we?' Balthazar asked.

There were limits to even Dantavakra's delusions. Balthazar's footwork, even in the tiny space, was a blur. Behind his sword, there were decades of experience protecting the most powerful men in the world. Some small, severed part of Dantavakra's mind coldly registered his own incompetence as he desperately flailed thrust after thrust. Dimvak would have jumped into a well on seeing Dantavakra chase phantoms while Balthazar's blade kept slicing his body, sinew by sinew.

'You need to spread your legs more to balance the weight, son. Now strike like you mean it.'

Did Balthazar just taunt him the way he had taunted the Moustache Knight? Fucker. His blood was up now. *This is your destiny, Danta.* After all, you don't become a legend by duelling losers. You become a legend by duelling Gods. Dantavakra walked towards Balthazar like he had three thousand lovers from the arena cheering him on.

He gifted Balthazar a flurry of strikes, and soon enough, the Iron Knight was on the retreat. Dropping back through moonlight, then darkness, then moonlight again from the open doors, Balthazar barely parried Dantavakra's frenzied, graceful thrusts. Their breathing, their urgent footsteps and the grinding sound of steel against steel echoed in the corridor.

'Here is the thing about honest duels. The most skilled swordsman wins,' Dantavakra said, 'not the most devout, no matter the charlatans he serves.'

The taunt at the Seven worked. Balthazar roared as he came charging. Dantavakra smiled as he feinted at him, felt his smile slip as it was this time Balthazar who laughed, when he bent low. There was something about the way Balthazar twisted his feet, the way he held the steel, the look in his eyes. Balthazar had read him like a large pamphlet, had known his taunt for what it was, aware of Dantavakra's mistake, had countered him with a flick of his wrist.

If that didn't hurt his ego, Balthazar had also been right – Dantavakra's legs were not spread wide enough. Just as the Moustache Knight hadn't listened to Dantavakra's advice, Dantavakra ignored Balthazar's. Falling victim to his own lessons? How humiliating. But worse was yet to come. He dodged Balthazar's attack, only to be shoulder-pushed just enough to stumble over a corpse.

Dantavakra lost his balance but found it again when he was pinned to the wall. Hot pain exploded in his shoulder as he stared down in horror at Balthazar's blade, sunk three inches above his heart. Shock cut deeper than the steel, but soon enough, the pain caught up as well. Warm blood flowed across his sweat-dripping skin, tickling his nipples something devilish inside his shirt. Surrender seemed the only option to escape out of this alive – one he was considering eagerly – especially given how there was no audience to witness his shame, those three thousand lovers all gone.

'Ser—'

Balthazar twisted his sword the other way, and he felt the blade grind into his shoulder, blood running down his arms and into his lap. Whatever Dantavakra was about to say in surrender came out only as a synonym of the sound *Aaaaaa*.

'A Contest finalist? A Rakhjai? A joke is more like it!'

'You would have been dead if not for armour!' Dantavakra cried. *What a perfect way to surrender, you fool!*

Balthazar relaxed his grip. 'Only they cry unfair who carry not the caution of coming prepared. You think I would have let my guard slip like you if I hadn't been wearing armour?' He twisted savagely, scraping bone as he withdrew his sword. The feeling of steel kissing your skin on its return journey is something only poets can describe well. It sent Dantavakra tumbling to his knees. Balthazar tossed a rag from his belt at him. 'Stuff it. It is laced with a numbing coagulant. So, what do you say? One-zero?'

When Dantavakra looked at him, confused, Balthazar picked up Dantavakra's fallen sword, its blade wet with the blood of the wrong man. 'I won the Imperial Contest in its first year... when real men duelled each other. How about we make it a contest of three points to see whether you are a man of steel or you are just what you appear: a man hiding in skirts?'

 MATI hid with Vahura behind the staircase leading onto the deck of the First Galley instead of returning to the Second Galley from the corridor between the galleys. Slipping onto the deck of the First Galley and making their way to the Third Galley from the deck above was their best shot at escape. Once in there, they could find some king or lordling to conceal them till they reached Airavat's Reach. The kick in her stomach shed light on what her baby thought of that. Mati... smiled at the knowledge that the baby was still alive. She would not admit it but the blood spotting had worried her.

Behind them, the sound of swords echoed up and down like bells in a temple. When an Iron Order knight came down the deck, passed them, oblivious, into the bridge of the Second Galley, Mati patted herself on the back for loudly declaring her plan to Dantavakra. She knew Balthazar's whistle had been to call on a colleague who had been waiting above deck.

'Before we head above to the deck, describe everything you saw while you were crossing it.'

Vahura recalled the deck, starting from the deserted aft to a shaman amusing himself with the useless steer, from the five guards engaged in a round of cards to what lay hidden beneath the blue-red tarp, from the stacked crates to the airavat silhouettes.

How about it? Asshaye had been right. It was here on deck just as the hag had suspected. Mati extracted the Rakshasan Key Relic from her pocket and passed it to Vahura, all the while explaining its potential use, while ignoring her widening eyes. 'There's a fair chance this won't unfold as we desire. But that's—' A sudden cramp wrenched her head back and it slammed into the wall.

'Princess!' She could feel Vahura's breath warm against her face. Mati swatted away her hands.

'There is... a...' Mati's words were caught on another cramp. Tears washed into her eyes. She wiped her runny nose with her sleeve. 'We need to. We need to wait here for a moment. You've got the Scrolls, don't you? Let's see what you can do with them.'

Vahura drew forth the Daevic Scrolls. They appeared to be a modest tome with not too many pages.

Vahura looked up, and Mati met her unsure gaze. 'Are you certain we should not be escaping now?'

'Red, read it now. And use that wretched memory of yours. Can't take the chance of losing its secrets if we were to lose the Scrolls,' Mati said and then sucked in a long, shuddering breath as a cramp twisted the muscles of her lower back.

Vahura nodded, tracing the spine with her finger, knocking on the cover, and then sniffing the block.

'What. Are. You. Doing?' Mati seethed. 'We haven't the luxury for such library superstitions!'

Vahura rolled her eyes. 'The book is bound in the shell of a *kurma*, a giant world turtle so long extinct that no trace of them survives unfossilized. With books bound so in hides of mythical beasts or unknown alloys, you have to be careful about how you open it. *The Time Traveller's Guide to Manu's Papers* is matted using the Sanjeevani herb from which springs a strange perfume. When I turned the first pages, I was taken hostage by chimeric dreams so vivid that I thought I was an oracle in the making. The things I saw,' she laughed, 'of a buried land where the sky was a mirror, where griffins flew the air and where buildings of glass soared into the sky,' she said, dreamily.

Mati coughed, noisily.

Vahura, chastened, returned to the Scrolls. 'Right. Yes, so where was I? Aye, it took me a week to recover. And look at this book. I have to be careful.'

Mati snatched the book and with scant ceremony, opened it with a single hand. As she anticipated, the pages had no scent to speak of. So no chimeric dreams for Mati this time around. But to be fair to Vahura, there were no pages in the book, either. Instead, they were substituted with delicate wafers of white ruby that somehow could turn, bend and fold. Magic, one might say. Daeva magic. The sheer gold this would fetch on the black market…

'Oh, my.' Vahura recovered from Mati's blasphemy and then cooed as she turned the second page. 'The Daevic Scrolls, written by Trisiras… a Danava? That doesn't make sense. Then they should be called Danava Scrolls and…'

As though in response to Vahura's blabbering, Mati's baby kicked hard, bringing an entirely unmotherly remark from Mati's lips. 'Don't mind her, little one. Red is in shock.'

'The baby?'

'Yes, it is asking you to hasten the fuck up.' And then seeing Vahura's curious eyes, she lifted Vahura's hand and pressed her palm against her belly. So much for a dramatic effect. Nothing happened. She turned to her baby. 'Don't tell me you suffer from anxiety before an audience – oh there! Did you feel it?'

Vahura nodded, eyes wide. 'It is… magical.' Vahura softened. 'I… really am sorry you had to put yourself in harm's way because of me.'

If only Vahura knew. There was not a single pit where Mati had fallen which had not been her own creation.

'Worry about the Scrolls,' Mati said, bent low. 'Dantavakra will die if you don't hasten.'

That had the desired effect.

'Oh, bless us!' Vahura squealed. 'This has a table of contents: the finest invention from the eyes of an academic, that is of course, until the Acharyas find a way to search for a word across the book in a heartbeat.'

'Good for you,' Mati said dryly as she shook her head and crawled to the side to relieve her bladder on the floor. *Hang in there, little one. I will get you out of this soon. For now, close your eyes.* As she peed, she plucked from her belt the bottle of the finest spirit in the world – the Blue Fairy – she had flicked from Sokarro's room and stashed in Vahura's satchel. She licked her lips as she did so, thirsty for a sip. Building a wall against temptation wasn't her finest skill, and she let it flood her as she opened the bottle. The fragrances of fennel, anise and wormwood greeted her with shields and spears. She felt far from being a connoisseur when she gulped the Blue Fairy directly from the bottle, but her wits needed a caress. The cold burn of the artemisia scalded her lips, laying siege to the tip of her tongue like a crocodile on heat. A fire spread like blazebane up her sinuses and burned through her nostrils, and through her throat at the same time. 'Oh, this is a delicacy stolen from the personal cabinet of the Ocean Goddess,' she wheezed as she kissed the bottle.

The world was already looking brighter by the time she reached the halfway mark on the bottle, when Vahura slammed the book on the ground. The Balkhan was ash-faced.

'The cure... doesn't exist?' Mati asked, feeling a flicker of pity for her.

'It does... What is that smell?'

'Piss. Now, go on.'

'Yes, right. The cure exists but it is safeguarded by the Seven. This... is in First Tongue script but I was wrong. It is written by a Danava, yes, but look, the scrolls end with an insignia of the Saptarishis and is signed by Maharishi Dadichi! I have petitioned them, and not just me, thousands and thousands have petitioned them over the years to help save a mother, a son, a brother... a sister... a city, and they lied to us. They said there is no cure when they not only had the cure but also a shield against it. They knew... but they not only let all those innocents die but they sent their assassins to make sure the diseased and their family were butchered. This... this exposes them. I...' She fumed.

'Careful now, Librarian,' Mati said, as she saw Vahura's hand almost crunching the precious sunstone sheets. 'Don't want to incur vandalism penalties now, do we? So *this* doesn't help you.'

'It... does, I think,' she said. 'There are more than a few cures.

'Marigold Mold may crawl through the eye, but it's the heart where it truly takes root. It accelerates the beating heart, driving the afflicted to the brink of madness. Before long, the heart races so fiercely that it tears through the blood vessels, sealing the victim's face with a fatal rupture. But not before those ensnared descend into a savage frenzy, tearing apart all in their path, a perfect way to incite these descendants of primates to tear themselves asunder.

'But there are sketches of this armour the Daevas and the First Vanaras forged to wrap the plague and suppress the beating heart. I will need to use other scrolls for reference to understand the minerals used, but this definitely helps. There is also a sketch of the alchemical blindfold my mother used to stall the spread of the Marigold. How she knew of it, I couldn't tell you, but from what I read here, Vauri only has two full moons left before the plague spreads to her mind, and then even a Daeva could not save her. So, yes! There is a cure! Oh, my father's army will descend on the so-called kingmakers and teach them what a kingdaughter can do. But Vauri. Will. Be. Saved. Oh, my imagination already runs wild.' Vahura looked back at the luminescent charcoal sketches again. 'Though I wonder how will she look in amber eyes and skin-pasted armour? Like a little Satyabhama, I wager.'

Mati's heart skipped a beat, and for a change, it was not because the little one kicked her. 'What do you mean *amber* and *skin-pasted*?'

'Aye,' Vahura said, showing her a page from the Scrolls. 'See, the armour is stitched over the skin to hold the plague in, but I reckon from what it says here that it turns the eyes of the plague carrier completely amber. It isn't a natural eye colour found in mortals.

I think that is wise so that the others can know, and be careful. Wouldn't want one to slice off the armour of one in a moment of passion, now, would we?' She laughed awkwardly at her joke when she saw Mati's horrified expression, before clamping her mouth shut. 'I am sorry. Was I too loud?'

Mati held Vahura by the collar against the wall. Her hand shivered. 'Tell me straight, Red. Does this blasted book say what the colour of the armour will be?

Vahura, shocked, struggled to reply. 'What are you—' She wriggled her neck higher to breathe. 'Sunstone!' she managed. 'It will be sunstone.'

She gasped when Mati released her grip. 'And what fucking colour is that?'

'Curse you! Old Ella was right. That poison,' Vahura pointed at the Blue Fairy as she massaged her neck, 'is clearly not good for your head. Sunstone is... well, sunstone... alright, let me try, think orange hued with topaz and tangerine.' She squinted as she pictured the colour. 'It is something like golden. Yes. A golden breastplate!'

Karna... The revelation slipped into Mati like a dagger.

 DANTAVAKRA withdrew a dagger in one hand and held the one-handed sword in the other. His heart was pumping fire. All the missed chances, the broken oaths, the lost lovers were nothing now. He was in the arena again, every detail of his opponent standing out like a candle in darkness. There was only win or shame. There was respect too, no doubt, as Magadh's Rakhjai met a Saptarishi's Angrakshak, a duel between dancers of death. Or so Dantavakra thought.

'Don't tell me you mean to duel in the Valkan style. I find that school vulgar,' Balthazar scoffed, his eyes as black and empty as a lizard's.

When Dantavakra just stood there, too taken aback by the disrespect to respond, Balthazar sighed theatrically and raised his sword, this time in the crane stance, springing forward before Dantavakra even registered his stance.

The force of Balthazar's thrust numbed his torso faster than the healing rag. Dantavakra stumbled back, gasping, into Bhagadatt's room. His training, skill and technique lost to the dust, he flapped his sword like a kitten as he tottered backwards, barely keeping Balthazar's blade at bay. Found a split-second gap. Tossed the dagger at him. Balthazar swatted it away with a flick of a hand. But the dagger found skin. Dantavakra had finally drawn blood.

His success earned a movement in front of him. Something bald. A sharp pain in his face. The sensation of flying. A sound of a howling wind, or a screaming girl.

Was he falling?

Balthazar's headbutt had no doubt twisted Dantavakra's face into a shape that diminished its aesthetic. He fell face first onto Bhagadatt's bed. Grateful for the Rakshasa's preference for satin sheets, he pushed himself up. Despite the soft embrace, spots of blood pit-pattered onto the green sheets below him. But he was still lucky, all things considered, for he had narrowly dodged cutting himself on a brass candle frame. But it wasn't a candle frame, was it?

When you can't bully your way, blast your way through. He let go of his sword.

'Is this what the knights of the South have fallen down to?' Balthazar laughed cruelly as he circled the bed like the lecherous villain in a play. 'No wonder the Iron Order hasn't seen one of your kind in our ranks. Now wake up, pup. It is two-one. I still have to fetch my winning point.' He yanked Dantavakra's leg off the bed.

Dantavakra turned, waving the brass frame like a scythe. Balthazar moved ever so slightly back. A graceful step. Almost an unconscious gesture – a movement of weight in space – he easily dodged it. Dantavakra then tossed the frame itself at Balthazar, but with such a heavy weight, it was almost as if he threw the frame to play catch with Balthazar. This time the Iron Knight struggled in tossing it aside. It gave Dantavakra the time to jump off the bed, and roll to the other side of the room, right behind Balthazar.

Balthazar smiled, and turned. 'Imbecile.'

Dantavakra was trapped, his back against the table. In a desperate bid, his right hand scrambled madly for a weapon. Balthazar's eyes tracked it like a condescending hawk.

'*You* imbecile!' Dantavakra cried, for with the left hand, he flung the contents of the vial on the table at Balthazar.

As Dantavakra expected, Balthazar lived up to the Iron Order's reputation as he deftly turned his wrist to swat the vial with the flat of the blade. Delicate chimes clinked as the vial cracked against the glimmering patterns on Balthazar's blade, shattering into tiny shards. Bluish black liquid slithered down the breadth of the Assyrian steel.

'Enough horseplay.' Balthazar raised his sword. 'You are such a disappointment.'

Dantavakra grabbed something with his right hand, charged at Balthazar in a mad rush to death. Balthazar scoffed as he brought his sword in a perfect, unblockable slash. It would have been, had the Assyrian blade not been frozen and eaten by the Frostwater alloy that had disintegrated Bhagadatt's Assyrian safe not too long ago. Only air slashed across Dantavakra's unprotected neck as Balthazar turned, the suddenly weightless sword carrying him more than he intended in his slash, launching him straight into Dantavakra's fist which held Vahura's safe hooks.

Dantavakra stabbed those safe-hooks into Balthazar's eyes, and without dropping a tune, used the flat of his right palm to slam those two hooks upwards into Balthazar's skull.

Balthazar croaked a tiny word out. 'Cheated.'

'Only they cry unfair who carry not the caution of coming prepared. Knockout trumps two.'

Balthazar fell.

Dantavakra jumped in excitement, turning, thumping his arms in the air victorious, and his grin slipped. The one time he used a badass comeback, there had been no bard to witness.

No one is going to believe me that this is how it happened. His shoulders sagged. *What is the point of a duel without an audience?* The wraiths of Vahura and Mati knocked on his mind's door. Right. No rest for heroes. He wearily retrieved his sword and made for the door when he stopped. *Come to thy lover, you sultry thing*, he smiled as he discarded his sword.

MATI could not believe she had fucked a lover with Marigold Mold and had lived to tell the tale. How many could claim that in the world? None, she wagered.

She crashed mid-memory against Vahura's back on her way up to the deck, and almost toppled back the stairs. 'Oi Land Legs! Can you walk – Oh!' Beyond Vahura, bodies lay everywhere. So this was how the Iron Order entered the First Galley. Probably waiting outside the City, saw their chance, jumped on deck? Sounded a little convenient, and in any case, something which she had no time for, especially given the scenery on deck.

Even in the dim moonlight, she could make blood out everywhere. On the deck, splashed high on the steers, and on the door itself, against which Vahura now stood. Around them, bright specks of gulls plunged down to the deck, to begin at long last their feeding.

'*Theyothealldeaad.*' Vahura said, shivering.

'Hold still your tongue, and keep walking.' Mati prodded Vahura ahead.

She stuffed the Blue Fairy inside Vahura's satchel, the mouth jutting out from an open space in the corner of the bag. She uncorked the bottle, tilted it ever so slightly, crying on the inside at blaspheming so. The liquid trickled behind them as they crossed the deck, as if marking the territory of a shadowcat. She then crossed Vahura, the sword she had picked from Sokarro unsheathed, holding Vahura's hand to find balance as her feet skidded to a stop on the blood-soaked deck. On the centre of the deck, lay a Grey Shaman. And on him lay a swan, spreadeagled, its feet and wings spiked into the the Shaman's chest, and... someone had dyed the swan black. Finally, Mati felt the bone-deep fear that had crippled Vahura moments before. It was plain as day. *This is not the work of the Iron Order.*

'We are going to die! We are dead, Mati! Dead!'

'Red, calm down or I am going to make your nose match your hair.' The last thing she needed was a woman in shock to babysit. Mati squinted through the darkness around until she found what she was searching for. It was time for the backup plan.

★

'How much do you think this might fetch on the black market? Just in case the plan goes into a kraken's arse?'

'Where did you find this?' Asshaye turned the Rakshasan Key Relic in her hand. 'Each curl on this is a testament to the meticulous craftsman-ship of Daevic smiths.' And she paused, tracing her hand on the symbols of wind around the glowing sapphire. 'You can't sell this, Swan.'

'Why?'

'Because if I'm right,' Asshaye said, 'which I always am, this is your exit plan if the soup sours.'

Mati stepped over the corpse, her eyes flitting everywhere to see if the culprits had stayed back to admire their work, while Vahura clutched the beads of her locket with her free hand, praying in urgent whispers. Beyond the deck, she saw business as usual on the Second Galley. A sparse crew was moving about on that deck, oblivious of how fortunate they were to not have been promoted to serve the First Galley tonight.

'The Iron Order are godless monsters.'

'They are, but this is not their handiwork, Red. The Iron Order has an unhealthy obsession with cleanliness. They... don't torture. Let's not wait to find out whether I am right, shall we?' Mati trailed off at the sound of oiled metal sliding on rope, unmistakable to anyone who had slid off the lines using a crossbow to cross from one ship to another. 'Or, I reckon we can say hello, considering they are here.'

Mati turned as a red-robed man landed gently on the deck and whipped out a shiny skewer on which shimmered kebabs, making her stomach grumble.

'Kindly don't bore me by running away,' he said.

Mati rolled her eyes. 'Well, too bad for I was just about to start because I clearly am in shape to win sprint races, Acharya Tapasa.'

'My bad.' Tapasa smiled, a smile that made Mati want to pee. 'Must say the witches make for excellent cooks,' he said as he tore a piece of grilled kebab from the skewer.

Another man emerged from behind, through the companionway they had used just moments earlier. She did not have to guess who. 'I owe you ten sovereigns.' Tamasa strode in, face grumpy, holding a backpack, made round as if it were carrying a stone ball. 'Should've known they would use the deck.'

'As we would have,' Tapasa said, the grin a mask. 'It is the wiser choice.'

'I took care of our Iron Brother who was chasing after them in the wrong direction,' Tamasa said, as he wiped his sword clean against the cloth of his backpack till he tossed the backpack away. It rolled over like a ball to the side. 'They do things so noisily.'

Mati wasn't listening to the casual way they were talking murder or paying attention to the possibility that she was no longer a widow or to the peril posed by the round backpack rolling about on the deck.

Her attention was on logistics. Two blades on one. Let's rephrase that. Two deadly, perhaps immortal, Red Acharyas against one pregnant Mati. If she were being honest, of all the deaths she might have chosen, this seemed like a fitting way for someone of her stature to go. If not for the damn baby, she would have accepted her fate without regrets and with a certain degree of pride. As it was, she wasn't going to let the fuckers touch her baby she had spent the last few months protecting.

She still had one card up her sleeve. The Red Order, like most men who were good at what they did, were unduly fixated with elegance in excellence. Fighting dirty always won against fighting elegantly, and there the Black Swan would always have an upper hand.

'Boys,' Mati said, a little unsure, caressing her stomach. She egged Vahura to move behind her, whispering to her words she hoped did not reach the Red Acharyas. Putting distance between Vahura and her, she took steps towards the two assassins. 'Surely you understand the drowning bit. Pregnancy. Mood swings. It is quite the curse of womankind.'

'A moodswing that involves leaving Acharyas of the Red Order and your own husband to jadesharks, poor man.' Tapasa exchanged an amused glance with Tamasa. 'Glad to know our Vachans of celibacy do seem to have a point.'

Vahura decided to turn this moment into one where she found her courage. 'Is this what the Red Order has fallen to? Use innocent little girls as weapons, and then go after pregnant women for vengeance.'

Tapasa ignored her. 'Do not be crude, Princess Vahura. Leave if you wish. We have not been tasked with your life. The Iron Order bore that charge, and they have failed.' He drew a line on the deck with the sword as if to drive home the point. 'We, of the Red Order, were sent by the Seven to bring your sister to the Conclave and then end you, Princess Mati. You were our true quarry on the ship.'

'I am honoured,' Mati said, the foundations of her usual cocksure certainty burning down to cinders inside her, especially when she heard Vahura inch away behind her, and then run away. 'Though I do wonder if I am deserving of it.'

'Oh, none better, I say,' Tamasa said, as he began to move to the edge of the deck, eyes on Vahura's retreating figure, no doubt in a bid to circle Mati. Though, given her state, why bother. 'You have singlehandedly made our Oracles feel unworthy, a feat for which I am sure some of the Seven are grateful. Modesty isn't the strongest suit of the Seventh Order.'

'Those tortured ducks?' Now Mati was genuinely curious. 'I have never had the fortune of meeting one.'

'Neither have they met you in their visions, unfortunately, or else we would not be here, would we? Every prophecy, every prediction the Oracles drew of the future, you ate through it with the acid that is your… personality. You are the patron saint of chaos, Princess. You and your impulsive actions have twisted the future times beyond counting. What do the Seven call you? Yes, an aberration, Princess, a star that never stays still for the ship to navigate its course by. Shipwrecks do not bode well for business, a sentiment you appreciate, no doubt.'

'I do, but I also know the sun stays true in a sky of fickle stars. And any captain worth his salt uses a compass to take him ashore. So, bad metaphors aside, Acharyas, how did *I* cause an inconvenience to—'

Tamasa interrupted her, anger colouring his voice. 'Karna was to die in Kalinga! But you saved him! Prakar Mardin would have returned peace to the East but you killed him! Arjun would have wed Draupadi to eventually become the heir to Panchal, and Yudhistir's jealousy would have eventually driven a rift between the brothers, but your hand tossed that plan to the fires when you burned down the Swayamvar. You even fooled the Bats of Magadh into believing you have surrendered to their Vachan.'

'Calm your heart, brother.' Tapasa smiled. 'Don't mind his tone, Princess. But he speaks true. You see, with Karna dead, Arjun would have had no archnemesis to amuse him, and he would have made one out of Yudhistir just for the fun of it. He is playful like that, our Arjun. Hastina would have had three contenders then, not two, and would have hosted the Conclave there and not allowed it to take place here in the Rectum of the Realm.'

'We would have released the Marigold Mold in Hastina as was predestined,' Tamasa said, 'and after the world had mourned the horrifying deaths of the hundred kings and queens of the realm, they would have begged the Magadhan Empire to take over. The Riverlands and the Realm would fall under a single man, answerable only to the Seven. One Empire. One Monarch. One Master. *Akhand Aryavrat*. A mighty fist in the hands of Jayatsena's heir to confront the true danger lurking in the future! But now, the Conclave finds itself in this dreadful Tree City, where most kingdoms couldn't even be bothered to send their sovereigns. All thanks to your meddlesome actions.'

Jayatsena? What? The Ehtrals and the Seven are hand in glove? Disbelief at the absurdity of what she heard made her slow on the uptake. She took it all in, chewed on it, didn't like it one bit. Sighing, she said, 'What can I say? Overplanning kills the magic.'

Tamasa looked ready to annihilate her, which made Mati wonder why had they not done so already. Tapasa laughed as if he had read her mind. 'Won't disagree with you there. It would have been a minute's work to remove your head from the rest of your unwomanly body in Magadh. But…' he leaned in as if confessing a secret, 'the kindness of our masters always causes them more harm than good. They wanted it to be kept quiet. What is the point of being puppeteers *behind* the screen if the world can see their hand on the strings?

So, they shifted the plan to Kamrup. Less casualties, yes, but no less effective.'

'Saham Dev knew of your plan, didn't he?'

Tapasa laughed. 'He was only too glad to be part of the plan rather than plan himself.'

Ingenious. A flawless scheme to stitch a new world without heirs, and without causing any wounds to the lands that matter. Meanwhile, the mutilators in Magadh would raise the Old Lion's lost Jayatsena to be a worthy puppet. Eventually, the path for this *Akhand* Aryavrat would be clear, with the East vanquished, the Rakshasas extinct and a pestilence successfully contained by the barricades the natural terrain of the East supplied. The Seven had left Krishna trailing in the dust when it came to thinking three hundred and seventy-five steps ahead. To be fair to Krishna, the Seven did have oracles on their side.

'Impressed, aren't you?' Tapasa asked. 'Kill three birds with one stone. Alas, it doesn't work, however, when one of the birds is…'

Mati smiled. 'The Black Swan.'

'Hope you realize why I have been so candid with you.'

A sound of crates crashing on wood echoed from the bow of the ship. Mati smiled back, taking a fighting stance, a sword in one hand and a dagger in another. 'Of course. You think you've won.'

Tapasa nodded, grinning. 'We took a detour, yes, but the destination remains unchanged.'

'Enough.' Tamasa drew his sword, silver glint of death against the murderous black sky. Noises of wood crashing against wood rose from the front of the ship but none of the three took their eyes off each other. 'You threaten the peace of the realm, Princess Mati of Kalinga, and for your crimes, the Seven has sentenced you to die.'

A door slammed open.

 Dantavakra slammed open the door, annoyed by the twitch of excitement he felt at the words he heard. He had been pleased when he had run into the Second Galley earlier, only to find a crowd gossiping around the corpse stashed in the luggage

stash room. The corpse's white cape and human face naturally made the gossip all the more salacious. None had paid Dantavakra any attention as he had slowly backed away into the First Galley. Not even the guards who were clearing their way through the crowd and saw him walk back to the First Galley. For the guards of the Second Galley, their jurisdiction ended there, and what happened outside their assigned galley might as well be taking place in another universe. Then, Dantavakra had the idea of returning to the deck to use the rope to climb back to the crossbeam above.

He had been pleased, had been happy, that the plan had worked, and for a change, he had made a sizeable contribution to it. Some might say it was the most sizeable contribution, considering it involved saving everyone's lives. He hoped someone else would say it eventually given that it would not carry the same effect if he were the one telling the story. But then he heard the words while climbing the companionway, words that carried violence from the deck. He knew the words were drawn against his friends, friends who would finally witness his glory in a god's weapon: a trident!

That was until he stormed onto the deck. Then three things happened in quick succession.

One of the red-robed assailants turned to face him, the shock from recognition causing Dantavakra to abandon his charge altogether.

Two, in his attempt to stop, he skidded on the slick deck, wet and greasy for some reason, and landed on his arse, legs spread wide.

Three, sparks danced from Mati's sword as she rang it against her dagger, kindling a fire that caught a liquid trail on the deck. It summoned forth a tiny hedge of flames partitioning the Twins from Mati. Unfortunately, the trajectory of the flames seemed to wind its way close to the vicinity between Dantavakra's spread-out legs.

Dantavakra whelped an unmanly cry, and rolled to the side, instinctively tossing a cushion cover to douse the fire ahead – a cover that carried the vials from Bhagadatt's room to be used against other Iron Order knights.

'You think fire can stop us!' Dantavakra heard one of the Red Acharyas scream, a scream that was soon lost to another sound. A sound of vials breaking.

 VAHURA could only hope she did not break Mati's trust as she fled from the Red Order. She waded in the darkness at the bow of the ship, towards the place where she had spied it from above. It was easy to follow the stench, strongest where the guards had made their last stand, when they had thought the Red Order had come to steal it. She wondered if the Red Order even knew of its existence, and then she wondered if Mati knew what she was talking about.

She picked her way round the corpses until she found refuge behind a sizeable heap of crates that she had spotted earlier from the crossbeam above. Mati's question again sent an excited lightning down her spine as she held the fluttering red-blue tarp.

'*Can you fly?*' Mati had whispered.

It took time but she flipped one side of the tarp out, where the wind caught it, and took it on a ride to the marshes outside the Earthship. *Well, finally a stroke of luck* – unbidden, tears streamed out of the corners of her eyes as her eyes beheld the treasure from an Age lost, an Age of Engineers and Forgers, an Age she had only read of her in her books and scrolls. An Age where mankind had wings. She traced the sigil drawn on the ship. Paint on the blackened bronze cast. Wolf heads, ten of them. The sigil of Raavan. She did not fail to notice how the sigil was drawn over the sigil of Manu: the Giant Fish.

'*Pushpak Viman*, as I live and breathe.' A beast of wooden beauty, fashioned in the shape of an enormous dragonfly, this was the last of the windkeepers that survived the First Age, Manu's windkeeper, the same windkeeper that was flown by Ravana of Lanka before his fall, thought destroyed by the Ayodhyans. But it had survived… survived the test of time. And in her hand, she held its key, a key that the Magadhans had found, unaware of what it was, just knowing it for a Rakshasan relic. She held… the key to the future.

She studied the windkeeper. A rigging, as complicated as astrology, knotted all over the place on the windkeeper, holding close to it its six great whalewings. Vahura guessed the whalewings must be used to take turns in the air. Above the rigging, lay a lifeless, enormous rag of cloth. She had no notion of its purpose. How fascinating. The deck itself was a wooden oval with railings around and a single *wheel*, for lack of a better term, at the helm.

Stop studying it, and get inside it, moron. Vahura shook her head and climbed onto the windkeeper. She pulled herself along the railing. Passed the four chairs to the helm. The helm was vaikunshard glass that faced the front and the bottom. Made sense. A captain would want to see what was in front and below her. As for the *wheel*, it was in truth a slab of a strange alloy laced with an assortment of six levers and three colourless crystals protruding out of it like sword hilts and tiny shields.

'*Can you fly?*'

It was a stupid question. What was she to say? *Oh, yes. It is like driving an ox-cart.* Not that she knew how to do that either. But since Mati was fending off certain death at the hands of the Forge-damned Red Order, Vahura was willing to step outside her comfort zone.

The levers must draw the six whalewings. Of that, she was reasonably certain. If her limited grasp of Daevic runes was any good, the panel marked with three horizontal lines had something do with air or ascending. *What is the Forge-damned procedure for this?* She looked under the panel for a manual but, of course, why would Ravana be so helpful.

A slit-shaped hole built into the underside of the panel caught the attention of her fingers. Could it be? Could it be that simple? Vahura slipped Mati's Rakshasan Key Relic into it, and it slid in with a fascinating murmur. *Lavannai, please.* Whispering a prayer, she turned her wrist. The windkeeper silently came to life with crystals on the panels glowing red. *What does that mean? Red is a good sign, right?*

The rigging and the yardlines of the windkeeper quivered in heat. The windkeeper cracked, creaked, wrenched as a tearing sound started on the windkeeper's deck and worked its way through

Vahura's body. The wires in the rigging around her grew taut as the dead cloth came to life to turn into an enormous elliptical balloon with large runes drawn on it that glowed blue.

A noise erupted inside the balloon, as if it had trapped a demon inside who fought against its bondage, or if she was feeling less dramatic, it was like the sound Vauri made when slurping the last of the tea from her plate, except this time, it souded as though *Vayu* himself was the one making the noise. It couldn't be... She couldn't be sure but her gut screamed at her that there was an Astra inside the balloon. A tiny shard at best, that caught the invisible Elemental of Wind coursing around them and began pulling Wind inwards. A real Astra... she gaped, her mouth hanging like a baboon. Astras were extinct. It was not possible. *So were windkeepers but here you are on one.* If only she could see it, but it was invisible to her eye, hidden in the folds of the balloon. *I. Cannot. Wait to unravel this.*

Blinding flash.

A detonation shook the Earthship beneath her. Smoke, rising in a column that billowed eastward, swallowed the black night in shadow. Ears ringing, nose stinging, Vahura coughed as she squinted through the grey-hued air to find Mati. A huge hole yawned in the deck where the Red Acharyas and Mati had been standing but a moment before.

 DANTAVAKRA dragged himself across the deck like a cockroach without legs, wondering where Mati had been standing, till he found her hanging, hands clinging to the edge of the hole like a strip from a tattered sail. With one hand to his shoulder, trying to keep the blood in, the other reaching out towards Mati's, he pulled her up with the last of his failing strength. Things were still raining from the sky. Small things for now – splinters, soot and fragments of rope. A few inches away from where he lay, the enormous hole widened as more of the deck fell below into the third room, destroying the precious artefacts of Bhagadatt's Garden.

Turning, he saw that the fused bridge between the First Galley and the Second Galley had been severed by the explosion. The Second and Third Galleys, now untethered, careened off the tracks and tipped to the side, no doubt moments from finding how long it takes for a ship to sink in a bog. *Fuck...* Dantavakra's eyes welled up as he lost sight of the two galleys when the airavats turned around a bend, dragging the First Galley along with them. *I hope no one is hurt.*

He pulled Mati up, Mati squealing as she rose, her eyes flickering open. She turned to look at Dantavakra. Heat had rolled over him from the left, his hair, parts of his cheeks, most of the armour he had borrowed, singed.

'Good,' Mati groaned. 'I would have mourned you if had you died.'

Soft chuckle. 'The Reds have fallen.' He pointed at the hole in the deck.

'Hope they stay there this time.'

'Agreed. But what now? The other galleys are gone. You can't climb the ropes... no matter how muscled those arms are. The airavats aren't stopping, I don't know why. Oh, of course. The Grey Shaman is dead. We have no legitimate means of escape,' Dantavakra said, when Mati held his hand, smiling, nudging him to look skyward.

'Impossible,' Dantavakra said. *And so... illegitimate. It should have been me!*

'Dantavakra!' came a familiar voice far above them. 'Are you both alright?' Shimmering in the moonlight was a small ship, its enormous wings on the side billowing, and a red-haired girl with braids staring down at them from over the side. Satisfied at seeing them safe, Vahura, the first human to fly in a thousand years, vanished from the side of the flying ship. 'Just wait, okay! Just wait!' her excited voice wafted down.

Dantavakra found Mati's smile was strangely broken. Before he could ask her, he was interrupted by a long rope ladder that tumbled from over the side of the flying ship above.

He looked uneasily at the ladder. It was unnatural. Ships that floated on land. Ships that sailed the sky. Unnatural! Not to forget sailing had not been the finest of his experience. He doubted flying would be any different. But, as usual – what choice did he have? Dantavakra looked back at the charred railing of the Earthship like a forlorn lover as he caught at the rope ladder with the hand of his good shoulder, and he held it steady while Mati pulled herself onto it, then he climbed on below her.

Vahura extended a hand. 'Welcome aboard,' she said. 'This is the Balkhan Ship *Vaurihura*, bound on an expedition to save the world. Captain Vahura, at your service.' Dantavakra coughed a laugh, deep from his chest, even as Vahura started laughing, almost jumping. 'We did it! We not only did it, we also found a lost windkeeper and a Forge-damned Astra! We can even go and call for help to save the passengers from the other two Galleys. Can you…' She stopped short when she saw Mati's face. 'Are you alright, Princess?'

'Fuck the other Galleys.' Mati held the railing of the windkeeper as if jolted by lightning. And then she… peed her pants. Though it looked worse. Liquids had just seeped through her trousers with the enthusiasm of an overturned bucket.

'You need more robust trousers, Princess,' Dantavakra observed.

'I'll knock out your crooked teeth one by one!' Mati screamed, 'Fool! The baby is coming.'

Dantavakra's jaw dropped like a drawbridge. 'The baby is… *What* now?'

MATI would have broken Dantavakra's jaw if two lives were not at stake. But they were, so she didn't. She knew it was bad timing. She did not need him drawing short, furious breaths as if he were in labour.

'Alright, what should we do?' Dantavakra asked Vahura as she struggled to manoeuvre the windkeeper around the rigging lines just below the Horn of the Earthship, the nostalgic venue of their spidersilk mishap. 'You're the book magician!'

'How should I know?' Vahura stared at him incredulously. 'I have not read… well, books on childbirth!'

'And clearly not one on flying!' Dantavakra said as the wind-keeper caught itself against another rigging, causing them all to sway sideways. 'Help, Vahura!' he pleaded.

'Stop shouting!'

'I am not shouting!' Dantavakra shouted.

Mati had again erupted into sobs, no doubt loathing herself for her body's instinctual reply to even the slightest weather shifts. 'No, no,' Dantavakra cooed. 'I'm sorry for shouting,' he murmured, gently guiding her to her seat. She followed like a lamb, making Dantavakra feel very uneasy with such uncharacteristic compliance.

'Ssshh, don't worry,' he whispered into her hair. 'We'll manage. You're the Black Swan, remember? Daughter of the Storm. Surely you must be able to remember something about having a baby? From the lectures in Magadh or perhaps even from your long voyages.'

Mati rubbed her snot on his sleeves. 'I suppose.'

'Try not to think of it as a pain of labour but just as a knock by your baby,' Vahura said, no doubt vomiting some filth she had read.

'Yes, in the way a tempest might be called a breeze, you fool!' Oh, this must be karma for her sins, a punishment too harsh by any standards of justice, to have Ser IWantToBeAHero and Princess BookDependent play midwives to her.

'And don't worry, Princess! I might not have books on childbirth but I've helped a cow give birth in our stables.' Vahura paused, no doubt trying to remember how it was that she had assisted in that bovine project, till she realized that Mati was staring at her with malicious intent.

'Oh, so should I go down on all fours and moo? Will that help? No doubt Dantavakra has been wanting to see me on all fours for a while!'

'It was Vahura who called you a cow! Not me! Unfair!'

'I... I did not mean to call you a cow. I mean, uh, what,' Vahura looked helplessly at Dantavakra but he had nothing to offer as poult-ice, 'I'm sorry!'

'No, you are right. Look at me. I am fat! So fat! Leave me, you guys! I will do it on my own,' Mati growled as she wiped her eyes on her sleeve and walked to the rear of the windkeeper, one hand on her belly as she heaved through her contractions.

By now, Dantavakra looked like he knew by the time he returned to Magadh his scalp would be too grey for anyone to recognize him. 'Princess...' And a flash of crimson almost severed his arm but the blade rebounded off the gauntlet Dantavakra had stolen off Balthazar. He did not have time to seethe at the thought that his guard had slipped, for the assailant was already behind Mati, that same round bag on the floor, one hand locking Mati's hands.

There was one of those silences, *pregnant*, was what they were generally described as. Mati looked at Dantavakra. Vahura looked at Mati. Tapasa looked at both of them. Vahura's spidersilk rope, which Tapasa had used to ascend to the crossbeam and dive onto the windkeeper, slapped against the windkeeper's side.

'You are all beginning to annoy me,' Tapasa said, his grin still plastered on his scorched face, as his free hand pressed a skewer against Mati's throat.

 VAHURA held Dantavakra's arm as the skewer pressed against Mati's throat drew blood. What could she do? She raced through pages and pages of books, of stories, trying to find a similar scene which could offer her assistance – where the supporting actors pulled off a feat of the wit to let the hostage turn a hero. But she came woefully short. Dantavakra was shaking, his hand gripped tight on a trident's hilt, but he knew even a slightest baring of the steel would lead to Mati paying with her life.

But surely, Dantavakra could beat the Red Acharya. He had vanquished three Iron Order knights! What would a Namin do against Dantavakra? But Vahura only now noticed the wound in Dantavakra's shoulder, a splinter jutting out of it. Parries blocked and prayers unanswered, left only pleading.

'Reverend Acharya,' Vahura said. 'Princess Mati carries the heir to the Empire. Prince Saham Dev lives no longer, and the child in Mati's stomach is the only survivor who carries the Emperor's bloodline. Surely...'

'Does it?' the man Mati called Tapasa grinned again. 'Captain, have you not confided in your friends that the whelp in your belly is a bastard, born out of the seed of perhaps a dozen men, whose father – while he could be anyone – was definitely not Saham Dev.'

'So?' Vahura asked, stepping aside the shock of that revelation. She was growing rather good at this. 'Do not the Seven preach that the illusion cast upon the ruled only be displaced when it can be replaced with another. Is there any other heir? No? So…'

'Clearly Princess Mati must have found the tale of Jayatsena too delicate for your ears.' The Red Acharya smiled. 'But Princess Vahura, you certainly live up to the rumours of your courage and wit. Fighting valiantly to save the life of this Kalingan. Why? You had never even met her until two days ago. Is it because she hatched this fool's errand to save your sister? It did not work, did it now? Mati brings ruin wherever she treads! Look around you, Princess. Look at this marvel of mankind, painstakingly built over decades – obliterated, all because of her. Mati is pure poison, corroding everything she touches. Best be purged.'

Mati was groaning in pain in his grip, the contractions no doubt growing worse. She had to find a way to distract him to help Dantavakra find an opening. 'What do you mean *it did not work*? It did work!' Vahura pulled the Daevic Scrolls and waved them at him. 'The Scrolls say…'

'Sagacious as a hawk, this one.' Tapasa laughed into Mati's ear as she struggled against the tip of the skewer. 'Mati still didn't tell you, did she? Not surprising. She would have hidden the truth from you till she squeezed out the last use from you, Princess.'

'That is not true…' Mati protested, heaving when Tapasa dug the skewer deeper.

'I had thought that is why you had asked the Librarian to run away – you know – to spare her, and not because,' Tapasa looked around, impressed, 'well, not to unearth this treasure and make it work. I thank you, Princess Vahura. I can't wait to take this windkeeper back to the Seven,' he remarked as he looked around the windkeeper like a Daeva museum curator. 'Think of it as spoils of war. Uh, uh,' he turned to Dantavakra, who had just taken a step forward, 'no funny business, lad.'

'Please...' Mati said, the word sounding alien on her lips. She whispered something to him but the winds maliciously carried the words to Vahura. 'Spare her...'

'The way you spared my brother?' Tapasa whispered into Mati's ears, the grin slipping from his face for the first time.

'Spare me *what?*' Vahura stepped forward, pulling away from Dantavakra's hold.

Tapasa turned to Vahura as if she had interrupted an important thought. As if only now remembering what Vahura was talking about, he winked and kicked his bag across on the deck.

'The smallest pyres sear the deepest.'

The bag rolled on the floor like a misshapen ball, its strings open, spilling its content on Vahura's foot.

Vauri's severed head.

 DANTAVAKRA sagged to his knees, his face hung loose with hopelessness and horror. Dread slowly spread out from his chest to the very tips of his fingers. Everything he had done, he had killed, he had cheated, all an utterly pointless waste. The little girl he wished he would find in his daughter – her head lay face down on the deck, still blindfolded, as if playing hide and seek the way she used to on the *Gilded Lion* – but the blood around her neck... the decapitation was a botched job. Not a clean cut. She would have suffered, gagged, blood spilling out of her mouth, till a second slash removed her head from her shoulders.

'To be fair, we did not kill her,' the Acharya said, grinning when Dantavakra looked up at him. 'Well, we just smuggled into the temple and found her chatting with the Tusk, Bhagadatt while he was bound securely in his manacles. Chatting something interesting about his feelings for her sister. It was adorable to be honest. All we did was open the girl's blindfold.'

No...

'The result was better than we expected, wasn't it?' Tapasa turned instinctively, expecting to be backed by his brother... who was absent. His grin slipped momentarily before returning. 'Rakshasa and a flock of Yoginis – all enemies of the Seven. It did not affect the Tusk quite the way it did the witches, but it was enough. The Yoginis, driven mad by rage, descended upon each other, clawing each other's throats out, drinking their blood, eating their filth, nothing they would not normally do, to be honest. It took two Yoginis to stop the massacre. Heroic stuff. They sacrificed themselves by severing Vauri's head, and then stabbed each other before the plague took over them. You had to be there to appreciate the sheer theatrical value of the carnage.' He pursed his lips as if to kiss in the air. 'While the surviving Yoginis circled around, killing off any of their infected sisters, I slipped away with the prize,' he pointed at Vauri's head, 'as a souvenir for a job well done.'

His throat closed up. Dantavakra's imagination, always vivid, was now a curse.

By now the horror had crept slowly through his body and mingled with the pain of his shoulders. Must have been, for he tried to wriggle his toes, clench his teeth, move his fingers – he could not. He was paralysed by dread. *Find rage*, he told himself, *find rage and it will steer you.* Deliver to him a death Yama's torturer would be envious of.

But he could not find it. He forced paintings of Vauri into his mind to let wrath be born again in the soles of his feet but sometimes even provocations can't wade through a sea of pain.

Dantavakra lay against the helm, defeated. 'I curse you to die a death of being eaten by a thousand maggots while you are alive!' He hoped that was enough, he hoped his curse was powerful enough to be a Shrap. But if it had been, he should not have been breathing.

'A life of moderation does not build up the *atman* you need to pull a Shrap off, lad. Why are good swordsmen always stupid?'

Dantavakra ignored him, for the first time realizing, if he was affected so, what would Vahura be feeling? She still stood frozen to the spot, eyes downcast, staring at the back of her little sister's head. Dantavakra opened his mouth, but no words came forth, and realized how grief tasted so much like fear.

 VAHURA opened her eyes but she was blind. Blinded with a carousel of what-was, what-is and what-could-have-been. She was vaguely aware of other mouths moving, weaving stories of horror about what happened to poor Baggy, driven mad because of her, of the poor Yoginis who helped her, slain because of her. She wondered if old Asshaye finally fell because of her misplaced trust in a librarian. Not a single thought about her sister, however, could claw free out of the prison of her mind. Was this the hysteria that she had read about? Felt strange. An endless tide of horror, crashing against her chest, a chest on a body pinned to the rocks on the shore. The tide crashed again and again, stripping her flesh to the bone. Why did she not die then? The tide was silent and deafening, full of blood and smile, of gaping mouths and quiet screams, all at the same time.

She was vaguely aware of drool dripping down her still-open mouth to the head of her sister below, a head of red, braided hair like hers, her pony tails lying over her blindfold that seemed to have been tied again in a different knot than what her mother had used. Vahura did not even realize when she sprayed vomit onto her boots and clothes. Clearly, an empty stomach offered no relief from loss.

'Princess Vahura, you are unusually silent. Are you alright?' The voice dripping with malice brought her back, rescued her from drowning in the sea of her thoughts.

Vahura raised her face to look at the Acharya. Her eyes were broken glass, bright with rage. She peeled her lips to reveal a dead smile as she picked up Vauri's head, her sister's face facing the Acharya, and... opened the blindfold.

 MATI shielded her eyes with one hand, wondering if a palm could ward off a plague. She did not feel any different. Just the normal amount of rage and discomfort one might expect from a pregnant woman who'd been tossed off a flying ship. But the eye is blind to itself. How would she know the colour of her eyes? It was not as if she could simply ask Dantavakra

or Vahura. The fools were still high up in the air on the windkeeper, no doubt still working on how to get the damn thing down.

As fragments of memory returned, carried on the currents of various aches, she remembered how Tapasa had nabbed Mati to use as his own shield before hurling them both overboard onto the deck below. *Oh, Red! This is 'cause of you!* Mati might nurse a grudge against Vahura for her reckless gambit, but, deep down, she couldn't suppress a swell of pride. It was exactly the sort of demonic deed Mati was renowned for.

Ow! Right. There is a baby on the way. As the waves of contractions intensified slowly, Mati tried to distract herself. That was all she could do to while the time away till Dantavakra rescued her and delivered her to the nearest Yogini. *Sink me!* Twelve to twenty hours of this pain! Oh, where were the handmaidens when you needed them?

She tried to slide away from Tapasa's body. Turning him at the last minute in the air to land on him was a move she had picked up from the oral autobiography of Dantavakra's *Life in the Arena*. Having heard his complaints against Eklavvya a thousand times over had finally been worth it when she had felt Tapasa's bones break under her. Bloody hell! Mati had influenced Vahura, Dantavakra had inspired Mati. What was happening?

Hope Danta does not catch the Marigold. Oh, Vahura...

Above them, the windkeeper jerked in the air, pecking at the Earthship's mast. She was sure they would figure out how to turn a windkeeper back but with every passing second, the ice below her certainty cracked a little bit more, and it finally shattered when rosaried hands clasped her waist tenderly.

'I hope you didn't think that little fall hurt me, Princess.' Tapasa grinned into her ear.

Mati realized he was toying with her. He could have killed her a dozen times already – which meant he wanted something – which meant there was still something she could offer him.

'You killed my brother, my companion of centuries,' Tapasa said, as if answering her thoughts, and suddenly it became clear why he was stalling.

He wanted uninterrupted time with Mati.

Despite the heat of the explosion on the deck, all Mati felt was cold.

'Acharya, please, let my child be born and then you can—'

'Now,' he ignored her as he unsheathed a jewelled dagger, 'this fine blade is an Astra, the only one on this side of the realm till I saw the one used to bring that windkeeper to life. But you know what is special about the dagger? It is attuned to the Elemental of Life. They say it traps the souls of the ones it stabs to remain sharp. Now, I have no idea whether this is true but, in your case, I am willing to take a leap of faith.'

Mati grappled with him, her grip feeble as he chuckled, rising to her side and gently lowering her head. 'Don't worry, Mati. The dagger comes later.' He withdrew his hand and belted the blade. 'It is a tool for the finale. Your death was always going to be enter-taining ever since you left us for dead in the sea. But then... you had to go and pull off the stunt and kill my brother. He lies down on the deck, scorched and lifeless. So, now you see, you made this personal.'

Mati curled up defensively, instinctively, both hands shielding her stomach. 'Just... let my baby be born, Acharya, just let her be born! Please... she is harmless! I'll do anything!'

'Hm. Alright.'

Mati blinked her eyes open to stare at his dark silhouette against the sky. 'Wh... what?'

'As you wish. I first need to have a look and see how far dilated you are,' Tapasa said in a matter-of-fact manner, smiling. Mati's eyes widened with equal parts surprise and fear as her thighs crossed and clenched. 'Do not flatter yourself, Princess. I have sampled pleasures for centuries. Do you think a woman who could not arouse Saham Dev would be of any interest to me? But then... on second thoughts. Who has the hours to waste waiting for you to push your baby's head out? Let's do it the easier way, shall we?'

Th... there was an easier way?

Tapasa lifted her shirt. Her belly, swollen like a moon about to wane, glistened with sweat. One rough hand held her down, splinter wood digging into her flesh. 'You will have to stay still, Princess,'

Tapasa said as he rummaged through the various pockets of his robes. Mati could not see what he was doing but for obvious reasons she felt she could not trust him.

Mati was right.

'Only the finest of Madjas can do this,' Tapasa grinned, 'and they only do this to save the baby's life when it is stuck in the woman's canal or has lost its way in the womb. That isn't the case here, but we are in a hurry, are we not? Smile, Mati. Time to meet your baby.'

A sharp pain, born of flesh as well as awareness, flared beneath her stomach when Tapasa made the first incision along the abdomen. The blade parted the skin with ease, leaving a crimson smile on her body. 'There you go! See, how easy that was.' Tapasa beamed as Mati screamed.

He sent the edge of the blade under her side and began to slice, back and forth, separating the meat from the membrane below. Blood flowed, making it hard for Tapasa to see the lines. He looked around, saw a small aleskin on Mati's belt and extracted it, his other hand still on Mati's wrists, holding her down.

'Tch, tch, ale even in your delicate condition,' Tapasa shook his head, 'Matakshara should have taught you better. Now, don't struggle! You want your baby out of you, don't you? Move too much, and I will end up cutting it by mistake. Yes, scream, scream as much you want,' he said as he uncorked the aleskin and poured alcohol on her stomach to keep the cuts clean and clear.

The fire from the ale sent a surge of pain violent enough to kill her. That had been merciful of Tapasa. Too much of pain, and your mind becomes fuzzy, it unlatches itself to let your body experience it alone, you don't truly experience the next cuts. White fire coursed in her eyes, swiftly darkening to black. She was not gone from her body, but in a strange way was detached from it. She knew she was screaming but she could not hear it. It was almost as if she had floated into the air and looked through the sky's eyes at a red-robed man dissecting a pregnant pirate alive.

'Oh, are you passing out on me?' Tapasa laughed as he held her nose, and applied pressure on two distinct points that woke her up

with a violent arc of the spine. 'Tiny Chakra points on the nose –
twisting them awakens you to every feeling, making every second a
lifetime. Devadasis use it to heighten awareness of each whisper of
pleasure. I have found it amplifies pain just as keenly.'

His hands moved with a practised precision, widening the incision, revealing layers of muscle and membrane, the shimmer like
wet silk. 'Now you'll sample every bite of pain as if it were the first
time you were suffering it – pure anguish till it lasts, no getting used
to it, no darkening of vision, no death till I permit it.'

She clamped her nostrils shut. *Please die, please die, please die,* she
begged her body the way one would scream *wake up* while suffering
a nightmare.

But her body refused to die, refused to surrender as she felt her
mind awaken, alive to every spore of pain on her muscle.

DANTAVAKRA wondered if he was alive. He carefully opened his eyes. The night sky whirled dizzily
overhead but he was alive. Judging by the nearby
groan, so was Vahura. Dantavakra blinked the confusion away, and then remembered why he was on
the floor and closed his eyes shut again.

'Shit!'

'As this story comes to a close,' Vahura's voice muttered somewhere in the distance, 'I see it now. I was the villain all along.'

Eyes closed, he called out, 'Is…' he gulped, 'Vauri's blindfold…'

'I have put it back on.' She spoke in a voice that shook.

He opened his eyes and found Vahura at the end of the windkeeper, her back turned to him, cradling something on her lap. But
he had no time to console her. No time to console himself. He heard
Mati's screams. He peered down from the railing and saw Tapasa
on top of Mati. Xath protect! He needed to save her. Dantavakra
climbed to the helm and looked at the assortment of levers. They
obviously controlled the whalewings to steer around. And he was
reasonably certain the crystals had something to do with the flying.

Nothing.

'Going down...' Dantavakra pulled a lever, and the *Vaurihura* rocked, '...is clearly something other than that. Oh, here we go.' He pulled another lever, and the *Vaurihura* evened out, then turned slowly in place as it continued to rise instead of descend.

Loath as he was to admit it, Dantavakra was shockingly not a natural at flying. 'Vahura! I need your help!'

Nothing.

How does this damn thing work? 'Yama, help me!'

It was as if his inner ear caught a song, and Dantavakra jerked his neck to the right. At first, the sky looked the same, dreadfully dull and dark. And then sudden green light, across from where the moon was setting, billowed across the black sky like ocean waves crashing upon the craggy shore. And was that a jade pillar in the sky? Mother of God! And those plumes of green poison spreading across the sky. It looked if it was caused by the reckless spill of an otherworldly paint.

'Vahura, are you seeing this?'

'Ser, are you seeing ahead?'

Dantavakra, alarmed, spun around. Before him, in the sky ahead, loomed a gate... a gate suspended in the air... a gate of coiling green around which countless human-like shadows writhed. Had he by mistake summoned Yama for real? Was that the gate to the after-life? *Oh, Yama – no, no, call some other God. Oh, Seven! Xath! Storm God!* He did not want to die!

And I will not.

He looked at the helm again. He was a hero. He was not built to break! He decided to dive onto the deck, but Yama had other plans.

 MATI'S throat was raw from screaming. Each cut sliced through taut flesh with grace, and each slice was a promise of pain. Blood welled up, dark and viscous till Tapasa ran his free palm over it. Mati did not even feel the ice settle in her veins as the river of blood pouring out of her turned sluggish.

Satisfied, he sawed her stomach from one side to another, then dug his fingernails into the gap and pulled, slowly at first to test whether the cut was at the right place. There was still some connective tissue so he had to burrow his fingers deeper and tug from the bottom. Blood splattered against his face and swirled down his chin.

Die, Mati! Please let go! Just die, dammit!

'If that feels undeserved from me, you can tell yourself it's a return gift from Panchal.'

The First Galley heaved and rolled beneath them as if the very wood recoiled from horror. Suddenly a breath caught in a throat, and Mati saw Tapasa bathed in a sickly jade sheen. And then suddenly, it blossomed green, as if the world had awakened to an alien sun. He paused for a moment, letting her draw painful, burning draws of air. But there was no momentary relief. Every second, Mati burned to death, and was resurrected to burn again.

'I cannot believe Parshuram failed to vanquish the Son of Darkness!' Tapasa muttered, his smile disappearing from his face for the first time. He squinted into the western horizon. 'By my calculations, that jade pillar is rising over Mathura, is it not? Oh, now, all the Dvārs around the world will be flung wide open. There is going to be so much work,' he groaned. 'So many people to kill. You were right, Tamasa. In this world, trust is a luxury we can ill afford. Have to do everything ourselves.'

Tapasa was still staring at the jade pillar rising in the west, mouth open, distracted. Had he glanced up a moment earlier, he would have spied a door of darkness yawn wide open in the sky above him, slowly thickening until it became opaque. The suspended frame of the door lingered briefly until it swallowed the windkeeper and Mati's last shred of hope.

When the jade pillar on the western horizon finally vanished, so too vanished the door above in the sky – as if it had never been, leaving behind a night swirling with colours, like shattered rainbows. Only then did Tapasa turn his gaze behind him to search for the windkeeper. He frowned at the shrinking hole in the sky, a ragged gap where the windkeeper had simply fallen through and vanished.

'Where did the windkeeper disappear to, Princess?' Tapasa asked, and then chuckled, his hand and his blade still inside her. 'They abandoned you? Aw. That knight deserves more credit than I give him. Sorry, I got distracted. Some mishap over Mathura. Eh, why interrupt our pleasure, no? We are so close.'

By the end, his hands disappeared up to the wrists in the gaping wound in Mati's stomach. Mati's body arched in agony. Amidst a ripping of skin shreds, and a flood of blood and fluids, the hand delved deep into her, searching. Digging. Pulling flesh out of her. Till it found what it wanted… His face beamed as if the fish had caught his bait. Breath hissing through his teeth, with a final, brutal tug, her baby was removed from her womb, leaving her burned and ripped.

She could hear crying. High and wild and desperate. A wounded cat, perhaps? Very loud. Was it on the deck? Was it her? Was it someone else on the Earthship?

She did not know how long it was but when she opened her eyes, through blurred vision, she saw Tapasa with a red bundle, wrapping a tiny squashed-in face.

'I'm a mother,' Mati managed to mutter, her breath rattling like wind through dead leaves, her life seeping away with the tide.

'Seems to be the only conclusion,' Tapasa smiled, 'for now. You were right. It is a girl.'

Just then Mati knew how she had been lying to herself all along. Of the lie that she did not care for her baby. Of how she had eaten those horrible foods, of how in every duel, she had angled away her belly even if it put her at a disadvantage, of how secretly before sleeping she ran possible names in her mind. She had never wanted to be a mother. But months had passed, and she had fallen for her baby, like two prisoners condemned to life. 'Please, Acharya, take care of her,' she said through fistfuls of breath as she prepared to die. Too much blood gone. And by that moment, she truly believed she had dug as far into pain as was humanly possible.

She was wrong.

'I took your baby out as I promised,' Tapasa said, clicking open the Chakra points in her nose again to awaken her, 'but I am sure you know the Elemental of Life is strongest in a life just formed. Flesh of the Gods, they called it in lore. Blesses you with a long, long age,' saying which Tapasa ate her baby.

 DANTAVAKRA wondered if the Dantavakra that he had left behind perhaps would have jumped in joy. For the Dantavakra who was resolutely not turning to look back at Vahura didn't even flinch at the mirror clouds offering flattering reflections of his face from all possible angles. 'I'd always believed all those tales of other realms were nothing but elaborate inventions of priests, meant to scare wives into sleeping with them.'

'I wonder if that ignorance lends you comfort or fear?' Vahura asked.

'Well, ignorance is like a glass palace, causes comfort until it breaks and leaves you surrounded with a moat of fear,' he shouted over the ashen rain, using his skirt as a rainshield over his head.

'Look at you, Ser. Heists can turn philosophers out of swordsmen,' Vahura chuckled.

Vahura had gone mad. But then again so had he. Reckon they both were going to die on denial.

'Beginner's luck,' Dantavakra rallied.

Vahura laughed, and he heard her cries in it, and wrapped the skirt tighter around his ears.

'What do you think we entered through? The Curator I met could not stop talking about ley lines, or Godstrings, claiming the rail was built on it to make the most of Earth Elementals.'

'That makes sense. The jade wound on the horizon must have caused a gate to open up. I have a theory – ah well, why bother now, eh? Look at this place. Echoes of death and destruction are suspended as if the place was trapped outside time itself.'

A place trapped outside time? He again remembered the Curator. The Asuran had waxed on about places that were corridors between worlds, where mortals who dared enter them died.

A lightning burst illuminated the land below in fits and spurts. His face, unbidden, turned below to see the world through the glass floor of the windkeeper. If they were going to die in the tempest, he might as well admire the view. If the trees below bore leaves, he imagined the view would've been shrouded under a green blanket. As it was, there were just thousands of blackened spears rising out of the earth, with marigold trees scattered here and there, to uselessly challenge the heavens. In between the corpses of trees and sentinels of marigolds, rose wraiths of towers, broken glass towers whose tips he felt the windkeeper could nudge any moment.

Still ignoring the knock of reality, he focused on keeping the windkeeper afloat. He knew he had taken his sweet time but he was finally doing a grand job steering the ship amidst a tangle of winds and mirrored clouds. He puffed his when he saw his reflection. If only Asanka could see him now. Dantavakra: the Sky Pirate.

Vahura stirred behind him. He would rather dive into the ruins below than turn and face the ruins behind. If only she could stop making those sounds. *They* all made sounds, small sounds that could deafen the thrum of the waterfall. The sound of Vauri's head rolling under a seat every time the windkeeper was tossed by the wind. The chatter of teeth that could only be from Vahura's shivering body. Perhaps the loudest sound was the silence of Mati's absence, biting at his ears, pulling it apart to scream into his skull, 'You did not save me.'

Ahead, something took shape in the storm, and as they drew closer, he could make out another colossal Gateway suspended in the air, similar to the one that had swallowed them up. Dantavakra straightened. It was not the Gateway that had him gushing but it was what he could see beyond the Gateway. Something so ordinary, something so in contrast with this world of mirror clouds, marigold trees and black rain, and now so special, that he would never walk under it without muttering thanks.

A dawn sky still unkissed by the sun.

A dawn sky of their world.

A dawn sky whose horizon was constricting as the Gateway began to shrink.

'Vahura! Look!' He turned. 'That has to be home! We might make it! Vahura… please, no,' he said. His voice quavered, each tone of his tonsils' vibration thick with fear. 'Don't do this to me…'

 MATI grunted, a grunt that became a groan, the groan became a shriek, the shriek, a rending howl as she saw him swallow the last of her baby. The wound to her mind was unbearable, her eyes now drowning in tears from the pain of something that was deeper than her skin, something darker – something that made her feel she could shred every soul in the realm.

She looked at her ruined womb one last time and whispered, '*May the Waves Carry You… into a kinder sea.*' Using strength she did not know she possessed, she snatched the Astra-dagger from Tapasa's belt.

No more revenge. Just release.

Mati stabbed herself in the chest.

The world shattered. The anguished screams of Tapasa broke the stillness of the night. She did not know if it was a desire at death or delirium of pain but the last sight she thought she saw was of Tapasa reaching up, as if to cover his ears. But he never completed the gesture as he imploded, as if under vast pressure from the inside, his skull horribly contracting into itself only to explode outward, spattering Mati and what remained of the deck in bloody pieces. And then that was all.

 DANTAVAKRA saw Vahura perched on the wind-keeper's railing, cradling Vauri's head in her lap, and stroking her wet hair, her legs turned to the deck. Vauri's face was pressed against Vahura's ribs, her eyes hidden away. Even in the storm's blur, he could make out Vahura tottering on the edge of the wind-keeper, holding gingerly against the rain's onslaught. Her face held a nameless emotion. An emotion that grew once anguish decided it was not enough, that grew in a bloodless way, in a cancerous way, eating away at will.

'Staying grows so very lonely when one stays all alone. But it is far, far lonelier when one has to stay with ghosts. Just like this black rain around us – I wonder in what language it is falling around us on this city of stained glass, shattered glass...'

'You aren't alone!'

'The Yoginis destroyed. Bhagadatt – the one responsible for all my laugh lines – no doubt dead, or worse, spreading the plague through the Tree City. Innocent people on the Earthship, and the Earthship itself, a marvel of mankind, split in half, and Mati and her unborn child... well, I doubt they are going to meet an enviable fate,' she chuckled again. 'All because of me. I told you. I am the villain. Me, and the Seven. Those fucking bastards!'

Dantavakra could swear this was the first time he heard Vahura swear.

'That felt good.' She grinned. 'Bastards! You fucking bastards! Ha ha! This feels good,' she stretched out the *good* as if she were savouring a wine, 'if I knew how to, I would burn my soul to Shrap the Seven.' She laughed now, a madman's laugh. 'Do you know the last thing Mati told me? She found the cure to Vauri's plague even though the... fucking... Seven had buried the cure. It lay in the armour of the only other known plague victim...' Vahura's eyes were blank as she spoke as if reciting a poem, '... a strange golden armour with stranger earrings. A beautiful man, a better soul. Tread softly, Mati said, for he is a child at heart. You will know him from his golden eyes. Said his name was Karna.'

Dantavakra was slowly inching towards Vahura, trailed by a crashing wind and a spray of rain, but he stopped in his tracks. 'That lowborn upstart from the North? What?'

'Or so Mati believes. Does he have amber eyes?'

'Isn't looking into a Marigold's eyes dangerous – Wait, how am I to know how Karna's eyes looked?' Dantavakra cried, almost offended. 'I have not met him, and even if I did, I don't go about noticing the colour of men's eyes.'

'Such a prude,' Vahura said, and chuckled again. 'Oh, you are a wall, Ser. A wall to lean on, not a wall that blocks. Thank you. But, if you ever meet Karna, well, take him to an Acharya of Balkh and perhaps we can save another Vauri...' her voice broke down as she laughed and sobbed, all together, 'and if you ever meet the Seven, kick at least one of them in the nuts.'

'Vahura, please come down,' he said, turning just slightly to reconfirm they weren't running into a cliffside. 'We can kick them in the nuts together.'

'Promise me!'

'Vahura, why don't we talk?' He was at a sword-swing distance from her. He blinked away the sheets of angry black rain. 'Just come down.'

'Promise me, and I will come down!' she screamed over the rain.

'Fine!' Dantavakra raised his hand. 'I promise! I see Karna, and I will take him to the nearest Acharya! I will take a Vachan to this when we find a damned Acharya. Now, I did as you pleased. Come down. See there is a Gateway! This windkeeper won't fly itself into it.'

'First, call it a Dvār. Not a Gateway. Second, a promise is a promise,' Vahura laughed, 'I am coming down,' she declared, swivelling her legs away from the edge, and toward the deck, almost climbing down before halting abruptly, 'but then, you neglected to specify come down on which side. Details, Ser!' With a laugh, she reclined gently, as though leisurely dipping into a pool, and then Vahura and Vauri, both, disappeared into the sky.

In the world beyond the Dvār, the sun rose in a scarlet-streaked hue like a public execution.

MARIGOLD WINTER
PART II

RAJGRIH, MAGADH

FINAL DAY OF THE BATTLE OF MATHURA

'Despite these ominous signs
Why has doomsday not come?
Why does the last trumpet not sound?
Who holds the reins of the final catastrophe?'
—Ghalib

ANAADI, the innkeeper of Tulips, knew it was hard to turn your back on a winning streak, but harder to walk away from a losing one. But he was a man under siege, and today was a day when destinies would be decided, debts would be settled, fortunes won and lives lost, depending on how the heads rolled. One false step, and it could be curtains! For it was the Night of Blood, the Night of the Imperial Contest.

The last time Anaadi had stood in this spot, waiting in the queue, had been the day he had lost his farms to a wagerwolf when Dantavakra had lost to Eklavvya. It still offended Anaadi that a nine-fingered tribal upstart from the forests or wherever he was from could have vanquished his beloved Dantavakra. Hard to imagine that this was little more than a year ago. So much seemed to have happened since. He had thought then that the Virangavat could not possibly have been more crowded, more tense, more excited. How wrong he had been.

Thanks to the rumours of Chalakkha's secret surprise, the queues for the free seats were crammed, and the air was dense with their eager, fearful whispering. An ash-smeared fool was already annoying the crowd about the evils of shedding blood for sport, while street girls sold skewered kebabs and melons to the hungry. Good thing Anaadi had stuffed a chapati roll of minced pigeon in his pocket, though he was too excited to be hungry.

He found the queue for his caste, and squeezed in between the wedged shoulders of smiling faces. Some, he greeted by name, and some he only knew as familiars from the gambling den. Most welcomed him cheerfully despite the earliness of the day. One even passed him a terracotta glass of cheap ale, and he took a swig, and turned to pass it along the Drachma queue when his gaze snagged on the aged sage and his daughter, renters of a room in his inn for the past week, standing in the Namin queue. Enlisting a friend to save his spot, he strolled over for a chat with his lodgers.

He hoped he would be able to get them to spare words this time after the favour he had done them, for the pair were always quiet. The few times Anaadi had eavesdropped during lulls in the inn, where purpose rather than panic guided his steps around the table, all they spoke of was some prophecy, someone called Masha and something called Machli.

But there was a certain serenity he felt whenever he spoke to the kind sage, and he could use some serenity after the wagers he had made. Though Anaadi did find it strange that the sage had brought his daughter to the blood sports. The marked education to the girl's manner had already told him the sage was illegally teaching his daughter the word of the texts rather than the way around the kitchen. No wonder the girl was scarred so, and always skulking. Motherless daughters are always doomed, and fatherless daughters are harlots: such was the way of the world.

'Sage Parshu,' Anaadi bowed, 'I did not figure you for a spectator of the sport.'

'Can hardly claim to have seen a new city without seeing what the bards say must be seen.'

'True, true.' Anaadi nodded. 'But the sport is a little too violent for certain eyes, no?'

'Lends me something to scare her with later if she misbehaves.'

'I hadn't thought of it so. Excellent notion. Oh,' Anaadi leaned in, 'need any more Abyss? My friends are here, and they would be happy to lend more aid.'

'We are amply provided for, thanks to your largesse, Anaadi. Yama bless you.'

Anaadi was on the verge of patting the sage on the back when he halted just short of his palm touching the sage's robe, held back by a primal caution unknown to him. He fumbled instead, using his hand awkwardly to scratch his neck. 'I hope the guard did not give you trouble accessing the cells. He is my wife's brother, a thorn in my arse, but it is good to know someone in the Imperial Prison, eh? That lowborn prisoner you met, Karna was his name, wasn't it? Was he a trusted servant from your village?'

'His mother was. Owed her a favour. We don't liaise with traitors.'

'Of course! My pardons if my words slipped. I heard Lord Dimvak tortured him personally.'

'Hardly a surprising epilogue to a treasonous life. Any word on...?'

'Alas, I wish I had good tidings. I still haven't gotten any word of anyone named Vyas or Ajath or, for that matter, any sighting of a Naga in the City. Shame that your caravan was separated. But then again, you just arrived here two days ago. We will find them. I am sure Indra – I mean, Yama – will keep them safe.'

'Maybe you should have killed the Imperial Guards when Chalakkha refused to meet you,' the girl chimed in, eyes half closed, giggling in a manner that set Anaadi's hair on end. He knew the signs. The sage had used Abyss to drug his own daughter. Poor man. 'Maybe they think you died in Iyran, and gave up on finding you, and returned North to prepare. Can hardly blame them. Time misbehaves, he knows, but even he wouldn't wait weeks for you, would he? Time and tide wait for none. Don't know why Hanuman did. Or maybe Chalakkha was the only one who escaped, and your friend is as dead as mine.' The girl laughed again, her eyes glistening in green, till the sage clubbed her on the ears, and she started to sob.

Anaadi left the pair silently to join his friends, lest the girl's Abyss-riddled ramblings sour his mood. He was already turning sober – beginning to wonder if he'd been careless with his wager. *Indra protect me.* He had no idea how he would pay the wagerwolves if he lost. *Think on that, or your wife's reaction later. You won't lose.*

'Who have you wagered on, Anaadi?' a friend asked.

'Isa,' Anaadi answered softly. He might have had little more understanding of duelling than a toad but even he knew this was going to be a monumental night in the history of the Empire. The first Imperial Contest with no clear favourites. With Eklavvya retired, Dantavakra had been a dull favourite but with his promotion and absence, Rajgrih was blue in betting fever.

But Lord Isa of Hehayas had won three of the last seven mock duels, and Anaadi had thrown all the rent he could not afford to lose on Isa. To assure him of his choice, Indra had also sent him a dream where he was locking a treasure in his safe, and the sigil of the Hehayas was three interlocked keys. He knew he would win.

By the time they were permitted inside the arena and shoved on to the Drachma Box, the sun had long since fled the sky. He knew many had grumbled at the astrologers deciding on predawn as the auspicious time for holding the Imperial Contest, but he was glad their fears were unfounded. Just look at the arena: parts of it stark and sharp in the silver light of the moon, while other parts were mellow and soft in the saffron light of fire. It would be breathtaking to see blood spill in such a beautiful arena, made more so by the colossal roofless cage of shimmering metal encircling the blood pits. The gaps in the cage's grids were spaced widely enough that only a few of those seated in the lowest tier grumbled. Anaadi chuckled. Look at them whining about a cage blocking their view. If he were in their shoes, he would be more concerned with why in the hells they needed a cage at all!

 THE ACHARAK wondered if he could cage in words the emotions he had on the day Yama rescued him. His adulterous wife had called him unfeeling that day, and his father, who he had found her abed with, had branded him a fiend. Contradictory compliments. For a fiend permitted feelings to torment him, to agonize him to fury. But Yama preached that it was not enough to be betrayed to be hurt but one should have to *believe* that he was hurt for the knife to find a nerve. Had his wife and his father succeeded in provoking him, he knew he would be a willing accomplice in the provocation. But Bhadrak was now Acharak in the service of Yama. He did not respond impulsively to impressions. He did not bludgeon his wife or burn alive his father as he wanted to. He took a moment to remember Yama, regained control and had them apprehended by the Ehtrals. It wasn't until weeks later that he learned of Justice's path. His father, castrated, was sent to serve in a leper prison, while his wife had been initiated into the service of Yama after being purged of desire. So, if there were any intrusive thoughts on discovering that it was his wife lighting incense sticks to mask the rank odour in the room, they did not penetrate deep.

Especially considering her lamentable effort. Despite the incense sticks, the reek of spilled wastes from the harlot remained over-powering. Being chained to the bed for weeks, defecation on the bed was only natural, almost symbolic of the holy work Yama had cast on them, and just like it, it stained and smelled unpleasant, but was necessary. So, he willed his nose into obedience as he stepped around the harlot's bed. 'Prepare the prisoner for questioning,' he ordered.

His wife, now shorn bald, nodded. She had not once looked up since his arrival. She set a saucer of gutter water to the prisoner's cracked lips and waited for her to finish sipping. She then set about washing her back down with the same water. The Acharak beamed at seeing the bed sores that had erupted on the harlot's bare arse, while ignoring the smell of ointment on the red welts surrounding the harlot's wrists where she had been pulling on her bindings to squeeze through the shackles. It was only when his wife began mopping the floor, did he realize that maggots had crawled out of the harlot's wastes. *The same way her secrets will.*

'Do not clean her,' he ordered, and his wife nodded, withdrawing to the shadows.

'*Devadasi* Marzana,' he said, 'time for us to have a conversation, again. Your days of spying are over but there is still a chance for you to walk again in Yama's darkness.'

Marzana opened her eyes to him, a strange heavy look to her bruised eyes. 'One only stumbles in the darkness, one-eyed fool,' she croaked.

'With sufficient distance in the sky even a peak could look flat, the valleys between them invisible. This is an illusion of light. The Ehtrals see the peaks, see the mountain ranges and see the valleys of civilization in the darkness, and guide it accordingly.'

'I have already confessed everything. There is nothing more I have to say,' Marzana said, and then through cracked, desiccated lips, she smiled and whispered in a croaking voice, 'Ah. But the torturer needs to pretend his victim always had more to shed, or else, what is the point of his profession? And Jhestal—' He struck her hard, her head snapping to one side.

Chest heaving fast, he cursed himself for loss of control. He hissed. 'Rail at me all you will, harlot! It is only expected. But not at our Great Priest. He is humanity's last true hope.' He inhaled deeply. 'Now, your confession so far surely has been helpful. A little disheartening that it took two days of our hospitality for you to admit that the man masquerading as Prince Duryodhan and the one called Karna are spies for Krishna, sent to abduct the future Queen and bring harm to the Crown Prince. A rather ill-conceived plan.'

Marzana said nothing.

'I still find it beyond belief that Krishna thought the Empire would believe *you* to be a Devadasi. And it's got nothing do with the fact that a Devadasi wouldn't even let a Resht's shadow fall on her, let alone fornicate with one. And it has nothing do with that raven we received from the Temple of Kaamah denying any link to a Devadasi by the name of Marzana. I know not who you waggled your arse for to get the mark of Devadasi but just look at you. You are a Mleccha, a fair-skinned bug, who would ever let a Mleccha wed those Gods, false as they may be. You, a Devadasi,' he scoffed. 'A better jest, I have heard not.

'But I'm grateful,' he continued. 'Your confession certainly greased the wheels for convicting those spies. It served as a nice complement to the Resht's confession to murdering the knight and the little serving girl to shield his stiff-jawed friend from blame. Loyalty amongst thieves – who would've thought?' he said even as Marzana winced. 'I must say, though, the other one we dredged out of the river still swears that he is the Prince of Hastina.'

'Lord Krishna is good at convincing people they are who they are not,' Marzana said.

'But then again, your confession did not spill any beans we hadn't already gathered. Our spies in Hastina and local ambassadors of the Union here had confirmed that Duryodhan left to attend the Conclave in the East so that ruse was easy to uncover, with or without your help. In sum, you have not done anything *yet* to earn Yama's clemency but... you can earn it. Riddle me this: who is Shon?'

Marzana's eyes widened first, and then she laughed, her laugh soon breaking into ragged coughs. 'You already know, don't you?'

'That he is the leader of the Red Blades, and the spy with the golden eyes is his brother. Yes, I pieced that together from his scrolls you'd stitched within the folds of your blouse.' When Marzana shot him a sharp glance, he laughed. 'Told you we don't let Light blind us. So, tell me this, Marzana. Why are the Red Blades, the Resht rebels, working with the Usurper? Is this Krishna's grand plan? To spark a Resht rebellion inside the Empire?'

Marzana just stared back at him, eyes full of murder.

'I reckon I am right.' The Acharak smiled. 'The High Priest will be most pleased. However, there is a matter I find perplexing about your plan,' he said, delicately wiping away a trickle of blood from her nose. 'This... Shon, he had already informed you that the Crown Prince and the Princess are not in Magadh, that they've set off for the Conclave. Then, why orchestrate this ruse of letting those two spies infiltrate the royal palace?'

Marzana flinched but she still did not answer.

'So be it. I envy the interrogators their job. Extracting the truth from traitors is the noblest calling there is. Farewell, Marzana. I must make haste. The Imperial Contest has already begun, and I would hate to miss the spectacle of your lovers meeting their grisly ends,' saying which the Acharak turned to issue instructions to his wife when Marzana spoke.

'The Imperial Contest has begun? In Virangavat?' Marzana lifted her head even if it was a struggle. 'And Karna is already there? Fighting?'

His steps slowed suddenly, as a cold dread swept through him at Marzana's tone. He dismissed it. 'Both were sentenced to death but the Ksharjan seized his chances in the Empire's new amnesty scheme while the Resht, well, the Resht enjoy no such favours. The Resht picked up a weapon – so he will be crucified in the arena. Why?'

Hacking laughter, a bubbling of red froth at the corners of her mouth, answered him.

He leaned over her, one hand searching for a tool of confession on the table and the other choking Marzana. '*Why?*'

'You are too late, Acharak,' came a wet cackle, madness grating out of Marzana's dehydrated lips. 'My work is done, and my son is saved.'

His thoughts wrestled with her revelation, struggling to retain foothold, to understand.

'The Ksharjan and the Resht in the fighting pits! *That* was your plan all along! By Yama! Why? Are they carrying Mathuran munitions inside their arse? Are there more spies? An assassination attempt on the Jhestal or the Emperor? No, it doesn't make sense!'

'You know what the finest lie is, madman: a truth spoken unconvincingly. They never were spies!' Marzana's made a hacking sound which the Acharak realized was more mocking laughter. 'Now your Jhestal can choke on your cock and—'

He struck her again, harder than before, and then winced at the pain. He examined his hand – it was trembling, a shard of Marzana's broken tooth jutting from one knuckle. Shame descended on him. Hitting with the hand was not the Ehtral way. It was base and cheap. And it did not help that his former wife, still standing in the shadows, had witnessed it. He wanted to strike her too. *No. I don't have time for this! I need to warn the High Priest before it is too late.*

 CHALAKKHA might have found favour back again with the Emperor but his new seat in the High Gallery of Virangavat felt decidedly uncomfortable. Even the reverence of his rivals in the Imperial Court lacked lustre. He had always anticipated his men and women would be martyred in his quest – it was a Ksharjan's noble destination – but there was nothing noble in the way Whisper died. *Murder most foul.* He was done with the Acharyas and their games. Still… refusing to meet Parshuram on a whim felt unwise. Why had he done it? Was it because he had been too shocked to learn Parshuram was alive? Was it due to a sense of betrayal he felt by not waiting for them when they hadn't emerged from Iyran Machil for a week? Or was it because the Bane of Ksharjas would usurp his glory? For no one would believe that Chalakkha had led the hunting expedition if they even got a whiff that 'the' Parshuram had been lurking around in Iyran Machil at the same time.

A lengthy howl from the arena pits disrupted his bout of self-pity. Chalakkha wrinkled his nose in distaste at the scene unfolding. In days past, the idea of men fighting wolves in an arena would have found him cheering himself hoarse but he'd had his full of inter-species encounters in Iyran. Still, he watched, for what else was left for him to do? He could only pray the wolves made short work of all the contestants so he could return to mope in his room. Chances of it, however, seemed less likely by each passing moment as he saw a warrior with a stiff jaw command the rest to arrange themselves in a formation.

Contestants could choose their weapons, and suddenly many of them mimicked the stiff-jawed warrior who had chosen a spear by hurriedly swapping their swords, battle-axes and rapiers for pole-arms, pikes and halberds. The Magadhan knights, the ones who had not withdrawn from the lists last week, were the only ones who chose not to follow the trend. Ego always leads the impudent astray. Long-stem weapons work best on wolves. *But I do not recognize him. Who is that warrior?* Chalakkha thought, a sudden interest putting some will to his eyes.

He was certain the betting guilds would be teeming with excitement. The sudden announcement that the Imperial Contest would be a Duel to the Death had seen more than fifty withdrawals of applications, reshuffling the list of favourites so dramatically that nothing of the original roster remained. Rumours swirled that while the announcement may have been sudden, the Ehtral's plan to make it so had been brewing for quite some time. Some courtiers had even insinuated that the Emperor had knighted Dantavakra as Rakhjai and dispatched him to the East to save his own favourite from an untimely demise in this Contest. Was this also why Eklavvya and Shishupal, former champions of this blood sport, were curiously absent from the arena? Was the Emperor's loathing for a duel to the death also the reason he chose to shun the Contest entirely?

Regardless, the Magadhan taste for blood, the absence of star fighters and a series of hasty withdrawals had prompted a surge of a new breed of contestants to join the Contest – prisoners on death row, mercenaries, paupers and desperates – all optimistic about their chances with last year's finalists out of the painting. It did not matter. For they were not going to face each other, not before they proved themselves against the beasts of Magadh.

It was as if that very thought had conjured the Unni Ehtrals forth.

Fortunately, the winter night's moon, the imported mothlamps and the firelight torches around the arena were bright enough to lend a silver-topaz hue to all their light touched. Commotion on the corridor around the arena below drew his eyes to where the black-clad priests were dragging a young man, a lean-muscled mass of gold and blood. A late addition to the sacrificial list, perhaps, but he looked different from the rest of the bodies crucified around the arena pits. Most were women, one child, but all of them were scholars. This man, on the other hand, seemed a warrior by the fire-light. A golden skinplate hung from his one shoulder like a strip from a tattered sail.

Chalakkha ignored him, and returned to wondering where Vyas had disappeared to after entering the Empire. Rajgrih was an ancient city, teeming with tales of strange underground temples to forgotten gods. The Virangavat was itself said to be built on hallowed ground though it was rumoured a curse of an Old God had thwarted its construction for years. That is, until the Ehtrals had buried virgins alive to lay the foundation of the arena on their living corpses. Perhaps Vyas was out with Ajath and Taksha to find other such lands. Maybe Chalakkha should have sent Whisper to trail them in case they found more treasure and then, as if just now remembering Whisper's fate, he settled back into his chair, his appetite for ancient relics all extinguished.

This was so frustrating! He was supposed to be joyous! The Emperor had brought him back to the fold. Everything was going splendidly. Then why did he feel so heavy, so low, so dejected and so... plain. Oh, just admit it! It was because of how Jhestal was treating his gift. He had imagined the bald-headed Namins using their alchemy to spawn hordes of dragons to flatten the Three Sisters of Mathura and make mincemeat of the Usurper's griffin. He had even gone so far as to imagine himself leading these dragons on their charge.

But to find out that the last dragon of the world was barren had driven a stake through his heart. No breeding was possible – the Ehtrals had ruled. They had acknowledged Chalakkha's contribution as grand in size but in terms of real value, it was as impotent as the dragon.

 DURYODHAN tried hard to not acknowledge the stake looming at the corner of his vision but his will was impotent. He couldn't look away. From it, tattered and bleeding, hung his only friend. Now there was no option but to win the Contest and ask the victory boon of the Emperor to rescue him.

Duryodhan could not wait to rescue Karna so that he could crucify Karna himself. In what world the idea of throwing a friend off a tower into a river would seem a fine idea was unbeknownst to him. Favouring his leg wounded by the fall, Duryodhan jogged ten paces behind the Magadhan knight with the sword. The spear the pitmasters had thrust into Duryodhan's palm was still in his grip, a detail he had to remind himself of every few moments since his fingers hadn't shed their numbness since his swim in the river.

He had already rallied a few of the contestants or convicts, he did not know who was which, and made them back away against the wall in a defensive formation. If the wolves did not see them as a threat, they would not assail. Wolves hunger for a meal, not a massacre. He would have then put his plan into action.

For Duryodhan had harboured grand designs when they had convicted him of espionage on Meenakshi's false testimony and condemned him to a trial by duel in the arena to decide his sentence. Nothing could be further from the laws enshrined in the Codes. Then again nothing could be further from civilization than the South. Humanity's lust for carnage had reddened so deep that it no longer distinguished between black and white. How foolish had the Union been when they had mistaken this bloodlust to be a symptom of the rise of Unni Ehtral. Gods were not the cause of violence, they were the excuse.

Exhaling his worries, Duryodhan commanded the lighter members of his new 'troop' to focus on slipping beneath the wolves to stab and slash from below and the heavier ones to aim for the neck. Some hesitated to follow commands from a stranger but, as it went in group discussions, so it went in gladiator duels – it was always the survival of the assertive. 'Stand and swing!'

Two spearwomen behind him, drunk by the looks of it, echoed the cheer, 'Stand and swing!'

As Duryodhan turned to face the innocent wolves, the words of law, of justice, of order froze dead in the space between his ribs. If he had to slay innocents in a contest, he would. Even if it meant flouting the Codes. Even if it meant butchering poor beasts who bore him no ill will. For when it came to Karna... *Fuck the law.*

 DIMVAK was a Rakhjai, a Man of Law, known for wielding discipline like a battle-axe, but when confronted with the Contest, he was as battle-drunk as the drunk gents in the gallery boxes. He did not care that the Ehtrals had intervened and introduced beasts into the noble sport. It did not ruffle his mane that the gladiators had to duel while crucified men and women and children wailed from their stakes. Such was the code of warriors. They suffered silently. They survived, no matter what you threw at them, no matter the toll on their soul and their body. They fought to honour the blood-stained sands.

Having been such a warrior himself, he couldn't help but be impressed with the spy. The whole arena still chanted that fool Isa's name, their voices rising like a war cry, eager to lend their strength to the gambling den favourite. They did not see or perhaps care for the way the Northman had rallied most of the other contestants. It was a show of leadership that seemed more fitting of a seasoned warleader than a clandestine agent of Krishna.

But Narag Jhestal had said the Northman was a spy, so he was a spy. After all, it was not his place to doubt the voice of God, the same way it was not Jhestal's place to dictate army formations. His place so reminded, these whispers of the heart were quelled before they turned into echoes.

Though, Dimvak did feel a pang. Loath as he was to admit it, he missed that simpleton, Dantavakra. His prized student had been destined to win the Contest, and would have won it if his silent protest had not been ignored by the Emperor. Heroes are not forged in safety. This kiln of challenge posed the risk of self-immolation, and Dantavakra had understood that, but the Emperor hadn't when in misplaced affection he had the fool anointed as Rakhjai. Oh, how Dimvak would have loved to witness Dantavakra face off against this Northman.

For now, he just resigned himself to wondering whether the Northman realized these were no ordinary wolves he faced, but trained wolves the Empire planned to unleash on Mathura in the next battle. This arena was a testing ground of their trainers.

Just look at the way the Northman had willed his formation to disorient the wolves, using their confusion to turn them into carcasses.

But the wolves had schemes of their own.

The leader of the pack growled when Isa broke away from the Northman to make it on his own, and two wolves, the black ones, broke from the pack to perhaps mirror him. Though the torches around the arena burned bright, the two stalked the ground in shadows, their movements difficult to discern, felt more than seen.

It was too late by the time it dawned on the arena that Isa, who'd charged the wolves head on and who they had been chanting for, had been already marked for dinner.

 ANAADI did not know when his chants for Isa turned to cries instead and when he emptied his dinner on the seats below him. No one complained. Most of their faces lay contorted in a ghastly grimace, as if hearing some dreadful jest. Anaadi's eyes only blazed horribly in his stricken face as he realized he had bet on the wrong horse.

Isa's armour might've blocked one wolf's attack had it not found a vulnerable spot between the straps on his ankle. A scream rent the air. Isa raised his head to the skies in agony. Mistake. In doing so, he exposed an expanse of his throat, a territory the other wolf was only too keen to conquer by clamping on it. Despite Isa's powerful punches to its belly, the wolf stubbornly held on, its upper jaw blocked by Isa's helm while its lower jaw gnashed viciously upwards at Isa's underchin till Isa lost his footing and fell, the wind swallowing his final words.

But, to Anaadi's shock, the two wolves retreated to their pack without even so much as sniffing Isa.

Wolves don't wage war. Wolves wage guerrillas. It was known. But the way the two withdrew so swiftly should have confirmed his suspicion: the wolves were trained. Only through their training would the will of the wolves supersede the wisdom of warriors.

Of able warriors, however, there was a deficit.

The northern spy's 'wings' scattered into a flurry of feathers when Isa fell. Taking advantage of the disorientation, the leader of the pack with the coat of burnished gold and scarred eyes set its sights on the northerner now left standing alone. He had not draped himself top to bottom with steel, bartering safety for speed, *and* he limped, making seemingly for an easy game for the leader, who sprang into the air, death in its jaws.

The spy dropped to one knee, bracing the spear upright, the tip pointed skyward. The shaft bowed under the wolf's weight, then snapped as the ironhead punched deep into the beast's groin, tearing flesh and bone asunder. Wood shattered, splinters flew, and the wolf crumpled with a choked howl even as the spy rolled aside, a spray of sand marking his narrow escape. People around Anaadi roared their approval, cheering the spy and chanting 'Northman' as if Isa himself had returned! As if they had not just lost all their savings on a wager! Or was it just Anaadi? Perhaps they were all simply numbed by disbelief, fear of the future flickering in the eyes every now and then, until their stupid refusal to accept reality forced them to witness someone else's carnage instead.

By now, the Northman had turned, just in time to see another set of gaping jaws hurtling towards him. He drew the shortsword from his belt with his left hand. As the wolf lunged, he sidestepped, holding the blade steady, letting the beast's own momentum do the work. The keen edge sliced through fur and flesh. The strain should have left the Northman's arms deadened but he still raised his hand high, and the arena loved it. As did Anaadi. *Marvellous! Absolutely marvellous!*

The arena was, however, not the only one marvelling at the Northman's mettle. Witnessing his feat against the wolves, the rest of the gladiators had rallied behind him again, doubts dispelled.

For a while, this plucky band of the Northman danced with the wolves. They feinted and struck, patterned and unravelled, in a midst of sweat, shield and steel. One by one, the wolves fell though not without cost. Half the gladiators lay whimpering on the threshold of death, bleeding from a half a hundred bites. Those who survived, noses and cheeks red with exhaustion, feet and hands aching, lungs a command away from bursting, received a thunderous applause from the arena but Anaadi knew it was far from over. In fact, it had just started.

The survivors, comrades in arms so far, now cast wary glances at each other, slowly waking up to the knowledge that while once bound by a common cause, they now stood on the precipice of a Duel to the Death, each realizing that they now had to kill their allies. With a wry sense of tragic amusement, Anaadi saw how most turned their blades to the very man who had saved them, and the Northman was keenly well aware of it. Anaadi could not help but boo alongside his brethren at the announcer who now rose in his pulpit, commanding the Contestants to stay their blades, hands raised in assurance at the arena.

His announcement, inaudible to anyone who was not sitting directly under him, was echoed by deputies stationed before each and every gallery box, till the announcement rippled across the arena as if magically amplified. Anaadi could bet the gladiators were not pleased with what they heard.

For just then, the sand pits trembled as a section of it separated, forming a slope that descended like a chariot ramp into the void below. And from that void climbed out a legend. A legend that drew each and every eye in the arena to the centre of the sand pits, lost wagers and crucified culprits all but forgotten.

 KARNA had been ready to die to keep the peace, and so he hadn't uttered violence when they had crucified him. They had done a horrifying but exquisite job of it, driving the nails through the holes in his wrists, arranging small grooves for his buttocks and feet so that he would not hang by his

arms and asphyxiate swiftly. The crucifix was designed for the crowd to savour human agony. If the Ehtrals let him, Karna would last for weeks there. They had even rubbed chilli powder on his wounds to keep him conscious somewhere between death and despair, and through it all, only silence left Karna's parted lips. But while being dragged across the corridor around the arena, Karna's eyes had fallen on his torturer.

Dimvak had been his name. When he had scored a strip of Karna's golden skin-armour from his shoulder and began to slowly pull it down, Karna had known then for certainty he was going to be skinned alive. Karna had experienced pain before, known it intimately, and so Karna had begged his torturer then. Not for mercy. But for Abyss.

He hadn't had such clean eyes for such a long time in a long while. The days in the dank prison had been hell. He had welcomed the beatings, welcomed the batons, the pain distracting him from his thirst for Abyss. But, after a while, even that did not suffice, leaving him trembling. Oh, Abyss. Nothing else could ever bring Karna such pleasure, such freedom, the power to talk and eat and practise, safe from the miseries of memories.

He had believed in Malengar that if he drugged himself enough, over and over, he'd emerge renewed, reborn. A whole new person, his mind resurrected so many times that the past became just distant, foggy memories. His favourite were the days when he used to dip three crystals into his eyes. Those days he barely even remembered he was Resht.

And now... he hadn't blinked a grain of Abyss in his eye for weeks.

The withdrawal had been excruciating. The entirety of his existence had flashed before his eyes in the worst way possible, his mind refilling itself with each detail that he had worked so hard to suppress.

Mother's murder. Three Shraps. Red Blades. Sudama... Oh Sudama...

Karna thought the torture would distract him but Karna remained Karna even as Dimvak had taken the knife and torn another strip of his golden skin-armour, wet with blood, in a crab grip to draw it down. On the contrary, with each slice of pain, visions of the havoc he had wreaked each time he had dipped Abyss flooded back.

Those Namin women in the woods. The Vishkanyas in the tavern.

Oh, Gods. He had slaughtered them all. All! How scared Marz must have been at seeing him unleashed so! How had the Hanged Man released himself without his knowledge? It was then he'd understood that Abyss was an acid corroding not just his memories but the locks placed on his soul. He had stopped begging his torturer for Abyss then, knowing he deserved to be skinned for his crimes, and just then, Dimvak's knife had paused.

Dimvak and Jhestal had been summoned away, leaving him to fester in the wounds and the guilt amidst fevered hallucinations. But that had been enough. His guilt was taut enough for the noose around the Hanged Man inside him.

But beast delayed was not beast denied.

Now, crucified on a stake, powerless, Karna had blinked through a dried web of blood to witness Duryodhan face certain death. The lark of evil, louder and louder it had sung then. Then song possessed his mind, and this time… he let himself heed its call. He was aware of the gamble he took by letting the noose free, aware of how the fire of his fury would make a pyre of innocents but he had no choice but to surrender. For when it came to his only friend… *Fuck mercy.*

'Come out,' Karna had whispered with baffled lips that had never thought they would dare to profane so again. And with those words of despair, his eyes, not just irises, but eyes, bright and gold as amber, opened to the world.

Twin voices trembled then, the two voices of Karna Thrice-Cursed, of the founder of the Red Blades, of the Hanged Man, of the man Parshuram had named: Mrytun Jay – He Who Enslaved Death, the greatest student of the Bane of Ksharjas.

'FINALLY.'

Caged as a wandering thought, now free as one, Mrytun Jay awakened his Chakras.

All of them.

 DURYODHAN scowled as he saw all the legends of dragons he had grown up listening to be mutilated before his eyes. Its body was like carved ivory in the moonlight though its movements were sluggish, as if sedated. Its arms seemed like stubs, its wings stunted, and its hide grey, a far cry from the multiple colours depicted on the ceramic vases from the Tree Cities. But that they faced a dragon, there was no doubt about it, even if it did resemble a colossal crocodile who had learned how to balance on his hind legs.

It bore several scars on his body, though none looked likely to reopen with a simple poke of a spear. Even a severed tail seemed to have been made whole by a steel appendage that turned it into the sharpest whip in the world – as if the dragon had needed any more killing instruments.

'Are my nerves playing tricks, or you can see that too, Itch?' the woman behind Duryodhan asked. 'Oh, why did we have to volunteer for this!? This reeks!'

The woman named Itch, with a resigned air, replied, 'We volunteered to save ourselves from rotting in the cell, Fidget! Not all of us are dangerous lookin' like Whisper and Sidestep to be employed by fat lords for treasure hunting. Maybe we could pet the dragon the way Vial pets Garud. It might take a likin' to us, eh?'

Their strange names betrayed them as members of the Silver Wolves, a fact that probably explained what was wrong with them. But at least they stood their ground. Many had fled, screaming.

'They have a blasted dragon!' one of the other condemned exclaimed, flinging his weapon aside to dash ahead and kneel in prayer under the Emperor's gallery, praying for mercy, but there was no Emperor present today. Meanwhile, two Magadhan knights hastened to the arena's edge instead, hands raised, wanting to exit the list, evidently in the hope that 'to the death' had been added to 'duel' by a drunken scribe. The crossbows they faced forced them back but none begrudged the pair their cowardice. For while everyone in the world dreamed to see a dragon, precious few ever wished to face one.

The dragon turned to the cheering audience, leaning forward as it ran on its enormous hind legs, its bladed tail thrust back for balance as he charged at the cage in what might have been a polite request for lowering the volume. But the cage withstood the dragon's assault, its bars shimmering blue every time the dragon's claws raked it. Duryodhan had overheard from the gaolers that the First Stone, Vishwakarman himself, had built the cage, and now he believed it.

Frustrated, the dragon opened its mouth wide, its throat bulging as it roared. The crowd behind the dragon cheered while the audience in front cowered, though none need have feared. Forget a burst of flame. Apart from noxious breath, nothing gusted out of the dragon, not even hot air.

'Glad the chroniclers got something wrong,' Duryodhan said to no one in particular, as he stood his ground despite his unhealed leg. 'Oh, Mati and perhaps even you, Divine Marzana, you would have relished witnessing my fate, wouldn't you?'

The dragon, who had been busy snarling in frustration at the cage, having no better alternative, turned to descend on the feast the Empire had so generously set out for it: the Condemned.

MRYTUN JAY'S blood flowed generously as he wrenched his palm free from the stake. With the bleeding hand, he wrestled easily with the remaining nails that bound his other palm and ankles. Once the rope around his waist fell away like a serpent shedding its skin, he dropped on the sand gracefully. Naturally, most in the arena had eyes only for the dragon, the arena's star attraction, and remained blissfully ignorant of this second act transpiring outside the blood pits. He supposed no one truly expected any further drama *after* a man was crucified. Their loss.

In the pits, one of the contestants was jerking on the sand, bright blood pouring from the ragged stumps of his legs. Another contestant was trying to throw javelins at the dragon from behind until the dragon swerved, caught him in his jaws and tore his windpipe out.

The one-eyed priest, lost in watching the contestants, couldn't have been older than fifteen summers. He didn't even notice Mrytun Jay stab the bowman by the stake. Mrytun Jay clamped a bloodied hand over the boy's mouth and pressed the sharp end of a stake nail against his throat. Frozen in terror, the boy squeaked, but who would notice a black-clad priest held hostage in the shadows over a dragon running amok in the pits.

'HAND OVER THE HONEY,' Mrytun leaned forward to hiss in his ear, a voice as grating as nails on a board. The boy-priest nervously groped beneath his robes, finally extracting the vial, only to clumsily drop it on the ground. Enraged, Mrytun stuffed the lad's throat with all the four long-nails from the stake, and forced him to swallow. He watched the boy kick and gurgle until finally becoming still. He took the broken vial, and scraped out what honey remained.

Sounds of screams drew his attention to the pits as he lathered honey on his wounds to staunch and pack them. Saw highborn warriors in the pit flinch on every side, recoiling away from a reptilian beauty on two legs. Spine almost horizontal, a long, black-scaled neck snapped forward. Jaws closed. Crunched. Tore loose. Blood sprayed, its mouth spitting out bone and meat. Pinned a man on the ground, its talons sinking deep, tearing armour and flesh to reveal a raked scapula and cut spine. Fleeing men and women were torn apart in a matter of gory moments as its bladed tail slashed left and right. The screams of the dying dimmed by sounds of cheering, closing in on the last three surviving contestants, the only three who had stood their ground. Two women. One man.

Mrytun Jay spared the arena a fleeting glance and was about to leave but then remembered Karna's debt. Oh, what a massive burden it was to be a moral creature.

 NALA elbowed a woman in the back to move out of the way for a better view of the creature. She pushed past a balding, fat priest, his jowls trembling with outrage till he saw the figure of Parshuram trailing behind her, and just grumbled under his breath. In this hostile manner, Nala forced her way through to the railing and glared down. Abyss may have had the memories in her mind pinned but her ears still hoarded the power to hear the wind.

'Should we go about what we are here to do, Fidget?' one of the women said.

'Kill the Emperor, Itch?' Fidget gripped her spear firmly. 'Did he finally turn up?'

Itch shook her head. 'One good throw, and end the war. Sounded too good to be true, eh?'

'Shame. I would have even settled with the Yaksha, truth be sayin'.'

'Well,' Itch said, wearily. 'Dragon it is. At least I am going to die following this handsome brute to the afterlife. Love the way he thinks he can command me.'

'Very Satyabhama, is he not?'

'Silver Wolves,' the Northman commanded, turning to look at Fidget and Itch who, surprised, stopped mooning over him. 'Someone captured that dragon and brought it here. Someone vanquished that dragon. Why can't that someone be us?' He turned his eyes away, pulled the fresh spear from where had planted it on the ground and raised his hands in the air.

Itch and Fidget nodded, exchanged a wink, and trailed after the charging man. They were faster, and soon they had crossed the limping man. Itch whistled, and it seemed Fidget understood. The two women split and stealthily circled the dragon to reach just outside its peripheral vision. What was their plan? Oh, Nala saw it. They sought to hamstring the dragon's legs while it nipped at the man.

'Oh, c'mon! This is unfair,' Nala cursed, no doubt mirroring the thoughts of those women when the dragon, despite its stunted wings and its enormous size, flapped its wings to climb the air to swiftly turn to face Fidget. The flanking failed. A scream followed.

The bladed tail of the dragon had slashed horizontally behind it. Itch's raised spear fell from her hand, her hands reaching to gather her uncoiling, tumbling intestines, till she sank. Nala froze, seeing the scene unfold from a distance, a distance not just in space but in mind, the Abyss in her veins doing its finest to keep the image of Masha, dying the same way, away. Memories found you often enough without you looking for them. She was grateful to Parshuram for knowing this beforehand, knowing how the violence in the pits would be dangerous to watch up close, and taking measures to help her.

A ragged moan distracted her. Nala saw the woman she had shoved past earlier collapse to the floor, fainting. A helpful soul dragged her away, fanning his orange scarf in her face, and the ill-tempered crowd pressed in tight behind to close the circle. *Fuck! Distracted me!*

She turned to find Fidget howling, wishing the others could have heard the valiant soldier's defiance as well. 'You overgrown fire-impotent lizard! Die!' Fidget hurled her own spear at the dragon's face. It flew straight and true to plunge itself inside the dragon's nose.

CHALAKKHA rushed to the railing when he saw the dragon pin Whisper's friend, Fidget, to the sands, undoubtedly preparing to shred her to ribbons. He should do something! He should have saved them! It was the least he could do to honour Whisper's memory. They were her friends, her cellmates, and Whisper gave her life for him! He owed her, didn't he?

Sadly, sometimes the hour was truly just too late. What could he now do for them when they had themselves volunteered like fools? This was not Iyran. Here, time was not something one could turn back.

It will be over soon, and it will be painless. After all, how many ways can a dragon use to murder you?

Apparently, quite a few.

The dragon grazed Fidget's ear with its snout, and then let out a roar that left her spasming in torment. A roar that had all the warriors, the priests, the attendees, the guards reaching for their ears. It burst into Fidget's skull with such fury that blood trickled out from her nose, eyes and ears. Her body thrashed like Matsya in the reverberations of the dragon's declaration till the world became silent. Chalakkha could not believe it…

Screamed –
Right into her ear –
Abomination.

Fidget's contortions ceased. Blood from her burst eardrums trickled down, pooling on the sand. Nala reckoned the roar ceased its sting once one turned deaf. The dragon must have reached a similar conclusion as it withdrew to squash Fidget with a colossal foot, a grim ending that would be mourned by all.

TAKSHA, on their grim journey from Iyran Machil to Magadh, had refused to mourn the loss of Parshuram, Nala and Masha. He imagined them as only delayed, not dead, and instead of worrying over them, he had devoted his time to mastering the tongue of the Softskins to study dragonlore.

Despite having quelled the immediate threat of a D'rahi army at the hands of Softskins by destroying its womb, Taksha had not wanted to depart the arena with Vyas and Ajath to wherever they were headed. Ever since he learned from Chalakkha that the Softskins had now the grand idea of using the D'rahi to duel humans instead, he had dedicated every waking hour to fashioning a locket out of the baby dragon skull he had claimed. He just knew, deep in his scales, that the moment his entire brood had been waiting for, for centuries, was here.

But as Taksha stood hooded from head to toe, by the enclosure from which the fighters had streamed out to the pits to meet their fate, by the same enclosure from where he had witnessed a crucified man savagely kill an archer and a boy, he realized he should have never left Pataal.

He should have perished with his home.

At least he would not have watched his hope, murdered.

The wisps gathered around that murderer's aura writhed about like maggots in search of flesh. The gold-flecked, purple light around him was almost muscular, like coiling roots of a banyan tree, and it somehow gave the impression of chains pulled taut under immense strain. Deliberate skeins were woven into the armour he wore as a second skin, and the rings on his ear, hidden by his hair, the threads of some elaborate, alien and ancient ritual. Taksha swallowed as he realized both the man's armour and his earrings were made of ancient blood and lightleaf and… Taksha had inhaled this flavour of air before – when Vyas had conjured that orb of light. His armour was forged of diptaloha, solidified Elementals! *Star-touched skin.*

Taksha's skin had begun to moult out of sheer fear. *The mark on the ear.* The strange rings carved into that man's ears. *The gilded gaze.* The amber eyes. This was their prophesied Messiah? This… force of rage! *No… it could not be. He is… pure evil,* Taksha thought as he desperately clung to the faint hope that this man was not the Messiah. For surely the last thing any Chosen One was expected to do, with a dragon about to squash a woman in your vicinity, was dance.

Moving their bodies in time to music amongst humans was a test of their mating prowess, was it not? A ritual in weddings, festivals and other pre-copulative environments. Then why was the most dangerous man in this world writhing alone? Human quirks made his head hurt.

 NALA felt her chest hurt as she saw the dragon's foot descend. It was quaint and barbaric at the same time, something to cheer at while looking away. A moment thwarted when the Northerner stood in its path, his spear raised to stab its underside the moment it landed. The dragon leaped back, almost as though it had been hurt by such an assault before. Unfortunately for it, dodging required grace, a quality not easily found in creatures as large as dragons. Beasts were not naturally inclined to walking backwards, much less leaping. The dragon

stumbled over its own bladed tail, and tumbled onto its side, like a tower falling on the road. The Northerner saw his moment.

'If you are planning to do something, Duryodhan, now would be the time,' Parshuram muttered, somehow drugged by the battle thrill.

Duryodhan? The Prince of Hastina! The Enemy of Bheem! Didn't that make Duryodhan her friend then? *Oh, Spirits! Help him!*

Duryodhan hobbled to the dragon's side. Face to face with the dragon's eye. Fuck. This was a once-in-a-lifetime chance, and he was going to do it! He was going to stab the damned dragon in the eye! *Yes! Do it! Kill him, Duryodhan! Kill the Stone Mother! Stab her in the eye!*

Spear thrust out from Duryodhan's hand, a duellist's lunge, completely extended. Beautiful to watch... until his weight pounded down on his injured leg.

His leg buckled beneath. Bone twisted. Pain on his face, and then sudden realization – the moment lost – as the dragon's fangs punched into his shoulder, sliding to his scapula, and clamping down like tines securing lamb meat. And before she knew it, she saw the dragon jerk its head. Duryodhan was thrown high in the sky.

And then the Hope of Hastina, the Prince Who Loved, the Breaker of Castes, fell from the sky.

Straight into the fucking jaws of the dragon.

PARSHURAM did not see the Heir of Hastina die. His gaze was crucified to the eastern corridor around the cage, shifting from recognizing Taksha standing in the shadows, to finding Karna dance. A smile crept. His faith was rewarded. It was Karna's destiny after all.

Parshuram wondered where the Emperor was. Such a day comes rarer than a comet. The Emperor should have been here to witness it. *Well, if not the Emperor, his Empire will be their witness.*

One could see why Parshuram craved an elite audience. There is nothing more gratifying for a teacher than to see his student leave a mark on the sands of time. And Parshuram beamed as he saw his finest student in the Art of the Sun. Limbs contorted and cavorted, forming grotesque shapes in the air and graceful shadows on the ground. To any civilian watching, it might have come across as a macabre take on the dance of the Devadasis but to Parshuram it was clear as carnage.

Sha's Beard. He figured out the steps on his own. Parshuram followed only two rules in his instruction: one, no Ksharjan would ever receive his knowledge. Two, he would never corrupt a pupil's mind with more than one discipline.

One Almanac for one pupil. Knowledge from other disciplines was forbidden.

So, while Bheeshma had mastered the Red Almanac: Art of the Sun, he did not even know the existence of the Grey Almanac: Dance of Shadows, which Nala now studied. And neither of them would learn the secrets of the White Almanac: Song of the Stars that Masha had spent time memorizing. In such blissful ignorance, their powers remained restrained and manageable.

Karna had been no different. Parshuram had tutored Karna in the Art of the Sun, but Mrytun Jay had somehow managed to weave the Dance of Shadows into his quiver.

'Mrytun Jay… we cross paths once more.'

Parshuram's words washed over Nala like ice-cold water. 'Karna… is Mrytun Jay! Your favourite student is Karna…' her voice trembled at the crossroads between shock and disbelief, '…and Karna is the Son of Darkness… who is Mrytun Jay.'

'I wouldn't go that far in calling him my favourite,' Parshuram's tone was reserved, but the ghost of a smile hovered at one corner of his mouth.

He had always wondered how their duel would be. For Karna was a berserker, a beast beneath human restraints and, above it, a god. Or perhaps he was both, given how he was cut off from all human emotions when he was in this state.

Now this god-beast, the Hanged Man, Mrytun Jay, was versed in the Art of the Sun, the warrior's path, and the Dance of Shadows, the assassin's path. Finally, on a par with Parshuram. *Proud of you, son*, Parshuram thought, truly regretting that he was moments away from slaying him.

 NALA would have never believed anyone was capable of slaying Parshuram till she saw Mrytun Jay urf Karna dance. A curious recollection flitted across Nala's eyes. Like a memory plucked from ether, a play by the Fifth Year students on the eve of the Seven Stars alignment, performed again in the mists before her eyes. It was a play on the forms of fighting in malla wrestling. All the malla forms had names: mountain names for the heavy and charged attacks, names drawn from nature to describe light and fluid moves, and from earth and silk for styles that absorbed damage. It was how they named what they did.

Except for the one they simply called *Naah* which meant Denial in the First Tongue. In the arena of forms, *Naah* meant something slightly more. It meant Denial of Pain. Lowering of the body temperature to stem blood flow and to numb nerve endings to pain. *Naah* was the last stage of the Dance of Shadows that Parshuram always dangled like a carrot before her.

Now, as she saw how Mrytun Jay sprinted ahead, bow in his hand, utterly unmindful of the holes in his palms and his ankles, Nala wondered if Mrytun Jay at Nala's age would have been able to save Masha, a thought that was pushed away as soon it was birthed into the abyss. She laughed morbidly at the mistaken pun.

Meanwhile, Mrytun Jay's sprint put him in the path of the spearwoman with the bleeding ears, her hands clutching them as she cried in the sand pits. Nala gasped as he squashed her head beneath his feet, silencing her, without breaking a stride, to face the dragon alone, his hair streaming behind him like a pennant of pure darkness. The crowd, the soldiers, the royal box, everyone was too shocked by the turn of events and the feral smile on this warrior's face to notice the mark of Resht on his neck.

'Do we stop him now, Master?' Nala asked.

'Not yet,' Parshuram said.

The dragon had still not noticed Mrytun Jay, its back turned to him. Mrytun Jay raised the bow and shot an arrow at the metal tail of the dragon. The arrow deflected, and bit straight into the dragon's rectum, the only un-scaled, fleshy part in its rear, lodging itself in there like an errant fish bone in the throat. The dragon recoiled, its swallowing efforts abandoned.

Mrytun Jay then rushed between the pillar legs, pulling the arrow off the dragon's arsehole, and then repurposed it to stab the fleshy part of the tail's base. The tail whipped upwards. Mrytun Jay, still gripping the arrow's shaft tightly, was lifted off the ground and onto the dragon's back. Wasting not a moment, he scaled the beast.

Just as the dragon twisted its neck to confront him, Mrytun Jay pressed his knees against the dragon's neck in a squat and propelled himself off to leap and catch hold of the spear lodged in the dragon's nostril – a grim souvenir of the woman who Mrytun Jay had killed not moments ago.

And then in a feat to rival the nimblest of acrobats, Mrytun Jay pendulumed himself up the spear, and scaled the dragon's nostrils to the ridge. He dislodged the spear, its tip dripping in dragon snot and blood, earning a lament from the beleaguered beast. Swiftly seizing the opportunity, Mrytun Jay expertly manoeuvred the spear, driving it deep into the dragon's gaping maw just as its jaws parted, piercing the tongue and pinning it to the lower mandible. Then, with the arrow he had pulled from the dragon's indelicate location, he stabbed the upper jaw from inside to dissuade the dragon from snapping its jaws shut.

But it was a dragon, not a puny crocodile. Defiant and un-deterred, it still clamped its upper jaw shut.

But it was the Son of Darkness, not an ordinary Ksharjan. Mrytun Jay tossed his bow down, and raised his hands and… And he caught the jaw. He staggered beneath the weight, sinking to a knee, and the air rang with the clang of fang against Mrytun Jay's armour. But he caught it.

'Fuck…' Parshuram swore for the first time.

 Duryodhan knew it wasn't exactly ideal to spend the last moments of your life being ingested by a dragon, but he thought to make the best of it by trying to slay it. Though try hard as he might, he could not move his hands. It also did not help that he could feel the edges of consciousness fraying as the dragon gulped, turning his mind into a miser with words.

Keep your eyes open. Fight your way out. But the dragon gulped again.

Ribs – cracking. Immense pressure – the suffocating, gelatinous substance blinded him. *Saliva?* He tried to wriggle again but his hands were completely immobilized under him. He just slid helplessly across the slimy, scalding surface into the belly of the beast.

With what part of his consciousness was left un-frayed, he tried to glean some useful intelligence from the surroundings of his soon-to-be viscous tomb. Alas, a dragon's insides were not the sort of place that lent itself to casual inspection in the absence of abundant light. Though Duryodhan did get the sense it was all walled in, filled with a general air of digestive intent. His time had come, and he should be happy that he died fighting, the Ksharjan way of death. Duryodhan could almost see Karna roll his eyes in heaven at that casteist remark. *Forgive me, friend. I could not save...*

A roar ripped through his legs, and through his senses, as he felt light seep around him to illuminate the charred tonsils of the dragon. The dragon had opened his mouth.

No.

Its mouth had been opened, and now it stayed open. He felt himself slither, this time backwards, as an unfriendly hand gripped the ankle of his broken leg. It was slow and painful but Duryodhan was not complaining. With a final tug, he was pulled clear of the dragon's maw to stare back at a pair of golden eyes upside down.

'With this, Karna's debt to you is paid,' a man said, as he flung him to the ground with a flourish. The fall broke his already injured shoulder blade but Duryodhan was alive and intact, which was more than could be said for the dragon's dignity.

Before the world turned dark for Duryodhan, he saw in a blur
the man still standing between the prised-open jaws of the dragon,
leaning out of it, one hand on the spear between its jaws.

Terror and happiness filled Duryodhan as he saw that man...
was Karna. Karna climbed from between the dragon's mouth to the
ridge to stand tall on its snout, looking down at its eyes, and asked
a question which Duryodhan could not believe a mortal could ask
of a dragon.

'PEACE OR PIECES?'

 TAKSHA could scarcely fathom this absurd, un-
believably strong, yes, but absurd Softskin was
meant to be the harbinger of peace and prosperity
for the Nagas. Taksha would have rather chosen
the slime-sheathed spearman. He could only hope
that the spearman had not died at the hands of his
saviour simply because of a clumsy landing.

But before he knew it, Taksha was running. Within moments of
entering the pit, he stumbled over a contestant's corpse and lost a
sandal. He did not stop running. He could feel the sand between his
toes, cold and rough. Softskins were calling after him. None dared
follow but he still ran faster.

By the time he reached the centre, the D'rahi was stamping its
legs wildly around, sending up a coughing gust of blood-stained
sand. Despite the sand in his eyes, Taksha was grateful for the cover
as he dived.

Above him, the D'rahi roared. The sound filled the pit.

As Taksha scrabbled in the sand, his fingers brushed against the
spearman's wrist. It was warm. He was alive.

By the time he had dragged the spearman to the cage, he had
imagined being set upon by Magadhans. But they were all still
looking at the D'rahi. Taksha decided then to take a stab at making
a poultice with his poison. It would not heal the spearman but
would make his heart forget that he was hurt and take away his
pain so that he might sleep and heal.

'Good gracious, is that lowborn madman talking to the dragon?' a Softskin in the red box above him shrieked.

Confused, Taksha turned even as he cupped sand in his palms and spat into it to make the poultice. At first sight, it seemed the golden-eyed Softskin was poised to fulfil the prophecy by slaying the D'rahi. All he had to do was take the straightforward spear-to-the-maw strategy to its logical destination... but instead, he withdrew the spear and ascended his snout to stare into the D'rahi's eyes, slapping the side of the D'rahi's giant face. Wait. Not slapping. Petting.

The prospective Messiah was petting the damned D'rahi!

The good folk of Virangavat, initially struck dumb by the sheer novelty of events, now rose in an uproar at what they perceived as an act of kindness. Taksha had to assume the golden-eyed Softskin was violating the arena's code of conduct where showing mercy was blasphemy. He couldn't tell but he did gather that, in an arena, bloodshed delayed is entertainment denied.

But surely there were other kinds of entertainment. The kind where you realize you're going to die when you see the flightless fireless dragon... fly.

 NALA could not help but chuckle madly at the way five thousand voices in her gallery stilled when they saw the dragon fly in the air, its stunted wings beating like strange drums and its bladed tail hissing in the air. 'What did you expect when you brought a monster for your delights?' Nala shouted at them, doing her best to ignore that she had just seen Taksha run into the arena. Seeing Taksha knocked on doors that Anaadi's Abyss had firmly locked. She put her hand in her pockets just to make sure she had another dose of Abyss should—

Not a monster.

Nala looked around, startled and sobered. That voice in her head... it reminded her of Matsya's or even Nomnom's. Who was it this time? *Is it... the dragon?* Nala's gaze shot upward, meeting the dragon's eyes. Impossible.

Another hallucination?

Or maybe she was just sleepy. By now, the hem of the night was slowly pulling away in the sky, taking stars with it one by one.

I had no desire for bloodshed, not even when they trapped me for endless seasons. I made peace with my cage till you wrenched me from Sanctuary, poisoned me and dragged me here, for what, to host a fair of my fury.

'I... Please forgive me,' Nala's eyes welled up as she realized she was talking to the dragon, 'I did not know.' Around the arena, soldiers who were adjusting their crossbows had paused on Chalakkha's orders to wait till the dragon rose to an uncomfortable height over the cage and posed an actual risk to the onlookers.

I gave in to this fate, to this destiny, but I am not what you call me. Monsters are made of will, and my will was taken from me.

Mrytun Jay had by now climbed to its skull, clinging with both hands to the spines on its head, and was shouting words of encouragement. Up, up and up in the air it went, rising an inch with each sweep of its stunted wings.

In this sweet man who wants to free me, some sweet hope lies, he will take me to a place, hidden from human eyes.

Oh... the dragon sounded so much like someone she knew.

Parshuram became aware of Nala's glistening eye on him moments later, and he finally relented. 'I'll pluck your eyeballs to make meditation easier for you if you keep staring.'

'Acharya, I just wanted to ask. Are you certain Mrytun Jay is the Son of Darkness? He... doesn't seem evil?'

'How would you know?'

Nala did not want to answer that. 'Isn't he prophesied to stir the Elements awake?'

'Why do you think I haven't slain him yet?' Parshuram said. 'Justice needs evidence.'

Evidence did show up moments later but not in the way Parshuram or Nala anticipated. For neither of them had truly expected the night sky to split and bleed poison at dawn.

THE ACHARAK hastened through the city slowly crawling out of darkness, a city from which the moon was withdrawing its guiding hand on this longest night of the year. He led a score of Magadhan Claws towards Virangavat, heedless of the grit, the dust and the stones' cruel bite on his unshod feet. His Eminence and the Emperor had to be reached before the harlot's machinations ripened. In his haste, the order to fetch Marzana to the arena for interrogation had slipped his mind. No matter. Minor oversight. Easily remedied. What would prove irremediable was how in his haste, he had not noticed the young soldier who was staring daggers at him from across the alley, the soldier who was now following him.

The Acharak was too lost in the expectations of the Emperor and Jhestal's approving nods for catching a conspiracy. The Crown Prince Saham Dev already held him in high regard. After all, it was the Acharak who gifted him the children he gagged on his bed to silence their cries. Purging children of their innocence was divine work, and Saham Dev destroyed the children with precision, leaving them a bright future as loyal servants of Yama. He was quite confident in his ability to charm Jayatsena, the eldest born of the Emperor, especially when it came to light that the Acharak had pledged his own soul in a Vachan to Mati to bring back Jayatsena to the fold. The Acharak was already Jhestal's most trusted, after all. Now, the only remaining challenge was to win over the Emperor.

With this fit of determination, the Acharak stormed the arena doors with the smirk of an invader, only to realize it was the wrong door. He had barged through the gate meant for Drachmas to reach their gallery while the Emperor's Box lay on the opposite side.

What was worse was that the Acharak had completely forgotten the Emperor was going to avoid the Contest today like a plague. The Acharak blamed the harlot's wiles for muddling his mind. How had he forgotten that the Emperor would remain absent from the arena until much later? For reasons the Acharak could not fathom, the Emperor held battles between man and beast in great distaste. It had taken a promise of assured destruction of Mathura by Jhestal to convince the Emperor of the necessity of such sacrifice but such a promise had not been enough to drag the Emperor to witness the sacrifice the Ehtrals had taken great pains to orchestrate for him.

No matter. He could see Jhestal sitting in the tier just above Dimvak's. He would convey his findings to Jhestal and they would together protect the Empire. He was just about to order the Claws accompanying him to clear a path through the gallery when the blackness of the night vanished.

He shaded his eyes against the stinging jade light that streamed from the Northern sky as he saw the heavens turn emerald, like the sun seen on the surface of an algae-ridden, murk-infested pond. The pillar itself was spilling upwards like a typhoon. All around them, the citizens, the priests, the nobles, were busy either clutching each other or wailing or throwing themselves to the ground, covering their eyes and calling for their heathen Gods. He could only hope what the harlot had planned had nothing to do with the poisoning of the sky.

MRYTUN JAY could see his own poisoned face floating inside the dragon's pupil, which had grown into a pool of emerald as the sky above misbehaved. Beneath the green sheen, its sandalwood horns, the fringe of spines on its back, and even its crown glimmered majestically. He gently pressed a hand flat on the dragon's damp scales and realized only later the scales weren't damp. Blood had oozed out slowly from the hole in his own palm like molten copper. But he doubted the dragon cared. And from what he had studied of them under Parshuram, dragons did not hear in the same manner as humans did. Touch helped them feel the vibrations of a human's voice, and right now Mrytun Jay needed the dragon to soar higher than the cages if he was to stand any chance of saving it.

'THE NIGHT IS POISONED,' Mrytun Jay said, 'OR THE STARS ARE CELEBRATING. YOU WILL SURVIVE. OR YOU WILL FALL. EITHER WAY, IT WILL BE OKAY. BUT YOU NEED TO TRY.'

The dragon replied in a dirge that was a whale song and a storm thunder rolled into one. Mrytun Jay could not translate the sound but his heart smoothed the hum into words like glass shaped in the belly of a volcano.

And what Mrytun Jay heard was despair.

'THE WINGS YOU ARE LOOKING FOR ARE IN THE WORK YOU ARE AVOIDING,' Mrytun Jay rasped as he stroked a hand over its scales to calm it. They should have gleamed like the scales of a fish but here they were hatched with scars, rent by arrows and blades.

Memory flashed before his eyes. Through the crimson haze, he remembered the words his mother had told him when they were exiled from Hastina, 'Now that we don't have to be safe, we can be free.' The memory made Mrytun Jay ache to be held.

He held the dragon.

The dragon let out the softest rattle through its teeth as it dipped in the air again.

Mrytun Jay agreed with it that its chances were slim. He leaned against the cold scales of the dragon, pressing his hands deeper into them, and whispered. 'BUT WHAT IS FUTILE EFFORT, IF NOT HOPE PERSEVERING,' Mrytun Jay said, 'LIKE A MOUSE RUNNING FROM A CAT THINKING IT'S JUST A GAME.'

A rattling breath passed down the dragon, right down the length of its body, as it flapped its wings harder and began to climb the air, its snout swivelling from left to right.

'WAS THAT A GIGGLE?' Mrytun Jay growled over the sound of gigantic claps. Glimmers of green hope swirled in those black eyes. 'Giggles, you will then be called. Now fly to freedom, Giggles! Winter is over. Now, dream of spring!'

 NALA looked at Parshuram, hoping the horrified look on his face had nothing to do with the spring blooms in the sky. She saw him close his two eyes and puff his cheeks. To a stranger, his face resembled a tomato struggling with choosing a side between the fruits and the greens. But Nala knew the look. He had closed his two eyes to open the third. In front of them, the

dragon only climbed the sky higher with stunted wings of bronze, now singing in an ancient language. Cloud smoked from its nostrils.

'The pillar is bleeding ancient power,' Parshuram said, without opening his eye. 'It is eating like acid into the clouds around it. Note these numbers, and tell me.'

Nala nodded, her mind drawing the lines, etching the circles and measuring the trajectory on her diary. Her calculations collapsed in a sigh of dreams and desires as Parshuram opened his visible eyes.

'It seems the pillar has risen two hundred leagues to the North,' Nala said. 'Over Mathura. This means it should have...' Something in Nala's chest ignited at the slow realization.

'In a wonder made by Ma■■■■an.
Will rise the S■n of Darkness'

'Mathuran... Magadhan... they are the same number of letters. The prophecy...The bard got it wrong. Acharya, have you...'

'Failed? Yes, it seems I have,' Parshuram sighed, and Nala heard with a pang how devastated his admission sounded. He still held his gaze fast on the jade pillar. 'The scars in the sky... this can only mean the Veins throb again. Ancient pathways, Dvārs, perhaps even Elementals. Have all the secrets resurrected? Nala,' Parshuram answered with a bitter scoff. 'Failed? I have failed miserably.'

 THE ACHARAK screamed at his soldiers who had failed to carve a path through the gallery. Evidently a pillar of green fire on the horizon and the sight of a dragon's pathetic attempts to fly made each step ahead a pitched battle as if the very stones of the arena had conspired with Marzana to impede his progress. He had commanded each man under him, whoever managed, to relay word to the Royal Box that the Contest should be stopped immediately, while his own eyes darted, seeking passage through the seething sea of moneycounters. At one point, he was jostled and jolted by three drunk Drachmas. When he barked an order to the nearest Claw to hew the three down, his words were lost in the clamour, as two sections of the crowd, one eager to escape the dragon and the other seeking a closer view, surged past.

After a point, the Acharak's body was buoyed solely by the press of other bodies, his eyes aflame as he sought a way out. And, in a miracle, he found the narrow, humble frame of Jhestal gazing in his direction. Could it be that Jhestal had foreseen, had known that his devoted aide would be trapped in the Drachma gallery? He was certain Jhestal could. That was the power of devotion. His Eminence would discern, would dispatch aid, and together, they would save the Empire, and none would dare question Xath and Yama's splendour, not even in the secrecy of their innermost thoughts. That is what true devotion is— The dagger slipped into the left armpit of the Acharak.

Eyes widened in sudden agony, sudden surprise. Traitors, here? He felt his head tilt to one side and before him stood a soldier with barely a whisker on his large-eyed face, a face that smelled of stables. Yes, he remembered now. His family ran the local horse races and – Oh.

Mair whispered into the Acharak's ears, 'For my sister, Milani.' He withdrew the blade even as he stuffed rags into the Acharak's mouth to muffle his shriek. Not that anyone would have heard him over the drumbeat of draconian wings.

The next thrust went in through his right thigh, missing his testes, tearing the skin that held the sack to his body instead. Blood gushed under his black skirts as if in a flood of constipation.

The Acharak had failed.

He felt himself slide against the grip of the young man, and then to the ground, his eyes to the sky, gazing up at the heavens, in the direction opposite to that of the green pillar. Being the only turned so, he was the first to behold a falling star

Look, Yama weeps for me.

But it was no falling star, was it?

 ANAADI, the innkeeper of Tulips, having nimbly scaled the blue gallery railing to escape the mad crowd, saw a falling star in the sky and made no wish. Lord Isa had died, and Anaadi had lost all his coin, certainly lost his inn, his days of living on false hope all gone. So there was naught to wish but for a great day of blood, a wish that had already come true.

He had drunkenly poised himself to witness the greatest show on earth in peace, even as a stampede claimed his friends behind. He could not fathom why they were fussing over the colours in the sky. Hadn't they all seen fireworks before? No doubt this was the Emperor's display of Magadhan might. Honestly, such superstition would be the death of the grand Magadhan civilization. 'Have a little faith, you bastards!' he shouted to everyone and no one.

If he had feared that a gallery-wide panic might put an end to the entertainment, those worries were swiftly dashed. No one resembling an authority figure seemed inclined to intervene. *Xath bless them!* Anaadi, for one, did not want this to pause! The greatest day of his life! He had never experienced such raging emotions. Never felt so alive! He was actually hard behind his breeches, not from a glimpse of a bosom, but from a glimpse of bravery.

Wolves! Grisly deaths! A dragon! And topping it all, an undead Resht warrior! Wager lost or won, Anaadi cared not. If death arrived now, he would welcome it with open arms, thankful for the beautiful sights he, an ordinary Drachma, had seen.

'Look!' Shouts reverberated over the shrieks across the arena, and Anaadi saw outstretched fingers point at the falling star, better visible now that the green fingers had slowly withdrawn from the sky. *Oh, my heart will burst!*

'A ship! It is an airship!' The cry echoed through the gallery in many forms, each and every one believing the scenery in the sky to be orchestrated by the Empire. The star was a ship! Xath, what power had the Emperor and Vishwakarman unearthed?

Anaadi was so torn between watching the dragon ascend and the flying ship descend that he ended up doing both, knowing full well his neck would be sore for days to come.

'Anaadi, you won't believe this…' his wealthy friend, a star cartographer, who had aped him by climbing to the other side of the railing, whispered as she looked through her eyeglass.

In a drunken haze, he liberated the eyeglass from her to see what the fool was prattling on about. *It could not be.* Anaadi gulped as he recognized the captain of that airship, peering over the railing, to look down upon the arena like a God on his faithful. *This was too much!*

Anaadi let out a squeal to rival the woman's but he could not have cared less. Anaadi knew it! He fucking knew it! He knew there was no way in Yama's hell that *he* would have sat this one out. The youngest fucking Rakhjai in the world! Anaadi wagered he would lose his voice if he shouted any louder but he was well beyond giving it any mind. His hero was here!

Dantavakra of Chedi was here!

 DANTAVAKRA'S hands flitted about on the knobs and levers like a disturbed butterfly, trying to wrest control of the windkeeper, as if he ever had control in the first place. When the windkeeper had whisked through the rent in that realm of marigolds, he had fancied he was headed to certain death, or worse, back to the Tree Cities where the Twin doubtless would be waiting for him. The odds in favour of certain death had risen significantly when he had seen what he imagined his most cherished place, the Virangavat, would look like from above. *I am in heaven, and the view is marvellous.*

By now the darkness of the night reluctantly surrendered to dawn's uncertain birth, allowing him an aerial view of heaven's Virangavat. The galleries around the fighting pits, carved from stone, rose like serrated teeth around it, a contorted girdle guarding the earth's maidenhood. Something glimmered. A cage? Oh, that was new.

Only when awareness shook him like a rag doll did he realize the scene below him was not a sensuous gift of the heavens for his heroism. It was Virangavat in the flesh! Or stone, whatever fitted the phrase.

'I am home!' Dantavakra cheered, weeping. Truly weeping.
Curiosity at how he had fallen from the world of Kamrup to the
world of Rajgrih in a matter of moments did not trouble him.
Curiosity was engagement, needing a mindfulness beyond that of
a mere witness, and Dantavakra, after the events of the last hour,
dreaded the revelations.

Moreover, there were bigger questions that loomed, starting
with: was that a fucking dragon?

Dantavakra extended the eyeglass Asanka had gifted him and
seethed. What was a dragon doing destroying his favourite sanctuary? And who was the poor man trying to hold on for dear life on
its head?

You still have a chance to be a hero, a voice whispered guiltily, a voice
Dantavakra closed the lid on swiftly. How could he still remain so
vainglorious? He'd forsaken Mati! Left Vahura to die! Failed Vauri!
Condemned the Crown Prince to sharks! A hero? Dantavakra
would count himself fortunate if they did not name a method of
execution after him.

Not that it mattered. Dantavakra was going to die long before
it came to that. The windkeeper was falling like an orange from a
tree, and Dantavakra would count himself lucky if they picked his
body up rather than sweep for his parts. Truth be told, he no longer
minded dying. He could not have handled the disappointment of
Dimvak, the scowls of Shishupal or the tears of his admirers when
he was rolled off Yama's Hands into the firepits. He had done his
best. Now all that was left was to crash. Quick, swift death.

A stray shaft from the rising sun caused the breaking dawn's light
to ricochet off something gilded, striking Dantavakra squarely in
the eye through his eyeglass. Dantavakra blinked, pulling himself
away, blinded, and then extended the telescopic limbs of his eyeglass
for a closer inspection. Just then, the man struggling for help on the
dragon shifted his gaze upwards to stare at Dantavakra, or rather,
stare at the windkeeper. Dantavakra dropped his eyeglass when he
saw the man's eyes.

Pupil and iris were no longer distinct in them, all enveloped in an
ocean that burned the shade of lava from a bursting volcano. And
he knew it then!

Was it mere chance?

Or was it the hand of destiny that had brought Dantavakra face to face, vertically speaking, with the only known survivor of the Marigold Mold? He remembered Vahura's last words.

'... *a strange golden armour with stranger earrings. A beautiful man, a better soul. Tread softly, she had said, for he is a child at heart. You will know him from his golden eyes. Said his name was Karna.*'

And suddenly doing the best was not enough.

'*Promise me, Ser.*'

Now he needed to do what was required no matter how afraid, alone, insecure, unworthy and incapable he felt. 'This is for you, Vauri and Vahura.'

 NALA could not believe how fortunate, blessed, lucky and star-touched she felt at seeing a skychariot. The men and women around her were wiping their brows, gasping and groaning as if they were the ones facing death. Perhaps some of them were. After all, the skychariot was swiftly losing altitude.

'How did he pop out of the sky?'

'If the jade spectacle is an omen of truth, the ley lines sing with newfound life, weaving their ethereal across heavens and land, awakening Gateways – the Dvārs – near at hand. Imagine, dear Nala. The man soaring above has journeyed from lands far away, crossing leagues untold in moments, riding the shimmering currents of the Veins, perhaps even over the ruins of Iyran Machil itself, only to appear above this arena as a falcon in flight. I may have failed but there is beauty even in failure, for it gifts me the grace to witness this grandeur. And you oaf, it is not called a skychariot but a windkeeper.'

Nala did not know what to say. Parshuram almost sounded senile. 'Skychariot has a finer ring to it,' Nala managed.

'I won't contest you. I seem to be getting everything wrong these days.'

DANTAVAKRA did not get much right about being a seafaring man, but he had, in his brief time in the air, discovered he had a taste for flying. And one of the important elements of flying, he determined, was learning the right ways to crash. He pulled two levers. Pressed the knobs. Three of the working sails fanned open. Soon enough, the windkeeper, though hurtling down at a pace to make his eardrums hurt, began to take a more active role in its fall. Drawing smoking circles over the Virangavat, it now spiralled down instead of just falling down. Peering down the windkeeper to check his angles, he found the arena looking up at him, cheering.

'Danta! Danta! Danta!' The wind carried the faint sounds of cheering. They were cheering him? They were cheering him! Virangavat was cheering its own as the windkeeper careened down in dangerous spirals. The dragon meanwhile was rising vertically like a tower – above the cages – and soon it would rise to a level to put the lives of innocent Magadhans in peril.

Steelsong surged through Dantavakra as he was moments away from his target. With a final downward spiral, the windkeeper hit – crashing – colliding – headlong into its destination: the dragon's maw.

But just before machine met monster, Dantavakra, remembering last year's Contest, decided to repeat history. After all, second time's a charm. Half chuckling at imagining Dimvak's expressions, he recklessly climbed the railing of the windkeeper. The wind tousled his hair and tugged fitfully at his Rakhjai cloak, making him feel rather legendary as he launched himself on the dragon, trident in hand.

ANAADI wept tears of pride as he witnessed history. Dantavakra leaped from the airship, silhouetted against the fading green sky, to land on the ridge between the dragon's eyes. With the dragon's head angled skywards, its back to the Namin Box, the Resht behind the beast's cranium was shielded from Dantavakra's line of sight. Not that it would have mattered.

Dantavakra was playing hero. He was unstoppable.

Twenty thousand throats around the arena roared out their approval. 'Danta!' they cried as they stamped their feet and slapped each other's shoulders, and shouted 'Danta, Danta, Danta,' until the whole arena seemed to tremble.

With grace that defied belief, Dantavakra balanced himself on the snout as he drove his trident in the dragon's right eye, pulling it till it came loose in a spray of blood and smoke. What sight met Dantavakra, Anaadi could only guess. But it made Dantavakra leap into the air over the dragon's ridge, and land again to lodge his trident deeper into the recently vacant socket. Anaadi cried, 'Dantavakra! You are a God, I say!'

The dragon and the airship now plummeted down.

Anaadi's drunken eyes traced their destructive path and knew two things instinctively. One, it would miss the cage. Two, it would land on the Namin Box. The orange-clads rushed to get out of the way.

But it was too little, too late, as the dragon and the airship slid into the Namin Box, crushing the congregation of Namins before sliding to rest amidst shattered stone seats.

'That was a lot less damage than I imag—' his friend murmured.

The ceiling of the Namin gallery on the second floor shattered and collapsed in the aftermath, and the entire section of Rajgrih's Namins, recently made powerless by the Ehtrals, were buried alive, including his two lodgers.

TAKSHA'S hope was resurrected and uncoiled to life as he half-danced on the spot. Of course, in the back of his mind, he did pray Parshuram, Nala and Masha were not crushed under the debris of the gallery but the front of it was just cosy nests and warm milk.

His scales thrummed with a vibrating eagerness.

'Did you see that, human!' Taksha called out to the injured spearman groaning on the ground beside him.

'Yes!' Taksha fluttered with anticipation. 'That foul, black soul man who saved you is not the Messiah! It was this Softskin from the windkeeper!'

The Messiah was destined to be the mortal who killed the D'rahi! It was this man – the man with the bubbling aura of pink, orange and sky blue who the arena was calling Danta! Yes! Danta was the hope of the Nagas, the hope that came with feathers.

 MRYTUN JAY'S hope to liberate Giggles was buried alive, like so many of his other dreams, and so many desires. For a fleeting moment there, he had believed. That he and Giggles, kindred monsters, would soar away together. This way, Mrytun Jay would have at least freed someone in his accursed life.

But just as Giggles was about to escape, the skies had opened and in had flowed a legend from the past.

The windkeeper had crashed into Giggles like an enormous boulder hurled by a God of Sea against a kraken on two legs. The collision made Mrytun Jay lose his hold over Giggles' scales, and he'd slipped down. He would have plummeted straight to the Namin Box if not for a whipping tail striking his armoured chest, throwing him against the cage instead to cushion his fall. Though the drop had knocked the wind from his lungs, it was nothing compared to the anguish that washed over him when he realized Giggles had, with his last act, saved Mrytun Jay from being crushed in the rubble of the Namin Box.

But this was unfair! The windkeeper had been a mere wisp compared to Giggles. How could Giggles have been bested by such measly a thing? *Who did this to you?* Giggles had only let out a mournful wail in response. And it was then Mrytun Jay had found one of Giggles' sockets impaled by a trident, making their last moment one of agony. It was truly a thing of tragedy that the most merciful thing Mrytun Jay could do for his friend was to make him sleep.

DANTAVAKRA woke up to the lament of a dragon swiftly silenced. Recollections trickled back of a daring leap from dragonback to the blood pits, mere moments before calamity struck, to roll on the corridor to safety. As he staggered through the wreckage, he found the gallery a scene of destruction. Death lurked beneath every rubble, the morning air thick with final gasps, and he could feel this assault on his admirers by his own hand like a clenched fist in his chest.

He needed to fetch help for the survivors. *But what about the dragon?* Its upper half sprawled across the corridor, its skull propped against the flattened cage at an awkward angle, while the rest of its body vanished into the wreckage of the gallery. If only he had judged the trajectory of his crash – well, then what could he have done? Yama's teats! He had truly been banking on landing within the blood pits.

'Danta the Dragonslayer!'

'Danta the Dragonslayer!'

'Danta the Dragonslayer!'

Dantavakra turned, confused, to the Ksharjan and Drachma galleries behind him. It wasn't his self-obsession playing tricks on his ears. They were indeed cheering his name! Not just his name. They had blessed him with a title that severed his ties to Chedi, to Magadh, to the Rakhjai, to any other attachments that weighed down warriors.

Now he was immortal.

He was the Dragonslayer. He might not have ever won the Imperial Contest but he was the last man standing in the arena after having vanquished a bloody dragon!

A noise of stones moving. A noise of hammering heartbeats. Dantavakra turned sharply, wiping his tears, fearing the dragon was rising from the wreckage. But it was only a human.

Through the clouds of dust in the wreckage behind the dragon's skull, rose a tall figure with a bow strapped across a gilded chest and Dantavakra's trident in his hand. He climbed over the dragon's massive skull, navigating the terrain without even a glance at where he was walking, his face set on Dantavakra. Standing thirty paces from him, the wind whipped the long hair across his pale, bearded face, and his eyes came into focus...

Yama take me...

Dantavakra was about to shield his eye when he remembered Karna was *cured* of the Marigold Mold. And if he wasn't, well it was too late for Dantavakra anyway for he had gazed into Karna's eyes for longer than he had gazed into those of women across the room in a ball. *Speak, dammit!*

'Karna...'

Dantavakra felt the wind whizz above his head. He looked up to find spears flying in the air over him to converge on Karna. *No!* But, turned out, Dantavakra need not have worried.

Karna parried them all aside, almost lazily, with Dantavakra's trident, one after the other, and with each clash of shaft against steel, the trident sang. Dantavakra almost felt envious of him until he remembered *he* had saved Karna from the dragon, not the other way around. *But it will be for naught if the Claws mow him down, fool.*

Dantavakra spun around sharply, coming in between Karna and the Claws, waving his hands like a madman. 'As Rakhjai, I command you to place down your arms and withdraw!'

The Claws it seemed had but awaited such a command for they broke into a rout without ceremony, making a beeline to the exits. *Cowards.*

Up ahead, on the Royal Block, Dimvak shot Dantavakra a glare that could only be described as a threat for the future. Dantavakra waved back at him and hollered, 'I'll explain later,' and then realized his words would likely not cover the distance. *Not your finest day, Danta*, he thought. *Oh, shut up! I killed an Iron Order Knight and killed a dragon. Finest of finest days!*

Turning back to Karna, who was now approaching, Dantavakra spoke, 'Oh, Karna, you have no idea how Fate has conspired to bring us together. I am a friend of Mati's.' He imagined he saw Karna's face flinch but Dantavakra's head was swimming too deep in the lake of applause to notice the ripples. 'I realize this is not the best time for revelations, and you have clearly been through a lot, and, I know you might just know me by name, but tell you what...' Dantavakra took a deep breath, 'I will explain everything once we have filled our bellies with food and throats with ale, and not necessarily in that order! And then I will tell you how I need your help in saving the world. The least you can do to pay back the debt of me saving your life, eh?' He winked.

The sound that erupted out of Karna was a growl, a sound so filled with malice that Dantavakra's blood turned to ice. It was almost nostalgic of Tamasa's silent grin. Dantavakra shook his head, watching, as Karna cast the trident at his foot.

'Oi! That trident is mine! Have some respect,' Dantavakra said, no longer feeling any camaraderie with this man, cure or not.

'YOUR TRIDENT?' Karna rasped and Dantavakra flinched. There was a physicality in Karna's voice, like a friction between two voices – a stone being rubbed harshly against a brick. Deep in place. Scratched apart in others. 'YOU MURDERED GIGGLES!'

'Murdered? What Giggles? Who is Giggles?' And realization dawned on Dantavakra, and he burst into peals of laughter. A dragon named Giggles! Dantavakra could not believe he was laughing so heartily in so heated a circumstance. Perhaps it was because all the pent-up tension in his muscles had been seeking a release, and he had just found it.

'I apologize,' Dantavakra, remembering the code of chivalry, managed to say, shoulders still shaking. 'I fear I've been wiped of my wits… but truly, Karna, *Giggles*. That brought a smile to my face, and by Yama's breath, I needed it. You are Karna the archer, right?'

'KARNA IS SLEEPING, CROOKED SMILE,' he eventually uttered.

Crooked Smile? Did he just call me Crooked Smile? Dantavakra was suddenly rather conscious about his misshapen tooth, which, by the way, women found endearing.

'You need to work on your nicknames,' Dantavakra said, slightly offended, though he supposed the man was just overwhelmed. He gestured to the crowd. 'Hear that name they're chanting? That's mine. Dantavakra.'

The man, in a sudden unsettling motion, cocked his head. 'ALL I HEAR IS DESTINY HISSING YOUR NAME AND HER BREATH REEKS OF BLOOD.'

 Mrytun Jay would not dance the shadows for Crooked Smile. Murderers did not deserve such honourable deaths. And to think he had demanded Mrytun Jay aid him without any preface was galling. But what else could be expected of a Ksharjan? The Ksharjans desired, and that desire invariably transformed into a moral right to own. No more. He placed his foot under the fallen trident and kicked it off to Crooked Smile.

'You disgraceful Resht!' Crooked Smile cursed as he reflexively extended both his hands to grab it.

Mrytun Jay hauled back his foot and kicked Crooked Smile between his legs. He felt balls squish and crack against his instep and saw the imbecile's eyes bulge out like a cock's bulb from its foreskin.

Crooked Smile missed the trident, sputtering, clutching Mrytun Jay's shoulder. 'Alright, alright, I am dreadfully sorry. Truth be told, this is not the first time I have been kicked in the balls but definitely the first time I was kicked by a man and the first time when I deserved it!' Crooked Smile heaved. 'That remark on the caste was unwarranted. And Giggles is an absolutely splendid name! It grows on you. I will name my daughter Giggles, okay?' Crooked Smile said, his fingers twitching blindly for his crotch, the awareness that the pain would only sicken more in moments to come making him clench his jaw in defiance. But to Mrytun Jay's surprise, Crooked Smile smiled. 'But I think we got off on the wrong foot. Oh, that was a bad pun! Listen, I am a friend. Ow! Pray you haven't shattered my jewels, Karna,' he said, 'or you will be cursed by the ladies of Rajgrih, the ones who haven't kicked me in the nuts, I mean.'

Curse. What did he know of being cursed? A voice inside screamed at him to stop. *He is a friend*, the voice said. *A friend*.

It was easy to ignore that voice.

'Now can we go for the drink or what? I need to see bottles and women now, Karna,' Crooked Smile asked, sitting on his haunches, heaving.

'I am Mrytun Jay. And where you're going, you won't need eyes to see.' Mrytun Jay dragged Crooked Smile's writhing body to the skull of Giggles, which lay, mouth agape, tongue lolling out, just beside the cage.

'What are you—'

Mrytun Jay said nothing as he raised Giggles' upper jaw with his free hand, this time a lot easier, and put Crooked Smile face to face with Giggles.

'Oh, that is a bestial stink!' Crooked Smile moaned. 'Oh, I will retch! This is no longer amusing. Not to forget, a punishment far exceeding the crime.'

'SAID EVERY RESHT BEFORE BEING BURNED ON THE STAKE.'

TAKSHA'S eyes burned as he understood what the Demon was about to do to the true Messiah. *It will be fine. Difficulty brings out the diamonds. This is the Messiah's test,* Taksha thought as he gripped tight the garland of skulls he had fashioned, gripping it harder when the man who the Messiah had called Mrytun Jay seized a handful of Dantavakra's hair. *Swallow your fear like water.* Fine silky strands that first slipped through Mrytun Jay's fingers. *Lack of faith kills more prophecies than fear.*

Mrytun Jay wound Dantavakra's hair around his own fingers, gripping it firmly, slowly adjusting Dantavakra's face. Satisfied, he lowered Dantavakra's eyes into the fangs. Just then Dantavakra's body thrashed wildly, perhaps finally realizing this was not a joke, that kindness was not reflected, that mercy had flown away from this world like doves in a magician's trick. Struggling against Mrytun Jay's life-stealing grip, Dantavakra lashed out with a hand. Too late.

Vitreous fluid spread copiously from the eye that burst. The other missed the sharp point. To stop Dantavakra from struggling, Mrytun Jay touched his spine with two fingers, plunging them into his back softly like spikes, pushing past skin, muscle, softly twisting the governing vessel points in the spine. His touch disrupted the flow of prana in the kidney and bladder meridians, putting an end to Dantavakra's defiance by paralysing him.

Anguished gasps rippled through the crowd. But it wasn't over.

For Mrytun Jay began to rub Dantavakra's face against the dragon's lower jaw like a bar of soap. Left-right, left-right, left-right in relentless succession – as though attempting to scrub stains from the dragon's fangs. Red oozed in every direction, the fangs slicing through the tendon and cartilage, which tore apart like eggshells. Flesh burst. More fluids sprayed. Where Dantavakra's temporal bone had been, grey flesh now sprayed out. The fangs caught more bone and hard cartilage, raking through Dantavakra's skull, spilling cerebral matter from the gaping space.

The air around Taksha was suddenly filled with people scream-ing. Men and women hissed a torrent of curses at Mrytun Jay. A sidelong glance revealed that a considerable number were reck-lessly trying to vault over the railings of their blocks to save their poor hero. The few remaining guards in the arena – the ones who had survived the stampede, the ones who had not bolted at the sight of the green sky, the ones who had not made a beeline for the exit when Dantavakra had commanded them, the ones braver than he was – now sprinted in Mrytun Jay's direction. But too little, too late.

Lifting Dantavakra's head from the dragon's lower jaw, Mrytun Jay brushed away locks of the knight's flowy hair to inspect the fruit of his efforts, and pleased, raised it aloft like a prized trophy for the charging mob to witness, for Taksha to see.

The shimmer of Taksha's Gehan faded.

Dantavakra's face was shredded into ribbons. Taksha tried to find his eyes but couldn't. Grooves had been gouged deep into the bone. Only the edges of Dantavakra's face – the ears, the hairline, parts of the chin – remained untouched. Within these borders, the pile of pink flesh, broken enamel, and splintered bones had been tenderized.

The arena roared their hideous grief while the Naga just stood by, a locket of a reptilian skull lying discarded on the sands. It was as if he had frozen, chilled with the knowledge that the champion of Nagas, the Messiah, the D'rahi-killer lay slain, and that he, Taksha, had done nothing, had not lifted a single finger, to stop the annihi-lation of hope. The hope that he had used as warmth on cold nights, he had let its stitching be ripped apart without a whisper.

 ANAADI screamed as Dantavakra's face was ripped apart. He sank to the floor and started bawling now. *My beloved hero, the youngest Rakhjai in the history of the realm, why did you leave us?* A flame amongst moths of men, he had loved women to madness, and painted taverns red. He was so young. He did not deserve this. He did not deserve to be butchered by the Northerner he had saved.

Anaadi did not care if he was weeping for someone he did not personally know except as a distant, heroic figure in the blood pits and a patron of his inn. The Ehtrals had the right of it. The Northerners, especially the Resht, were ungrateful scum, the scourge on this world, who had forgotten their place. And the Emperor, in his naïvety all those decades ago, had opened the City to this godless and malevolent breed. Just see the way ill luck breeds when these blasphemous Reshts from the North hold a weapon! Just see how the Namins of the Empire were crushed alive.

Anaadi whispered, 'Look, even Dimvak sheds tears while smiling.'

'Those are tears of pride, Anaadi,' the woman said, crying. 'Ser Dantavakra finally won an Imperial Contest, and he did so by slaying a beast that makes a griffin look like a cat. My hero! Magadh's Martyr! Dantavakra the Dragonslayer Extraordinaire. Come now, friend. Let us avenge him!'

'Avenge?' Anaadi wiped his tears, looking around as others leaped over the railings, faces brown with rage, white with fury, blue with sadness, shaking fists, crying, all of them, without a doubt, drunk, all of them hungry for the Resht's blood.

A desire, Anaadi realized, that was moments away from deliverance as the arena came alive with the descent of a silent, towering silhouette from the royal gallery. It was not the first time Anaadi had seen him but the dawn's angle made him seem so tall. Hugely boned, the skull under the bare crown was bestial, made more demonic by the red in his gait and the length of his mace.

Justice was here.

But the arena was too enraged to wait.

Anaadi watched, as a Ksharjan, having leaped from the Red Box, charged at the pits only for the unholy Resht to laugh. Disbelief at the absurdity of the challenge made the Resht's moves lethargic but still lethal.

The sight of the Ksharjan walking drunkenly back the way he came, the fragments of scalp and bone leaving a trail behind him, froze many in their tracks, including Anaadi.

He was still frozen, unmoving even, when he saw the Resht draw three arrows and tauten his bowstring at the mob, at him.

Might as well die at the hands of Dantavakra's murderer than between the jaws of the wagerwolves. At least then, he would die sharing something in common with a hero, rather than as an insolvent who threw his family into poverty.

I join you in death, Dragonslayer.

But just as the Resht was about let loose the arrows, he dropped his bow and leaned back, narrowly avoiding an airborne axe and a whistling mace as they collided above where his head was, before crashing to the ground mere inches from where he stood.

Rising back to his full height, the Resht turned his head sideways, once left, once right, to see whose aims had been this true, and was pleased with his discovery, as were the wronged citizens of Magadh, and as was Anaadi.

'Karna, that will be enough. Stand down,' Sage Parshu ordered the Resht.

Anaadi was stunned. How did Sage Parshu know the murderer? He knew something had smelled of rot in his lodgers.

'I owe you gratitude for saving me the time in finding you, master,' the murderer said with a smile, and then turned to the other side and growled at the man clenching his fists. 'And you, who are you?'

The Contest was clearly not over, Anaadi realized with a thrill, as the Resht picked his bow to face off against Sage Parshu and… Jarasandh, the Emperor of Magadh.

Marzana was grateful that that she never had to face Karna, that she was spared from seeing Shon's plan unfold, from seeing Karna's memories return in drowning tides, dragging him into the darkness where it would be swallowed whole by whatever it was unseen forces sought to unleash.

But the puzzle remained: how had Shon found his hands on an oracle? She had heard tales that the Seventh Order did not take chances with even a single child cursed with the gift of sight. But then how was each and every betrayal of hers choreographed by Shon way before Marzana had even seen the man she would destroy? Were the Red Blades a tool? A tool used by the Rakshasas? The Westerners? The Greeks? The possibilities poking into her mind were legion. Too many theories, each theory warring with the next, but she let them tussle, for without them, she would become too aware of where she was, too aware of her smell.

Footfalls approached – joined by grunts and the clatter of bars. Back so soon? She could not even raise her neck and see for herself for even her neck was bound. She could only stare at the darkness of the ceiling, a canvas for her haunted thoughts. The only sanctuary, filled with light, was the world she willed to creation when she closed her eyes.

A callused hand settled on her brow and softly cut at the rope around her forehead. She opened her eyes. Soft white light, gentle as whispers, came from an orb of light suspended in the air. Looming over her was an old and weathered face with eyes shimmering with tears. Despite the tears, his nose wrinkled, and the old man turned his face away, a reflexive gag clawing his throat, revealing the mark of Namins on his neck. 'Are you well, Lady Divine Meenakshi?'

The kindness in the voice almost crippled her. 'Apologies, Revered Namin,' she said, her voice a dry croak but dignified. 'He has not cleaned me for days, now. He does not let me—'

'You've nothing more to explain. I am Acharya Vyas,' Vyas said as he began releasing her from her restraints. 'I am a friend of Shon.'

A clarity washed over Marzana. 'Not a friend,' she croaked, 'employer.'

The hands working at her manacles paused briefly but then resumed their fiddling. 'Very little escapes your eyes. Shon chose well. You would be glad to know your sacrifices are yielding fruit.

But... I beg your forgiveness, child, for being late to rescue you. I promise you, the Acharak will burn for this. I already sent a devoted knife his way. Come.'

Release? Truly? Could it be possible? Could she see her son again? Marzana began crying though it was hard to tell, given she had no water to let loose from her eyes.

'No, no,' Vyas soothed, softly caressing her brow, 'you have done so well. Here, come, lean on me while we walk.'

Marzana had lost so much weight that even the old man was able to hold her up easily. But the movement caused her limbs to draw inward, and the pain arrived, in every joint. Legs and hands, stretched for so long, now began contracting like snakes being burned alive. And the bedsores on her back burst where Vyas held her – *oh, Kaamah, take me!* Watery wastes trickled loose from her legs into Vyas's feet but he did not even flinch.

'Just a little longer,' Vyas said, his voice soothing as they shambled along outside Marzana's private torture room. No other guards stirred. No black-clad priests brandished their staffs. The body of her caretaker – the bald woman – lay on the floor, face crushed. All the rest lay dead or unconscious at the temple entrance but Marzana did not know that then. Even if she had, she would not have cared. All she wanted, desperately, was to ask Vyas about Karna but she was scared of the revelations.

She knew Karna had died in Panchal. Or rather, his self had died there. The rest had died in her arms in the months after when she had raped his mind. Devouring his memories, stealing his locks, spreading ink by drowning him in Abyss to obscure his idea of himself, of his plans to change the world, of all the meaning that he, like any other man, used to use to anchor himself in the ocean of hopelessness. Shon had told her the Karna she loved was a lie, and that his true self was what lurked beneath the surface. A lie that Karna had told himself often enough to believe it.

So what? Isn't everyone a mirror of their desires rather than their dreads? Isn't that how anyone changes or evolves, by imagining a life different from the one we are leading now, and pretending to live it long enough for it to become reality.

Drawing fire from that thought, she asked, 'Acharya, please take me to Karna.' If Karna could pretend to be good, Marzana could pretend to be strong.

 VYAS was tired of pretending to be the grandfather-figure, a well of confidences and cosiness. Sometimes he felt envious of the fear that surrounded Parshuram like a quilt. He had only sampled that taste once in the face of Chalakkha on their journey back from Iyran Machil. But Vyas had been lost then in the ramifications of abandoning Parshuram on Hanuman's beckon.

For the most part of his life, Vyas was someone approachable, someone people were not intimidated by, the affable teacher, the realm guide, the helper. None knew Vyas for what he truly was: the Spider, as the Rose Coterie called it.

The thing is, a prophecy written down with a date becomes a goal. But a goal becomes a plan only when dissected into assassinations, planting murmurs, covert manoeuvres – each a step in a calculated succession. Vyas was the architect of these steps, the steps that would guide Aryavrat out of this labyrinth of chaos.

Step one: Clear the Path. Parshuram was trapped back in Iyran Machil, likely dead, and if not, likely late, given how the sky above had already bled green. Parshuram's blunder would haunt him enough to remove him from the game.

Step two: Spread Alarm. By now, Mati and the Twins had probably let Vauri loose and unleashed the Marigold in the Conclave, snuffing out the future of half the hundred kingdoms of the realm. Given the East's isolation, Vyas did not expect the plague to cross into the Riverlands, and even if it did, the blockade maintained across the Eastern borders by the Empire to stop Mathuran trade could be alerted to turn the East into a containment zone. Either way, the Seven held the cure.

Step three: Tame the Unpredictable. The most important step of all. The headache of Mati would finally be over.

Step four: Cue the Villain. With Jarasandh absent from the arena, there would be no one to pose a challenge to Parshuram's finest. Karna would be unleashed in the arena, finally giving the world a long-awaited villain. For, without a villain, could a hero rise?

Vyas was pleased, and perhaps it was his joy at his plans unfolding like a well-tailored curtain that allowed pity for Marzana to grow in him. Or else there was no need to save her from the mad dogs of Unni Ehtral. Though he knew it was less pity for her but rather a feeling of recklessness, of a man riding high on a good gambling spree. So, save her he did, but he did not rescue her. The moment he put her near the exit, he scarpered back to the entrance of the temple, leaving Marzana with nothing but a black Ehtral robe to keep her modest. Now chaos would be the compass of her fate.

Only step five was left. He had a hero to give birth to, a hero who would unite *Akhand* Aryavrat.

 ANAADI spared precious breath to curse the lowborn who had felled his hero as he fled for his life. Twisting while avoiding the poking spears, he glimpsed for the last time the Emperor resolve into form within the dust cloud stirred to life by the pursuing Crimson Guard's boots. Dimvak and his soldiers had after all sealed off the pits, driving the citizens out of the arena. Where was the blasted Northern scum? Anaadi could not bring himself to run with resolve without looking at Dantavakra's killer one last time but his hunt ended when he tripped and pitched face first in the sand instead.

An emaciated woman, one of the Bats who had been comforting the mob, rushed to Anaadi. She raised her hand at a pursuing Crimson Guard soldier and surely shielded Anaadi from an army of purple bruises. Anaadi might have been distraught but the fear of Bats had been drilled into him by witnessing repeated executions. He wiped at his eyes, and bowed awkwardly while lying on the floor.

Her face came closer. Those eyes, the dull green of counterfeit emerald.

'My name is Sarai. I know there are emotions in you that you need to vent, to take vengeance against the outsider,' said Sarai, probably a decade younger than Anaadi, as she cradled Anaadi's head in her chest, and suddenly it became too much for Anaadi. Anaadi cried like he had never before.

'The lowborn outsider killed... Dantavakra,' Anaadi sobbed.

'Exactly. *They* did,' Sarai murmured, as if struck anew by sorrow. 'This Resht will be dealt with by the Emperor. But he is just one, isn't he? The scourge of these foreigners needs to be rooted out, base and stem, to retain our purity. We are losing our inheritance to them, are we not? Come.'

Anaadi rose with her, wisdom dawning upon his head and blood-lust returning to his ear. Without any word spoken, Anaadi walked side by side with the rest of the mob, into the vastness of Rajgrih beyond the Virangavat, to participate in what the Ehtrals would call later 'the Reckoning'.

NALA reckoned a giantess must have birthed Jarasandh for he was vast. The width of his shoulders was equal to the length of Nala, his thighs as thick as a young tree. And those colossal arms were disproportionately long, a mace in one of them, scraping the ground behind him. As Jarasandh strode past the corpses, his gait was strangely fluid for a man so large. If ever a man deserved to be crowned Emperor on the basis of appearances, Jarasandh's clay model would be the guiding anchor for the judges.

'He is mine to torment, Parshuram,' Jarasandh said as they met at the centre of the blood pits, even as Mrytun Jay stood on the opposite end of the arena to face them. 'He killed my ward.'

'He is not himself, Jara,' Parshuram said in a tone of familiarity. He then used the cloth Nala proffered to wipe his face clean of the dust from the wreckage. 'Something you would have known had you graced your own barbaric Contest. Can you not hear the infected heartbeat, faint though it is? Can you not see his marigold eyes?'

Jarasandh's dark eyes stared out of darkened hollows above a mane of grizzly black beard. 'So, he is the one. Your favourite. The pupil you cursed.'

Parshuram nodded.

'And the armour...'

'Keeps his heart from beating itself to death.'

'It doesn't matter. He skinned my ward's face. He will suffer.'

'Was it not a duel to the death by your decree? No rules were broken. Killing him won't be justice,' Parshuram said.

'Justice is a conceit,' Jarasandh scoffed.

'Then why does Karna need to suffer?'

Jarasandh fell silent. Finally, he relented. 'Need aid?' His tone bore no slight.

Parshuram nodded. Nala cocked her eyebrows in surprise. As did Jarasandh. Parshuram needed help? Just how strong was Mrytun Jay? 'Vanquishing someone is rather difficult when you don't want to kill them,' Parshuram said, as if explaining.

'I wish to help, too, Acharya,' Nala said.

'You can serve as the diversion,' Parshuram said.

'And who might you be?' Jarasandh asked.

'Acharya Parshuram's apprentice,' Nala said, proudly.

Jarasandh shook his head as he looked at Parshuram. 'You never learn.'

 AJATH learned first of the seething violence in the mob from the acrid scent of embers and cinders. She saw the rioters only later, most of them Magadhan Drachmas or Ksharjans with black-clad priests moving through them, who seemed to be hard at work stoking the mob's ire with well-timed proclamations and provocations. The orange robe around Acharya Vyas and the twin swords at Ajath's belt, however, encouraged a lack of attention from the mob, which was good, because Ajath was tired after her fight with the guards and priests of the underground

Ehtral temple just to cross the last name off her list – the bald woman who had handed over her sisters to the rapists and killers. Ajath had been surprised to find her in service to the Ehtrals, and had almost considered sparing her, given what she knew of the induction ritual. Almost.

By the time Ajath had lifted her mangled body off the ground only by her neck, little remained of her nose and teeth. She had died too soon, too easy. Disgusted, Ajath had turned her over mid-air and slammed her skull-first onto the stone floor. The sickening sound of her head smashing should have comforted her but it didn't.

It was only then she realized she was distracted by her worry about Taksha, hoping the fool was safe. Vyas had insisted that Taksha was fine but still, Vyas had taken long enough down below, letting Ajath imagine the worst to befall the Naga.

And she could not let anything foul happen to him.

He was her ward now, the way her nephews had been, the same nephews who she had failed to protect from being butchered. *You better not have tried something heroic... again.*

 TAKSHA knew that not even trying made him a coward, but when he saw Nala charging with a weapon against Mrytun Jay, he realized what a burden it was not to be a hero. Especially when your friends rose against the same evil, uncaring, unflinching. Why did she find the will in her feet, and not him? His small spirit was left feeling even smaller, and he chose to deny it. He blamed the courage on Nala's training, blamed it on the immortal pillar of safety beside her. But in the end, even he could not believe his excuses. Dishonoured by his cowardice, he withered.

Taksha knew he should flee the arena before they found out he was here, rush for safety, join the exodus of the mob and find Ajath. But he did not. Why did he linger? He knew not, but in a strange way he stood his ground and witnessed.

Nala surged ahead, the Acharya and the Emperor spreading wide to come at Mrytun Jay from three sides. Mrytun Jay's hands danced over his bow as he pivoted, the bowlimb thudding into Nala's ribs – just enough to stun, not to break. In that heartbeat of stillness, with the bow braced against Nala's side, he drew the string back and let two arrows fly at Parshuram rushing in from the left.

Without a glance at the arrows' flight, Mrytun Jay let the bow's tip bounce off Nala's ribs, spinning to the right. The bow caught Nala's face in passing, snapping her head back just as the Emperor charged into range. Bigger men made for easy marks.

Two arrows soared.

The Emperor batted one aside with a sweep of his arm, but the other found its mark, pinning his ankle to the corpse he'd just stepped over. He stumbled, a grunt of pain escaping as the arrowhead threatened to tear the tendons from his bone.

Mrytun Jay grinned his berserk smile as he completed the spin to face Parshuram, who had seemingly batted away the earlier arrows with his battle-axe. Parshuram slipped through the arcs of Mrytun Jay's bow with fluid grace – deflecting the bow with his left hand, brushing aside the arrow with the axe in the other, never so much as breaking a sweat. Taksha had never seen Parshuram fight but he could never imagine seeing this level of skill from even the finest of Naga elites.

But Mrytun Jay moved with instinct... no, something deeper guided his movements. He truly danced around Parshuram's axe, the air wrapping around him. It was as if every limb of Karna now had a mind of its own, untethered by the need of commands from his mind.

It was the only way Taksha could explain how Mrytun Jay caught Parshuram's wrist just in time, the bowlimb slamming against the sage's arm before the axe could slice clean through his own. He twisted the bow, just enough to let the axe slide past, close enough to feel the wind of its edge. Parshuram's own momentum betrayed him, dragging him forward, right into Mrytun's space, the bow drawn back, arrow aimed straight at Parshuram's unguarded chest.

PARSHURAM stood aghast, unable to believe how he had let his guard down so easily. He should have seen it coming. No matter. Parshuram's Third Eye was Turning, and his chest muscles had already, on their own, no thanks to his mind, *Hardened* against the onslaught of arrows – which never came.

Why didn't Mrytun Jay release the arrows?

A memory swooped down like a winged demon. Mrytun Jay, the White Eagle and the Rosary were masters of the Art of the Sun, a teaching based on the Fire Asanas of Yoga. Haisun and Amba excelled in the Dance of Shadows, a teaching rooted in the Water Asanas of Yoga.

But there existed another Art, a war stance even Parshuram had only heard rumours of for he had never witnessed Hanuman duel in real life: the Breath of Wings, an art evolved out of the Air Asanas of Yoga.

As Parshuram's keen eye failed to predict the energy currents in Mrytun Jay's attacks, he realized it was because they were so unhinged, so formless, like trying to predict chaos itself. Mrytun Jay's moves burned and extinguished like the birth and death of stars, out of nowhere, into nowhere. Could it be? Had Mrytun Jay learned the Breath of Wings?

He knew now that it had been a mistake. He should have killed his student when he had the chance.

For Parshuram, the greatest warrior in the realm, who had destroyed armies singlehandedly, had his glory earned over thousands of years stolen by Mrytun Jay in ten heartbeats.

NALA, emerging from the sands, probed her ribs and then her cheeks, wondering if someone had stolen time. Had she fainted? No, she would have remembered. But could it be? Might a mere ten heartbeats be enough for her teacher to fall?

Parshuram had Hardened his chest against arrows that never came. But in doing so, he had let his focus flicker away from the rest of his defence.

Misstep.

Mrytun Jay spun around Parshuram, twisting, hopping on his side, circling him in impossible asanas of the body, too close for Parshuram to swing his axe, too damn fast for Parshuram to even land a kick, till Mrytun Jay snatched Parshuram's quiver from his back.

Parshuram's quiver which held seven arrows.

Mrytun Jay leaped back, sand spraying in his wake, gaining precious distance. He must have known Parshuram would Harden his chest, a trick that might have made the Acharya tough but not nimble. In ten heartbeats, Mrytun Jay let loose all seven arrows, each with violent intent.

The first struck the base of Parshuram's neck, severing the muscles that kept his head held high. The second sank into the back of his knee, hamstring torn, his leg buckling. The third struck the shoulder joint, leaving his left arm hanging uselessly.

The next arrow slipped just under the ribs to make trouble for his lungs. The fifth pierced the back of his other ankle, slicing the tendon. His stance collapsed. Nala did not even see when the sixth punctured Parshuram's wrist, robbing him of his battle axe. The final arrow lodged above the collarbone, right into the knot of valor, severing nerves, cutting Parshuram's control over his limbs, or whatever remained of them.

Blood began to drip from his knee, his shoulder, his wrist, his ankle, and his collarbones. The sands beneath eagerly drank it all till Parshuram fell to the side, stiff straight, eyes shocked wide.

Mrytun Jay had sliced only muscles and ligaments. No major vessels. Only flesh and veins. And in sculpting him so, Mrytun Jay had paralysed Parshuram.

Mrytun Jay made a sound that might have been laughter which startled Nala to her very roots. 'YOU UNDERSTAND NOW.' Mrytun Jay spoke, and Nala regretted ever lending an ear to that voice. The way he uttered 'understand' sounded like nails scratching against a board.

'A SHRAP? THAT WAS YOUR GIFT TO KARNA, WAS IT NOT? YOU TURNED ALL OF HIS DEVOTION VIOLENT.'

'Mrytun Jay...' Parshuram tried.

'IT WAS YOUR CURSE THAT BUILT MY CRADLE OF FIRE. THE HATE WHICH BECAME MY LULLABY.'

'Karna, if you are inside, if you can listen—'

'I OWE YOU PAIN, PARSHURAM, AND I HAVE COME HERE TO PAY. YOU WILL NOW NOT ONLY SUFFER FOR ETERNITY BUT SUFFER ETERNITY IN EACH MOMENT OF YOUR EXISTENCE.'

Mrytun Jay's fingers curled around the hilt of Parshuram's axe, his eyes tracing its edge. 'THIS AXE HAS SIPPED ON THE BLOOD OF YOUR MOTHER, HAS IT NOT, MASTER?' He trailed off, a grim admiration in his tone. With deliberate slowness, Mrytun Jay inserted the handle of the axe into Parshuram's gaping maw. 'NOW IT THIRSTS FOR—' Mrytun Jay's words were cut short as he spun, barely in time to block with the axe-handle the onslaught of Jarasandh's fist. A blow cracked the very handle Mrytun Jay held. The impact sent Mrytun Jay careening across the sand, his footing slipping beneath him.

'If you surrender, I will spare your life, lad,' said the Emperor.

'IF YOU BEG, I WILL MAKE IT HURT LESS,' said Mrytun Jay, rising.

The Emperor chuckled as he cracked his knuckles. 'So be it, student of Parshuram,' he said as he glanced at Parshuram's unmoving body. 'I am not weakened by mercy like your Master. Your final lesson is at hand.'

 DIMVAK had always scorned arrows, seeing them as a weak's tool, not a man's weapon. But could he cling to such conviction in the face of what he had witnessed? That Dimvak still drew breath after the torment he had unleashed on that Resht was a miracle. To have disrespected that warrior, the one Acharya Parshuram had called Mrytun Jay, Resht or not, spy or not, was a transgression Dimvak would have to plunge in the river Ganga to cleanse himself of. Dimvak would remember and honour his name till he died: Mrytun Jay.

For now, Dimvak had halted the advance of his soldiers outside into the city to quell the small riots in a bid to honour this duel. Riots may flare and fade but the lessons hewn from this clash of wrath and worth would endure.

Though the truth was that the desire to see vengeance had swallowed Dimvak in its grasp. He wanted to see Mrytun Jay suffer for what he had done to his student. Dantavakra, who had never harmed a soul out of malice; that spoilt brat, who never learned to keep his guard up, who trusted too soon, did not deserve to be skinned alive. So, try as hard as Dimvak could, the cords of his soul were too entangled with Mrytun Jay's fate to let go.

And unlike his soldiers, he was not the least bit worried for the Emperor's safety. The matter would be settled soon. The Resht's quiver ran as empty as his veins, and the Emperor had never known defeat in a contest of raw strength. Even now, a mere flick of the Emperor's wrist could send Dimvak sprawling, and Dimvak had giant blood in him.

'Our Emperor is in no peril. But keep your eyes peeled. Watch his steelsong and glean.'

They could see how the Emperor stood in the stance of malla, a battle form reserved for those who had awakened their Solar Plexus Chakra, his skin Hardened from within and, unlike the warrior sage, the Emperor had the bulk and mass to Harden every sinew, and still not lose his swiftness, evidence of which was soon laid bare.

Mrytun Jay flung the axe at the Emperor; the Emperor seized it mid-air and tossed it away with contempt. Mrytun Jay, growling, charged at the Emperor, who lowered his stance.

The moment Mrytun Jay came in an arm throw's distance, the Emperor moved in a blur to cross his right arm under Mrytun Jay's left shoulder, placing his side against Mrytun Jay's groin, his body a living counterweight. In one powerful sweep, he heaved Mrytun Jay's left arm up and over, flipping him over and smashing his body to the ground. *The Washerman Slam. From here on it was a swift descent to a neck—*

But Mrytun Jay headbutted the Emperor before the Emperor could even complete the neck choke. *How did the Resht recover so fast!*

The headbutt, however, did little to make any impression on the Emperor's face.

Dimvak's eyes pleasingly took in how the colour of the bruise on the Emperor's face from Mrytun Jay's head strike spread from the point of contact, across his face and neck before fading away like spilled ink on wet cloth.

'The Emperor is able to shift the harm across his frame, spreading it thin and so diluting its effect,' he explained to his men. 'Now, the Emperor's turn.'

The Emperor cleaved into Mrytun Jay with a barrage of punches.

Mrytun Jay Hardened, catching his fist. When Mrytun Jay's wrist broke, there was the golden breastplate. When that cracked, Mrytun Jay punched desperately at the Emperor's elbow with his working hand. That slowed the Emperor's fists down for a fraction of a heartbeat before the Emperor's punch caught him in the skull, and Mrytun Jay slammed into the pit, kicking up a cloud of sand.

This time, Mrytun Jay was not impressed. He started laughing. Grunting, Jarasandh rained down blows, but the laughter only died when Mrytun Jay, out of the blue, clapped his hands on either side of Jarasandh's face. Jarasandh leaped back instinctively to escape that. The clap, if it had landed, would have deafened Jarasandh for it was impossible to Harden the ears.

Mrytun Jay had been baiting the Emperor!

But it did not work. For the Emperor, unlike the warrior sage, did not underestimate Mrytun Jay, not once. Overconfidence never marred his movements. Mrytun Jay must now know that this duel was a foregone conclusion. An infant trying to bite a lion had better chances than a man trying to beat Jarasandh in a contest of strength. Only a man as strong as Jarasandh could hurt Jarasandh.

It appeared Mrytun Jay arrived at that conclusion as well for he went mad. He began to… dance.

Back on his feet, the Emperor drew a deep breath and delivered a final bone-shattering punch to Mrytun Jay's face. Mrytun Jay smiled as he met it with Wind Palm, an arcane asana, that deadened his nerve endings. Dimvak could only imagine the violence of the Emperor's strike running through Mrytun Jay's nadis, his energy lines, as Mrytun Jay flooded it with his own strength before channelling all of that force to the base of his other palm. For when Mrytun Jay touched the Emperor's skull, the Emperor was already backpedalling. But at that touch, the Emperor's head wrenched back as he was thrown off his feet and onto the pits.

Had Jarasandh remained standing, or had he been charging ahead instead of retreating, his skull would have shattered.

'Should we go aid him now?' a Rakhjai asked, disbelieving what he saw.

'The Emperor... is fine, he is fine,' Dimvak said, stuttering. 'Look, he stands.'

The Emperor rose somehow only to falter, and then collapse on one knee. Consciousness began to slip from the Emperor like a receding wave after a flood. He looked at Mrytun Jay with respect and nodded, willing all his strength to talk.

'Parshuram was wrong. *You* are the finest warrior of our time. You win the Contest,' Jarasandh said through bloodied teeth. 'Ask your boon.'

Mrytun Jay's lips curled into a bloodied, ghastly smile as he drew his face close to Jarasandh, close enough to kiss him. 'DESOLATION,' saying which Mrytun Jay ensnared Jarasandh's neck in a chokehold grip.

Dimvak's commands thundered! His soldiers formed a loose circle around Mrytun Jay. If it looked to a spectator that Dimvak's men had trapped Mrytun Jay, that impression would be mistaken. It was the other way around.

'Stay, stay there, Resht!' Dimvak shouted, hand to his belt. 'We will do what you seek. Do not hurt the Emperor. Just demand what you want. You will be pardoned. Your friend, too. Is that what you want?'

'WHAT I WANT? I WANT REDEMPTION FOR RESHTS? REHABILITATION OF RESHTS? RESTITUTION FOR RESHTS?' Mrytun Jay paused, his grip tightening around the Emperor's head, seconds away from wrenching it. 'NO? THOUGHT SO. RETRIBUTION, IT IS...' Mrytun Jay looked up.

Dimvak witnessed a Claw in the ranks behind Mrytun Jay tumble as the largest woman he had ever laid eyes on barrelled through, brandishing a monstrous sword – a sword Dimvak now recognized because he himself had gifted it to her. Her eyes were afire, her blackened teeth belonged to Yama and her height cast a bestial shadow, as she brought her sword down on Mrytun Jay, who only managed to evade the blow by relinquishing his death-hold on Jarasandh.

Her fist thundered again on her armour, and that caught Mrytun Jay's attention. Those who did not understand the language of sign, squinted. Those who understood, gasped. For the words may have been silent but their echo would remain in the hearts of those who witnessed this for a long, long time.

'*How dare you strike my father?*' Jarasandh's firstborn daughter, Jayatsena urf Ajath, signed.

MRYTUN Jay decided he would first wrench the daughter's neck before the father's eyes, and then dismember the father before he died. He gathered his withered body up, aches filling the holes where they had crucified him. He was on borrowed time now, thanks to Karna's love for bearing torture without complaints. But he was not going to fall before slaying these two.

Mrytun Jay staggered as he stalked towards the half-giantess when the sands turned into a market place. He was tossed to and fro, as vast waves and billows of ocean rolled around him. He was on an island. Karna took in the ocean and surrounding palm trees. Off in the distance he saw gulls going about their pointless lives. This looked so… normal. Except the colours. Everything looked washed out, grey and faded like life had been sucked from the scenery.

In all that anguish, his mind latched on to the scaled hand around his ankle. *A Naga?* He caught the wrist, a tiny thing, like a parched snake, and the scene before his eyes burst into the sands of the arena. *Illusion?* He tightened his fist, and felt the Naga's bones behind the scales crack, an awful grinding sound.

Just then, the half-giantess was upon him, her blade falling. Mrytun Jay left the Naga to raise his hands and slap them together.

Catching the black blade between his palms, just inches away from his nose.

He flicked his wrists, and wrenched the blade to toss it away.

'*Messiah Killer!*' The Naga, refusing to surrender, jumped over the half-giantess's shoulder and sprang off the balls of his feet and in a somersault, landed on Mrytun Jay's shoulders this time, straddling his neck, hands grabbing his forehead.

The arena before him changed again, this time to another arena. A burning one. It was filled with silhouettes. Some fighting. Some clambering over each other. This time Mrytun Jay knew it for an illusion and his hands reached to crush the Naga once and for all. Only Mrytun Jay found his hands yanked back, held fast, not just by sinews or strength, but by a familiar voice.

'Karna,' Duryodhan said. 'Stop it…'

Was Duryodhan's voice a hallucination? Or did he somehow recover from his fall? The very name of Duryodhan in his thoughts was enough for Karna to stir inside him.

Karna's face surfaced from the black sea, struggling against Mrytun Jay's grip on his neck. *I AM NEVER GOING BACK. I WILL BURN THEM ALL!* Mrytun Jay screamed in his mind.

Mrytun Jay, eyes closed, refused to surrender to the Naga's illusions, the giantess's punches, the friend's call or his inmate's rebellion, but when a woman's callused hand swept his over nose, he lost. As if prodded by muscle memory, Mrytun Jay opened his eyes, and his pupils ended up sipping Abyss.

Marz… I thought you had left me.

Mrytun Jay's mind melted as Taksha's magic flooded now into his eyes without barriers.

In the deluge of Abyss-stained illusions, Mrytun Jay spied a tiny silhouette emerge from the throng of black shapes to stand still before him. And then the silhouette turned sideways, the outline of the arrow jutting out of his little skull, stark against the cage behind him.

'Sudama…' Mrytun Jay just stared at his nephew blankly behind closed eyes, his face slack, as he fell, heedless of the large black sword glimmering above his head.

Duryodhan dragged his friend away, rising to the half-giantess till the edge of that sword stopped just above Duryodhan's shoulder, a shoulder still bleeding from the hole a dragon's tooth had left in it.

'*Try that, My Lady,*' Duryodhan signed with his free hand, '*and you're not going to like what happens.*'

'Jayatsena,' Jarasandh tapped, wheezing on the ground, signing and speaking at the same time. 'Daughter, don't! Yama will have him… when he earns him.'

'Princess Ajath,' a Namin's voice said out loud and slowly, too slowly so that the giantess could read his lips. 'Do not kill him! He is needed,' he cried. 'Remember our deal.'

The sword never fell. Denied death again. Of course, they needed him. No one wanted him. They all just needed him. Like a tool. No one wanted him but Marzana. If not for Abyss…

Marz, you saved me… again. Karna smiled silently behind trapped eyes even as Nala stowed Anaadi's Abyss into her cloak's folds.

 MARZANA knew mercy to the guilty was cruelty to the victims. So, she did not grudge Vyas for abandoning her. He at least gave her a chance to redress her wrongs, and she would do just that. Marzana crawled up to a crooked alley. She could see the arena's looming towers from here. Soon, she would be there.

In her painful journey, she had come upon many roving bands who, seeing her robes, had given her a wide berth, and if some got curious, they had been chased away by her foul stench and fouler laughter, making her more afraid of sniggers than swords. But she cared not.

She would save Karna. Tell him everything. Heal the scars of his mind as he healed her mangled body. If the beast had indeed been freed of his cage, she could coax him back into it. She would love him, and be his, and worship him. She would tell her daughter and son the truth, and they would leave for the mountains that Karna used to speak of so fondly.

Reaching the mouth of the alley, she dragged herself out of it, pleased to be out of the gloom and into dawn's grey caress. *A little longer.* She crawled over the slick, moss-slimed cobblestones. She could still hear thousands in the streets she had left behind, their rage against whoever they were purging not yet quenched. Some name called *Dantavakra* was being cried out like a chant. She found herself slipping on wet cobbles. There was a growing stream of water that was working its way down the alley, the touch reminding her of the times she had soiled herself on the Ehtral bed. And then the smell made her realize it wasn't water but ale. She tried to climb to her feet to avoid it, when from up ahead came a loud sound of a bottle rolling down her way.

 ANAADI scowled at his sloshed friends, who had sent his precious bottle rolling down the alley. He had scowled at everyone. Scowled at the fawning women, their thieving hands all over the Claws too drunk to stand. Scowled at the painters, their shoddy representations of Dantavakra the Dragonslayer taking shape by candlelight. Scowled at the salesmen who had appeared out of nowhere, selling items they had stolen from houses they had burned. Scowled at the joyless cheers and drunken babble.

'S'posed to be revolutionaries, no' drunk,' he said.

'You worry too dan' much, Anaadi,' his friend, a former stable owner, now horse tender, Sayana said. 'We revolutioned all night. We deserve this! For the Dragonslayer!'

'Deser what? You rolled down our last... Oh!' Anaadi swished whatever was left in the aleskin in his right hand, then tilted it back to drink deep. Then, wiping at his mouth, he jumped down by Virangavat's East Exit and climbed down the alley to retrieve the bottle.

'For pet or pot!' a boy shrieked on the way, thrusting up a stolen puppy at him. Anaadi ignored him.

They'd been revolution-ing for the last hour, that was true. The rage awakened. The rage against rising prices, rage against loss of living, rage against loved ones lost in a war, rage against starvation, rage against the war itself, all of this rage had bubbled over the decade-long Yamuna War. But rage needs victims. Without, it is just a bunch of dried reedsticks. Dantavakra's death was the spark that brought flames to a roar, the word of *Justice for Dantavakra* raced mouth to mouth, hungry as lust.

They had gutted so many migrant quarters, left so many windows soot-stained, Anaadi wished he had started a count when he had started. His clothes still smelled of ash from the Broom Quarter where they had descended on the migrant labourers encroached there – well diggers, weavers of saddle bags, an old man who healed hoof-sores, little girls, angry boys, tired grandmothers and grandfathers, all had been dragged from their illegal houses, and after seizing their no-doubt illegally gained possessions, disappointingly scant though they might have been, they had set fire to those hovels. The families then had been herded into the street and surrounded, and given how there was no cart available to ferry them to Yama's Hands, they had been torched alive in the public square to dispense swift justice.

When Anaadi grew exhausted, he had returned to Virangavat to find out what had happened to the murderer. The spectators who he met outside Virangavat were celebrating, celebrating the death of the murderer and return of Jarasandh's eldest, his daughter, Jayatsena, the Guardian of Rajgrih. Turned out it was Jayatsena who had slain the murderer in single combat, and then in Dantavakra's honour, given crates of ale away to the citizens to rejoice. And Anaadi had only been too happy to join them. Free ale meant the news was truth. They all shouted 'Glory to Jayatsena' before diving into the bottles off the crates.

As Anaadi swayed in his attempt to stop the last bottle from rolling down any further, he found a woman attempting to climb against the wall. A glimpse of what she wore revealed her to be an Ehtral priestess. By now, Sayana had joined him.

'Ap-apologies for touching you, Acolyte, but be assured I wear gloves.' Anaadi bowed deep as he helped her rise, till he spied lines of blood and waste on her bare ankle. The smell of faecal matter then assaulted his nose and Anaadi blanched but for some reason Sayana did not mind it.

'She makes my loins stir,' Sayana said, 'and she is too powerless to resist.'

Anaadi was horrified by even the suggestion. 'You can't... she is... look at her. She can't even stand.'

'Which only means that she had already been used. So she would definitely not mind another,' Sayana said as he lifted the robe of the screaming woman and fell back when he saw a back ridden with bedsores. But it was the large butterfly mark behind the bedsores that finally made Anaadi stir to act.

The mark of a Devadasi.

The mark of a whore.

But there are no Devadasis in Rajgrih after their expulsion. He may be drunk but he well remembered what he had heard from his wife's brother – the warden. That Resht, the golden-armoured man in the jail, the one who slew his hero, this Resht had infiltrated Magadh with the help of a Devadasi! This was that woman!

'WHORE! SPY!' Anaadi screamed.

'What are you doing!' Sayana gritted through clenched jaws. 'We need to run away!'

Anaadi held Sayana's collars and shook him. 'She is the spy!'

'Sssh, please, ssh,' the woman begged, falling to her knees again, holding his feet. 'I am a Devadasi! I am a victim of the Ehtral—'

'Victim? Ehtrals are our saviours! You are not their victim, you are their prisoner, and you have escaped. It is because of you,' Anaadi wept, 'because of you... Dantavakra is dead. You! The murderer escaped us. But not you!'

'Listen, you walking vomit,' the woman rose to her feet, painfully, revealing her true nature, 'I am a Devadasi, graced by the love of Kaamah, you hairy-livered Drachma! Now close that stinking mouth of yours, or I will give a Shrap that will turn you into such a vulgar little maggot that even lepers will avoid you—'

Anaadi sent the bottle flying for the spy's head, knocking her down. He then spat on her face. The thick gob of ale-ridden phlegm clung to her cheek even as Anaadi dragged her to his friends, shouting all the way.

It was not long before a mob gathered. There were no Ehtrals on this alley to guide them this time but they had lived in Rajgrih long enough to know the procedure.

Anaadi was the first one. Just like a children's game, he thought as he hurled a stone. It struck the side of the whore's head. The woman screamed but it was drowned by the startled 'Oooh' sounds made by the justice-mongers.

'Who else wants a stone! Get in a queue! For the Dragonslayer!'

The mob took their seats around the spy excited for their chance to finally do something right.

 MARZANA sought to climb to her feet after they stopped but something was wrong. Her legs were not responding to her. Why were they not responding? She was a Devadasi, the dancer of all forms. Why were her feet not moving! *Kaamah, what is happening?* She looked up, her vision blurry. Men, women and even children around her, all laughing, none helping. But none wore black. They were ordinary folk. Good folk. Why did no one help her, then? Why was she on the ground?

Most of her teeth were shattered. Her lips were drenched and swollen. Her nose was broken. Only one eye blinked open. But her hands worked fine.

She felt a trickle down her neck, and her hand tracked it to her once lush, now dried hair. Not dry any longer. It was wet. She parted her hair on instinct, as if searching for lice, and found one third of her skull was entirely gone. *Karna... will you forgive me?*

Her fingers, involuntarily, probed deeper, and touched sticky, pulped matter, and then a hard, pebbly surface. A stone. *Will you find me in the sky?* Marzana's trembling fingers plucked the stone out of her exposed brain, and Marzana died.

High overhead, the heaven and its audience of unblinking stars had witnessed their fill, and the sky paled, as if washed of all blood, as if drained of every drop of the will to live.

AFTERMATH

RAJGRIH

2 DAYS AFTER THE BATTLE OF MATHURA

'Only the dead have seen the end of war.'
—Plato

CHALAKKHA

Those busy in mourning may have failed to spy the fluttering standards of monarchs being flown on the ramparts of the Imperial Fort but it was only a matter of time before they heard. The regents of war had been summoned to a hunt. *To what end?* Chalakkha wondered. Revenge, of course.

The Emperor had been the first to send an arrow flying true to pierce a large eagle that was just about to clutch a hapless rabbit in its talons. The eagle had, much to the shock of the kings, turned its ire on the Emperor, uncaring of the arrow lodged in its neck. Such treason met a swift end when the Emperor, with his gloved hands, ripped its wings apart from its body. As the eagle lay still in his hands, the Emperor turned to face them all, face bruised, ankle bandaged, looking every bit the warrior who had brought them all to their knees.

Jarasandh the Conqueror.

'As long as are we all here,' he said, 'let us rest. I have words to speak.'

The chatter faded, and the noblemen and royals shuffled around to face the Emperor, every face taut like a bow drawn to maximum tension. Looking around, he realized that even the clearing where they stood now was probably not a matter of chance. Was it only luck that Jarasandh had spotted an eagle to hunt down here in this very spot? It was, wasn't it? Or was it a symbol of things to come?

With the air of ascending a throne, he sat down on a fallen log. His squires approached the log bearing satchels, and on his nod, took out scrolls and parchments from them to be spread out on a makeshift table while the Emperor pulled off his feather-laden gloves to reveal a heavily bruised knuckle.

Chalakkha felt a sweaty shiver run up his back when he saw Acharya Vyas stand beside the Emperor. The familiar face was anything but a comfort. He looked around him, at the faces of the great men who had helped guide the course of the Empire for the last decade ever since the Emperor had shut himself inside a room, each of them perched on razors, at least the ones who had not deigned to travel East to the Conclave: Bhimsaka, the King of Vidarbha, whose daughter had eloped with Krishna to become his first wife, a shambling skeleton leaning heavily on a twisted cane; Chitragandh, the King of Kalinga, a heavy robust man with wind-weathered skin; and even Desra, the Prince of Kasmira, fair, clean shaven and sweating, recently given the charge of overseeing the construction of the Dragonslayer's statue in the arena.

Chalakkha on the other hand skulked in the dappled shadows of the trees. Rumours had lately swirled around him, accusing him of thwarting the Claws from unleashing their arrows to save the beast on the Day of the Dragon. Eager to evade the light, he chose to return to the shadows he had spent half his wealth trying to emerge out of.

'War,' Jarasandh said. At the mention of war, eager nods rippled through the assembly. Those few who had thought they would find answers to how in Xath's name a flying ship had come out of nowhere would have to wait a little longer. 'Dimvak, enlighten them.'

'Mathura has fallen,' Dimvak said. 'The Mleccha, Archon of Yavanas, Kalyavan, betrayed our trust and launched an assault on Mathura alone with the aid of Bhagadatt's airavats. The Three Sisters no longer stand.'

A tide of near-hysterical whispers swept over the forest.

'The Sisters were breached!' Desra squealed in a tone of disbelief, as if calling Dimvak a liar.

'A great victory for the Emperor, Yama be good,' Bhimsaka said.

Chalakkha wondered what the Emperor had to do with this. Not to forget it was the Emperor himself who had built those walls.

'Reports are unclear. What we do know is the War Mistress is dead. Kalyavan is missing. Losses were heavy on both sides, but in the end while Mathura was flooded, the Mathurans were saved by Hastina forces who annihilated the Greeks. The Mathurans won.' Dimvak wiped his brow. 'I would be remiss if I did not state the Hastina Forces were led by the House of Pandavas, the ruling family of a new kingdom, Khandavprastha. It appears the Union has partitioned, split, not an even split, but split nonetheless.'

A raven's cackle spilled into the silence following Dimvak's revelations which had exploded like Mathuran munitions in their minds. Despite the fraught, worn emotions in the assembly, Chalakkha smiled. His botch-up with the dragon faded in comparison to Kalyavan's folly. He stepped forward, unable to resist himself as he said, 'But with Mathura flooded, and the Sisters fallen, it is a victory for the Empire.'

'That is most unfortunate, indeed,' the Vidarbhan King said, ignoring Chalakkha. 'Not only have we lost the airavat as an advantage along with an ally but now the Union has thrown in their lot with Mathura. This could see the realm riven again for years.'

'That green sky was because of Mathuran munitions, wasn't it?' Desra asked, his eyes shifting nervously. Even the bravest Ksharjans, who would run into a sword happily, feared the sorcery of the munitions.

'It is important we do not take out the meat before it is boiled,' Dimvak said. 'Our bravest soldiers, Lord Shishupal of Chedi and Eklavvya of the Valkas were undercover in Mathura, and we can only hope for their wellbeing, Xath be blessed, and we can know more only when—'

'If Mathura has indeed fallen the way the scouts report,' the Vidarbhan King said, not realizing he had interrupted Dimvak, 'the Hastina Union will grow strangler's fingers round the Yamuna–Ganga confluence. With Panchal's strength added to their own, it would become bothersome. Truly bothersome. The eagle and the cow and the stag might already be in bed together for aught we know, Your Grace.'

Jarasandh's face gave no hint as to his feelings as he steepled his fingers beneath his chin.

'Why would the Tusk aid Kalyavan with his airavats in such a foolhardy endeavour?' someone else asked.

Chalakkha stiffened at that insult to his Lord. 'I can assure you Lord Bhagadatt is a man of his word! He would never!'

'Then why has no raven left the East?' another voice raised itself. 'We have heard no news from the *Gilded Lion* since it entered the harbour of Airavat's Reach.'

'No,' the Emperor finally spoke, 'I do not think we would find any blemish in the Tusk. But if Bhagadatt has meekly dipped his banners to a conspiracy against the Empire, it would not bode well for the Prince to show his cards and risk himself. The Empire can ill afford the issue of a royal hostage complicating matters. But do send a raven, Dimvak, asking the Prince to return forthwith. Claim I have fallen sick, and I need urgent counsel with him.'

'Your will, My Emperor,' Dimvak said.

Chalakkha watched the Emperor closely. *There is something he's not saying. Something going on in the back of his head.* And then he saw a shadow fall on the Emperor, and found it birthed from Vyas. Suddenly Chalakkha remembered Vyas's words when Parshuram had dismissed oracles when they had first met. *Our plans are measured in centuries.*

'I am certain the Usurper would not want to relinquish the Queen of Trade Routes,' Chitragandh said. 'No, it is plain, he would solicit the help of his magical jewel, that Syamantaka, or take another loan to repair Mathura, join his forces to the Union's against the Empire. That is what *I* would do.'

'What matters is,' Jarasandh spoke, 'Krishna lives, and has found an ally in this new King Yudhistir.'

'What do we do, Your Majesty?' Bhimsaka asked. 'Our treaty with the Union forbids us from stepping into their borders as it deters them from the South, a bargain which had seemed better for the Empire then given how the South was more than half the realm. Not to forget, we are also not at our full strength. Having lost one, or worse,' he eyed Chalakkha, 'two allies.'

'The Empire might have lost two allies,' Vyas said, smiling the way an artist might smile at seeing how beautifully his painting has come together. 'But it has gained two in their stead, an Army of Nagas and the Hastina Union.'

'Your Grace,' Chitragandh asked, 'pardon my impertinence, but if the House of Pandavas is against us, how have we gained Hastina as an ally?'

'The same way allies have been forged since time immemorial, My Lord,' Vyas said. 'Wedding. Wedding of the Heir of the Empire, Jayatsena to the Heir of Hastina Union.' Concerned gasps from the Ksharjan Kings. Sighs of astonishment from the Drachma lords. Heavy silence from the Unni Ehtrals, every eye fixed on Vyas's pointing finger. The Northman stepped into the light, and Chalakkha saw his cloak was black rimmed with red.

As the shock ebbed away, Chalakkha's mind began to churn. *So that is why Vyas was so adamant on keeping Ajath close. That is why Ajath shadowed Vyas for vengeance in the name of her sisters –* by *sisters,* she meant the twins of Jarasandh who were violated in Mathura and whose children were butchered by a mob. That was why Vyas even sought Chalakkha out years ago to intercede on behalf of a woman accused of adultery and beseech the Ehtral to induct her instead. Could it be? Had that woman been one of the perpetrators of the crime against Jarasandh's kin? Had Vyas depicted that woman as the perpetrator of the anguish caused to the Emperor's daughters, Chalakkha would have delivered her personally to the Emperor. But rescuing someone accused of adultery stirred sympathy, not more suspicion. No… this was Vyas's hunt, and Chalakkha had been his dragon.

'Prince Duryodhan,' Bhimsaka asked, 'are you truly prepared to wage war against your own? Your own cousins.'

'Kingship,' Vyas answered on behalf of Duryodhan instead, smiling, 'knows no kinship.'

KARNA

The last of the morning was slanting down through the blue-green-coloured glass of the windows to dapple the white marble floor with diamonds of a dozen hues. Scented candles, already lit, flickered in niches cut from the thick stone walls, doing their finest to keep the reek of pungent potions and burning balms at bay.

Karna woke to the drawing of curtains, his senses still clouded by the fever. 'Just once I would like for our reunions to be when one of us is not laid low on a deathbed,' Karna said with a raw and hoarse voice.

'One of us?' Duryodhan shook his head sternly as he handed Karna a glass of water. 'I only ever recall *you* dying.'

'You're a dreadful friend.' Karna took a sip, the water so tart with lemon squeezings that he spat half of it out.

'Says the one who chucked me off a height,' Duryodhan said, and then rubbing his bandaged shoulder, added, 'twice.'

'I am grateful to the Lions they did not toss you in my dungeon when they caught you. I no longer look forward to this reunion.' Karna suddenly frowned. 'Talking about dungeons,' he said, his voice dropping, 'I… seek your pardon for Marzana's…'

'Betrayal?' Duryodhan asked.

Karna sighed. They didn't know for certain if the priests had not relied on the spectre of death to wrench out those lies from her. Why else would Marzana brand them as spies of Krishna, instead of revealing who they truly were. But Duryodhan was a man of straight lines. He wouldn't see the grey.

'Forgive me,' Duryodhan said. 'I shouldn't have. You were saying?'

'Is she… safe? I am surprised she has not come to see me.'

'Got word from the High Priest that once she'd confessed, she got the boot from the capital with a bag of gold and a back of scars,' Duryodhan said, 'long before our time in the arena. She is like to have nestled back in Malengar safe, sound and wealthy by now.'

Marzana had left? Oh. Karna let out a breath he hadn't realized he'd been holding. But it was for the best, he reckoned. She could find solace with her blood, far from any deranged friends, he thought and chuckled.

'Talking about reunions,' Duryodhan changed the subject, 'there will be no more of it. For we separate never again.'

Karna scowled at Duryodhan. 'You just reused the line you had planned to use on Princess Mati, didn't you?'

'It was a good line. Seemed a crime to let it rot. Talking about rot, do you remember?'

If only Duryodhan knew then how Karna's mind had woven tapestries again to hide the rough, chipped walls which bore evidence of his savagery. The last thing Karna remembered was being crucified on the stake, and releasing... well, *himself.* It seemed today was the day Duryodhan would finally choose a thread from the tapestry, and tug at it to reveal to Karna the hard truths behind. He did not. He spoke instead of what they had missed.

Duryodhan spent the better part of the next hour weaving the tale of the Trial of Arjun in Hastina, the Partition of the Union, the Battle of Mathura, the events at Virangavat. Karna asked nothing about Mati. Duryodhan said nothing about Karna's murders. Their friendship was not the kind to itch open wounds for nostalgia's sake even if they knew they both were haemorrhaging from wounds a healer could not see.

'Nothing good ever comes out of us leaving Hastina.' Duryodhan gave a weary smile, as he began changing the bandages on Karna's palms and feet.

'Won't go that far,' Karna said. 'You came to steal a Princess from the Crown Prince and you are returning with his father's army instead.'

'Not just his army...' Duryodhan said, not looking up, beads of sweat on his forehead sparkling in the firelight, like so many little wet gems. '*My* army.'

Karna knew that look. 'What. Did. You. Do?'

'By law, I won the Imperial Contest. I was the last man standing, after all. So... I asked a boon.' Duryodhan laughed without laughter in it. 'I am to be wed.'

Karna shoved himself up, ignoring the stabs of pain through his shoulders. But Jarasandh's daughters were dead. Karna squinted at Duryodhan and his words grew shrill with alarm as he remembered what Duryodhan had told him about the events at Virangavat.

'Of all the eligible women in the world, you chose the one woman who beat me bloody to death.'

'That was main reason, honestly, the pinnacle of her allure,' Duryodhan said. 'Though I gather she is not very enthused.'

'Did you speak to her? What is her name?'

'Jayatsena, though I hear she prefers Ajath. And, no, I haven't. Then again, she is deaf and mute. I suppose she'll get on famously with my blind father.'

Karna laughed, his ribs hurting. 'Then how do you know she is not enthusiastic about it. This would be the alliance of the century, and she would be fortunate to have you. I must confess though I had not known the Emperor had sired a fourth child.'

'His first, rather. I am unclear on the details but I heard rumours that she had been banished by the Emperor years ago, long before the coup in Mathura. But given how she has been imprisoned in her room along with her Naga ward has me doubting her commitment to this.'

'She is a woman, older than you, so your principle against marrying a just flowered girl is preserved. She is of your station, and so she is fit to be wed. You only need to breed an heir, the earlier, the easier it will be, to put any future succession rights to rest. Do remember, Yudhistir must be doing the same with...' Karna could not take her name. 'After that, if you both prefer to wait a year or two before bedding each again for another heir, you would be within your rights as husband and wife.'

'You've been spending too much time with Uncle Shakuni, Karna.'

The mention of a torturer finally pushed him into the alley he had been avoiding. 'Prince... will they hang me for my crimes? I would rather not be burned alive by these black bats.'

'Mrytun Jay – a drab moniker by the way – committed those crimes. Not you, Karna.'

'They are not carved spirits within me, Prince. They are the same. It is just suppressed. It is…'

'Beast and human are in constant conflict within every mortal, and the conquest of human over beast is an eternal struggle that defines our journey to be above the food chain,' Duryodhan said when Karna raised a brow. 'I read it somewhere. Your beast is just… a tad dramatic. I only wish I saw how you bested Acharya Parshuram and the Emperor in one go. I reckon I will hear an embellished version of it soon.'

'Doubt they will paint me in a flattering image.'

'Reckon at least six hands and two heads. Would be an improvement. Do you… remember?'

'Some bits of it,' Karna said. 'Unfortunately.'

'Sounds cosy. You should be thanking my future wife for your life. I asked a pardon for you as dowry. Didn't even have to bargain. Most likely they considered you would be dead but they saved you, though. The same old men you embarrassed. You were so pale, a woman might be forgiven for thinking you had a Rakshasi for a wife. Blood, you had none, but pus, too many. Your flesh had mortified. I heard the healer claim even the maggots would not touch the foulness in your veins. I thought I had seen the last of you but alas, Fate has plans of tormenting me a little longer.'

'My heart wails for you,' Karna said, coldly. 'How did I survive, then?'

'You have your teacher, Parshuram, to be grateful to. I still find it hard to believe you learned from the legend himself. Now, don't ask me how he saved you. I know not the details, for despite my looks, I am unversed in black alchemy,' Duryodhan said, frowning. 'First, he softened the malignant veins around your eyes by leeching them. All the leeches died, you know. For the loss of blood, well, he transferred some.'

The revelation cut short Karna's seesaw of thoughts. 'Transferred blood? That is not possible.'

'Worry not, friend,' Duryodhan said. 'Not mine, but I volunteered, mind you. I would have been humoured to see your face sour at the idea of a little bit of me running through you.'

'Whose blood courses through my veins, then?'

'Jarasandh's.' *Impossible.* 'Something about a similarity, I know not the terms he used, only that I was even more indebted to the Emperor then. You know, after the royal pardons and his daughter and his army and all of it. By Vayu, is this how it feels to be you?'

'Welcome to the beautiful life of insolvency,' Karna said, absently.

'I reckon that has made the Ehtrals' job of disparaging Reshts from the North a tad tougher if their glorious Emperor's blood was seen mixing with a lowly Resht's, but we are supposed to keep it a secret. Maybe the Emperor will adopt you as a son and you could be his Heir to the Empire. The world knows he is no fan of Saham Dev.'

'Something you share in common.'

Duryodhan scowled at him. 'Though given he has found his long-lost daughter, Jayatsena, I suppose your chances don't look good. Jayatsena is already a hero. The story is running wild that Jayatsena was the one who avenged the fallen by slaying you, or rather, your more charming version.'

'But I am alive.'

'The ones who fought in Virangavat were not Karna or Duryodhan. They were spies of Krishna. Saves the Empire and the Union some embarrassment. Saves you from a fire. Those were nameless villains who met the fate they deserved.'

'The crowd needs a villain.' Karna nodded. 'But I... murdered that boy.'

'Again, not murdered. Vanquished. It was a Duel to the Death. Murdered doesn't apply. Not to forget, the boy killed an entire legion of Namins with his ship.'

'Will you tell me?'

'Fine. But just to get it away with once and for all, yes, you slew a guard and a priest, a civilian from the mob, and yes,' Duryodhan hesitated for a moment, 'Lord Shishupal's brother.' Duryodhan illustrated the events. He held nothing back. When all was said and done, Duryodhan was still a man honest to the bone, unversed in sweetening harsh truths.

Karna was torn apart in his descent through the records of his rampage. His guilt was fire, silent screams and noiseless thunder but it was something that Duryodhan heard.

'I will leave you alone to wallow in unnecessary guilt,' Duryodhan said.

'May I recommend apprenticing under an Acharya to learn the thesaurus and use kinder synonyms,' Karna said, eyes brimful with tears.

Duryodhan shrugged, went back to a table and poured a glass for himself and for Karna. The one for himself, he watered. 'You saved your Prince, Highmaster. You saved your friend, Karna. Tell me. If given a chance to reverse it, would you?'

'No.'

'Good. And, as I take it, it evens you with Shishupal for his sin.'

Karna's voice wavered, 'You know I never blamed Shishupal for what happened to Sudama.'

'Doubt he will lend you the same clemency. But I think you're lucky. Surviving a thrashing without a scar on the face to show for it,' Duryodhan drawled as his fingers traced a gash from cheek to beard. 'You think dragons are a terror. Try wolves. But... word has it that Shishupal met his end in Mathura. So, I don't expect he will be marching in for revenge anytime soon.'

'My luck...' Karna laughed through his sobs, his ribs hurting. 'The most exquisite luck in the world.' In the shared laughter, un-noticed by them both, a female praying mantis, green and graceful, alighted on the other side of the window pane.

The windows themselves had gone dark, and the faint light of distant stars had ripped the diamonds off the floor. The sun had set for good, the stench of death growing only stronger, despite the scented candles.

'I am sorry, by the way,' Duryodhan said, 'for... Divine Marzana. You don't love her back, do you?'

Karna was silent for a breath. 'I LOVE HER ENOUGH TO LET HER GO.' When Duryodhan said nothing, Karna cleared his throat and asked, 'So what now? Another abduction?'

'Of a throne, this time.' Duryodhan smiled as he nodded. 'We head to war.'

EPILOGUE

A FEW MONTHS AFTER THE BATTLE OF MATHURA

'This is where Manu made the choice between saving his people and saving his race. Or so he claimed,' the Keeper of Scrolls said, dusting her cloak in vain. Staying spotless was a fool's errand in a realm where ash had long since dethroned the dewdrops.

'*So, what's the lesson? A person relying on foresight always regrets in hindsight?*'

'Not sure I like that, Sister Marigold.' She laughed, though it came out more like a wheeze, her face twisting with the sting from her still-raw arms. 'Especially since our plan for teaching the world some manners relies a fair bit on your eyes.' She turned, staring out the window, the view baked grey by the skin of stone that cloaked the thousand faces beyond. 'Are you certain, you want to stick with this name? Marigold? Your name at birth was a fine one.'

'*The fate of the world denied me the indulgence of my Chosen Name after initiation,*' Sister Marigold signed. '*It seems now that the omission was for a purpose.*'

There was a noise—a noise that sliced through the quiet like a knife through flesh. One of the massive doors crashed open, and in came a girl, stumbling in a manner that suggested her sword was doing its best to outwit her ankles. The girl took another awkward couple of steps before she finally managed to stand still. Her entire left side—from the jacket to her neck and face—was a ruin of charred flesh, twisted and fused with the tatters of her clothing, melted and mangled by some ill-tempered magic. Which was just as well, considering that a good set of scars seemed to be the chief qualification for membership in their merry band of vengeneers.

'Welcome, Storm. We have been expecting you... and your friend. No trouble on the journey I hope.'

'Not particularly.' Storm looked around the Stone Men with naught a fear in her eyes. 'Came across a thrashing fish, and that was interesting. We do appreciate the hospitality of the hippocras,' Storm said, raising the drained goblet of emerald and gold that matched the dented goblet in the Keeper's hand, 'even if it did taste like iron. Oh, but the bard you sent to present us the drink with and escort us was most painful to bear. Why do you think I'm panting? I couldn't get away fast enough.'

'The bard is an acquired taste, I'm afraid,' the Keeper said with a smile, glancing at Sister Marigold, both of them realizing they liked this Storm.

'I thought I was walking into a hornets' nest,' announced the warlord's deep voice from behind Storm, 'only to find two girls busy plucking their wings.'

'How else can we make certain they only sting the friends we choose?' the Keeper replied, watching the warlord and the bard enter behind Storm.

The bard crossed the passage to stand beside her, but she barely noticed. Her eyes did not leave the warlord. Rough like a chipped dagger, this outlander from another time, his skin pale as ivory except around that scar, a black ring around his neck, like a noose that had failed its job. The man's carriage already named him warrior, especially the way his arm seemed ready to dart for a sword with a hand that was no longer there. Scars, indeed.

'I must confess I am surprised at seeing the throne of Iyran Machil occupied,' the warlord said.

'*Finders keepers,*' Sister Marigold signed from the pool, the red from the ruby wedged in her throat casting a malevolent glow to the smile on her face.

'*The Language of the Sign,*' the warlord grinned. '*At least something survived from my time.*'

'I do not know this finger dance. Does she not deign us worthy to talk?' Storm asked.

'A half-eaten windpipe does not for fine conversation make,' spoke the bard. 'Muchuk Und of the Ikshvakus and Storm of the Silver Wolves, you are in the presence of Sister Marigold, Sister of the Black Order and Realmseer of Iyran Machil and she is the Keeper of—.

'Realmseer?' Muchuk Und interrupted. 'Last I heard, the Realmseer was a doddering old bastard with that bloody great gem in his skull.'

'Old fashions must pave the way for the new, and you'll find us girls far more motivated to the cause of mayhem,' the Keeper said.

'S'pose, I'll find out,' Muchuk Und said, and then he turned to Sister Marigold. 'So, you saw me coming, and you know what I want,' he said, his eyes crucified on the Orb of Agan Mian lodged in the Sister's half-eaten throat where blackened nerves bulged out like veins on a marble statue. 'What now?'

'*We need another helping hand.*'

'Sister Marigold has a candidate in mind,' the Keeper said, 'but the shaping towards the opportunity remains distant. Nor do I think her pick will please you. For now...'

Sister Marigold signed to chime in. '*For now we had best hope that interested entities remain adequately distracted,*' saying which she reached a tiny-fingered hand down to the water. They watched it vanish beneath the surface, but it was the scene in the waters that seemed to waken, a faint turbulence, the hint of ripples. '*Until then, you need to trust me.*'

'You ask me to trust you,' Muchuk Und growled, 'where no trust has been earned.'

'*You forget your past holds no secret from me, and neither does your future,*' Sister Marigold signed.

'Do you see me stompin' on your pretty face then?'

The Keeper decided to step in. 'Warlord, we have a long list of enemies. Common ones. Sister Marigold wants her friends destroyed for abandoning her, your friend wants...' the Keeper looked at Storm, and smiled, 'you want Lord Krishna, dead, don't you?'

Storm stopped playing with the empty goblet in her hand. 'How did you know that, Keeper?'

The Keeper smiled, turning to Muchuk Und. 'And you want—'

'The Children of Light,' Muchuk Und answered before she could finish.

'What if I were to tell you that in the War to end Wars, they all stand on one side.'

'Makes it much easier to knock the cunts down,' Storm answered.

'That depends on who stands opposite them,' the Keeper said, and then looked at Muchuk Und. 'Say, for example, an Army of the Undying, the Warlord of Lore and the Realmseer together? That'd be a thing no one could dismiss, not even the Daevas.'

'I suppose,' Muchuk Und said, looking up to Sister Marigold, and then glancing back at the horde of growling but well-behaved Stone Men and Stone Women. When he turned, he found Sister Marigold standing in front of him. The Sister set a gentle damp hand on Muchuk Und's arm, steering him towards the window of the hall.

Nar Ad, running his fingers over a lyre he could play no longer, nudged her. 'Can I ask you a question, dear Keeper?'

'Apparently,' she replied.

'Always the barbs for this bard,' Nar Ad chuckled. 'Continuing from where we left off, can you still, true to heart, deny the role of luck in bringing us where we are?' *Here we go again.* 'Masha not being up to the culinary standards of Stone Baby—'

'Because a man she trusted used to poison the Sister's soup,' she said.

'The magic of the Orb of Agan Mian keeping Masha alive,' Nar Ad rallied.

'With a slit throat and no voice and no friends.'

'Or me surviving,' Nar Ad puffed, 'because of a ceiling that fell in the most aesthetically concealing angle.'

'That depends on whether you're looking at your luck or ours.'

'Ouch. Fine, what about you landing on the highest tower of the world,' Nar Ad reminded, 'with only a broken hand to show for it.'

'It is a bleak day when you consider a lady in luck for merely shattering every bone in her arm,' the Keeper chuckled, remembering that day, that sky, the man she left behind. She wondered if he had survived, and then slapped the thought away like a bothersome fly. Hope was now a volume perched on a high shelf she couldn't reach.

Before Nar Ad could try again, she asked, 'Your point? That luck is the residue of prophecies, the charioteer that cannot be captured, the prayers of the meritorious answered.'

'Yes! Exactly! But tarry there. I know that line. It is a quote from...' Nar Ad gasped, 'from my book! It is my quote! I love your mind, *Flames!*'

Vahura, the Keeper of Scrolls for the new Realmseer, smiled, taking a sip of the blood again from her goblet. She felt the iron tendrils of its taste wriggle through her throat as she swallowed.

'Come, My Lady, the time draws nigh,' Nar Ad said as he beckoned her to the window where Sister Marigold was showing Muchuk Und her gift for him. *I am the luckiest woman in the world, indeed.*

For the gift was a little girl's head, wreathed in copper locks and neatly severed. Maroon aprons under closed eyes, pink rims round her nostrils and contorted cheeks laid undeniable evidence of the suffering the little girl must have felt in her last moments. For now, it swung carelessly from Sister Marigold's hand. The Sister tipped the girl's head forward and pried her eyelids open in the direction of the Stone Kin, and moved her hand slowly from left to right, and again from right to left, spilling the seeds of Marigold amongst the morbid.

It took a while for the song to play but play, it did. Nar Ad called it the 'Raag of Rta'.

The hearts of the Stone Kin closest to them in the garden began to pound, almost as if the sound was trying to claw its way out of their chests. They thrashed, their skulls a host for pleasure and ecstasy. Their shrill moans echoed through the ruins of Iyran Machil, as the Marigold seed spread its roots from the dead girl's eye to theirs. And just like that, this garden, a mausoleum of petrified souls for millennia, was now a maelstrom of life.

The Stone Kin felt. The Stone Kin hungered. The Stone Kin thirsted. No more a withered husk of life, the Stone Kin lived. At least, temporarily.

'An Army of Stone,' Storm said as she peeped over Muchuk Und's shoulder. 'Bet you didn't plan on winning an army when you came for the red gem, did you now, old man?'

'Vetaals,' Nar Ad said, smiling at Sister Marigold. 'I found a name for them,' he explained. 'Stone Kin lacked a certain ring. They are the Army of Vetaals.'

'But,' Muchuk Und turned to Sister Marigold, 'how?'

Sister Marigold tapped at the Orb of Agan Mian in her throat, the goblet in his hand and then turned to point it at *her*.

'That wasn't hippocras we drank, was it, Keeper?' Storm asked her, gulping.

Vahura smiled faintly. 'The magic of Orb of Agan Mian keeps the Stone Kin from dying but does not keep them truly alive. Now what does the Marigold Mold do? In its essence, it makes a mortal heart pump so much blood that it drives them berserk, causing them to slaughter everything in sight, until their heart gives out. But... when it comes to hearts of stone, the Marigold reanimates them. Temporarily. For mortals, it is a plague. For the undying, it is a drug.'

'And what does *this* have?' Storm asked again, shaking the goblet pointedly.

'Manu's blood,' Muchuk Und answered gruffly instead. 'It is a shield against the plague. So, you do know that Trisiras concealed the shield and the sword against the Marigold in Manu's blood.' Muchuk Und scoffed. 'He had tried to barter this pearl of wisdom for a lease on life.'

'I reckon you agreed,' Nar Ad said.

'Oh, I agreed, yes. I pocketed those pearls, and then rather unsportingly, separated his head from his shoulders for the Daevas. The cunning plan was to return home and use this little secret as a weapon against the Daevas...' Muchuk Und said, a nostalgic gleam in his eye, 'but karma's got a swift chariot for people like me. So, tell me this, if you see everything, do you see us win? Do you foresee a Daeva's throat struggling in my grip? Or do we cross that bridge when we burn it?'

Sister Marigold signed, '*Anyone who overestimates the importance of visions undervalues the comfort of an existence free from the sights of burning cities, hanging Gods and dead cats.*' Muchuk Und raised an eyebrow when Sister Marigold added, '*But comfort isn't our currency, is it?*'

'It isn't.' Muchuk Und grinned. 'Well, lead on then, Sister Marigold.'

'Dead cats, Keeper?' Storm asked.

'Told you *all* our enemies are on one side,' replied Vahura as Mister Nomnom squeaked his assent from the pocket in her satchel.

ACKNOWLEDGEMENTS

Once again, to Mahwash, a Farishta masquerading as my friend – thank you for being the Chandler to my Joey, the Aragorn to my Legolas, the Karna to my Duryodhan. Without you, I cannot fathom being a writer. Just. Cannot. So please, do not let your future husband distract you from your best friend duties of partnering with me in all my adventures.

To GRRM, whom I thanked in my first book, where I wished I would meet him someday. Evidently, the manifestation gurus got something right because I did meet him (though 'chased him down' at Worldcon might be more accurate, in true Mission Impossible style) to thank him for inspiring me to create *ASOIAF* in Ancient India.

To my editors, Shona Kinsella, for demystifying biology, and Stephen Black for being the Dimvak to my Dantavakra in the arena fight scene.

To the Head of Zeus Team, who make me feel I'm collaborating with a merry band of rebels than a stiff-suited corporate machine. Nic, thank you for championing my book and for keeping me from wandering into perilous alleys in Scotland. To Sophie (for brightening up my Gmail), Charlie (for your Vimeslike patience), Polly (for being a great travel guide), Jade (for that magazine surprise), Jessie (for conspiring behind covers) and everyone else, thank you. You've all made me feel right at home with Pringles, freezing AC setups and signing pens. Thank you.

To my long-suffering agent, Oliver, who is so deeply invested in the stories I write that I often mistake him for my editor, thank you for being my therapist and whiskey specialist.

To Dad, for being the book's best stalker and marketer online, and to my brother, for handling the chores and emotional heavy lifting so I can be the fun son.

To Micaela Alcaino, my Michelangelo, for continuing to make my books, masterpieces before anyone's even turned a page. To Gauri for inspiring Vauri, and for that I am sorry.

To Awantika, who saw the colors between my lines and painted them true.

To Matt from The Broken Binding for changing my life with your wand.

To the unsung heroes from Barnes & Noble who loved this book enough to recommend it for a special edition, I tip my hat to you. Thanks to you, I am able to pay my bills and keep writing with reckless abandon.

To Prachi, who, poor soul, is usually just minding her own business when an incomplete chapter is thrust upon her, accompanied by my plea, 'Please assure me this doesn't bring dishonour to my ICSE legacy!' I suppose I could manage without you, but it would be a miserable process, considerably less enjoyable, and frankly, nowhere near as good. Thank you for helping turn this book into something I'm truly proud of.

Gigantic, d'rahi-sized thanks to all my readers who rush to order and review the books – it helps more than you know. And to all the kind souls on BookTwt, Booktube, Bookstagram, and hopefully Booktok (I wouldn't know as TikTok is banned in India), without whom I would have been forced to return to the courtroom for good (as a lawyer, not a criminal, just FYI). Heroes without capes, every one of you. Especially you, Mihir and Petrik.

And finally, to all the artists and writers from South Asia and beyond, all the marginalised creators with a red line under their name in Microsoft Word, thank you for continuing the fight for the sun that others receive without question. Today, you are more necessary and powerful than you could possibly imagine.

GLOSSARY

Akhand: Undivided. Akhand Aryavrat is the ambitious dream of uniting the realm under one empire, sort of like trying to herd cats and baboons under one roof.

Arangetram: The debut performance of a classical Indian dancer. Expect emotional matriarchs and desperate guests.

Asana: A yoga pose with the idea to balance, stretch, and bend oneself into positions that would make a contortionist raise an eyebrow.

Chakra: Mystical wheels of power turning within the body to align one's spirit with cosmic forces, assuming, of course, you've had enough meditation and not too much mead.

Dvar: Doorway between realms, the veil between worlds.

Janeu: A sacred thread that chaps of the Namin persuasion wear across their person. A sort of club tie for the devout.

Mangalsutra: A sacred necklace worn by married women, symbolizing their marital status and doubling as a protective charm to keep their husbands in one piece.

Nadis: Counterpart to arteries and veins, nadis are highways through which the life force (prana) flows assuming there are no other spiritual roadblocks.

Nritya: Indian classical dance in honour of the Gods.

Padams: Slow, lyrical dance compositions in Nritya focused on emotional storytelling through subtle gestures and expressions in the dance.

Sessed: Stretching your awareness out to assess and absorb energy currents.

Shrap: A curse that slams fate's fingers in the door, draining the caster's prana. Only those with prana to spare dare cast it.

Urf: Alias or 'also known as'. Used when your real name is too problematic to pronounce.

Vachan: An unbreakable vow that makes you think twice before committing – because if you break it, your insides will burn like a tapestry torched by a tipsy candle.

CASTES

Namins: Caste at the top of the social ladder – priests, scholars, and general know-it-alls, given to advising kings, studying ancient texts, organizing pujas and sacrifices.

Ksharjas: Sword-wielding, shield-bearing, war-whooping weapon wielders – royalty and soldier class.

Drachmas: The merchant class – farmers, traders, and other haggling folks.

Reshts: Lowest rung of the social ladder who keep the whole show running – craftsmen, cremators and cleaners. Salt of the earth sorts.

DEITIES

Indra: God of Thunder and Wielder of Lightning (Vedan).

Vayu: God of Wind and Master of Skies (Vedan).

Agni: God of Fire and Lord of Hearth and Sacrifices (Vedan).

Prakioni: Goddess of Earth and Keeper of Soil (Vedan).

Yama: Bringer of Death and Judge of Darkness (Ehtral).

Xath: Breath of Life and Giver of Light (Ehtral).

Storm God: Tyrant of Tempests and Turmoil (Kalingan).

Ocean Goddess: Mistress of the Deep and Ruler of Tides (Kalingan).